ROSEMARY ROGERS

"The queen of historical romance."
—*New York Times Book Review*

"Returning to her roots with a story filled with family secrets, politics, adventure and simmering passion, Rosemary Rogers delivers what fans have been waiting for."
—*Romantic Times* on *An Honourable Man*

"Her novels are filled with adventure, excitement, and always, wildly tempestuous romance."
—*Fort Worth Star-Telegram*

"This is exactly what her many fans crave, and Rogers serves it up with a polished flair."
—*Booklist* on *A Reckless Encounter*

"Ms. Rogers writes exciting, romantic stories… with strong-willed characters, explosive sexual situations, tenderness and love."
—*Dayton News*

"Her name brings smiles to all who love love."
—*Ocala Star-Banner*

Also available from MIRA Books and
ROSEMARY ROGERS

AN HONOURABLE MAN
BOUND BY LOVE
A RECKLESS ENCOUNTER
RETURN TO ME
SAVAGE DESIRE
DANGEROUS SURRENDER
SCANDALOUS DECEPTION
JEWEL OF MY HEART
SAPPHIRE

ROSEMARY ROGERS

DANGEROUS SURRENDER

Quills®

First Published 1982
First Australian Paperback Edition 2010
ISBN 978 0 733 59863 0

Published by
Harlequin Mills & Boon™
Level 5
15 Help Street
CHATSWOOD NSW 2067
AUSTRALIA

Printed and bound in Australia by
McPherson's Printing Group

DEDICATION

To the youngest female in my family,
my granddaughter Reina—
and to all women who are trying to
find themselves; and to the men who
are strong enough to understand and help us.

PART I

1

The heat in Colombo, capital city of the British Crown Colony of Ceylon, seemed especially oppressive on this sun-scorched August afternoon. As their carriage jolted and rumbled over a newly paved street, Alexa Howard surreptitiously opened one more button on the front of her gown, thankful that Aunt Harriet appeared to have fallen asleep and wouldn't notice.

And even if she *had,* Alexa would not have cared! It was ridiculous, Alexa thought mutinously as she felt unladylike rivulets of perspiration trickle down her sides and between her breasts, that women should be expected to keep up the English fashions in a hot, tropical climate. Far more suited to the prevailing temperatures was the simple costume worn by the native Sinhalese women—a piece of cotton material wrapped twice around the waist and knotted at the hip, reaching to just above the ankles, known as a "camboy." And their only other garment was a very brief and low-cut bodice that more often than not exposed a bare brown midriff. In fact, when Alexa was in the privacy of her own room at home, that was all *she* wore. But now here she was in Colombo—too many miles and far too many hours away from the comparative coolness of the hill country, and encased in a steel and whalebone corset that cut into her flesh, as well as layers of stifling petticoats under a gown that was supposed to cover her from neck to wrist.

The sharp clatter of horses' hooves on either side of the carriage made Alexa wish enviously that she too could have made this journey on horseback wearing practical breeches instead of a hampering skirt. She knew the two young officers who had volunteered to act as their escort and *they* knew as well as she did that she could outride and outshoot either of them. Hadn't she proved it only three weeks ago at the boar hunt up on Horton Plains? How cool it had been that day. She remembered the feel of the fresh wind in her face and the mounting sense of excitement that kept building during the chase with the dogs leading the way—the challenge of danger that was always present on one of these hunts. Why couldn't *she* have been born the male instead of her brother, Frederick, who hated getting dirty and turned pale at the sight of blood, preferring to read books and practice on the pianoforte for hours on end when he could have spent the time outdoors enjoying all that life had to offer instead?

And what does Freddy know about running a coffee plantation? Alexa began to fan herself vigorously with the newly acquired bonnet she had positively *refused* to don before they had set out early that morning. Why, *I'm* the one who acts for Papa when he has to go away, and I can keep the ledgers and talk to the overseers in their own language and...and they respect me too, even if I *am* a woman! Freddy doesn't even care about learning things like that even though he'll need to know them some day, and Mama coddles him far too much, of course! But then, rather guiltily she caught the thought back, remembering how precious her only son was to poor Mama, who had lost three other children in infancy. And that was the reason it was Aunt Harry and not her mama who was to be her chaperone at the Governor's Ball tomorrow night. Freddy had developed a fever—a *slight* fever—but of course Mama couldn't dream of leaving his side! She had been quite preoccupied with instructing the cook exactly how to prepare fresh beef tea when a sullen Alexa, hurried along by Harriet, had left the rambling bungalow at five that morning.

"*Do* have a wonderful time, my darling," Mama had said earlier. "And do try to *smile* instead of frowning in that forbidding fashion. It was so very kind of the Governor and Mrs. Mackenzie to invite you to stay with them in Queen's House—really quite an honor, dearest, and I'm sure you'll make both your papa and me very proud of you. Who knows, you might just meet some nice young man in the Civil Service, and..." But at that moment Freddy had called out for Mama, and she had hurried away after bestowing a quick kiss.

Perhaps it had been just as well, Alexa thought now. Sometimes she had to almost bite her tongue to keep from arguing vehemently, especially when the conversation turned to "suitable" young men. And that was another of the things she resented. Why was it simply taken for granted that every woman's ambition must be to "catch" some man and be married? And yet it was usually either that or end up as a governess or an unwanted poor relation hovering in the background, hiding in the shadows—eternally grateful, constantly self-effacing. Alexa fanned herself even harder, feeling her lips grow taut with anger and frustration.

"*I* am going to be different! Why must I be forced to choose from such poor alternatives? I'll find *some* way!" Alexa remembered herself saying that, the words spilling from her hotly; and she remembered even more clearly her aunt's cool, measured voice replying.

"My dear Alexandra, I can only hope that besides giving you an education that most young females of your age are not fortunate enough to receive I have also taught you that you must learn to be *practical.* Logical and reasonable in your thinking, if you prefer. At any rate I'm sure you're intelligent enough to realize that there are certain inescapable facts of life that have to be accepted, like it or not, my dear. You were born a female—and you have no other alternatives save even more unpleasant ones that we need not discuss."

Oh, how fiercely she had argued, and how intensely she had felt the pain and frustration of the *injustice* of it maul her like the claws of a leopard before she'd been forced to concede to what Aunt Harry had called the inescapable facts of life—if you were a *woman,* that was. She had been allowed the taste of freedom for as long as she could remember, allowed to learn and think for herself and express her own opinions—to "run wild," as some of the neighboring planters' wives put it. And then...

"But *why* have I been allowed to have such freedom if I was only meant to lose it some day?" Alexa never cried, but the words had been a cry of despair in themselves. "You know Freddy doesn't know *anything* about running a plantation, and he'll never take the trouble to learn about it. I could help him, couldn't I? I could..."

"Could be his right-hand man until he takes a wife, who will hate you and want you out of her house? Yes, *her* house, Alexa, for all that you've looked upon it as your home for most of your life. Freddy will inherit the plantation, and when he marries it will be his wife's home, not yours."

All it had amounted to was that Alexa should be *practical* and think *logically* and should begin to prepare for what her future must be. It was after their talk that Alexa had finally agreed to accept the invitation to Queen's

House for the Governor's Ball, which would really be a birthday ball held in her honor—like a "coming out." But snatches of that unusually frank conversation with Aunt Harry still floated through Alexa's head.

"There have been women throughout history, my dear, who were clever enough and wise enough to rule countries and empires through their men. You might remember that." What a strange thing for Aunt Harry to have said.

"There's the main gate of the Fort up ahead of us now. It won't be too long before we arrive at Queen's House!" One of the young subalterns who had escorted them leaned down from his horse to give the young woman he usually called "Alex" a grin and a wink. He grinned even more broadly when she gave him one of her famous scowls. "It'll be a lot cooler there, you know. Sea breezes and all that. And you'll save me a dance tomorrow, won't you?" Seeing Alexa's eyes narrow dangerously, he winked at her again before he straightened up hastily, turning his grin on his brother officer. Poor old Alex! She must be furious, suddenly being turned into a female. He couldn't even recall, come to think of it, that he'd ever seen Alex in *skirts* before. Wonder if she knew how to dance? Well, at any rate he and Eric had talked about it in the mess last night, and they'd decided that since she was such a good sport it would only be the proper thing for them to help her out; and they'd taken a solemn oath *not* to laugh and tease her if she tripped over her flounces and furbelows—for one thing, she'd probably come after both of them with a pistol if they did, and, female or not, Alex had a damned cool head and a deadly aim! He'd seen that for himself, and they'd all heard the story of how she'd finished off a wounded and enraged bull elephant in mid-charge.

"Did that young man say we were almost there? Lord, I cannot believe that I actually fell asleep in spite of all the rattling and bumping around!" Straightening up, Harriet delved in her reticule for a handkerchief to mop at her face with. "I hope to goodness it'll be cooler once we get closer to the ocean. Such heat! I'd almost forgotten how hot Colombo can be."

Alexa had been gritting her teeth so hard that she was surprised to find her jaws were not locked together. She said with syrupy sweetness: "And were you giving me an example of how to rattle on like an empty-headed young thing, Aunt Harriet? Since I'm up on the auction block now I suppose I really must try *harder,* mustn't I?"

"Oh, for heaven's sake, Alexa, let us not become dramatic!" The snapped-out reply sounded more like the Aunt Harry she was familiar with, at least. "And shake out your sleeves. They're looking positively *wilted* in spite of the lining I had that stupid tailor stitch into them. And put your bonnet on at once! It was *not* meant to be a fan, you know. I don't know who else will be staying with the Mackenzies, but I do want everyone who might be there when we arrive to know that even in the hill country we try to keep up with the latest fashions."

Alexa's slate-colored eyes, so dark they could look almost black, flashed dangerously even though her voice remained sweetly docile. "The *latest* fashions? But all the journals we receive from London are at least four or five months old! If *I* had been consulted I would have begged Mrs. Mackenzie to make it a fancy dress ball tonight; and *then* I could have attended as a Sinhalese woman and be cool all evening."

Realizing the girl was riding on a short rein, Harriet was wise enough to shrug and say only, "Well, I'm sure that the ball gown that Sir John means to surprise you with will be truly exquisite and in the very latest style, so that you will outshine every other female there. He has such good taste!"

At the mention of her adopted "uncle," who was one

of her father's best friends, Alexa could not help but lose some of her earlier feeling of resentment, even if he *had* been one of the instigators of this birthday ball for her. How could she not continue to love and respect her beloved Uncle John? It had been Sir John who had presented her with her first thoroughbred and had taught her to ride it like a man—Sir John who had taught her about guns and how to shoot and not to flinch even from the kick of a heavy elephant gun. And how she had loved being allowed to listen when Sir John and Papa would begin talking about the wars they had been in and the exciting battles they had fought under Wellington.

"I'll wager that *you* wish you'd been there too, don't you, Alex?" Sir John would tease her sometimes, but he never teased her in the condescending way of grown-ups; and Alexa would nod vigorously, her eyes wide and shining as she imagined how it must have been—the noise of cannons and the smell of powder and the keening sound of a musket ball whistling past your head; the excitement of a charge with your sword drawn, facing a screaming foe, and hand to hand combat; and if you died you died gloriously and with honor, and if you lived you always knew you had been there, so close to death that you had brushed shoulders with it and had still survived.

It was only to Sir John that an older Alexa, only a few months ago, could confide seriously: "I know it's probably only because I've been hearing the stories for most of my life—yours and Papa's—but sometimes I really feel as if I *have* lived through wars and battles. It seems so *real,* as if I know what it's like. Even to the smell of horses and dust and blood, and the sounds of clashing swords, and how you feel *inside* in battle..."

He hadn't laughed—she remembered that. "Well, my dear, I lived in India for quite some time, as you know, when it belonged to the old John Company, and the Hindus there, they believe that souls are born and reborn over and over again. And that it's possible for some people to remember past lives. Who knows, my dear, who knows? It's something I've often wondered about myself.''

Harriet, of course, could hardly know of the thoughts that had raced across her niece's brain during the past few seconds. But by mentioning Sir John Travers she had done exactly the right thing, she recognized with relief, seeing the almost imperceptible relaxing of Alexa's tensely held shoulders. Sighing, Harriet said, ''I really hate to admit how weary I am. All those miles and miles of traveling and the change of climate—I'll be glad of a nice cold bath, I can tell you that!'' She noticed with relief that Alexa was actually putting on her hated bonnet, although she did so with a wry face, adjusting it over her decorously pulled back hair and actually tying the wide ribbons in a bow under her chin.

''If either Eric or Basil make *any* comments when they see me in this...!' Alexa sounded so fiercely threatening that Harriet had to force back a smile. In spite of the fact that she would be eighteen years of age tomorrow, Alexandra could sometimes sound very much like a hoydenish little girl. But the child must face the fact that she was a woman now and a whole year older than her own mother had been when she had carried her. Poor little Victorine, so helpless, always so pretty...

As she usually did, Harriet closed her mind firmly on unwanted memories of the past. No point thinking back, was there? Victorine was safe and content now. She had a loving, considerate husband, the son she'd always craved, and she had security. The future belonged to Victorine's daughter, and now, although she was not overly religious, Harriet thought, Pray God I've taught her enough and made her strong enough to survive and go forward. To be a victor instead of a loser.

"Well, ladies, here we are at last!"

The carriage had actually come to a stop, and the feeling of not being in motion was almost strange.

"Aunt Harry? Are you unwell? You looked so..."

"Nonsense! I was just thinking, that's all. And there's the Governor himself waiting to greet us, and Mrs. Mackenzie. Shake out your skirts, dear. And smile. It lights up your whole face when you do."

One of the young officers had dismounted quickly enough to open the carriage door for them, and taking a deep breath Harriet squared her shoulders before she accepted the hand he proffered. Behind her Alexa too had drawn in her breath, holding it inside her until she felt calm enough to breathe out again. Yoga. She had learned about that from Sir John. And it was comforting to think that of course *he* would help see her through the whole ordeal ahead.

There was actually a smile on Alexa's face that showed off the dimple at one corner of her firm young mouth, Harriet noted relievedly. And the sprigged muslin had held up remarkably well after all with its wide "Mary Stuart" sash that made Alexa's small waist seem quite *tiny*.

Lady Mackenzie, who had had her misgivings about this whole idea and had only acceded to her husband's request to please Sir John Travers, gave a tiny mental sigh of relief. The young woman was quite charming after all and seemed well-mannered too—which only went to prove that one did best not listening to gossip spread by jealous older women with daughters of their own. Why, she could see nothing *mannish* or forward about this very feminine young creature who actually dropped a small, old-fashioned curtsy while making her thanks for the honor being shown to her. Remembering the days when she had been married to that insufferable bore Sir Samuel Hood and had been gossiped about because she enjoyed smoking a hookah, Mrs. Mackenzie decided immediately that she was going to *like* Miss Howard, and would, moreover, make her coming-out ball an event that would be long remembered in Colombo.

2

When at last they had been shown to their spacious quarters and the door had closed behind the last obsequious servant, Alexa could relax again. She felt by this time as if her face ached from smiling while she uttered simpering insincerities. Thank goodness they were to be allowed to rest for the remainder of the afternoon and that at last she could take off the constricting muslin gown she already detested, as well as all five petticoats and the corset that seemed to cut off her breath.

"Oh, at *last!* Did I behave well enough to suit you? But I do not think that I can stand another minute—no not another *second*—of being smothered in all these layers of hypocrisy! I would like to *tear* myself free! Thank God it is cooler in here… I was beginning to feel as if I could not *breathe* any longer. A few more minutes and I would have…"

Used to handling her charge, Harriet faced the challenging glower directed at her with a raised eyebrow. "My dear Alexa, don't you think that you are by now a trifle past the age for childish tantrums? I was proud of the way in which you conducted yourself just now, and I'm sure you lived up to everything Sir John must have told the

Governor and his wife about you. You're not going to let down the people who believe in you from lack of self-control, I hope?''

For a moment Alexa seemed to stand there poised like a hummingbird caught in mid-flight, and perhaps even *she* did not know whether she was on the brink of rebelling or running away. But then, to Harriet's relief, the rigid young shoulders seemed to slump, and the slender fingers that had already began to claw at the neck of the offending gown dropped away.

Not defeat, Harriet warned herself. With Alexa, born under the zodiacal sign of Leo, the lion, there would never be the concession of defeat, only an occasional retreat, perhaps. Putting aside her own weariness, Harriet came forward briskly, commanding a suddenly woebegone-looking Alexa to turn around.

''No need to tear a perfectly good dress, what with the price of fine materials these days. Here, I don't suppose you want me to send for one of those chattering little maids, do you? So I'll undo you myself, if you'll hold still. And do try to remember, my dear, that losing your temper is the same thing as losing your head—or losing the advantage, if you were engaged in some kind of a contest. Do you imagine you'd be any good on a hunting trip if you stopped using your head and gave in to blind panic?''

''I…I suppose I never thought about all *this* in the same light,'' Alexa confessed, with her head bent. And then, throwing it up almost defiantly, she said, ''Keeping a cool head… A *hunt*—is that what I am supposed to be engaged in? But who is the quarry, Aunt Harriet? The eligible man I'm supposed to capture with my false, feminine wiles? Or *I* myself?''

There had been an edge of cynicism and perhaps even of desperation in Alexa's voice that forced Harriet to answer with studied brusqueness. "My dear child, I hope I did not make you imagine, with all my sermonizing, that you are being abandoned to the wolves. You must not feel that you must immediately find yourself a husband, or think that this will be your only opportunity to meet eligible men. All I meant to say was that it is more than high time you thought of yourself as a beautiful and feminine young woman to whom men are bound to be attracted and *not* as a sister or a plucky comrade, as some of the young officers stationed upcountry seem to regard you! Oh, for heaven's sake! I really can't seem to recall now *what* I started out to explain to you in the first place. There, that takes care of your corset. And I'd have you know that I am many years older than you are and just as hot and sticky and tired!"

For once Alexa did not kick aside each garment, as it dropped around her ankles, with a smothered, under-the-breath military oath that Harriet always pretended not to hear. She had been standing as still as a statue, and just as silent except for a slight sigh of relief as the tightly laced corset was loosened. And now, to Harriet's disquiet, Alexa actually bent down to retrieve each offending article, one by one, something that she, used to doting servants waiting on her from babyhood, had never deigned to do before.

Alexa's voice sounded rather smothered for a moment until she straightened, still with her back turned to Harriet. "Well, I suppose that *you* did not want to make this journey any more than I did, Aunt Harry, especially with Freddy being sick and Mama all flustered, and nobody to help Papa out with the ledgers and to see that he eats enough. And I suppose that I *have* been spoiled and allowed to run wild, and...and have thought only of myself all this time without any sense of responsibility towards other people. While everyone else around me, like *you,* Aunt Harry..."

Alexa swung around abruptly with her untidy bundle of clothes clutched before her, a naked pagan goddess with the sheen of unshed tears making her widely spaced storm dark eyes appear even more brilliant under uncompromisingly straight dark brows. "We all take you for granted, don't we? But what of *you?* Why didn't *you* ever marry? Didn't you want to, ever?"

Harriet had always taught Alexa to be honest, to tell the truth and take the consequences if she had to, no matter what the cost. And now, without making herself too much of a hypocrite, how could she give this child-woman standing before her anything less than a direct answer to a direct question?

Harriet heard herself say in an oddly stiff voice: "The man I imagined myself in love with fell in love with someone else and married her. And I...I could never settle for second best. I think that is enough for one afternoon. Even old memories can bring painful twinges, as you might discover for yourself some day."

Her back, as she turned to walk through the archway that led to her own connecting room, was as uncompromisingly straight as Alexa's had been earlier; and it was only after she had pulled the heavy curtain closed to shut her into privacy that Harriet permitted herself the rare luxury of flinging herself onto her bed fully clothed and giving way to tears.

Alexa could turn into a raging termagant at times, with her volatile temper that matched her lion's mane of gold-threaded auburn hair; but she could never bear to see suffering or pain, much less cause it herself. And she sensed only too late that her thoughtless, *prying* questions had somehow hurt Aunt Harry. She would have given anything to take back her words if she could, as soon as she noticed how her aunt's face had whitened and seemed to grow stiff all of a sudden. But Aunt Harry was a trooper, and of course she would feel that she had to answer honestly, even if it hurt.

Alexa kept staring at that firmly drawn curtain that had become a barrier keeping her out, keeping her from trying to comfort her aunt in order to assuage her own feelings of guilt. The tears that she too had stubbornly been holding back had begun sliding down her face in warm, wet rivulets, but Alexa did not try to wipe them away. She almost never shed tears, and then only in private. No telltale sobbing and sniffling to give herself away to other people. Tears were punishment, assuagement, relief from tensions. Let them come now. Tomorrow she would make Aunt Harry happy and proud of her—even if the effort killed her! Yes, she'd even let her hair be tortured into those ugly, fashionable ringlets, and she would flutter her fan and giggle and even bat her eyelashes, if that was what it took to take the stricken look off Aunt Harry's face that had been put there by her thoughtlessness.

Like the sudden tropical cloudbursts that were so common in Ceylon—never lasting too long—Alexa's torrential flow of tears soon dried up, leaving her feeling drained and weak, as if her legs could no longer hold her up. Dropping her bundled-up clothes where she had been standing, Alexa stretched like a cat, her arms over her head as far as they could reach and then behind her back and to either side until she heard the tiny cracking sounds along her spine and shoulders that always brought comfort when she was tired or tense. And now that she had made herself relax she had barely enough energy left to slide her body between cool cotton sheets and turn her face against the pillow before sinking into the soft nothingness of sleep.

When Harriet, who had *not* been able to escape into sleep, came in an hour or two later, she shook her head as she looked down at Alexa's sleeping profile, still stained by the telltale trace of tears. Automatically she reached down and pulled the covers up over the girl's nude shoulders while she thought to herself, How resilient the young are! When Alexa woke up she would be smiling and sunny-tempered, eager to make amends for everything. That mood would last for a day or two perhaps, and then who knew what might set her off next? The pity of it was that Alexa had almost begun to think of herself as a young boy, running free. Was she really ready yet to turn into a woman?

Fortunately for her own well-being, Harriet Howard was a woman not often given to introspection. Emotion, as she had often pointed out to Alexa, was all very well *sometimes,* but *reason* and practicality had to come uppermost. One did the best one could—without being completely heartless, of course—and one survived, somehow. She had taught herself these things, and had immersed herself in books that had broadened her tiny insular world into a veritable universe, and she had learned, and had survived too, hadn't she? Obviously, there was no such thing as a broken heart, or she would have died on that incongruously bright summer's day when her best friend, eyes sparkling, had whispered her ''secret'' and had kept talking on and on without noticing how still and quiet Harriet had suddenly become. Turned into stone and just as cold by a Medusa with short, shining curls crowned by a filet of pearls and a pointed chin and red, pouting lips that men stared at. Even *he.* But no one had known her feelings. She had not let anyone see, even when the pain inside her screamed for release. ''That's nice. Of course I'm so happy for you. And of *course* I'll be one of the witnesses.'' Smiling, sensible Harriet.

Ceylon had seemed a long way from England, thank God, and unlike the other planters' families *they* had never felt the urge to go ''home'' on leave or even to visit. Home to what?

Besides her brother, Martin, and the man whose name Harriet never permitted herself even to *think,* the only other human being that she had let herself love was Alexa. Alexa had needed a strong influence in her life—someone who would concentrate on *her.* It had not been difficult to take Alexa away from Victorine, who tended in any case to regard a baby girl as a burden inflicted upon her by fate. Victorine was a *silly* woman, and a helpless one—the kind of female who would cry and wring her little hands and do nothing at all to help herself even if it was a matter of survival.

Alexa, Harriet had decided a long time ago, would be brought up differently; the way Harriet wished at times that *she* had been brought up. Strong, self-reliant, not afraid to demand whatever she wanted, or to reach out and *take* it if she had to. Not above playing a role in the charades imposed by men if she had to, but always letting her head rule her heart. Hearts, they said, broke too easily, and giving way to emotion invariably made matters worse instead of better.

Alexa really *must* learn to control her temper, Harriet thought fretfully before she managed to regain control of her own emotions. Patience and self-control were the hardest lessons to learn, after all; but Alexa had always been possessed of a very quick mind. And if she could be brought to see tomorrow night as a challenge, it might well turn out to be the proving ground that might transform the young Amazon of the hill country into the sophisticated young lady.

The soft chimes of a clock reminded Harriet that dinnertime (and it would be an early dinner tonight, Mrs. Mackenzie had announced) was less than two hours away. Alexa had not stirred, and indeed seemed to be sleeping so soundly that Harriet could not help thinking it would be almost cruel to wake her now and have her hurry to get ready while she was still in a stupor. In fact, it would be much better to let the poor child sleep tonight and *then* spring her on the assembled company tomorrow when she would be rested, refreshed, and at her best.

Her mind made up, Harriet pulled briskly at a velvet bell rope that summoned at least three servants within minutes. She was in her element giving orders. A tray with an assortment of fresh fruit and a carafe of cold water that had been *boiled* and filtered (one couldn't be too careful here) to be left for her niece in case she woke up, with perhaps a decanter of dry white wine as well. And for herself, she must have bath water immediately. Her authoritative commands resulted in the delivery of everything she had requested, and in less than the time she had allowed herself Harriet was bathed and dressed in a dark purple watered silk that was sedate without being dowdy.

She had already prepared the excuses she would offer on Alexa's behalf—the strain of a long journey coupled with the excitement and natural anticipation, and a degree of nervousness, of course. The Mackenzies, who had eleven children between them, would surely understand. As Harriet descended the stairs, escorted by no less than two turbaned house servants wearing red cummerbunds over their spotless white camboys, she prepared herself for an evening of pleasant conversation and no doubt a discreet exchange of gossip once the ladies retired after dinner, leaving the men to their port and cigars.

Hearing the subdued sounds of laughter and voices, both male and female, as she descended a second flight of stairs, Harriet was doubly pleased that she had allowed Alexa to remain asleep tonight. Small, private dinner, indeed! There must be at least twenty people here, if not more, and all dying from curiosity, no doubt. Well, they would just have to wait until tomorrow, wouldn't they, Harriet thought before she composed her features. Tomorrow we'll show them all, Alexa and I!

3

Alexa had never been able to fall asleep easily, usually not drifting off until she was completely worn out and hardly able to keep her eyes open. But then, once asleep, she slept as heavily and as deeply as a child. There were weeks on end when she would only catnap—an hour or so in the afternoon because it was required of her, and perhaps four or five hours at night after she had finished reading whatever book she had become immersed in. Always active and used to spending as much time as she could outdoors, she seemed to exist during these periods on nervous energy alone. And it was during these times too that she was most reckless—whether she was riding by herself or hunting with the pack of hounds she had trained, or else challenging some of the young officers stationed in the district to a race over the most difficult terrain imaginable or a wager as to which of them could bag the most dangerous animal during a hunting trip. She was like a young, healthy animal herself and seemingly indefatigable, until there came a time when she would become irritable for no apparent reason and snap at everyone around her before retiring, finally, to her own room to "meditate" as she called it.

Harriet, who always recognized the signs, would usually give Alexa an hour or two before she would open the door to find her sound asleep, sometimes with her head down on her desk and sometimes sprawled out on the floor. Her sleep at such times was almost like a trance, and Harriet would have her carried to her bed and order her old ayah to sit with her, and then the girl would usually sleep from twelve to eighteen hours or more at a stretch.

''Oh! I feel reborn!'' Alexa would laugh, stretching her arms high above her head. And for a while she would act as if she had in truth been renewed—sunny-tempered, easy to please, and wanting to please everyone around her, even to the extent of reading for hours on end to her brother, who adored her at these times and avoided her at others.

Usually, when Alexa had one of her ''deep sleeps'' as Harriet called them, she did not dream. Perhaps on this particular occasion it was the doing of the young, barefoot maid, who had drawn apart the heavy drapes that were meant to keep out the sun, and then pushed open the heavy wooden shutters to let in the smell and the sound of the restless surf along with the cool ocean breeze. But in any case, Alexa did not lie in bed as inertly as a toppled marble statue, and the habitual blackness of her sleep was laced through with strange dreams that made her twist and turn uncomfortably even though she did not want to wake up just yet.

Riding into battle, always as a man. And Uncle John asking her, ''Well, Alexa, have you made up your mind yet?'' About being reborn, he meant of course; and she could hear herself answer: ''No, not yet. But I think I should have been born a pagan woman who would delight in nothing more than *feeling* without having to think; and then perhaps being born a woman would not be so bad without being hedged about with rules and regulations and people who are always telling you that to be happy and enjoy yourself is wicked!"

"Were you ever a pagan woman before? In what countries were you born as a woman?" She did not recognize the voice that had asked her that question. Perhaps it had only floated in on the sea breeze that carried with it the scents and sounds of a myriad different countries touched by the same ocean moving back and forth and back and forth uncaring what names it was given because it knew it was life and beginning and end and always.

Not wanting to dream so deeply even in her fragmented dreams, she almost surfaced as she thought...countries? Spain...why did she think Spain? Papa had fought in Spain..."bitter-sweet," he had said of the music. Moorish influence..."they call it flamenco"...in her dream she saw herself dancing by herself in a red dress with only the sound of a guitar...then a voice...hers, somehow. Why would she sing when she was so sad? Sad...waiting...never, the words of the song said. Gone...gone...never... It had nothing to do with *her!*

Alexa almost woke then, but not quite. Floating between sleep and wakefulness, she heard someone playing minor chords on a guitar, a voice singing in Spanish. The almost cloying perfume of night-blooming flowers drifted into the room. Queen of the Night, Jasmine. Temple Flower. Gardenia. Alexa, knowing Spanish (as well as four other languages), understood that the song was a cry of unrequited love—of happiness followed by sadness—until it ended on an ugly, discordant note. "So, enough! There are too many centuries of bitterness embedded in the music of Spain. An English song, perhaps?"

There were more voices and sounds now, drowning out what she had almost felt and almost reached. Turning over on her side, Alexa burrowed her face into a too-soft pillow, still not wanting and not prepared to wake up quite yet.

She was drifting as lightly as a lotus blossom on the surface of sleep when she heard Harriet come in, followed by a servant. A tray was to be removed and another with fresh fruit and fresh, cool water and wine brought in to replace it. She felt Harriet bend over her, pulling up the cotton sheet that had slipped down to her waist. Poor Aunt Harry. An uneasy mixture of conservative and liberal. Think free, but *do* conform on the surface. What had happened to the man she had loved who had married her best friend?

"Have all the young missy's clothes been pressed before they were hung up?"

"Oh, yes, lady. I look after everything. I sit up all night if young missy want something."

"Good. Thank you—Menika, was it? I'm sure you'll see to everything. And *I* intend to go to sleep myself. No, I don't need any help. Well, just the buttons at the back, perhaps, and then I shall manage quite well."

Breathing evenly, Alexa floated in and out of sleep in spite of the fact that the sheet Aunt Harry had pulled up as far as her neck felt scratchy and far too hot. Poor Aunt Harry. Poor dear. She needed her sleep too.... She could hear the faint sounds of the sea from outside, and over that the sounds of carriage wheels and horses' hooves and voices calling out good-byes. Soon everything would be quiet and the night would belong to the sounds of the sea again. The faint aroma of a cigar made her wrinkle her nostrils, and she thought: Smells like one of Uncle John's. He always smokes the very best. And he had given her the very best of himself too. His wisdom, his understanding...

How pleasant it was to lie like this and drift along the borders of sleeping and waking. So many thoughts floated in and out of her mind without ceasing, one dream thought melting into the next. She saw herself as a rebellious, questioning child who resented the hampering skirts she was supposed to wear—until Aunt Harry took her side. And then in her next dream picture she was a pirate on a ship that rocked under her bare feet, fighting with a cutlass until the last and then, with a laugh of defiance, turning to plunge into the sea. How cool and pleasant it was, the sea. Like a friend she had always known. Green or blue or grey shading to black. Foam-tipped and salty. Both friend and foe. Nemesis or lover.

What a strange and almost startling thought. It must have been *that* and the chimes of the clock on top of the mahogany bookcase that made Alexa start upright in bed. Twelve. Somehow, she knew without counting how many times the same note had repeated itself. She was wide awake, all of a sudden, and she was hot and thirsty as well. The unfortunate young maid who started up almost as soon as the ''English missy'' did had no way of knowing at that moment, of course, that Alexa was also used to having her own way. Or that she had learned to speak both Tamil and Sinhalese, the major languages of the country, and was accustomed to getting into heated arguments with some of the young English officers who grinned and made comments like, ''Alex has a way with the natives, all right. Can't understand it.''

''Natives?'' she would say, flaring up. ''I suppose that's how the Romans and the Danes and the Saxons *and* the French who invaded England referred to our ancestors! This is *their* country and we're just visitors here—uninvited, I might add. And the civilization of the 'natives' of this island dates back to a time before Christ was born! You—*we*—all of us should be *learning* instead of trying to tear down in order to substitute...well *look* at us! Look at our *clothes,* look at... Have you ever wondered how primitive *we* must seem? As primitive, perhaps, as the barbarians who overran Rome, in the end.''

''Can't stop Alexa when she gets on her soap box!'' How it infuriated her when they wouldn't listen, or did not *want* to listen perhaps, and would sometimes deliberately incite her into "laying down the law" as they called it.

But on the other hand, when it suited her Alexa could not only act but sound as imperious as any haughty English madam.

"I'm thirsty. I'll have a very little of the wine, thank you. No fruit—I'm not hungry. And then I'd like a bath."

"A...a bath *now,* Missy? With hot water brought up?"

Even in the dim light shed by two candles, Alexa could see the dismay on the girl's face, making her relent slightly.

'No, I don't want hot water by any means; not in *this* heat. But isn't there a bathing place here? Where do *you* go to bathe? In the hill country..."

The Sinhalese people made it a point to bathe at least once every day and sometimes more often if it was exceptionally hot. At a well, or a stream, or under a waterfall. Alexa looked questioningly at the pretty young woman who had to be close to her own age, and repeated her question in Sinhalese.

Understanding, the girl shook her head as she tried to explain. "Not *here,* Missy. There are only bath tubs and the Governor's pool. But it has water from the sea, not fresh water. And *this* Governor and lady never use the Governor's pool."

Alexa flung aside the sheet that was supposed to cover her and swung her legs off the bed, stretching as she rose to her feet and pretending not to notice the amazement on the face of the young maid, who had obviously never seen an "English missy" naked before. "It sounds very inviting to *me,* at least," she said pleasantly. "And while I drink some wine you must tell me about the pool. Is it quite private? Is it very close to the house? How long would it take for us to get there?"

Menika had been newly promoted from her hitherto

lowly position of helping to make beds and fold linens, and her mother, who had served several former governors, had instructed her strictly as to what her duties were. She must obey orders, and she must never let her tongue chatter until she sounded like a mynah bird; also, she must remember that anything she heard or witnessed was never to be repeated. Did she understand? Never!

The girl understood well enough, as she always had. She knew very well too why her skin happened to be a much lighter shade of brown than her mother's skin was—and why her eyes were hazel instead of being black. And also why her "father" was supposed to be dead. Sometimes she would wonder which Governor was her real father, and then push the thought away. Most likely he had been a guest. *This* Governor and his lady made sure that Menika attended only their women guests; but before there had been times when she had been obliged to lie with some drunken, bad-smelling Englishman who would use her body without any consideration before sending her away with a slap on her bottom and perhaps a few rupees, if he was sober enough to think of it. For as long as she could remember, Menika had always understood what life was and had accepted both its cruelties and its rewards. In her heart she was a Buddhist, although like her mother and the rest of the servants who served the English Governors who came and went at Queen's House, she had to pretend she was a Christian convert in order to keep her position. It did not matter—the ritual she had learned to repeat parrot-fashion held no meaning for her. It was what people thought and believed inside themselves and how they lived their lives—never consciously harming any living being—*that* was all that really counted.

Usually, when she attended the Governor's guests, Menika merely obeyed orders and answered questions as briefly as she could. She had never encountered a guest before who could speak her own language, or who was not ashamed of standing naked before a servant while she sipped wine and asked to be told more about the Governor's pool.

"Oh, did you unpack for me? Thank you! I must find something cool to wear..." From one of the sandalwood-scented drawers Alexa took out her most comfortable costume—the camboy and brief, low-cut bodice of the Sinhalese peasant women. She could detect no change of expression in the face of the young servant woman who stood waiting respectfully for her next command. Menika. Yes, that was her name; she had heard Aunt Harry say it. A pretty name that meant "precious gem." And Menika herself was pretty, and deserved more than a life of waiting on other people. But what other alternatives did *she* have either? I wish I could talk to her and find out how she feels and what she thinks, Alexa thought; but there was a barrier between them that had been put there by circumstances and a rigorously enforced system of etiquette and convention that bristled with rules and reminders of what was *done* and "simply *not* done."

So instead of saying what she really wanted to say, Alexa walked to the opened windows and looked out, asking over her shoulder, "Is tonight the night of the full moon?"

"It is the night after the *Poya,* as the Buddhists call the night of a full moon." Menika corrected herself quickly, hoping her slip had not been noticed. She had stolen a few minutes to visit a temple yesterday—*Poya* Day to the Buddhists—and even her mother knew nothing about it.

"My ayah is a Buddhist and I've gone with her to temple on *Poya* Day a few times," Alexa said mildly. "*Our* temple has a pet cobra who likes milk, of all things! He's really quite affectionate after you get to know him." And then, so unexpectedly that she reminded a confused Menika of a striking cobra herself, Alexa went on to say brightly: "But of course an almost-full moon on such a clear night as this means that we should find our way to this bathing pool quite easily, don't you think?" She added patiently, noticing the look of shock on Menika's hitherto expressionless face, "The Governor's pool that you were telling me about."

"The missy is joking, surely?"

"I most certainly am *not!* I want to swim in the moonlight without any clothes on, like a pagan! And I *can* swim—very well indeed—so you need not be afraid that I will drown and they'll blame *you.* Also..." Alexa sighed, "do you think as long as we are alone you could stop calling me missy and call me Alex, or Alexa instead? In any event, I must tell you that I am determined to go anyway, with or without your help, now that my mind is made up. Although I promise I'll be very discreet and not get you into any trouble. Well?" And then: *"Please?"*

On the verge of offering Menika a bribe of a gold bracelet or several rupees, Alexa thought better of it and instead used the courteous word *karunakolla,* which also meant *please* but was for the most part used between equals and implied respect for the other person at the same time.

"You shouldn't ask such a thing of me. If the other lady wakes up she will be very angry and blame *me!* And it might not be safe to swim there alone. Colombo is full of thieves and bad men who might think, seeing you dressed like...not like an English lady..."

"We are surely not going to be troubled by any desperate characters in the gardens of Queen's House? I remember seeing uniformed guards everywhere when we arrived." Alexa's voice went from coaxing to teasingly mischievous. "Oh, *do* unbend for once, Menika! Have you never been tempted to do something forbidden? Isn't there any special friend that you sometimes slip out to meet? I'm sure you know how we can avoid running into any of the sentries, who are all probably asleep or playing cards at this hour anyway. And I'll go barefoot, and be very quiet, I promise you. Look, I'll even take my little pistol just in case we run into a snake—of any species! And I can use it too. I never miss.''

Caught between what Sir John Travers, who was a scholar, would have termed ''Scylla and Charybdis,'' poor Menika found herself left with no real choice after all. She could hardly let this unusual young Englishwoman try to find the tiny natural inlet known as the Governor's pool by herself, for if she got lost or something happened to her, she, Menika, would be blamed for everything. But on the other hand, *this* young Englishwoman wore the costume of the people without a trace of awkwardness, and she had just proved by the swiftness and ease with which she had loaded her pistol that she was quite familiar with such weapons, *this* one now carefully hidden in the folds of a lace shawl.

If I do as she wishes perhaps it will not turn out badly after all, Menika thought consideringly. After all, she acts as if she can take care of herself as well as any man, and there is no soft fat on her body. Perhaps, once her wish is gratified she will grow bored and want to return. And besides, hadn't she actually *asked* her politely instead of *ordering?*

Sensing surrender, Alexa smiled at Menika, impatiently running fingers through the heavy mass of her hair before twisting it into a knot at the nape of her neck.

''Come, let's go quickly on this adventure, and I promise not to take too long. And as for my aunt, I know she'll sleep soundly until morning. She's probably taken one of her headache powders as she usually does when she is tired and wants to sleep without interruption.''

Resigning herself, Menika bowed her head. ''If you are determined, then it would be better, I suppose, if I took you by the easiest and safest way. There is a back staircase that is used only by servants, and it is very narrow—you will have to watch your footing. And there is a secret path. I have never used it myself, but my mother who has worked here for many, many years showed it to me once. There are no guards posted along that path or about the bathing pool either. A previous Governor gave the order...'' Menika's eyes darted to the face of her unlikely companion, and detecting no shock but only a lively curiosity, went on in a soft voice: ''He was a man who, like most men, enjoyed women. Others, beside his wife.'' Speaking in her native tongue instead of the pidgin English she had acquired, Menika seemed much more at ease. Now she said hastily, ''But please, from this moment we must be very quiet. There are guards close by.''

Hurrying along on bare feet over dew-damp grass, feeling and relishing with a mounting sense of exhilaration the freedom from the restriction of layer upon layer of heavy clothing, Alexa wanted to laugh out loud. With Menika leading the way they slipped between tall hedges that shut out most of the moonlight, following a path that was almost completely grassed over so that it was now a mere track. An owl hooted from somewhere close by, and the fragrance of flowers lingered in the air. Some people would have called this a romantic night, but to Alexa it was only another example of the beauty of nature itself. And now, sensing the nearness of the ocean, she began to long for the feel of silky-cool water against her skin...to be floating on her back while she watched the moon float above her, and feeling herself rocked gently by the motion of the never-still sea.

''The...the cry of the owl...it is supposed to be a bad omen!'' Menika was obviously nervous.

''Nonsense!'' Alexa said as bracingly as Harriet might have done. ''The owl is only awake at night. Does the twittering of birds in the daytime alarm you? There is nothing frightening or mysterious about the night; it is merely a time when the sun is shining on the other side of our world...when the sun is *resting,*" Alexa quickly amended, catching the puzzled look Menika threw over her shoulder.

"I had never thought about it that way," the girl said with a note of surprise in her low voice. And then she broke off suddenly to point ahead. "That is the place. It was not made by any person, but by the sea itself, slipping through that narrow opening there to form a protected bathing place. But the former Governor I told you about had rough steps cut into the rocks. See? On this side. The pool, however, is quite deep, so I have heard."

"How beautiful! And especially under the moon! Don't you want to come in too? I could teach you how to float if you'd trust me."

"No...no!" Menika stepped backward apprehensively. "I cannot swim, and I would not dare try the water. It frightens me. Please, perhaps we should return to the house? The water looks so black where the moon does not touch it, and it keeps moving as if it was breathing..."

"Well, *I'm* going in, and this is probably the last opportunity I will have to swim out in the open—under the sky—without all the hampering clothes I shall be expected to wear all the time now, I expect. Oh, how I hate clothes, and everything they represent! Repression—hyprocrisy—sham!" Alexa was talking to herself, almost, as she removed the skimpy bodice and tossed it aside before undoing the carelessly tied knot that held her improvised "skirt" about her hips. She stood there in the moonlight like a naked Greek goddess carved out of marble, stretching her arms out wide over her head with an almost primitive sense of ecstasy she did not quite understand herself as she paid homage to the moon and to the ocean—both female like herself. And then she said carelessly, "Are you sure it's deep?" and dived in without waiting for a reply, her body cleaving through black and silver with hardly any splash at all—coming up for air with her hair dripping and hanging heavily down her back; the reflected shine of the moon gleaming off her wet skin as well.

"Ohh! It's wonderful! And actually quite warm too. Do join me, Menika. Be daring just this once! I can swim and I promise to look after you." But the girl only shook her head, backing off as she glanced nervously behind her.

"Please, if you do not mind I will wait here for you and watch." There was no budging her for all Alexa's coaxing; and all she would say, stubbornly, was, "I will wait, and guide you back when you are ready."

In the end, seeing Alexa begin to swim back and forth—sometimes diving under water like a fish and coming up some moments later to shake back her long, strangely colored hair—Menika decided resignedly that she might as well rest for a while, since she *was* tired and had hoped to snatch a few hours of sleep tonight. Retreating a short distance into the shadows thrown by the shrubbery that had been allowed to grow wild at this particular place, Menika leaned her back against a tree, tucking her feet under her. Oh, but she *was* tired! She had been awake since five in the morning and had been working ever since. Perhaps if she could just close her eyes for a few minutes…

Poor little thing, Alexa thought contritely as she came up for air, delighting in the salty tang and taste of the sea. Perhaps she should forgo her own selfish pleasure and go back for Menika's sake. But then, watching the riding lights of a ship that was anchored some distance away, beyond the coral reef that protected this part of Ceylon's coast from sharks and enormous breakers that could crush any unwary bathers, Alexa decided that she might just as well enjoy herself and the glorious feeling of freedom that bubbled in her veins. She had never done anything *this* daring before. Swimming stark naked in the Governor's private pool on a moonlit night. What if the Governor himself had the same idea? She had to resist the impulse to giggle at *that* thought. *Not* the Right Honorable James Alexander Stewart Mackenzie, most certainly! Balding, bespectacled and quite overshadowed by his wife, whose name he had adopted upon their marriage, he was hardly the kind of man who would dare to stray—and especially since he was devoutly religious as well. Or so Aunt Harriet had warned her, begging that Alexa should on no account enter into any kind of discussion on religion or *religions,* as the case may be.

Well, I did promise everyone that I was going to behave and be a credit to them all, Alexa reminded herself stoutly. But *that* is tomorrow, and tonight is mine alone…my last secret adventure, perhaps. Just for tonight I can be what I feel and what I am. Turning on her back, Alexa floated lazily again, letting the slight swell of the water rock her while she stared back at the silver face of the moon and let her thoughts wander as they pleased.

4

How gentle the ocean was tonight, with hardly a wave to break its smooth, swelling surface; and how bright the moon, splintered into a thousand, a million tiny silver fragments that danced along the gentle swells. A magical, enchanted night with the moon a fairy godmother who could turn every hidden, secret wish into reality for just a few precious hours. Alexa knew that Harriet would have frowned and told her that she should think *rationally.* Learn to be more *practical.* But how she hated that word! Ah, tonight was meant only for fantasy…was only a fantasy, perhaps, as she felt herself caught up in a silver-spangled web that transported her into a magical place where wishes came true and anything was possible if you closed your eyes and believed hard enough.

Almost mesmerized into believing she could disappear into the silver eye of the moon as she stared into it, Alexa found herself remembering the fairy tales that Mama used to read to her when she was very young and Freddy hadn't even been born yet. Stories of handsome Princes, and Princesses with long golden hair that could be let down castle walls. Of dragons that could spit fire, and tall giants and twisted gnomes. Enchanted forests and bramble bushes that could grow in the twinkling of an eye to shut in a sleeping beauty who could only be awakened from her slumbers by a kiss. "Stuff and nonsense!" Aunt Harry used to scold. "The child's head shouldn't be filled with fantasies and falsehoods that have nothing to do with real life!" But what was wrong with escaping from real life sometimes into the magic world of fantasy where anything was possible? To imagine herself the fairy princess held captive by the spell of the wicked magician—waiting, wrapped about in her silver-webbed sleep for the Prince who was destined to rescue her. Or a pagan sacrifice like Andromeda, waiting for her Perseus. Waiting, like a moon-silvered statue, for…it did not matter. She felt herself flow into the moon and felt the moon flow into her, and she *was* magic and part of the night itself that was the birthday gift of her fairy godmother. A gift of magic…

Still floating languidly, Alexa suddenly felt a different, almost agitated motion of the water beneath her. A sudden wave that had managed to force its way in through the tiny entrance to this miniature bay? A splash…? No, her own moon-fevered imagination. What had she expected, a sea monster? She should not have let herself stare so hard at the moon that she became altogether lost in the fantasies her imagination surrounded her with. There was no one, and nothing here but poor sleeping Menika and herself. Annoyed at herself, Alexa closed her eyes for an instant against the silver brightness that seemed reflected everywhere, and began to tread water while she pushed annoying strands of wet, clinging hair from her eyes. So much for fantasy!

And then, on the very heels of that particular thought Alexa almost felt her heart stop as she felt something touch her. Seaweed? Then the strangest sensation of having her skin stroked underwater, all the way up from her calves to the length of her thighs. Not a *shark?* No, only some large fish that had somehow managed to find its way in here through the narrow opening that separated this pleasant little pool from the sea beyond it? Suddenly frozen and losing all power of motion for some seconds Alexa felt herself sink under water, to come up gasping and spluttering and blinded momentarily again by her water-logged hair, which clung to her face and neck like choking strands of seaweed. Helplessly, and *unbelievingly,* she could feel herself being moved backward in the water until her back scraped uncomfortably against a rocky-surface—one of the ''steps'' hewn into the rock here on the land side of the pool. She was still quite incapable of speech, having accidentally allowed herself to swallow a considerable amount of salty water, and barely capable of thought either until she heard an unmistakably *human* voice that held an annoying undercurrent of amusement.

''Well, well! I seem to have caught myself a mermaid! Or is it a sea witch? One of old Neptune's wicked daughters?''

It was also, Alexa realized belatedly, unmistakably a pair of human hands that held her hard, and far too familiarly about the waist at this moment. And if only she was not still choking and coughing in a most unladylike way she would have used some of the barracks slang she had picked up from some of the young officers who sometimes forgot that she was a female. Oh damn, *damn,* she thought; why did her *damned* hair always have to get in the *bloody* way? How often she had longed to be able to crop it off! She shook her head fiercely, pushing heavy tangles back from her temples, and found herself looking into a face that was far too close to hers—a face she could hardly see, because the moon was at his back.

Alexa had not, until tonight, ever really believed in superstition or ancient legends; but now without her willing or her wanting, the sudden memory of her earlier fantasy thoughts raced through her mind. A *man* (and she knew instinctively that he was as naked as she was) who had risen out of the sea—or so it seemed. Had she managed, by some impossible accident, to conjure up some dark spirit from the ocean depths? Poseidon? No, Lucifer himself—no fairy prince! She could only see him as an outline against moon-bright sky and water…archetypal *man,* as pagan and primitive as the night itself. Alexa felt spellbound; and she had never known the meaning of that word until now. As if she too had been turned by a silver-tipped wand into someone else. As if, while she had lain floating on her back and offering herself to the moon she had suddenly had her offered sacrifice capriciously taken up and had lost herself. Even her voice, since her vocal cords seemed to have become frozen and immobilized like the rest of her senses as she stared into the darkness of a face she could not see.

"I never thought to wonder whether mermaids could speak or not…and perhaps it's better they don't. Is that why you're such temptresses?"

The man's voice was rough, because he had had time to study her face in the moonlight, and he did not like to admit, even to himself, the unwanted emotions it aroused in him. It was a *different* face, one which might indeed have belonged to some mythical creature, whether sea nymph or siren. Wet hair always looked dark, but hers seemed to have strange shimmers of light shot through its wet, curly masses wherever the moon happened to touch it. Well-defined dark brows were etched against the pale oval of her face; and her eyes? They reflected the moon in miniature, but were they black? Dark grey? He had the instinct that they would be, even in daylight, the kind of eyes no one could read.

He had spoken to her twice and she hadn't answered—had just continued to stare at him with those strange dark and silver witch-eyes. Was she only held transfixed by terror, or was it possible that she could not understand English? Perhaps she was the pretty Eurasian mistress of one of the English officers or the Governor himself; or a trespasser afraid to be found swimming in the Governor's private pool. Whoever she was he hadn't meant to scare the poor girl out of her wits when he'd navigated that little channel underwater. He'd meant to come to this place late tonight to swim in privacy, and then he'd seen her, hardly believing his own eyes. A naked pagan goddess under the moon, as open and unashamed of her nakedness as the women of Tahiti and the Sandwich Islands; women who had not yet had civilization trap them and change them from natural to artificial products of an unnatural society. Who was she? Ah, but did it really matter?

Almost unconsciously he had been looking at her parted lips, noticing that they were chiseled and well-shaped. Tempting lips. And so, without thinking, he bent his head and kissed them, acting purely out of instinct, his hands sliding up from her waist to her shoulders to bring her body closer against his. He wanted to taste and feel the texture of her lips, her mouth, to feel the pressure of her high, pointed breasts against his chest as they rose and fell like the sea itself with the motion of her breathing. He wanted much more than that, and his loins told him so; but he did not relish the thought of rape, and enjoyed seduction and the building up of desire that was mutual—the long, lazy enjoyment of lovemaking. So all he did for the moment was enjoy kissing his captive mermaid, who, as he had already discovered, possessed two long, sleek legs instead of a tail. And he kissed her gently at first, savoring the salt taste of her, the faint answering tremor he felt under his seeking mouth in the beginning and then under his hands. He could sense that she was like a shy, only half-tamed animal that might spring away in panic or begin to struggle desperately to escape if he moved too fast. But God, she had the sweetest, most temptingly perfect body in the world; and when at last her mouth yielded to him and her head fell back against his arm it was hard to remember patience.

And as for Alexa herself, she was still in a kind of trance. A dreamlike feeling of unreality had taken hold of her, while in the depths of her mind she wondered if, like some bold Greek maiden of ancient times who had dared challenge the gods, it was her fate to be held captive forever in the silver-webbed spell spun by the moon while strange sensations she had never experienced before chased themselves up and down her spine before spreading all through her body; making it feel unaccountably weak. She had never been, never *wanted* to be, kissed by a man, and yet it was happening and she was enjoying it! Even when she felt his hands caress her body, touching her everywhere like an exploration, it was as if the slightest brush of fingers over her skin explored her senses as well—evoking feelings she had not known existed within herself, making her feel breathless and no longer in control of anything that was happening to her.

She heard him whisper against her ear as his lips left her mouth and moved there on a trail of burning kisses, "I want you, sea witch. Silver moon maid. But you know that, don't you?"

He "wanted" her? What did he mean by that? Did he mean to carry her off with him somewhere into the depths of the sea or wherever he had come from? Who was he, what was he? And what was it she was supposed to know? With a concentrated effort that cost her almost all of the strength she had left in her, Alexa tore herself free and dived back into the water, swimming vigorously as she tried to gather her already scattered wits about her. Moon maid, he had called her. Moon mad was more like it! *Lunatic*...now she realized how the word had been coined.

When she came up for air, shaking wet hair away from her face, Alexa found him before her again. Without her knowing it, she was playing the coquette—going from the innocent playfulness of a moon child to deliberate teasing. The cynical side of the man's mind told him that she was playing a calculated game with him. Of course! Wasn't that what most women were taught from infancy? Sweet deception. Blow hot, and then cold. Tease and pretend while you played "catch me if you can"; a game guaranteed to drive a man to his knees. But the fact remained that she was here like a fantasy turned flesh and blood—a naked nymph whose shoulders gleamed like silver in the light of a sinking moon—and he was the mortal man who had come upon her by accident, overcome by desire for her, as she probably knew very well!

Alexa *still* could not make out his features too well, although she could at least see that he was dark-complexioned. And although his English had been impeccable, he had a slight accent she could not quite recognize. Was he a gentleman? But then, how could he take her for a lady? It suddenly occurred to her that in spite of all the books she had read on almost every subject under the sun and in so many different languages, there were still many things of which she remained ignorant. Like...well, how *did* one act if you found yourself alone with a strange man on a moonlit night and neither of you had any clothes on?

Irrepressibly, Alexa started to laugh, perhaps as much from nerves as from the awkwardness of the situation she found herself in. But *he* did not laugh with her. In fact his voice sounded as if he was gritting his teeth while he spoke.

"You find something laughable about this?"

"I'm nervous! I always laugh when I'm nervous. And none of this seems quite *real* yet..."

It was the feeling she had that his body was suddenly *poised*—for attack? Assault?—that made Alexa suddenly break off in mid-sentence and turn in panic to swim for the steps again. But as she had half-dreaded and half-anticipated he was there before her to bar her way to safety and security. Ridiculous! She, Alexa Howard, had never been cowardly enough to run away from danger, and of course she was *not* afraid! And yet, when she felt his arm go around her, she could not help the sudden tremor that ran up under her skin.

As if they were merely continuing a polite conversation he said casually, with his head bent to hers, "What is it, mermaid? What did you suddenly think of? And were you thinking or—calculating?"

"*Calculating?* And what do you mean by that?" Indignantly, Alexa tried to shrug off his arm as she added, "Not that it matters in the *least,* of course; except that you have intruded upon my privacy, and you..."

"Indeed?" His drawling voice made her hackles rise instinctively as he continued sarcastically: "But then, you see, *I* had counted upon having some privacy myself tonight, and I happen to know that you are not the Governor's wife nor the wife of the Lieutenant Governor either. In fact, I really cannot imagine you as the *wife* of any one of the very proper British gentlemen I've met, for that matter...having the courage to go out swimming under the moon without a stitch of clothing on! Which makes me wonder about you, sweet sea nymph..."

"Oh!" Alexa felt her face grow hot and was glad he could not know it. It was quite insufferable, as well as ungentlemanly of him to *mention* it, of course. Sitting one step lower than he was, she slid herself deeper into the water until her shoulders were safely covered; and hearing his soft, amused chuckle at her strategy, Alexa would dearly have loved to use her nails on him. But instead, controlling herself with an effort, she said stiffly: ''Since I happen to be a *guest* at Queen's House, I can only believe that *you* must be the trespasser here. And if you had any decency you would leave at once! In fact, I don't even think you are *English!* Where did you come from anyhow? I'm sure you have no rights to be here, and if you are wise you'll leave before...''

She did not quite like the sound of the short laugh that cut off her half-uttered threat as he said: ''Before...what? Would you call the sentries and let them see you as you are now? A guest at Queen's House? I had guessed you for some lucky man's light of love, not His Excellency the Governor's, for I don't think his wife would permit him such an indulgence; but perhaps one of his senior officers? Obviously one of the *older* ones, or you would not be out here by yourself to seek your solace from the moon and the sea, would you?''

Her volatile temper boiling to the surface at last, Alexa snapped cuttingly, ''By God! And now you've made it obvious that you are not only without manners but a depraved, degenerate...''

''You left out *pervert* and *libertine,*'' he pointed out in a casual tone of voice that took Alexa by surprise. And then he said savagely, almost beneath his breath, ''But if I'm no gentleman and all that you think I am, my little mermaid, then neither are you a lady! I think you're a flirt and a hypocrite.''

''That's not true!'' Alexa flared up.

''It isn't? Then why are you afraid to prove it, little liar? Or are you going to seek safety behind the convenient wall of convention and mortal sin?'' His voice, deceptively calm to begin with, had suddenly turned into an animal snarl that almost frightened her. But then, before she had time to think further, his arms captured her again; and he began to kiss her, sliding his body against and over hers until she was held trapped and helpless. And this time his kisses were not gentle as he cut off her half-formed protests by the pressure of his hard mouth over hers. They were demanding and almost savage, these kisses; and when she fought, almost by instinct, to free herself from the encroachment of his body over and against hers, it was only to discover that he was much stronger than she was—and in the end, and even more frighteningly, that her body did not, inexplicably, really *want* to escape.

He was touching her everywhere—*everywhere,* even though she wriggled and tried to twist and turn herself free. And nothing in her upbringing or her schooling, as unconventional as it was by the standards of the day, had prepared Alexa for the wild and almost overwhelming tumult of emotion and sensation that raced through every vein in her body and rendered all the rational, *practical* commands of her mind futile. She heard herself moan and felt the shudders that shook her whole body when he touched her in certain ways, despising herself with the one small detached part of her mind that remained sane and actually relishing all the new sensations that had suddenly begun to erupt in her with all the force of a volcano. What was happening to her? What did it mean? How could she *let* it happen, this feeling of senses taking over from mind and reason until thought was only a vague pinprick?

Caught and trapped in a daze of unfamiliar emotions and feelings, Alexa was only half-aware of leaving the softly undulating coolness of water for the wetness of dew-damp grass. They had climbed the steps, still holding on to each other, and had almost fallen down together soon after.

The moon had slipped even lower in the blue-black sky, moving inexorably towards the horizon that was defined by the dark line of the Indian Ocean. Silver reflections still danced and shimmered off the surface of the pool they had just left and the sea beyond it; and Alexa could still see the twinkling orange riding lights of the ship she had noticed earlier, anchored at Colombo Roadstead. She saw without really seeing because for the moment only *feeling* was uppermost in her.

The grass had not been cut for some time, and it felt scratchy and coarse against her skin. And with his hands roving over her body—seeming to know, diabolically, just where to linger—Alexa found her breath first coming faster and then catching in her throat as she began to wonder helplessly what she was doing lying here with a stranger and allowing him to take such liberties with her. Harriet had never warned her about *this*—no one had! He was lying on his side with his body touching hers along its length; and when his fingers began to play teasingly with her breasts—making taut, aching points of her nipples before he bent his dark, wet head to kiss each one in turn—she wondered why she did not seem to have the strength to roll her body away from his and thought that she must have been made mad by the moon. Because she was suddenly frightened by so many strange feelings inside herself that she did not understand—this sensation of being swept away on a surging tide she could not control, making her body ache and tingle and want...? That was what *he* had said before. Want *what?* She was afraid—of *him* and of everything he was making her feel in spite of herself.

"No!" Alexa heard herself moan softly in protest. "No...no more...*please* stop!"

"And why is it that women always cry 'no' when they really mean 'yes'?" He reared himself up on one elbow to look down at her, and the meaning of his caustically uttered words acted like a glass of ice-cold water thrown in her face.

With a catlike swiftness that took him by surprise Alexa twisted away and sat back on her haunches as she glared down at him. "I suggest that you go find these women you are so familiar with who say no when they mean yes and do as you please with *them!* But as for me, I detest that insufferably superior attitude of yours, and you can..."

By now he had sat up too; and unfairly, she still could not read his shadowed face as he held her wrists for a moment and said: "Listen, moon maid...mermaid...witch...whatever you are. Why should we waste time on questions or arguments on a night like this? We're strangers brought together by Fate and we'll probably never meet again. But why not make the most of the present? I could not fall asleep tonight, for some reason, and so I decided to swim out here and try out the Governor's pool, and I found you. And I want very much to make love to you, moon maid. Right here and right now."

His hand reached out to touch her face, and Alexa flinched away nervously, never wanting to lose herself again under the touch of a stranger's hands. Within an hour's time he had used her far too familiarly and had turned her into a shameless wanton—a bold, reckless hussy. Her hair lay in tangled, sea-wet curls about her face and shoulders, and although she could not know it, the way in which she stared at him in startled silence reminded the man of a frightened doe—and was unaccountably annoying to him. *Now* what was she playing at? She had yielded, teased coquettishly and then yielded again before this latest display of temperament. How dare she suddenly glare at him as if he had mortally insulted her?

"For Christ's sake! What is the matter with you now? Or is it that you dislike plain speaking? Should I have seduced you *without* words instead? When I first saw you, swimming naked under the moon so naturally, I had the feeling that you might be different. Why must you suddenly insist on playing a game of charades?''

Each contemptuous word was like a stone that had been flung at her, sinking into vulnerable, sensitive flesh. He thought...but of course he *would* think the worst, and no wonder. She had allowed him to think, all this time, that she was one more of the quick, easy conquests he was no doubt used to. How humiliating the thought was!

Almost unconsciously, Alexa's small white teeth had begun to worry her lower lip, and her eyes had narrowed dangerously—both signs that would have made her Aunt Harriet watchful and that made *him* aware intuitively that he had said something to make her as furious as a spitting cat, suddenly. He watched her warily now, outwardly relaxed but half-expecting her to leap at him like the wild creature she had begun to remind him of at this moment, when only seconds before he could have sworn she was one of the few women who might appreciate honesty and openness in place of flattery and guile.

Breaking the tensely-stretched silence between them, he said quietly, ''I have the impression that I've said something to make you angry, even if I did not mean to do so. What was it?''

Instead of mollifying her, his speech only seemed to make her even more angry, her lips drawing back from her gritted teeth as if she belonged, in fact, in the depths of some primeval forest—an animal as wild and as untamed as every other that lurked there.

''Why should your 'plain speaking' make me angry? Or your 'seduction without words'? I wish you could repeat your speech so that I could learn it by heart! Is it one of your favorite gambits when you think you are dealing with some gullible female?''

Oh, hell! he thought disgustedly, all the more annoyed

at himself for letting the advantage slip so easily into her grasp. He should have been more cautious, more careful with her; and most of all he would have liked to act the brutal savage and snatch her into his arms without thinking about seduction, wrestling her into submission while he kept kissing her into silence and caressed that magnificently long-limbed body of hers that gleamed like polished marble in the moonlight. Making her as wild with desire as *he* was, although he had sensed instinctively by now that it was too late for that. Damn!

"Do you make up a new speech for every occasion that arises?" Her overly honeyed voice cut through his thoughts, and he gave her a considering kind of look that made her scramble to her feet rather too hastily to match the air of cool, detached dignity she belatedly tried to portray. "Not that it matters.... It's time I returned before I'm missed...." And where was Menika? She had been sleeping (supposedly) right *there* in the shadow of the tall hedge. Where had she gone? How much had she witnessed?

"Are you sure you don't need an escort? A beautiful young woman can never be certain what kind of depraved monster she might run across on a night like this!"

"Thank you, if that was meant to be an offer; but I have a pistol," Alexa said coldly. "And I am accounted an excellent shot by everyone who knows me. On the last hunt we were on *I* bagged the most game...." She wished that he would not watch her so intently as she attempted to knot the camboy around her waist while holding the pistol she'd grabbed up hastily from the folds of her discarded shawl in one hand. And fastening up tiny buttons across her breasts proved even more difficult under his interested survey.

"If you need any help I should be glad to oblige

you...*without* any more attempts on your virtue I assure you. Pistols have always made me cautious.''

''I don't need *anything* from you!'' Alexa snapped waspishly, wishing he would not lie there so casually, as if he felt quite at home, and watch her in a suddenly detached fashion. And damn and double damn! The silly little buttons on her bodice wouldn't fasten easily, and holding the pistol made it even more awkward. In fact, she had almost fired it accidentally a minute ago while trying to get one arm at a time into the short, tight sleeves. He *could* have tried to make a grab for it if he had really wanted to, she supposed resentfully, but quite clearly he had already decided she wasn't worth either the effort or the risk. Forgetting herself, Alexa swore under her breath—one of the very *worst* oaths she had overheard.

''Are you sure you don't need help? Or an escort? Unless, of course, you happen to have a jealous husband or lover waiting for you...?''

''That's enough out of you!'' Alexa said furiously, leveling her pistol at him, and angry enough to fire it too. ''What I do and where I go is none of your business; and since you are an obvious trespasser, why don't you go back to wherever you came from?''

''I suppose I might as well, since you are so plainly capable of looking after yourself.'' His drawling voice sounded almost indifferent as he came easily to his feet without any signs of embarrassment and stretched, making Alexa remember guiltily a picture she had once seen—a painting of a naked man that Uncle John had told her was a reproduction of a sculpture by Michelangelo. There were the muscles rippling under smooth skin, the width of shoulders narrowing down to the hips. And she remembered unwillingly and far too well the hardness she had felt pressing along her thighs. Although she had not been told too much about what Harriet termed ''certain unpleasant topics,'' she had lived for most of her life on a plantation, and the South Indian laborers were remarkably open and uninhibited about every facet of their lives. Since she understood their language she had heard many things she had not quite understood until now. Until tonight...

''Good night, sweet moonwitch. Or should I say good morning? You really should hurry back before they send a search party out for you.''

She would have dearly enjoyed the pleasure of shooting him if he had given her only the slightest provocation, Alexa thought. How dare he pretend to *tease* her in such a familiar fashion?

''Oh, go away! And I hope you drown!''

''You really *are* a vicious little bitch, aren't you? Well, don't worry, I'm a good swimmer, and my ship isn't as far away as she looks. Adios!''

She might have actually fired her pistol at him after that impudent speech and the crude expression he'd used to describe her; but his body was already cleaving the silver-black surface of the water by the time she thought of it, disappearing underneath it and staying under long enough to make her stand there irresolutely while she wondered if perhaps he'd dived into a place that was too shallow and was drowning...?

And then she heard a low whistle and saw him, well beyond the inlet now and out to sea, turning lazily onto his back for an instant to lift one arm in a mocking salute before he began to swim in earnest again, making for the distant-seeming ship whose lights she had noticed much earlier.

So he was nothing more than a common sailor, with a different woman in every port, no doubt! And thank God I am not likely to set eyes on him ever again, Alexa thought guiltily, not wanting to be reminded of her own weakness. It had been her fault for giving in to ridiculous flights of fancy, a willing victim caught in a moon-spun web of dreams. *Practical*—Aunt Harry was right, of course. Only children allowed themselves to play at games of make-believe.

In spite of all her self-castigation, Alexa could not help turning to look after him just once more—an unwilling glance over her shoulder. But the moon was dipping low over the horizon by now and turning to gold; and she could make out nothing at all against the pewtered surface of the sea.

As if she had been a wraith, Menika suddenly seemed to materialize from nowhere as Alexa turned back again.

"I waited here for the missy, where the light of the moon did not shine in my eyes and blind me. But please, we *must* hurry now!"

It was much wiser and much safer not to ask questions, Alexa supposed as she followed the girl silently. Not even of herself, perhaps; like wondering how she might be feeling now if she had yielded to the temptation of a devil moon and a man who had reminded her of Lucifer himself.

5

Both silent, each wrapped in her own thoughts, the two young women, who were so unlike each other except for being about the same age, were fortunate enough to regain the safety of Alexa's room without being discovered. Luckily for them the young soldiers who had the night watch were too busy fighting sleepiness at this hour of the morning to be as alert as they were supposed to be; and even more fortunately, Aunt Harry was still asleep and snoring lightly when Alexa finally went back to bed.

Alexa had already decided, very firmly, that *nothing* had happened. She had slept the night through, with Menika watching over her, and even if she had dreamed occasionally…well, dreams were nothing more than figments of a fevered imagination and had no significance at all.

After going down alone to an early breakfast, Harriet shook her head at finding her niece still asleep when she came back upstairs. Alexa's pillow was hugged to her and the rumpled sheet barely covered her hips. Really, Harriet thought exasperatedly, I *must* try and make Alexa understand that young ladies—any *lady* for that matter—do not go to bed quite naked. Alexa possessed at least four pretty nightgowns, none of which she had ever worn yet. What must the servants think?

Looking about the room, Harriet's observant eyes had noticed that there was fresh fruit and a fresh carafe of water placed by Alexa's bed, and that her rumpled traveling dress had been washed, starched and pressed already before being carefully laid across the back of a brocade-covered chair. Well, at least they were efficient here. And they ought to be, Harriet thought grimly; with more than a hundred servants running about, each trained to do but one particular task. Even at informal meals there was a servant stationed behind the chair of each guest, ready to spring forward if necessary. *She* thought it a ridiculous waste of government funds, but of course the governors of a British crown colony were supposed to keep up certain standards of style and elegance, and the ball tonight, she hoped, would prove an example of both.

Alexa stirred and mumbled in her sleep, burrowing her face against the pillow she hugged so fiercely. What a child she could be sometimes, while at others... But it was high time the girl woke up and took some nourishment. Why, her hair alone would require hours of careful detangling and brushing out before it was ready to be styled. Bending down, Harriet shook the sleeping girl's shoulder firmly.

"Alexa! Out of bed with you quickly, before they bring up the breakfast I ordered for you. Please have the good taste to wear a nightgown and that pretty wrapper your mama had made for you. And it's no use your pretending you're still too fast asleep to hear me, either. Up this instant, my girl!"

Recognizing, even in her drowsy state, a certain note in her aunt's voice that meant she would brook no more procrastination, Alexa sat up at last, still yawning and rubbing at her eyes. She had been dreaming of something quite pleasant, and now she could not remember what it was.

Why did she have to wake up so early? Sullenly, she found herself almost forced out of bed while Harriet moved her this way and that like a rag doll, scolding all the while.

"You know very well that too much sleep always spoils your disposition! Here, slip your arms into the sleeves, and I'll tie the sash for you since you seem incapable of making the slightest effort on your own. Mrs. Mackenzie offered me a personal maid to take care of you, but I had to refuse, of course, because of your immodest habit of walking around your room with nothing or hardly anything on. And you must understand, my dear, that even though we have allowed you a certain amount of freedom at *home,* other people will hardly understand or condone such pagan habits. Why, not even husbands and wives..." Harriet bit off her words sharply but not soon enough, for Alexa had thrown back her head and was regarding her curiously.

"Do you really mean that people who are *married* and have children, perhaps, do not see each other without their clothes on? Why, *I* think that not being naked and free together is the more barbarous custom. And..." But now it was Alexa's turn to cut short her indignant flow of words and blush as the one memory she had sworn to put completely out of her mind came back with startling, unpleasant clarity.

"I should *think* you'd have the grace to blush!" Harriet snorted. "And I certainly hope you will never dare attempt to air *those* views in polite company! I suppose it's because you spend too much time talking to those coolie women who walk around half-naked themselves. I should have gone along with your mother, and had your papa forbid you...but then..." Harriet suddenly sighed heavily. "I have never believed that females should be kept overly protected and *ignorant* either, and that is why I have been so free in my discussions with you and have allowed you to read certain books which although they are considered *literature* are also thought to be not fit for ladies to read."

"Aunt Harry, I..."

"I do hope, my dear Alexa, that I have not been wrong to bring you up in the way I did. You are eighteen today and still more than half-child, in some ways, but I always wanted your eyes to be *open* when you became a woman."

Alexa threw her arms around her aunt, hugging her fiercely. "Please don't, Aunt Harry! I'm so glad and so lucky that I was brought up by you as I have been, with my eyes open. And in spite of the silly tantrums I throw sometimes and the angry things I say, you must believe that I will never let you down; especially not in public. I feel so sorry for those poor women who know nothing at all beyond how to sketch or paint with watercolors or play a tune on the pianoforte, and cannot even carry on an intelligent conversation with men on politics or hunting or horses..."

At this Harriet had to repress a smile, although she said with her usual brusqueness: "Well, I do hope you will speak with a little less *frankness* than usual on the topic of horse breeding and refrain from joining in arguments that concern politics or religion. And now get on with you and wash your face with some cold water. Your eyes are quite puffy from oversleeping."

While Harriet bustled about the room Alexa's muffled voice came from behind the lacquered screen that hid the washstand with its china pitcher and basin. "I promise that I will be charming to everyone tonight, even the *bores,* and that I will be decorous and demure and seem helpless and even a little *silly,* since that is what's expected of a *proper* young lady." She emerged toweling her hair, with those strange slate-colored eyes of hers sparkling in a way that Harriet mistrusted. "In fact, do you think I will find a 'catch'? It might be an interesting experience to have a suitor, even if I might not decide to marry him in the end. But I suppose I really must learn how to be a *flirt,* even if it is only to find out if I can turn men into my *slaves* or not.''

''Alexandra!'' Harriet's voice carried a warning note, but Alexa only laughed, making a turban of her towel as she twisted before one of the full-length mirrors so that her silk skirts swirled about her long legs.

''Oh, but you must not worry that I shall do something to disgrace you. For since I have, thanks to you, dearest aunt, a passably good mind, I have decided to follow your advice and use my feminine wiles to the greatest advantage possible.'' She was studying herself in the mirror as she spoke, especially her face. She looked so different with all her hair tucked out of sight. Was it possible that she could ever pass as a man? And then, sighing, Alexa decided not, putting aside one more childhood ambition of hers.

''Well? Trying to decide if your face is your fortune?'' Despite her dry tone of voice, Harriet had come up to stand behind Alexa, watching, with a strange tug to her heart, the changing play of expression on the girl's face as she stared at herself.

''I suppose I'll never be a raging beauty, will I?'' Alexa said diffidently. ''Not one of the fashionable kind, anyway, with tiny rosebud mouths that simper instead of smile and faces like pink and white china dolls that don't show *feeling*...''

''Sometimes it's just as well *not* to show one's feelings too openly,'' Harriet said quietly, but Alexa was too caught up in her game of self-assessment to pay more than token attention.

''Oh, I think I know better than *that,* of course. But now you must please tell me *frankly* if my nose is too short—and too thin as well? And my eyebrows—how I wish they were more arched than *straight.* And...you see how they actually *slant* a little bit at the temples? But I suppose there is nothing very much I can do about all my *defects,* including the fact that dark eyes are hardly in fashion at the moment; unless I can manage to make myself *all the rage* by making every man think I am fascinating!''

''Well...'' Harriet cocked her head to one side, studying Alexa's eager face almost as critically as the girl herself had done, before she said judiciously: ''At least you have quite an *arresting* face, my dear, which *I* consider the next best thing to being thought fascinating. You have white, even teeth and an attractive smile when you *do* smile, as well as nice high cheekbones and unusual hair-coloring...and that is quite *enough,* I think, since I do not on any account want to turn your head.''

''Oh, you could never do *that,* but you have paid me the greatest compliment in the world by telling me that I have an *arresting* face. Do I *really?* Perhaps I need not feel quite so nervous now that you have told me that. And at least I do not freckle under the sun. But...''

''Enough!'' Harriet said sternly. ''I want you to sit down and eat *all* of your breakfast before it gets too cold; and at once! There's a lot to be done before we get you quite ready to be the belle of the ball tonight, my dear.''

''Belle of the ball'' indeed. For all of her surface bravado, Alexa could not help the feelings of uncertainty and something akin to fear that stayed with her, making her wish fervently to be anywhere else but *here,* on exhibition before scores of watching, curious, critical eyes. But she wasn't a *coward,* she told herself over and over again. And even if this ordeal seemed worse than facing a charging bull elephant, well, it would be *over* eventually, and until then all she had to do was to *act.* Pretend that she was someone else much older and much more experienced who was used to making slaves of men, that was all.

Pretend—an amusing game like ''charades.'' What role

would she play? Cinderella? Cleopatra? Diane de Poitiers? Or innocent Little Red Riding Hood? Her hands felt clammy as she stood in front of the mirror as rigid as a statue while Harriet gave orders to four chattering "sewing women" who had been summoned to make last minute alterations to her ball gown. It had taken at least two hours to subdue her unruly curls into a fashionably sleek coiffure—looped braids on either side of a prim middle-parting threaded with pearl encrusted gold ribbons—a matching "ferronière" around her forehead.

Faint strains of music drifted up through the open windows, and Alexa could not help whispering, "We are not *late,* are we?" while Harriet was still trying to decide on what jewelry she should wear. From the case she had brought along with her Harriet produced several items, now holding them against Alexa's bare throat and then discarding them.

"Not suitable...too opulent...*not* sapphires with a gold and white gown..." And then, irritably, "Of course we are not late! The musicians are merely tuning their instruments, that is all. As if I would allow you to be late!"

With a sigh of resignation Alexa returned to studying her mirrored image once more, hardly caring by now if she wore any jewelry or not, for the fairy-princess gown her dearest Uncle John had magically produced for her seemed more than enough to help her feel like an enchanted princess tonight. Arresting. Would they really think she was arresting? The very latest fashion in Europe, Uncle John had assured her with a twinkle in his bright blue eyes. And it had been especially created for her by the leading designer in Paris—all in white and gold—white silk overskirt delicately sprigged with gold fleur de lys opening at the point where her tightly fitting basque dipped into a vee to reveal shimmering cloth-of-gold—a gossamer-delicate fabric that Sir John had obtained in India.

Rows and rows of tiny ruffles all about the full skirts, which almost swept the floor, and matched those accenting a bateau neckline that left most of her shoulders bare while allowing her short, tight sleeves to barely peep out beneath. And there were knots of gold ribbon to further ornament her overskirt as well, and gold satin dancing slippers...

"Here! I think I've found just the right thing at last. This pretty and unusually designed gold necklace of your mother's that matches the bracelet she gave you on your seventeenth birthday. *Exactly* right. Alexa, you are not wearing your bracelet, and I know that I reminded you to do so just before we left. Surely you cannot have *lost* it, especially when you know how much it meant to your mama! Please try to think where you might have left it. I could have sworn I noticed you wearing it yesterday. Oh dear—this room is in such a state of *confusion*..."

Harriet, preoccupied and edgy, did not notice how white Alexa had suddenly become in spite of the red rose petals that had been vigorously rubbed along her cheekbones to give them a glow. Her bracelet! She *never* took it off, and she clearly remembered seeing it reflected in the moonlight before her whole night had been spoiled by something she'd much rather not remember. But *when* could it have fallen off?

"Well? For heaven's sake, *do* try to remember. It's almost time we should be downstairs to join the Governor and Mrs. Mackenzie when they begin to receive their guests."

Alexa found her voice with difficulty. "I *know* it is somewhere here, Aunt Harry. I think I took it off before I had my bath, and...but how can I remember *now?* I promise to find it later—I *know* I shall—but not *now* when I can hardly think and it is almost time..."

To her relief she heard her aunt snap: "Oh bother! I suppose you are right and we *do* have to hurry just now.

Here, let me tie this gold ribbon around your wrist to make do for the moment. And now turn around..." As Alexa moved automatically, almost like a puppet, Harriet contemplated her critically before saying, "Well, so you are finally ready, I suppose. Here, take your silk shawl just in case you might need it later—and do remember to hold your head *up!*"

There was nothing to be nervous of. She must remember what Sir John had told her earlier. Courage. Once you *faced* what you had thought of as an obstacle as squarely as you would face a challenge, it would never seem insurmountable. And yet, as Alexa descended the stairs with her aunt, everything about her seemed to have become hazy and unreal, like a blurred scene watched through a gauze curtain. Her skirts, with the starched and stiffened petticoats she had been made to wear underneath them, seemed heavy and cumbersomely wide as well as being *hot.* She held on to the polished wood banisters and saw, looking down, the flashes of gold made by her pretty dancing slippers.

"How lovely you look, my dear, and what a beautiful ball gown! They're all going to envy you; and you're *not* to mind, d'you hear?"

Alexa barely remembered to curtsy her thanks to the Governor's lady for her generous compliment.

"You look just as exquisitely beautiful as I knew you would when I first pictured you in this dress, Alexa." Sir John kissed her cold cheek lightly as he gave her icy hands a reassuring squeeze and whispered, "And remember, you have a mind that matches your beauty; so be sure of yourself, as you have every reason to be."

Alexa found that even helping to receive the seemingly endless number of guests that had been invited to the ball this evening did not make her feel awkward with Sir John standing next to her; and by the time they had all sat down to dinner she had already begun to feel a little more self-confident. Course followed course; but all she had to do was push the food around on her plate after she had taken a bite or so and then *that* particular course would soon be cleared away to make way for another.

As the guest of honor, Alexa found herself seated to the right of the Governor himself; but since Sir John was seated on *her* right, she managed quite comfortably. In fact, she found that the Right Honorable James Alexander Stewart Mackenzie was a *kind* man in addition to having fathered seven children (all away at school in England), which she felt made him all the more understanding. Not only that, but he was quite a scholar; being particularly learned in Latin and delighted at *her* knowledge of the language, as well as the literature of ancient Rome.

In time, Alexa's smiles became genuine instead of forced, so that her dimple showed. Studying her while she listened and laughed over some dry anecdote the Governor related, Sir John Travers reflected that it was in some ways a pity she did not realize how attractive she was—this child-woman he had watched grow up. Had she lived in Europe she could have become all the rage; but with a little more experience and polish, of course. There was the almost unique color of her hair, with its variety of shadings; and the startling contrast of those slate-dark eyes against a pale gold skin of the kind that welcomed the sun instead of having to hide from it. She had the supple, athletic figure of a young Amazon as well, and it was a pity that women's clothes these days were meant to disguise and conceal every natural curve and line of the feminine body. In fact, the thought that his little Alexa's free, bold spirit would some day be caged and confined by the stays and corsets of convention and what was supposed to be *fashionable* was almost intolerable. But perhaps he could do something about it? A challenge, that was what he needed at this point in his life, when all of the vast fortune he had accumulated over the years merely for the fun and adventure of it could not buy him health or happiness or an extension on life itself. A challenge…stimulation…a *rescue?* And why not? Ah yes, why not indeed?

"Uncle John? I've been chattering my head off for the past few minutes, practicing on you, as you said I should do. But you haven't heard a single word, have you? Did I sound too vapid and inane? Or just too *boring* to be worth your attention?"

Alexa's reproachful voice made Sir John chuckle as he patted her arm and said, "Not at all, my dear! Just had a lot on my mind, that's all; and some of my thoughts concerned *you,* as a matter of fact. But I see Mrs. Mackenzie giving the signal for all you ladies to retire; so we'll talk about it later, shall we?"

There was a rustling of long skirts and the scrape of chairs as all the ladies rose in concert to follow the Governor's wife; and Alexa, reluctantly, had no choice but to do likewise.

As they walked out Mrs. Mackenzie made a point of holding Alexa back for a few moments; her smile kind and almost conspiratorial.

"I just wanted to tell you, my dear, that you're doing very well indeed, and you mustn't let being thrown in with a crowd of women intimidate you. Makes me remember my own coming out ball, y'know! I was as nervous inside as *you* must be, but I didn't let them see it either. And—ah yes—what I really started out to say was that I don't want you to think there will be a lack of young men to dance with later on. The dinner was for the pillars of society here, if you know what I mean, but once the dancing begins I'm sure they'll flock around you like flies—all our eligible young officers and Civil Servants. And we're to have distinguished guests from at least two of the foreign ships anchored at Colombo Roadstead as well—at least one British title among them! We had some of them to dinner last night; a pity you were too tired to join us. But I see all the ladies watching us curiously, and the last thing I meant to do was to make you feel conspicuous. I only meant to tell you, my dear, that I *like* you because I can tell you've got spirit; and that I want you to enjoy yourself tonight. You're only young once, after all, and why not?''

Having delivered her speech in a rapid undertone, Mrs. Mackenzie swept a somewhat dazed Alexa ahead of her into the drawing room, where she found herself seated between the Governor's wife and a milky-faced blonde of about her age who was gowned in ruffles and flounces from her hem to her neck and down again to her elbow-length sleeves.

Charlotte Langford had attended an Academy for Young Ladies in England before her formidable mother had decided that it was time she found herself a suitable husband. And here in Ceylon, where there were not very many blond and blue-eyed young English girls to be seen, she could have her choice of the most eligible bachelors—as long as her mama approved, of course.

Her mama had very decided opinions on everything, and Charlotte had always been guided by her; but in the case of Miss Howard she had not been quite as forthright as she usually was.

''Now remember, Charlotte, that if you are introduced to her I will expect you to keep a detached and *Christian* viewpoint. You know what I mean?''

''Oh yes! Of course, Mama!''

''Good! And I am trusting, of course, in the way in which you have been brought up and the education you have received back home. It will disappoint me if you should show any signs of being *patronizing* towards a young woman who has *not* been fortunate enough to have gone back to England since her birth, poor child. And as for the kind of schooling she might have received, I have no idea of it. But if Sir John Travers is sponsoring her it must mean, I suppose, that at least she is presentable enough…''

''Yes, Mama. But I am afraid I do not quite understand if I am to make friends with Miss Howard or…or not.''

''Oh heavens, Charlotte! Don't you listen to anything I tell you? If she has been accepted by the Governor and his wife as well as Sir John, I see no reason why you should not make her *acquaintance* at least. And I'm sure that I can trust you not to…well, not to be influenced in any way your papa and I might not approve of; and to find out for yourself if Miss Howard might prove to be a suitable friend or not.''

''Oh *yes,* Mama!''

Charlotte had found out long ago that it made life much more pleasant to say ''yes'' to Mama. Even Papa did so, and he was a colonel and used to giving orders. But now that she was seated right next to Miss Howard, what would Mama expect her to *do?* The seemingly self-possessed and fashionably gowned young woman who had been able to carry on an animated conversation with Sir John Travers and Governor Mackenzie could surely not be the same person who, according to the gossip that filtered down from upcountry, went riding dressed like a man and hunted wild game in the company of the young officers stationed nearby her father's coffee plantation without the benefit of a chaperone? Used to her mama's close guidance in everything, Charlotte could not help but feel rather nervous at being left on her own, so to speak. She was not used to anything or anyone out of the ordinary and had no notion of how to deal with Miss Howard and keep her mama happy at the same time, although she had to admit to a certain degree of curiosity….

Suddenly, taking Charlotte quite aback, Alexa turned to her with a bright smile that Charlotte could not know was pasted on.

"I'm so sorry if I have appeared rude! But this is my first experience of such a formal gathering, and I have not yet discovered what is considered *correct* and what is not—so I hope you'll forgive me for introducing myself to you, since nobody else has troubled to do so. I am Alexandra Howard, and you...?"

Charlotte's mouth had dropped open with surprise at such an unexpected and unconventionally forthright approach, and she could not help but dart an almost desperately appealing look in her mama's direction before she managed to stammer: "I... Oh, I *do* hope you will not think... Since we are seated next to each other I should perhaps have made an effort.... I am Miss Langford, you see. Colonel Jack Langford is my father, and that is my mama across the room. I had been quite looking forward to making your acquaintance, Miss Howard, since we have all heard so much about you."

"Have you? What have you heard about me?" Under straight dark brows Alexa's storm-cloud eyes gazed with uncompromising directness into Charlotte Langford's reddening face, never wavering while Charlotte began to stammer awkwardly again, her cheeks looking positively blotchy by now.

"I hope you did not think I meant... All the young officers who have been transferred here from upcountry are always so full of admiration for your courage and...and *daring,* you see, and of how well you ride and *shoot...*"

"How nice of them to be so flattering!" Alexa said in a noncommittal voice, discovering nastily that Miss Langford had particularly ugly teeth that looked yellow, and watery blue eyes that kept dropping before hers. How she hated gossip and gossips!

* * *

"They are actually staying with Uncle John—in his guest house! He is a good friend of her papa's, Miss Langford informed me condescendingly. And I'm sorry, Aunt Harriet, but although I *did* manage to remain *polite,* I cannot like her. You should have noticed the way she kept glancing towards her mama for approval every second we were engaged in conversation; and in any case she *has* no intelligent conversation at all. All she does is quote her mama or pretend to pity me because *I* was never packed off to school in England as she was."

Alexa had for once been relieved to catch her aunt's imperative eyes and follow her dutifully upstairs to their rooms when Mrs. Mackenzie had kindly suggested that some of the ladies might wish to make use of some of the retiring rooms that had been set aside for them before the dancing began.

"You are going to appear fresh and sparkling when we go downstairs again, my dear," Harriet had said firmly. "Some more of that rose cologne on your wrists and temples perhaps, but not so much as to be overpowering of course. And perhaps some rose petals rubbed on your lips and just a slight touch of vaseline to give them a slight shine; although you must never tell your mother I suggested such a thing. And let's shake out your gown at the back…and yes, I noticed you were talking with the Langford girl—Charlotte, I think her name is. It might do you good to have a *female* friend of about your own age for a change, you know."

Although Alexa had forced herself to be still and allow Aunt Harriet and the two attendant servant women to do as they pleased with her ever since they had come upstairs, she had found it harder and harder to subdue the rebellious side of her nature that was already simmering under the politely simpering, naive surface she was supposed to present. And then her aunt's expressed opinion that she might do well to make a friend of Miss Langford had brought all her smouldering feelings of resentment tumbling out into passionate speech.

Her uncompromising brows drawn together in a dangerous scowl she was not even aware of, Alexa paused only long enough to take a long breath before continuing: "And what is more I could never even think of becoming friendly with anyone that *silly*—who is not capable of carrying on an intelligent conversation and thinks that *gossip* is a substitute. Why, I doubt that the poor creature has a thought in her head that wasn't put there by her mama!"

Harriet, realizing the danger signals belatedly, said sharply: "Alexandra! You'd better wipe that ugly look off your face before we go downstairs, my girl, or you'll be certain to give all the spiteful gossips such as Mrs. Langford the satisfaction of nodding their heads and repeating that you're obviously unused to being in polite society. And that would be a great pity for all of us who have faith in your strength of character, as well as for yourself, don't you think?"

Realizing that Aunt Harry had as usual managed to say exactly the right thing by subtly putting her on her honor while showing her a challenge at the same time, Alexa could only fall silent, gritting her teeth with the effort. Even if she could not make *friends* with Charlotte Langford or any of the other young women she might meet, she could and would show them that she, Alexa Howard, could play any role she chose to play and do much better than they could. Hadn't she promised herself that she would be a success tonight and make all the nasty old gossips eat their words?

With a sudden whirl of skirts Alexa turned about to face her aunt with her scowl replaced by a brilliant smile.

"Don't worry, Aunt Harriet. Tonight I promise I'll make

you all proud of me; and I won't lose my temper either, no matter how provoked I feel. And what's more I'll be polite to *everyone,* even those people I don't like; and I won't appear *too* intelligent for their liking either. In fact they're all going to end up saying what a well-brought-up young *lady* I am—you'll see!''

6

As she walked downstairs again with Aunt Harry's rather dour "Hmphh!" still in her ears, Alexa felt almost the same way she felt before putting her horse at a particularly difficult jump, or when she had to face a charging wild buffalo with blood in its eyes. "The only way to meet a challenge is head on," Uncle John had told her a long time ago; and remembering his words, she lifted her head defiantly. Tonight was hers, and she would make it so—no one else could.

She looks as regal and as self-possessed as a young queen, my little Alexa, Sir John Travers thought as he waited at the bottom of the marble stairway. And so lovely too, reminding him for one painful instant, as her hair caught the dancing candlelight of the chandelier above, of someone else.... And then, sternly pushing *that* unpleasant memory out of the way, he returned her rather tremulous smile and lifted her cold hand to his lips in a courtly, old-world gesture of gallantry that came almost automatically at this moment.

"Ah...I knew that if I was patient enough *I* would be lucky enough to have the privilege of escorting both you ladies into the ballroom, where I'm sure your arrival is eagerly awaited. My dear Alexa, Mrs. Mackenzie is quite taken with you—as I knew she would be. And she is waiting to introduce you to all the latest arrivals. You *will* save at least one dance for your old Uncle John, won't you though?''

Some of Alexa's newly found bravado deserted her as they walked into an already crowded room where all the chattering ceased for a second as curious eyes were turned on them. She was relieved that Sir John had asked her a question, and said in a slightly panicked half-whisper: ''I think I would like it above all things if I could dance as many dances as possible with you—and especially the first waltz—that is, of course if you are not already engaged to dance with someone important, like Mrs. Mackenzie, or...''

''But, my dear, don't you know that tonight *you* are the most important lady present? And I'm sure you'll have most of the young men here clamoring for the honor of a dance or even half a dance. Of course it would give me the greatest pleasure to have the first waltz with you; although I should not blame you in the least if you should change your mind, you know, and lose your heart to some dashing young blade between the lancers and a sprightly polka.''

''How *could* I? Most of the young men I've met are so *silly,* in any case, and I'd *much* rather have the chance of talking to you while we dance!''

They had come up to where the Governor and his wife were standing, and both ladies made their apologies, Harriet melting tactfully into the background soon afterwards with Sir John while Mrs. Mackenzie took Alexa's hand with a smile and said kindly: ''D'you think that *I* don't remember how much time it took me to primp when I was your age? But you're here now, and I'll let you have enough time to get your bearings before we begin with introductions again. And if there is not enough time to get to all of them, well, it will be quite proper for you to agree to dance with any of the young men who might ask you, providing they ask permission of your aunt or me first—and depending on whether you think you might enjoy dancing with them, of course. If you don't care to you can always make some excuse, you know. Tiredness or thirst or whatever excuse comes into your head first. I'm sure you'll soon learn exactly what to say. But come along with me now and remember that there's no need to be at all shy, because they're all quite dazzled by how lovely you are, my dear."

Mrs. Mackenzie's hair was arranged in a formidable headdress of peacock feathers and purple orchids, and following in her wake Alexa could not help feeling very much like a tiny rowboat being towed along by a majestic ship of the line. Then the Governor's lady stopped so suddenly that Alexa almost cannoned into her.

"Ah! And here is a gentleman you *must* meet, for his mother and I once attended the same school and his father was a friend of my late husband, Admiral Hood. May I present to you, Miss Howard, Charles Lawrence, Viscount Deering. You *are* a Viscount, aren't you, Charles? Of course. I thought that was one of your father's titles. Well, anyhow, *this* is Miss Alexandra Howard; and quite apart from being an uncommonly pretty girl she's an heiress as well. No need to blush, my dear, for Charles knows I've always called a spade a spade. Known him since he was on leading strings, which gives me the right to be familiar. Well, Charles? Lost your voice as well as your manners?"

Alexa had almost begun to get used to Mrs. Mackenzie's forthright manner of speech; but at this particular moment, feeling the eyes of the whole assembly watching, she could not prevent her cheeks from growing hot with embarrassment. In fact, it was only with a supreme effort that she managed to retain some semblance of composure; and obviously the young gentleman to whom she had just been presented was just as embarrassed as she was, for *his* face had also become flushed before he bent gallantly over her hand, lifting it to his lips.

"A pleasure, Miss Howard. I must confess that I had been looking forward to meeting you. Everyone here has been singing your praises."

"Oh please! That is flattering to be sure, but you must not embarrass me by saying such things."

Was that really *her* voice, responding so glibly with stock phrases? But during their brief exchange Alexa had been studying Lord Charles from behind the shield of her demurely lowered eyelashes; just as she knew very well that he was studying her.

He had chestnut-brown hair parted to one side, and a somewhat ruddy complexion. About four inches taller than she, he was slimly built and impeccably dressed by the right tailor, as even *she* could tell at a glance from the fit and cut of his clothes. And he was quite nice-looking—handsome, in fact—especially when he flashed her a conspiratorial smile that actually reached his amused brown eyes.

"Now that I have had the envied privilege of being presented to you, Miss Howard, I wonder if you would consider it too bold of me to importune you for the honor of a dance? I have to confess that I am hoping to be ahead of some of my shipmates who have been eagerly waiting for the guest of honor to arrive."

Was it proper for her to accede to his request so soon after they had met? Alexa's inquiring glance met with a smiling nod from the Governor's wife, and she was able to turn back with a smile of her own to the young man who waited for her reply and to say without any of the usual coyness he was used to encountering from most of the young women he met, "I'm sure I shall enjoy dancing with you—and especially since you are the first gentleman who has had the initiative to ask me for a dance."

She was quite enchanting, Lord Charles thought, as he said eagerly, "A waltz?"

He was rewarded by the sight of that tantalizing dimple of hers again and the flash of pretty white teeth. She seemed to hesitate for an instant before saying, "Oh yes! But not the *first* waltz though, for I've promised that to my adopted uncle."

"The second waltz then...?" When she gave a slight inclination of her head in assent, Lord Charles looked into her intriguingly shaded eyes and murmured fervently, "I shall count each second until then, Miss Howard!" To his own surprise he found that he had, for a change, actually meant what he had just said.

"Well! And now *that's* settled, Alexandra and I must be moving along. You young men of today take so long to come to the point! Can't understand it!"

Alexa caught a long, almost caressing look from Lord Charles that should have made her blush, but instead only made her feel quite elated. *Lord* Charles. A Viscount, no less. (*That* ought to please Aunt Harriet!) And he seemed very nice too, and quite taken with her. Suddenly Alexa felt positively *giddy* with a rising sense of power as she thought: Shall I try to make him fall in love with me? And what if he does? There's not much to *flirting,* really...it's like acting out a part in a play. And in a way it's such fun—finding out how easy it is after all to *manipulate* men, and finding out as well that they are not the omnipotent beings they *think* they are!

Alexa's eyes had begun to sparkle and her cheeks to glow; and even Harriet was surprised at this sudden transformation in her wayward, recalcitrant niece who had stormed and sulked earlier at being forced to take part in some ''silly charade'' as she had termed it then. *Now* this new Alexa Howard was surrounded by a bevy of eager young men who were almost to the point of quarreling with each other as they begged for dances—or for even half a dance. And how quickly she séemed to have learned and adopted the coy arts and mannerisms of a born coquette, too, Harriet reflected. Unless it was in her blood, passed down to her by her mother, Victorine, who had seemed always to have known how to make men fall in love with her and never cease craving her. Even now, and after so many years, wasn't her brother, Martin, still completely besotted by her? If Harriet had not made herself useful to Victorine, there was no doubt that her brother would have let her go out of his house and his life without qualm. A witch of sorts, Victorine had been, and perhaps still was. Some women seemed to have a power over men that was impossible to explain or to analyze. Helen of Troy...Cleopatra...Delilah...Madame Pompadour. And some of the most famous and sought-after courtesans, who could have anything they desired from their men except marriage. But why on earth were her thoughts suddenly taking such a strange direction when Alexa was only following her advice after all? Alexa was only eighteen and playing a make-believe game because she had promised to make everyone proud of her tonight. Tonight she was Cinderella at the ball, surrounded by would-be Princes, but tomorrow she would probably be back to her old self once more.

I should be pleased and happy! Harriet reprimanded herself as she noticed that while Alexa led a reel with the Governor himself the young Viscount had not taken his eyes off her for one moment. A Viscount—young and single into the bargain. And every mama there with a marriageable daughter was gritting her teeth, of course—particularly that detestable gossip, Mrs. Langford. Alexa herself looked happy, and as if she was thoroughly enjoying herself. There was absolutely no sensible reason, therefore, Harriet thought, for the strange feeling of anxiety—almost of foreboding—that stayed with her like an uncomfortable weight she could not shake off. No, she was being completely ridiculous!

"I suppose I do not need to ask if you are enjoying your first ball or not," Sir John Travers said, smiling down into his young partner's flushed and glowing face as they waltzed. "In fact, I can almost feel the jealously hostile looks that are aimed at my back this minute! Do you realize, my dear, that you have taken them all by storm? From now on you will have to make plans for every hour of your time; allotting just so many minutes to each different swain!"

"Never! Oh, Uncle John, *do* stop teasing, for you know me better than to think I would.... Why, most of them are far too silly to bother with; especially some I used to think of as my *friends,* who called me "Alex" and never bothered to act so *gallant* before. And now they are suddenly making calf's eyes at me and swearing that they have always been in love with me and acting as if—as if I had suddenly become someone quite *different* when it is *they* who have changed. Just because I am all dressed up like a lady for a change and have been playacting! One would think... But do you think it is because men too feel obliged to playact? Do they feel obliged to flirt and flatter merely to prove that they are masculine?"

Sir John expelled a slight sigh before he answered a trifle ruefully: "I am very much afraid so, my dear. Especially the young men—*most* young men, one must suppose—who are influenced by the example set by their elders or by superior officers. Pursuing an attractive young woman is looked upon, I'm ashamed to say, as another form of hunting; and the larger the field, the greater the challenge. Even courtship has developed into a form of ritual these days, with so many prescribed moves to be made—the correct things to say and do to which a woman is supposed to respond correctly also. It has become almost like learning the steps to the latest dance, and it is called 'polite etiquette'..."

"Oh," Alexa said thoughtfully before Sir John added hastily, not wishing to dampen her high spirits with philosophy at this time, "But that is not supposed to mean that a man may not be utterly sincere when he expresses his feelings. Men too have been known to fall madly in love at first sight, you know."

He had to admit to himself that Alexa's rather matter-of-fact response took him by surprise.

"Well, I think that anyone who professes to fall in love at first sight must be extremely silly. Why, some of the young men I've met tonight have only just met me, and know nothing of *me*—only this Cinderella creature they have glimpsed for the first time tonight. So perhaps what is termed "falling in love" is a ritual too? For how could anyone know what I am like, or what I think, and what kind of a *person* I really am? At least *you* know how hard I fight to get my own way, and what an abominable temper I have—because you know *me*—but *they* don't. And they don't really care about that either, do they? As long as I show myself to be what I am *expected* to be, I suppose, and don't show myself to be too intellectual or too *clever...!*"

Sir John's mouth quirked as he shook his head at her, but his eyes remained serious as he said quietly: "You mustn't become cynical too soon, Alexa, not before you've given yourself time to experience more of life and understand more of human emotion. Try to enjoy tonight for what it appears to be on the surface and for the learning experience it is proving to be; no more and no less for the moment at least. You're the most popular, the most sought-after, and the most envied young woman here tonight, you know. Why not savor it to the fullest extent? There's no need for haste, my dear."

Long after he had escorted Alexa back to her seat beside her Aunt Harriet, only to have her hand claimed almost immediately by an eager young captain of the Dragoons, Sir John Travers continued to watch her and to remember the first time he had set eyes on the skinny beanpole of a child she had been and the strange sense of affinity he'd felt for her even then. Her bare brown legs had been all scratched from thorns and the sharp leaves of mountain grass, but she had been defiantly riding bareback a wild pony she had actually tamed herself; and there had been an air of almost arrogant triumph about the little wild thing she had been even though she must have known the punishment she faced for having slit her dress up on both sides in order to ride astride. He had interceded for her that day and had introduced her to thoroughbreds and to saddles—but never a decorous side-saddle for Alex, who had always wished she had been born a male. Until *now,* perhaps, when she had suddenly discovered the feminine side of herself?

Under the crystal chandeliers Alexa's auburn hair with gold streaks interwoven in it shone like burnished bronze and drew almost every masculine eye, although she herself was not aware of it. Seating himself beside Harriet in the chair her niece had barely sat in all evening, Sir John became engaged in a low-voiced conversation with the older Miss Howard that had her shaking her head at first and then nodding it resignedly. He was right, of course, Harriet had to concede. Now that Alexa had been introduced to society and had proved a *success,* she needed to follow up that success by spending more time in Colombo, meeting more people.

Alexa had not failed to notice that Sir John and her aunt were engaged in what was obviously a deep conversation. At first she had thought Aunt Harry seemed doubtful about something, from the way she frowned and shook her head; but then she had begun to nod in a somewhat resigned fashion, which was unusual for *her* and had to mean that Uncle John had some exciting scheme in mind. When would she find out what it was? For it *had* to concern her, of course. Alexa could tell that much from the many times they glanced in her direction, and she was so full of curiosity that she was barely able to respond to the stilted conversation forced upon her by Captain McLeish. At least she had learned in a very short time that she was not really required to do anything more than *listen*—and to smile or lower her eyes occasionally while breathlessly murmuring innocuous words like "oh!" or "really?" or "please, do go on!" even if she was unutterably *bored* by every pompous word her partner uttered. Lies and pretense were the foundation of this new social world she found herself in, and honesty would only make an outsider of her. But how strange it was—and how paradoxical—to be brought up as a child to tell the *truth,* no matter what the cost, and to despise dishonesty and *cheating;* and then suddenly to be thrown into the adult world where those were the very things expected of you if you were to be considered "grown up"—and where everyone played at "Let's Pretend" and took it seriously.

After Captain McLeish had reluctantly escorted Alexa back to the seat Sir John had just vacated, she said as much to Harriet. "It is all like some tremendous *game,* isn't it? But once you learn the rules it is almost too easy, and hardly fun any longer—not if you can predict everyone else's moves and beat them at their own game! And every man I have danced with so far—except for Uncle John, of course—has been so predictable and so boring! It's as if they have all been cut from the same pattern.''

Harriet snorted her disgust. ''Hah! So you're bored and quite blasé already, are you, with the evening not even half-way through yet. My advice to you, miss, is to develop some humility for your own good, and not become too cock-a-hoop. 'Cut from the same pattern' indeed! And what, pray, if you should happen to come across some completely unpredictable man who does not fit into any prescribed pattern? There are men who are...well...*blackguards*—although I hate to use the word. Men who might come from the most exalted stations in life and might use all the right words and pay lip service to etiquette and convention; *and* be admired and well thought of by their colleagues and cronies too. You must remember that men will stand up for each other, and it's always a woman who is blamed if she makes a mistake.''

Alexa's eyes widened as Harriet pursed her lips over the euphemism she had just used, and then she shrugged impatiently and somewhat resentfully before saying: ''I am not so naive, I'm sure, that I will not be able to recognize a man who is a *blackguard,* if I should meet one. And even if I should, I am surely more than adequately chaperoned tonight, am I not? And thank goodness I am a little more sensible than most of the poor, simpering females here; so that I hardly think...''

''And how sensibly do you imagine you'd continue to think if you should ever imagine yourself to be in *love?*'' Harriet's voice, as she broke in abruptly, was caustic. ''Yes—in love. Madly and unreasonably in love with a man. Happy when he smiles at you and comes to call. Desperately miserable if he smiles at someone else or you do not see him for days. And *then?* No, don't shake your head at me in that decided fashion, my dear, for it could happen to *you* just as easily as it could to anyone else. And pray do not commit the dangerous error of imagining that you are the only female to be miraculously exempt from such a *sickness*—for that is what it can be like.''

Alexa's voice sounded almost startled as she said, ''Why, Aunt Harry...!'' And then, happening to catch Lord Charles's eyes for an instant, she was able to look back at her aunt with a brilliant smile before continuing: ''Believe me, you can be sure that there is not the slightest danger that I will ever fall in love. How foolish that would be—to become a willing slave to some silly, pompous man and have *my* happiness depend on *his* smiles or frowns—for all the world like a fawning hound. Never! You can be assured that you have taught me *that* much at least! I would much rather have it the other way around and make a man *my* slave—make him fall madly in love with me....'' Lord Charles had begun to make his way towards her in a purposeful manner, until he had been stopped by one of his friends, who had put a hand on his arm. But Alex had not failed to notice that he had watched her all this time and had not danced with any other woman but the Governor's wife so far.

Harriet, following the direction of Alexa's wandering eyes, sighed inwardly, although her dry voice betrayed none of her concern.

''All well and good, my girl, although I hope you will try not to make your ambitions and your intentions *too* obvious!'' In a milder tone she said, ''What *I* would wish for you is a husband who will understand you and indulge you as well as love you; and that he will be, hopefully, a man that you can respect and care for as well.''

''Oh yes, I've already decided that,'' Alexa said a trifle absently. ''If I decided to marry I would have to *like* him of course, or it would never do. And he must be enormously rich into the bargain—otherwise there would be no point in my marrying him at all!"

"Very sensible! But I do hope that when you make your final choice of a husband it will be after a period of time in which you can come to know each other. There's an old saying that 'a bird in the hand is worth two in the bush,' and that applies to men as well. Especially those, titled or not, who might only be visiting Colombo for a day or two at the most."

"A day or two? But plans can be changed, can they not? After all, there are always ships that drop anchor here on their way to England." And then, losing her attitude of confidence, Alexa suddenly stiffened and shot her aunt a dismayed look. "Oh! Oh dear, I had almost forgotten that *we* might not be staying in Colombo for more than a day or two!"

"Yes, I thought you might have overlooked that fact while you were so busy plotting and planning. You should have remembered that we were supposed to return home the day after tomorrow."

"Were?"

"Ah! So you caught that, did you? I thought you might, with that sharp mind of yours. Well, I suppose I might just as well tell you now before that poor man you sent off to fetch you a glass of punch returns." Harriet sent Alexa a silencing look before continuing. "Sir John was kind enough to suggest that you might find it enjoyable to spend a week or two in Colombo as a guest in his home. He thought that you might, in that period of time, have a better opportunity to—shall we say—*winnow* out those particular young men you might want to allow to continue dangling after you? Hrmph! All of them that *I've* noticed so far act like silly, moonsick calves, but I suppose that's neither here nor there. In any case, I don't suppose a short sojourn here would do any *harm;* and it might prove to be a useful experience—for *everyone* concerned,'' Harriet finished significantly.

But by then Alexa's eyes were already fired with excitement and anticipation. ''Oh, how I *do* love Uncle John, and how kind and understanding he is! Do you think I'll be asked to more balls and parties? And if I am, I don't think Papa would mind very much the expense of two or three more new gowns, do you? I'm sure there must be excellent tailors here in Colombo.... How long do you think we can stay?''

''Alexa!'' Harriet shook her head, stemming the flow of words. ''You must understand that it is quite out of the question for *me* to stay on here for longer than we had planned. Your mother will need me to see to the household while she is busy nursing Freddy, and your father will need assistance with those tiresome ledgers as usual. And there's no need for you to wear that martyr's look, because you know very well that it was *I* who took care of everything before you were old enough to recite your multiplication tables. No, it has been decided, and you are to stay. I will explain everything to your mama and papa and I am sure they will approve.''

''But...''

''If you are wondering if you are to be left without a chaperone, you may put *that* thought out of your head at once! As you know, the Langfords are presently occupying Sir John's guesthouse, and I'm quite certain that Mrs. Langford will prove more than adequate as both chaperone and mentor, while her daughter Charlotte...''

''Oh *no!* Not the *Langfords,* of all people! That thin-lipped dragon of a woman who kept looking me up and down as if she wished that she could find some positively dreadful fault in me so that she could gloat over it...and that mealy-mouthed daughter of hers with all the sly insinuations she makes in a sickly sweet voice while she watches me all the while to discover if her barbs have drawn blood...why, I remember saying to you only a short time ago that I could not possibly..."

Harriet said sharply: "Well, my dear, then you must remember what I said to you in reply. I can only tell you that if you wish to stay on in Colombo you will have to put up with the Langfords or you may choose to turn down Sir John's offer and return home with me instead. I daresay that in time you're bound to meet some nice young planter..."

Alexa had been worrying her lower lip with her small, white teeth while Harriet had been speaking, a sure sign that she was attempting to make up her mind. And now, when Harriet paused significantly, she said in a rather sullen voice, "But the *Langfords!* Why couldn't it have been anyone else?"

"Well, my dear, if you could take a completely *objective* view of the situation, you might be able to consider it a kind of *test,* perhaps?"

"A test? I cannot imagine..." Harriet met Alexa's rather suspicious look with a studiedly impatient shake of her head.

"Surely you're sensible enough to realize by now that not everyone you meet will like you or be likeable to you. And yet society and good manners demand that we must be polite and *not* allow ourselves to be goaded into losing our tempers, which only serves to give others the advantage over us. In other words, you might look on your stay in Colombo, if you choose to stay, as a test of your self-control, perhaps? And of your readiness to go out into a world of other people and survive its perils and pitfalls by being *clever* enough to use your intelligence instead of being swayed by mere emotion; but perhaps you don't feel yourself to be ready yet?"

Harriet saw the effect of her cunning speech as Alexa's

vividly expressive face seemed to harden; and behind the cover of her fan she leaned closer to the girl in order to drive her point home as she added in a low, and almost fierce voice: "You see, my dear Alexa—and you must see, must understand if you are to survive and still remain wholly your own person—the most important lesson of all is *control* over all the emotional weaknesses that mankind has been cursed with: rage, hate, blindly misplaced pity, and—obsession. Which is merely another and more descriptive term for the sorry state of 'being in love.' But if you have enough strength of character to resist giving in to such weakness, then you might achieve anything you wish to achieve because you will always retain the advantage!" Taking a deep, rather uneven breath, Harriet sat back again, composing her features into their normal, almost forbiddingly austere lines.

She had said too much to Alexa perhaps. Almost without volition she had opened up old wounds that were still far too tender and released, like oozing pus, too much bitterness. And yet Alexa, so young and lovely and full of the joy of living, had become over the years much more Harriet's child than Victorine's; and this was the time that Harriet hoped she had prepared her for—*armed* her for—the time when she would have to take her own first steps by herself into the world of her future. Whether Alexa would use what she had been taught—let her *mind* rather than her heart guide her—remained to be seen and was beyond Harriet's control now.

She heard a hard little voice that was scarcely recognizable as Alexa's say softly at her side, "Thank you, Aunt Harriet, for *reminding* me of everything. And now I am not even *afraid* any longer of anyone or of anything; so you must not continue to worry about how I shall get on. I shall do very well indeed!"

"Hah!" Harriet, with an effort, managed to sound like

her usual self. ''We'll have to see about that, shan't we? But for the moment I wish you would try to smile and show off your dimple, my dear, for I think I sense a collision, if not a confrontation, between two of your admirers. Here comes your Viscount with a determined look in his eye, and the Governor's junior aide with the glass of punch you requested some time ago. And don't look to *me* for help; I intend to sit back and observe for myself how well you manage to deal with such crises.''

7

Smile, Alexa, smile! And try to be, at least on the surface, exactly what they expect you to be—*want* you to be. An arresting face and a passable figure, with nothing *behind* the face to think or question. Don't, by all means, forget to show that dimple of yours men think so enchanting, and don't forget to flatter them—lords of the universe! Above all, never be foolish or daring enough to forget that you are, after all, only a poor silly, helpless, dependent female. Belonging to your father until you are *fortunate* enough to find a man who wants to marry you—and the property of your husband after that, like your fortune, should you possess one. For women were not supposed to have the brains to handle money, of course, and needed a strong, dictatorial male in their lives to guide and instruct them in every way! And once a woman passed from her papa's keeping into her husband's, she belonged to him in the same way as his horse or his favorite hound or any of his other possessions.

Disgusting. The mere thought was *degrading!* Alexa's teeth gritted for an instant under the cover of her bright smile and interested look. But—even if she could not change laws and customs, she reminded herself that she had been trained to *think;* and that gave her an advantage. Did the secret of the few powerful, successful women she had read about lie in finding a weak man? Alexa pondered that for a moment and then decided to let it be for now, although she meant to find out eventually. Aunt Harriet was right—she tended to be far too precipitate at times, a fault she must learn to beware of and curb. One step at a time—until she had had sufficient opportunity to study the people she met and could determine how best to deal with them. That was the best and the safest way to proceed.

"Miss Howard—excuse me, sir—but I believe this is *our* dance?"

"Oh, but of *course* it is. The second waltz. I had not *really* forgotten, of course, but Mr. Sutherland's account of his wonderfully interesting duties as aide to the Governor had me *so* fascinated that I did not even hear the musicians strike up, I'm afraid."

Alexa had managed to keep Lord Charles at her side for the past few minutes by explaining apologetically that Mr. Sutherland had been *so* kind and gallant—forgoing the dance she had promised to him in order to fetch her a glass of punch to assuage her thirst—but the glance she had given him from under quickly lowered lashes while she played with her small ivory fan was enough to make Lord Charles think that she would much rather have been engaged in conversation with *him,* although sheer politeness forced her to pretend to listen to the pompous and boring Mr. Sutherland. While Mr. Sutherland, on the other hand, felt that the interest Miss Howard had shown in his conversation, in spite of the fact that she had a Viscount standing behind her chair in attendance, was a sure indication of which gentleman she *really* preferred. Of course she had turned her head away occasionally to engage in some polite exchange of words with Lord Charles, but *that* only proved that she was mannerly as well as being well-bred.

As Alexa left on Lord Charles's arm to join the dancers after a softly murmured apology to *him,* Mr. Sutherland gazed after her with a fatuous smile that made Harriet want to snort explosively again as she thought what arrant fools men could be.

Viscount Deering wore a rather rueful smile as he looked down at his partner. "What a soft heart you have, to be sure! But I must confess that even I had to feel sorry for the poor, pompous young man."

"Yes, he is really *very* young, isn't he? Just a few years older than my younger brother, Frederick. I daresay poor Mr. Sutherland must miss his home and his mother."

"Well, I beg that you will not think about him any longer or my feelings will be quite crushed! Do you know, Miss Howard, that I have been counting every minute until this moment?"

"I think you're *flirting* with me, Lord Charles."

"I suppose I must confess that I was trying to. Do you mind very much?"

"No—I don't think so, really. Especially since you have been so honest about it. I wish..." She hesitated, but Charles, quite charmed, prompted her gently.

"And what is it that you wish, Miss Howard?"

"Well, to tell the truth—and I don't quite know why I should be saying this to you when we have only just met—I have often wished that people could always be honest and straightforward in their dealings with each other. Haven't *you?*"

Her unexpected question had taken him by surprise, and Lord Charles in his turn hesitated a few moments before he answered it.

"I suppose... Yes, to be truthful, I too have often wished that such a thing could be so. But since we live in a world with other people who do not think the same way and might mistake honesty for weakness or mere stupidity—what is one to do? But we are being far too serious, I think! Please, I wish that you would tell me more about yourself, Miss Howard. Where your home is; the things you enjoy doing…"

"I am afraid I have led a very sheltered life here in Ceylon, and I have never traveled abroad in all my life. But surely Mrs. Mackenzie must have told you everything she knows about me and about my background already? I'm afraid that a dull account of a very quiet life on a coffee plantation in a remote province far removed from Colombo can hardly interest *you;* especially since your life must be so different and so exciting in comparison. Have you traveled a great deal and had all kinds of strange adventures? Does life here seem very slow and backward to you in comparison to life in England and Europe? Oh—I do hope you don't mind my asking so many questions?"

Lord Charles, who was considered quite an eligible catch by London's matchmaking mamas and had been glad of an excuse to flee from them for a while, found himself frankly intrigued by this exceptional young woman who swung so lightly in his arms. Exceptional—yes, she was that, and more. A treasure he would never have expected to find here in this small crown colony of all places. Different—with a certain air of poised self-assurance that was lacking in most young women of her age and protected background. And spirited too; he had already sensed that under the ladylike exterior. He had owned a little mare once, whose glossy coat reminded him of Miss Alexandra Howard's hair. All docility and sugar-and-spice until, if her rider wasn't careful enough to keep a firm rein, she might suddenly decide she wanted her head. The resemblance was there too in the way this young woman held *her* head; in her slate-dark gypsy eyes, and the very slight flare of her delicately formed nostrils. She was a rare find indeed, and a real prize for any man lucky enough to take her before anyone else did—and tame her.

Lord Charles masked his thoughts with an engaging grin as he said: "What man could possibly mind talking about himself? Although I must warn you that once you get me started you might have to promise me the dance after this one and a few more afterwards as well—unless I succeed in boring you too quickly! And as for exciting adventures, I find myself forced to admit that I have not been fortunate enough yet... If you are really interested in hearing tales of that kind, you should ask my newly-discovered and very distant cousin whom I had traveled all the way to the North American continent to find, and finally did so in one of the former Spanish colonies there. I believe, though, they broke away from Spain and transferred their allegiance to Mexico several years ago. Am I confusing you?"

"No, at least not yet!" Alexa said with a shake of her head and a dimpled smile. "But you *have* succeeded in fascinating me, for I have always longed to find out more about the Americas."

"Well then...on condition that you promise to interrupt me as soon as I begin to bore you..." Lord Charles continued in the same light tone he had adopted earlier. "I hardly know where to begin, without sounding like a geography tutor, you know. But this ex-province of Spain is called California, and I found the style of living there different from anything I have experienced in Europe—or anywhere else, for that matter. It is a mixture of wildness and freedom and feudalism—a huge, vast land that has hardly been mapped yet; where the great landowners think nothing of owning hundreds and thousands of acres; can you imagine that? My cousin's father was a sea captain from Boston in the United States of America who happened to anchor in one of the California ports to trade for hides and tallow. There he met a pretty Spanish girl of gentle birth—an heiress, I believe—whose family was and still is ranked among the richest and most influential in that part of the world. Why, *I* was feted and entertained there in the most lavish and generous style imaginable! It's a lush and promising land with all the extremes of climate you could possibly imagine, from snow-capped mountains to burning desert and ocean. In fact, I might have been tempted to stay there myself except that there are also great, furious bears that stand tall enough to dwarf a man, and predatory mountain lions—not to mention fierce Indian tribes. Not being the kind to thrive on danger and adventure like my cousin, I must confess that I decided to settle for Europe and the tameness of civilization instead; and the only adventures I can relate, therefore, are secondhand. I hope I have not made you despise me!''

''Of course not!'' Alexa responded quickly. She flashed him a smile before saying lightly: ''I daresay adventures are all very well to read about and hear about, but to actually live in constant peril must be a very different thing and not what one could call exciting at all. I hope this distant cousin of yours lives in a *safe* part of California, for his sake.''

''Oh, I managed to persuade Nicholas to come to England with me, and you'll meet him later on, I'm sure. He's taking a promenade with the Governor and is involved in some deep discussion with him. But I should warn you, I suppose, that he is not an *easy* man to understand! He is somewhat of a cynic, and has a rather abrupt manner, besides being completely indifferent to what anyone may think of him. In fact, I can hardly wait to see what London society makes of him!'' Lord Charles gave a rather boyish chuckle before continuing: ''What a great lark *that* should be! Although you must not think he is some half-civilized colonial from my rather forbidding description, Miss Howard. Nicholas can adopt a polished air when he chooses to, and he has traveled in Europe before. But when we were in London together *this* time…'' Lord Charles broke off suddenly, realizing he had monopolized the entire conversation, and that the dance was almost over, before he could ask Miss Howard if she would be his partner for the light buffet supper that would be served later. ''I say, I really *am* sorry for going on and on,'' he exclaimed ruefully, and shook his head at Alexa with a smile. ''It must be *your* fault, Miss Howard, for being such a good listener.''

Miss Alexandra Howard, who, he learned, preferred to be called ''Alexa'' by her friends, had begun to interest Lord Charles more and more as the evening progressed. According to his mother's friend Mrs. Mackenzie, she was accounted an excellent shot and an accomplished horsewoman; and actually enjoyed reading books, in addition to being fluent in at least five languages. And yet, she was certainly no bluestocking either. So far, he had not managed to discover any flaws in her—a fact surprising in itself, the Viscount (who considered himself quite blasé when it came to women) could not help thinking.

Lord Charles did not have to pretend that he was delighted when Miss Howard accepted his escort for the brief intermission, during which a cold supper was served for the benefit of those who wished to avail themselves of the enormous variety of dishes arranged on long, damask-covered tables that had been set up against one wall. All the more so because he saw an opportunity at last to remove her from under the eagle eye of that forbidding-looking aunt of hers, and from the assiduous attentions of all the other men who flocked about her.

Small groupings of tables and chairs had been arranged on one of the wide, covered galleries that overlooked the lush gardens, with pretty colored lanterns hung everywhere to add to the beauty of the warm, perfumed night and create an atmosphere of intimacy as well. Softly treading servants dressed in the scarlet and white livery of Queen's House carried silver trays bearing tall-stemmed glasses filled with chilled champagne and white wine among the throng of guests, and it seemed as though no sooner was a glass drained than another was being proffered by one of the ever-present servants. Alexa had been allowed to drink an occasional glass of wine or dry sherry at home after she had passed her sixteenth birthday, but she had never taken a drink in public before, and now she wondered—did she *dare?* She had inspected the buffet because she thought Lord Charles, having missed dinner, might be hungry; but although the thought of food did not tempt her in the least, Alexa could not help looking quite longingly at the sparkling glasses of champagne that were constantly being offered to her. What if she were to take one?

As if he had read her thoughts Lord Charles said suddenly: "Have you ever tried champagne, Miss Howard? No? But then of course you *must*—especially on the occasion of your eighteenth birthday." Without waiting for a reply he took two glasses off one of the trays, his eyes twinkling down at Alexa as he lowered his voice to say: "And if you are worried that you might not be approved of, allow me to tell you that ladies in the very highest social circles in London—and all over Europe, for that matter—sip the bubbly, as it is called; and it is quite acceptable. You *could* say, if you were questioned, that you could not refuse to respond to the toast I proposed without appearing rude, couldn't you?" And then, teasingly, "Well, are you game? Please say you are."

Accepting the glass he handed her, Alexa could not help but laugh at the rather audacious way he had teased her into it. "And the toast, Lord Charles? Just in case I am asked?"

"The only toast that no loyal British subject could refuse, naturally. To the Queen—and her forthcoming marriage!"

A *lady* could not drain her glass off in one swallow, but she *could* take rather large sips once she had begun to acquire a taste for champagne, couldn't she?

"Do you think you like champagne?" Lord Charles had prompted after Alexa had taken a few sips of that first glass.

"I like its dryness! I remember reading one of Papa's books once that was all about wines and different vintages and where the best wines come from. It's the *effervescence*—all those little bubbles—that take getting used to at first, I suppose; although I daresay that with enough practice one would no longer notice."

By the time she had drained a second glass of champagne and found herself holding a third, Alexa wondered, with a sudden return to caution, how Lord Charles had managed to maneuver her out through the French doors and onto the gallery. She *must* be careful or she would spoil everything, and Aunt Harriet would be disgusted with her.

Alexa had turned to place her back against the polished wooden railing, and in her white and gold ball gown she seemed to be framed by the pattern of trees and lawns and a dark night sky studded with a profusion of glittering stars. How much Lord Charles wanted to seize her in his arms and kiss her, knowing that of course he did not dare try to do so, at least not yet. He must be careful not to startle her or scare her off; and there was that aunt of hers to be reckoned with as well.

There was an unaccustomed stammer in his voice when Lord Charles said: "There *is* a slight possibility…Miss Howard, I am very much aware of the fact that we have only known each other a few hours, and I am only too well aware of manners and *convention,* believe me. But I have so enjoyed conversing with you and, well, what I mean to say is that if our ship should happen to be delayed in Colombo for a few days, I would deem it an honor to be permitted to call on you. You did mention that you would be staying with Sir John Travers at his residence here, did you not? I would naturally request *his* permission first, and your aunt's as well; but if *you* would have no objections to our meeting again, I would like that above all things!''

''At least you had enough sense to come back inside before your absence could be remarked upon. It would never do, my girl, to let yourself become conspicuous!''

Harriet, fanning herself vigorously, had given Alexa a very thorough scrutiny when she had returned to sit demurely at her aunt's side again while the young Viscount took himself off to procure her a dish of fresh fruit and cream. At least, Harriet had thought then, she did not *look* as if she had been kissed; and her ball gown still looked uncrumpled and had no stains from food or drink upon it. She grumbled. ''But what on earth made you suddenly decide you were hungry at this late stage in the evening, just when the dancing is about to begin again?''

Alexa gave Harriet a mischievous smile. ''Two and a half glasses of champagne, I'm afraid! I really do not feel at all hungry after that enormous dinner; but I remember listening to the boys talk, and they all agreed that it was most unwise to drink on an empty stomach.'' Catching Harriet's expression she added quickly: ''Please don't think that I am in the least *intoxicated,* Aunt Harry, even if this *was* the first time I have tried champagne. I understand that it is quite *de rigueur* nowadays for ladies even in the highest circles, and that even the Queen does so occasionally. So you see there's no need for you to look at me that way or to scold; for I might just as well get used to it and learn to hold my liquor, as the boys up-country would say.''

''Hold your liquor indeed!'' Harriet snapped. ''And if you keep talking of those harebrained young officers you used to ride and hunt with as 'the boys' you could very well be misunderstood by someone who does not know you. *Champagne!* Nasty, fizzy stuff—I never did acquire a liking for it. Tell me the truth now, because I won't have you making a fool of yourself when the evening's gone so well until now. Do you feel at all dizzy? Does your face feel abnormally hot? You look quite flushed...''

''Oh *please,* Aunt Harriet!'' Alexa could not help the note of impatience in her voice. ''I *have* told you the truth; and you have been reminding me all evening that I am a grown-up young woman now and not a child. I do *not* feel dizzy and if my face appears flushed...'' She broke off when Harriet nudged her ankle with her foot; and looking up saw Lord Charles return, followed by two servants.

''Hah! I'd like to see you put away all *that,* my girl!'' Harriet whispered from behind her fan in a grim undertone. Her look was dour, for she would have liked to say much more to her headstrong niece on the subject of *drinking;* especially champagne, which was said to have a very insidious effect.

There appeared two small gilt-edged tables and a large silver platter holding every imaginable kind of fruit, together with pitchers of thick cream. But even as the servants began to arrange everything before her, Alexa's eyes had already gone beyond them and past the smile on Lord Charles's face to rivet, without reason, upon the man who walked at his side. She had thought the Viscount Deering tall, but *this* man was taller yet by at least four inches and had broader shoulders. His formal evening attire fitted him so closely that it had obviously been made for him—long, tightly fitting trousers (Aunt Harriet called them ''unmentionables'') that matched the black double-breasted jacket cut short in front to display a richly embroidered satin brocade waistcoat fashioned of varying shades of reds and golds and dark green; a strangely glowing dark green that seemed to match exactly his dark-lashed eyes. Animal eyes, Alexa thought inconsequentially. Like some she had seen glowing out at her from the dark in the sudden flare of a campfire. And there was something dangerous and almost barbaric about him that she could *sense* without quite understanding why or how at first: that sunbrowned face that was as dark as that of any native, with curly black sideburns sweeping down rakishly from temple to jawline and serving only to emphasize the harsh planes of his face. Even though he wore an air of easy assurance and civilization he was—in some strangely indefinable way—*different.* Like a primitive tribal warlord of ancient times who had chosen to masquerade in modern clothing; at least, for as long as it suited him.

Alexa discovered almost immediately that she did not *like* him, and that she especially hated the insolent way in which he looked her over without seeming to. She could almost *feel* his eyes on her mouth, her bosom, her… And now, unfortunately, she could not help the flush that colored her cheekbones while she thought angrily that the man was obviously a *cad,* and she was amazed that Lord Charles would associate with such a person.

It was all Alexa could do to keep up an appearance at least of being poised and unconcerned while the Viscount Deering proceeded to introduce her and her aunt to his several-times-removed cousin Nicholas. De la Guerra. Puzzlingly, a Spanish surname, although it was the *mother* who had been Spanish, according to Lord Charles. Not that it mattered to her—she only knew what her senses *felt* and wondered why her hands suddenly felt so cold and clammy, while she wished at the same time that he would walk away instead of continuing to *watch* her—for all the world like a leopard eying its prey.

"The Misses Howard live on a large coffee plantation in the central, mountainous part of Ceylon where it gets quite cool at certain times of the year, so I understand."

"But I suppose that Colombo, in spite of the heat and humidity, must have its compensations. Do you visit here often, Miss Howard?"

Suddenly, Alexa found herself clenching her hands under the folds of her skirt, her first stirrings of disquiet growing into ugly suspicion that kept expanding and expanding. His voice, with an edge of cynicism underlining each overtly polite word… She had the feeling she had heard it before. That… Oh, please God, no!

"No!" Alexa said the word aloud without meaning to, and far too abruptly, judging from the Viscount's rather startled glance. "That is—" she amended quickly "—we do not visit Colombo often at all. Do we, Aunt Harriet? *This* time it was only because… Of course it is so *kind* of the Governor and Mrs. Mackenzie…"

What on earth was wrong with the girl? Harriet thought irritably. She had behaved so well and with such poise all evening; and now, all of a sudden, she had begun to stutter like a schoolgirl. It had to be the champagne she had indulged in.

"We arrived only yesterday," Harriet interposed smoothly before Alexa could say another word. "And it is really such a long and tiring journey—especially since we had to be up well before dawn. My poor niece was so worn out by the time we arrived that I had to send her directly to bed."

"Why, *we* arrived only yesterday too!" Lord Charles exclaimed.

"However, since Colombo Roadstead is best approached in daylight we were forced to drop anchor some distance out to sea. Quite frustrating, in a way, since we were close enough to see the lights and even to make out which belonged to the Governor's mansion, with the aid of a glass. In fact, if either of you ladies had happened to be wakeful enough to take a moonlight stroll last night I am certain you would have noticed our riding lights.''

As she listened to that slightly drawling voice Alexa had begun to feel slightly nauseated. How...oh, but how unspeakably *low* and *vile* he was! He wanted her to know that he recognized her, of course. Like the predatory jungle feline he had reminded her of from the first, he wanted her to suffer the torture of anticipation while he continued to play his cruel game with her. Perhaps he hoped to see her crumble before him, losing her poise, her pride and her courage.

''I am afraid that both my niece and I must have been already sound asleep by the time the moon was up.'' Thank God for Aunt Harry! ''In fact Alexa slept so late into the day that she missed both breakfast and lunch before I decided to wake her,'' Harriet continued.

With a grateful smile for Lord Charles that excluded her tormentor, Alexa had begun to take tiny nibbles from the mountains of food that had been set before her. Fresh pineapple, mango and papaya topped with thick cream had always tasted delicious before; but now she hardly tasted anything at all; eating only because it saved her from having to engage in conversation or look in *his* direction. What a detestable, despicable man he was, this ''Cousin'' Nicholas that Lord Charles seemed to admire so much. It was quite apparent, for all his surface playacting, that he was by no means a gentleman and was obviously unused to dealings with *ladies.* A gentleman would have acted as if nothing had happened—and of course, thanks to *her,* nothing *had* taken place between them, Alexa reminded herself. She had sent him away, hadn't she? And had decided to forget everything that had happened last night, had quite succeeded in doing so, until now. Why didn't he go *away?* Or—a thought alarming enough to cause her heart to pound—what did he hope to achieve by playing cat-and-mouse with her?

"Is everything to your satisfaction, Miss Howard?"

Lifting her head, with a mixture of defiance and bravado arming her, Alexa managed to produce a brilliant smile for Lord Charles. "It was *exactly* what I had been craving all evening, and I *do* thank you for your kindness and consideration."

He sent her a relieved smile in return. She had been so silent for the past few minutes that he had begun to wonder uncomfortably whether she had been offended in some way, perhaps by his introducing his cousin without first requesting permission to do so. And then, of course, Nicholas tended to be rather *overwhelming* when one met him for the first time. Sheltered young ladies especially could not be used to the kind of man who disdained what he referred to as "silly parlor games"; usually with a dangerous glint in those strange eyes of his that boded no good. But on *this* occasion Nicholas had laughingly promised to either behave himself or take himself off as soon as he felt it a strain to do so. To sheathe his claws, in fact.

"You won't use that certain tone of voice on her, will you? She's quite young and has been very sheltered. Never even been home to England, so I understand, even though she was born there. And this is her first ball—celebrating her eighteenth birthday, Mrs. Mackenzie told me. She's really quite different, you know."

"My dear Charles! Why on earth should I take the trouble to—sink my claws in her, did you say? Into some guileless little thing who probably won't even recognize sarcasm if it's directed at her? Believe me, I don't bother to waste my time on giggling young innocents. I've lived long enough to discover that only *women* present a challenge worth taking up.''

Sometimes—perhaps most of the time—Charles didn't understand Nicholas at all, even though they had become companions and even friends of a sort. Different countries, vastly different backgrounds—for all that the same blood ran in their veins, and for all that Nicholas was well traveled and had been in Europe several times as well as to China. The *real* difference between them was that Charles was truly civilized—innately polite—whereas Nicholas was well mannered only when it suited him and did not feel himself bound in the least by either custom or convention. But tonight at least he seemed to be comparatively well behaved, Lord Charles noted with a feeling of relief. Why, he was actually being obliging enough to engage the *older* Miss Howard in quite an animated conversation, which was unusual for Nicholas.

Seizing his chance, Lord Charles asked in a low voice, ''Would you consider me too presumptuous if I were to beg for the honor of another dance? That is, if you have not already promised them all...''

Without really *wanting* to listen, Alexa had not been able to help overhearing some of the conversation between Aunt Harriet and Señor de la Guerra. Something to do with growing coffee and the way the berries had to be processed before they could be shipped. Hypocrite. *Viper!* What was he really up to?

Pushing her thoughts aside as decisively as she pushed away the gold-trimmed plate before her, Alexa decided to concentrate all of her attention upon Lord Charles while she ignored his so-called distant ''cousin.''

''Oh! And now you are going to think poorly of me, and my aunt will scold and say I have disgraced her; but do you know that I cannot *remember* if I promised this dance to anyone or not?''

How adorable she was, and how frank and open in contrast to the practiced debutantes he was used to who had been trained to keep careful tally. And of course she was probably quite overwhelmed by the attention *he* was paying her, the darling innocent that she was.

"If you do not see any man with a happily gloating look upon his face who is hurrying in this direction—*then?* After all, Miss Howard, no *real* gentleman would allow himself to be even a minute or two late in claiming his dance, and you would be quite within the bounds of propriety if you were to accept the offer of *another* gentleman under such circumstances."

"Are you teasing me or is it really permissible?" Alexa risked a hasty glance at her aunt who, surprisingly, seemed quite engrossed in whatever subject she was expounding upon. She should not agree to dance too many times with the same gentleman because it would only serve to make her appear *conspicuous*—how many times had Aunt Harriet told her so? And yet she *needed* to escape from the almost palpably physical presence of the man whose hard green eyes suddenly seemed in one flashing look to see right through her—through everything she wore to the warm flesh he had touched so intimately last night and with such sureness that he had, for a few moments, made her feel as if everything he was doing was both natural and right. Oh God! To think how close she had come to utter degradation!

"Word of honor, Miss Howard. There are some things I would never tease about, I assure you."

Alexa said hastily and almost mechanically as she sternly pushed aside her wild thoughts, "It is just that I would not want to be considered *fast* by everyone else, you understand."

"How could anyone possibly think such a thing of *you?* Miss Howard, I..." Lord Charles was forced to cut himself short when a rather breathless young man in military uniform came up at that moment to claim his dance, full of profuse apologies for his tardiness.

Unable to hide his disappointment, Charles was quite aware of his cousin's cat-eyed look; but he pretended to ignore it, even when Nicholas said lazily: "How difficult it must be to have to play chaperone, or *dueña* as we say in Spanish, to such an attractive young woman. I have two younger sisters myself, and my poor mother is forever worrying about them and nagging, which doesn't help. But perhaps customs here are not quite as strictly rigid? I have tried to persuade my mother that even well-brought-up young girls should be permitted a certain degree of freedom, so that they do not feel stifled by the restrictions that they are surrounded by—although to no avail so far, I must admit!"

When he shrugged, one could almost sense the ripple of muscles under skin beneath the closely fitting jacket he wore. And Harriet was immediately horrified at herself for even *thinking* such a thing. It had been more years than she cared to remember since she had noticed anything about a man beyond his manners, his clothes and his outward appearance. She must be on the verge of senility!

"Even in *this* remote part of the world we try to conform to what is proper and *safe* when it comes to the upbringing of a young lady," Harriet heard herself say rather stiltedly. "I have had the charge of my niece's education for the most part, and I think I have taught her what I consider most important of all—the difference between right and wrong. At any rate, she has seldom disappointed me so far."

"And *I* have heard nothing but the most flattering comments on both her appearance and her manners," Lord Charles interjected emphatically, deliberately ignoring his cousin's cynical look. Damn Nicholas and his infernal air of detachment anyway; and let *him* make his sly assignations with the kind of *experienced* woman he preferred. But as for himself, *he* preferred the challenge of innocence that was so rarely to be found—a girl who was untouched and natural and still on the threshold of womanhood, full of ideals and expectations. Like Alexandra Howard. Alexa, her aunt had called her. And although he could only say her name in his mind for the moment, he hoped that before long, when she had learned to trust him, she would grant him that right.

Taking the seat that Alexa had vacated, Charles set out to be charming to her aunt, sending a defiant glance in his cousin Nick's direction. After all, it wasn't as if Nicholas was his *guardian,* dammit, just because he happened to be a few years older, and "The Pater," as Charles usually called his father, the Earl of Atherton, had requested embarrassingly that Nicholas keep his son out of "any unsuitable entanglements." Well, Miss Howard could hardly be called "unsuitable," and in any case, at twenty-six years of age Lord Charles considered that he was wise enough in the ways of the world to be capable of managing his own affairs without interference from outsiders. Alexa... Why, he could easily fall quite madly in love with her! And there was no reason why he should not stay on here in Colombo longer and catch the next ship that sailed back home. With *her* to accompany him, perhaps. It was quite a titillating thought.

Rather belatedly, Charles noticed that his cousin was about to leave them, and was making his polite excuses to the older Miss Howard. Meeting the ironic look in those dark green eyes and a lifted black eyebrow, Charles put on his most pleasant smile as he murmured, "Are you deserting us, Nick?" How well he knew how his cousin hated that particular shortened form of his name. "Well, I think I will stay where I am and converse with Miss Howard, and hopefully win the honor of another dance with her lovely niece!''

''Oh, good heavens!'' Harriet snorted uncontrollably at that, drawing a quite *natural* grin from the dark-visaged Señor de la Guerra for the first time. ''I *must* say that I have never received such devoted attention before in all my life! It's enough, I vow, to make me wonder if it could possibly be true that women, like select wines, become more sought-after with age and maturity. Perhaps you will be able to enlighten me?'' And then, catching Lord Charles's rather dismayed expression, she laughed shortly and said more kindly: ''Ah, well! I'm afraid I'm one of those perfectly obnoxious old ladies who insist on sharpening their tongues occasionally at the expense of the young. And since I was never either an heiress or a beauty in my day, I was forced to fall back on my cleverness or my wit, neither of which ever brought me such marked attention as I have received *this* evening, though.''

''Then all I can say is that I pity the men of what you call *your* day who obviously had not the wit themselves to appreciate such a rare treasure as an alert and intelligent mind,'' Lord Charles said quickly, with the winning smile that never failed to charm all of his mother's friends. ''I have always thought it a shame that too many young women in *this* day and age are only capable of carrying on a conversation that consists of mere banalities.''

''Then I must say that you're different from most young men of today,'' Miss Harriet said after giving him a piercing look.

Lord Charles kept an attentive smile on his face while he settled back to listen to her expound on what was obviously one of her favorite topics. Nicholas had wandered away to seek his amusements elsewhere, and Charles could not help a feeling of relief at not being under the surveillance of that mocking and somehow skeptical gaze that always made him feel *young* and vaguely uncomfortable. Dammit, why should *he* become a cold-blooded cynic who trusted in nothing and no one just because Nicholas was that way? There was no fun to be found in picking everything to pieces, he felt, and life and its pleasures were meant to be enjoyed. Like the lovely Alexandra—Alexa—even while he continued to listen to her aunt with half his mind, Lord Charles had begun to picture *her* at his side, elegantly gowned and hung with jewels that would show off her beauty. How jewels would glow against the rich bronze of her hair, lie heavily about her slender neck, gleam at her ears. And she should wear bracelets about her wrists and above her elbows as well, to emphasize the slimness of her upper arms. Rings on her tapered fingers too. And how he would enjoy dressing her—taking her to the most elegant modistes in London and Paris for her gowns—and how much more he would adore undressing her! Naturally, she would be afraid and even overwhelmed to begin with, but he would teach her, gradually and gently, to overcome her fears, teach her to love him. All he needed was enough time to spend with her, and he meant to make sure of *that.*

8

Gala festivities in Colombo, since they occurred so seldom, usually lasted until the first mother-of-pearl shades of dawn pinked the sky defiantly and gradually faded the stars until they disappeared completely. Following a ball given on such a grand scale as this one, there would be a sumptuous breakfast served to all those who stayed on until the very end; even if the host and hostess had already retired to their beds.

Harriet had already warned her niece that *she* had no intention of keeping such *early* hours and that as soon as the Governor and his wife had begun to make their excuses, Alexa might take that as a signal that they should do so too. "And I'll tolerate *no* dillydallying and procrastination either, if you please, once I have announced that we too should retire. Also, I shall expect you in future to *refuse* champagne when it is offered to you and to ask for fruit punch or lemonade instead; for you may take my word for it that even if a young gentleman *does* offer you wine or champagne he expects you to refuse it. Self-restraint, my dear Alexa, is a lesson you might learn and find useful in the future."

"*Yes,* Aunt Harriet." Alexa's deliberately widened eyes

and false smile caused Harriet to award her a grudging, if somewhat sarcastic nod.

"Very good, my dear, although the smile *might* have appeared less artificial if you had remembered not to grit your teeth together at the same time. And just one more word of advice—you would do much better *not* to show yourself too eager to accept the attentions of any *one* particular gentleman and give him too much of your attention, even if he should court you with posies and pretty speeches. As far as men are concerned it's the thrill of pursuing the unattainable that keeps them interested; and an easy conquest is just as boring as a suggestion of uncertainty and competition is a challenge. For your own sake, you might remember what I have just told you."

She *had* danced at least four times with Lord Charles, Alexa thought resentfully, but it did not really *mean* anything significant beyond the fact that she found him interesting to talk to as well as attractive and understanding. She was sure *he* did not misunderstand or think her too easily available; so why should the fact that *other people* might think this or that be a matter of concern to her? Before Alexa could say anything in reply to her aunt's warning speech, however, she was approached by her next partner; an extremely bashful young man who had no conversation whatsoever, as she soon discovered. But that was *her* fault for feeling so flattered at being surrounded from the beginning by so many eager gentlemen begging for dances that she had recklessly promised almost all of them before realizing her own foolishness. The *next* time she would know better and would pick and choose; but perhaps… By the time she was being escorted back to her seat by her red-faced, perspiring partner, Alexa had begun to wonder thoughtfully if perhaps she *should* deliberately sit out a few dances. The *next* dance, maybe? Especially if it happened to be a polka and her partner an energetic military man. She must learn how to make excuses gracefully.... Beginning to fan herself in anticipation of announcing regretfully to her *next* prospective partner that she felt *so* overheated and could not possibly dance another step until she had managed to regain her breath, Alexa suddenly realized that her treacherous foot had started tapping in time to a lilting Strauss waltz. Her very favorite dance of all. And oh dear! Here was the Viscount Deering bowing before her again while he begged for the honor, if she had not already promised this waltz to some other more fortunate gentleman.

With an apologetic smile in the direction of the wooden-faced Miss Harriet Howard, Lord Charles explained that he was forced to leave the festivities earlier than he had anticipated in order to return to the ship to supervise the unloading of a few personal items too valuable to be trusted to anyone else; and *that* was why he dared to be bold enough to importune Miss Howard again so soon after their last dance. "Mrs. Mackenzie has been kind enough to invite me to stay *here* for as long as our ship will have to undergo repairs to the damage incurred during a particularly nasty storm we encountered last week; and my cousin has informed me that by tomorrow she will be positively crawling with workmen, so..."

Avoiding her aunt's eye, Alexa returned his almost pleading look with a smile that showed her dimple, and was actually about to extend her hand to him when he suddenly moved aside with a bow and a murmured apology. The *Governor* of all people! Alexa swallowed uncomfortably, thinking how close she had come to committing a *faux pas.* How *could* she had promised the fifth waltz to her host? Her Aunt Harriet would *never* have forgiven her!

"Well, young lady. Hope you didn't think I'd forgotten our dance, eh? Quite the belle of the ball, you've been, and I was almost afraid that some bold young buck might have been quicker than I.''

Perhaps it was in some ways just as well that Lord Charles should feel slightly thwarted, Alexa thought, remembering Harriet's lecturing. He would probably be all the more eager to meet her again; and after all, he *had* made it clear that he would be staying on in Colombo for a few more days at least.

His Excellency the Governor, Alexa rediscovered, was quite a Latin scholar and seemed to enjoy testing her vocabulary; but it was soon obvious that his waltzing was as stiff and jerky as his manner of speech. Poor man. He would probably have felt much more comfortable as an Oxford don rather than filling the post of Governor of a British crown colony. As he guided her through one or two turns about the room, Alexa tried to respond as best she could to the occasional questions he directed at her—rather as if she had been a student he was testing, she thought with rueful amusement. But at least he seemed pleased at her replies, and even went so far as to compliment her on her knowledge of Latin grammar and the extent of her *reading* in that language.

''I've often wished *my* daughters would take more of an interest in learning and reading, but my wife tells me that's not considered an essential part of a young female's education any longer. Pity! *They're* more interested in learning the latest dance steps—and in young men, of course! I suppose they think I'm an old fuddy-duddy, and perhaps I am in some ways, only I haven't *quite* forgotten how it felt to be young. And because *you're* young—and pretty into the bargain—I'm sure you must be wishing you were dancing this waltz with someone nearer your own age who can whirl you around until you are dizzy—am I not right? Well, even if you're too polite to admit it, I suppose I'm still young enough at heart to sympathize with the young, my dear. And so I have a surprise for you. Young fellow who arrived late and wasn't fortunate enough to beg a dance from you earlier. *Nice* chap, though, or I wouldn't do it. Spent an hour or more with him talking about gardens and different varieties of plants, and I could see right away he knows a lot. Gardening's one of my pet hobbies, you know. But anyhow, I'm sure *he* can lead you through a waltz much better than I can, at any rate; and when I asked my wife what she thought, she agreed there would be no harm in it, especially when the poor young man admitted he was quite bowled over the first moment he set eyes on you."

The Governor's sudden burst of speech at first puzzled and then quite confused Alexa, especially in view of the fact that when he concentrated on *speaking* he tended not to keep time to the music, which forced *her* in turn to have to concentrate on trying to keep up with his somewhat eccentric progress about the floor. And perhaps that was why she was so utterly unprepared for his "surprise"—feeling for some moments as if she had been stunned by a sudden blow that left her too dazed to speak or think coherently, even while her limbs continued to move quite mechanically in time with the music.

"I believe that you have already been formally introduced? Enjoy the rest of the dance!" Suddenly, she was no longer dancing with the Governor. He was surrendering her, with misguided gallantry, to another partner.

Alexa's heart had begun to pound so hard from a mixture of emotions she hadn't yet had the time to examine that she could hardly comprehend what had happened, at first; or how she suddenly found herself turning around and around like a porcelain ballerina poised atop a music box—dancing a waltz with *him.* The one man of all men that she had hoped never to encounter again.

It was only the hard pressure of his hand against the

small of her back that forced her to keep moving mechanically in time to the music. Alexa remained silent for such a length of time that it was *he* who had to speak first.

"I do assure you, Miss Howard, that there is no need for you to look up at me like a terrified little rabbit caught in a bear trap. What do you think I might do to you in the midst of this public assembly, ravish you? Wring that slender white neck, out of disappointment that I was not able to do so last night?" The silky-sarcastic tone of his voice deepened into what seemed almost a dangerous growl, for all its deceptive softness, before he continued more impatiently: "For God's sake, what's the matter with you? When I took pains to arrange to dance with you I thought I might see some show of *spirit*—or at least some *natural* and unstudied reaction that came from the free and half-wild creature of the elements I came upon by accident last night. *Then* you did not seem afraid to give way to your instincts and your feelings. Even that violent fit of rage when you wanted to shoot me with your little pistol was something real and unfeigned, at least. But tonight..." His eyes narrowed wickedly as his glance swept up and down the length of her body with deliberate, insulting slowness before he said softly: "Or is it only tight corsets and stays and too many layers of petticoats that restrict you? Would you like me to free you by removing every garment you are wearing one by one?"

Alexa discovered that she must have been holding her breath when she heard herself gasp as she released it, along with the pent-up fury that made her voice shake when she was finally able to address him.

"You...! How dare you presume to speak to me in such a fashion! Or to *force* yourself upon me by...by using deception and *trickery* on other people who are too honest and...and too *decent* to recognize how *depraved* you are? Any *gentleman* would never... I wish I *had* killed you! If

I had a pistol tonight I... Oh, I can assure you that I happen to be an excellent shot, *señor,* and I would *not* miss!''

''It has been *my* experience, moonwitch, that the best way to insure *not* missing is to keep a cool head, especially if you're in a tight spot. And perhaps I should advise you also that if you *do* allow yourself the luxury of losing your temper, you should really try to control the stutter you seem to develop when you do. To some people it might seem to point to a limited vocabulary, you know. That is, of course, if you worry about what other people might think of you! And there's another thing—when you keep your lips parted the way they are now, I should warn you that most men, even if they are *gentlemen,* would be sorely tempted to kiss you and might even imagine that you are inviting them to do so, especially when your cheeks wear such an adorable flush of what might even be attributed, if a man was conceited enough, to excitement.''

''Ohhh!''

''I'm sorry...there was something you wanted to say, Miss Howard?''

''You are the most *despicable,* the most *hateful*... You're... Oh, how I wish I knew the kind of words that would really describe what you are, you monster of depravity! If I had any kind of weapon I would kill you without a qualm!''

''I'm quite sure you would! But then, what would all these nice, decent people think of you? What kind of story could you make up for them without giving yourself away?'' He seemed to have become amused by her venomous outburst of rage; just as if she had been a little spitting kitten he could tease and play with and manipulate by stringing her on with his mocking, deliberately inciting words.

Belatedly recognizing his tactics, Alexa forced herself to take a deep breath before she said in a calmer voice:

"Very well. Since I have no pistol on me and you're really not worth the scandal it would cause if I were to kill you, do you think you're ready yet to come to the point and tell me why you have chosen to *bait* me? What is it you have in mind? If it's blackmail, I don't have any money of my own yet and no jewelry of anything but sentimental value; and that only to *me.*" And then, encouraged by his sudden silence into plucking up her courage, she said more strongly: "And in *any* case, no matter *what* nasty things you might choose to say about me I think, Señor de la Guerra, that people *here* would believe my word over yours; and especially since I will be able to prove, if I had to, that I have not…that I am still…"

How his voice could change! Now, as he interrupted her, it had become deceptively silken again. "Allow me please, Miss Howard, to save you the embarrassment of saying it aloud. You *were* struggling for exactly the *proper* words to make it clear that you're still a virgin? How admirable! Saving your—er—*virtue* for the lucky man who legally weds you, and then… But never mind. I suppose I should pay tribute to your strength of character, as you deserve. I humbly beg your pardon, chaste Diana, for having doubted your purity even for a wicked instant! And as a token of my repentance, I have a gift to offer you. A little trinket that you might be pleased to get back without having other people know where you lost it or how it happened to fall into my possession."

"I don't know *what* you can be hinting at *this* time, and what is more, I no longer give a *fig* for any of your sly threats and insinuations!" Alexa retorted hotly. "And if you do not take me back to my aunt this *instant…*"

"Before I return your pretty gold bracelet to you? Or haven't you missed it yet? I saw it gleaming on the bottom of the pool, speared by a stray moonbeam. That was after your dangerous-looking pistol had made me think better of continuing in my efforts to seduce you. And then, since I sometimes have an unfortunate tendency towards being rather sentimental, I decided to keep it as a souvenir of my encounter with a mermaid on a moonlit night. In fact, I have it with me now. But perhaps you don't particularly care if you have it back or not?''

In a low, choked voice, Alexa barely managed to articulate, ''You're…you're even lower than a…a snake…a viper! You're *vile!* And completely without scruples or…or *conscience,* aren't you? I wish…''

''Be careful of what you wish, or it might come true!'' The false smile he gave her was slightly twisted. ''I seem to have heard or read that somewhere, a long time ago. And I won't remind you of another old saying about finders being keepers if *you* will continue to…why, what a light dancer you are, Miss Howard. Such a pleasure to lead! And do you not agree that it is much cooler out here where we can see the stars and watch the moon as it begins to sink? You can always scream for help if I make an improper move, you know. And will it make you feel even safer if I promise not to make any attack on your cherished virginity?''

She did not feel at all safe out here alone with him on the gallery, Alexa discovered. Not even when he released her and pointedly stationed himself at least a foot away from her with his back to one of the gleaming white columns that helped support the roof of the gallery. He was a barbarian, that's what he was! Donning the outward guise of being civilized like a leopardskin cloak that could be thrown aside or worn again to suit his own ends.

''I don't…'' Her breathing quickened by anger and frustration, Alexa had to make an effort to steady her voice before she could continue scornfully, ''I suppose you will only feel *flattered* if I am forced to admit that since I have unfortunately learned that I cannot trust in any *gentlemanly* instincts you might possess, I... No! I do not feel any safer in your company, Señor de la Guerra, than I would if I should have found myself locked into a cage with a tiger! But at least with *animals* you know where they are—they are either hungry or they are not; whereas *you* have done your best to try and *frighten* me all evening long with your *hints* and your veiled threats, haven't you? But *why?* And to what end? You have practically forced me out here in order to reclaim a little gold bracelet of no great value that was my mother's before she gave it to me, and means much more to *her* than it ever could to me. *Why?* You must surely have realized by now that I am no match for you with your clever, sarcastic speeches that are meant to leave a sting and the way you have of manipulating people and circumstances to suit yourself. You must have known *that* all along! I cannot understand either you, or the motives for your calculated cruelty, or...''

Alexa had turned her face away to stare blindly out into the night while she delivered her furious little speech; and now suddenly she was utterly surprised when she felt him reach over to run one long finger lightly over her averted cheek.

''Poor, frightened little virgin! You don't really understand anything about life yet, do you? You're a product of your upbringing and your environment, I suppose, for all that you're daring enough to take a few risks now and then. What do you do about those certain emotions that run far deeper than the surface ones you're *supposed* to display? Have you ever wondered, poor little lost mermaid, about what *you* might really want or need; quite apart from what you have been told you *should* want? Did you imagine that you had committed some mortal sin merely because you enjoyed the way I touched your body and made you feel as if you wanted to experience even more? Is that the only reason why you hate and fear me so much now—

because I gave you the yearning for forbidden fruit? Damn you, sea witch! Will you *look* at me? For God's sake! Do you really, in your most secret heart, believe that what happened by chance between us—two strangers meeting naked on a moon-enchanted night—was not natural and normal, but something *bad* and *sinful?* Christ! Must the naked truth be constantly cloaked by evasions and euphemisms in order to satisfy the hypocrisy of *others?*''

Even while he exploded at her and goaded her, Nicholas could not help wondering, with some detached part of his mind, why he should take the trouble to do so. Whether she was actually a virgin or not, it was clear that she was inexperienced at least—and, as she had pointed out, no match for his cunningly thrown barbs. Damnation! She was barely *eighteen!*

But last night she had seemed ageless. Aphrodite rising from the sea. Mermaid...moon goddess...sea nymph. Temptress-witch. *Last night. He* was the one who should have known better than to expect whatever the hell it was he had expected when he had recognized her tonight.

Nicholas had been almost ready to back away from her when Alexa suddenly whirled her body around to face him as he had demanded earlier—for all the world like an animal at bay. Her storm-dark eyes were pinpointed by tiny red flames, reflecting the light of the crimson-shaded lantern that had been placed in the center of one of the tables. She reminded him, in that moment, of a cornered vixen—all eyes, claws and teeth; and in fact the angry vibrations that he could almost *feel* emanating from her tense body were all animal. A vixen all right! The impression was heightened by the somewhat pointed, high-cheekboned face and the way her thick hair sprang back from her temples, escaping winsomely at the same time in tiny, curling tendrils that clung to her forehead and her cheeks.

''How can you possibly preach to *me* about honesty and

truth and what is *natural* when you are such a hypocrite yourself? I think you have learned only too well to use certain words and catchphrases in order to achieve your ends, and to *twist* things about until... Well, I don't care *what* you say any longer, or how you taunt me, because I... Oh! I may be naive and silly and all of the other things you've implied, but at least you have opened my eyes to... Why, you are nothing but a disgusting *lecher!*"

"I must admit that *lecher,* especially delivered in that particular tone, sounds positively *cutting!* In case you should be prompted to use the word again, that is. But on the other hand, if you should really want to sound insulting, you might try 'bastard,' or even..."

"I would really prefer *not* to hear any more!" Alexa interrupted acidly while she tried valiantly to hold on to her treacherous temper. "In fact, you surely *must* be quite aware that the only reason I am still in your company is because... Well, I don't care! If you do not have the decency to return my mother's bracelet to me, then I have no choice but to consider it *stolen* and you the thief. And moreover, if you will not immediately escort me back inside I am quite capable of finding my own way! By now my aunt..."

His sudden laugh was unpleasant and made Alexa start nervously before she could prevent herself from doing so. "*Dios!* Why should I give a damn, after all, about what you seem to be and what you turn out to be? As you have reminded me, Miss Howard, I am old enough to know better than to believe in illusions. Mermaids and sea nymphs are only myths, after all, and the magical, ethereal qualities they are said to possess merely a product of man's wishful imagination. Surrendering one's rational mind to the spell of the moon is as foolish as believing in chaste young goddesses who come to give themselves up to the moon and are surprised by vile man with all his base instincts!''

''I don't... *Please!*'' Alexa did not realize that she had whispered that last word almost pleadingly until she heard herself.

''Of course. My apologies. You want your mother's bracelet back since it has such sentimental value. Don't worry, you shall have it back as soon as I... Ah, here it is.''

Most of the candles that had made the gaily colored lanterns glow had guttered out by now; but as if to compensate there was the yellow-gold light of the setting moon slanting dimly across the gallery from the west as it seemed to search out a hiding place in the moving, restless sea.

Hiding? Was that *really* what she was doing? Hiding from whatever was her *real* self? And who *was* her real self? She would find out for herself some day. In any case, it certainly wasn't any of *his* business!

Stiffly, Alexa forced herself to say: ''Thank you. And I suppose it was rather rude of me not to say before how grateful I am that you...'' Behind her awkwardly stammered words a picture flashed through her mind of the shape of a body cutting through black water to rise suddenly and after almost too long, to break through a moon-silvered surface. An arm—uplifted for a moment in a mocking salute. He must have been holding her bracelet then!

''Your fingers feel as cold as ice, Miss Howard!'' The rough impatience in his voice stiffened her spine, even as he added, ''Here, let me fasten the clasp for you. I suppose you're used to having your maid perform such tasks, although you might remind her the next time to be more careful...''

With her precious bracelet fastened safely about her

wrist once again, sheer relief if nothing else made Alexa say snappishly: "I do *not* have a maid who waits on me hand and foot, and I am not so helpless as to expect someone else to clasp a bracelet about my wrist! And besides, I do not possess many pieces of jewelry either!"

"No? But what a pity! Although I'm quite sure that you soon will have if you follow all the rules and catch yourself a wealthy husband who will be able to provide you with every luxury you might desire."

"*Catch?* What a denigrating word! And why, pray, do you imagine that I should need to *catch* myself a husband? I am sure that if it comes to that there will be more than enough men who would want to catch *me* for me to choose from when the time comes!"

"Ah! A flash of honesty at last!" Alexa could almost *sense* the lift of one patronizing black brow. "But it's very wise of you, moon maid, to let *them* do the chasing, without committing yourself too soon. It puts the price up as well, although I don't mean to sound crude."

"But of course you *did.* And far from being in the least honest yourself you're a *hypocrite,* which is even worse. And..." Alexa's unruly tongue ran away with her as her volatile temper passed boiling point, and she almost spat out the ultimate insult that *he* had taught her. "You're... Why, you *bastard!*"

"You certainly pick things up quickly, I see," he drawled aggravatingly. "And don't think you'd get away with going for me with those sharp little claws of yours, because I can move faster than you can and as you've already surmised I'm not your usual polite gentleman—I don't possess too many scruples either."

"You've certainly made that much *quite* obvious, haven't you?" Breathing deeply, Alexa made an attempt at icy coldness, although her voice still shook slightly. "And you're a cruel man as well. I think you *enjoy* fixing others on the sharp pins of your ridicule and your sarcasm, just to watch them squirm. Well, if I've provided you with enough sport for one evening I should like to be escorted back to my aunt, if you please. I am *not* enjoying myself—or your company either."

"No? But then, since I *am* a bastard, why should I let that make any difference to me?" Suddenly, the mockery in his voice deepened to harshness as he added, "And *that,* little virgin bitch-goddess, is why I intend to claim my forfeit for returning that precious bracelet of yours before I return you to your *tía dueña!*"

Without warning he had grasped her roughly by the shoulders; his fingers pressing into her flesh as he bent her backward against the railing; and during those first few instants Alexa thought fearfully that he meant to break her in two. And then his lips descended over hers with all the fierceness of an eagle swooping on its prey, cutting off her breath along with her reason, so that for some moments she actually thought that he meant to kill her as Othello had killed Desdemona—with a punishing kiss.

Was it only terror that held her still after her first, shamefully brief attempt to tear herself free? Alexa felt her head fall helplessly back against his arm as he forced her lips apart to explore her mouth, and almost instinctively she raised *her* arms, meaning to beat against him with her fists before *it*—the same strange thing that had happened to her before—seemed to take hold of her. That frightening, helpless feeling as if all her bones were melting and running together, so that she could hardly stand and needed to hold on to *him* for support. Heat—suddenly flooding through her to make her face, her breasts, her whole body burn and tingle as if she had a fever that had rendered her mindless and incapable of resisting either him or her own worse instincts. She felt the rippling movement of the muscles in his back, even under the jacket he wore, and remembered without shame how he had looked naked—the feel of his flesh under her hands. And now her fingers touched his hair, wanting on their own to memorize its texture; and if she didn't know what she was doing or why, she wasn't sane enough to care at that moment. Not even when he brushed his fingers gently and teasingly down from her temple and along the arch of her neck—and even further down to touch her breasts, seeming to burn through the stuff of her gown and knowing exactly where to linger.

Why was she encumbered by so many layers of clothing anyhow? Alexa realized suddenly, or rather her *body* did, that she wanted the feel of his fingers against her skin, touching her everywhere, not stopping. No thinking to cloud this surge of pure, primitive *feeling.* She felt like a pitch-soaked torch, suddenly ignited and flaring into brilliant life; and yet at the same time she had no real understanding of why she felt so, or what it meant, or even of where such feelings might lead her. She had not even asked herself why she had so recklessly allowed herself to be carried beyond caution and carefully set boundaries as her body arched eagerly and almost fiercely against his and the sea-murmuring in her ears was the sound of their breathing, his and hers, as he held her and took her even more closely against himself until Alexa could almost feel that she was melting into him. Melting—dissolving…

It was Nicholas, in the end, who broke away; firmly disengaging her clinging arms from about his neck while he cursed himself for having allowed himself to be goaded into yielding to a wildly irrational impulse. Christ! *He,* at least, was certainly old enough to have known better and to have thought of the possible consequences. What if someone else had decided to come out here for a breath of the cool night air and had seen them? Unfairly enough, it would have been *her* reputation that would have been ruined, and he had neither reason nor any right to do that to her, after all.

She was staring up at him in a dazed fashion, her eyes wide and uncomprehending, her mouth… But he had better not start thinking along *those* lines again, Nicholas warned himself grimly. She was passionate, and obviously man-ready, as he had already gauged; and he could not prevent himself from *almost* regretting that he could not be the one who would take her for the first time, making her like it. But she'd probably end up marrying some clumsy oaf who wouldn't take the time or the trouble to discover what a prize he had; and in the end she'd turn cold and hard, substituting expensive trinkets, which could be shown off, for feeling and emotion. For all that she seemed to be possessed of a daring and adventurous spirit *now,* there was no doubt that in the end she would be made to conform and would turn out exactly like all the other young women of her class and background.

Poor, pretty, ingenuous Alexa! A mixture of both pity and regret made his voice unusually gentle as he touched her face and was not able to resist lightly tracing the contour of her soft lips with one finger.

"Dammit, I suppose I should tell you how sorry I am for having allowed myself to get carried away; but that would be hypocritical, for I thoroughly enjoyed kissing you and I would have liked even better to have been able to make love to you, little moon maid. But I suppose that *would* have created quite a scandal, and I'm not as completely devoid of scruples as you accused me of being."

"Stop it! Stop talking *down* to me as if I'm a child, even after you… Yes, you *are* a hypocrite of the worst kind, Señor de la Guerra, and I wish…I wish… No, don't!" Alexa's shaking voice suddenly became fierce, warning him to silence. "There is really no need for you to *explain,* or to say anything more. I think you proved whatever it was you meant to prove *quite* well, didn't you? And I suppose I should be grateful to you for being so *instructive* in showing me the dangers of giving way to *weakness.* I shall certainly be much more careful and less *trusting* in future, I assure you! And now do you mind if we went back inside before my aunt begins to worry?''

9

Nicholas de la Guerra was a base, despicable libertine of the worst kind and had almost succeeded in spoiling for her the whole exciting occasion of her eighteenth birthday ball. Thank goodness he had decided to make himself scarce following the scathing setdown she had given him after he had *dared* to force himself on her, Alexa thought. She would dearly have loved to have said even *more*—to have told him in the most *cutting* tones exactly how much she disliked and despised him and how much the very memory of his insolent boldness in taking advantage of her embarrassment and fear of scandal *disgusted* her. But of course he was hardly worth thinking of, and since it was fortunately not likely that she would ever set eyes on him again she must really learn to put him firmly out of her mind like any other unpleasant or irksome thought that only served to disturb her. *Some* things were best left in the past where they belonged, and she should remember only that what was done could not be undone—although she had certainly learned a lesson that should serve her well in the future.

Her color high, Alexa tried to force herself into concentrating only on studying herself critically in the mirror. Her new riding habit, just made up for her, was a dark forest green. Not a color she particularly cared for, but Uncle John, who had helped her pick out the material and style, had told her emphatically that it was flattering to her and set off her hair to perfection. And after all, it was Uncle John who had *paid* for it, the darling. Turning around to view herself from every angle, Alexa thought that the tailor had done very well considering the short notice he'd been given. Of course he'd been paid double his normal charge, but that was still less than a *tenth* of what one would have had to pay one of the fashionable *modistes* in London or Paris.

Am I becoming as *worldly* and blasé as Aunt Harriet feared I might? Alexa wondered as she tried to perfect a *bored* expression before she started to smile irrepressibly at her own silliness. But she *had* promised her aunt that she would not let herself become too spoiled during her stay in Colombo with her indulgent Uncle John; and in fact she had even promised recklessly that she would at all times be unfailingly polite and respectful to the ferret-faced Mrs. Langford, who for her part couldn't *quite* manage to disguise the fact that she disliked Alexa and would dearly *love* to find as many faults and flaws in her as she could to relate to her cronies. As if *that* promise wasn't hard enough to keep, she had even had to give her word that she would try *very* hard to make friends with that silly ninny Charlotte Langford and would include the girl in as many excursions as possible; even when she was invited to go riding with Lord Charles. Hemmed about…! Alexa began to scowl at her reflection that scowled back. *That* was how she had begun to feel, surrounded by Langfords! And it was all the fault of that certain vile, inconsiderate *wretch* who had kept her out on the gallery with him for far too long a time, and against her wishes too. Otherwise she need never have been forced into making so many promises to Aunt Harriet, who would otherwise have continued to insist that since Alexa had proved how irresponsible she was and how easily she let herself forget everything she had been taught about decorum and what was proper and what wasn't, they would *both* return home the very next day.

"But all we did was *talk!* About California and what life is like there!"

"Huh! I know very well that that was the excuse *he* offered—with that twist of his lips that's supposed to pass for a smile and that irritatingly sardonic look on his face that seemed almost to *challenge* me to make an obvious fuss. But I'll have *you* understand, miss, that I don't accept *excuses,* as you should know very well. And even though *I* might have found this Señor de la Guerra quite an interesting conversationalist, you might recall that we conversed *here,* in public, and *not* alone with the night and the stars." Harriet had snorted again before adding: "And you can spare me that look of injured innocence too, my girl, for I've known you too long for you to fool me. I was young and foolish myself once, believe it or not! The man's far too old for you in any case, and far too… Well, never mind. I am sure you know exactly what I am driving at."

Stubbornly, Alexa had managed to keep to her story, staring angrily down at her clenched hands while she wished she could let her temper explode along with the resentment and positive *hatred* she felt towards Nicholas de la Guerra, who was the cause of her aunt's wrath. It really wasn't fair or *just* that *she* should be the only one to shoulder all the blame, and to be punished by being marched upstairs to bed by her aunt after being allowed only two more dances ("only in order to squelch any gossip!" she had been reminded), just as if she had still been a *child.*

In the end it had been Sir John who had persuaded Harriet to relent. Alexa never learned just *how* he had managed to convince her aunt that she deserved another chance (just as if she had been a *criminal,* she fumed inwardly), but at least she *had* been allowed to stay behind in Colombo—after all sorts of solemn promises had been extracted from her first. Not *fair,* when it hadn't been her fault at all; and in any case, why was it that her every action and her life should be controlled by a nebulous "they" who had made up all the rules that were supposed to govern what everybody could or could not do? And what made "them" qualified to decide what constituted "sin"? It wasn't considered a sin if an angry planter beat one of his coolies to death for what *he* thought of as insolence; but to lie naked with a man or to allow him to kiss you or touch you in certain ways was the unforgivable sin! Hypocrisy. That was one of the things that *he* had spoken of, of course; but obviously it had been only in order to gain his own ends, Alexa thought darkly. Part of the insidious poison he had tried to feed her—as dangerous as the sudden rush of unwanted memory-pictures flashing through her mind.

Annoyed at the wayward direction her thoughts had begun to take, Alexa scowled at her reflection in the mirror and snatched up her hat, adjusting it at a jaunty angle on her head so that the feather that adorned it curled enticingly about the brim before it swooped down to almost brush her cheek. She could only *hope,* of course, that Lord Charles, who was doubtless used to moving in much more sophisticated circles than *this,* would not find her too unstylish; and if he did not it was again due to her dearest and most understanding Uncle John, who had, like a benevolent magician or fairy godfather, arranged for both the new riding habit and the hat as well.

"Oh, Alexa!" Alexa swung around angrily with her straight dark brows drawn together; but Charlotte Langford never seemed to realize that she was intruding when she burst unannounced into Alexa's room without so much as a perfunctory knock. "He's here! The Viscount Deering, I mean. And on such a magnificent horse, too! Don't you think it so *exciting* that it is us he has chosen to honor with his attention? How envious every other female in Colombo will be, to be sure!"

"Oh? Do you think so?" Alexa managed to respond coolly enough as she turned back to the mirror to make sure her hat was pinned securely on her coiled up hair, stepping back to study the effect of her whole outfit taken together.

"Oh, but of *course* we will be envied and thought lucky. I suppose, living upcountry you could have no *idea* how people gossip in a city like Colombo. A *Viscount*—asking *us* to go riding with him in *public,* just as if we had a Rotten Row here in Colombo! And especially after all the *marked* attention we've been paid during the past few days—his *calls*..."

How was it that Charlotte always sounded so *breathless* while she rained spun-sugar inanities on her unfortunate victims? On the verge of gritting her teeth Alexa surprised herself by managing to say in quite a *civilized* voice, "And I suppose that since Lord Charles has been so kind and attentive it is the least we can do not to keep him waiting, don't you think?"

From Charlotte's giggles and pink cheeks it might seem as if it were really Charlotte Langford that Lord Charles had called upon almost daily and not Miss Howard. There had, as a matter of fact, not been a single minute when Alexa had been left alone with the Viscount, for Charlotte's redoubtable mama had always made sure that Charlotte sat with them in the parlor or out on the verandah; ensuring that all their conversation remained stilted and formal. And it had been difficult indeed to carry on any kind of intelligent conversation at all when Miss Langford, who lacked both tact and sensitivity, might interrupt during any slight pause to comment on the continuing good weather or the bazaar her mama had recently organized to raise money for Christian orphans. There had been moments when Alexa's unruly tongue and temper had almost burst out of control, and she found herself grinding her teeth together much more often than usual. But at least she had earned herself the right to enjoy *this* particular outing, which she'd looked forward to almost greedily for the past few days.

As she leaned down to pat the arched neck of her horse, Alexa realized how much she'd missed her daily rides on horseback. Her favorite out of all the horses in Sir John's stable, the high-spirited chestnut mare she rode had been foaled at his horse farm in the hill country, where Alexa had already ridden her several times before. Although, she could not help thinking almost painfully now, it had been so different there! Cold, dew-pearled mornings with the smell of woodsmoke in the air and the excited yelping of hounds waiting to be let out for their morning run. She could ride comfortably astride, and without a hat; her carelessly finger-combed mane of hair tied back with a ribbon and the weight of a pistol at her side to remind her of the dangers she might encounter at any time. A poisonous snake, an enraged wild boar…

But not *here,* in Colombo, on such a very decorous outing as *this* one had turned out to be, Alexa thought with mounting indignation as she listened to Charlotte Langford's high-pitched voice chatter on and on between giggles and pronounced sighs and could not help wishing that she *had* brought a pistol with her after all. Not only had *Charlotte* been inflicted upon her but two other men of Mrs. Langford's choosing as well—a middle-aged and terribly boring major who was a friend of Colonel Langford's and Mr. Sutherland, the pompous young man who had bored her with his solemn relation of all the duties of an aide to the Governor and the importance of such a position. The two native grooms trailing behind their party made them seem an *entourage,* and it had not been meant to be like this! Lord Charles had asked *her* to ride with him, without making mention of anyone else, and his surprise had showed in his eyes for an instant or two before he had masked it with his usual polite manners.

Manners! Alexa thought rebelliously as she toyed with the wicked idea of pretending her mount was running away with her, just in order to enjoy a real gallop instead of being forced to conform to a sedate trot for Charlotte Langford's sake. Why is it considered good manners to be sickly sweet to a person you really despise and dislike? Why are people never supposed to be completely honest and truthful with each other? Stripping away dishonesty and lies like so many unnecessary layers of clothing and being able to face together the naked reality of truth? I shall *never* understand—and least of all why I must let myself conform and pretend and *be* all those things that I despise the most. It was not fair that now, too suddenly, she was expected to make her *real* self disappear behind a decorous social mask. To *act* instead of reacting. Not *fair!*

It was perhaps fortunate, considering the angrily mutinous trend of Alexa's thoughts, that Lord Charles's voice broke in just then.

"I say, Miss Howard, I've just hit on a capital idea, you know. That is, if you don't *mind...*" Viscount Deering's rather diffident voice was belied by the almost conspiratorial smile he wore, as Alexa discovered when she glanced at him in an almost startled fashion. She had almost forgotten, in her preoccupation with her resentful thoughts, that he had quite cleverly contrived to be the one to ride beside her when the riding path had become narrower. Until now, barraged by the bright flow of small talk kept up by the others in their party, both Alexa and Lord Charles had remained comparatively silent; and she had almost begun to imagine that he had begun to think of her as being far too provincial and naive to be worth his time and attention. Now, however, his next words belied *that* fear as he continued with a twinkle in his expressive brown eyes: "D'you think perhaps that this might be a suitable opportunity to practice our French and Italian on each other? I seem to remember your mentioning that you did not have many opportunities to converse in those languages in order to keep *fluent,* and since I too have the same problem I thought... *Do* you mind?"

Charlotte had admitted only two days ago, with a sniff, that *her* mama had assured her that English was spoken everywhere in Europe by the *better* class of people and that it was quite unnecessary to try to learn some foreign language that might well contain certain words and phrases that were *not* considered polite in English. So much for Charlotte! And it was even more unlikely that Major Doyle or Mr. Sutherland knew either French or Italian. Lord Charles was being cleverly inventive, and an appreciative sparkle lit up Alexa's eyes, relieving some of the tension that had shown in her face as she had contemplated the hypocrisy of "good manners."

"Mind? No! I should enjoy trying out my French and Italian very much indeed, if you will only promise to correct all of my mistakes."

What a difference it made when she smiled and let that charming dimple show, Lord Charles reflected in a rather fatuous fashion. *She* was really quite adorable, with a touch of naiveté he found quite unusual and intriguing. If only he could have had enough time to spend with her, and without the constant and vigilant chaperones she was always surrounded by...! He had done nothing but dream of her for the past few nights, and had imagined, when he was *not* asleep and dreaming, everything he would like to share with her and *do* with her. Teach her everything. Arouse her virginal senses and take her, step by step, to the knowledge of passion and sensuality. Dammit, she seemed to offer both a promise and a challenge that were almost worth staying for, if only his dark-visaged "cousin" Nicholas would not continue to be so obdurate about leaving in two days from now and did not insist on reminding him that his parents expected him back in England before Christmas. Two days, and he had begun to want her quite badly. Not that Nicholas, being the cynic that he was about women, would give a damn about *that,* of course! He respected nothing at all—not even the purity of true innocence—and talked contemptuously of normal human emotions and feelings as if they were merely weaknesses that should be controlled and pushed out of existence. Well, the devil take Nicholas *and* the coldly detached calculation he preached. He, for his part, preferred to enjoy the hedonism of giving way to feeling and impulse!

Yes, why *not* act on impulse after all? Especially since it was obvious by now that he had not much to lose except perhaps a few hours spent too well chaperoned in *her* company. Manfully, Lord Charles plunged into speech, hoping he would not have to regret his impulsiveness later, although, of course there were always ways *out,* weren't there? He had decided on French to begin with and then switched quickly into Italian when he remembered uneasily that French had become almost *too* fashionable these days.

"I hope my little ruse did not anger you too much? But if you could only know how much I have wanted to engage in a *real* conversation with you and to spend much more time in your company *without*... That is... All that I meant, of course, was that, well, I had very much looked forward to getting to know and understand you much better before... Believe me, I am not usually as tongue-tied as some adolescent schoolboy, Signorina Howard! And—with your permission of course—not quite as boldly precipitous. Please. If I were to beg your indulgence and your *forgiveness,* could you possibly grant me such a favor?''

And what could Lord Charles possibly be leading up to with such difficulty, for heaven's sake? With a show of insouciance Alexa answered brightly that of course he had her permission to be quite frank with her, because she infinitely preferred honesty and directness to the polite insincerity that *most* people practiced. She could only wonder why he felt he had to ask her *forgiveness* first, as she questioned, ''Is whatever it is you want to tell me so terribly bad?''

''For *me* at least it is. And especially since I have met *you.* To learn that we are to leave for England within two days, when I have not even had the opportunity to speak with you and meet with you as often as I would have wished... I am afraid that I'm not the kind of cynic my cousin the Spaniard would have me become, and that I cannot help the way I have begun to feel towards you. I admire you and respect you and I wish... Ah, at least perhaps you will believe me when I say I am sincere in my feelings, *bella, cara signorina!* and that I would give anything to be granted just a few precious moments of *private* conversation with you so that I could speak to you more freely and with less constraint. To know that you would *trust* me enough to feel safe and at ease in my company if you should ever... I hope I have not made you angry with me?''

It was perhaps unfortunate that Charlotte, who must have been listening to their exchange with a growing sense of frustration, should have chosen that particular moment to chime in archly from behind, protesting that they really weren't being fair at all in excluding the rest of the party from sharing *secrets.* And then, with one of her high-pitched giggles that always set Alexa's teeth on edge, Charlotte had to add coyly: "Of course Mama has always said that one *should* try to remember a few commonly used French words that have been absorbed into the English language; but..." with another rather embarrassed sounding giggle this time, "I understand that... Well, at least Mama has always given me to understand that certain reading matter that would *never* find its way into decent English... Mr. Sutherland has just been telling me that he agrees with Mama that certain books that are published abroad in other languages might be far too easily available, under the guise of *literature,* of all things, and could corrupt Innocent and Unspoiled Minds. *Not* that I meant..."

"Oh, but I'm sure I can *quite* understand Mrs. Langford's natural anxiety, and she's right, of course." Even if she gnashed her teeth mentally, Alexa's tone was dulcet. "After all, I'm sure that a mother is always the best judge of her own daughter's susceptibility to certain reading matter! And you mustn't worry, Charlotte dear, that *I* will ever tell Mrs. Langford that you have actually discussed such topics with a *gentleman.* In fact, I shall continue practicing Italian grammar and diction with Lord Charles and pretend that *no* discussion of improper literature ever took place!"

Charlotte's only half-smothered gasp and the rather choked sound that Lord Charles quickly turned into a cough came at about the same time, Alexa remembered later. At least he had a sense of humor, she thought, and he was, at the same time, a *gentleman.* So very much the complete opposite, thank goodness, of his uncouth cousin from California, that panther-eyed adventurer who possessed neither manners nor morals nor scruples either and certainly did not deserve to be received by polite society. Lord Charles, on the other hand, was entertaining, polite and obviously *sincere;* and what, after all, could be so very wrong with meeting and conversing with him alone for a few minutes? *He,* at least, was not the kind of bold rogue who might, without warning, force her into an unwanted embrace that was as much a punishment as it was an insult, his hands taking casual liberties with her, just as if she had been some coolie woman who was supposed to feel flattered by his disgusting advances!

In any case, I *trust* Lord Charles, and it *does* rather sound like a daring adventure as well as a challenge, Alexa thought defiantly afterwards when she recalled her rash promise to meet him on the private strip of sandy beach at the bottom of Sir John's garden. He was going away, and he wanted to talk with her—had given her his solemn word that she would be perfectly safe in his company. As of course she would be, for he was far too honorable to try and take advantage of her trust in him. And what *fun* it had been to progress from arguments to arrangements right under the stolid noses of the others; particularly Charlotte's, which had been pink with indignation during the rest of their ride. She didn't really care a jot what Charlotte or Mrs. Langford thought or speculated about either, Alexa decided firmly. She would pretend to have developed a headache and retire early tonight, and then… Lord Charles had said that he had something very important to ask her. Was he thinking of proposing to her? And suppose he actually *did,* how should she answer him? It was all very exciting, and helped to push other, less pleasant thoughts from her mind.

10

That night, at dinner, Mrs. Langford seized on some flimsy excuse to hold forth at great length on the subject of the correct and proper *training* of pure, and yet far too impressionable, young minds. She had a rather high-pitched voice that grated on Alexa's nerves, and a consciously affected turn of phrase as well; being overly fond of throwing in quotations at random from either the Bible or one of her favorite sermons to illustrate her every point, or pointed comment.

"...The unrestricted reading for books, for instance, and especially *novels....!*" Here the lady's rather thin lips had puckered, as if she had just tasted something unbearably sour, before she continued in rather heavier tones that were meant to convey the extent of her disapprobation: "And especially the kind written by *foreigners,* in their languages...ah, how important some gentle but *firm* guidance in the right direction is, in order to prevent the *corruption* of a young mind that, as our dear and *learned* Dr. Jennings has often said, resembles a clean slate waiting to be written upon and is open, in its innocence, to every influence. Parental supervision—constant advice and guidance—how important they are, and most especially in the case of a young female, delicately nurtured and of a tender susceptibility! 'As the twig is bent...' I know I need not complete the phrase, for my Charlotte has heard her father quote it many times. Colonel Langford also believes very strongly in the importance of *disciplining* as well as instructing the young, immature mind; along with, of course, the social graces such as manners and proper deportment and behavior—so *essential* for a young woman who dreams of being the perfect wife and mother when the time arrives for her to be passed from the benevolent guidance of her loving parents into the keeping of—her *Husband!*"

If she continues in this vein for much longer... If I have to listen to that voice and those smug platitudes and watch how Charlotte preens herself without realizing or even *caring* that she has been brought up and *trained* like a show pony or a brood mare; only in order to be passed from the hands of one *owner* to another...! I wonder what she would do if I suddenly gave way to a violent fit of hysterics? A headache? But then Uncle John would start to worry and concern himself needlessly, and *she* would probably think...

Alexa forced herself to look down at her plate while she pretended to occupy herself with cutting into her slice of boiled mutton surrounded by carrots and potatoes. But in spite of all her efforts her mind seethed rebelliously. Slavery! That was what it amounted to. Passed, like a possession, from one *man* to another; and yet most young women thought like Charlotte, who would consider herself *honored* if some pompous jackass should consider to ask her father for her hand in marriage. And after that, instead of "Yes, Papa!" and "Of course, Papa!" it would be "Oh yes, Mr. So-and-so!" or "But of course, Mr. So-and-so, you always know what is best for me." How could any human being with a mind capable of reasoning submit *will* as well as person so unquestioningly and so *passively?*

Thankfully, Mrs. Langford had interrupted herself in order to enjoy her third course, and the sudden quiet that seemed to descend encouraged Alexa to change the angry trend of her thoughts. In *that* direction lay frustration, she reminded herself wisely. And she had more immediate problems to deal with tonight. *Planning*—or should she be prepared to improvise instead? It was certain that she would have to wait until the servants had been dismissed to their quarters for the night and most of the house lights extinguished before attempting to slip away. And what should she *wear?* Something cool and light and not too encumbering nor too showy either. A gown she could feel *comfortable* in without appearing too dowdy or *shabby.* Her green cotton with the lace inserts, perhaps? It was at least two years old, of course, and the style had been copied from a fashion journal of the early 'thirties but at least it *did* flatter her figure as well as show off her shoulders and ankles to advantage. And being a man, Lord Charles probably would not notice in any case. Yes, the green dress would be exactly the thing—not that it *really* mattered of course, because she had no intention of staying out beyond half an hour at the very most, even if he *did* propose!

During the rest of the meal, Sir John, who had noticed and understood the dangerous gleam in Alexa's slate-dark eyes, made sure that their conversation was steered into safer channels, leaving Mrs. Langford and Charlotte no choice but to follow his lead. Alexa's mood lightened noticeably and her whole manner became quite animated when the discussion turned to horses and a lively argument ensued regarding the merits and shortcomings of cross-breeding.

The entrance of Sir John's dignified-looking butler, carrying a silver tray bearing decanters of port and brandy and a beautifully carved rosewood box containing a variety of the very finest cigars, filled Mrs. Langford, for one, with a feeling of profound relief. She had noticed that her poor Charlotte, like herself, had barely *toyed* with the last two courses, and had not even had a second helping of the chocolate soufflé. But now, at last, she could with all propriety give the signal for the ladies to retire—and high time too! There had been moments, she thought with an inward shudder of taste, when she *knew* that she could not prevent herself from blushing at what she could only dare describe, even to herself, as "stable talk."

How she had *longed* to be able to cry out that Charlotte should instantly clap her hands over her ears when certain unpleasant subjects were being discussed far too freely! She could only hope and pray of course that dear Charlotte's carefully nurtured innocence would protect her; and it was with considerable relief that she had noticed Charlotte's rather *puzzled* expression when there were subjects mentioned and *blunt* terms used that no well-brought-up young *lady* should have any knowledge of. And that *any* young woman of good background should actually sit and discuss with such ease and familiarity such *unsuitable* topics not only reflected badly on her unfortunate parents but was enough to make any other person forced to listen and observe such behavior positively *recoil!* The blame did not lie with Sir John Travers, who had been a bachelor all his life and was more used to *male* company, poor man. No, it was the responsibility of a female, if she was indeed a *lady,* to make haste to change the subject to a more tasteful one. It certainly did not speak well for the *education* of women if *this* was its result. Foreign languages, the reading of novels, far too much *freedom* of both action and thought—all insidious poisons that twisted and corrupted. No wonder poor Charlotte had been almost distraught when they had returned from their excursion on horseback; so *torn,* the dear soft-hearted creature, between loyalty to another of her own sex and the high moral standards *she* had been taught.

"I vow I do not mean to sound *uncharitable,* Mama, but I have to confess that I could not help *longing* for the time when we would turn back, in spite of the fact that Mr. Sutherland was *so* kind to me and showed himself to be so *understanding* of how I *had* to feel, and was *made* to feel. Mama, you *know* how hard I have tried to make a friend of Miss Howard and to *guide* her, as you told me I should. But today, why she was *flirting* quite boldly with Lord Charles, and *monopolizing* him! Even Mr. Sutherland admitted to me that he could not help being disappointed and rather *surprised* at her behavior. And then, to make things worse, they began speaking in… Oh, I don't even know what it was. Some foreign language that sounded like gibberish that none of *us* could understand; and when I only tried to *hint,* tactfully, that it was rather *rude,* she actually *snubbed* me, Mama! And turned back to him, laughing! And you should have seen the *looks* they kept exchanging all the while. I have *never* been so embarrassed in all my life, and my *head* aches so badly from the strain of it all that I can hardly bear to lift it!"

At least she could be thankful that Charlotte, poor disillusioned child, had seen for herself the consequences of too much freedom, Mrs. Langford reflected grimly. But even if she put her natural maternal feelings aside, there still remained her Christian Duty towards the young and unfortunately misguided female who had, after all, been placed in her care. Yes, a few words of wisdom and of *caution* could not be amiss.

Following her mother's example, Charlotte had already risen to her feet with alacrity, but Alexa, on the other hand, tried hard to pretend she hadn't noticed. How on earth, and *why,* had such a silly custom become established? *She* didn't in the least mind the aroma of a good cigar, and she would *much* rather have continued her interesting conversation with Uncle John instead of being forced to retire with the Langfords.

"Miss Howard? Will you not deign to join us?"

Alexa had begun to rise, slowly and unwillingly, when Mrs. Langford's rather sarcastic reminder of her *manners* made her angry enough to sit down again and *defy* both custom and silly women. But in the end, after only an infinitesimal hesitation, her head went up defiantly while her eyes took on a pewter sheen that would have warned anyone who knew Alexa to caution. Even her face seemed to have changed in some subtle way, appearing suddenly older and harder, while her voice seemed to have crystalized into dry ice.

"I do beg your pardon for being a few seconds tardy in joining you, madame. Thank you for the tactful reminder."

So his young Amazon was primed to give battle? Sir John Travers spent a few extra seconds staring thoughtfully at the double doors of polished satinwood bound with brass that had just closed behind the ladies. He was sure that Alexa, with her clever mind and gift for ingenious argument, could hold her own against Mrs. Langford quite easily, if only she could manage not to lose her temper to the extent that she also lost all power of reasoning.

Sir John sighed rather heavily as he turned back to his brandy and cigar, thinking ruefully as he did that it was a pity indeed that the young had everything except experience and the wisdom and ability to exercise self-control, whereas those like himself who had learned life's hard lessons no longer had youth or time enough to use the knowledge they had gained. Youth and knowledge and wisdom. Ah, to possess all three gifts at the same time was to rule the world, and perhaps that was why it so seldom happened that way.

Alexa. A small smile tugged at the corners of his mouth

under his greying mustache as he remembered the leggy colt of a girl she had been when he first encountered her. Even then she had had spirit, an eager, questioning mind, and *courage* as well. She, and not poor delicate Freddy, should have been the boy, of course; but what was the use in regretting what *was?* Alexa was no longer a girl but a grown young woman—an attractive young woman too, with a kind of *aura* about her that made her somehow unique, although she herself was as yet quite unaware of this special quality in herself that would always cause her to be noticed and singled out wherever she went. She was still quite immature, for all of her book-knowledge and education and that quick mind of hers. But there was so much potential there! Potential he had helped to nurture and had hoped to see realized some day if only... Well, what was the point in thinking about it now? His doctors had decreed otherwise, and mortal man cannot circumvent fate. So be it! At least he had been able to arrange that she'd always have enough money, so that she need never have to feel herself obligated to sell herself on the marriage market, even when Freddy inherited. Beyond that, his greatest hope was that when she was ready she would find the *right* kind of man for her—one she could converse with, who would appreciate her intelligent mind and free spirit and love her for what she *was* and not for what he thought he could make her into.

Sentimental old fool! You can only do the best you can and hope for the rest; and since you won't be around to see how it turns out in the end, there's no use worrying about it, is there? Clearing his throat fiercely, Sir John relit his cigar and dragged on it far too deeply, forgetting his doctor's orders. Even though he had chosen an exceptionally mild one, it made him cough, and he swore inwardly. When he looked up at last after his coughing fit had ended, Sir John realized with disgust that his butler was hovering over him while pretending to rearrange everything on the silver tray in an ostentatiously significant manner that obviously called for comment.

"Well?" Sir John grumbled testily. "And what the devil d'you think you're up to, fiddling about like that? If you've anything to say to me, be out with it!"

Velu, who had run his master's house in Colombo for over fifteen years, merely turned down the corners of his mouth with a look of patent disapproval.

"I hear doctor say only half cigar, and much better Master take no cigar!" And then, noting indications of an imminent explosion, Velu went on hastily and with some relish, "But I come to tell Master that it is better, maybe, that Master retire to Study Room with door locked? Ladies make many arguments and the big lady is very angry. With mouth open like this..."

Velu's imitation of Mrs. Langford actually left speechless for a change tempted Sir John to chuckle, and he was not able to compose his features quickly enough to prevent the sharp-eyed Velu from noticing his mouth twitch before he said drily: "I see. And I won't ask you how many times you invented excuses to go in there, you old rascal, but I'm sure you didn't miss anything, did you, eh? What of the young ladies?"

"Ah..." Velu rolled his eyes with pretended concern. "Big lady's young missy crying and *our* missy Alex she smile but speaking sharp like knife. Good thing she have no knife or gun or maybe I think big lady be dead! Too bad!"

"I won't ask how that last pithy statement was meant to be taken," Sir John said after he had cleared his throat loudly to cover his involuntary chortle. He added thoughtfully, "But I suppose you are right in suggesting that I'd do well to take myself off to my study, where I have urgent correspondence to deal with and must on *no* account be disturbed.''

As Velu sprang to pull back his chair, Sir John reflected with a grim kind of amusement that this was certainly the first time anyone could have accused him of running away from a battlefield. But under the circumstances, and in view of his decided partiality, there could be no question that in this case at least discretion was most definitely the better part of valor.

''Oh, and Velu...'' Settled before his desk with the open French doors bringing in the night-smells of dew-wet grass and frangipani and jasmine, Sir John held up one hand to halt his servant. ''If by some chance you might have reason to visit the drawing room—perhaps to ask if the ladies need anything before they retire—you might just say a few words to Miss Alexa in *your* tongue, perhaps a mumbled undertone. You're good at that when you imagine you've something to grumble about, eh? Tell her... The devil take it! Just make sure she's not about to lose her temper and start throwing things, you hear? You might move my Ming vases out of there. *That* ought to give her a hint. Tell her those were my orders and she'll understand very well what I meant. That's all. And since I might go outside for a stroll later on, I don't want you sitting up for half the night either. That clear? *You're* getting to be an old man too. Hah!''

Poor faithful old Velu! He'd be getting a pension, of course, and enough money to buy himself that land in Jaffna he'd always wanted, as well as a young wife to give him children before it was too late. Too late... You spent your time and energy accumulating money and possessions and forgot why you were doing so in the process, until suddenly it was too late to enjoy their use and you saw them for what they were—more clutter and *things* to leave behind when you had to go.

No, dammit! Sir John slammed down the glass he had been holding and began to pace about the large, shelf-lined room as he usually did when he was deep in thought. Dammit, he thought again, I haven't gone *yet!* Still got some time left to me if all those doctor chaps were right and if I don't overdo things. Time enough, perhaps to make sure it wasn't all for nothing after all, not just *wasted!* Made use of—*enjoyed.* That's what money was for, and possessions. And why the deuce should the Crown get any of it, anyhow?

11

By the time Sir John had stopped his pacing back and forth, Alexa had already regained the comparative sanctuary of her bedchamber, although she had had to spend several minutes leaning with her back against the door she had slammed shut behind her before she managed to catch her breath. These silly, tight corsets she was supposed to wear in order to be fashionable… And that even more ridiculous woman who reminded her of an ugly old crow with her taste for carrion…!

Oh! How dearly I should have loved to *indulge* myself by flying into a simply towering rage, when I might really have said or done something quite outrageous. How I would have loved to see their faces *then!* Why, if Velu hadn't appeared…

Even in the midst of thinking such dark thoughts Alexa's sense of humor interrupted for long enough to make her start to grin unwillingly. For she *had* been eying one of poor Uncle John's precious Ming vases consideringly when Velu had sidled in to remove them, muttering what sounded like incantations under his breath until she understood that instead of praying to his Hindu gods he was trying to warn *her.* Something like "lose mind, lose all," which may or may not have been an old Tamil proverb. But at any rate Velu had been just in time to prevent an outright disaster, which would have ended, Alexa thought ruefully, in her being sent home in disgrace—even if it hadn't been at all her fault.

Thinking back to her confrontation with Mrs. Langford made Alexa scowl all over again, and the nervous ayah Velu had sent to her to help her undress became even more nervous, so that her fingers fumbled over their task at first—until she realized that "Alex missy's" glowering look was not meant for her.

Charlotte, Alexa was thinking, was merely a nasty little gossip and a tattletale who didn't like to be ignored, as well as being her mama's very echo. But Mrs. Langford...! Alexa's lips curled in a most unpleasant way as she recalled how Mrs. Langford had started out with her condescending, hypocritical little speech that was meant to put Miss Howard in her place while exalting Miss Charlotte Langford as an example she should try to model herself after. Snatches of that speech flashed back into Alexa's memory now, together with the mind-picture of Charlotte sitting next to her with modestly bent head, trying hard not to preen herself.

"My dear Miss Howard. Although I have hesitated before, my sense of duty *forces* me to speak out now; and I do hope you will take some well-meant advice from a mother with a daughter close to your age in the spirit in which it is intended. A few pertinent words of *caution* from someone older and more mature who is used to moving about in *Society* and much more aware of the dangers and pitfalls that await one too inexperienced and too impetuous... *Guidance* of the young is so necessary; that and constant, loving *supervision...*"

While Alexa listened almost unbelievingly, Mrs. Langford had gone on and on until at last she had been forced to pause long enough to draw breath. Alexa had thought to herself—*now* I suppose she is bound to throw some solemn quotation at me!

"And after all, as the saying goes, 'a stitch in time saves nine!' Dear Charlotte embroidered that very motto for me on a sampler when she was barely six years old, and I still have it, framed, of course. So..."

"I'm sorry, Mrs. Langford, but I really fail to understand what your favorite motto has to do with *me,* since I usually do those things that I *must* do very quickly in order that I might be finished with them, instead of trying to put off the inevitable. I'm afraid I cannot see..."

The natural ruddy tint of Mrs. Langford's complexion had become quite mottled as she girded herself for battle almost visibly; drawing herself up as she cast Alexa a look that was meant to *reduce* her.

"I can only *hope,* Miss Howard, that you did not deliberately choose to misunderstand me when you interrupted what I had begun to say. 'Children should be seen and not heard'—and for all that you have reached eighteen years of age it cannot fail to become very soon apparent to the bystander who watches and observes that you, Miss Howard, are a mere child in experience of the Ways of this World. And while *children* may be allowed a certain amount of... Well, let me be brief and say merely that what can be forgiven in a child who does not know any better can never be quite as easily passed over when one is considered to be *grown-up* enough to enter society. Any foolish or unthinking action that could be misconstrued by others, even the slightest indication of being—shall we say—a little too *free* and *easy* in one's manner towards the opposite sex... Perhaps you may not know it, Miss Howard, but once there is *Talk* about a young woman it is too late for her to try and retrieve her mistakes! She will soon find that she is no longer accepted in the best circles, where once she might have been welcome; and all too soon…''

Mrs. Langford had paused to take another deep breath, and seizing the opportunity, Alexa had almost sprung to her feet, with her impatience and rage showing in every movement—very much the young lioness her birth sign symbolized. That horrible, *ugly*-minded, petty woman! If she didn't *move*—find something to do with her hands—she might give way to the impulse to…to… How fortunate that Velu, on one of his suspiciously frequent trips into the drawing room, had placed a small tray bearing a decanter of sherry and some glasses on one of the sideboards. It was just what she needed at this point to calm her nerves.

Taking long strides that she knew would be considered *unladylike,* Alexa crossed the room before saying over her shoulder, ''Sherry, anyone?'' When she heard only horrified gasps in response, she shrugged as she lifted the decanter to pour out a glass of sherry for herself, turning immediately afterwards to face them defiantly as she raised her glass with pretended insouciance. ''Well, *à votre santé,* then! Or, translated into English, to your good health! Mmm! This is an excellent sherry, and you ladies really should try it.''

Mrs. Langford had recovered herself sufficiently by then to utter in a choked voice: ''*Sherry!* Another intoxicating beverage, is it not? And you must not think that I didn't notice that you sipped from your wineglass at dinner, young woman! It was only out of a spirit of Christian forbearance that I refrained from making any pointed comments before *now.* But to have my Charlotte subjected to witnessing a young woman of tender years indulging boldly and far too indiscreetly in what is even considered a vice in *men…!* Ah, Miss Howard, I pity your poor parents!''

''*Do* you, Mrs Langford? I shall be sure and tell them

so.'' The sherry she swallowed down far too fast because she was angry warmed Alexa's throat like liquid gold and fortified her spirits with a rush of energy and strength that allowed her to say quite calmly: ''But apart from the fact that I enjoy a glass of sherry occasionally, what other shocking crime have I committed? Please feel free to be quite direct with me, for I appreciate *honesty* above all things.'' Another sip, and Alexa was able to smile quite composedly and almost cheerfully into Charlotte's gaping face before she added with mock concern: ''Or is it that I have, quite unwittingly, upset poor Charlotte by practicing my Italian on Lord Charles? If so, you should have said so to *him,* Charlotte. But you may have Mr. Sutherland all to yourself if you like him, and I promise to keep out of the way. In any case Lord Charles will be returning to England tomorrow, so you see...?''

Charlotte's mortified ''Ohh!'' was drowned out by Mrs. Langford's rising voice as she pronounced in a strident tone: ''Why, you brazen young hussy! And to think that I actually encouraged my poor daughter to try and make a *friend* of you! Thank God there has not been time for her to have been *swayed* by what I see before me! A young woman—surely too young to have been allowed to indulge in every vice known to... Surely not a *second* glass of sherry?''

''Indeed, yes! And it really *is* an excellent sherry too, in case you might wish to change your mind and join me in a glass.'' While Mrs. Langford searched in her reticule for her vinaigrette, almost panting from emotion, Alexa continued in a deliberately questioning voice: ''But Mrs. Langford, surely you must know that for a lady to partake of wine or sherry is considered quite the done thing in the highest social circles everywhere in Europe? So Uncle John was telling me at any rate, and I am sure that he would know. In fact, I understand from him and from Lord

Charles that even the Queen has been observed to partake of wine or champagne. But perhaps this is not my only *vice* in your eyes? Have you managed to discover any other vices I should be called to account for?''

Having delivered her speech, Alexa had lifted her tiny glass of sherry to her lips and sipped from it deliberately, her dark brows lifted in question; and it was at that point that Mrs. Langford forgot herself as she almost gasped out: ''Why, that you *dare* to mention our angelic young Queen as an example—an *excuse* for your own... And what will you do, pray, when Lord Charles has left—and left *you* with a reputation for allowing gentlemen Too Much Familiarity? Ah, it is too late, Miss Howard, to *cringe* from the last of Truth, I am afraid! For a woman's reputation follows her everywhere, and once she has allowed certain... Take care! For you will find that once the word is out every *other* man you meet will—although I shudder to say it—Expect the Same Thing! And they might even...''

Emptying her glass for the second time before setting it down with such force that Charlotte jumped and gave a small scream, Alexa advanced to stand directly before Mrs. Langford; and there must have been something in her almost feline manner of walking and her stance that startled even *that* thick-skinned lady into sudden silence.

''And what exactly do you mean by 'The Same Thing'? For you must understand, Mrs. Langford, that in spite of my 'free and easy manners' and the—the *familiarities* I supposedly allow gentlemen to take, there are still some things I remain ignorant of. But I am sure that you, ma'am, with your obvious worldly experience in such matters, could instruct me?''

It was perhaps fortunate for all concerned that Velu had made his entrance at that point, while Mrs. Langford was still gasping like a beached fish and her daughter hovered on the brink of hysterics. Just as well too, Alexa thought darkly, that the dirty-minded old *witch* had decided to beat a hasty retreat while she could; sweeping her precious Charlotte ahead of her.

"*Come,* Charlotte! And you may rest assured, Miss Howard, that I will be speaking to Sir John as soon as possible."

"I had hoped that you would, ma'am! For then *he* could explain to me the exact meaning of some of the expressions you used!"

One of them had been "brazen hussy." Dismissing the sleepy-eyed ayah, Alexa stared at her own reflection in the looking glass while she attempted to tidy her hair. She should have let the maid, Karuna, brush it out for her as she had offered, but it had seemed more important that she be left alone with her thoughts at this time—with herself. *Was* she a brazen hussy? Well, better that than a pious hypocrite putting on mincing little airs and mounting trivial, meaningless words.

And why should I care what people like *that* might think of me or accuse me of being? Swinging angrily away from the mirror, Alexa began to search determinedly for her favorite green dress, and finding it, slipped it on over the single petticoat she had kept on. No corset or stays to cut off her breathing. And if Lord Charles didn't like her the way she really was, then *his* opinion didn't matter to her either.

A glance at her small clock told Alexa that she had already delayed longer than she had meant to, but if she *ran* part of the way... She paused again in front of the mirror to take one last look at herself, and then, acting on a sudden, wildly defiant impulse, she took down her hair and shook it free, letting it run down like a bronze rivulet to her waist. A brazen hussy, was she? Well, she would find out soon enough if Lord Charles thought so too.

The young creature who sped barefooted through a night

brightened by the light of millions of stars and flickering fireflies, with her dainty slippers carried carelessly in one hand and her mane of hair swinging between her shoulders, was a very different Alexa from the fashionably gowned and coiffed Miss Howard Lord Charles was used to seeing. Tonight she more resembled a half-wild gypsy as she ran as swiftly and as soundlessly as the jungle predators she was used to stalking; relishing the sudden, almost heady sense of freedom that filled her and would make this wild, rash escapade seem worthwhile even if he had decided not to wait for her. She had regained her sense of belonging only to herself—of being capable of daring anything and facing anything at all—and what *fun* she was having!

Having run all the way, using the shortcut she remembered from past visits here, Alexa arrived at the small grove of coconut trees that fringed the beach and found herself quite out of breath, so that she was forced to pause for a minute or two in order to regain it. She seemed to have forgotten how long it had always seemed to take to arrive at the beach from the house, even if they *did* take the narrow and rather zigzag path that cut between trees and tall shrubbery. But at *least* she'd been lucky enough not to encounter any reptiles along the way or hear an owl issue its mournful cry of warning tonight!

She had leaned her back against a tree while she caught her breath, and now Alexa shook her head impatiently to ward off her own thoughts. There was no sound to be heard except for the rustling of leaves overhead whenever a slight puff of sea breeze brushed against them and the endless soft sighing of the sea waves as they slid up the closely packed yellow-and-blue-tinged sand and retreated. Back and forth and back and forth... Of course he wouldn't be here, still waiting. He had probably become discouraged by now and had left, thinking that she had not been able to manage to escape from the house after all; and he wasn't well enough acquainted with her to know that if Alexa Howard made a promise she would keep it.

Ah, well, at least she still had the night and the ocean all to herself! Straightening, Alexa stretched her arms above her head before lifting the weight of her hair off the back of her neck. How hot and heavy it felt since she'd stopped to rest. Reaching in her pocket for the green velvet ribbon she'd snatched up just before leaving, Alexa contrived rather impatiently to tie back her hair in a careless fashion that she decided would have to do for the present, even if the bow *was* knotted rather clumsily. She found herself longing to wade in the ocean again and to run along the beach playing tag with the waves as she'd done as a child. And why not? But first she must make quite certain that poor Lord Charles was not still waiting for her after all.

Still carrying her soft leather slippers in one hand and pulling her gown calf-high with the other, Alexa left the sheltering darkness of the coconut trees to run lightly over the damp sand, sometimes letting tiny wavelets lick at her heels. When she glanced out to sea there were only the tiny, flickering lights of native fishing boats to be discerned; and above the darker, undulating surface of the ocean the myriads of stars seemed tumbled in their bright clusters against midnight blue velvet.

How beautiful nighttime was! And here by the ocean there were different smells to be breathed in and savored, while the night sky seemed to arch and stretch ahead forever without the stark-black outlines of hills and mountains or densely growing jungle vegetation that always seemed to limit or take away from the vastness of the sky. Without her quite realizing it, Alexa's steps had slowed, then paused, as she gazed at the dark, wavering line of the horizon. *Her* horizon—the furthest she could remember seeing. Would she ever go beyond and see the horizon continue to stretch and stretch ahead of her until she sighted other lands and other oceans? Would she ever get the chance to sight flying fishes and great whales and see ice floes floating on cold black seas, or watch the seasons change and feel what snow was like? Ah—for all of her *reading* about other countries and distant places whose very names spelled enchantment and mystery and her viewing of paintings and sketches and listening to descriptions, she had still not truly experienced anything beyond this small tropical island of about 25,000 square miles that was known as the Pearl of the Indian Ocean. Or Lanka…Serendib…Taprobane…Zeilan…so many other names from times long past when merchants and explorers from all corners of the world had traveled here; some to pause and to trade and some, caught by a certain spell, to stay. Perhaps Ceylon was the fabled land of the Lotus Eaters described in Homer's *Odyssey,* Alexa thought suddenly. For even if distant horizons could beckon on a night such as this with questions and images and promises of rainbows'-ends, there were still the hot golden-and-green-shadowed days that slipped languorously by like water ripples in the wake of a slow-gliding canoe; making it far too easy to allow yourself to be lazy and dream life away without realizing it or even, in the end, *caring.*

"Why don't *we* ever go to England to visit? Everyone else we know does."

"For one thing, because your father is far too busy to leave the plantation. And for another, because neither you nor Freddy could stand the cold or the dampness."

"Well, *France* then! Doesn't Mama have any relatives or friends there? Or Spain. I know from my geography book that it is always hot in the south of Spain. Or…"

"Alexa, that is enough! Your poor mama has no family

left alive in France; and in any case you know very well she'd never leave your papa to try to manage alone; and neither would I. Perhaps one day when you are grown up and married you will travel..."

Dialogue from the past, suddenly returning to her mind as she stared at the distant, moving line between sea and sky. And when had she stopped questioning and become quite happy and content with her life and the activities she filled it with? Why, she had even been reluctant to leave home in order to come to Colombo, where she would have to face new people and new experiences. Thoughtfully, Alexa dug her bare toes into the sand before she moved back to watch a wave smooth out the impression she had left. So much for her impression left on Colombo society—if that nasty Mrs. Langford could have her way!

Suddenly remembering why she had ventured out here in the first place, Alexa pushed straying tendrils of hair off her forehead and temples crossly, annoyed at herself for dallying to indulge in fanciful thoughts. She had promised Lord Charles that she would meet him by what she had always called "the sea wall"—that section of high stone wall marking the boundary of Sir John Travers's property that extended all the way down to the ocean, reserving a pretty stretch of private beach for his use.

"A wall!" Lord Charles had chuckled, delightedly. "Why, it reminds me of *A Midsummer Night's Dream,* although I hope we will not be forced to converse only through a chink in it!"

Alexa remembered laughing at the suddenly dismayed look that had clouded his expressive features for a moment before she had relented enough to explain that their bridle path would take them past the wall in question and that although it was high on *this* side her Uncle John had had rough steps built on *his* side of the wall in case any of his more curious guests might wish to observe what went on beyond it.

"Ah, then you *are* determined to keep a wall between us!"

"Well...perhaps only until I am *quite* sure I can trust you—or until you're ingenious enough to think of a way of scaling it from *your* side!"

It had probably been that particular bit of teasing conversation that had driven Charlotte Langford to distraction because she could not understand a word of what they were saying, Alexa thought, a fleeting smile touching her lips when she remembered the *look* poor Charlotte's face had worn. Well, both Charlotte and her mother would probably swoon from sheer horror if they could have known exactly what the brazen hussy with free and easy manners was up to *this* time! And as for poor Lord Charles... Alexa had started to run again, but now she slowed her steps deliberately as she thought, If he's been patient enough to wait all this time, a few minutes longer won't make too much difference—and I certainly don't want him to think I'm too eager! But I wonder if he *is* there, waiting?

As Alexa approached the stone wall it seemed to look much higher than she remembered it, slicing darkly against the starbright sky. Goodness, the poor man! Why hadn't she thought of suggesting a small boat instead? Unless he'd brought a *ladder...!* Suddenly nervous and uncertain of herself Alexa had to catch back an almost hysterical giggle at the thought. Ladder indeed, as if they were planning an elopement! And of *course* he wasn't still there on the other side of the wall. He had probably given her up a long time ago!

Halting irresolutely once she had reached her destination, Alexa decided against attempting those shallow indentations that passed for steps in order to peer over the top. Not when she was hampered by a skirt. Looking up, she hesitated another moment before, with a slight shrug, she cupped her hands about her mouth and emitted a low but carrying whistle. She knew well enough that ladies never did anything so vulgar as to *whistle,* but if Lord Charles *was* there and heard he would surely be broad-minded enough to understand. Would he guess that it was she and not some night bird? Rather impatiently, Alexa gave the same low whistle once again, this time adding a trilling note at the end. She had suddenly begun, for no sensible reason, to feel uneasy, and found herself almost eager to end her adventure now and return to the house. In fact, she had already picked up her skirts again in preparation when she received the response she had only half-expected. Only—it was neither a straightforward whistle nor a birdcall but something different—something that sent involuntary shivers up and down her spine and seemed to freeze her into stiff stillness for some moments. The hoot of an owl! And there it came again, much closer this time, and of course it could not really be an owl because she knew very well that there were no trees nearby. Such an eerie kind of sound! It's no wonder the natives call it the devil-bird, Alexa caught herself thinking almost superstitiously. And only a short while ago I was telling myself that... She shook herself mentally the next moment, thoroughly annoyed at herself for reacting in such a silly fashion. After all, the cry of an owl was a normal night sound, and that, no doubt, was why he had chosen...

She was on the verge of being daring enough to call out softly when a slight sound made Alexa lift her head sharply, like a young doe scenting danger on the wind; and it was at that moment that she saw a dark shape detach itself from the top of the wall to land before her with a soft, scrunching sound as feet hit sand.

"Oh!" Alexa could not stop herself from gasping before

she tried to recover that involuntary show of weakness with a relieved bubble of speech that was quite unlike her. "How *ever* did you manage *that?* I'd forgotten that this wall was built so as to render it practically impossible to… And I'm sorry I am so late in getting here, but it was more difficult than I had thought it might be to leave without anyone knowing, and I really could not have blamed you in the *least* if you had grown tired of waiting or surmised that I might not come at all! And I am still not quite certain if…if this meeting is quite *wise,* you know…or sensible either! And I do *not* usually keep rattling on in this ridiculous fashion, I'd have you know, but you *did* startle me a little bit, by appearing as suddenly as you did. For heaven's sake! Why can't *you* find something to say? Even if it is only to keep *me* from going on and on… You… Ohh!"

Suddenly, and with shocking unexpectedness, Alexa found her flow of words cut off in the middle of a startled exclamation as she felt herself seized roughly into a far too close embrace while he began to *kiss* her into silence—and very thoroughly too; but how *dared* he? And especially after making her such solemn promises, the very first thing he had done was to try to take immediate advantage of her foolish trust in his word as a *gentleman!*

Filled with righteous indignation Alexa began to struggle and twist furiously against the almost hurtful pressure of his arms and this kiss that bruised her lips against her gritted teeth until she actually tasted blood. Who did he think he was dealing with? Some timid village maiden who might feel flattered by a young Lord's crude attentions? Well, she was capable of fighting back, and he'd soon find *that* out, to his cost!

He had managed, by the sheer unexpectedness of his *attack* on her, to capture both of her hands between their bodies; but now, as Alexa was transformed into a raging virago who kicked viciously at his shins with her bare feet at one moment and then arched her body backward while twisting her head wildly from side to side at the same time, she managed to inch one hand free at least. The lying, cheating reprobate! She'd *show* him! Like a maddened wildcat Alexa tore at him with her nails, wishing only that they had been knives as she ripped furiously at his shirt until it tore and she was clawing at his flesh now; feeling it catch under her nails until the blood flowed. She told herself that had she been able to reach his face instead of his back, she would have slashed it to ribbons! But at least she'd made sure that he'd bear some scars to remind him another time not to mistake the kind of quarry he thought to trap so easily.

They were both panting by now, he with the grim determination to keep her captive and she with an even greater determination to fight herself free. Whatever he had expected when he had yielded to a sudden impulse, it had not been a battle with a female mountain cat with a supple, athletic body that would not stop twisting and turning almost frenziedly—a cat with sharp claws she used with a vicious ferocity he could hardly believe, even when he first felt them gouge and rip at the flesh of his back. Christ! The damned little bitch-cat was liable to rip his flesh to ribbons if he couldn't get her calmed down enough to listen to him.

Had he but known it, Alexa was in such a desperate white heat of fury that she could not have heard, let alone understood, anything he might have said over the pounding of blood in her temples that drummed against the roaring in her ears. She was, in fact, not even herself at that moment—not the Alexa Howard who could behave like a lady if she had to—but a purely primitive creature who would use tooth and claw to kill or maim. Even the stifled noises of protest she made under the gag of his mouth had begun to sound more like growls of rage and hate; and when he lifted his head for a moment to say something to her, she gathered what spittle there was in her mouth and spat into his face with a hiss that reminded him even more forcibly of a cat. And when he would have attempted to silence her wild and almost incoherent cries once more, she drew her lips back from her teeth and tried to bite him. Dammit! Something had to be done with her, and quickly too, before *she* got the best of him.

Alexa had started to kick at him wildly again when suddenly—too unexpectedly for her to be able to keep her balance—she felt herself released; only to fall sprawling backward onto the hard-packed sand with enough of a jar to shock her into momentary silence. Blinking her eyes back into focus again, she saw a dark, menacing figure loom over her and tried to push herself into an upright position without being aware that she was panting out loud; each indrawn breath sounding almost like a sob.

"Oh for Christ's sake! You couldn't have hurt yourself falling back onto the sand.... Not that you don't deserve much worse, you vicious little hellcat, all claws and teeth! I've begun to wonder why in hell I troubled to come out here and wait a good hour at least, just to make sure that *you*... And now what the devil ails you?"

"Ohhh! Oohhh!" As her initial feeling of shock was replaced by renewed fury, Alexa found herself incapable of coherent speech for some moments while her mind adjusted itself to what she had belatedly discovered. *Not* the Viscount Deering at all but *him!* The Spaniard—her saturnine, cynical *bête noire,* of all people! Why hadn't she guessed right away?

And now, after his insultingly cavalier treatment of her, he had the supreme effrontery to pretend some *concern* for her, even to the extent of offering her his hand while he said condescendingly in that drawling accent of his that she *detested:*

"I'm sure you'll find that there's nothing wrong with *you* except for a few well-deserved bruises, you little vixen! Here...let's find out if you can stand..."

Before she had the chance to protest Alexa felt herself positively *hauled* to her feet in a manner that jarred her all over again, while Nicholas de la Guerra dared to add fuel to her fury by suggesting that instead of just standing there like a ninny she might as well brush some of the sand off her gown while she held her tongue and *listened* for a change.

A red mist of pure rage fogging the rational part of her mind, Alexa sprang at him again, fingers curved into talons as she clawed for his eyes—that hateful, mocking face she remembered all too well. And if he had not been as tall as he was or his instincts as sharp as they were, she might have *found* his eyes instead of merely gouging the side of his neck—and barely missing the jugular vein.

Nicholas's reflexes had always been fast, and he had lived the kind of life where survival depended upon finely tuned nerves and senses; but if he had not also developed a certain measure of control over his purely reflexive reaction to any sudden attack, he might easily have killed her, as he had killed before. Fortunately for Alexa he had felt wary of the way she had stood looking at him through narrowed eyes soon after he had helped her back onto her feet. She had reminded him of a mountain cat that settles back onto its haunches just before it leaps for the throat, and it was just as well that even while he spoke to her with deliberate brusqueness he had continued to watch her carefully. How fast she had moved! Fast, and out to kill! Bracing himself just in time, he had managed to seize one of her wrists even while he felt her nails tear at his neck.

The little...! Angry now, he gave the slim wrist he held

a sharp twist that made her cry out with pain, and caught her other wrist when she tried to claw at him again.

"You...you! Let me *go!* I'd like to kill you! I..."

"I'm sure you would indeed, you goddamned hellcat!"

With a painful swiftness that forced a cry of protest from her, he pinioned both of her wrists behind her back, holding her helpless and almost spitting with frustration before him while he continued between his teeth, feeling the warm ooze of blood crawling down the side of his neck to soak into his torn shirt: "And now that I finally have you quietened down for the moment, are you going to hear me out? Or will you force me into snapping the bones in your wrists in order to keep you still? You may be certain that I would have *no* compunction about doing so if you push me to it!"

"I don't care. I don't *care,* do you hear?" So furious and frustrated that she could hardly bring the words out, Alexa's voice sounded choked and almost hoarse. "I will *never...* You can *kill* me if you wish, but I will not submit to your...your brutality! And I won't listen to you...I won't let you force me into...into..."

"Dammit, you hysterical little bitch! Do you think I need to take my women by *force?* Or that a stolen kiss is a natural prelude to rape? I do not know if your *other* experiences have led you to believe so, but in this instance I think you flatter yourself, Miss Howard!"

Her response to his sarcastic comment—first astonishing him and then enraging him—was to scream. Fortunately, because she was overwrought with rage, it was not loud enough to carry too far; but he had an unpleasant impression that she was gathering up all her strength and her energy for another, piercing shriek which might well arouse the inhabitants of every house in the vicinity and their servants as well.

Alexa had, in fact, opened her mouth to do exactly as

he had feared she might when Nicholas said in a deliberately cutting voice, ''If you think to provoke me into kissing you again in order to silence you, I'm afraid it will not work *this* time, you conniving baggage!''

He noticed with a feeling of satisfaction he managed to keep well hidden that his ruse had worked, for instead of a scream he heard a gasp of sheer outrage before she sputtered: ''Con...*conniving* did you dare to say? To...to insinuate that *I* deliberately provoked you into...ohh! But you are...''

Pressing home the slight advantage he had gained, Nicholas drawled: ''The trouble is, my girl, that I'm not Charles, and not as easily taken in by outward appearances and fluttering eyelashes. You see, I've met your kind before—full of teasing tricks meant to lead a man on before you dance back, *just* out of reach. Until, I suppose, you get exactly what you set out to get.''

The *contempt* in his voice made Alexa's own voice rise, and she could not prevent it from shaking as she repeated almost unbelievingly: ''Teasing *tricks?* My...my kind? Do you *dare* mean to imply that *I* attempted to *entice* Lord Charles here in order to...to...''

''You took the fullest advantage of his obvious infatuation with you when you suggested this romantic starlit rendezvous in a very private place, did you not? And then, I suppose that once you had tempted him into kissing you, poor Charles would find, as I did, a veritable virago on his hands. Insulted beyond measure, fiercely guarding your so-called virtue. A scene. An unpleasant scandal... But what did you hope to get from it? Money to hush it up? You didn't set your hopes as high as *marriage,* I hope for your sake, for he'd never go so far as to think of *marrying* you, of course—infatuation or not! Or were you prepared to settle for a slightly lesser position?''

12

For a long time after he had uttered those cold, contemptuous words in a tone that was worse than a slap across her face, Alexa thought she could hear them echoing and re-echoing in her head like the hollow reverberation of bells in a bell tower.

''What did you hope to get from him? Money? He would never dream of *marrying* you, of course. Were you prepared to settle for a slightly *lesser* position?''

No—no! But Lord Charles had not come. He had sent his cynical, cruelly overbearing cousin in his place to…to make it *clear* to her that… Dear God, so *that* was what they thought of her! *He* had called her a ''conniving baggage'' before he'd said the rest. Twisting everything around to make it sound warped and ugly; to make *her* seem ugly and somehow soul-stained.

''Let me go.''

She had remained almost startlingly silent and still in his grasp, with her face in the starlight looking like a pale mask with holes for eyes. So silent that Nicholas could not help feeling what was almost a stab of compunction for having gone quite as far as he had in his indictment of her. Damn her for staring up at him that way, as if *he* had been the one to draw real blood!

"I asked you to let go of me, Señor de la Guerra." Her voice was no more than a whisper, as it had been when she had first spoken a moment ago, and Nicholas frowned down at her suspiciously, exasperated at himself for feeling almost guilty and at her for making him feel that way. Damn her, she was as volatile and hard to grasp as quicksilver!

Making his voice deliberately rough, he said: "Let you go? Why? So that you can go for my eyes again when you think you have me off guard? Those sharp nails of yours are dangerous weapons and deserve to be clipped."

"If I could be sure that I'd succeed in blinding you then I *would* try!" Alexa snapped with a renewed show of spirit, throwing her head up defiantly before she sucked in her breath and said in a voice that shook with frustration, "But...but since you have managed to prove all too *clearly* to me that I am no match for your...for..." And then, to her utter horror, and as if to add to her humiliation, Alexa felt it happen. Like the fit of blind fury that had seized her earlier, closing her mind to all reason, she felt herself and her will overtaken and almost drowned by the sudden storm of weeping that seemed to bubble up from somewhere deep within her with such force that she was powerless to control it.

She wept as wildly and as loudly as an angry child; her mouth open as she tried to scream out her incoherent accusations between large, gulping sobs that shook her whole body. Tears streamed in floods from her eyes and even her nose; Nicholas, staring down at her with shocked fascination, had never seen anything like it.

These were patently no squeezed-out feminine tears that were carefully calculated to soften a man's heart or loosen his purse strings. He could feel her body quiver and vibrate with the fury of her weeping, as if she had been a small boat tossed about by rough seas; and even after he had released her and moved back she did not, as most women would have done, attempt to wipe her nose or knuckle her eyes. No, not *this* one, for Christ's sake! She continued to stand there, rubbing at her wrists almost unconsciously, while she rocked back and forth like a professional mourner; and the noisy sobs were turning into angry wails that seemed to grow increasingly louder by the minute, he noticed grimly.

The devil take her! What had set her off so suddenly? And why didn't she make some effort to control herself? She was acting like a spoiled, frustrated child taking refuge in a temper tantrum when she couldn't have her way—*that* was it! He'd observed the spoiled younger son of one of his mother's friends cry in much the same manner once—throwing himself on the floor to lie there drumming on it with his heels and striking out wildly at anyone who approached in an attempt to soothe his ruffled feathers; squalling all the while. And no doubt that was exactly what *she* would do at any moment now—kick her heels in the sand while her weeping and wailing became even noisier and more hysterical. Well, damned if he'd stand for it!

His jaw clenched, Nicholas grabbed her roughly by the shoulders and shook her as he growled: "You'd better stop your damned caterwauling this minute, do you hear? And temper tantrums won't get you anywhere either, let me tell you! Control yourself and quiet down at once, or I'll be forced to treat you like any other hysterical female!"

"Ahh…aahh…" Christ, he thought disgustedly, was she going to start off again? "Ahh…can't…sto…stop!" Alexa wailed, gasping, and the way her voice had risen dangerously made Nicholas drop his hands from her shoulders before he ran tense fingers through his hair while he eyed her grimly and found himself almost wishing that he *had* broken her neck after all—as he'd been tempted to do when she first ripped at him with those sharp talons of hers. But what should he do with her *now?* Slap her face? He would have enjoyed doing so if he hadn't had the unpleasant feeling that such an action would only succeed in making her cry harder and even louder. If only there had been a bucket of cold water handy he would have thrown it right in her face—exactly what he had done to Fernando when he had grown bored and heartily annoyed by the little brat's screaming; and it had worked like magic, too.

Cold water...dammit, he had reached the limits of his patience with *this* ill-tempered, sharp-clawed brat who stood there bawling with frustration because he'd foiled her attempt to catch herself a Viscount. And if he'd had her on his ship he'd damn well have no compunction at all about giving orders that she should be keelhauled, or thrown overboard for that matter! His mouth hard with determination, Nicholas needed only to take one long stride to reach her before he scooped the startled and still sobbing young woman off her feet and into his arms with as little care or consideration as he might have paid to a bundle of old rags. Only five more furious strides took him thigh-deep into the ocean, unmindful of his polished leather boots or his expensively tailored fawn trousers. And then, still without uttering a word, he looked down just once to make certain the water was deep enough before he dropped her into it.

That should cool her off, and teach the little wildcat a lesson as well! In fact, Nicholas told himself grimly, as he turned about and made for the shore without a backward glance, he didn't really care what happened to her now—or whether she might sink or float. The devil take them all—Charles and his anxious, overly protective parents included! Dammit, Charles was not exactly an inexperienced boy any longer, and was hardly in need of protection or unwarranted interference in his affairs either. Already angry at himself for ignoring his own earlier resolution not to meddle in anything that might transpire between Charles and Miss Howard, Nicholas found his foul mood accentuated by the squelching sound made by his waterlogged boots with each step he took back to shore. Ruined, of course, like his newest pair of trousers and his fine linen shirt, which had been a present to him from his last mistress.

Halting to look down at himself once he had regained dry ground again, Nicholas scowled blackly as he growled a lurid Spanish obscenity and then swore again when he heard himself take another step. He refused to *squelch* every time he set his foot down, goddammit! His teeth gritted when he thought about the time and the careful effort that had gone into the making of these boots. Made of the finest, softest leather obtainable and handstitched by a master shoemaker known throughout Europe, his closely fitting Wellington boots were his favorite footgear as well as being the envy of his friends. His trousers, his shirt and his mistress could be replaced quickly and easily enough; but not the boots! His expression darkening even further, Nicholas sat down on the closely packed sand and began to remove his now-offending footwear; experiencing considerable difficulty in doing so, to make matters worse. Swearing under his breath each time he was forced to tug and wrench at his own foot, he did not feel inclined to pay any attention to the splashing noises he had begun to hear, accompanied by gasps and sputters. At least she wasn't weeping and wailing any longer, and even if he hadn't managed to drown her he hoped that her salty bath had served to cool off her nasty disposition. In fact, if she knew what was good for her the little vixen would do well to slink back to her lair and *not* make any further attempts to provoke him!

Having managed to get *one* boot off at last, Nicholas turned it upside down and watched the water run out of it, cursing under his breath. Damn her! This was all *her* fault! And what was more, he had absolutely no intention of making any apologies for his somewhat rough treatment of her. The deep gouges her nails had made in his back and along the side of his neck had begun to sting and throb quite painfully, and for all he knew he might develop blood poisoning and die from it; and *then* how the bitch would laugh, no doubt, to think she had obtained her revenge on him for confronting her with the truth about herself—with the fact that she was, for all her pretenses and protestations, no more than a sly, teasing coquette who enjoyed taking risks now and then. The half-shy, half-wild child of nature he had thought he'd discovered that moon-bewitched night had been only a figment of his own imagination, making *him* the damned fool for wanting to believe in the impossible—he, the cynic, who of all people should have known better!

In the act of attempting to tug off his other boot while he gave full rein to his dark and angry thoughts, Nicholas suddenly happened to look up, and the apparition that met his eyes was sufficient to stop both thought and motion for the moment. In fact, he remained half bent over, with both hands still holding on to his wet and slippery boot and his head lifted, while he continued to stare, fascinated, at the strange *object* that looked as if it had been washed up on the beach by the playful waves. A bedraggled, forlorn-looking sea waif! Or...no, more like a half-drowned kitten! In any case, the sorry creature he saw before him bore no resemblance to the temperamental virago he'd just tossed into the ocean—or the calculating adventuress of his brooding thoughts just moments ago.

Alexa, if she had known what he was thinking, would probably have turned and crawled back into the sea she'd just crawled out of; but at that moment she hadn't yet thought of what she must *look* like, because she felt almost dead with exhaustion from the effort it had taken her to struggle back to shore. The fact was that she had been so distraught and tear-logged when he had heartlessly thrown her into the ocean that she could easily have drowned, especially since she had swallowed great quantities of salt water before she came spluttering to the surface and realized that she could actually *stand.* Swimming would have been almost impossible with her water-soaked skirts to impede her; and as it was, it was only with the greatest effort and difficulty that she had, almost by instinct, managed to half-stagger and half-crawl out of the tugging, insidious pull of the waves in order to regain the beach once more.

All she wanted, all she cared about was to let herself crumple somewhere *dry,* where the waves couldn't reach her and grasp at her skirts any longer. Almost beyond thought, Alexa felt as if all emotion had been drained out of her, leaving her so empty that nothing mattered except finding a safe place to lie down and rest—her appearance the least of all. Her hair hung in straggly rattails about her face and down her back, with the sad-looking velvet ribbon all entangled in it; while the prettily becoming green dress she had always liked so much bore no resemblance to what it had looked like before. Both the gown and the one petticoat Alexa had conceded to wear tonight had become quite transparent from the soaking they had received and clung far too revealingly to every curve and hollow of her supple young body, drooping off one shoulder to bare a pointed breast. And since Alexa had unthinkingly tugged her skirts up almost as far as her knees in order to make her stumbling progress easier, she now gave the impression of some rain-wet stray out of the gutters of London or Paris who hopefully displayed everything she had to offer in order to earn the price of a meal or a bed to sleep in.

Completely unconscious of the appearance she presented, Alexa continued her haltingly erratic progress up the slight slope, staggering like a sleepwalker; and as he continued to watch her as if he had been rooted in place, Nicholas suddenly found that his earlier feelings of disgruntled rage had been wiped away by the almost overwhelming urge to burst into laughter. A waterlogged sea waif left stranded by the tide! Actually forgetting his ruined boots, he could not help grinning while he waited for her to come up closer. If only she could see herself as she was now, she would never dare to give herself airs and graces again. He had, with unsympathetic amusement, watched her crawl out of the water on her hands and knees before she had managed to clamber onto her feet again; but now, quite suddenly, Nicholas discovered that he no longer felt like laughing derisively at her plight. His eyes narrowed thoughtfully as they took in every detail of her appearance at closer range. Leaning back on his elbows with one leg negligently cocked, he continued to study, as closely as the starlight allowed, the unstudied grace of her body—all the way up from her slender ankles and bare legs to the curve of her hips that accentuated the natural smallness of her waist. And her breasts, as he had noticed before, were high and firm, tapering to tiny peaks that could tempt even a saint into wanting to feel their growing tautness against the palms of his hands, or under his lips....

Without surprise, because he had been *willing* her to come to him, to offer herself to him, Nicholas became aware that, having come abreast of where he lounged, she had let herself drop to her knees, her star-sheened eyes seemingly slightly glazed, as if she too had become mesmerized by the sudden pull of passion between them. Her skin seemed to have taken on a shimmering glow from the combination of salt water and fine sand that contained even finer grains of mica—fool's gold some called it—which could reflect even the faintest light. Leaning forward, she seemed to be offering him her bared breast, with the material of her gown still selfishly clinging closely enough to partly cover her nipple.

His fingers itching to pull down her gown all the way to the waist, Nicholas started to reach out to her when she spoke in a husky, small voice.

"I...I think that I'm about to be quite *sick!*"

Forgetting himself, Nicholas swore in Spanish. "*Maldición!* I should have..." He rolled sideways and out of the way just in time, coming to his knees while her shoulders still heaved and her body rid itself of all the sea water she had managed to swallow.

By the time it was over Alexa had barely enough strength left to drag herself a few inches further up the sloping beach before she collapsed face down onto the sand, to lie there in a kind of swoon. She had forgotten about the events that had led up to this moment and about *him*...forgotten everything but the ghastly feeling of nausea that had suddenly assailed her. But now, as she continued to lie still and limp with her mind emptied of any conscious thoughts, she remained aware of other small and inconsequential things—like the sound of the waves lapping innocently against the beach, and the gritty feel of sand against her face and outspread limbs that seemed to be weighed down by her water-soaked garments and the heavy mass of her wet hair. She neither wanted to move nor to think. She wanted only to be able to fall asleep and to wake up in her own bed at home, discovering with relief that she'd only been having a nightmare. Home—with all its familiar sounds and smells and mornings cool enough to force her to pull her blanket up to her neck. Sometimes over her ears to shut out the noisy birdcalls outside her open window and the plaintive, quavering songs of the Tamil coolies who worked among the coffee shrubs. But it was usually the familiar, tantalizing odors that woke her up in the end: the scent of blue-grey woodsmoke from the kitchen that would be overlaid by the spicy aroma of curries, and the smell of steaming hot black tea when her old ayah carried in the tray and lifted off the tea cozy to pour out her first cup, tempting her into wakefulness. Her thought-dreams suddenly seemed so strong and so clearly defined that Alexa almost expected to hear her ayah's voice scolding her for lying abed so late and reminding her cunningly the next moment that her horse was already saddled and becoming so restive that the muttu found it hard to control her and threatened to ride her himself if the missy didn't come soon.

"He had better not *dare...!*"

Starting up, Alexa discovered that she had spoken the words aloud, so convinced that her wishful imaginings were indeed true that the feel of a wet rag mopping roughly at her face came as quite a shock.

To add to her feeling of disorientation a drily caustic voice that seemed unpleasantly familiar said, "I do hope I have not become the spectre of your maidenly dreams, Miss Howard?"

"I...what...? What do you think you are doing?" As her eyes became focused again and her mind dropped back to ugly reality with a dull thud, Alexa jerked her head back instinctively and found herself looking into the one, dark-shadowed face she had hoped never to set eyes on again. Cruel...hateful! Even if she could not see him very well in the faint light, she could picture his face all too well. The Spaniard, as his cousin laughingly called him, with that dark, harsh-planed face and his hard mouth that never really smiled but only curled mockingly in an unpleasant travesty of a grin. He'd almost succeeded in *drowning* her a few moments ago. What did he intend to do with her now?

Caught in the whirlpool of her own fearful thoughts, Alexa hardly realized for some moments that he was addressing her again in the same dry tone he had used before. ''What do you think I'm doing? I thought that cleaning off that grimy face of yours might do some good, unless you don't mind being taken for a strayed guttersnipe when you decide to return to your lodgings. That is...'' Alexa could feel her face begin to burn with humiliation as his eyes flicked over her in the most *obvious* manner before he continued smoothly: ''That is, of course, if it *was* your intention to return? Forgive me for being blunt, but I do hope that for your own sake you did not do anything so silly as to leave a note or anything of the sort behind saying that you planned—or *hoped*—to elope with Viscount Deering?''

''I did nothing of the sort! And how *dare* you insinuate that I might as much as *consider* doing such a stupid thing? I had no intention of doing anything more than *converse* with Lord Charles, whether you choose to believe so or not. And I am not...not...ohh!'' Almost breathless with rage and mortification, Alexa's words trailed off into a furiously protesting cry as something about the way in which his eyes seemed to dwell significantly on her made her suddenly aware of her appearance. Tugging futilely at the shoulder of her gown which seemed in imminent danger of slipping down to the elbow, she panted, ''You...you unfeeling...*beast!* You *cad!* Have you no conscience at *all?* This is all *your* fault! Ohh...!'' Alexa broke off, speechless with raging frustration when she noticed that he had begun to shake with soundless laughter.

''I'm sorry!'' he managed at last. ''But it was that particular word you used—'cad'—that set me off, I'm afraid. Although on more sober consideration I suppose it might be said to apply, even if it *is* rather mild in comparison to certain more colorful adjectives I've had used on me before.''

''And if *I* was acquainted with such terms of verbal abuse as you seem quite accustomed to, I would indeed use them on you!'' Alexa's voice shook with suppressed emotion. ''But it so happens that my main concern at this moment is *not* you—as vile, as loathsome and without conscience as you have shown yourself to be. It is...''

''Ah, you're doing much better now.'' He applauded sarcastically; but with her distress overriding her fury as she glanced down at herself, Alexa managed to ignore his barbs this time.

She blurted out: ''Oh, *stop* it, can't you? Since you're so anxious to be rid of me and since it was *you,* you brute, who caused this predicament I find myself in, please tell me how I'm ever going to explain this to that nasty old Langford woman when I get back? She's such a wicked, evil-minded *gossip,* and we had quite a set-to this evening so that she... Why, there's nothing she'd like better than to create a great scandal if she could. What am I to *do?*''

She noticed his shoulders lift in a shrug before he said in an unsympathetic, almost bored voice: ''I should think, my dear, that if you were resourceful enough to slip away from the house unnoticed you should be able to manage getting back the same way. And if someone should notice how *wet* you are, couldn't you explain it by saying you decided to have a nocturnal dip in the ocean? After all, you *are* wearing a trifle more than you had on the other night under the moon, aren't you? And I presume you managed to get away with *that* particular escapade without any unpleasant repercussions?'' Before Alexa, breathing hard with fury, could interrupt, he continued caustically, ''I am quite positive, Miss Howard, that you possess a clever and inventive mind that will continue to serve you well, even in your present predicament. And now, if you will excuse me..."

"You have ruined my very favorite gown—and you deliberately tried to *drown* me, you murderer!"

He had made as if to rise, dusting his hands off, but now he stiffened before saying in a positively dangerous voice, "And *you* have caused me to ruin my favorite pair of boots, which not only meant a great deal to me but were probably worth at least ten times more than an old-fashioned rag short enough to show your ankles."

"*Rag* indeed! What would a...a *barbarian* like you know about fashion? And as for your silly old boots, I don't give a *fig* for them, since it was *your* fault entirely! And what's more, you don't know how *silly* you look right now with only one boot on and the other off...and...and as for my showing my *ankles,* why you sound exactly like Mrs. Langford, you...you *hypocrite!* Or do you think by attacking *me,* to make excuses for your own despicable behavior? And what right do you have to *judge?* I came here to meet Lord Charles, and that cannot be any concern of yours, surely, nor any reason for you to try to *force* me to submit to your crude advances! And then, when I disappointed your expectations by attempting to *resist,* you...you would have drowned me if you could! Oh...there are no words vile enough to describe you, believe me. And as for..." Since he had surprisingly remained silent throughout her tirade despite the tension Alexa could sense in him, she paused only long enough to take a gulping breath before sweeping on scornfully: "And where is your *cousin,* I wonder? Is it a habit of his to plead for private *conversation,* giving his word as a *gentleman,* and then send you in his place? Is it an evil game the two of you play, *señor,* because your manners are too crude and too abrupt for most feminine sensibilities? To think that *you* spoke to me once of *honesty* and directness...!"

His voice cut through her accusing speech like a steel blade, silencing her in spite of herself. "Enough, Miss Howard! You should learn not to belabor a subject once you've made your point. Ah yes—like a veritable Portia, your eloquence has touched even *my* black villain's heart, I must admit; and because of it I must confess that when I left poor Charles he was quite drunk and snoring loudly! There was a party at an officer's mess we were both invited to, and I must admit I encouraged him to drink far more than he could hold. And then I went so far as to have him carried back to the ship and given a nightcap that should keep him sound asleep until late afternoon—by which time I expect we'll be well out to sea." Ignoring Alexa's gasp of outrage, he continued ironically: "And since you have succeeded in moving me to *honesty,* Miss Howard—or may I call you Alexa, since we have come to know each other so well?—I found that once I had disposed of Cousin Charles I had time on my hands, you see, and I felt it a great pity that you should be kept waiting out here alone, with your little heart all aflutter in your pretty bosom."

As Nicholas had anticipated when he began prodding at her simmering temper, she lunged at him like a maddened mountain lion, all claws, her teeth showing too, as she spat, "You cruel…*devil!* By what right…"

Poised and ready for her, Nicholas trapped both her wrists with ease, forcing her backward in spite of her struggles and leaning the weight of his body over hers so that she could not wriggle free nor escape from hearing what else he had to tell her. Ignoring her gasps that sounded almost like sobs and the way her head tossed back and forth, he grated between his teeth: "By what right, did you say? By God, if you didn't have such a vicious temper you'd remember that Charles and I are related and have become quite well acquainted these past few months. And you might also have asked yourself how *I* came to know just where and when you two young lovers had planned to meet!'' Still holding her arms pinioned above her head, Nicholas felt the sudden stiffening of all her limbs as he went on harshly: ''You *did* ask for honesty, did you not? And perhaps it is time you learned that the truth is not always pleasant to hear, besides being twice as hard to swallow. If it's any consolation to you, Charles was, in fact, quite taken with you—to the point of infatuation, as I'm sure I mentioned earlier. But you must also understand that like many other young men, Charles makes a habit of falling in and out of love quite often—and sometimes, so his parents warned me, with the most unsuitable females.''

Alexa had, while he was speaking, ceased her frenzied struggles and her efforts to interrupt; but now, sensing a fresh revolt, Nicholas added harshly: ''There's no need to act offended, I assure you! For in *your* case I happened to develop the mistaken notion that perhaps you were not aware of the plans Charles had for you. *Did* you know, Alexa? Or did you imagine that it would be a great adventure to be carried off on horseback and smuggled aboard a ship bound for England? Did he promise to have you fashionably gowned and dripping with jewels so that he could show you off to his friends? Well? Is that the extent of your ambition? It's your turn for honesty now, I think—that is, if you are capable of such a thing.''

In a cold little voice that took him slightly aback she said: ''Why is it that you seem impelled to *snarl* at me and insult me at every turn? If you had only *let* me I would have answered you before. Because of *course* I had no idea that Lord Charles planned to try and elope with me; and even if he had asked me to I would have refused, in spite of the jewels and fashionable gowns he might have offered me. I would have insisted, if he was serious, that he must speak to my father as well as to my dearest Uncle John, who understands me better than anyone in the world.

But I do not think that I am quite ready to be married yet, even if Aunt Harriet keeps telling me I should be... And what have I said *this* time to make you laugh in that ugly, evil fashion?"

"Oh, Christ! Did I laugh? If I did it must have been because I *am* all the things you've called me, as well as being a confirmed skeptic, and that is why I can hardly believe you did not understand what I meant when I... Or could it be that you are trying to have a joke at my expense? Pure little Alexa, who would battle to the death to save her virtue. But why no pistol to protect yourself tonight?"

"Because this gown has no pocket large enough and I had no load for it!" The words slipped out involuntarily, and Alexa could have bitten her tongue when he laughed shortly in the same nasty manner once more. She snapped, "If you are quite done with laughing at everything I say, I wish that you would let me up. You're hurting my wrists, besides being so heavy that I can hardly breathe!"

"Ah, sweet Alexa, now you hurt my feelings. Must I pretend to be sorry that I'm lying over you? Such a sweet pillow your lovely body makes. Why, I could lie on you and *in* you for hours on end if you would only let me—which is also exactly what Charles wanted."

"Stop talking in that silky-nasty, hypocritical tone of voice! And I don't understand *anything* you're saying and I feel stifled besides!" Trying to cover her disquiet with a petulant tone of voice, Alexa eyed him warily. What cruel game was he indulging in *this* time? She was, by now, only too aware of her complete vulnerability to his strength, and even being found out by Mrs. Langford seemed infinitely preferable at this moment to being held captive by a savage Spaniard who possessed neither decency nor conscience.

"You do not understand *anything,* you say? Then perhaps I should be more direct, in order to make sure that you *do,* and so that there can be no further misunderstanding. You see, my dear, Charles never wanted you for his wife. Wives, in his circles, are carefully chosen from the *right* families, and such matches are usually made with the idea of breeding sons to carry on the family line and bear the title; whereas *mistresses* on the other hand... Among his friends a man is admired for the beauty and *dash* of the mistress he keeps and the style in which he keeps her; and in some ways I suppose a mistress is one of the more cherished of a man's possessions until he decides he is tired of her, or *she* decides to move on to greener pastures. I wonder if I have managed to make myself plain enough, or would you prefer that I elaborate further?'' In spite of Alexa's violent head-shake he seemed almost obsessed with the need to go on tormenting her, adding to the agony of shamed degradation that tore at her already frayed nerves. She heard his harsh voice continue almost tauntingly: ''You know, come to think of it, you're pretty enough and have a magnificent figure, so that I cannot really blame Charles for wanting to carry you off with him to London! With a little town polish and a few lessons you could probably soon have your pick of wealthy protectors—unless you continue to be naive enough to set your sights so high as to entertain the notion that one of them might actually *marry* you. But you seem to be a clever enough wench when you use your head. You had Charles persuaded that you are actually a virgin, you know. He enjoys deflowering virgins—'breaking them in' he calls it. I wonder how long you would have been able to keep up a pretense of shy, untarnished virtue within the close quarters of his cabin?''

''Oh *please!* Please—you've said quite enough!'' Alexa whispered in a tortured voice, turning her head aside so that he could not see the sheen of tears that filmed her eyes.

"Have I? Perhaps you're right, for there *are* some occasions when sparring words and playacting only waste time that could be spent much more pleasurably." Although his voice had softened and become almost teasing, Alexa suddenly found herself seized by a feeling of unreasoning terror when she felt his body move over hers in a subtly *different* way from before. It was as if he was *fitting* himself to her—cunningly making her all too aware of the shape and feel and contours of his body, of its hardness and its strength, so that she felt as if there was not one inch of *her* body that was not touched by his and possessed by his. *Possessed?* Dear God—after everything he had said, had accused her of, had insinuated; now *this* ultimate humiliation as well, of being treated like...like a...

"Don't...*don't!*" Alexa moaned before she summoned up enough strength to blurt out with desperate defiance: "If you do not let me go this *instant* I swear that I will denounce you! I'll tell my uncle—tell the Governor himself, if I have to—that it was *you* who enticed me here in order to take advantage of me! I'll—why, it will be quite obvious to anyone that I tried to resist you! And I'll tell them, too, how you tried to *drown* me in order to keep me silent. I..."

"Before or after?" The lazily drawled question, delivered in a tone of mild curiosity, took Alexa so much aback that she found herself stammering.

"What? What do you mean?"

"Am I supposed to have attempted to drown you before or after I took *advantage* of you? And how will you explain being alive to tell your pitiful tale?" She could have sworn that he was laughing at her again—*damn* him!—before he shook his head and added in a hatefully condescending voice: "I'm surprised that you could not do better, you know. Up until now you struck me as being a most resourceful young woman, quite used to nocturnal expeditions on your own where most females would swoon at the very idea. Surely you can think of something more dramatic? For instance, that I had, since our first moon-bathed meeting, become so enamored of you that I deliberately arranged to take my cousin's place tonight in order to..." Bending his head, his lips brushed hers with a teasing lightness before he continued softly, "To kiss you again and find out if your lips were still as soft as I remembered and to..."

"No..." Alexa's despairing whisper was lost under the gently exploring caress of his lips, which seemed to plant a myriad kisses as light as the brush of a butterfly's wing on her trembling mouth—from the arch of her upper lip to the fullness of the lower, and then to the very corners of her mouth and back as he whispered between kisses: "And to discover if I—would still want you—*dulce* Alexa—as much as I did that first night—and the second—and that I found you just as irresistible and desirable—and—you had better stop squirming under me in that suggestive fashion or be answerable for the consequences."

"Please, you mustn't! You're... Don't make me... I don't *want* to...." Why must he continue to kiss her? Not only her mouth but the tip of her nose, her chin, her damp cheeks and the very spot where her dimple showed when she smiled. And back to linger over her mouth, silencing her last, despairing protests with a kiss that was no longer light but fiercely demanding.

I'm lost! A small voice cried in the furthest reaches of her mind. Ah, it's too late now and I can't help myself. I..."want," he had said. What had he meant? What was this strange, helpless feeling of... Alexa had not been aware that her wrists had finally been freed until she felt the muscles in her arms begin to ache when she lifted them to clasp them about his neck. It didn't matter, when overriding everything else was the warm, tingling feeling that made her breath come shortly and her heart pound as his hands touched her body—moved over her flesh; each movement a lingering caress as he leaned over her.

"Oh God, you wild witch of the sea, how I want you!" Somehow his impatient hands had freed both her breasts now and he made the words sound almost like an oath before he bent his head to kiss each peak in turn until Alexa felt as if she could not bear any more—and would not be able to bear it if he stopped. "Have I made you want me too, little firebrand?" Alexa hardly realized what he was saying as she felt his warmly caressing fingers on her leg, pushing up her wet gown to above her thigh before sliding down to stroke, very gently and unhurriedly, up and down the length of her inner thigh, from just above her knee to… She should stop him, but she didn't want to any longer. "I want you to want me as strongly, and as achingly, and as unreasoningly—damn you—as I want you! Do you understand what I am saying yet? *Can* you?"

Biting off his own forced-out words, Nicholas fastened his mouth over hers again as he felt her body begin to arch and shudder while she moaned uncontrollably; her fingers almost clawing at his back as she clutched at him fiercely. She wanted to scream, and she wanted to go on and on, wanted him to keep touching her in that particular way in that particular…*wanted!* Feeling his tongue begin probing her mouth as he kissed her in almost the same way as his finger had begun, very gently, very slowly, to probe inside her.

Lost to everything but feeling and the sudden heat that seemed to spread all over her body, Alexa offered no resistance and no protest as the first slight discomfort she had experienced soon passed and she arched her hips up almost demandingly against his hand. Her head was flung back now as her whole body became rigid, seeming to vibrate from within as ripple after ripple of sensation grew and grew and became more intense each second while she made gasping, incoherent sounds in her throat.

What a contradictory creature she was, Nicholas thought, kissing the sweet arch of her throat and feeling the tiny pulse that throbbed beneath his lips. All fire and fury one moment, then wildly, passionately responsive the next. Clinging to him and pressing her body eagerly up to his in wanton invitation almost as fiercely as she had clawed and kicked at him before; her thighs parting easily to make way for him now as he felt her open like a tightly budded flower under his hand. Ready for him at last—and God, how much he wanted her! It was, by now, as if he *needed* to bury himself in her, feeling the heat and the tightness of her close around him, before the quick, convulsive contractions when she… Damn the troublesome encumbrance of breeches! He wanted her badly, wanted to take her *now.* She was so velvety-soft and so *tight* in there, almost as if she was still a… And then, while a disbelieving voice in his mind kept saying, "no, dammit to hell, no!" his exploring fingers encountered an unexpected barrier to any further pleasurable exploration. Or to anything else, for that matter, unless he forgot himself sufficiently to make short work of her offending maidenhead. And why not, for Christ's sake? She was hot-blooded and passionate and *ready,* and if it wasn't him tonight it would be some other man some other night soon. Why not take her now, without thinking, while they were both hot for each other?

13

Alexa kept her eyes tightly squeezed shut even *afterwards,* while she continued to savor the sensation of delicious, satisfied languor that made her feel as if she had become as light as a feather—still floating...drifting.... Why had she fought against giving in to her instincts that had led her to such exquisite pleasure as she had just experienced? A *feeling* that she could never describe, even to herself; or rather a complexity of myriad sensations felt all at once that seemed to move both outward and inward until... At least she *knew* now what "wanting" and "making love" meant. How strange and wonderful and almost *frightening* at the same time to feel yourself disappear into a million tiny sparks of light before coming back together again. Was she a Fallen Woman now? She didn't care. I feel *happy,* Alexa discovered, beginning to smile and then to laugh from sheer enjoyment and lightheartedness.

"Well? And what ails you *now,* for God's sake?"

Wondering why his voice had sounded almost like a snarl, Alexa blinked her eyes open as she turned languidly onto her side and discovered that he was lying on his back with his arms crossed under his head, a scowl on his face. "Well, what's wrong with *you,* for that matter?" she murmured in a husky, unconsciously coquettish voice as she ran one exploring finger teasingly down his bare chest that was all roughness and smoothness over hard-muscled strength. But instead of responding he caught her wrist with unnecessary roughness and moved her hand away.

Puzzled, Alexa looked inquiringly at him. "Was it too bold of me to touch you like that? I only wanted to..."

"Alexa! Dammit!" His voice sounded as rough as his touch had been as he rolled over impatiently onto his side to face her, propping himself up on one elbow before he continued almost angrily: "One of the many things you obviously have yet to learn is that there are limits to the exercise of self-control. And *mine* I can assure you, has been strained to the breaking point already! Do you understand me?"

"But...but I wasn't trying to...Nicholas? I did not mean to make you cross with me again! Only to show you how wonderfully happy I feel all of a sudden. Please don't be angry! And if you will only *tell* me what I did that was wrong, I will try not to make the same mistake ag—"

"*Will* you be quiet and listen to me for a change?" The sheer fury that charged his voice was enough to render her speechless as she stared wide-eyed into the dark blur of his taut-muscled face; and Nicholas forced himself to suck in a deep breath before he managed to continue in a more controlled and reasonable voice: "I'm sorry. Hell, it's really not *your* fault that I'm in such a vile mood! And it has nothing to do with anything *you* did, although in a way you damn well *caused* all of this with your... No, please try to restrain the flow of words I see trembling on those delicious lips of yours, *querida mía,* and hear me out. Nights can seem all too short sometimes, and I have to get back to my ship before she misses the tide. And although I'm not usually given to making speeches or to diplomatic words and phrases, I feel, for some irritatingly inexplicable reason, that it is almost my *responsibility* to warn you against..." He swore under his breath. "Christ! I begin to sound like an uncle or a Mrs. Langford, I suppose! But since I have already said too much..."

All her newfound happiness seemed as ephemeral as mountain mists that stayed for only a few seconds before vanishing under the onslaught of the sun; leaving nothing behind to show it had ever been there except a curious little ache of misery that she would never, ever show. In a flat, dead-sounding voice Alexa said, "Yes, please do go on. And pray do not hesitate to be blunt, if you must."

"All I meant to say was that every man is different. And that few men would hesitate to take what they may imagine is being offered to them. Dammit, there is a difference between being innocent and being naive, as you'd better learn quickly; and *gentlemen* do not, as a rule, either respect or expect to find virginity in a young female who agrees readily to a clandestine meeting in some isolated place." Nicholas found himself wishing that the golden rind of the same moon he'd first met her under had not had the temerity to show itself, allowing him to see the expression on that transparent face of hers. She looked as if he'd just slapped her, and he would have infinitely preferred to be any place but *here* with a half-finished lecture on morals to deliver. Clenching his jaws, he said between his teeth: "If you hope to get yourself a husband and respectability, my inquisitive little virgin, I would advise you to force yourself to conform to the rules that govern the society you must live in. For as unfair as it may seem, and *is* in fact, those rules are too easily bent or stretched or even ignored where *men* are concerned. To make it even clearer, an act of mutual passion only enhances a man's reputation when he boasts of his latest conquest to his cronies, but the unfortunate female will have lost hers. Do you understand what I am trying to explain to you?"

"I...think you have indeed managed to make yourself...*more* than clear, thank you." Alexa found she had to lick her lips, which suddenly felt stiff and cold, before she could get the words out. "But you..."

Sitting up with one fluid, easy motion that had put his back to her, Nicholas seemed to ignore her now; tugging viciously at the boot he had forgotten to remove until it came off and he flung it aside. It was almost, Alexa thought with a sudden stab of pain, as if he was throwing *her* off as well, now that he'd done what he'd obviously considered his duty. And now at any second he would stand up and dust the sand from himself before he turned to walk away from her as if she no longer existed for him. Leave her. She'd never see him again. And she should be glad, glad!

"But you said...you told me once before that being my *natural* self was more important than other people's rules." Why did she persist when he was already on his feet?

Hesitating almost unwillingly, he looked down at her with expressionless eyes that seemed as dark as hers in the faint light. "Another lesson to remember, I'm afraid. Men will say—and promise—almost anything to a gullible female in order to get what they want from her, without meaning a word. I'd advise you, my too-sweet Alexa, to be careful in future to remain an *elusive* quarry and to save your virginity for your husband to take on your wedding night. Men are *very* insistent on virgin brides, for some ridiculous reason!"

While he had been speaking to her in a drawling, indifferent voice, Nicholas had proceeded to turn his wet trouser legs up to mid-calf, looking very much like a Spanish buccaneer as he straightened and turned to walk away from her without another word.

Finding her voice at last, Alexa flung her last question

almost desperately at his retreating back as she scrambled to her feet, wondering why her legs felt so weak under her. "Wait! *Damn* you!" Ah, at least that had halted him—his shoulders stiffening before he turned his head. Only that small concession, forcing her to go on speaking without being able to choose her words more carefully: "Why did you go on and on about...saving my *virginity?* I thought...I thought that after you...that I had nothing *left* to save any longer. How can..."

Grimly, he waited until her hesitantly spoken words began to stumble and falter before saying in a caustic voice: "My sweet, provocative sea nymph, had I *not* discovered that you were still *virgo intacta* I would have gone very much further than I did, believe me! But since you *were* and since I had promised myself long ago that I would never take a virgin again... No, I assure you that you're still unsullied and virginal. All I did with you, sweet innocent, was relieve as best I could the tension that I was responsible for building up in you. And now, if you'll excuse me, I think I will leave to seek some sweet solace for my *own* tensions before it's time to board ship. *Señorita,* I leave you to your prayers! *Adios.*"

While he had been speaking Alexa's limbs had become so weak that she had collapsed to her knees; and now, after he had left her with a strangely formal sketch of a bow, it seemed as if everything around her had suddenly become very still; almost as if time itself hung suspended like the pitiful splinter of a moon hanging above the horizon—a candlewick about to sputter out. The only sound she was conscious of for a while was the repeating echo of his harshly delivered words in her head; until suddenly her ears picked up the faint drumming of a horse's hooves, fading away almost instantly into the distance. He'd have to have brought a horse in order to scale the wall, of course, and to take him back afterwards. But what did that matter to her now? Slowly, turning her head to look about her with an effort, Alexa became conscious again at length of her surroundings, and of her own sorry state.

Most of the stars that had seemed to glow so brilliantly earlier seemed to have faded into obscurity, and the rising tide had already begun to inch its gradual way up the sloping beach. His ship would sail out from Colombo Roadstead at high tide. What time would that be? She had no idea of how late or worse, how *early* the hour was; but if she hoped to regain the comparative haven of her room Alexa knew she must hurry and run all the way back.

Gritting her teeth with determination, Alexa managed to get to her feet again and began trying to shake as much sand as possible from the folds of her damp, crumpled dress. What a fright she must look! At least he'd pulled down her skirts and...but she could not think of that part of it just yet; must remember only that she'd been taught a lesson—several lessons in fact. Pulling her gown up further in front, Alexa began to make her way back, fixing her mind only on remembering the path she had taken earlier and on making up some excuse in case she happened to be found out. At least they couldn't know she had met someone—or anything else that had happened. Perhaps she could say that her confrontation with Mrs. Langford and the accusations that had been made had so upset her that she'd decided to drown herself. A story she'd thought of using in a different context earlier, Alexa remembered with an involuntary pang. But in this case it *might* work. Mrs. Langford would certainly relish the dramatic effect of her lecturing! It might even make her think more carefully before she launched into one of her sermons in future. Yes, unless she could think of a better story, it would have to do. She had tried to drown herself, but the ocean was too shallow and the water too salty and cold, so that in the end her cowardice had got the better of her.

While she had been forcing herself to keep her mind busy, Alexa's bare feet had found her shortcut almost by instinct, running as soundlessly and lightly as she could to avoid disturbing any small nocturnal creatures or sleeping birds. Slowing down after a while to catch her breath, she guessed that she could not be too far from the safety of the house now; and she had seen no flickering torches nor heard any anxious voices calling in search of her. Perhaps she would have no need for made-up explanations after all. Only a few more yards to traverse *very* quietly, and then she would soon see the outline of the house, and after that it would only be a matter of…

Alexa had begun to move forward again, at a slower pace this time; but in spite of her bravely optimistic thoughts her nerves, already exacerbated by what had taken place earlier, were as tautly strung as thin wires on the verge of snapping. When she rounded a sharp bend in the path and almost ran into a dark shape that seemed to loom up from nowhere, she almost fainted from shock and could not repress a small, startled "Ohh!" before she recognized Sir John's urgent whisper and felt his hand grip her arm warningly.

"Alexa, hush! Sorry I had to startle you this way, but there was no help for it. Knew I had to stop you before you got as far as the house, my dear."

"Oh!" This time it was a soft, guilty whisper.

"It's that damned meddling Langford woman again. And that sly-puss daughter of hers. Never could stand namby-pamby, sniveling young women! But to get on with it—the way *Charlotte* told it to her mama was that she couldn't fall asleep without apologizing to you for having *unwittingly* caused trouble. Went to your room, she says, and looked in quietly in case you were asleep, and… Well, I'm sure you can guess the rest, my dear."

From Sir John's concise account Alexa gathered that

Mrs. Langford had decided to keep vigil in Alexa's room, to "catch the little hussy when she comes sneaking back," according to Velu, who could repeat whole sentences verbatim even if he didn't quite understand some of the words used. And it was Velu who had found Sir John in the garden and had told him everything; being promptly given instructions that if Mrs. Langford should ask for him his master could not be found either—he was fond of taking long nightly strolls. But now Mrs. Langford had begun to demand that Velu find Sir John *immediately;* huffily refusing to believe that a man of his age should prefer to linger until past two o'clock in the damp night air when he had a perfectly comfortable bed to sleep in.

"And so now there's the devil to pay and it's all my fault," Alexa whispered contritely. "Oh, Uncle John! I'm so *very* sorry, and especially if I caused *you* any anxiety."

Sir John made as if to clear his throat before thinking better of it and saying abruptly: "As a matter of fact, after your set-to with the Langford female it didn't surprise me when Velu told me you'd run off somewhere. Couldn't blame you for needing to breathe some fresh, clean air into your lungs, my dear, and knowing you as well as I do, I guessed where you might have decided to go. Fact is, I thought you might want to talk it out, y'know. Help get things off your chest! Only reason I decided to take a stroll down to the beach, just in case. But… Well, didn't feel I had the right to interfere, really. Meddling…"

Alexa could not help her shocked intake of breath before she managed to whisper, "You…then you must have… You *saw?* Everything?"

"Didn't mean to play the voyeur, my dear. Or to… Well, what I'm trying to say in my clumsy fashion is that I only stayed long enough to feel sure that you were not…that you weren't being *forced,* dammit!"

Alexa could feel her face growing hot and cold in turn.

He'd *seen!* Her willingness—everything. Seen her lying there on the sand with her skirts up and her breasts bare; lost in the throes of that shameless, abandoned ecstasy that had made her forgetful of all else—including the consequences! Why, *anyone,* some trespasser, some curious fisherman, might have watched too, for all that *she* had thought, or cared either. Because during that space of timeless time that might have been moments or minutes or even hours, she had not belonged to herself any longer—had not even *been* herself. She would have allowed him to do anything at all—anything he wanted to do with her. Would have let him take her anywhere he pleased with him, forgetting shame or conscience—if he wanted her…

Ah, don't think about it. You mustn't; it's over, her mind warned her as she struggled to find words. "I… How you must despise me now. And oh, I am old enough to realize that to say like a child 'I did not *think*' is no excuse at all! Aunt Harriet was right. I am too rash, too impetuous, too unmindful of… I suppose I *should* have drowned myself after all! It was what I had planned to tell Mrs. Langford in case she… Oh, but I think I could bear *anything* except that *you* should think badly of me and be disappointed in me, although I cannot blame you for it."

"Now just you look here, my girl—that's quite enough out of you along *those* lines, do you hear?" Alexa had never heard Sir John speak so roughly to her before, nor had he ever grasped her by the shoulders as if he meant to *shake* her. "Dammit, I won't have you turning into a whining, self-flagellating… And why the blast should you think that after I've done my best to teach you to think for yourself I should turn about and *despise* you for doing so? Eh? Or blame you for being young, and human, and impetuous? *You've* been brought up differently from the likes of those *others*—" he gave a jerk of his head in the direction of the house "—and thank God for it. But because you've got a *mind,* my girl, you'd better use it before you think up any more *explanations,* because your drowning story won't do, you know. Hah!'' He shook his head disgustedly. ''No one's going to believe you were trying to succeed in drowning yourself for the past three or four hours—not even Mrs. Langford.''

''Oh! I suppose I didn't think of *that.* But...but you see, I *did* go in the sea, not that I *meant* to, but...'' Alexa was glad Uncle John's sharp eyes could not see her flush as she went on hurriedly, ''But since I *am* quite soaked through and my hair is still so wet...it was the only explanation I could think of.''

''Hmm!'' Sir John's voice was dry. ''Bathing in the ocean is supposed to be good for the health—and I'm sure it was wise of you under the circumstances. *His* idea I take it?''

How could he have guessed? And what had he meant by... But Sir John must have taken her puzzled silence for assent, for he nodded in a satisfied way before his manner suddenly changed; becoming unusually serious and almost solemn as he caught both of her cold hands in his before saying gravely:

''Alexa my dear, we've known each other for quite a few years now, haven't we? Let's see, the first time I met you, you were seven? Eight? Hard to remember exact dates at my age.''

''It seems to *me* as if I have known you *forever!*'' Alexa said in a fierce whisper, squeezing his hands back. ''And you've always been my very best friend in all the world—the only person I can talk to about *anything* at all.''

''Do you think you can trust me, Alexa? Completely?''

''But you *know* I do! Only I don't understand why...''

''I know you don't understand, my dear. Not yet, anyhow. But I promise you that after we have dealt with Mrs. Langford together, we'll have a chance to talk. For the moment, I'm asking—and hoping—that you trust me enough to be absolutely sure that I'd always do only what's best for *you.* I've had a few hours to think things over, and... Well, the most important thing of all is that even if there are any *consequences* of what took place tonight, you'd be protected. No slurs on your good name or your parents' either. And in case you don't... Well, you won't be *held* to anything, you know! I've made you my heiress in any case. Meant to tell you before you had to go back home, of course, but now's as good a time as any, I suppose. Now—what do you say to facing the music and getting it over with?"

"But I...but Uncle John, I don't quite *understand* yet. What am I supposed to say to Mrs. Langford? And what..."

"Don't want *you* to say anything at all. A few maidenly blushes would do, and if you can't force the blushes you can look down modestly and twitch at your skirts. I've seen that particular trick work very well. But just you leave the speechmaking to me, and try *not* to show that you're either shocked or surprised when you hear what I intend to tell Mrs. Langford, eh? Put a stop to any gossip at all. Even *she's* not going to dare say a nasty word, I promise you. Only solution, my dear, so come along now!"

PART II

14

The skirts of Alexa's new black taffeta dress, belled out from her tightly corseted waist by six starched petticoats, swished and rustled with every step she took; and even when she sat or stood. Now, as she stared back at her reflection in the mirror, it was like observing a stranger, only slightly resembling the old Alexa who had looked back smiling and merry-eyed, sometimes even going so far as to pull a face or stick out an impudent tongue. But *this* sober-looking person she saw would never do anything so childish or look so happily carefree either. Looking back at her was a somberly clad woman who might have been thirty years old, with a pale, drawn-looking face and slate-grey eyes that seemed enormous and quite blank, as if they had been painted on. The colorless lips that were held firmly together had surely never learned how to smile. Only the bold, dark slash of her brows belonged to that *other* Alexa, who would never have worn her hair in such a severe style either—all pulled back from her face and parted in the center with tightly woven braids coiled into a heavy knot at the nape of her neck. Every curl or riotous tendril that tried to escape had been firmly pinned in place.

Why, it's not *me* at all, she thought involuntarily before

the treacherous thought too was firmly caught back. The *me* of only a week ago no longer existed; changed irrevocably by a cynical, jungle-eyed stranger who had invaded her life for a short time and had caused almost everything that had happened since.

She *must* learn to control her thoughts, to prevent them from straying in spite of herself. Suddenly, Alexa had to squeeze her eyes shut, gripping very tightly at the edge of her dressing table. How unreal, how *impossible* it still seemed that so many shattering events could have taken place within the space of *hours*—altering her whole existence and leaving her with this cold numbness that seemed to come from somewhere deep inside her to freeze even her mind. She moved about and ate without tasting anything and slept when she was told to and even spoke when she was spoken to without remembering afterwards what had been said or what *she* had said. Everything familiar and comfortable that she used to take for granted was so different now. Even her relationships with the people she had been closest to seemed to have changed, and sometimes she felt as if *she* wasn't real either but caught up in a bad dream she couldn't wake up from. She was sleepwalking, as Freddy used to… Alexa's mind pulled quickly away from that thought, and she chose instead to remember the look on Mrs. Langford's face when Sir John, holding her firmly by the elbow to keep her from turning coward, had led her into the house that night.

"So you have found her after all. You cannot imagine how sick with worry we have been, Charlotte and I, as the long hours ticked by. Naturally, neither of us could sleep a wink! I must tell you that I *did* try to make your servant understand that you *had* to be informed, but he… Ohh!" Belatedly taking in Alexa's bedraggled appearance, Mrs. Langford had gasped as if she was choking, her hand going to her throat. "Oh, dear heaven! I cannot *believe* that I am seeing... *No!*"

By then, Alexa had begun to feel very strange, as if all the voices she heard were coming from some distance away and had nothing to do with her. But she would *not,* at any cost, give Mrs. Langford the satisfaction of seeing her fall into a guilty swoon at her feet.

Breathing deeply, as she recalled doing *then,* the young woman dressed in black let herself sink onto the padded stool before her mirrored dressing table, keeping her eyes fastened shut as she tried to remember everything that had been said. But only snatches of the conversation that had gone on over her head and some isolated phrases came back to mind. "Compromised"—she remembered *that* word very well, and what it seemed to mean. Uncle—oh dear, she really *must* remember to call him *Sir* John—had explained that he and Alexa had been strolling on the beach together, talking of the future. *Had* he used her story, in part at least? That part was hard to recall now, but she *did* remember the look of venomous chagrin on Mrs. Langford's face and more tears from Charlotte. And Mrs. Langford had actually kissed her wetly on both cheeks as she almost *hissed* with deadly sweetness, "So *lucky!*" Alexa had almost laughed. If Mrs. Langford only knew that her dearest, most gallant Uncle John had gone to the length of pretending he wished to *marry* her only in order to save her reputation!

"Alexandra has had quite enough nervous strain for one night, I think. Must insist she go off to bed at once—Velu!—while you and I continue our discussion, eh, Mrs. Langford? Know I can count on you to help out, of course. Colonel Langford's a lucky man, and I shan't fail to tell him so when I see him next. Hope he might consent to being best man at the wedding—unless Alexandra changes her mind before then. Woman's privilege, you know!"

"Oh, but I'm positive Miss Howard would never *dream* of doing so, not when...one of our most eligible and *elusive* bachelors, if I may say so."

Words had followed her, but she had been, by then, wrapped in a cocoon of sheer exhaustion, and nothing made sense or mattered either. She'd had a hot bath and several cups of hot tea, and had felt relieved that all responsibility had been taken from her; that she could escape, for the moment, from the effort of explaining, thinking, remembering anything she would rather *not* remember. She had still been the old Alexa, whose moods were as different as sun and shadow and who could push carelessly out of her mind anything she did not care to think about—occupying it instead with something else, something new. In that "then" time, there had been nothing capable of keeping her upset or depressed for too long, and oh, why couldn't she have continued that way? Why couldn't everything in the enchanted garden she once lived in have remained unchanged and unchangeable? Who needed Princes to break down fairy walls meant to keep all who dwelt within their magic boundaries safe? Because when the walls collapsed and crumbled she had been unprepared and unready—helpless and far too vulnerable.

When Alexa's eyes opened to look into their own reflection, they looked almost black, tormented and staring as her clenched fists pressed into her temples as if to grind out all sound and thought. But how could one stop *thinking?*

Thoughts formed pictures in her mind. Sir John's study and herself seated comfortably in one of his wing chairs. "You'll join me in a spot of cognac? Despite the fact that it's called after that blighter Napoleon, it's excellent stuff. Although you needn't mention that I offered you any."

Even then, she had not taken any of it *seriously* but only a ruse to save her, *and* her reputation, from Mrs. Langford's vicious tongue. Until Sir John had made her realize, although in the gentlest and kindest way possible, what kind of predicament she might have found herself in if he had not stepped in.

"But I've heard you say so many times that you *enjoyed* a bachelor's life and would *never* marry! How could I let you *sacrifice* yourself just because I was so stupidly thoughtless?"

"And, my dear, I wouldn't dream of expecting *you* to sacrifice your youth and beauty and capacity for living for an old fogey like me. I've always wanted the best for you—every opportunity life has to offer, freedom of choice above all. You'll have it, too. Either way, I mean to make sure of *that.* Only, getting back to what's more urgent, there's always the *possibility,* you see? Finger-counting—not that I'm trying to tell you conception is as easily and quickly accomplished as *some* think. But if it *should* happen, then...romantic elopement, you see!"

"But, I do not think you... That is..." She had *tried* to tell him that his sacrifice was needless, that she was still... But *was* she? "Men will say anything..." he'd said. Could he have lied to her, in case she accused him? What did she really know about him?

While Alexa stammered with embarrassment and hesitated over her choice of words, Sir John had stricken her into silence with his brusquely delivered speech.

"My dear, I want you to know that... Well, to put it quite bluntly, even if it comes to pass that we *are* married there'll be no question of...hrrm...conjugal rights, you know. Not possible in any case—battle scars! Explain it later, if you don't understand. And as for the rest of it, well, you might want to know you won't have to worry about being tied to an old codger for too long. Wouldn't want you to tell anyone else—our secret, eh?—but the damnfool doctors tell me I'll be gone in a year—eighteen months if I'm lucky and take care of myself, hah! Point is, though, that you'd be a very rich young widow. Able to pick and choose from the very best, live in any way and any style you choose.''

Choose, he had said. At the time she had not wanted to *think* of the meaning of what she had been told and had put all her efforts into *not* letting him see how deeply upset she was. But already—she could see it *now*—the safe, solid foundations of her life had started to crumble and nothing would ever be the same again. Never, ever! What she had left was choices. Belatedly, too many different choices.

''Alexa!'' She heard Aunt Harriet's voice, impatient and brusque, and the sound of her black leather boots going along the polished wood floor of the passageway. ''I trust you will be down in a very few minutes. They are all here.'' Thank goodness Harriet had gone on instead of opening her door to discover her staring into the mirror.

With an effort, Alexa lowered her fists from her aching temples and unclenched them, wiping her clammy palms down the sides of her rustly black gown that was buttoned all the way up to the high neck where she had pinned an ivory and jet brooch. Black was such an unsuitable color for a young woman, she had always been told. And she had never liked black, for it reminded her of the carrion crows who hopped along the tree branches outside her room and watched her with their beady black eyes. Oh, she hated black! But today, wearing black suited her mood—and after all, black was also the color of mourning.

Downstairs the usually sunny and airy morning room that had been her mama's favorite room in the house looked so different with all the wooden shutters tightly closed and black crepe draped over the delicate white and gold French Provincial furniture that had been brought here all the way from England. Entering to take her place between Harriet and her father, Alexa found herself wondering almost savagely why everybody felt they must converse in hushed whispers. Did they imagine that the dead could hear and might be disturbed in their permanent sleep? The *dead.* What difference could it make *now* if they all sat here with their hands clasped together and their heads bowed while the bishop, who had come all the way from Kandy, and the little bald vicar from the church in Gampola read the funeral service? The dead couldn't hear. The dead couldn't know or care!

"It will be just the family and a *very* few close friends. That's the way your father wishes it." Aunt Harriet, in her usual competent way, had taken charge and seen to everything while their whole private little world was collapsing about them. Her father looked as if he wasn't really *here* with them. He had been locked in his room when Alexa had arrived from Colombo yesterday, and she had not seen him until now. Harriet had said it was better so. In his black suit, with his shoulders hunched and his eyes unfocused, he had not yet shown her any sign of acknowledgment or recognition; a sad stranger who had taken the place of the confident, joking Papa she remembered.

The bishop cleared his throat as a signal that the service was about to begin, and Harriet pushed a leather-bound prayer book into Alexa's black-gloved hands. She could not help glancing sideways. Was Papa really aware of anything that was taking place? Was he actually reading the words in the book he looked down at? Or was he thinking as she was that solemn phrases and responses read ceremonially out of a book could not assuage grief, any more than words of comfort and reassurance, no matter how well meant, could ease the pain of loss. The so-called "barbaric" customs that prevailed in other cultures and other parts of the world were surely more natural. What was more natural after all than to weep and wail and tear your hair and your garments until all the feelings of pain and anger at Death the Robber were spent? And to Buddhists and Hindus death was not an end but a new beginning, like passing through a doorway into another room.

The monotonous buzzing of a fly somewhere in the room seemed to form a counterpoint to the droning voices and hushed responses. A funeral service, not a burial service, for the climate of Ceylon did not allow for delays and opened coffins that friends and relatives could parade past dutifully. No, the burial had already taken place by the time that the mail coach had delivered a dazed and confused Alexa back home. By then there had already been two freshly dug graves in the Gampola cemetery, and only Martin Howard and his sister Harriet had been present to watch the moist earth cover up the coffins that contained the mortal remains of Victorine and Frederick Howard, deceased.

Measles, Harriet had said. "Measles, of all things! First a feverish cold, and then… Your mama never said a word about not having had the malady herself, and of course she insisted on staying up night and day to nurse Freddy. Martin and I had it as children, and neither of us thought that *she* might not have. I suppose her system had become too weak to resist the sickness from all the sleepless nights and not eating properly, and she would *not* have the doctor over until they were *both* so ill that I took matters into my own hands. By then, of course, there was nothing he could do. Brain fever. How could any of us have guessed? I saw no point in sending for *you,* since you have not had the measles yourself and it would have done no good to have had another patient on our hands." Ah, strong, always practical Harriet.

Alexa's fingers had begun to ache from gripping them together. Her neck and her shoulders ached as well—physical, *outside* hurts that even helped in some peculiar way. But inside herself she felt as if her heart had turned to ice. Perhaps Papa felt that way too as he stared vacantly down at his prayer book without turning over the pages while his lips moved automatically when it was time to make the responses. She had noticed how bloodshot his eyes were and how his hands shook as they held the prayer book; and she had wanted, for an instant, to fling her arms about him and bury her face against his shoulder that had always seemed so strong and reliable while she let the ice inside her melt into tears. But he hadn't even seemed to *see* her or realize that she was standing there beside him, and so she had said nothing and done nothing, suddenly understanding in a painful, *adult* kind of way that he needed the protection of his self-imposed isolation that detached him, for a time at least, from the unbearable agony of reality.

"He's going to need you more than ever now, Alexa," Harriet had told her. "Especially when he comes out of the daze he is in. But until then we'll have to manage on our own. Thank God you're levelheaded and strong!"

Strong, Aunt Harriet had called her. But was it strength or only a self-induced feeling of numbness that kept her from breaking down and made her *seem* strong? Perhaps real strength lay in being able to disassociate yourself from anything too unpleasant to be faced; in being able to *pretend* successfully.

Pretending that she was the strong and levelheaded person Aunt Harriet expected, Alexa managed quite well during the funeral service, which seemed interminable, and even during the light luncheon that followed. No one expected too much from her, and even Harriet did not nag at her for merely playing with the food on her plate instead of eating it. As if she was in a kind of trance, Alexa was able to *react* to anything that was said to her, to answer questions, to thank friends for their condolences and even to give the necessary orders to the servants while Harriet was occupied with seeing everybody off. How *odd* it was that Mama wasn't here too, standing by the doors that led out onto the verandah, laughing. Mama loved visitors! And there was no familiar sound of the piano from the other room—Freddy practicing his endless scales and arpeggios that used to annoy her so at times. No, she was only having a nightmare, and if she closed her eyes and opened them again everything would be back to normal.

"My dear, I'm going to leave as soon as the carriage is brought around. Perhaps you should go upstairs and lie down?"

Alexa had not realized that she had swayed slightly on her feet until she heard Sir John's concerned voice and felt his supporting hand take firm hold of her elbow. He had traveled with her from Colombo, making all the necessary arrangements, soon after Harriet's brief message had been delivered; and during all of the time it had taken them to finally arrive here he had not tried to press her into conversation, although he had listened intently when *she* felt like speaking and had limited his speech to brief comments on something she had said or to answering her questions. Her dear, wonderful, understanding Uncle John, her best friend.

"I don't really *need* to lie down, not yet. And if you must leave at once then I'm going to see you off, of course." Alexa tried to make her voice bright and cheerful, although from the sharp look he gave her she could tell that he was by no means taken in. Were they actually supposed to be *engaged?* Somehow the idea seemed as unreal and as impossible to believe as everything else that had happened recently. And *now* of course there could be no question of anything of the kind—anything *official,* at least. He'd only come up with the idea to save her from the consequences of her own foolishness, her unforgivable *weakness.* And because he'd wanted to make sure she would be taken care of and comfortably off, so that she need never be forced to marry for reasons of security alone. But everything was different *now,* and there was no need for poor Uncle John to make the supreme sacrifice, was there? Even Aunt Harriet had admitted that she was needed here, and Papa needed her most of all, for comfort.

When she saw Sir John off at the verandah steps Alexa reached up quite naturally to hug him and kiss his cheek as she always did when he ended one of his visits, saying, as she usually did. "You'll come back very soon, won't you? Will you *promise* you will?"

"Of course I promise. But, Alexa, I want *you* to make me a promise too."

She looked at him with a slight frown of puzzlement drawing her dark brows together, wondering at his sudden seriousness, and he said quickly, trying to make his voice sound light: "It's nothing you need frown over, I assure you, my dear. Just promise me—as your best friend in all the world, if you still think of me as such—that you will not hesitate to send me word if you should happen to need a friend. Or anything else, for that matter. You understand? Not *too* hard a promise to keep, is it now?"

Walking back into the cool stone house with its wood-paneled walls and floors that always smelled faintly of lemon wax, Alexa had to pause a moment to let her eyes adjust to the sudden contrast to the bright glare of the sunlight outside. Everyone had left, and how silent the house seemed, suddenly!

"Alexa? Oh, there you are. I was hoping you had finished with your farewells by now. There is a great deal to be done, and I am going to need your help." Aunt Harriet's brisk voice put everything in place as it *was,* bringing

Alexa sharply back from her impulse to daydream herself into the past again.

"The sun was so *bright* outside I... But where is Papa? I cannot believe that I have not spoken a word to him since I have been back. Nor *seen* him either, until this morning."

Her impulsive words brought a strained, impatient sigh from Harriet. "I know, my love. I *know.* And that is only one of the things that we will have to talk about, you and I. But for the moment there are a countless number of things that have to be done and orders to be given, the accounts to be gone over as well. I've tried to do the best I could, along with everything else that needed attention, but it has been getting harder and harder as things seem to keep piling up."

Alexa said stubbornly: "But what about Papa? Surely he needs to throw himself into anything that might take his mind off... Oh, I do understand how very lost and bereft he must feel, because I feel exactly the same way too. And perhaps if we could *talk* together, he and I... Aunt Harriet, don't you think it would help him to *talk?* And to realize that at least we still have each other?"

"Alexa, please. I know you mean well, but we are all under such *strain* that we are none of us our usual selves. What you must try to understand is that some wounds go deeper than others and that everyone grieves in his own fashion. Your papa needs to be left to himself for some time; and in this you must allow yourself to be guided by me, since I have known him since we were children together and have grown to understand his moods. As you have seen for yourself, he has chosen to shut himself off from painful reality; and until in his own time and his own way he is able to accept what has happened, we will just have to be patient and try to *manage.*"

After a slight hesitation Alexa's battle-squared shoulders slumped and she sighed. "I'm sorry. I suppose I did not quite understand and was being too precipitate, as usual. But I *do* want to be useful, and to help *you*—and Papa too, of course.'' She managed a falsely cheerful smile with an effort. ''Won't he be surprised and glad to find—when he feels better, of course—that we haven't let everything go to rack and ruin? Tell me, what needs to be done *most* urgently of all?''

15

There was more than enough that had to be done, Alexa soon discovered, to occupy both her mind and her time for most of the day and leave her, thankfully, almost no opportunity for morbid introspection. Not since that first afternoon when Harriet had thrown open the door to Papa's small office, gesturing wordlessly at first, until Alexa's shocked eyes had had enough time to take in everything.

The rolltop desk, usually so tidy and neat with papers and correspondence stored in the correct pigeonholes, was now all cluttered with sheets of paper and open ledgers that had more papers piled on top of them; and the wooden cabinets where Papa had kept his files were all standing open, while some of the files themselves had been left lying on the floor.

"And now you can see for yourself how difficult things have been." Harriet's grim voice had aroused Alexa from a state bordering on stupefaction. "*I* have no head for figures, as you well know; and of course Martin has not been himself since your mama took ill. With harvest time approaching I really do not know *how* we might have managed to muddle through for the past fortnight if Letty Dearborn hadn't been kind enough to send her own foreman over to help us out! But of course she has her own coffee crop to see to as well and we cannot continue to impose. I had thought that if we divided between us the list of things that have to be done we could probably manage to scrape through, at least until Martin is himself again.''

Would Papa ever go back to being his old self again? Could *she?* Or Harriet? Would *anything* ever be the same again?

''Of course Martin will emerge from his state of depression soon, and neither of us should think otherwise. But you must realize that he—forgive me for being *blunt,* my dear—he loved your mama to a degree almost amounting to *obsession.* That is part of the reason why it is taking him so long to... Martin was always so *sensitive!* When our parents died I was afraid for a time that he might never recover from the shock. But life does have to go on, and we cannot turn back the pages or change what is written on them. You might remember that, Alexa, if you can. Because *your* life is just beginning, and you'll soon learn that mistakes are meant to be learned from and not to be repeated, if you're intelligent enough to realize that. Alexa, look at me!''

Still busy with sorting out the confusion of papers, Alexa had almost unconsciously spoken her thoughts out loud when Harriet entered the room to find out if she was ready for a cup of tea; and now, almost unwillingly, she lifted her gaze from the papers clutched in her hand to meet her aunt's eyes.

''You think I'm still too naive and impractical because I like to indulge in wishful thinking sometimes? But what's so wrong with doing so?''

''What have I taught you? Why do you think I've tried to open your mind?'' It was not until Harriet suddenly reached down to grasp her wrist that Alexa realized how seldom her aunt had actually *touched* her; for she had never been given to any outward show of sentiment. ''Opened your mind...'' Harriet repeated in a strangely harsh voice. ''Yes, that's what I did for you, even if I had to fight them every step of the way! Your mama—and even my own brother. And God knows why I felt compelled to do so, unless it was because I thought I saw, perhaps, something in you that reminded me of myself in earlier days. I was something of a rebel too in my time, as surprising as it might seem to you; but I learned *my* hard lessons too late for them to make any difference. It shouldn't be the same with you—if you've *learned* anything, that is. The important thing is to keep emotion and reason apart, always being able to distinguish and separate the two in your mind. It's the only way, my dear Alexa, that you will always remain in control of your own life and your destiny, whatever it might be.'' With a short, discordant laugh, Harriet dropped her wrist as suddenly as she had grasped it. ''As you'll discover in time, one's destiny is always a surprise, for all that we dream and plan and aspire—or even *hope!* But if you're sensible enough you won't take anything for granted, or let yourself be taken by surprise either.''

As if she had said too much already Harriet stopped and shrugged, raising one eyebrow when she noticed that Alexa's forehead had puckered thoughtfully. ''Here I stand making speeches while there is so much that has to be seen to. And I only meant to pause long enough to remind you that we shall probably have guests for dinner tonight—Letty Dearborn and her latest foreman, the young man who's been such a help. He's Portuguese, or something of the sort, I think she said when I spoke to her last. In any case, it's her usual night to come to dinner and I've already reminded the servants to make two guest rooms ready.'' Aunt Harriet's rather wooden expression and deliberately noncommittal voice reminded Alexa immediately of all the whispers she remembered overhearing about Mrs. Dearborn and the succession of young, nice-looking foremen she had employed to help her run her estate since her husband had been trampled to death by a maddened rogue elephant he had shot at and failed to kill. Anybody who did not know *exactly* what they were about and were not crack shots had no business trying to shoot elephants, Alexa remembered thinking unsympathetically when she heard what had happened. And since then Mrs. Dearborn had confounded the gossips and the pessimists not only by managing to run a large coffee estate efficiently and profitably but by showing her indifference to what anyone might whisper about her. She was a rather tall woman who wore her hair cropped short in the style of at least a decade ago, and on occasion she even smoked a cheroot. Even though she was considered eccentric and rather *fast* she was also known as a kindhearted woman who would do anything to help her neighbors if she liked them. And although the young foremen came and went, Alexa remembered meeting and quite liking Mrs. Dearborn herself on several occasions after she had been considered old enough to join the grown-ups for dinner.

Aunt Harriet seemed to be waiting for her to make some comment, Alexa noticed, and so she said with an attempt at brightness, "It will make a pleasant change to have guests for dinner again, don't you think? I remember Mrs. Dearborn as being quite nice. Is her foreman a nice sort of man too?"

"Nice enough, I daresay. And at least he seems to know what he's about. Letty Dearborn tells me he was brought up in South America, where I understand they grow coffee quite successfully." Harriet gave a disparaging snort before adding briskly as she turned to leave: "Well, since you can't seem to make up your mind I'm going to send in a pot of tea and some nice buttered scones, in any case.

And don't stay poring over those books for as long as you did yesterday if you don't want to be wearing spectacles before you've turned twenty."

As soon as the door had closed behind her aunt's rigid back, Alexa gave an unconscious sigh before she turned back to her mound of papers and ledgers. Thank goodness she had always been good at figures and had been used to helping Papa before, or she would not have known where to begin. And thank goodness for any task that would keep her mind occupied. There was nothing that demanded more concentration and was so *impersonal* at the same time as balancing books filled with row upon row, line upon line of figures—some red and some black. Income and expenses. Money on paper. Numbers on paper that had never seemed quite real. Bank accounts. The money from some trust fund or annuity that Papa received from England every quarter—quite a tidy sum. Money put aside every month that would have been used for Freddy's grand tour. "Of course, *you'll* inherit everything now," Harriet had reminded her bluntly only yesterday. The plantation, the house with all its furnishings, the money. She was an heiress now and did not *need* to look for a rich husband to support her. She could stay home and be a support to Papa and everything could go on *almost* as usual. Mama was gone and poor little Freddy, who had not lived long enough to *enjoy* life at all; and it was only because of that double tragedy that *she*...

Alexa's eyes had begun to sting with treacherous tears when she was rescued from allowing herself to become what Harriet would have called "morbid" by the entrance of a servant carrying a tray bearing the tea and scones that Harriet had threatened her with, a second servant following close behind with two glass-chimneyed lamps that glowed brightly even in the daylight. As she had half expected, Harriet herself glanced in not too long afterwards, awarding her a brief nod of approval when she noted that at least two of the scones had disappeared along with at least half a cup of tea.

"Good! And don't forget to allow yourself time to bathe and dress for dinner tonight. We're having oxtail soup as a special treat, and steak and kidney pie as a second course to follow the curried chicken. And trifle for dessert. It's Letty Dearborn's favorite."

"I'm glad she's coming. I like her, you know, and there's so much I want to ask her about everything. In fact, I think I shall go out riding tomorrow morning and keep her company for at least part of her ride back home. Would you mind telling Muttu?"

Her head bent in concentration over one of the thick ledgers when Harriet looked in, Alexa had glanced up only briefly before returning to her task again; but the casually authoritative manner in which she had spoken without being consciously aware that she had done so made Harriet lift her eyebrows after she had closed the door behind her. So! She had not expected to see it so soon, in spite of all her lectures and admonitions, but whether Alexa herself realized it or not, she had already begun to make her own decisions. And to give orders expecting without question that they would be obeyed. Power. Ah, the girl obviously had not realized it yet—her full potential now that she and not her sickly, overly pampered little brother would be in charge of everything. Poor, soft, *weak* little Freddy had been Victorine's child in every way, taking after his mother in his looks as well as his nature and constitution. Pretty, silly Victorine, whose only talent had been her ability to attract men with her wide eyes and her helplessness that made them want to protect and cosset her. Just as she had done in her turn with Freddy, the son she had always yearned for. Weakness nurturing and encouraging weakness, that's what it had been. But *she* had made Alexa hers—*her* child much more than she had ever been Victorine's. Strong, willful, intelligent, with a mind that she, Harriet Howard, had helped develop. Alexa was her father's child and Harriet's child, and that it had turned out to be so was not revenge, for revenge was too petty. Justice, rather!

There was a small mirror in a carved gilt frame on the wall just outside the office. Victorine had wanted it there so that she could make sure she looked pretty enough before she knocked and then went in there to sit on Martin's lap and chatter about foolish trivialities, disrupting the afternoon's work he'd planned. So that in the end it was usually Harriet, or more recently, Alexa, who ended up finishing what he had begun.

On this particular afternoon Harriet paused before Victorine's mirror and looked back at herself without flinching, as she had learned to do quite some time before. "A handsome woman," they used to call her after the word *pretty* had gone out of style. "A bluestocking." She'd heard that too. And later it had been "old maid." Well, by God, at least she had chosen her own fate and her own path. She'd had her choices—several of them—but Harriet Howard, who had once had one of the most eligible bachelors in all of London at her feet, pleading for her favors and calling on her almost every day, could never have settled for second best! Just for a moment she almost imagined that she could see the girl she had been smiling back at her from the dark mirror. Riotous brown curls spilling over a gold headband—"à la Tite," they had called that particular style in her youth. A full, smiling mouth and eyes that could laugh, or so *he* had said several times during the months he spent courting her. And what if she had said yes to him instead of playing a tantalizing game of hard-to-get? Said yes while he still wanted her and pursued her—and before he had become acquainted with her new best friend, the little *émigrée* from France?

Annoyed at herself for indulging in such ridiculous, pointless flights of fancy, Harriet frowned loweringly back at her reflection. Over and gone! She wasn't a silly young girl any longer, and lost chances could never be retrieved. She was a middle-aged woman with greying hair severely parted in the middle and scraped back from her forehead; stifling corsets and voluminous skirts over six or seven starched petticoats replacing the short curls and clinging muslins of her youth.

In spite of herself, Harriet could not help sighing shortly. What a different world she had lived in when she had been just Alexa's age! Wars—or the constant threat of war—and the ever-present threat of Old Boney just across the channel. A sense of breathlessness and urgency—men in their dashing military uniforms who knew they might never return from some foreign battlefield and wanted to live life to the fullest while they could. And ah, the beautiful simplicity and elegance of the clothes that women had worn *then!* Thin, almost transparent materials that were sometimes dampened so that they would cling to the body—banded under the bosom and falling straight to the ankles—sometimes slit up at the sides to show one's legs, if they were shapely enough to display. Muslin, tulle, gauze, and the very finest, thinnest silks and taffetas. A woman had to have a figure in those days to carry off the latest styles; but *today* who could know what kind of figure might be disguised under layers upon layers of petticoats?

Shaking out her own detested skirts, Harriet squared her shoulders before she made her way upstairs to look in on Martin and make sure that he had eaten something off the tray she had carried up to him earlier. After that she would choose something suitable for Alexa to wear tonight and make sure that it was pressed and laid out across her bed by the time the girl remembered that she should change before dinner.

As it turned out, Harriet found herself obliged to remind her niece of the lateness of the hour and the imminent arrival of their dinner guests.

"Oh dear! Is it almost dinnertime already?" Alexa flexed her aching shoulders and stretched widely before adding with a glance at her ink-stained fingers, "I suppose I should go upstairs and make myself a little more presentable."

"Your bath is ready for you, and I had your ayah press a suitable dress for you, so you have no excuse for dawdling, my girl."

"Suitable?" Alexa murmured with a grimace that made Harriet snort.

"Yes, indeed! Or had you forgotten that even plain upcountry folk usually dress for dinner when they are expecting guests? You haven't been paying very much attention to your dress or your appearance of late, I've noticed, and it's high time you did. I thought your dark green velvet might be just right, since the color is so dark it looks almost black by lamplight. And it should fit you perfectly now. I have noticed that since you have stopped eating sensible meals at the proper times, you have begun to look positively *gaunt.*"

Did she look gaunt? Alexa was annoyed at herself for continuing to study herself critically in the mirror while her grumbling ayah tugged at the ribbons that laced up her corset. Nonsense! It was true that she had lost some weight, but it certainly did not show in her face yet. At least the green velvet fit her perfectly *now,* where before it had always been just a trifle too tight. It had a tight waist that dipped into a vee in front, a fashionable bateau neckline, and puffed and banded sleeves reaching to her elbows. And Harriet had been right about this particular color; it *did* set off her hair, somehow.

Although she derided herself for bothering about her appearance, Alexa made sure that she surveyed herself from every angle before she went downstairs, a slight flush coloring her cheekbones at the thought of her own ridiculous vanity. She hoped that she was not late enough to appear *rude,* for Aunt Harriet had informed her that poor Letty Dearborn had grown rather sensitive to *slights* in recent times.

So the gossips have been at work again? I wonder what they will have to say about *me* in the end. Cruel, nasty-minded females like Mrs. Langford who shed crocodile tears while they tear you to pieces with their claws. Hypocrites! Fortunately, none of Alexa's thoughts showed on her face.

"And this, at last, is Alexandra. I'm sure you must find her greatly changed since the last occasion you saw her."

As Alexa dropped a small, polite curtsy almost by habit, she felt Mrs. Dearborn take her hand in a warm, firm grip and give it a squeeze before releasing it. "My dear," she said in a husky, almost mannish voice, "you've grown into a ravishing beauty! And with pretty manners too. Don't you agree with me, Paul?"

The young man who rose to his feet gave Alexa a rather diffident smile along with his polite bow. His deep, pleasant voice held only the very slightest trace of an accent. "I am deeply honored to make your acquaintance, Miss Howard."

"*There.* I knew you two would like each other." Letty Dearborn gave one of her loud, rather raucous laughs as she winked significantly at Alexa, her eyes twinkling. "Didn't I say so, Paul? He's an absolute love, you know. Don't know what I'd do without him."

Later, after the decanter of sherry had been brought

around and the conversation became general, Alexa had an opportunity to study Mrs. Dearborn's latest foreman from under the shadow of her lashes when he did not happen to be looking in her direction. He was quite a handsome man, she had already decided; well-built and muscular, and of medium height. He had brown, sun-streaked hair that was slightly wavy and hazel eyes that could look quite *green* from certain angles. In fact, his eyes and olive skin had given her a sudden, almost unpleasant start when she had first entered the room. But the Senhor da Rocha, who had been born in Brazil of Portuguese parents, not only had charming manners but was obviously a *gentleman* as well. His father owned a large coffee plantation in South America, and he knew almost everything there was to know about the cultivation and harvesting of the coffee bean, Alexa soon discovered.

Aunt Harriet had faded rather purposefully into the background soon after Alexa had entered the room; almost forcing her to play the hostess. After Alexa had, rather defiantly, imbibed two glasses of sherry, it did not seem hard to play the part. In fact, by the time that dinner had been announced and they went in to take their places at the large, formally laid dining table, they were all talking as comfortably together as if they had been friends for many years.

Until tonight, Alexa had not realized that the formal dining room was such a very *big* room or that the mahogany dining table, even with all the extra leaves taken out, was quite so large. By habit, she had taken her usual place, and now she turned to Mrs. Dearborn rather apologetically.

''Perhaps we should have dined more informally in the parlor, as Aunt Harriet and I usually do. I feel as if we shall have to positively *scream* at each other in order to continue our conversation.''

''My dear, I *love* to have the opportunity to dine formally and to get all dressed up, and in any case I *always* scream, as you should have discovered by now. The loudest voice at any gathering, I'm afraid!'' Letty Dearborn gave one of her shouts of laughter again before she added, ''Now I'll be able to talk the rest of you down, won't I?''

Thanks to Aunt Harriet, everything was just right, from the silver place settings to the arrangement of crystal wineglasses by every silver-rimmed dinner plate. And Alexa had no doubt that the cook and the houseboys had received careful instructions on how each course was to be prepared and how it was to be served. There were so many things that *she* would have to learn if she was to play the hostess more often.

''But where is Martin? Don't tell me you are still allowing him to mope and remain shut up by himself in his room like some desert hermit? God's sake, Harriet. I'd have thought that *you* of all people would have shaken him out of it by now. Life must go on in spite of everything, mustn't it? And death's something we should all learn to accept before it's *our* turn, eh?''

Trust Letty Dearborn to speak out with blunt frankness, no matter *what* the subject might be, Alexa thought wryly during that first frozen second that followed her speech. Even Aunt Harriet could not seem to find the right response, so that Alexa felt almost compelled to say *something.*

''I'm afraid that Papa is still far too...'' Hesitating over her choice of words, Alexa suddenly felt, for a frozen moment, her breathing stop.

''You're afraid Papa is what? Well, Letty, so here you are, always to be counted on, thank goodness. Wouldn't miss dinner with *you* for anything, my dear. Apologize for coming down so late, though. Damn stupid boy didn't have my clothes ready.''

Papa? Alexa's head turned stiffly, as if she had been

turned into a wooden marionette. It *was* Papa, but he looked so *different* somehow. His dinner jacket was slightly creased and he looked as if he might have started to grow a *beard,* as many men had begun doing since it had become fashionable. And he had grown so *thin!* His formal evening clothes that used to fit so perfectly now seemed almost to hang on his gaunt frame, and his eyes were still red-rimmed as they had been on the last occasion she had set eyes on him. But...but oh! Alexa thought suddenly with a rush of emotion, what did *anything* count for beside the fact that he had *roused* himself out of his stupor of grief somehow, and was *here?*

"Martin! Why—I suppose I just did not think that..." Alexa had never heard Aunt Harriet *stammer* before. And the next moment she found herself unutterably thankful again for Letty Dearborn, who shouted cheerfully across the room in her usual down-to-earth fashion and gave them all time to recover from the shock it had been.

"Well, here you are at last, Martin. Was just asking about you! Harvest time's almost here, you know, and we've missed you at our meetings!"

Out of the corners of her eyes Alexa could see the confused servants scurrying about quickly to set a place at the head of the table where Papa always sat. She saw him frown when he noticed, but as always he was too much of a gentleman to deliver a reproof before guests, although he mumbled almost under his breath, "Can't understand what's got into the lazy blighters! Act as if they've forgotten everything they've been taught." And then he said to the head boy in an irritable voice: "Yes, yes! Of course you may bring around the wine. But you can bring me a glass of brandy, if the ladies will forgive me, of course? Very warming, brandy. Isn't that right, Mr.—? Have we met? Letty, you're forgetting your manners again. Haven't introduced us yet."

"Well, I'm sorry, Martin. But you know what a scatterbrain I can be sometimes. This is Paul da Rocha, my new foreman. He's from Brazil, where his father owns a very large coffee plantation."

"A pleasure, sir."

Why, Alexa thought suddenly—while *dear* Letty Dearborn kept up a flow of brisk, loud chatter—why, Papa's *drunk!* Quite drunk. Seated at his side, she could smell the almost overpowering fumes of alcohol on his breath. And although at this moment she did not *dare* attempt to catch Harriet's eye, she realized that of course her aunt had to *know.* She must have known all the time that he'd been sitting there in his room trying to drink himself into a state of forgetfulness, poor Papa!

"Well, Martin, and what do *you* think of the latest prices they're offering us?"

"What? Beg your pardon, Letty, but it seems as if I forget things too easily these days; must be getting old. Victorine always tells me..." And then, as if with an effort, his head seemed to swivel around as his eyes, glazed and unfocused, became fixed on Alexa's whitening face. His voice sounded puzzled and rather querulous. "But my dear, why are you sitting *here?* You know you usually sit at the head of the table when we have guests—or did they forget to set *your* place too? Can't understand what's got into them! Boy!" He rose rather clumsily, extending his hand to her; and like an animated puppet Alexa rose too, feeling the sudden silence grow and grow all around them while her mind almost forgot to function. "Blast your hide, Carolis, you've been with us long enough to know better. Set Lady's place at once, d'you hear?" And then, with one of his old, merry smiles and an apologetic shrug he murmured "Sorry, Letty. Got to put them in their places sometimes when they need reminding, eh? I want to hear about the latest prices again though. Can't understand why the figures seem to have slipped my mind."

He thought... Papa actually *imagined*... Alexa's hands had turned ice-cold and even her lips felt as if they had been frozen, so that she could not move them except with an effort. Only her legs seemed to move on their own as Papa escorted her, with old-fashioned gallantry, to her mother's usual place at the bottom of the table, pulling back the heavy chair for her.

"*There,* my dear. And *now* you're in your rightful place."

All she could manage to do was incline her head slightly. Perhaps she had smiled; she could not remember. But suddenly she felt as if she was living a nightmare. What should she do or say now? How was she supposed to act?

Once again Alexa had cause to feel grateful towards Letty, who immediately embarked on an animated discussion as soon as Papa had returned to his seat again. And this time the young foreman also joined in, enabling Alexa to risk glancing, at last, in Harriet's direction, finding that her aunt's face was as paper-white as hers must be, although Harriet of course was watching Papa and Alexa could not catch her eye.

The servants, not understanding too much beyond the fact that the missy was now in the place that had been the lady's, were now looking to Alexa for the little signals that her mother used to give when one course was to be removed and the next served or when a wineglass was to be filled. She discovered that fortunately her memory served her well; or else she acted on instinct alone as she managed to do what was suddenly expected of her. *That* much she could manage—but she could *not* force herself to eat, although she was able to make a pretense of doing so by pushing her food about on her plate and occasionally lifting a fork to her lips.

Dinner had never seemed so interminable, Alexa thought, especially since she longed for it to end. But *how* would it end? She had not been able to help noticing how many times Papa had signaled to have his glass refilled; and she had even begun to hope that he would drop off to sleep in his chair. Almost anything would be preferable to the ordeal that this evening had turned into.

But somehow, in spite of all her hopes, he managed to stay awake and even reasonably alert; and Alexa found in the end that just as she had feared and dreaded, there was still one more act of what had become a ghastly charade to be gone through.

"My dear?" Papa was giving her that quizzical look which meant... Oh, God, what should she do now? What *must* she do? Now at last she finally caught Aunt Harriet's eyes and the *speaking,* almost pleading look in them that made her force a smile somehow and draw in her breath before saying brightly, as she had heard her mother say on so many occasions before, "Will the gentlemen give us leave to retire?" She could not help it if her voice sounded strained and brittle, even in her own ears. As strained as her nerves, which might snap at any moment and had almost reached that point when she heard Papa use the same words he had always used, accompanied by the same loving smile.

"With regret, my dear. With regret."

Now the two gentlemen rose politely to their feet (Papa was swaying slightly) and the ladies could leave the table at last. Alexa had never felt such profound relief and *gratitude* for the existence of a custom she had always bitterly despised before.

16

In the end it took the concerted efforts of Senhor da Rocha and two of the servants to carry Martin Howard upstairs to bed after the brandy had finally overcome him and he had fallen asleep with his head down on the dining table. And, as Alexa said fervently to Harriet afterwards, she felt that she would always owe a debt of gratitude to Letty Dearborn for having carried everything off in such a matter-of-fact, *ordinary* manner.

"She is the dearest, *kindest* woman imaginable, and so understanding. Did you notice that she never said a word about Papa afterwards, and never once asked a single prying question? And we can be quite positive of course that neither she nor Senhor da Rocha will mention anything of what took place to anyone else. I think people who are honest and naturally direct themselves never stoop to idle, vicious gossip."

Harriet, who had also been more shaken than she cared to admit by the implications of her brother's strangely erratic behavior that evening, said more sharply than she had intended: "Well, I'm sure *I* never said anything to imply that Letty Dearborn is a *gossip* or anything but a good-hearted creature and a helpful neighbor, did I? But there's no use your trying to make a *saint* out of her either, just because she did her best to help us all through some very trying moments. I daresay you or I would have done the same thing under similar circumstances. We're all merely *human,* with faults and failings, my dear Alexa, and Letty has hers."

Alexa had appeared to be *attacking* her tangled mass of hair rather than brushing it when Harriet had entered her room to talk with her a short while ago; and now, still far too tense and overwrought to remain calm, she flung her tortoiseshell-and-silver-backed brush away from her and sprang to her feet with her eyes flashing as she confronted her aunt.

"And if by faults and failings you mean to remind me of the nasty rumors circulated by those busybody women who are discontented with their own husbands and jealous of the freedom that Letty Dearborn has, I must tell you that I don't give a *damn* for them, even if it *is* true that she takes lovers; for that is her own *personal* life, and what difference should it make to anyone else? And what is more I don't even care if Paul da Rocha is her lover or not. He is a *gentleman,* and he too is kind, and intelligent, and—and I like him very much indeed and enjoy conversing with him."

"Alexa!" Harriet started to interrupt warningly, but Alexa merely swept on defiantly, "And I might as well tell you, Aunt Harriet, that I have already accepted Mrs. Dearborn's invitation to go to *her* home for dinner next week and to spend the night there, naturally!"

"*Have* you indeed, miss?" Harriet snapped back tartly. She snorted as she gave Alexa's anger-flushed face a narrow-eyed look. "Hah! So you're suddenly beginning to feel your oats now, are you, and want to prove how independent you're getting to be? Well, my girl, let's hope for *your* sake that you're wise enough to understand that there's a great deal of difference between freedom and license; and let's hope that it's not the thought of that young Portuguese *senhor* of Letty's that's the *real* reason for this sudden show of spirited independence! Because *that* would never do at all, as you should be well aware. And even if all you're after is intelligent conversation and the company of someone young and closer to your own age than most of our friends, you'd *still* do best not to encourage a friendship to develop there, my dear." As angry spots of color stained Alexa's cheeks and her lips tightened mutinously, Harriet raised her brows before saying in an acidly sarcastic tone: "I am *quite* aware in what very low esteem you hold *gossip* and those who spread it, of course; but I must hope that you are also *intelligent* enough to realize that *other* people might not hold the same opinions. Even *you* have proved from your quick defense of your new friend Mrs. Dearborn that you've heard all the rumors and sly whispers that have been going the rounds, eh? So you must obviously realize that whether you like it or not people *will* talk and whisper and make ugly insinuations that others might choose to believe."

Unable to remain silent any longer, Alexa burst out angrily: "But why should I be concerned if other people who don't matter to me choose to spend their time twisting the truth into ugly lies if *I* know that everything they say is *untrue?* People like Mrs. Langford and her daughter, who *enjoy* making the very worst out of nothing more than the exchange of a *smile* or a few words in a language *they* couldn't be troubled to learn. Why, I..."

"I hope that when your temper cools somewhat you'll realize that you too are choosing deliberately to evade the truth, Alexa. Or certain inescapable *facts,* if you will." Harriet's voice was cold and her face hardened as she continued: "I only wish to remind you that to give people an *opportunity* to spread their poison would not only be a foolish and childish act of defiance that you may very well regret bitterly some day, but that you would only succeed in hurting and affecting deleteriously the very people who love you and care about you the most. And if you are not concerned for your papa's feelings or mine, then you might think of Sir John, at least. You'd make *him* a laughing-stock—have you thought of *that?* An older man with a young fiancée who shows a decided preference for a handsome and much younger man soon after their engagement? Your Mrs. Langford would make capital out of *that,* I've no doubt!'' Seeing the color recede from Alexa's face as she bit down on her lip, Harriet gave a disgusted snort and marched, stiff-backed, to the door before turning with her hand on the latch for one parting shot. ''If *I* were you I'd be *honest* enough to play fair by Sir John and think up some tactful excuse to break off this *engagement* of yours *before* you start making a fool of yourself. Good night!''

How *dare* Aunt Harriet be so *unfair* as to jump to all kinds of conclusions merely because she had mentioned that she *liked* Paul da Rocha and had enjoyed his company? And then speak *down* to her in such a cutting, contemptuous tone, as if she took it for granted that Alexa would... No, almost as if she had already *done* something terrible that put her outside the pale of society and brought disgrace and shame to her loved ones. Fists clenched at her sides, Alexa continued to glare at the door for some moments before she remembered herself and turned away abruptly, thereby avoiding the urge to *throw* something at it. Why, it was almost *unbearable* to be reminded that she should accept society's edict that if a young man and a young woman were allowed to meet alone and unchaperoned it was inevitable that they would *sin!* Even *he,* that night on the beach, had had the insolence to imply the same thing, the hypocrite! Feeling the blood heat her face and neck, Alexa slammed both her clenched fists down on her dressing table with such force that the small crystal bud vase Mama had given her one Christmas almost toppled over. *No!* she told herself fiercely. No, I will *not* allow myself to think of it. It never happened, any of it. Only a bad dream. I will *never* think of it again and let *those* thoughts spoil everything for me. All men are *not* the same, thank goodness.

In an attempt to calm herself Alexa sat down on the edge of her bed and began to braid her still-tangled hair while she deliberately made herself conjure up the young Senhor da Rocha's face in her imagination. He and Letty Dearborn had been given connecting rooms with only a door that locked on both sides between them. *Did* they lock it? Would that door have been quietly unlocked by now? Strange thoughts that made her uneasy and angry at herself for indulging in surmise. She didn't want to think of anything at all tonight, not even of poor, unhappy Papa, who had to drink himself into a stupor in order to stop himself from thinking of anything painful.

Letty Dearborn, in her usual understanding way, helped Alexa to understand Papa better as they rode together the next morning. Tactfully, Paul da Rocha had dropped back some distance when Letty, riding abreast of Alexa, leaned closer to say in a voice that was soft for *her:* "It might help you to understand, my love, that sometimes it is so much easier to push away certain things that are too painful for the mind to accept. Deep wounds take time to heal, you know, and some find it harder than others to face what they don't *want* to face. But in time..." Straightening up, she had returned abruptly to her usual cheerful manner, giving Alexa a wink before saying, "At *my* age, though, thinking of *time* only reminds me of gather ye rosebuds while ye may!" Laughing and turning her head to look back, she said, "Eh, Paul?"

While she was riding back home with Muttu still trailing

her at a respectful distance, Alexa felt even more grateful to Letty Dearborn for helping her to understand the *reason* for Papa's strangeness last night. Why, he hadn't really seen *her* at all, because in his poor drink-befuddled mind he had managed to conjure up the image of his beloved wife in place of her daughter. No wonder he had looked so dazed, and stayed shut up in his room with his decanter of brandy to help him forget that Mama was gone. Remembering how *close* they had always been, Alexa felt a rush of compassion that helped erase the horrid, strangely frightening feelings of last night. I'm going to try not to think so selfishly from now on, Alexa resolved firmly. And I'm going to do all I can to help and to encourage Papa to get well again. I'll never leave home as long as he needs me.

Time, Letty Dearborn had said. As well as all the patience and understanding we can give him, Alexa had added to herself. Alexa was to recall Letty Dearborn's words and her own inward resolve that very afternoon when the sound of the office door opening made her look up from frowning over one of the daily account books to discover Papa standing there.

For just an instant, Alexa could feel herself freeze with inexplicable apprehension, hating herself for it soon afterwards when he said with a slight smile: "So there you are, my serious little Alexa. Poring over the books as usual, eh? Clever little mind for figures too. Can't deny what a help you've been! You're a good child, and always trying to make yourself useful, aren't you, my dear?" He looked so tired and *sad,* Alexa thought painfully, but at least this time he *knew* her.

"*Papa?* Oh, Papa, I...Aunt Harriet and I have done the very best we could but we've needed your strength so!"

As she started to rise from her chair, Alexa found herself stayed by the pressure of his hand on her shoulder, giving it a slight squeeze before he said almost absently: "Strength? Ah, you're kind to say so, dear, but I've never possessed a really strong nature, I'm afraid. Not like your Aunt Harriet. Not a *physical* coward, mind—cannon balls and shells never made me afraid. But there are other things...." He had begun to wander aimlessly about the small, cluttered space with his hands thrust into the pockets of his old shooting jacket that needed patching at the elbow, his shoulders slumped. "Harriet's always told me I wasn't capable of facing reality, you know. Suppose she's right as usual. I..."

"Papa, you *mustn't* think that way. I *love* you and there's no need to explain or to apologize for anything to *me.*"

"Yes..." He had patted her head almost absently in the way he used to when she was much younger. "You're a kind-hearted girl, my dear. A rewarding child. Always quick at picking things up—a great help with the accounts. Afraid I'm not quite up to them yet; my head sometimes seems to get... But perhaps soon, eh? Can't keep you slaving away indoors all the time, can we? Harriet was just saying that I must begin to...think the word she used was *'involve'* myself in work again. Very forceful woman in her way, my sister, Harriet, although she's a tower of strength when you need her. Your mama..."

He had stopped his pacing abruptly, and Alexa's breath caught in her throat when she saw his mouth work slightly. Should she say something very quickly to redirect his thoughts before he became too upset again? Or should she...

"I had almost *forgotten,* you know. Promise I made to her just before she began to ramble in her mind. The fever. Well, I suppose Harriet is right in saying there is no point in dwelling on the *sadness* of the past when I have so many beautiful memories to sustain me. More than most men can say, I'm sure. But here—before I forget again—she asked me to give you this key, my dear. It unlocks the old tin trunk she's had since she was a girl. Souvenirs—the usual girlish mementos, I suppose. Pressed flowers, old sketch books, favorite gowns she couldn't bear to part with, those little kid shoes..." His voice shook before he cleared his throat loudly. "Well, she wanted *you* to have it. Her only legacy, she said. You may do as you please with everything, of course, but perhaps...perhaps you would not mind..."

"Yes, Papa?" Alexa felt her voice sting and her throat contract achingly so that her voice emerged almost as a croak. No, she had to warn herself sternly. It would be the very *worst* thing she could do—to *cry.*

Clearing his throat again, he said in a diffident, almost pleading voice: "Perhaps one night at dinner—when there will only be ourselves, naturally—it would please me very much if you wear something of *hers.* I don't like the ugly way women dress these days. *She* always looked so lovely, so ethereal almost, in the classical simplicity of the Grecian style. But I suppose I'd better leave you to the accounts, eh? Think I'll go back upstairs and lie down for a little while. Seems to help...."

The key felt warm against the coldness of her palm as Alexa remained staring sightlessly at the door Papa had just closed gently behind him. A small, silver-colored key. Her fingers had closed almost convulsively over it when he had given it to her off his key ring. All of her mother's girlish souvenirs, her dearest memories. Favorite gowns and shoes, pressed flowers. Had Mama ever kept a diary? Had she been silly and giggly and dreamed of knights in shining armor? Mama had always been *Mama;* and before now she had somehow never thought of Mama having once been *her* age, with the same uncertainties and questions about life and the same feelings. Had *she* ever experienced the frightening, overpowering sensation of being lost to everything but a strange inexplicable *need* for…for…

No! With an effort, Alexa opened her cramped fingers and looked down at the key that lay in her palm. Mama's memories would all have been sweet and pretty and *clean.* She and Papa had loved each other, and theirs had been a perfect love. All Mama's souvenirs would also be souvenirs of her papa, of course. Letters they had exchanged when he was off to the wars—perhaps a locket containing a lock of his hair. Her own wedding dress that she had kept for her daughter to wear some day; a symbol of the kind of true love every woman dreamed of finding.

Why, Mama had almost never spoken of her girlhood or her young womanhood or of anything that had happened before she had met and married Papa, Alexa realized with a feeling of surprise. She and Mama had hardly ever had any *real* talks at all, for it had always been Aunt Harriet she had turned to for advice and guidance, and Aunt Harriet who had taken charge of her education and had made the *decisions.* I never really *knew* Mama, she thought suddenly and felt her eyes sting again before she squared her shoulders determinedly and took a deep breath before slipping the little key into the pocket of her gown.

Later, when she had had more time in which to prepare herself, she would open her mama's small trunk and… ''*Burn* everything, my dear!'' she knew Harriet would say in her usual decisive fashion. ''No sense in being *morbid.*'' Aunt Harriet had no patience with what she had always called ''sickly, sentimental twaddle.'' But her mama's few treasured possessions were *hers* to do whatever she wanted with, Papa had told her. No, when she went through the trunk she wouldn't even tell Aunt Harriet. Why should she?

Alexa had not meant to postpone doing what had to be

done for longer than a day or two at the most, but it was getting close to harvest time and there was much more than usual to be done and seen to at that time. The accounts had to be done each day and the coolies paid and supervised to make sure they did not grow lazy or careless. Every coffee bush had to be carefully inspected each day until the coffee "cherries" had turned from yellow to purple-red and were ready for picking at once. And after that there was the rest of the lengthy process that was involved—the "pulping," the period of fermenting, and then the washing—before at last the beans could be dried and packed for shipping to the rolling mills in Colombo. Papa continued to have his good days and his bad days, and both Alexa and Harriet were kept so busy that there were literally no moments to spare for anything that did not *have* to be done at once. I'll do it later, Alexa promised herself. After all the cherries have been picked. But in the end she almost forgot about the key and what it was meant to open, and the days continued to race by; each with their different crises and problems to be dealt with.

"Didn't I hear Sir John Travers say something about coming up here next week when he was here for the services?" Harriet said over breakfast one morning, adding in a sharper voice: "I suppose you'll insist on doing as *you* wish about it, but if he's coming up only to speak to your papa about wishing to make matters *official,* then I do hope you will consider very carefully the fact that your papa is still not quite his normal self and might find the idea of losing *you* as well too much to bear at this time."

"I *know,*" Alexa said a trifle tiredly, looking up from her plate of freshly sliced fruit topped with cream. She was in no mood to enter into an argument with Aunt Harriet this morning when they were both so much on edge. "Poor Papa.... Of course I would not dream of deserting him while he needs me. In fact I have already written to

Sir John explaining matters to him, so you need not worry. Muttu took the letter down to Kandy to catch the mail coach very early this morning.''

Poor Papa! By now Alexa had had enough time to grow used to his changing moods, which seemed to depend on the amount of brandy he consumed. Sometimes he came downstairs to wander about aimlessly, and sometimes he would remain all day locked up in his room until it was time for dinner, if he chose to join them. On some occasions he would call her ''Victorine'' and ''my love,'' but fortunately *those* were the times when he was so inebriated that he would soon fall asleep at the table and have to be carried up to bed. Now that she was able to *understand* so much better, Alexa did not let herself become upset at such times; but for the most part he knew who she was and would speak to her kindly, if a trifle absently. He too seemed to have forgotten about the key he had given her and his rather hesitant wish to have her wear one of her mother's favorite gowns to dinner one night. And if she remembered the key at all she always thought quickly that it would be much better to wait a little longer.

With the passage of time would come forgetfulness and healing in the end. Perhaps it was what they *all* needed.

17

"So you're determined to go after all? Hah! All I can say then, since your mind seems made up, is that I *hope* you remember to exercise some discretion, my dear. I'd go along with you myself if I could feel comfortable about leaving your papa alone in his condition."

"Aunt Harriet..." Alexa caught herself sighing impatiently. "You know *quite* well that I have already postponed going to dinner at Mrs. Dearborn's place *twice* and that it would seem unconscionably rude and almost like a *snub* if I were to do so again. Besides, I have both Muttu and Ayah with me as chaperones, and haven't I *promised* to act with the utmost *discretion?* Goodness, you never used to *fuss* so when I used to go on hunting trips with the boys that were far more dangerous than traveling a few miles to have dinner with a neighbor we have all known for years."

"You know *very* well that there's a difference," Harriet snapped before she sighed and said almost resignedly, "Oh, go on and get on your way then, and I hope that at least you'll make sure of being back before dark tomorrow. It's difficult enough as it is without having you off gallivanting."

Aunt Harriet had sounded quite *grumpy,* Alexa thought resentfully after she had started out. As if she was letting her down by leaving for a few hours. But she was not for the world going to let her aunt's sourness—or anything else, for that matter—spoil this evening for her. Her first formal call on her own. Her first step towards becoming independent.

To Alexa's secret relief she was the only dinner guest that night. She had been hoping that there would not be too many other neighbors there, or any young officers; but this was even better than she had anticipated and she soon felt quite at ease and *relaxed* with Letty Dearborn and the Senhor da Rocha.

"Do you like curry? I've developed quite an addiction to it, I'm afraid, and the hotter the better! But there's chicken stew with boiled vegetables too, just in case." The way her hostess screwed her face up at the mention of chicken stew made Alexa burst out laughing.

"After *three* glasses of sherry and now wine into the bargain, I do not think it matters in the least what I have to eat, as long as it is *not* chicken stew and boiled vegetables."

"Ah! You see, Paul? A female after my own black heart. Didn't I tell you so? She's not a bit like those namby-pamby creatures who are all false smiles and ugly whispers—are you, my dear? And *now* they have it that poor Paul is a result of one of my late husband's indiscretions. Little do they know! I was a dutiful wife while he was still alive, because I didn't know any better at the time, I suppose. But Samuel was much older than I was, and the poor dear could *not*... Well, never mind. Never speak ill, as the saying goes. Kept his Eurasian mistress hidden away somewhere because all his friends were doing the same, but couldn't beget children! Anyhow, I remember saying to Paul—didn't I, love?—wait until you meet Alexa Howard. She's different, independent. Got a mind of her own too. Hope they don't have time to get their knives into her in Colombo, though. *I've* managed to develop a hide as thick as an elephant's by now, of course, but, well, I'm glad you didn't let them change you, my dear. I *like* you, you know."

As the meal progressed Letty Dearborn's lack of formality and her direct manner of speech made it easy for Alexa to talk quite freely and honestly herself, not only to Letty but to Paul as well.

They had soon progressed to first names. "*Miss* this, *Mister* that; always thought it was ridiculous among people who feel comfortable enough with each other to become *friends. You* don't mind, do you?"

She did not mind in the least, Alexa thought, enjoying being able to sit together with *both* her new friends after dinner instead of retiring while Paul indulged in a cigar and port by himself. In fact, Letty actually lighted up a cigar for herself after she had ordered cognac for all of them.

"Another silly custom!" she'd said. "Like not being able to smoke if you're a female. But don't *you* try a cigar if you're not used to it, my dear. Make you very sick indeed!"

They sat around the table talking for what seemed like hours, while Alexa took small, careful sips of her cognac and the cigar smoke swirled under the punkah fan. Paul spoke of his life in Brazil and the influence of Portugal there, and Letty related some of her experiences when she had first begun to manage her husband's estate on her own. "You'll probably face the same thing some day, love. Women hate you and the single men without prospects want to marry you; at least until you get as long in the tooth as *I* am now. And the married ones want to bed you, thinking you ought to be *grateful.* Glad you're not shocked by my bluntness but I thought you should be *warned,* at least. Of course, I keep forgetting, don't I, that *you're* still single, and can pick and choose, eh? Still young too. Plenty of time ahead of you yet, and you'll have all the choices in the world. Don't even have to stay *here* because there's no other place to go and England's too damn cold. *You* could probably live anywhere in the world you decide to live, if... Think you'll marry Sir John in the end? No. I apologize for *that!* Prying...detest *prying.* But I always tend to talk too much when I've had more than enough to drink, as Paul will tell you.''

''Oh, but of course I don't mind anything you say...'' Alexa began, but Letty had risen abruptly to her feet, coming over to lean down and give her a perfumed hug.

''I *know* you don't, love, or I wouldn't have apologized, you know. Never apologized to any of *them* for anything! But I *do* know when I've had enough and should go upstairs to sleep it off. Doesn't mean you two young people have to waste the rest of the evening though, does it? Have Paul take you for a stroll in the new rose garden while the moon's still up. Think it was full last night, wasn't it, Paul? Well, good night, my dears.''

After Letty had kissed them both and departed with a casual wave of her ring-bedecked fingers, Alexa found herself rather confused and uncertain of what she should do next until she heard Paul say quietly, ''*Would* you care to stroll outside for a while, or would it make you feel uncomfortable to be alone with me?''

''I...'' Alexa met his gravely searching eyes and suddenly gave a shrug and a small smile as she extended her hand. ''But why should I feel in the least uncomfortable being alone with you now that we have become friends? And I do not even care if there *is* a moon tonight.''

That last defiant comment had burst from her spontaneously, and soon afterwards Alexa could have bitten her tongue for saying something so *pointless.* She was relieved when Paul, instead of questioning her, merely helped her to her feet, offering her his arm before saying with a humorous quirk of his lips, "I am glad you trust me, because I am afraid your *duenna* has fallen sound asleep."

Her poor ayah, who had been sitting on her mat in one corner of the large dining room all evening, had fallen asleep quite early, as Alexa had not failed to notice with relief. And now she said with her dimple showing, "Oh, it would be quite *cruel* of us to wake her, don't you think?" Poor Elisa was growing old, and once she had closed her eyes almost nothing could wake her until dawn, as Alexa knew very well and her aunt did not. And she meant to make the most of this one lighthearted night of feeling *free,* a free spirit among kindred free spirits.

Outdoors lay a different world from the orange lamplit dining room. An enchanted fairy world of silver light sliced through with black shadow; and damp earth smells mingling with the heady scents that drifted from flower beds, and thick vines that clung to bowers and hung from trees. And perhaps, Alexa found herself thinking almost defiantly, she needed to be walking outdoors with a man whom she could trust not to take advantage of her ignorance and her untried emotions. Perhaps she needed to prove at least to herself that she had changed and become stronger—no longer a weak, helpless creature who allowed her intellect to be ruled by her senses and the cloying, insidious lure of a moon-bathed tropical night.

As if he had sensed some of her secret thoughts and reservations, Paul da Rocha continued to talk easily as they strolled along the crazy-paved path that led to a small summerhouse in the center of the sunken rose garden. He spoke of his childhood and his parents and his sisters who had all been married off by the time they were fifteen years old. "And by now—Luisa is only twenty—they are all three like old women, even to look at. Sharp-tongued and nagging, with nothing to converse about except children and servants and other domestic matters. I felt desperately sorry for them at first; sold off like cattle to men they had barely met and did not *know.* I can still remember how Luisa, who was closest to me in age, cried bitterly all night before her wedding day. She thought she loved a friend of mine she had once exchanged glances with. But within a day or two afterwards, how she preened as she showed off her wedding gifts—her large new house with so many servants to do her bidding, her jewels and new finery.''

''Oh!'' Alexa cried, puzzled as well as revolted. ''But *I* never could… Only, I suppose that your poor sisters had no choice in the matter and so there was nothing to do but make the best of things. They could not be *really* happy, could they? Sometimes even *I* hate being a female and being so *limited* in every way. You should count yourself lucky that *you* were born a male, you know!''

''Ah, but you can have no idea what our Portuguese-Brazilian families are like. Marriages, even for sons, are arranged very early, almost from the cradle, in fact. And being the third son of my father, my only prospects lay in marrying a girl with an extremely large dowry. Only—my future bride was as fat and ugly as she was rich, you see, and she had been chosen for me by my father when I was not yet fourteen years old!'' Paul gave a short laugh as he shrugged his shoulders, looking down at Alexa with a half-bitter, half-humorous twist to his mouth before he continued more lightly: ''So to make a boring story short, I decided to use my father's generous allowance to make my escape before there was any talk of our formal engagement being announced. I decided, in fact, to seek both adventure and my fortune at the same time by embarking on a ship bound for Australia.''

''But…''

"Ah, the reason I ended up *here* is nothing to be proud of, I'm afraid. I was bored on that ship and took to gambling to while away the time, losing a good portion of my passage money; and the deposit I had put down was only sufficient to bring me as far as Ceylon. Fortunately for me I had the luck to meet with some kind souls who advised me that since I had some knowledge of coffee planting I should have no difficulty in obtaining employment here if I looked in the *Gazette.* And as you see, I was lucky again, for Letty happened to be visiting Colombo at that time, and here I am! Fortunate once more in that I have had the pleasure of making *your* acquaintance as well."

"Letty is indeed a very wonderful and exceptional woman," Alexa said rather too quickly. "I shall always love her for her kindness and understanding. But does she know that you are on your way to Australia and do not mean to *stay* here?"

"She's not the kind of woman one might feel inclined to keep things from, is she? I have always been honest with her, and she with me. I have promised her that I will see her through until the end of the season, at least, and she pays me very well indeed. You are right; she *is* a most exceptional woman, and I feel enriched by having had the privilege of knowing her. But tell me..." He had stopped suddenly and the abruptness of his question took Alexa by surprise. "*Are* you in fact planning to be married soon?"

"I..." Striving for honesty to match his, Alexa found herself almost stammering at first. "I do not really *know* yet. I know I mentioned something about it over dinner, and...but you see, what makes it so difficult to conceive of is that I have always called him 'Uncle' John, and everyone knows that. And then there is Papa, who needs me so desperately now, and Aunt Harriet, and the estate, and—Uncle John only offered to marry me because he wanted to protect me from gossips like that nasty Mrs.

Langford, of course! He said it would be a...a marriage in name only and that he had already decided that *I* was to be his heiress in any case. But he's so ill, although he doesn't show it, and the doctors have told him he's *dying.* And... Oh, you don't know how good and kind he's always been to me, ever since I can recall! If he might need someone to be with him and look after him, if I would be helping him by *doing* something for him... Oh, I really don't know *what* I should do!''

''So you are torn between duty and destiny, are you, Alexa? And after all, who can tell which choice is which? You will have to make your own decisions in the end, you know. It is very much like the toss of the dice, I'm afraid. But once a decision is made, *then* it will become easier, I think. Knowing that right or wrong, the choice you have made is of your own free will.''

Long after Paul had taken her back to her room, kissing her hand at the door before he left her, Alexa found herself lying awake with her thoughts turning cartwheels in her head. How much they had talked about, she and Paul. And how frankly. Two hours or more must have passed until she had mentioned almost timidly that perhaps Letty...

''Part of Letty's beauty is that she understands everything and condemns nothing. Yes, we are lovers, Letty and I, but only on those occasions when we are both of the same inclination. And it is not as incongruous as some may think, for Letty *is* a beautiful woman, and a giving one as well. A combination of mother and friend and courtesan all in one, although I do not think that you can completely understand yet what I am saying. I can see that you are not quite ready yet to be able to give with joy instead of guilt; with laughter in the midst of loving. Ah, I am sorry, Alexa. Sometimes I tend to say far too much!''

But what *had* Paul meant to explain to her? She had longed to ask him, but a sudden fear that he would think her silly and naive if she did had held her back; and he had casually steered their conversation to other, safer topics as he guided her back to the house—holding her arm. Not once had he attempted to make love to her, although she knew somehow, without knowing *how* she knew, that he would have liked to have done so. Why, he had already made sure that she knew that *Letty* wouldn't have minded, because she was not jealous or possessive and would never even dream of asking questions. But then he had told her that she wasn't *ready* yet. How different Paul was from…

Nicholas. The Spanish cousin. She had actually managed to forget what his last name had been, although she remembered too many other things about him. His manner of walking—the deep-forest greenness of his eyes against sunbrowned skin and his smile that wasn't really a smile at all. The unfamiliar, lazy drawl of his speech and the dark thickness of his hair. Even the very feel of his skin and the way his muscles moved under it. And most of all—oh, *worst* of all—she remembered what she wanted most to shut out of her mind forever. The way he had kissed her everywhere and touched her everywhere in such a diabolical manner that she had lost both reason and will.

Dear God—*why* did she continue to remember everything so vividly? Stirring restlessly in bed Alexa pulled the thin cotton sheet over her head to shut out the silvered moon-streaks that had crept in through a half-closed window to lie against the polished floor. It had been the moonlight…Paul…the turn of their conversation.… But then why, even if she did succeed in not thinking about *him,* did she have those certain dreams to haunt her on some nights?

I *hate* him. Oh, I despise him, her mind repeated like a familiar litany until she heard herself sigh in the darkness and thought at last, Yes, I hate him—but I want him too, at the same time; want everything he made me feel and crave and…oh, most of all *I* want to be the one to turn and walk away without a backward glance! She welcomed the gathering of anger that warded off other thoughts as she told herself fiercely, Some day perhaps I will have my chance! Some day when I have *learned* enough…when I am *ready*…

18

"I must say I'm quite relieved to see you back *early*. Your papa was rather upset when he discovered I'd let you go alone. Perhaps you might make some small extra effort to please him tonight? You know he has grown to depend on seeing us both at the table when he comes down."

"Yes, I know," Alexa said evenly as Muttu helped her dismount. "Should I go up and see him now, do you think?"

"As you ought to be aware, he's usually asleep at this time," Harriet said acerbically. "And for *his* sake we really should try to keep to a familiar routine during the next few months. You have not made any more dinner engagements, I hope?"

She had never realized before how *domineering* Aunt Harriet could be at times. But then she had never been away from her aunt's influence for long enough to think about what she had always taken for granted. Aunt Harriet had always been *there* as a part of her life, Alexa thought later when she had gone up to her room to change. Like Mama's fluttering sweetness and the sound of a piano somewhere in the background. Was it only because Mama and Freddy were no longer with them that everything seemed so drastically changed, or had the greatest change really happened within herself? Suddenly she had become irritable and even *critical* of things she had always accepted before; and now, with a feeling of being hemmed-in somehow she understood that the freedom Aunt Harriet had talked to her about and that she'd thought for a while she really *had* was not real freedom at all. Rather it meant the taking on of responsibilities that would eventually absorb more and more of her attention and her time until in the end it would be the business of the plantation that would be running *her* instead of the other way around.

I won't be manipulated into feeling *guilty* if I'm away for just one evening! Alexa thought rebelliously while her drowsy-eyed ayah helped her change into one of her old cotton gowns that had faded from brown into an indeterminate, rather muddy shade. I refuse to give up my options and turn into a sour, self-sacrificing martyr just to please Aunt Harriet.

"I'll see you for tiffin," Harriet had said in parting. "No doubt you'll want to change and lie down in the meanwhile." Arranging her hours for her, reminding her of the daily routine she was supposed to fall into. And now, after poor Ayah had gone off with her rolled-up sleeping mat to catch a nap in some corner, Alexa's dark brows drew together in an unconscious frown while she considered the consequences of avoiding tiffin *and* Aunt Harriet's inevitable questions as well. She would send word that she was not hungry...was too tired...had a headache. She did not even feel like sitting down to the daily accounts as she usually did after tiffin or like performing any of the other *usual* tasks, for that matter. Even if it was only to prove something to herself, she would do something different for a change. Something... Almost absentmindedly Alexa opened the lacquered jewelry box that had been one of her Christmas presents last year in search of her favorite garnet earrings as a change from the jet she was wearing and had begun to detest. And there, right on top, lay the small key she had tossed in there and forgotten about—the key to her mother's battered tin trunk that held her girlhood memories and secret, youthful dreams—Victorine Howard's only legacy to her daughter. Almost involuntarily, Alexa's hand went out to it, picking it up. Now, while she was feeling strong, was perhaps the best time to go through it—to begin, at least, to sort everything out. Suddenly, filled with a strange, new feeling of *separation* from Harriet, she felt an impulsive need to understand Mama better and to know more about her.

The trunk had always been kept in Mama's room, under the broad window seat that opened outward on hinges that squeaked. Inside the same boxlike cavity, Alexa remembered that along with the little faded blue trunk there had been several old boxes tied about with string. Hatboxes containing some of her favorite bonnets that Mama had explained once she could not bear to throw away.

"But what is in the trunk, Mama?"

"Oh, nothing in particular, dear. Old clothes and letters and papers—more things I could not bear to part with, I'm afraid. And now you must stop being so inquisitive!"

Strange, how small, tucked-away memories could surface quite unexpectedly, Alexa thought as she found herself hesitating before the closed door that had never seemed forbidding before. Strange, how suddenly, clearly, she could recall every detail of Mama's room, like seeing a picture in her mind. Mama had died in this same room, in the bed with its pretty covers and soft sheets that always smelled faintly of violets and Mama. Sometimes she had taken Freddy into her bed with her, but never Alexa, who had always wriggled and thrashed about in her sleep, so

Aunt Harriet had said. Before her thoughts could wander further or her courage fail Alexa turned the brass knob on the outside of the door and was almost surprised when it turned easily under her hand.

Pushing the door open, Alexa stepped barefooted over the threshold, forcing herself to look about her, her jaw squared. She had half expected to be greeted with the familiar smells, but now she found her nose wrinkling at the strong odor of carbolic. The bed looked bare with only a thin cotton blanket thrown over the mattress; no pretty covers and dainty satin throw pillows to add what Harriet had called with a sniff a "frivolous look." No pretty ruffled curtains at the windows, no gaily colored rugs on the floor. This was a different room from the one she remembered so well; a room that looked as if no one had ever lived in it, like one of the many guestrooms before they had been made ready for visitors. And the connecting door that led to Papa's room and which had always stood open for as long as Alexa could remember, was shut and bolted.

Harriet, of course. Her practical, levelheaded Aunt Harriet, making sure that there were no traces of that warm vivacious presence that had been Mama left behind in that room to remind Papa and make him even more distraught. Everything *personal* was gone—burned, most likely. Had the blue trunk and the hatboxes been thrown away too? Almost sure now that she would find nothing, Alexa crossed the room, pushing closed shutters apart to let some light in before she looked. And there they were, after all! The trunk, and the hatboxes as well; all dusty and cobwebbed. And when she reached down a trifle gingerly to push one of the boxes aside, an enormous spider ran out and almost scared her to death. She had always hated spiders! And no doubt there were probably a few centipedes lurking in there as well. She should have thought to bring one of the servants with her to poke about with a broom first just to make sure, or else have had the trunk dusted off and carried into her room, where she could look through it at her leisure.

Sitting down on her haunches as comfortably as one of the native women, Alexa grimaced with distaste as she peered into the dusty aperture. Spiders! Huge, hairy, loathsome creatures that had always made her flesh crawl, even though she *knew* that most of them were quite harmless. Perhaps this was not a good idea after all. With another grimace, Alexa had just started to rise to her feet again, dusting off her hands on her skirt, when Harriet's voice from behind her made her whirl about with a jump of her heart.

''And might I ask what on earth you're up to this time? You couldn't come down to tiffin because you were too tired after your long ride and needed to *rest,* and now here you are poking about and meddling with...''

''With my *mother's* few personal possessions, which are all I have left of her? I do not think of it as either 'poking about' or *'meddling,'* dear Aunt!'' The taken-aback, almost shocked expression on Harriet's face encouraged Alexa to continue in the same stiffly cold voice. ''It was *Papa* who gave me the key to my mother's old trunk and told me Mama wished me to have it to do as I please with its contents. Under the circumstances, you'll forgive me for saying that I saw no reason why I should ask *your* permission to enter my mother's room to look for something that now belongs to *me.*''

''Harriet, why what is the matter? Heard loud voices. ...Ah. You *did* find it after all, my dear, so I must have remembered...wanted you to have it. No one else. Promised Victorine. Harriet, what have you done with her? Put her out of her own room...?''

As Papa stood there swaying as he peered into the room, his brow creased with puzzlement that was turning to annoyance, Harriet put her hand on his arm and almost shook it as she said quickly: "Hush, Martin! And try not to make a fool of yourself, pray. You should remember very well that I *told* you the doctor ordered everything possible taken out and burned to prevent the infection from spreading to others. Like Alexa, who did not have the measles in childhood!"

"Oh..."

With his shoulders slumping again as the distant look returned to his eyes, Papa had already turned to leave when Harriet looked angrily at Alexa and hissed under her breath, "You see how easily upset he is? Now he'll probably forget—" She broke off when her brother turned back again to smile somewhat pathetically at Alexa with his head cocked inquiringly to one side.

"Ah, but there my sister's wrong. Some things I don't forget, eh, my dear? Promises, for instance. Promised me you'd wear one of your mama's pretty gowns down to dinner one night, you remember? The pale green, my favorite! Little bronze slippers she'd wear with it and an embroidered reticule to match. Quite the thing, you know; and how proud I was to be escorting her the first night she wore it. Think every other man envied me! *You* remember, don't you, Harriet? You were there that night too, with—"

"*I* have never chosen to dwell in the past, Martin, as you should know very well. But I'm sure that if Alexa made you a promise she will surely oblige you tonight, now that she has found what she was searching for at last." Turning to Alexa, Harriet added expressionlessly, "I'll send one of the servants upstairs to carry the trunk into your room for you, shall I? You might find it easier that way. And *then* I think we should all take a nice long nap before dinner. Don't you agree, Alexa?"

In spite of her brusque, almost caustic tone, Alexa noticed with a slight, unwilling pang that Harriet's face had suddenly begun to look grey and pinched and *old;* making her swallow the words she had meant to blurt out and say stiffly instead, "Yes, of course, Aunt Harriet."

"Well, if *Victorine* thinks I should rest, then perhaps I will. Perhaps I will."

"Papa...!"

"*Will* you let him alone? He'll be changed again by tonight if he's allowed to rest!"

Harriet's fingers grasped Alexa's arm, halting the rest of her impulsive speech until he had wandered away and she could argue. "But don't you *see* that if I do wear one of Mama's gowns it might only help to make matters *worse?* And I did not really *promise.* I just...did not say anything when he suggested it."

"Then if you had really hoped that he would forget about it, perhaps you should have waited longer before claiming your mother's legacy. We can only hope, I suppose, that it doesn't turn out to be like Pandora's box." Harriet's face had become stonily expressionless again to match her voice as she continued without inflection: "But I suppose it's too late for regrets *now,* and if Martin believes you made him a promise, I think you had better humor him, or he might become even more upset—and *angry,* as well as hurt. I *do* happen to understand my brother much better than you do or ever could, my dear Alexa—as I've said before. I'll have the trunk brought to your room at once, and if you will find the green gown and give it to Ayah I will see that it is pressed for tonight. And I'll come up early to help you with your hair, if you'd like. Your mother never would cut hers, even if it *was* the latest fashion, and I can remember helping *her* quite often."

I wonder if I ever really *knew* Aunt Harriet either? Can any human being really *know* another? The trunk had been carried into Alexa's room, all dusted off; but now, even after inserting the key into the rusting padlock, Alexa felt curiously reluctant to turn it. Pandora's box, Harriet had hinted grimly. And suddenly it seemed almost like an invasion of privacy, even though it had been Mama's last wish that Alexa should have her pathetic little trunk and all its treasured contents. Not Harriet, not even Papa, as close as they had always been. Alexa, the daughter who had always been more Harriet's than Victorine's. But even after *that* thought had driven her into opening the trunk with some difficulty, Alexa still hesitated to touch anything inside as she deliberately procrastinated by choosing to recall the dialogue between Harriet and herself just a few minutes earlier. Following in the wake of the servant who had carried in the trunk, Harriet had actually sounded quite affable as she said, "Well, here you are, my dear! You'll want it placed under that window there where you'll get enough light to see what you're doing, won't you?" And then, after they were alone, she had offered in her usual brisk tone. "D'you want me to help you unpack? The clothes at least will need to be shaken out and pressed before they're hung up, I'm sure. The materials that were fashionable in those days, like muslin and tulle and gauze, for instance, always *did* tend to crease dreadfully after they'd been packed."

"Thank you for offering, Aunt Harriet, but there's really no need to have to start unpacking *everything* right this minute, I suppose. I think, if you don't mind, that I'd rather have my nap first, and then perhaps..."

"Well, have it your own way. But do try and remember to hang the gown you will be wearing for dinner on the back of that chair by the door so that Ayah can have it pressed and ready for you in time."

With a shrug of her spare shoulders Harriet had already turned to leave the room when Alexa's sudden burst of speech had halted her.

"Aunt Harriet! Please, there is something I feel I must say to you *now*—before we go down to dinner. Because—well, *you* have always reminded me to be practical, logical; to face the...the realities of life, have you not? And that is why I..."

"I hope that I have also taught you to come quickly to the point you wish to make without having to stammer awkwardly over every sentence, my dear Alexa. Well, what is it you find so difficult to come out with?" Harriet's sarcastic tone and raised eyebrows made Alexa flush with anger before she made herself pause long enough to take a deep breath, trying to choose her next words more carefully. This time, she found herself thinking fiercely, I will not let her intimidate me or make me angry enough to stutter! "*Well?* Or have you changed your mind?"

"No, I haven't, Aunt Harriet." Somewhat to Alexa's own surprise, her voice sounded quite even. "What I wanted to say was that even if I am to wear fancy dress to dinner this once in order to humor Papa's whim, I feel that I cannot... I *will* not sit silent and allow him to imagine that I am...his *wife!* Don't you see that for his sake as well as mine he has to start seeing me *all* of the time as myself, as his *daughter?* As Alexa, not his Victorine. I only wanted you to understand, don't you see? You *know* I wouldn't for the world do anything to *hurt* Papa—I love him as much as you do! And that is why he has to be led back to facing and living with what *is;* instead of being allowed to keep on *pretending!* You *do* understand don't you? Aunt Harriet...?" Stretching out her hand appealingly, Alexa had let it drop in the face of her aunt's stony look.

"Since you have made it more than clear that your mind is made up, then whether I might approve or disapprove of your decision is surely irrelevant. Do as you will—and as you think fit, Alexa. The responsibility is yours."

Responsibility. The word reminded Alexa of what she had to do at *this* particular moment. No more procrastination. But at least she did not have Aunt Harriet looking over her shoulder!

Lifting off several layers of yellowed tissue paper, Alexa's first discovery was a white muslin gown with tarnished silver spangles and a small train. Mama's wedding gown? Shaking it out, she saw that the material had yellowed slightly along every crease and fold, and felt a sense of sadness. How sheer and how pretty it must have been when it was new, with its low-cut, high-waisted bodice and tiny puff sleeves that would be considered daring today. There were dainty silver slippers in a satin case tucked to one side; and just beneath the dress, also wrapped carefully in tissue, a pretty silk shawl with fringed edges.

As Alexa laid everything carefully aside, the faintest scent of violets drifted to her nostrils. How strange that perfumes could linger for so many years! Carefully lifting off more layers of tissue paper, she found herself wishing fervently that *this* would be the green dress Papa had spoken of with such nostalgia, so that she would not have to delve any further this afternoon. But revealed, instead, was another muslin gown cut more plainly than the first, with tiny sprigs of red and yellow roses against a pale pink background. Two more pairs of shoes—pink satin slippers and soft kid boots. A calf-bound volume of verses wrapped in a silk scarf. Feeling slightly ashamed of her curiosity, Alexa could not help opening it to glance at the flyleaf. "To my Dearest and Only Love, from One whose Heart is Forever Yours..." The untidily scrawled words were almost indecipherable, and the single initial at the bottom of the page, while it could have been an *M,* might also have been any other letter of the alphabet. The affectionate inscription had been dated 1819—two years before she had been born, Alexa thought; carefully rewrapping the small volume before she tucked it away once more in a corner of the trunk and lifted out a scrapbook. She glanced through it quickly and without too much interest. There were yellowed clippings from old newspapers that told of old battles and listed their casualties. A few pressed flowers and autumn leaves. All of the pages had not been used up, so Mama must have become tired of cutting and pasting in the end! The war between Greece and Turkey—Lord Byron—he'd been the fashionable poet of the day, of course, and the author of the book of verse she had just set aside.

Closing the scrapbook impatiently, Alexa replaced it and picked up a folder containing several sketches done in charcoal as well as pen-and-ink. Why, here was Papa, looking quite boyish in spite of dashing side-whiskers and a high uniform collar. And Mama herself—so pretty and young, with a half-smile on her lips that made her dimple just like Alexa, her hair secured by a band across her forehead that did not prevent it from spilling over in a froth of curls. There were several other sketches as well, but all of people Alexa did not recognize until she came to one of Aunt Harriet, of all people, and thought, staring down at it, Why, how pretty she must have been once! Short dark curls framing her face provocatively, and an open smile that showed her strong white teeth. A high collar setting off a slim neck. How was it possible that *this* happily smiling young woman had turned into the Harriet that *she* knew? Sour, mistrustful, her lips tight and permanently turned down at the corners; how sad it seemed! Turning quickly to the last sketch, Alexa found herself gazing down at the face of an exceptionally handsome young man—an officer, to judge from his uniform collar. Clean-shaven, with curly hair cut short in the fashion of the day. Intense eyes that seemed to look right into hers under straight, well-defined brows, and firm lips that almost smiled. A face that arrested Alexa's attention for some reason, and made her frown suddenly when she found herself wondering irritably how she could have thought she'd felt, even for a fleeting moment, the strangest sense of recognition or something familiar in those regular features. Impossible, of course! Catching the faintly penciled dates in one corner of the sketch, Alexa shook her head at her own silliness. "1798–1821." Poor handsome young officer! Such a short life he'd lived.

It had all happened such a long time ago—and she mustn't allow herself to become morbid, Alexa reprimanded herself. Putting aside the folder of sketches with decision, she also laid aside several packets of letters tied with ribbon, gauze scarfs, a pair of satin dancing slippers with the soles almost worn through, and a little round music box that played a tinkling waltz tune when she opened it and which was crammed with all kinds of trinkets and sparkling ornaments for the hair. And here, at last, lay the pale green dress with its matching silk petticoat that seemed to be as sheer as the thin lawn dress itself. It had been laid under some fashion journals of the same period, with the satin case containing the bronze kid slippers and matching, prettily embroidered reticule tucked in beside it. And now, as she shook away more tissue paper, Alexa discovered a wide ribbon of a darker shade of green embroidered with bronze and gold thread that must have set off Mama's dark curls to perfection on that evening that Papa remembered so well.

I have accomplished quite enough for one afternoon, Alexa thought to herself. I can go through everything else later when I have more time. Keeping out only the pretty green dress and its accessories, Alexa dropped everything else back into the trunk before closing the lid; and then, after hesitating a moment with her teeth worrying her lower lip, she locked it again.

19

"Well, here I am, Papa! And how do I look in Mama's pretty green dress? Goodness, I had no idea that dressing up could be such fun!"

With a forced air of gaiety she was far from feeling, Alexa performed a light pirouette for his inspection and was relieved to hear Harriet put in quickly, "Can you believe that Victorine's dress, and even her shoes, fit Alexandra as perfectly as if they'd been made for her?"

"Alexandra? Oh yes, of course! Considerate of you to indulge me, my dear. Always been a good, considerate child, haven't you? Reminds me of *her*—doesn't she, Harriet? And especially tonight. She was about your age, I believe—first time she wore that gown. Wasn't she, Harriet?"

"Yes indeed, I believe she was! But do permit Alexa to take her seat now, Martin, before the soup becomes cold."

Thank goodness Aunt Harriet was being *helpful,* and was adhering to the terms of the unspoken truce they had established between themselves earlier while her hair was being arranged in the artfully artless-seeming disarray of curls and escaping tendrils that had been fashionable twenty years ago. Thankfully Alexa sat down, wondering almost incredulously if her shy, sedate mama and even *Harriet* had actually dared to wear such diaphanous garments in public. Why, even *she* had felt strangely embarrassed and almost *naked* when she had made herself leave the sanctuary of her room this evening, although Harriet had told her with a snort of impatience that *some* young women of her day, like Lady Caro Lamb, had even gone so far as to dampen their gowns and petticoats so that the outline of their legs and breasts could be more clearly noticed! "And except for a few old dowagers, no one seemed to think *that* was too shocking either, so you have no reason to keep studying yourself in the mirror while you *blush!* After all, it's not as if you'll be seen by any *outsiders,* my dear. I've seen you wear much less around the house when you choose to go native on hot afternoons!"

Taking small sips of her chicken broth gave Alexa an excuse to keep her head bent so that she did not have to look up and discover that Papa had started to drink too heavily again. She remembered suddenly that Aunt Harriet had asked her casually if perhaps she had found some pretty earrings or other trinkets of her mother's that might go well with the green dress. "I seem to remember a pair of jade earrings that I cannot remember her wearing since..."

"Oh, I was feeling so sleepy that all I bothered to look for was this dress and the shoes and reticule Papa described. I'll have plenty of time later, I daresay." She had been equally casual, and Harriet had not pursued the subject further.

Perhaps I am becoming overly suspicious, Alexa thought contritely now as her aunt began to engage her in a flow of inconsequential small talk while their soup plates were whisked away to make room for the next course. The small activities of the day were reviewed in order to take up time and make it seem to move faster. There had been a family quarrel—two of the coolie women had delivered themselves of their infants at almost the same time and not more than a hundred yards or so away from where they had been working. "And as hard as it is to believe, they were back at work before three hours had passed—just as if nothing untoward had taken place at all! Like healthy animals!"

"Well, perhaps they are luckier than most *civilized* women..." Alexa had begun when Papa interrupted in a reproving voice that took her by surprise.

"Hardly a suitable topic for the dinner table, surely, Harriet? And especially not a fit subject for discussion with young, gently-reared females, I should think! Let's change the subject, shall we?"

"Certainly!" Harriet snapped back. "Shall we discuss the harvest instead and how we are progressing? Alexa and I have been thinking that we might have to hire more coolies this month. The ideal weather we have been blessed with..."

"Oh yes, Papa!" Alexa broke in eagerly. "I believe that all the 'cherries' will be ready for picking at about the same time this year, which is quite unusual, as you know. And Paul was telling me that in Brazil..."

"*Paul?* And who, pray, is this *'Paul'* you appear to be on such familiar terms with that you use his Christian name so freely?"

Quite taken aback by Papa's frown and unwontedly *angry* tone of voice, Alexa found herself almost stuttering. "Why—Papa! You must not think... We are only *friends* and...nothing else! And I did not mean...mean to..."

"Harriet? I am waiting for *you* to enlighten me and tell me what this unwonted familiarity *does* mean! What kind of freedom—or should I say *license* instead?—have you permitted an innocent and inexperienced young female left in *your* charge to become exposed to while I have been ill? Ah, I remember all too well that *other* time before when I became so ill, and you..."

While he was speaking, Harriet's fingers seemed almost to claw at the high neck of her dark taffeta gown, her face becoming blotchy and her voice strident as she broke in: "*Before,* did you say, Martin? Is it possible that you still choose to blame *me* for what happened, when in spite of your self-deception and purposeful *blindness* you must have known very well that I would have done anything—anything in the world, to prevent what happened!"

"Oh please!" Although she did not understand what the words that Papa and Aunt Harriet flung at each other *meant,* Alexa could not help feeling guilty for being the cause of their argument. She leaned forward now, as they both looked towards her, and said urgently: "Papa, please! You must believe me when I say that my familiar use of a man's first name does not denote any *further* degree of familiarity! And Aunt Harriet is not to blame for anything because I have done nothing wrong, I promise you! Paul da Rocha—Senhor da Rocha, if you prefer—is every inch a gentleman and has offered me nothing but *friendship,* that is all. The same sort of friendship that I feel towards Letty—Mrs. Dearborn, that is. Papa—you know I am no longer a *child,* and I can only wish that you could trust me!"

"If you remember, Martin, I told you that Alexa had gone to dinner at the Dearborn place, and that Muttu and her ayah accompanied her," Harriet said in almost her normal tone of voice before she added more strongly, "and *you* said nothing at all when I came up to ask your opinion—merely nodded your head as if it was of no consequence to you!"

Papa acted as if he had not heard anything Aunt Harriet had said, Alexa noticed with a sudden sinking feeling in the pit of her stomach. He drained his glass of brandy and signaled impatiently for it to be filled again before he said with a frown. "*Letty,* did you say? You refer to that Dearborn woman who dyes her hair and hires herself a new young man every season?"

"Papa!" Alexa could not repress her puzzled, almost shocked exclamation. "How *could*... Why, I always thought you *liked* Letty Dearborn! Why, the first time you joined us for dinner since...in *weeks* was when *she* came. And you seemed to like the Senhor da Roçha too."

"Have to be polite to neighbors, my dear. But that's got nothing to do... Yes, yes! You can fill my glass again; and set the decanter down here while you're about it! Inefficient— Might have trained them better, eh, Harriet?" Martin Howard turned from his glass and shuttled his gaze from Harriet to Alexa and back again; his eyes narrowing slightly. "*You* should understand perfectly well what I mean, dear sister! Letty Dearborn's a clever businesswoman and knowledgeable enough about coffee planting, I suppose. Neighbor, as I said. Tradition of hospitality— have to be *polite!* But I can't have any of the women in my household associating with her on a *personal* level, after all—what? Surprised at your attitude of *laxity,* Harriet. I'd hoped you would have explained *why* too close an association with the wrong *kind* might..."

"I'm *sorry,* Papa! And if you wish to send me to my room I'll gladly go." Pushing back her chair clumsily, Alexa sprang to her feet; her color high and her eyes as dark as storm clouds. "And I'm sorry, too, if I've spoiled dinner for everyone, but I...cannot *bear* to hear good friends vilified! Mine—and yours too, Papa, even if you have been too ill to remember! For while your other, *respectable,* hypocritical friends might have offered lip-service, only Letty Dearborn *did* something to help us! While I was in Colombo and Aunt Harriet was kept so busy, Letty sent her own foreman over to help. And we might not even have a coffee crop to send to market this year if not for her! Papa, surely you must understand *that?*''

Alexa stayed defiantly on her feet even though her knees had begun to shake after she had finished delivering her explosive little speech. Surprisingly, Papa had not said a word, although for a few moments she had noticed that he stared at her with his mouth slightly open as if he had not seen her before. She had shocked him, she supposed. And then he quickly raised his glass to his lips and swallowed half its contents, still without saying a word or taking his eyes from her face.

In the end it was left to Harriet to break the tense silence, as she said matter-of-factly: ''Well! And now that you've had your say and have not been banished to your room in disgrace, I suppose you might as well sit down and continue eating your dinner! Yes, boy, you may as well take away the plates and bring us the next course. Please make sure it is still warm.'' And while Alexa subsided into her chair rather sullenly, feeling slightly deflated, Harriet turned back to her brother and said thoughtfully, ''Do you think we could afford another hot plate soon? Cook broke one the other day and we are down to just two.''

The meal progressed in comparative silence, just as if nothing had happened. Alexa looked stubbornly down at her plate, her face still rather flushed. She might have spoken a little *too* strongly to Papa, she supposed, but on the other hand he had been wrong and unfair to speak of Letty in such denigrating terms. At any rate, he had not reproved her for speaking out; but Alexa could see from beneath the cover of her thick lashes how many times he refilled his glass, and she began to feel a trifle guilty. Papa wasn't well, and perhaps he hadn't realized what he was saying.

Perhaps she should have made allowances for him. Oh, she hadn't *meant* to upset him!

"Alexa, if you have quite finished playing with your fish, perhaps we can go on to the roast? Martin, will you carve or shall I save you the trouble by having Cook do it?"

"Of course I'll carve. What do you think? Can't have a perfectly good roast ruined by that old butcher!"

At least he *acts* as if he is quite sober, Alexa thought relievedly as he began to carve the juicy roast with all the expertise she remembered from so many other occasions.

"Here we are! Harriet, you prefer your meat not *too* rare, don't you? Two slices? And…" Catching his inquiring look, Alexa felt a sudden rush of affection mixed with contrition towards him for having forgiven her for her outburst.

She said quickly, with a small, tentative smile, "*Very* rare, please, Papa. The way I always like it. And just *one* very thin slice, please."

"What's this? *Rare,* did you say? But, my dear…why, you've always said you could not bear the thought of…well…red meat!"

"But I've *always—*" Alexa began before she suddenly broke off. It had been Mama who could never stomach rare meat and always begged for the slice at the end.

While she looked up dismayedly, searching for words, Papa said benignly, "No need to feel you *must* try it rare, my love, just because everyone teases you. Here you are—your very favorite part of the roast!"

Alexa remained silent as the houseboy set her gold-rimmed plate before her and while Harriet passed her the gravy with a grimly warning look. She was even able to help herself to a square of the Yorkshire pudding and a serving of boiled cabbage and potatoes. Once Papa had eaten something he'd be himself again, of course. Surely it wasn't because of *her* that his mind had chosen to regress again; although Harriet would probably say so, of course.

"Well? Shall we begin before our sumptuous repast is cold? Ah, very good indeed! Must remember to tell Cook he's really outdone himself this time, eh? But, my dear! Is *your* portion not quite to your liking? Would you prefer that I give you a slice from the *other* end?"

Alexa had opened her mouth to say hastily that she was quite satisfied with her slice of roast beef when a sudden, stubborn instinct made her pause instead and take a deep breath before saying in as *normal* a voice as possible, "It is a very *nice* slice of beef to be sure, Papa, and just thin enough; but I had hoped you might remember that I prefer my roast beef as rare as can be—just as you do."

"But I don't understand!" Papa said querulously as he put down his knife and fork and knitted his brows in a confused fashion before looking towards Harriet as if for support. "Harriet, *you* can confirm it, can you not? Hasn't Victorine *always* preferred the slice at the very end? Surely..."

"But, Papa—Papa, please *look* at me! Please *see* me! I am *not* my mama!" Disregarding Harriet's warning exclamation, Alexa left her seat and ran to him, bending over him urgently. "I'm only dressed up in one of Mama's old gowns to please *you,* Papa, but I'm not...Victorine. This is *Alexa* you see, and I am not your *wife,* dearest Papa, but your *daughter.* I *know* you understand!"

"What? What? Victorine...?" When Papa looked up at her his eyes seemed glazed and puzzled, and his mouth worked.

"*Alexa!* Papa, please *look* at me! I am your *daughter,* Papa!"

"Daughter?" He looked from her to Harriet, his voice

turning petulant. "I have no daughter, have I, Harry? Stillborn, they told me. Both of them. My poor Victorine..."

Strangely enough it was to Alexa and not her brother that Harriet directed her angry reproof as she burst out, "Don't you think you've stirred up enough trouble for one night? Be silent now, for God's sake, and leave him alone!"

But it was too late now to stop herself from saying what she felt had to be said; for Papa's sake and for *her* sake, Alexa thought stubbornly as she held onto the arm of his chair as if for support and went on speaking as if she had not heard her aunt.

"You listen to me, Papa, and try to understand that it is only because I *love* you so that I... Oh, *Papa!* I am your Victorine's *daughter,* don't you see? I am a part of her, that is why you see her in me. And you haven't lost *me,* any more than you have *really* lost Mama, because...because she'll always be close to us and live with us in the memories of her that we carry in our thoughts. Don't you see? Even if Mama had to go, she left me behind to take care of you and comfort you—if you will let me. But you must see me for who I *am,* Papa! My mother's *daughter,* not my mother!"

"See you? See? Ah yes...I suppose...the eyes. Not Victorine's eyes, are they? Victorine's pretty ball gown, but—but you *are* my Victorine's daughter, aren't you? That's right! Part of *her.* Of course! She wouldn't leave me all alone. I should have known it, shouldn't I? She had to go because of little Freddy. Softhearted, wouldn't want him to be alone! But she left part of herself behind, didn't she? Victorine wouldn't leave *me* all alone either—I should have had more faith, shouldn't I? Why, I feel as if she's so *close* sometimes! *Feel* her. Sometimes think I hear her voice..."

"Papa...!"

Alexa had not realized that she had been clutching at the arm of his chair until he suddenly patted her hand with a faint sigh.

"Yes. Thank you, my dear, for helping me to understand. Of course. Victorine's *daughter.* Her flesh and blood. Support and comfort. I should have known my Victorine wouldn't leave me *quite* alone, shouldn't I? 'Ye of little faith...' My apologies! And now, why don't we do justice to this excellent roast, eh? Have boy bring your plate back to me, my dear, and you shall have a slice of beef as rare as you please!"

20

After that night even Harriet had been forced to admit, albeit a trifle grudgingly, that Papa had changed for the better and become more like his old self. He had begun making an effort to leave his bed early enough to ride out and inspect what was being done on the estate, and he came down to dinner every single night and talked quite sensibly of business matters. Sometimes, he even made an effort to be humorous and to tease Alexa, especially when he found her hard at work in his office. He would pat her on the cheek or on the arm in an almost absentmindedly affectionate manner, as if he wanted her to know that he noticed her; and he had got in the habit of expecting her to be ready to pour out his tea for him in the morning room when he returned from his daily tour of inspection.

"Your mama always sat in here waiting for me, looking so fresh and pretty. Insisted on pouring my tea herself, too. You remember, don't you, my dear? She wouldn't want you to wear black either—never wore it herself. 'Reminds me of those ugly old carrion crows!' she used to say. You should wear *her* colors; she'd like that. Pretty pale greens and pinks and lavenders; yellow too."

Of *course* she wanted to please Papa and to show him

how happy and grateful she was to see him making an effort to take up the threads of his life again. And if all he asked of her was to wear her mother's favorite colors and take over some of her mother's duties... Alexa reminded herself frequently that it was little enough to ask of his only child and heiress, after all.

Suddenly, and almost without being aware of it, Alexa found that she had fallen into a kind of set routine that ruled all her time and all her days. It was her *duty* to be a comfort and support to her Papa, just as she had promised. Aunt Harriet reminded Alexa of it whenever she showed signs of restlessness and spoke impulsively of visiting Kandy or going hunting with some of her old friends.

''Perhaps when everything has gone back to being more *normal* and we all have more time to ourselves...'' Harriet would say vaguely after Alexa had admitted that perhaps she *was* being selfish and inconsiderate after all.

Perhaps...perhaps...? As one day followed another with an almost agonizing slowness and *sameness,* Alexa realized that those nebulous *perhaps* were all she had to look forward to. After her morning ride with Papa—*sidesaddle* now, because she was a young lady and not a gypsyish hoyden—they would go upstairs together to change; and then she would run down to the morning room to sit behind the dainty little table with its silver tea set and pour out tea for Papa and Aunt Harriet. After that it was accounts and then tiffin. Her afternoon nap—even if she didn't really take a nap at all and tried to read a book instead. And *then*...

When she started thinking along *those* lines Alexa had to catch herself back sharply. ''Stop it. You mustn't think that way!'' There were a few occasions when she almost said the words aloud, to startle the inquisitive birds and squirrels who hid in the trees outside her open windows. She told herself that she was restless because of the heat.

September was harvest time and one of the hottest months of the year, each day seeming hotter than the day before. Far too hot to wear layers of clothing in the afternoon, especially in the privacy of her room; but since Papa had taken to popping his head in unexpectedly to ask her some question about the accounts, Alexa found herself forced to wear some light garment at least; usually an old cotton petticoat that had seen better days.

Papa *needed* her, and she had promised not to desert him. But what about *her?* What about *her* life, *her* friends? Would she ever belong to *herself* again? Like a caged, restless young lioness Alexa paced about her room from door to window and back again with her thoughts troubled by conflicting emotions. She had tried telling herself that it was the unusual hot spell that made her feel so irritable and unsettled. And she had *tried* not to make too much out of what had happened when Letty and Paul had come for dinner a few days ago. After all, Papa had not been *rude,* nor had he *said* anything specific to cause the feeling of constraint that had prevailed throughout the whole evening, making it a stiff, uncomfortable occasion for all of them. No, Papa had seemed to make an effort to keep up a stream of pleasant conversation which he directed to Paul as well as Letty. But all the same, dinner had suddenly become a *formal* affair, as if they had all been polite strangers who were not quite comfortable with each other. And when Letty had pressed Alexa warmly to call on *her* again soon, it had been Papa who answered for her to say that he couldn't spare Alexa during this particular time, although perhaps later on…?

"We are fortunate indeed," Papa had said with a smile, "to have in you a friend understanding enough to overlook a breach of etiquette that was committed, of course, quite innocently and unknowingly, by my headstrong little miss here. Naturally, the next time Alexa goes calling she will not be unchaperoned. As *you* know, it takes precious little to get a young girl talked about in an undesirable fashion. Too many jealous mamas, eh?''

Alexa bit her lip as she paused for a moment before resuming her almost frenzied pacing back and forth. It was not as if Papa had said anything *outright* of course, but all the same she hadn't felt quite comfortable. And then, just today...

The two young officers who had called had been her hunting companions as well as her closest friends. Was it possible that it had only been less than three months ago? Papa had politely invited them to dismount and come into the shade of the verandah, but he had *not* invited them to sit down. And when one of them had rather stammeringly suggested that perhaps Alex—beg pardon, *Miss Howard*—might care to go riding some day or join them on the hunt they were planning next month, Papa had gently but firmly put a stop to that as well.

''Very kind and thoughtful of you young fellows, of course. But you'll understand, I'm sure, especially if you have sisters of your own, why I cannot permit a young *lady* to go about unchaperoned as she might have done when she was *younger,* eh?'' And then after the awkward, stammering leavetaking had left them alone again, Papa had patted her cheek affectionately, giving her a quizzical smile.

''There, my dear. Aren't you relieved that I got rid of those bothersome young fellows for you? Hunting indeed! Far too rough and dangerous, and certainly not a suitable sport for a young lady!''

It's only because he's afraid of losing me too, she'd told herself then, letting pity drown her first instinctive feeling of resentment. For after all, Papa had begun to *depend* on her so and, in fact, almost to cling to her as if he needed the constant reassurance of her presence somewhere close to him. He made her feel protected and cherished—and...and *caged!* Pausing in mid-stride, Alexa bit her lip as the word she had tried to avoid came into her mind and suddenly filled it with unwanted images that only made her feel guilty. A pet mynah bird with its wings clipped to keep it from flying too far away. Her days planned for her with loving benevolence, her time measured out. Oh no, it was not fair of her to think along such lines, and she ought to be ashamed of herself!

"Alexa?"

Whirling around on her bare feet, she wondered why her heart should have suddenly started to pound.

"Yes, Papa. I'm here."

"I didn't wake you up, did I, my dear?"

"No, of course you didn't. It's far too hot to fall asleep." And oh, how could she possibly, even if it was only for an instant, feel as if she actually *hated* poor papa?

"Feel the heat myself! Thought I'd ask if you'd like a pitcher of cold water brought upstairs since I was going down in any case. But—my *dear!* That's rather a skimpy garment you have on, isn't it? And your windows open wide too! I mean, one of those damned coolies might take it into his head to..."

He was her *father.* Why should he need to knock before he entered her room? He needed patience and understanding...but all the same Alexa could not prevent her voice from sounding a trifle strained and impatient as she said: "Oh, *Papa!* You know very well that all the coolies are probably hiding in the shade somewhere, and in any case my windows are far too high up for anyone to see in! I think I'd suffer from heatstroke if I wore anything heavier than this old petticoat; and even *this* makes me feel so..."

"Heatstroke? My dearest child, you don't feel... Are you sure you do not feel ill or...or *weak?* The heat... Perhaps I should call Harriet at once..." His face had turned quite pale with fear and concern and Alexa felt as if she could have bitten her unruly tongue.

"Of course I am not ill or weak in the least! I should not have spoken so carelessly when I only meant to say that I would feel far too hot indeed if I..."

"I understand, my dear, I understand. And you must forgive me for my old-fashioned attitudes. Privacy of your own room, after all, eh? Anything allowable in *private,* what? Innocence is its own protection, I'm sure—so many things you cannot understand yet! But you're my good, sweet, innocent little girl, aren't you? My Victorine's daughter—Alexandra Victoria. You were named after our new Queen, did you know? And after Victorine too, of course. See more and more of her in you each day, it seems." He touched her bare, damp arm gently and lovingly while he looked searchingly into her still face. "And it was *you* who helped me understand, my dear. Opened my eyes. I should have known she wouldn't leave me *quite* bereft, if she had to go away. Left *you,* didn't she? To make up for... Well! But I mustn't stand here keeping you from taking your nap, must I? Must promise me you'll lie down and rest; you look quite drawn and tired. Perhaps a tonic might do some good. I'll go and ask Harriet at once; she'd know!"

She had worried so much over Papa, and now he was worrying over *her.* And that was only natural, wasn't it? He was *Papa*—familiar and beloved—hovering over her only because he was afraid of losing her too, that was all! He was concerned for her—loving...

Sitting on the edge of her bed, staring at the door he had closed gently behind him, Alexa tried to control her own strange, wild thoughts by telling herself that it was the heat that had affected her without her realizing it; making her imagine the strangest things. Like seeing a *stranger* look out at her from behind Papa's eyes when he'd stroked her arm affectionately, as he'd done so often before. There was no reason for her to have had the sudden, violent instinct to snatch it away—or to have the unreasoning fear that perhaps he meant to keep her here with him for always; never letting her out of his sight, always hovering, always fussing over her—keeping her away from everybody else and only to himself, only *for* himself.

The *heat!* An over-fevered imagination that let all kinds of irrational, nonsensical thoughts into her mind. No wonder Aunt Harriet was always reminding her to think logically, to be *practical.* Sanity and sense!

Alexa flung herself down on her bed and lay there with her fingers pressed against her temples; concentrating only on breathing in and out until her ayah came in to remind her that it was almost tea time and she was expected downstairs.

So *hot!* It was enough to make anyone's mind play strange tricks. By the time she had been sponged all over with cool water and had slipped into a pale yellow cotton batiste gown with a skirt that was made up of tier upon tier of pretty ruffles edged with dainty white eyelet embroidery, Alexa had begun to feel more like her usual self.

She even made plans as she walked downstairs. A trip to Colombo as soon as the beans were ready for despatch to the mills. If it would not be considered quite proper for her to stay with Sir John, then perhaps they could take a hotel room, she and Aunt Harriet. Papa would surely be quite himself by then.

It was not quite as hot on the shady verandah as it had been upstairs, Alexa found to her relief. And after tea had been poured and the tiny sandwiches and light tea cakes handed around, she actually felt her spirits rise. The conversation was light and innocuous and dealt mostly with the garden and the planting of the new roses that had been ordered.

"Perhaps a small fishpond might be quite pretty—if it's put in a shady spot, of course. With a fountain, if you think it can be contrived."

"But what does *Alexa* think?" Papa turned to her with an indulgent smile. "After all, this is *your* home, and the gardens *your* concern now. Everything belongs to you now, my dear, just as *you* belong here—eh, Harriet? And of course you must tell me if there is anything you want changed in the house—new furniture for your room perhaps? New curtains— Oh, we can afford it, my dear, so you need not look so worried!"

"But you have already been more than generous, Papa. Why, think of the cost of all the pretty new gowns I took with me to Colombo! If you continue to lavish so much on me I'm sure that when I marry my husband will accuse me of being far too spoiled to afford!" Alexa had spoken lightly and almost teasingly, with a smile that showed her dimple, never imagining for an instant that her innocently spoken words might cause a thunderstorm to erupt out of the clear sky.

"*Marry,* did you say? *When* you marry? What kind of talk is this I hear? How did you get such notions in your head? Well, miss? You need not keep staring at me in that *guilty* manner now that the cat's out of the bag! Who is he? Who have you been meeting on the sly? By God, I'll have his name, or..."

Thunderstruck, Alexa could neither move nor speak, even when she felt his hands grab her shoulders with a roughness as shocking as it was unexpected and his voice continued to attack her as well. "I'll have the truth from you for a change, girl! Tell me—tell me how far you let him go! How many favors did you grant him, or let him *take?* Answer me! Or is it *guilt* that holds you silent? Has he—this man you speak so loosely of *marrying*—has he defiled you yet? Do you still have your virtue? By God, I thought you innocent—*good*—answer me!''

In the end, Alexa recovered her senses at about the same instant that she heard Harriet cry out sharply, ''Martin, stop! Stop this madness at once, I tell you! You're...''

With all the suddenly mustered strength of her young, athletic body, Alexa sprang up from her seat, twisting herself free of his almost feverish grasp at the same time and almost falling to her knees before she managed to surge to her feet, panting—the chair toppling with a crash between them.

''Don't! I haven't...oh, but you have no *right,* no right to...''

''Martin! For God's sake, have you taken leave of your senses? You must know very well that Alexa has hardly left this house for over a week!''

Harriet had spoken at almost the same time as she, but now Alexa said in a constricted, almost gasping voice, ''Papa, how *dare* you! And I do not care at this moment that you are my father, for that does not give you the right to...*accuse* me and make vile insinuations without any foundation or any *reason!* Ohh!''

Her pretty yellow dress was actually torn at the shoulder, and she felt *bruised,* both inside and out. She would have given anything in the world to turn and run and to keep on running blindly, if only she had a place to run to. And now, unable to help herself, she watched *him* through narrowed, hostile eyes as she might have watched some stranger; even when his mouth began to work and his eyes filled with tears. Strangely she felt no pity at all on this occasion—feeling like a stranger watching a stranger.

''But you talked of *marriage!* Husband, you said, just as if it was already settled! Unless it was only to make me jealous... Was *that* it, my dear? You promise me there's been no one? Haven't been with a man yet? That greasy foreigner who shares Letty Dearborn's bed— You used his first name..."

"Stop! Please...!" She had to control her breathing before she could manage to go on in a calm enough tone of voice: "If you find it difficult to believe that I am still a virgin and cannot take my word for it, then I suppose you could have me examined by a doctor if you choose. You have the legal right to make me submit to even *that* degradation, as I am quite aware."

"My dear—don't! Don't look at me like that! I wouldn't... You *know* I didn't mean it all, don't you? Only, when I heard you speak so lightly and casually of marriage and a *husband,* just as if you had one picked out already... Why, my dear, if you were only *teasing* me, surely you understand *now* how cruel it was? Wasn't it, Harriet? And you haven't let a man touch you, have you? My own dear Alexa—my Victorine come back to stay with me—so pure and untouched— How should you know what some men are really like? Faithless...liars...ask Harriet, *she* knows! Don't you sister?"

"Martin, please! Don't you think... The *servants!* We..."

"I pay them well, don't I? Pay them well enough so they won't eavesdrop or gossip, and they know it! And Alexa—my dear, you'll understand and forgive me for doubting in the end, won't you? Understand that I only mean to protect you and keep you from being sullied by filthy, treacherous hands! You'll have everything, anything at all you want—*here,* where you're safe and watched over. You love me, don't you? Said you did, didn't she, Harriet? You mustn't be angry with me— You know I mean well! Shall I buy you a pretty ring to make you smile again? A brooch? You shall name what you want and I'll give it to you—make you happy!"

"I only want... Papa, if you mean what you say then

the only gift I really wish is *freedom.* The right to choose my own friends—and your *trust* as well."

"Freedom? Own friends? I don't understand! You don't mean *men,* do you, dear? You don't know what they're like, and you'll thank me some day for saving you from the pain—the shame that comes with remorse and disillusionment. Ah, my poor Victorine! *She* could have told you—warned you! But I always loved her, you know. Never stopped; would have taken her on any conditions. And since then she ever made me jealous, never gave me cause. *You* wouldn't either, would you, Alexa? We have only each other now, you know. You and I. Alexa—no. Don't go from me! Where..."

"If you will excuse me, please? Because—as you see, my sleeve is torn and...and I must go upstairs and change...mustn't I, Aunt Harriet? If I may be excused?" Alexa felt as if she had been turned into ice, even the blood in her veins. And if she had to beg to be excused again she knew that her teeth would start to chatter uncontrollably.

"Of course you must change at once, before your dress slips off your shoulder and you catch a chill in this suddenly cool breeze! Yes, do run along, dear; and I'll send Ayah up to help you."

21

How could what had to be a nightmare continue and continue? Why couldn't she force herself to wake up? Alexa leaned her back against her door, hardly realizing that she was shaking as if she had the ague. She had to grit her teeth together to keep them from chattering so loudly that she could not even hear her own thoughts. Words, phrases, hints, insinuations came back to her mind like poisoned darts that kept spreading their venom in spite of all her efforts to think clearly.

What did it all mean? Oh, but perhaps she didn't really want to know! Perhaps she would be better off to try and convince herself that nothing had happened at all. Her breathing sounded like sobs; and her eyes kept hunting about the confining space of her room almost desperately, although she had no idea what she was looking for. Oh God! All her worst imaginings then were true and he—she could hardly bear to call him Papa any longer—he did not mean to let her go. "We have only each other now, you and I." He meant to keep her from—*defilement.* "Pure and innocent." Keep her away from all men save himself. Alexa could almost have laughed with bitter amusement at her own naive stupidity. Why had she not *sensed* something wrong before? He had not really come back to his senses as she and Harriet had thought. He had slipped even further into the depths of—what had to be *madness,* without either of them seeing it. Where before he had occasionally taken her for her mother, *now* he saw her as—even if her mind shied away from the ugly thought, she felt compelled to answer it. A gift to him from his Victorine. Her own mama's surrogate! Trained to grace his dinner table and to pour his tea and be always *there,* so that he would not feel lonely.

Oh, I *must* run away! her mind cried feverishly. But where and to whom would she go? If she went to Letty it would only make trouble for her friend, and he—Papa—would think she had gone to *Paul.* She almost shuddered when she thought of what he might do in a demented rage. No, she could not endanger her friends. And if she had her horse saddled and rode to Kandy, what would she do there without any money of her own? She was only a female after all, and how clearly all of Harriet's old speeches came back to taunt her now. Papa was her legal guardian, with all rights over her. He could beat her, keep her locked up in her room on a diet of bread and water; and if she tried running away he could have her brought back in disgrace, as if she were a common criminal. And if she should marry, then her husband would have the same rights over her property and her life itself. Unless... Unless...! With the thought that had come to her, Alexa's mind seemed to clear slightly. Sir John! Dear, dear Uncle John who had offered her *real* freedom without conditions. *He* would help her. Oh why, why had she ever sent him that letter putting him off?

Alexa had never bolted her door before, but she did so now before sitting down at her small escritoire to write. Her pen sputtered and her usually neat hand had turned into an untidy scrawl, but no matter. He'd understand and he would come at once. She would not try to think further than that for the moment. A very *short* letter. Muttu would be taking the dogcart into Kandy with Cook for the next week's supplies, and he was fond enough of her, she thought, to see that her letter was mailed; especially if she promised him a reward when he returned.

"Please come at *once* if you possibly can. I cannot explain what prompts me to write such a frantic kind of letter, but I think you know me well enough to..."

"Alexa? Alexa, why on earth have you bolted your door?" Aunt Harriet sounded slightly out of breath from the stairs, and annoyed as well, and Alexa's heart had leapt into her mouth for a moment.

Recovering her wits the next instant, she called out in a sulky-sounding voice that she only wished to be left quite alone for a while until she felt less upset. She could almost *feel* Aunt Harriet's hesitation before she said at last in an exaggeratedly patient tone, "Very well, my dear. I suppose you *will* have it your own way, as usual. But I did want to have a little talk with you before dinner, and I am quite sure you must agree that we have much to discuss."

"Well—perhaps. But only if I feel I am in a better frame of mind."

"I *hope* you are not going to throw one of your childish tantrums again, Alexa. This is *no* time for that. Very well, I will come back in an hour then."

Footsteps retreated, and with a ragged sigh Alexa turned her attention to finishing her letter. It was only when it was addressed and sealed that she had slipped it under her mattress for safekeeping that she remembered with a sinking feeling of dismay that she had no money for postage. Nor could she suddenly *ask* for money after the scene that had just taken place.

Alexa started to rack her brains, almost driven frantic with frustration by now. The servants? No! Too embarrassing, and they would probably not have enough saved up, not even her faithful old ayah who sent all of her meager salary to her only son and his family. The housekeeping money that Harriet always kept in her desk? But that would be *stealing,* and if she was discovered... No! Well then, perhaps she could find some change in one of her dresser drawers? In the pocket of a dress perhaps, or in one of her reticules. Alexa began to rummage through all of her possessions, uncaring of how Ayah would grumble when she had to tidy everything up again. Nothing—except for a few pennies.

She had begun to think, driven by sheer desperation, that perhaps if she could somehow get her letter to Letty or to Paul along with a note begging them to have it mailed for her, she might yet be *"saved"* (such a *Gothic* word!). Then a sudden thought—a faint recollection—made her narrow her eyes thoughtfully. She had gone through all of *her* reticules of course, but—the trunk! Mama's blue trunk! And Mama had *always* left change lying about everywhere, in *all* of her reticules as well. Why, Alexa and Freddy used to play "treasure trove" when she would sometimes allow them to search for and keep whatever coins they could find. And the little bronze leather reticule that matched those bronze slippers had felt... Yes, when she had opened it to slip in her handkerchief, she was positive she'd heard the jingle of coins at the bottom.

Alexa had carefully put the key to the trunk into the pocket of one of her oldest gowns; and now she retrieved it, thanking her good memory while she twisted and turned until she heard the tiny click as the lock opened. It should be right on top, along with the slippers. And there it was! Opening the drawstring top, she put in her hand and began to take everything out, item by item. A handkerchief—*hers.* A small enameled snuffbox. Had Mama *really* indulged in such a nasty habit? A silk and lace handkerchief... But wait! It was knotted at one end to conceal something heavy. With some difficulty Alexa managed to untie the knot, and a heavy gold ring fell onto her lap. There was no doubt that it was *gold,* of course, both from its weight and... But it was a man's signet ring. Far too big for a woman's dainty fingers. And here was a crest she did not recognize, circled with tiny diamonds set cunningly into the gold to form the shape of a shield. Alexa frowned down at it. A very costly ring, a *man's* ring. But how on earth had her mother come by it, and why had she left it here so carelessly? Was *this* the legacy she had meant? But even a ring of gold set with diamonds will not serve my *present* purpose, Alexa thought crossly. Perhaps later she might sell it if she had to, but not until she had found out whom the crest belonged to. She knotted up the ring again and then, with a burst of impatience, turned the reticule upside down onto the carpet. Ah, here *were* a few coins after all! They were all English coins, of course, but they would probably do. Silver shillings, more pennies, and here—a real treasure trove indeed—was a golden guinea! Setting the coins aside, Alexa began to thrust everything else back into the purse, including a folded piece of parchment that had been right at the bottom. How *official* it looked, despite the fact that it had been folded so many times that it almost looked crumpled.

In spite of her hurry, Alexa felt herself hesitate; and then, not quite knowing *why* she suddenly felt impelled to do so, she began to unfold the parchment. How creased it had become! And slightly yellowed at the edges as well. All the creases made it difficult to read at first, and even the ink had faded from what must have been black to a brownish shade. But it was still quite legible, especially when she held it closer to the lamp.

''Certificate of Marriage,'' she read. At least *that* was printed clearly enough. Her mama's marriage certificate?

But what a place to keep it! ''Victorine Angelique Bouvard, seventeen years of age.'' Only seventeen? But there must have been a mistake. This wasn't Papa's name at all! Perhaps the clerk at the registry had not heard right and had had to draw up yet another Certificate of Marriage; and Mama had kept *this* as a joke. Alexa read it over again. ''Gavin Edward Dameron, aged twenty-two.'' But how could there have been a *mistake* when there were the two signatures at the bottom? And the signatures of two witnesses as well, one of them... This was surely a day of surprises! Surely that was Sir John's familiar signature?

Alexa sat back on her heels, beginning to feel numb. In January, eighteen hundred and twenty-one, her mother had married—*not* Martin Howard, her papa, but an utter *stranger* whose name she had never heard mentioned before. Gavin Edward Dameron. This same creased piece of paper she held in her hand had made those two man and wife. And in August of eighteen twenty-one Victorine had borne a daughter who had been named Alexandra Victoria. Not Dameron, but *Howard.* But how could that be *possible?*

Gavin Edward Dameron. Alexa remembered the scrawled initial that could have stood for almost any letter in the alphabet; but now, with his signature under her eyes, she knew that that initial had been a *G.* Almost without her own volition Alexa's cold hands rummaged in the trunk and brought out the slim volume of poetry, opening it at the flyleaf. ''To my Dearest and Only Love, from One whose Heart is Forever Yours!'' Passionate, if rather flamboyant, sentiments, scrawled in Gavin Edward's sprawling hand. Her... Even though her mind hesitated over the word, she had to think it. Her *real* father? It would account for so many half-finished sentences, so many other hints she had not noticed before. ''Daughter? I have no daughter. Stillborn—both of them.''

"Victorine! God, how I loved her. Would have taken her under *any* conditions."

What had Martin Howard meant? *Was* he her father after all? If Gavin Dameron had *died* in the wars or in some tragic accident soon after their marriage, then her mother could very well have turned to Martin Howard who had "always loved her" for comfort and solace.

But I *have* to know, Alexa thought fiercely. I won't be able to *rest* now until I know everything. *Now* she understood Harriet's warning about Pandora's box and the *intent* way Harriet had studied her face for a while. Harriet had been afraid she might *find* something. But why did they not want her to know the truth?

With a cunning that was quite foreign to her nature, Alexa folded up the precious document carefully and returned it to its hiding place before she carefully closed and locked the lid of the trunk. They must not know yet. And for the sake of her own peace of mind, *she* must somehow find out whose daughter she really was.

Strengthened now by her feeling of *resolution,* Alexa began to strip off her yellow dress with a shudder of distaste. She *hated* that particular shade of yellow! And all those ruffles, row after row of them, had made her look and feel like a china doll. Fragile, docile, and above all, *virtuous,* because that was what every young *lady's* dear papa expected of her, was it not? And what would he do if he knew how very close his pure and innocent little Alexa had come to losing her so-called virtue to a dark-visaged stranger on a moonlit night?

"Alexa, my dear, why do you shut me out? Didn't I make you understand *why* I said all those things I said? It is because I *care* for you so much—because I could not bear to see my Victorine's innocent child tarnished and besmirched. You won't stay angry at me, will you? Please, my dearest..."

Alexa could feel an involuntary shudder coursing up her spine again, and she had to close her eyes tightly before she could answer that pleading voice. "I—am not dressed. You *tore* my pretty new gown, you know."

"But you can have *two* new gowns—*three* more, if you like—to replace that one. You know how sorry I am, and that I did not mean anything I said. Surely you know it? Don't—don't draw away from me now! I need you, don't you know that? Would never hurt you—only protect you! Please, my dear, won't you let me come in?"

"I *told* you, Papa—I am—I am not dressed. I am trying to pick out something to wear..."

"You're *alone,* my dear? Got the curtains tightly drawn? Well it doesn't matter if it's your papa who comes in, does it? You'll still be in *private,* won't you? Know you're a *good* child, my dear. Modest too. But you mustn't feel that way with *me,* you know. Little Victorine..."

I am going to be *sick!* Oh God, I know he is drunk from the way his words slur and run together, but I cannot stand anything more! If he...

"Martin!" Oh—Alexa thought, almost abruptly—oh thank *God* Aunt Harriet had come! "Martin, what do you think you are about? You are making such a racket that I could hear you halfway down the stairs. And you are quite intoxicated again, aren't you? You had better come back to your room with me before you make a complete fool of yourself."

"But I have to talk to her, Harry. She's angry with me now. Can't have her staying that way—*Victorine* never stayed angry! Why isn't *she* more like my Victorine? Victorine *trusted* me with her, didn't she? Must make sure *Alexa* won't be led astray. Women—so weak!"

"You can tell me about the weakness of women when we have both arrived in your room, Martin. And in the meantime, you mustn't frighten Alexa with all these wild, drunken speeches. Come along, Martin, you can talk to Alexa later. Isn't that so, my dear?''

''Yes—and thank you, Aunt Harriet. We *will* talk later, won't we? After I have found clothes to put on.''

Through the door she heard protesting mumbles that were drowned out by Harriet's sharp, imperative tones; and at last, while she held her breath, footsteps that moved away—followed within a minute or so by the slamming of a door.

It was only then that all the stiffness left her body, and Alexa crumpled where she stood like a rag doll with the sawdust running out of it.

22

Dreams were such pleasant escapes, like fairy tales one chose to believe in as a child; all peopled with pretty spangled princesses and handsome princes. And in dreams, as in fairy tales, everyone lived happily ever after. Why, then, were dreams as tenuous as those little wispy swirls of mist that clung for such short moments around the hilltops before they vanished as if they had never existed? Why did nightmares never seem to end but go on and on? Dreams seldom came back, but the nightmares did—forcing her to relive everything, hear everything over and over again until there were words and phrases that seemed scorched onto the very tissues of her brain.

In all of Alexa's nightmares there were doors. Long, dark passageways and doors. Voices behind doors—calling, crying out, quarreling. ''Alexa! Alexa, don't shut me out! It is only your loving *Papa,* my dear! You can be quite private with Papa, can't you? No one shall defile you, my good, innocent child. No one but...'' *Papa?*

Voices tearing away veils, opening up Pandora's box that was so pretty on the outside to reveal all the ugly hidden things inside. Secrets, covered up and put away in a box, but always lurking there beneath the pleasant stage-set facade.

The nightmare had already begun, although she hadn't known it at first. She had been puzzled, she had been angry, she had been almost frantic with frustration and an almost unreasoning kind of fear that urged her to run—run barefoot and alone into the night and keep running anywhere at all as long as it was *away*. But no, she had always been used to *facing* her fears instead of running away. And that was why she had opened her own safely bolted door and walked barefoot along that wood-floored passageway that led past Harriet's room and what had been Freddy's room, past the empty space that had been her mother's and to the next door, which was the very last.

She had been wearing a white cotton gown that needed pressing, but it was not one of the *new* doll-dresses that were so pretty and ruffled and laced. White for purity, she remembered thinking. And again and again in her nightmares she would feel under her bare feet the worn place in the thin coconut fiber matting and see the line of yellow lamplight that crept from under the door. Hear the voices, holding her there a listener, silent and motionless.

"Martin, for God's sake, come back to your senses! She's Victorine's daughter, not Victorine! She looks on you as her *father*, not…"

"Be careful, Harriet, be careful what you say! Victorine's daughter—part of my Victorine, all that's left of my only love. But not *my* daughter, sister dear, as you well remember I'm sure. *Gavin's* daughter! You remember your old beau Gavin, don't you? Sure he was going to marry you, the way you kept him dangling in spite of my warnings. So sure of yourself and him you let him meet my Victorine. Did you know you were playing *procureuse* when you did, Harry? Did you?"

"Martin, there's no use in going over and over the dead past. *Dead,* brother. Like Victorine."

"No! D'you understand that? No! She'd never leave me—promised me. She loved me—ah yes, she *did* when she knew how patient I could be, how gentle with her. When she knew how much I loved her *she* started to love me too! Did that make you jealous, Harriet? That why you hated my Victorine so? Gavin wasn't *her* fault. Yours! She was so innocent; not at all worldly wise as *you* were, even then, with your books and your clever tongue and the *bon mots* that made everyone laugh. But what did that get *you?* You let Gavin seduce my pure little angel, and you were so damned blind you did not even see what was happening under your nose until it was too late!"

"You're losing control of yourself, Martin. Victorine's gone and the past with her. Alexa..."

"Alexa? Ah yes—my little Victorine. Still unspoiled. Still untouched. Still is, isn't she? You watched over her in Colombo? You didn't let any man get too near her? *Alone* with her?"

"Martin, don't you see that you have to—you *must* forget this—this unnatural obsession of yours. Yes, it *is* unnatural! I cannot allow..."

"*Allow,* did you say, sister? And—'unnatural'? Alexa's not *my* daughter, is she? Not *my* name on her birth certificate as father, is it? *Not* incest, my dear Harriet, if that's your devious meaning. And it's not for you to allow or disallow me anything! You understand? Do you?"

She was backing away from the door, step by step. Hands over her ears to cut out the sound of the voices. In her nightmares Alexa always tried to put up her hands to block them out *before* they could begin, but the words came through her damp palms to fill her ears. Halfway down the hall there was *her* door, standing open. Ayah standing there shaking her head at her, her grumbling scold like a rescue. She would keep Ayah with her. ''Quick!'' she told the old woman. ''Bring your sleeping mat up as quickly as you can to missy's room. Yes, *now!*'' She must sleep here all night. If he came—if his voice came through the door, pleading and wheedling and calling her ''little Victorine...''

But it was only Harriet's voice that called, ''Alexa? Alexa, you *must* let me in,'' through her bolted door *this* time.

''Alexa, there are certain things that you do not understand yet, but I can only hope that you still retain enough trust in me to do as I must advise you to do, without asking too many questions.'' Harriet's face, so gaunt, suddenly so *old*-looking. She had never really *looked* at Harriet before, had she? She had always been just ''Aunt Harriet''—always there.

''I was outside his door when you were talking. So I think I *do* understand now. I have to go away.'' Alexa's voice, even in her own ears, sounded dead. In her nightmares the *other* voices were still beating against her mind, crawling into it like the ugly coconut beetles with their spiky, clinging legs.

Harriet's voice seemed to rise and fall like sea waves or the sound of the wind outside in the monsoon season. Now only certain words, certain phrases repeated themselves in her nightmares and her memory.

''I was afraid this might... For the last few days I have been... Letty Dearborn...''

''Letty?''

''Yes. I suppose she had started to—*wonder.* Wrote to him, I don't doubt. Not that she has any right to interfere, but what's done... Anyhow, he's staying *there* instead of coming straight here as he usually does. Had a note by one of her coolies a while ago, but of course I did not tell

Martin. It's the best thing for you *now,* though. Never mind anything I said *before.* It's all changed now...."

"*He?* I don't know who you mean!"

"I *do* hope you have been paying *attention!*" A return to the old, acid-tongued Aunt Harriet. "I just told you, I'm sure. Sir John Travers. *Must* have been Letty, but anyhow he's here. Wants to call tomorrow. And better *he* than... At least I'm sure he'll be kind to you. And you'd have everything you want too, as Lady Travers."

"Lady Travers? Lady Travers! Ma'am?"

Alexa started up in bed, wondering why there was no movement beneath her with some part of her mind while the *rest* of her reveled at escaping from the nightmare.

"Ma'am? I wouldn't have awakened you except you told me eleven o'clock..."

When she opened her eyes with slow, deliberate anticipation she was back to the present again, thank God. She *had* escaped after all and she *was* Lady Travers; sitting up in bed in her sheer silk nightgown and stretching arms luxuriously above her head as she smiled at the worried face of her maid.

"Was it another one of those nasty nightmares, ma'am?" Bridget had been with her for a little over three months now, long enough to know that sometimes her mistress had nightmares that made her toss and turn violently and moan out loud in her sleep, the poor young lady. And so young she was; to be married to a man old enough to be her father; but they always seemed to be more than happy in each other's company, at least, with never a lack of things to talk about for all that they didn't share a bed nor even the same room. None of *her* business, Bridget always told herself. All she knew was that if they hadn't *rescued* her that time in India, only God knew where she'd have ended up by now. There were some things it was better not to think about, Bridget believed fervently, and it was a real pity that her poor young lady had the nightmares to haunt her with whatever it was *she* was trying to forget.

Bridget was fiercely loyal, and closemouthed into the bargain. The first morning glimpse of Bridget's round red face with straying wisps of red hair escaping from under her carefully starched white cap was always capable of lifting Alexa's spirits; especially after one of her nightmares.

"Oh, I'm so *glad* to be awake and know that *this* is real!" Alexa glanced around the room with its pale brocade-covered walls and exquisite furniture and with what seemed to be a whole *wall* of windows that opened out onto a small wrought-iron balcony. Gauzy curtains blew inward before a soft breeze, and the smell of *breakfast* assailed her nostrils. Coffee and croissants. She was in Paris!

"Your bath's ready for you, madam. And hot enough so you can enjoy your breakfast while it cools a trifle."

"Do you know, Bridget, for a moment I imagined we were still at sea. It seems as if I've hardly been off a ship since I left."

"Well, it's glad *I* am, milady, that we're off that ship. I'd never have made a sailor if I'd been a man."

Immersed in her copper bathtub behind the gold and ivory screen that matched the walls of her room, Alexa frowned a trifle thoughtfully as she stretched first one leg and then the other out of warm, scented water and began to soap them. Man. Sailor. Why did she have to remember with almost startling clarity a certain moon-bright night, a rock-circled pool, the riding lights of a ship beyond the reef. And a sailor from the ship (or so she had thought) who had called her a mermaid and a sea nymph while he kissed her; their wet, naked bodies lying against each other. And the next time—and the last time after that when the whole chain of events that had brought her here had begun, in a way. Nicholas. She preferred his full name to the crudely American short form "Nick." What was California like?

"Shall I be bringing you a towel now, milady?" Perhaps it was just as well that Bridget's voice from behind the screen changed the train of her thoughts. Later—Alexa thought. Later! For in herself she knew that it was not finished between them yet and that she would encounter him again some day. But this time, now that she knew and understood so much more—this time they would be on equal footing!

"Do you know if Sir John is up yet, Bridget?" Lady Travers sounded rather breathless as Bridget tugged valiantly at ribbons, her face becoming redder than ever. Corsets! And she knew her lady hated them too, even though she always wanted hers done up until her waist looked so tiny you could hardly believe it.

"He was up before you were, ma'am. Mr. Bowles told me he was expecting his Lordship back by lunchtime."

"Well, I won't put my gown on yet, I don't want to look too crushed before we go shopping."

When she had sent Bridget off to get herself a cup of tea, Alexa sat rather gingerly on the straight-backed chair by the desk, with its inkwell and heavy paper with matching envelopes bearing the hotel's name and crest reminding her of letters. Letters and papers. Part of the secret that had been hidden for years. The proof of her mother's marriage—her only *legal* marriage. Alexa had found *that* out too, when she was already too numb to understand what it might have meant if Mama and Freddy had still been alive.

"His name was *there,* on the list of English dead. Lord Gavin Edward Dameron, Viscount Dare. And there *she* was, half-crazed with grief, and there *you* were, an infant only a few months old. No one to look after either of you. If you'd been a *boy* and a possible heir to the title it might have been different, but as it was.... Martin had always loved Victorine—and you know the rest of *that* part of it by now, don't you? When we heard that he'd only been left for dead and had actually been taken prisoner; that he was still alive and back in England—it was more than two years later then, and Martin and Victorine had already been *married* and there was another child on the way. The child didn't live, as it turned out, but what difference would *that* make anyhow? Bigamy. Scandal. Victorine had got over everything and was happy with my brother by then. And there was the money coming in every month. As long as we stayed out of England—that was the only condition *she* attached to the money, and it *still* comes in. Oh, for all that you look at me with those stony dark eyes of yours *now,* my dear, you'll have to admit that it wasn't *all* bad for you, was it? *I* saw to your education and your upbringing and manners, and there wasn't too much you'd have lost by *not* knowing, if things hadn't happened as they did. Even *you* wouldn't have wanted your brother branded as a bastard and your mother as a bigamist, would you? And there's one more thing I'll tell you, and I hope you'll take it as a warning. Be careful, my dear. Be very careful of the old Marchioness. You'll laugh *now* when I say it, but she's an evil woman with no scruples at all when it comes to what *she* thinks is best for The Family. Sons, daughters, nephews, everybody. She wouldn't permit any scandal where *they're* concerned."

Now that she was far enough away from *that* part of her past, Alexa could feel sorry for Harriet. Poor Aunt Harriet, who would end her life in exile. Poor *young* Harriet of the flashing smile and clever *bon mots* who had lost everything at once. Harriet *had* been kind to her, kinder than she need have been; and it had been Harriet after all who had opened her mind and taught her to use it.

"Is there any record of my birth?" Even though she asked the question Alexa had not really expected that Harriet would, without another word, produce her birth certificate, from her own box of papers.

"Here you are. *She* was too ill soon after you were born to remember what to do with anything, so I kept it for her, and she never did ask for it either. You'd have been able to get a copy made at Somerset House in any case, I expect. But it won't do you any good without a *marriage* certificate my dear; and for all I know *he* might have kept that himself, if he had time to get to know her scatter-brained ways at all."

Perhaps it was because she had ceased to trust Harriet by then that Alexa had never told her of her find. Perhaps Harriet really thought that Alexa had gone through all of her mother's meager keepsakes without finding anything of note. But at least Harriet had made no objection to Alexa's taking the tin trunk with her when she had left in the dogcart late that night, while Harriet's *brother* (Alexa could not yet bear to call him anything but that) slept heavily still, from the effects of the laudanum his sister had contrived to add to his decanter of brandy.

Sir John had ridden over by himself the next day, and Alexa had never yet asked him what had transpired between the two men. But there was no move made to stop her when she and Sir John were quietly married in Kandy that same evening, with Letty and Paul as their witnesses.

"Lost in dreamland, my dear? I'd quite expected you to be dressed and pacing the floor quite furiously because I was a few minutes late."

"Well, I thought that *I* should really be the tardy one, you see."

Jumping up, Alexa hugged her husband while she tilted

up her face for his brush of a kiss. How much she loved him—her dearest and best friend—and how much she owed him. It seemed as if he had transformed her life into a magic, fairy-tale existence and had changed *her* into a princess at the same time. A *wise* princess, however; under the tutelage of her indulgent fairy godfather, who was teaching her something new every day. And today she was going shopping in *Paris,* where it was spring, and she could buy anything and everything she might fancy.

"And when I have my *new* wardrobe I will give *this* gown away to Bridget, although it's beautiful and I love it—*today* that is."

In a fit of childish exubcrancc Alcxa threw her arms wide and twirled in a waltz step around the room before she stopped before the mirror again to put on her ruched silk bonnet. For the next few days at least, she told her reflection silently, she was going to enjoy Paris and all the new things she would learn and the new encounters it would bring. Later there would be enough time to read again the little packet of letters tied with blue ribbon that had revealed to her that her mama had actually had a *sister,* who might still be alive. Later, she would think very carefully about what she would do when she was back in England, where she had been born the *legitimate* daughter of Gavin Edward Dameron—now Marquess of Newbury.

PART III

23

"By the time I will have to *leave* you, my dear, you will be well equipped with the knowledge of almost every art and artifice that the female sex has had to learn and use to gain their ends from time immemorial. *And* you have so far managed to keep your mind detached enough to *use* your weapons effectively. But have you quite decided exactly how and to what ends you will use this armory of worldly wisdom?"

Alexa swirled around in a froth of skirts and petticoats to shift her contemplation from the bright blue Mediterranean sea to her husband.

"*Don't* I *know* and you know that I know what must be in the end, but I don't want to be reminded of it. And especially not on a day like *this.*" And then, with a sudden surge of alarm, she ran to him where he sat in his chair on the sunlit terrace. "You are not feeling *ill* are you? Or in pain? You did promise to tell me if you felt..."

"My dear, I assure you that I feel quite the same as usual, and it was not my intention to worry you. I am afraid that I could not resist letting my sense of curiosity get the better of me, if you'll forgive an old man who ought to know better than to pry."

"Then you also ought to know very well that I could never consider any question that *you* ask me as *prying.*" Although she spoke with mock severity Alexa sank onto the low velvet-covered stool by his chair and rested her head against his thigh. "I suppose you only asked me what you did to remind me in your subtle way that I should ask some questions of myself. And I think I know what I want to do—not just for the sake of being *revenged* alone, but for the satisfaction I would gain from knowing that *they* will not be able to sweep me under the carpet or *wish* me into not existing!" She looked up at him with a half-smile. "But perhaps I do need a devil's advocate, for I do not wish to make one single wrong move in the kind of chess game that I intend to play!"

"There have been chess games played many times where human lives were the forfeited pieces, my dear, and I hope you will never forget that. If *you* are the red queen, the old Marchioness—grandmother or not—is the black. And she has had many more years of experience at this kind of match—and is used to winning! If you mean to go through with your plans—if you do not change your mind—then you must remember at least three things. Never underestimate your opponent, never allow yourself to be distracted from concentrating, and never trust; particularly not those who flatter you or offer their help against your adversary. And as for the rest—your young mind is far too quick and agile for me, I'm afraid. You'll have to give me more time out here in the sun to think carefully of all the objections I should throw in your path and the difficulties you might encounter." Touching that thick, glowing hair of hers that almost seemed alive under his fingers, Sir John could sense that she was already preparing her answers for any question he might ask her. With one of those impulsively affectionate gestures that he had grown to treasure in her, Alexa seized his gnarled hand and kissed it before she turned her cheek against his palm.

When you were as young as she was you were invincible and immortal—or so you felt. And how strange that the older one grew the more vivid became the memories of all the seasons and the sensations of youth. Ah yes—once he, even he, had made plans and believed in ideals and idols. He had never feared death and had always gone to battle with a sense of embarking on some exciting adventure. In the end he would either be one of the victors or one of the vanquished; or one of the glorious dead. Youth knew only extremes, and there had never been a moment when he had imagined there might be alternatives. Or that there would be a time when he might actually choose life—even a conditional kind of life—over quick, clean death.

Well, in the end he had chosen—or rather, his *body* had made the choice for him. And here he was on a sunny terrace in the south of Italy, an old man with a young and lovely wife that other men envied him.

"Are you still thinking of all the pitfalls I might encounter?" There was a note of teasing laughter in her voice that made him smile too.

"Well, for one thing, my dear, you will have to learn patience. Yes, I am still thinking! And should you discover that I have closed my eyes, I would want you to realize that I think even better with my eyes closed!"

"Before you start to think, then, can *I* ask a question? Do you believe that the lawyer you hired will really be able to find my mother's sister? My *aunt,* I suppose. My *real* aunt. How cruel and unfair of Harriet to keep those letters from my poor mama, who must have thought her own sister had forgotten her!"

"You are not being impartial, my bright Alexa. How could Harriet risk the possibility that your Aunt Solange might let it slip that your *real* father was still alive, considering all the consequences that would have arisen? Being a pragmatic soul like myself, she did what she felt she had to do. And you cannot in all honesty blame Harriet for concealing the real facts from you without blaming me as well. *Do* you resent that, Alexa?''

He felt the slight, restless movement of her head against him before she said in a muffled voice, ''No. You *know* that of course I could never blame *you* for anything. And *you* were never hypocritical, as *she* was. But you're right, and I must really learn to be impartial and not swayed by *emotion.*''

Half-asleep already, Sir John recalled the question she had asked him and said suddenly: ''Getting old! You were asking about your Aunt Solange, weren't you? Well, Jarvis is a good chap. Very shrewd, very clever. And most useful of all, he has connections everywhere. Underworld, half-world—highest circles as well. Younger son, you know. Eton and Oxford. Quite the rascal in his day, and his family never quite forgave him for taking up a *profession.* But he's the very best, and I know him personally as well as on the professional level. If this Aunt Solange who liked young Guards officers is still alive, Edwin Jarvis will find her. And what's more, *he's* the one you should retain to handle all the business affairs, because he's honest and he's blunt. He'll tell you to your face that you're a damned fool if he thinks so.''

''Then I hope…I *know* that I will never give him the opportunity to say so. Mmm! Oh, how deliciously warm it is out here. And how glad I am that your friend the Conte was kind enough to lend us his villa. And—would you prefer that *I* should try to think hard too?''

When she was answered by a grunt that was followed soon after by a slight snore, Alexa patted his knee with an affectionate smile before she stood up again and went back to the warm stone wall and her contemplation of the sea below and the terraced hills that marched down to meet it. Tiny fishing boats bobbed up and down, punctuating the vivid blue swells with their colored sails. She could see, further off, the tall masts of some of the ships anchored in the harbor. The faint strumming of a mandolin floated up to her, accompanying a clear tenor voice singing of unrequited love, and jealousy and passion. In spite of the Neapolitan dialect, she found she could understand most of the words. Passion! Alexa thought, while her eyes narrowed reflectively against the dipping sun. I wonder if that is what I gave way to that night? Passion—or *lust,* as some might term it—was all too easily aroused, she had learned. And men, when their weapons of seduction were used against *them,* could be brought to fever pitch and rendered mindless by desire. A glance from beneath lowered lashes, a teasing smile. An "accidental" touch, a sigh through parted lips. Invitation and then rejection, followed by invitation again. That was the coquette's way. But there were also other ways to make slaves of men that were practiced and had been perfected by the great courtesans of the world, who could pick and choose their own lovers and their price and could incite proud men to fight duels over them and to beg like fawning hounds for their favors.

How warm still was the slowly setting sun! And how sweet the plaintive ballads of the singer! Alexa turned her back on the sun and the blue and white sparkle of the sea to feel the warm caress of the sun across her shoulders; but the words of the songs the unknown tenor sang continued to penetrate into her thoughts and stir them. Music should always be an accompaniment to the game of lovemaking, she had been told. And there were a myriad, endless ways of making love, although that expression meant nothing more than the arousal and exciting of the senses up to a certain point; and there were *some* men, she had been told, who preferred harder, coarser words. There was also a great deal more that she had learned, for all her "teachers" in these particular matters were considered the best and the most sought-after courtesans in each country they had visited so far.

There had been a certain elegantly decorated house in Calcutta, which was frequented only by Indian Princes and rich and titled Englishmen and whose talented inmates had come from almost every Eastern country—Java and Penang and Siam and China and Japan—as well as from all the different provinces and kingdoms of India. They had all been young and supple and beautiful; and in addition to being accomplished in the dances and music of their homelands, each one was renowned for a certain specialty.

When their ship had turned about after picking up its quota of passengers for England, they had visited many other ports and places—Mauritius, Madagascar, Cape Town and finally Le Havre and Paris. Everywhere there had been something new to learn, and especially in Paris, where they had remained for two weeks. The most famous demimonde in Paris, a slim, elegantly gowned woman in her early thirties, numbered Kings and Princes among her lovers and was known for her exquisite taste. She had taken quite a fancy to Alexa, and it was from Leonie that the young woman had learned of *subtlety* and its importance, and how to make a study of each man—learning his habits, his likes and his dislikes, not only in the bedroom but also in his choice of cigars or clothes or horseflesh. One also had to learn everything about the best wines and vintages, and how to set an elegant table and act as hostess to an informal gathering that might consist of royalty as well as some of the oldest and most distinguished titles of Europe. Also about food, about art and furnishings; not to mention being able to converse intelligently and with knowledge on any number of subjects that might range from politics and international intrigue to great music and literature.

"In short, *chérie,* you can never allow yourself to become—how shall I put it?—*jaded,* perhaps. Stale, like cigar smoke from last night. You have seen the visitors in my home, yes? Sometimes it is a salon where every subject may be freely and openly discussed. And I know something about everything, my dear, because I have made it my business—that is a good word, no?—to do so. When I am with a lover I become almost like his reflection. When he invites his friends to dine he knows that everything will be exactly right, from the meal itself to the wines and cigars and the musicians I hire for the evening. I not only know all his desires and needs, but I anticipate them. So, you begin to take my meaning?"

Some men wanted a tigress, some a temptress-siren, others a harem odalisque. Alexa had learned as much from talking with these women who had been her instructors as by watching their often lively demonstrations of the arts of love and reading certain *Editions Privées* of books on the same subject which also contained beautifully colored, carefully detailed illustrations to accompany each topic. None of the women she had met had been ashamed of their profession, but rather were proud instead, of having reached the highest pinnacle possible. Indeed, Leonie had, with a typical shrug and a wave of her thin, gold-edged cigar, admitted that she could have made a successful marriage on several occasions if she had wished to but had chosen to be as she was instead.

"A wife? And why should I go from pampered mistress to household slave? It is not these poor *jeunes filles* who are married for their family name, a dowry, or to beget heirs, who really *know* their men, but women like *me.* And while my lovers court me with gifts and words of flattery and adoration, their *wives* receive formal politeness and a grudging household allowance. To give *me* pleasure in bed they will expend a thousand kisses and caresses and tender embraces; with their *wives* it is quite different, of course. A hasty fumbling in the dark under her flannel nightgown and a few snores. It is only to get children and not out of *feeling,* you understand? And in making love—well, it is the feeling, the *emotion* that is shown that makes your lover yearn to come back again and again. You comprehend?''

Since they had left Paris there had been first Lisbon, then Cádiz, and finally this retreat in Naples where they could both rest in the sun for a week or so before visiting Rome and the Vatican. And then it would be London, but only if *she* wished it. While Sir John still slept with an occasional peaceful snore, Alexa frowned rather uncertainly until she remembered, with a rueful smile, to smooth out her brow. A woman's looks—her complexion and her skin—were assets to be carefully protected with creams and oils and lotions in the same way that her figure, if it was good, must be kept supple and slender with certain exercises performed daily and followed by a warm bath perfumed with richly emollient oils to soak into the skin; imparting a glowing sheen to it.

So many things to learn and remember, Alexa thought. And so far, she had not yet had the experience of putting everything in which she had received instruction into practice. Ironically enough, she was still—her lips twisted in a bitter grimace at the memory the word recalled—*''virtuous,''* if no longer *innocent,* but she was certainly not ignorant either, and thanked God for that. It appalled her, even now, to think how little she had really known or understood about the realities of life and even about her own body. In the kind of society where innocence and ignorance were considered to be synonymous with virtue, it was no wonder that so many young girls fell easy prey to seduction by an unscrupulous male. And no wonder either that brothels flourished; for once a girl had succumbed without first getting a ring on her finger, she was no longer "good" and there was seldom any other course open to her.

With her eyes closed and the sun still warm on her face, Alexa leaned backward against the stone parapet and felt its roughness under her elbows. Oh, to be able to give her body completely to the sun and feel its seductive heat penetrate every inch of her skin until it turned bronzed and glowing, like the skins of the village women she had sometimes come upon during her rides over the patnas of Ceylon, giggling together as they bathed under a small waterfall with their wet black hair sleeked against their bodies, down to their waists. As for *her* hair— She had merely swirled and twisted it into an untidy knot at the back of her head before coming out here, and now, without thinking, Alexa pulled out the few pins she had secured it with and tossed them over the parapet before she let her heavy mass of hair fall down behind her. If it had not been so late in the afternoon she might have been tempted to fling off all of her clothes and lie naked atop them like an offering to the sun. And run down the marble stairway still naked, and into the pool whose waters had been diverted from a mountain stream that ran through the property and watered the olive orchards. Swim there with the sun still pouring its hot gold honey over her as she lifted herself out of the coolness of the water and lay back again for the sun to dry.

"I do hope, Alexa dear, that you are not practicing how to fall asleep standing up?"

Opening her eyes, she straightened up and stretched her arms widely. "I was imagining myself a pagan sacrifice to the sun god and wishing I could take all of my clothes off!"

Sir John gave one of his short laughs. "You can and should do anything you wish to, my dear, as long as you remember that you have promised to see me through dinner this evening. But as a favor to my old ears, I wish that you would throw that poor young man who is serenading you in such a *loud* voice a flower or some such thing to render him soundless with happiness."

24

Later, those slow-moving, drowsy days in Naples were remembered by Alexa as her "golden days"—lying naked under the sun with her body gleaming with sesame oil that had been perfumed with Attar of Roses until her skin became almost as bronzed as her hair with the gold laced through it. She and Sir John saw no one and entertained no one and talked to each other a great deal.

"Why, I do believe that she's really in love with Sir John after all," Bridget told Mr. Bowles when he had gallantly offered to take her for a stroll in the garden. "And he's a fine man, don't you think I can't see *that,*" she added quickly before she was misunderstood. "It's just that I thought, what with *her* being so young and all and so pretty too, that well, maybe it was something fixed up between *families,* like they do among the gentry. But the more I see them together and the easy way they'll be talking to each other and laughing, well, I... Well, that's why I think what I just said I thought!" she finished triumphantly.

"I'm sure I—er—quite take your meaning," Mr. Bowles said after a slight pause. Reaching the edge of the rather overgrown rose garden, he turned back majestically, steering a rather disappointed Bridget with him. "However," he added after another pause during which he cleared his throat emphatically, "however, Miss Culligan, I must say that I *do* think a certain degree of—er—*restraint* might... Those *fishermen* keep singing their songs so *loudly!* And the *gardeners* keep carrying those very large pottery *urns* back and forth from the garden to the courtyard. The blighters always pretend they can't understand me when I try to tell them they are dismissed."

"Oh! You mean when the madam is swimming to get herself cool from that hot sun?" Bridget was now no longer shocked by anything at all, although she sometimes wondered what it all *meant.* Her voice sounded cheerfully unconcerned, almost shocking Mr. Bowles into stopping in mid-stride to stare at her. "Well, as to that now," Bridget continued in the same tone, "I suppose she knows very well what's going on and doesn't care and neither does Sir John—so I've always thought that it's no one's business but *theirs.* You'll be agreeing with me, Mr. Bowles?"

"All *I* can say is," he uttered rather frostily, "that I, for one, am quite relieved to be leaving for Rome tomorrow. They are a little more civilized there, I understand."

The silly, *obtuse* woman! he had begun to think with annoyance until to his further annoyance his thought was interrupted by a loud thumping at the wooden gate that was set in the imposing archway they had just drawn abreast of. "Now who, I wonder, can *that* be—making such a racket so late in the afternoon? It had better not be that persistent fisherman fellow with another of those ugly sea creatures that look all legs."

"At the *front* entrance?" Bridget breathed, looking quite awed. "Why even he wouldn't dare to do such a thing, the poor young lad. Perhaps it's the Count who's the owner of this place come back?"

As the thumping on the gate was followed by loud and obviously drunken voices that threatened to get louder and ruder by the second, Mr. Bowles disengaged his arm firmly from Bridget's nervous clasp.

"Miss Culligan, if you will excuse me. I suppose that since *I* am here and that lazy gatekeeper is probably asleep somewhere, it is left to me to take care of this unwarranted intrusion into our privacy."

Leaving Bridget round-eyed and openmouthed by his vocabulary, Mr. Bowles strode purposefully towards the massive wooden gate that had now actually begun to shake from the force of the kicks that assaulted it from the outside.

"There is no need for such a *violent* announcement, gentlemen—or whoever you might be! I am here." When Mr. Bowles's loud pronouncement brought a sudden silence, he nodded in a satisfied manner and slid back the long and heavy metal bolt that locked the two halves of the gate together.

Immediately, and quite without either consideration or politeness (as Mr. Bowles was to say later), two laughing young gentlemen who were obviously in their cups surged through the opening, closely followed by a third, somewhat older man with a dark, boldly defined face and a saturnine look who could quite easily have been taken for one of the natives except for his modish and well-cut clothing. He gave the astonished Mr. Bowles a twist of his mouth and a rather resigned lift of his broad shoulders while his boisterous companions tried to outtalk each other with a mixture of questions and orders flung in Mr. Bowles's direction.

"I say! When did Damiano get himself an English gatekeeper? Don't *dress* like a gatekeeper, I must say. Have to tell him."

"Used to go to school with Damiano. Promised to look

him up. Want him to meet our friend—another Viscount. We're *all* Viscounts! You *are* a Viscount, aren't you, old man?"

"*He* won't expect us to stand on ceremony, you know. Remember the way."

"Thought we'd surprise him. No need to announce *us*. You'll see to our horses?" A golden guinea tossed in Mr. Bowles's direction bounced off his heaving shirtfront to lie in the pinkish dust.

By the time he had recovered his voice sufficiently to pronounce, "If I might just *explain* to your Lordships that a *Mistake* has been made," the two younger gentlemen were already striding across the gently sloping grass lawns and up the steps leading up to the terrace that Mr. Bowles always called "the courtyard."

"Your Lordships! A mistake..." He had begun to follow them when he noticed that their rather unsteady progress had been halted while their heads swiveled to watch Bridget, who ran with remarkable swiftness ahead of them with her apron clutched in her hands.

"Not at all old Damiano's type, is she?"

"Maid perhaps. But didn't you think *she* looked English too?"

"I should not be too alarmed, unless your master happens to be entertaining some of his older relatives."

Until then Mr. Bowles had almost forgotten the presence of the third gentleman, who had remained behind, while he debated frantically as to what he should do to avert a terrible contretemps. And now Mr. Bowles turned to him with relief.

"Sir! I'm sorry, your Lordship. I beg you to... This is *not* the residence of whomever..."

"It is *not* the home of the Conte di Menotto, even though his family crest is prominently displayed everywhere?"

In his acute distress Mr. Bowles ignored the slight sting of sarcasm, almost wringing his hands as he stammered out, ''But...but the Conte is not in residence at the moment. He has rented this villa to Sir John Travers, and *Lady* Travers, who...who would not—oh, definitely *not,* my lord—wish to be disturbed.''

''You did say Travers? Lately of the city of Colombo, in Ceylon?''

''Yes, that's quite correct, your Lordship. And if you would *please,* your Lordship, be kind enough to...''

It was at that very moment, when Mr. Bowles had begun to wonder why this gentleman who spoke with an unfamiliar accent had suddenly begun to scowl in a very dangerous manner, that he now noticed with a sigh of relief that the two young Lords were now retracing their footsteps in a slower and more sober fashion than before. And it became apparent, as they drew closer, that their countenances, so much alike to look at, were quite flushed.

''Well? It seems your visit was so brief that I did not get my promised introduction to your friend.'' Why, Mr. Bowles thought quite indignantly while his eyes traveled from one countenance to the other, one would think he had not heard *a word* I said—or believed me either!

''I...we... Sorry old chap, but I think we...''

''Committed a *faux pas.* Found...''

''Soon found we'd made a mistake. Eh, Roger? Saw no one, of course.''

''No. No! It was the—the maid. Told us Damiano has the house rented out for the month. Better go now, I suppose.''

''I suppose we had better, now that you have discovered you made a mistake. Our apologies, please, to your employers.''

I don't know where *he* comes from, but he's not English! Mr. Bowles thought as he bolted the gate again with noisy force. And I wouldn't trust him either, for all that he dresses like a gentleman. There's what he said at *first,* and the sudden way he changed about, with his voice sounding like a knife blade hidden under velvet. Dangerous, he is.

It was only after he had started back towards the welcome coolness of the house that Mr. Bowles began to wonder why the two younger gentlemen had returned so quickly and in such an abashed manner. Surely *Bridget,* who was only an Irish country girl after all, could not have turned them around in such a hurry? But the only other alternative that came to his mind made him shudder, especially when he tried to think of what he must tell his master.

"Bridget was such a heroine. You should have seen the way she dashed up all those steps and *flung* her apron over me as if it had been Sir Walter Raleigh's cloak."

"Gallant Bridget!"

Alexa had dallied in her scented oil bath for longer than usual; and to make up for it, she had decided to put the last touches to her evening toilette in Sir John's room so that she could converse with him at the same time. Now she turned from the mirror to regard him with her clear, level eyes. "Are you angry? Because you *must* tell me if you are. Have I disgraced you, do you think? They *did* seem very much ashamed of themselves in the end; and they did promise—'word of honor!'—that they would not breathe a word. They were really quite *harmless* and rather stupid young men, you know."

"I think I recognize their names," Sir John said with a twinkle in his eye that made her relax immediately. "And I am sure your summing up was quite correct, my dear, except for your imagining that I might be either angry or *disgraced.* Please go on with your diverting story. You have me quite fascinated! So? Your gallant Bridget saves your modesty by flinging her apron over you as you lay sleeping as usual in the sun. And...?''

Alexa had begun to laugh by then. ''I'm sure I do not deserve such a wonderful and understanding friend as you are. And how very much I love you and appreciate you.''

Her voice sounded light as she related the whole incident and made it all sound quite amusing and droll. But when she had been awakened by Bridget, panting and puffing as if she had been running for miles, and had had an *apron* of all things dropped on her... It was a small wonder that when she sat up to find what had caused such a commotion, her eyes had flashed with anger instead of amusement.

It was only when she saw those two faces that looked so similar as to be almost identical, *gaping* at her with popping blue eyes that seemed unable to believe what they saw... Only *then* had she remembered rather belatedly to snatch the apron up before her, hoping as she did that it covered as much of her body as possible.

''Good—God!'' one of them said fervently.

''Say *that* again!'' the other echoed in a rather fainter voice.

They were obviously brothers, alike enough to be twins. And obviously quite young as well. Sent down from Oxford, she guessed. But they were not *so* young that they had not yet discovered women; and that fact was quickly apparent to Alexa, who had learned to look for certain signs.

''I *beg* your pardon?'' Her voice carried all the frosty dignity of a Dowager Duchess and had the immediate effect of making both young men stutter and avert their eyes.

''Oh, beg *yours,* I'm sure. Didn't know...''

''Didn't intend to *intrude,* that is. Looking for Damiano, you know...''

"I am afraid I do *not* know! And if by 'Damiano' you mean the Conte di Menotto, then I must inform you that he was kind enough to rent his home here to my *husband;* with the *assurance* that we would have absolute privacy!"

"Mistake! Never dreamed... Terribly sorry...!"

"What we *mean,* er—madam—is that—most abject apologies! Husband..."

"My *husband,* gentlemen. And you *are* gentlemen, I trust?"

Into the delicate pause she left open, both voices blundered at once.

"*Assure* you, madam—Ladyship...?"

"Viscount Selby. This is m'brother—Viscount too..."

"Rowell. We're twins, you know. Fortunate there were enough titles to go around."

"And now that it is established that you are twin brothers *and* gentlemen, I trust that you will leave me to my privacy and remember only that my maid explained the mistake you made? I am *quite* sure that would be what you father *and* your mother would advise; although of course they need not know that their sons have been guilty of such a breach of good manners and good taste, need they? I'm sure my husband must know them well—he knows *everyone!*"

"No! Not for the world! Saw nothing—did you, Roger? Mistake!"

"He's right. Blind. Deaf. Quite dumb. On our way back home. Never saw you before!"

"Quite so, gentlemen. And you'll excuse me if I don't wake my husband up to show you out? We tend to become *too* informal here, I suppose."

They had stuttered and stumbled over their booted feet and their shamefaced apologies as they left, and she had heard the slam of the gate that must have followed their departure. But it had been another lesson for her, Alexa confessed when she had finished. ''I should not have been so careless as to fall asleep in the sun, and especially *there,* when we have our own *private* terrace up here. Should I be worried about meeting them again *socially?*''

''My dear, you should not worry about anything at all. And I am quite confident that you are perfectly capable of carrying anything off—even to the point of acting as if you have never set eyes on each other before.''

''Of course I would. And oh, how glad I am now that we shall be going to Rome tomorrow.''

For the rest of the evening Sir John made an effort to appear as cheerful and lighthearted as *she* had become, although his mind continued to mull over everything that Bowles had imparted to him with that purposefully *impassive* look he sometimes adopted to hide disapproval.

His suspicions might not be correct, Sir John told himself. And if, by some unfortunate and untimely coincidence they *were*—well, *suspicions* were not enough reason to spoil Alexa's last evening in Naples, especially after she had felt so guilty.

So, when they went down to dinner, he made an effort to keep the tenor of their conversation as light as possible; and by the time they were back upstairs to prepare for bed, he had become convinced that he had done the right thing. After all, he was probably quite mistaken in imagining, from poor Bowles's rather indignant description, that the *third* gentleman who had lingered by the gate engaged in idle conversation with his valet could possibly be the same man that Alexa had told him of. And once she had begun to trust him enough to lose her reserve with him, she had told him almost everything that had transpired between the two of them—from their first moonlight meeting to their last, with all its fateful consequences.

Ignorance! Sir John had thought then, with a surge of silent anger. Keeping young girls unaware of the facts of life and reproduction and even their own bodies, and leaving them so damned vulnerable! When Martin went off the deep end that way, there could have been developments that would have left her scarred for life—and still in ignorance! Even after it was all over and she was safe with *him*—even then she had not really understood what might have happened. Intuition—and a sense of something not healthy—that much she had only sensed, without knowing anything about the *physical* aspects involved nor their possible repercussions.

It was for this reason, believing firmly that *knowledge* was not only the greatest defense but the best weapon of attack as well, that he had arranged for Alexa to be educated and instructed in certain realities. She had been eager to learn and quick to absorb everything; and he had with a sense of satisfaction seen in her a new sureness and poise. But—and this was the only thing to disturb him slightly for *her* sake—she was still so very young, and still vulnerable merely for that reason in spite of all her recent "education." The Spanish cousin of Lord Charles who had refused to take her once he found she was a virgin, the same man who had taught her what pleasure of the senses was before he had warned her harshly against succumbing to such weakness... There was still some strong attraction there that made her constantly remember and promise herself revenge. Attraction or urge, it was all the same thing. He, even he as he had become, could still remember sometimes how it had felt to desire blindly with the loins in spite of all the protests and objections of a rational mind. It was irrational, and you knew it; impossible—you knew that too! Something as primeval and unexplainable as the effect of the waxing and waning moon on ocean tides; and sometimes this kind of passion was as inescapable as it was inevitable. He could only hope that this was not the case with Alexa and wonder at the same time what would happen between them if they ever met again.

25

Rome! Crumbling walls and palaces side by side with marble monuments and piazzas made cool by fountains. Sun-drenched days and warm nights and music always and everywhere. Rome was a city of feeling—an *experience* rather than a series of sights to be seen. They had been in Rome for only three days, but already Alexa felt as if she would like to remain here forever if she could.

They were staying in the villa of an extremely old Italian Duca and his considerably younger English wife, Perdita, both friends of Sir John; and Perdita had already taken Alexa everywhere that she could think of on their sightseeing excursions.

"You have seen the Colosseum and the Circus Maximus and the Sistine Chapel—not to mention the catacombs and the famous Caracalla baths. But my dear, would you not like to see something of the more modern side of Rome?"

Giusto, Perdita's husband, had been engaged in a political discussion with Sir John, but now he suddenly looked across the room and gave a high-pitched chuckle. "Aha! You see how well I know my Perdita? I had been wondering how long it would take her to broach the subject." He chuckled again at Alexa's puzzled expression before he explained kindly: "The Temple of Venus, my dear. And it is well-named too, I can assure you. Most exclusive—most discreet. We usually make a habit of calling on our friend Orlanda at least once a week." Surprising Alexa even more, the Duca actually winked before he added, "But you must let Perdita describe everything to you, for she will do much better than I could; and then you may decide, *si?*"

"Of course I can describe it all!" Perdita had a ribald twinkle in her eye as she leaned closer to Alexa. "In fact, I used to work there myself until my dearest little Giusto insisted it was time that we began to present a reasonably respectable facade. When the French were here it didn't matter, but the English—good heavens, they have become so *stuffy!* On the surface, that is. In any case, I always wear a cloak when I visit now, and a hat with a veil or even a mask. Most people do these days, even the men. Don't want to be recognized!" Catching Alexa's rather wary look, Perdita shook her head with a laugh. "No, no, my dear! I know that by now you must feel as if you have seen all there is to be seen, eh? But I can promise you that the Temple of Venus is quite unique. For one thing...you won't find the usual house girls *there.* Some of the young ladies come from the best families in Europe—convent runaways, unhappy wives, divorced women, ruined governesses. They dress like demure young misses and usually speak several languages, as well as being accomplished in many other ways as well. And they all enjoy what they do. You've read about the priestesses of Aphrodite?"

In spite of the fact that Alexa had by this time begun to feel that there could be nothing that could surprise her any longer, she found herself intrigued by Perdita's veiled hints and roguish smile. Directing a questioning glance in Sir John's direction, Alexa discovered a slight twinkle in his eye; and with a mental shrug she thought that, having seen the ancient and *respectable* side of Rome already, there could be no harm in discovering the other, more raffish side of the city. In any case, they were guests of the Duca and Duchessa Atanasio, and guests were supposed to fall in agreeably with plans made for their entertainment, were they not?

She would remember all too vividly afterwards that the night air had felt as warm as a caress against her face, and that the color of the silk gown she had worn under her hooded black velvet cloak had been a shade of scarlet interwoven with gold thread that could change color in different lights. The sound of horses' hooves on the uneven cobblestones of the Via Condotti had made her picture the horses and chariots of ancient Rome that must once have traversed this very same street, and she had felt relieved that Sir John seemed less tired tonight than he had been since their arrival in Rome.

"Ah, there is nothing quite like a Roman night!" Perdita said as the Duke's private carriage pulled up before a deep archway that was almost a tunnel, guarded by a spiked metal gate with a gold-painted reproduction of Botticelli's Venus done in bas-relief against a deep blue background serving as a lock. The same emblem was also embedded in the brick arch above the gate, Alexa noticed as one of the footmen used the enormous silver key that the Duca handed him to unlock the gate for them. Almost at once, or so it seemed, two stalwart men clad in blue and gold livery appeared with torches to guide their way through the shadowed archway and across a small open courtyard with a fountain in its center, until they reached the imposing pair of carved marble columns that framed an ebony door bearing the same gold Venus they had encountered before, this time in the shape of an enormous door knocker.

They could very well have been entering the grand palazzo of some noble Italian family, Alexa thought as they entered a hall that was as large as a reception room, with its white marble floors scattered with oriental rugs and an enormous crystal chandelier overhead. And indeed, Madame Orlanda—dark-haired, slender and exquisitely gowned—could very well have been a titled hostess greeting guests arriving for a masquerade ball. There were a few other people about but they also were cloaked and masked and seemed to know in which direction they were supposed to go. In any case, Alexa noticed no display of curiosity or heads turning to stare as Madame Orlanda led them upstairs into her own private parlor to partake of some refreshment while she undertook to describe to the newcomers some of the exotic pleasures and pastimes available to guests at the Palace of Venus.

By the time they had gone upstairs and were comfortably seated, Alexa could not help but notice with a feeling of uneasiness that Sir John had begun to look tired and drawn again, although he brushed aside her concerned whisper with pretended harshness as he growled that he did not need a nursemaid at his time of life—a glass of the best cognac the house had to offer would do nicely instead.

"And after that I think I'll take a nap as I usually do. Can't keep up with active young fellows like Giusto here any longer!"

The Duca, who was at least fifteen years older than Sir John, chortled shrilly at this, while Madame Orlanda immediately invited Sir John to take his ease in her own sitting room, leading him there herself with a twinkling look over one elegantly clad shoulder while she invited the rest of them to make themselves quite at home until she returned.

Almost immediately the Duca put down his wineglass,

and after a perfunctorily murmured apology he took himself off with the air of a man who knew exactly where he was going and what he wanted.

As the door closed behind him, Perdita lifted her glass to Alexa with a smile and a slight shrug. "Well, here's to you, my dear! And to new experiences." Her look held open appraisal as she studied the younger woman in her flamelike gown with the black velvet cloak now slipping off her shoulders. "You're very lovely, Alexa," she said in a softer voice. "And especially in that gown. What colors one can discover in it every time you move!" As Alexa lifted her glass with a guardedly polite smile, Perdita gave a sigh. "But—you *do* happen to prefer men, do you not? I can usually tell. Have you ever found yourself curious, though, about having another woman?"

"No," Alexa said bluntly. The veiled admission that Perdita had made with her questions had not shocked her; she had been approached by other women before during the past few months when women had been her teachers, and she had learned to be direct. Now, because she really *liked* Perdita and did not wish to hurt her feelings, she smiled at her over the rim of her glass. "I suppose that might be so because there are very few things left for me to feel curious about since I began my *education,* as Sir John calls it. And *that* was in order that I could learn to defend myself."

Putting her glass down abruptly, Perdita crossed the room to where Alexa stood, touching her cheek with a strange, almost pitying laugh. "Ah, my dear, don't you think that *all* of us would like to guard ourselves against our feelings? But emotions can rise up all too easily to trap us unawares, like a sudden summer squall that comes from nowhere to whip a calm sea into a whitecapped frenzy. Be careful, for I do not think you have become a *real* cynic yet."

Alexa might have argued the point if Orlanda had not returned to them at that moment with the announcement that Sir John was quite comfortable and had already fallen asleep.

"Well then," Perdita said with a mischievous look as she drew her cloak more closely about herself, "*I* for one am going to find—whatever I might be in the mood to find tonight. Do enjoy yourself, love. There's nothing wrong with *that,* is there?"

Quite *unreasonably,* as Alexa had to admit to herself, she felt a little annoyed at being left to her own devices, even though Orlanda proved more than gracious and not at all impatient or condescending as she poured out a glass of sherry for herself and asked Alexa if Perdita had told her anything about the Temple of Venus.

"Only that it is quite unique, I'm afraid. But I hope that will not make you feel obliged to waste too much of your time in..."

"Ah no, *cara!* I do nothing I consider a waste of my time. And since I also believe in frankness, as your husband tells me *you* do as well...you do not mind if I say that what I have heard about you is most intriguing?" When a slight smile and a shake of Alexa's head answered her, Orlanda's own smile widened to show small white teeth that were still pretty. "Good! So, shall we sit here for a few moments while I tell you a few things about this house of pleasure? For you must understand from the beginning that here we only cater to pleasure and nothing else. There are no questions asked here and the only boundaries are those that are self-imposed—not by our guests only but by the young ladies who choose to please them as well. I do not permit that anything should be inflicted on an unwilling partner, you see. Those who visit the Temple of Venus and return again and again do so because here it is all discovery and excitement; an exploration of the senses and an intensification of feeling. And because not only most of our guests but several of the young ladies too prefer to remain masked, it gives a sense of *freedom.* You comprehend?''

Alexa did indeed comprehend before *too* long, especially when Orlanda, with a rather roguish smile, led her into her own bedroom, which was dominated by a massive bed that was canopied and curtained with tassel-edged satin.

''Come. I promise that you will not be bored by the *usual* peepshows.'' A sliding panel to the right of Orlanda's bed revealed a rather narrow aperture that led them into a narrow corridor that was thickly carpeted, the walls on either side covered with a heavy fabric that felt like velvet to the touch. The only faint light came from red-shaded oil lamps that burned dimly in the niches that were set into the walls at intervals and from thin pencils of light that seemed to come from within the walls themselves.

Alexa had played the reluctant voyeur before, never being able to feel quite comfortable about observing certain acts that would normally take place in privacy even after she had been laughingly assured that some men were actually more stimulated by the thought that they might be observed.

''Most of my guests prefer to participate rather than to merely observe,'' Orlanda whispered. ''And it is very seldom that I bring anyone along *this* particular passageway, unless they are close friends of mine and...'' she turned her head to look back at Alexa, who was following her, before adding with a strange kind of significance, ''in the same profession as I am.'' Before Alexa could think of a response to that rather enigmatic statement, Orlanda drew her attention to one of the tiny openings with the casual comment that she might be amused by *this* particular piece of theater. ''He enjoys playing the Turkish sultan surrounded by odalisques, and he pays very well for each of them."

A plump man wearing a domino mask that concealed all of his face except for his eyes sat naked and cross-legged upon a pile of cushions, surrounded by five young women clad in costumes that were as transparent as the flimsy gauze face veils they wore. One of them fed him grapes from a silver dish while another offered him occasional sips of wine from an ornately chased goblet. While a third young woman strummed on a strange-looking musical instrument and sang with suggestive smiles and movements of her hips and eyes, the other two who reclined on either side of him occupied their crimson-tinted lips and hennaed hands with pleasuring him.

"He visits us quite regularly," Orlanda whispered before she led the way once more. "And so do many others—both male *and* female—who can afford to pay the prices I charge to have their secret fantasies fulfilled. With the masks, as you can see, they can become themselves! Paradoxical, is it not? I have known great ladies of the highest degree—well known for their coldness and arrogance—who come here to offer themselves to any man who approaches them with a certain crudeness of manner. And gentlemen whose wealth and positions make them envied and looked up to, who seek the most unexpected kinds of satisfaction. Orlanda's slim shoulders lifted expressively. "But as you have seen already, peepholes can only provide a student of human nature, shall I say, with such a very limited field of vision; whereas the same performance on the stage of a theater or opera house... You can imagine the difference!"

Even while she had been straining her ears to try and follow Orlanda's low-pitched stream of words, Alexa found herself becoming more and more puzzled as she wondered why *she,* an utter stranger, should be taken into her hostess's confidence without questions or reservations.

"But now this is what I really wanted to show you." Orlanda paused so suddenly that Alexa almost bumped into her. "There is a curtain here which I will draw aside to reveal another kind of stage. I tell you this before because you must know that neither you nor I can be observed from the *other* side of what appears to be a wall of mirrors. So, now you will see my private theater and enjoy the performance that is offered tonight, I hope. This is the room to which my young ladies bring the men that *they* choose—customer or coachman. And they do so with the understanding that should I, or any personal guest of mine so choose… Ah!" Orlanda's soft, throaty laugh suggested infinite possibilities before she said: "If *you* should like to join the two on the bed or take the woman's place, the choice is yours, of course! And I will even promise you privacy from all prying eyes—even my own!"

Even while she made that last provocative offer Orlanda had begun to draw aside the curtain with short tugs on a velvet cord, revealing at last a stage set of mirrors lighted by crystal lamps that hung from gold chains in every corner of the enormous room. Dominating everything else was the only item of furniture in this particular chamber of Venus—a bed so large that it could easily have accommodated three couples at one time on its sheets of soft, oyster-colored velvet that almost seemed to glow.

A performance indeed! Without her realizing it, Alexa's fingers had suddenly tightened against each other while her eyes dilated. Why, this was almost like looking through a shopwindow! But with what a difference, for these were certainly no dressmakers' dummies swathed with lengths of material.

Both naked and both unmasked, they sat opposite each other—the man's sunbrowned back to the mirror while the young woman faced it. She was quite lovely, leaning slightly forward, her full red lips parted and her silvery-blonde hair covering just enough of her breasts to make her pose even more provocative as she deliberately invited the caress of the fingers that pushed aside strands of hair to find crimson peaks which seemed to quiver as the woman's breathing quickened. Her hands clutched fiercely at his shoulders as she whispered something and almost flung her body against her dark-haired partner, straddling him while her pale-ivory legs wrapped themselves about his hips.

"She is always hungry and always impatient, that Maddalena!" Orlanda whispered at Alexa's side as the man brought his hands up to the young woman's shoulders and pushed her backward while she continued to cling to him, her hips moving and now arching upward to answer thrust with counterthrust.

Alexa could feel her face becoming hot as her own breathing quickened unwillingly and her heart began to pound. The bed became an arena as the couple, like lusty young animals, playfully grappled with one another and changed positions, the man moving onto his side first and then onto his back with his hands as dark as mahogany against the pale flesh of his partner's hips as he controlled her wild, writhing movements and her silver hair swung back and forth between them like a wind-tossed banner. At the next instant Maddalena had suddenly flung her head so far back that the veins became ridges against the arch of her throat, her mouth open and contorted as if she was in the throes of acute agony. And it was between that tautly held moment and the next, when the woman let her body collapse limply forward over *his* that Alexa knew for a certainty what the purely intuitive part of her mind had guessed from the very beginning; holding her rooted in place by a sick kind of fascination that forced her to watch the whole obscene ritual of abandoned depravity.

Her sharply indrawn breath sounded more like a hiss as furious thoughts clashed against each other in her mind. Libertine! Lecher! Whoremaster! Debauched, profligate, hypocritical swine! And to think that this same infamous *animal* who frequented whores had dared to try to seduce the naive innocent she had been at the time, and his hands had actually touched *her* flesh with the same casual intimacy and the same calculated caresses he bestowed on his paid harlots! Why, if *she* had not learned by now how to exercise some control over her baser emotions, she would have been sorely tempted to…to…

''My dear! I had no idea that you would become quite so enthralled by my private theater. Or could it be that it is one of the performers who has managed to hold you spellbound?'' The rather archly uttered question in Orlanda's low, throaty voice broke into Alexa's baleful thoughts, bringing her back to caution as well as reality. Still it took some effort to pull her gaze away from that rumpled bed and its lust-sated occupants—ivory-white against copper-bronze and sun-dark fingers tangled in a web of pale silver. Before Alexa had found a suitably convincing rebuttal Orlanda was already continuing with a hint of teasing laughter underlying her words. ''If your hesitation is because of what you just witnessed, I think I can assure you with almost complete certainty that *he* has held himself back from…complete fulfillment. I myself have encountered only a very few men who have this kind of control; and I should warn you that should you meet one you might find yourself exceptionally fortunate or exceptionally unfortunate! But now, while Maddalena is still limp with satisfaction, would *you* care to take her place? I hope you must know by now that there is no need to feel *shy* here.''

During Orlanda's suggestive little speech Alexa had managed to regain some *semblance* at least of her usual detachment. Keeping her back firmly turned on that garishly set stage, she said cuttingly: "Oh, I am really far from being *shy* by any means, but I myself believe that *he* must be one of those unfortunate males who can manage to give women a certain amount of pleasure without attaining completion themselves. Poor devils, how frustrating it must be for them!"

"Do you *really* think so?" Orlanda did not sound convinced in the least, although Alexa saw her give a slight shrug, as if to say that it was quite unimportant. "Ah, well, if you do not feel curious enough to want to find out for yourself which one of us is the better guesser, is there any other kind of spectacle or experience that might appeal to you?"

"Well, perhaps I really should look in on my husband before I think of how I might indulge myself," Alexa said quickly, hoping she did not sound *too* sanctimonious. He had actually begun to make love to the more than willing Maddalena *again!* Were there no limits to his vile lechery? If she could have run away from the disgusting spectacle without making a complete fool of herself, Alexa felt that she would have done so. As it was she had to force herself to walk slowly enough to let Orlanda think she was reluctant to leave her theater of fantasy.

"I must admit that your idea of a mirror that becomes as transparent as a pane of glass on *one* side certainly provides one with a different perspective," Alexa managed to say as they reentered Orlanda's opulent bedroom. "And it was more than kind of you to allow me into your confidence."

She was obliged to pause while Orlanda stopped before a mirror to pat at her hair and touch her cheeks with color that made them seem to glow with healthy vitality. "My dear,'' Orlanda said casually over her shoulder, ''I must admit that I cannot accept the credit for *that* particularly clever idea. It was one of my closest friends who thought of it first. Have you heard of a Madame Olivier?''

The suddenness of that seemingly innocuous question took Alexa by surprise, so that her straight dark brows puckered slightly before she said inquiringly, ''No. At least I do not *think* so. Should I know her?''

Orlanda continued to study herself in the mirror quite unnecessarily, with her beringed fingers still touching a ringlet here and a curl there; but Alexa, standing behind her now, noticed that those dark eyes were watching *her* now, even though she used the same lightly casual tone of voice as she replied.

''Well, my dear, I had *wondered,* you know. And especially since I have been asked so many questions of late.'' One shoulder lifted in a shrug as Orlanda finally turned away from her mirror to face Alexa's frowningly questioning look. ''Lawyers!'' she uttered contemptuously, with a slight wrinkling of her nose. ''Why should I tell *lawyers* anything at all? And especially when after all these years I am told they are trying to find one of my closest and dearest friends? There are very few people I trust, *cara,* and lawyers least of all. But when Sir John—yes, your husband—also asks me similar questions, then I find myself wondering. Even quite curious; I must admit it. I began to ask myself why, after so many years, people are trying to find the whereabouts of Solange Bouvard?''

26

Afterwards, when her mind had had the time to adjust itself to all of the startling revelations she had been subjected to in one evening, Alexa would often find herself wondering how she had prevented herself from bursting into peals of hysterical laughter as Orlanda, after scanning her face intently, had finally explained all her mysterious allusions. Solange Bouvard, the long-lost Aunt Solange she had become so anxious to find, was in fact now known as Madame Olivier, notorious all over Europe for running two of the most expensive and exclusive Fancy Houses in London. What subtle irony! And all the more so since it was in a Roman bordello that Alexa had first heard of what her mother's sister had become.

Oh yes—if she had not been so *stunned* for several moments after Orlanda had made that first bluntly uttered revelation, Alexa was sure she would not have been able to control herself. But as it was she must have looked quite uncomprehending, so that Orlanda, with a rather impatient shake of her head, had gone on to enlighten her even further.

''How could I be certain, after all, how much you had already been told by *those two?* That Martin Howard who was always hanging about after Victorine, and his sister Harriet, who pretended to be Victorine's friend and Solange's as well when all the while she was eaten up with jealousy and hate because *she* had always wanted Dare—and it was Victorine *he* chose to elope with instead. Ah, if *you* could have been there to see her face when she heard of their elopement, as Solange and I were that day. 'Be careful,' I warned Solange later. 'She has decided that *you* are to blame for everything, and now she hates you!' And of course I was proved right later, after Dare had suddenly turned up from the dead—or so it seemed to all of London. I had already come to Italy by then, with my first Conte..."—Orlanda grimaced wryly—"or, believe me, I would have warned her once more—especially against seeing Dare again, or the Marquess of Newbury as he had become by then. My poor Solange had a weakness for the very good-looking men in those days, and she had always had eyes for Gavin Dameron, even after she knew he was after her younger sister. Ah, yes..."

Orlanda had, while she had been speaking, produced a slim cheroot from a thin gold case; and now, after sending Alexa a questioning look, she shrugged as she lit it and inhaled deeply, then exhaled a spiral of smoke with a sigh. "Yes," she repeated, her wise eyes resting thoughtfully on Alexa's set face, "if I had been there I would have reminded my friend to be careful—very careful—of bringing herself to the attention of the Witch, as we used to call the Marchioness Adelina. A very evil woman. And one that you too must be very careful of."

There was much more to the story that Orlanda related, of course, and by the time she had finished Alexa no longer felt like laughing. Indeed, she had by this strangest of coincidences found out much more than she had bargained for. Enough to make her wonder bleakly if she might not have been much better off being born the natural daughter of Martin Howard, instead of being of the warped stock she had sprung from. Her paternal grandmother was a completely amoral and unscrupulous woman who was capable of doing anything, including brushing people who annoyed her out of the way as casually as if they had been no more than buzzing flies; capable, in fact, of going so far as to get her son's *legal* wife safely out of the way with the threat of *bigamy* in order that *he* should contract a bigamous marriage with a Duke's daughter, by whom he had already had three daughters. And as for Gavin Dameron himself, Alexa found that she could not bring herself to think of him as her *father* any longer. What sort of a man could callously discard a young, newly wed wife with an infant daughter, allowing her to believe him dead and then turn around and ''marry'' within two years another woman his *mother* chose for him? And there was more—even worse than *that,* if such a thing was possible and Orlanda was to be believed.

When Orlanda interrupted her narrative in order to light up yet another of her cheroots, she lifted inquiring brows at Alexa as if to invite questions; but the younger woman remained silent for so long that she might have been transformed into a marble statue.

''My dear, I hope I have not said too much? But if you are planning to go to England, where you might meet all these people, you will be very much better off knowing everything *before.* Do you not agree?''

''Tell me, please. My...I suppose they *are* my half sisters, as strange as it seems! Do you know anything about them, or what they are like? I suppose they must still be quite young, the poor creatures!'' Her face hardened suddenly. ''And *he,* the Marquess of Newbury. What of him *now?*'' When Alexa saw that instead of choosing to answer all of her blurted-out questions immediately Orlanda was leaning forward to offer her a cheroot, she hesitated only momentarily before accepting one this time, although she had never *smoked* before.

"Here, let me light it for you...." Orlanda's rather amused look told Alexa that she had already guessed at her inexperience, even before she warned her not to try to inhale the smoke at once, especially if this was the very first time she had tried a cheroot. "Watch me, and try to do as I do, but instead of pulling the smoke into your lungs you would be much wiser to blow it back out gently, like so. Otherwise you might soon begin to feel quite sick." Then, while Alexa tried determinedly, glad to have something different to concentrate on for a few moments, Orlanda said abruptly: "You must not think that I am trying to evade your questions, *cara.* I will tell you as much as I know, if I can do so without breaking confidences. But no more tonight, I think. Too many shocks are never good for the system, and I think you need time to absorb and think about everything you have just learned. And also..." Orlanda leaned back with a roguish smile and gestured with her cheroot as Alexa almost choked on a mouthful of smoke. "Also, you see, perhaps I also need time in which to ponder over what I have learned about *you* tonight." Catching Alexa's rather startled look, she chuckled. "That surprises you? Ah, my dear, those of us lucky enough to have reached *my* position in our profession do so because we have learned almost everything there is to know about human nature, and especially its weaknesses, I am afraid. But I am an *observer,* and there are many I can also *sense* as well as see. A good madame should understand women and their emotions as well or better than she understands men."

Stubbing out her cheroot in a silver and brass ashtray, Orlanda met Alexa's suddenly wary eyes with a teasingly mocking smile that was almost a challenge, then rose to her feet and shook out her skirts. "Sometimes I am afraid

I chatter on far too much, and that was a habit that Solange always chided me for.''

It was almost unwillingly that Alexa followed Orlanda's example and rose also, feeling herself abruptly dismissed when there was still so much left unsaid and far too much *implied.* After all, *she* had not been the one to initiate what had turned out to be a series of unpleasant disclosures. And now, even though she had extinguished the cheroot she had accepted far too daringly, Alexa felt as if some of the smoke she had tried hard not to inhale had become trapped in her head, making it swim quite alarmingly as soon as she stood up.

How she had always hated admitting to any weakness in herself, and disliked most of all to feel *pitied!* Orlanda would almost likely begin fussing over her if she realized how easily she had been overcome by just a few puffs of smoke. Taking a deep breath and holding firmly on to the back of the chair she had just vacated, Alexa decided to buy herself a few more minutes in which to recover her equilibrium by asking one last defiant question.

''Please...'' About to lead the way out of her room, Orlanda paused, allowing Alexa to continue in what she hoped was a steady voice: ''Since you have shown me enough consideration thus far to be direct and open in your speech and manner, I hope you will not mind too much if I beg that you will grant me the same consideration just once more and tell me, if you please—'' after a slight hesitation Alexa forced herself to go on stubbornly ''—in what way I might have betrayed myself? I have been making great efforts to guard against showing my feelings too openly, and had actually begun to think that I had succeeded in controlling any telltale reactions that might too easily give me away. Was I badly mistaken?''

Orlanda regarded her steadily for a moment before she said with a slight smile and a shrug: ''I think you know, *cara,* that I only referred to what *I* believe I could sense in you. There were no others about to observe you and draw their own inferences, as you know. What would you like me to tell you? And are you sure that you might want to hear me say it out loud?''

Alexa's eyes wavered uncertainly, and she bit her lip. Then her head went up almost defiantly. ''I think, after all, that I *am* quite sure I would like to hear what you thought you could sense in me, apart from a certain amount of *lewd* curiosity, I suppose. I have seen many similar exhibitions on many other occasions.''

''Ah?'' Orlanda said mildly. ''And—if you'll forgive the directness you begged for—did you always, on such occasions, wish that you were the woman being made love to?'' Ignoring the flush that came up in Alexa's face and her startled expression, Orlanda went on pitilessly: ''What I *know* I sensed, my dear, was that you longed to be Maddalena tonight. You wanted the man with her to do the same things with you that he did with her—touch you in the same way and in the same places and give you the same kind of pleasure that *she* enjoyed.''

Alexa's face went from red to white, and her fingers tightened on the back of the chair as if it had been a life raft that could save her from drowning. She felt totally incapable of speech as a shiver that was half-despair and half-apprehension darted through her body. How was it possible that her darkest, most carefully hidden thoughts could have been so easily read? And, oh God, now that they had been plucked out into the light, she could not deny that everything Orlanda had said was the truth.

Orlanda's manner seemed to change in some subtle way as she studied Alexa's white face and dilating eyes. She said in an almost speculative tone, ''You saw his face. Do you know who he is and what his connections are? Ah, now you *do* have me curious!''

As if she had suddenly been released from some spell, Alexa stammered, ''Con...*connections?* I don't...''

''Perhaps you do *not* know after all.'' Orlanda suddenly gave a strangely mirthless laugh before adding: ''Ah well, my dear, since you *are* Solange's niece perhaps this once I will break one of my strictest rules for you. When I spoke of 'connections' I was speaking of family connections. On your *paternal* side, that is. Why, Maddalena's guest tonight happens to be none other than your father's heir, the future Marquess of Newbury. Although, of course, he is presently Viscount Embry. Lord Nicholas Dameron, Viscount Embry, to give him his full name. And he's quite the stud too, in addition to being a well-built figure of a man, wouldn't you agree, *cara?* I cannot help but think of how amusing as well as ironical it might have been if you *had* taken him from Maddalena. But I daresay that *your* mind is not as devious as mine is...and in a way that's a pity, I suppose. For if *I* were in your shoes I would have made the most of the situation and all its deliciously intriguing *possibilities*—in more ways than one!''

As the meaning and significance of those casually uttered words penetrated the numbness she had felt at first, Alexa heard the blood start pounding in her temples, so loudly, it seemed, that she was almost deafened. From the very beginning, then, he had lied and pretended and deliberately deceived her, even going so far as to call himself by a false name! And for what reason? Could *he* have known even before she did whose child she was and the kind of embarrassment her very existence might pose to certain people, *especially* if she learned of her antecedents and might turn up in England some day to claim her rights? Ah, how clearly she saw now why he had prevented her from meeting Lord Charles, and perhaps eloping with him.

The very thought of the *extent* of the monstrous deceit

he had practiced made Alexa begin to grit her teeth and actually *shake* with such uncontrollable fury that for some moments even Orlanda became alarmed that she was suffering from some kind of seizure. Quickly putting an arm about the girl's waist, she exclaimed with genuine concern, "My poor child! If I'd had any idea of what a *shock*...perhaps you had better sit down again for a while, yes? A glass of brandy..."

"No!" The sharp, almost harsh voice that Alexa heard from somewhere outside herself did not sound in the very least like *hers.* "No, brandy is not what I need at all! A devious mind—isn't that what you said? A mind devious enough and clever enough to conceive of ways whereby deceivers might be duped themselves!" She gave a laugh filled with such bitter rage that even Orlanda stepped back to stare at her strangely while Alexa, not quite aware of it herself, suddenly began almost to *prowl* back and forth with her hands clenched into fists at her sides. "Oh, how I hate and despise them all! And thank God I don't bear that cursed name any longer! Damerons—with their arrogance that sets them up above everyone else, and their false pride and their damned hypocrisy! But before *I* have finished with them they will have neither pride nor position nor arrogance left—I swear it!"

Alexa gave that short, almost ugly laugh again as she suddenly stopped her frenzied walking back and forth and stood still, staring narrow-eyed at Orlanda, who had found herself almost frozen into silence. "Do you think that I could learn to be very devious indeed? And a good *actress?* I know now that I could learn anything and do anything that would help me to accomplish the revenge that I plan. And *you* hate them too, don't you? But if you won't help me then perhaps my aunt Solange will, once I have met her and explained everything to her. And if not, then I have been made wealthy enough to hire lawyers and anyone else I might need to help me. But I *will* do it, you know!'' Her voice suddenly quietened, but there was a note of hardness underlying it that had never been there before. ''They will not be able to get Lady Travers out of the way as easily as they did my poor mother and aunt and God knows how many others who were thought to interfere with the old witch's plan. Didn't you tell me that was what you used to call her? Ah, perhaps I *am* enough like my grandmother to be the one to defeat her by using *her* weapons! What do *you* think, my wise new friend? And will you help me with your advice and your guidance?''

During all of this impassioned speech Orlanda had been regarding Alexa with enigmatic eyes that gave nothing away, and now she merely gave a shrug and a resigned, somewhat impatient sigh before saying with a wave of her hand: ''Well then, I suppose we might as well sit down again while we talk, for I must tell you that your prowling back and forth like a caged leopard was beginning to make me quite nervous, and I do *not* think very well when I am set on edge. Please…!'' Another impatient wave of her hand made Alexa sink back into a chair rather reluctantly while Orlanda walked over to a glass-fronted cabinet containing glasses and several crystal decanters. She said over her shoulder: ''*I* for one am going to indulge in a glass of brandy. Shall I bring you one as well?'' Without waiting for Alexa's reply she had already poured it out; and now she carried both glasses back, handing one to Alexa before she sat down herself and leaned back comfortably. She looked across at the young woman's rather flushed but determined face with a slight smile. ''So you want my advice and my guidance, you say. Hmm…'' Holding her glass up, Orlanda pretended to study the sparkling amber liquid with concentration before she looked at Alexa again and said: ''In that case, *cara,* I *do* think that the first thing

I will have to learn from you—before you make certain explanations that I'm sure you'll agree you owe to me—is—'' and now her eyes met Alexa's measuringly ''—if you'll forgive the blunt question...exactly *how* far are you prepared to go in order to attain your ends?''

27

If they were not finishing each other's sentences, the twin Viscounts, as they were popularly known in their circles, were usually engaged in an argument, as they were now.

''Tell you, it *was* her! Wasn't foxed enough at the time to mistake it!''

''All covered up, Myles old fellow. No way you could possibly tell, you know. Wasn't *before,* was she?''

''Makes no difference! Hair—not a common color, you'll admit. Hands too. Always notice hands. Fingers. Wore the same ring, too! Ruby, I think. Remember the setting, though. Unusual.''

''Well, *I'm* not convinced yet! *Think* about it. Hardly the kind of place a *lady* would visit, what? And this is Rome, *that* was Naples. Unlikely, you'll have to admit! Both agreed at the time, didn't we, that *she* had to be a lady? Spoke like one. Sounded too much like Mama when she decides to put us in our places. And you know as well as I do Damiano wouldn't rent the family home to just *anybody!* No, no, old boy. Not possible! Imagining things.''

''Know when I am and sure when I'm not, Roger! *Was* her all right, likely or not. Anyway, remember what

Grange told us after *he'd* been here last year? *Ladies,* he said. Why else would they wear masks when the *others* don't?''

''Still don't convince me, Myles. Not the *type,* in spite of...''

''In spite of what?''

The twins, comfortably seated on lawn chairs that had been placed in the shadiest part of the flagstoned terrace overlooking an ornamental garden complete with statues and fountains scattered among carefully trimmed grass and shrubs, now started almost guiltily as they looked up, their mouths falling open with dismay.

''I suppose I should apologize for interrupting such an interesting conversation?'' Viscount Embry drawled as he walked up the steps that led up to the terrace from the lawn below. Two pairs of slightly protuberant blue eyes topped by straw-colored hair seemed to become even more protuberant when they noticed that he was not only bareheaded under the hot sun but shirtless and shoeless as well, his closely fitting fawn trousers carelessly rolled up to just below knee level. As usual, that darkly saturnine face of his remained completely unreadable as he surveyed the twins through narrowed, lazy-lidded eyes that went from one red face to the other before he added pleasantly: ''I *had* been trying to get some sleep in the sun, you know; but once the sound of your voices had waked me up, I must admit that I could not help becoming quite intrigued. Unusually colored hair, didn't you say, Myles? Hands—or no, it was a finger, wasn't it? With an unusually set ruby ring. And you *did* mention your friend the Conte di Menotto, didn't you? The same one whose villa in Naples we committed a *faux pas* by visiting, even if it *was* only the lady's maid you encountered—or could it have been the lady herself? I am afraid that my memory sometimes plays tricks on me, so you *will* correct me if I'm wrong, won't you?''

''Ah—uh—sorry if we woke you up, Embry! Didn't know you were trying to catch a nap. Would *not* have argued so loudly if we had.'' The Viscount Selby spoke rapidly, casting his brother a significant look as he did.

''That's right. Couldn't know you were taking a nap, could we? No one told us. In any case—not safe to take naps in the sun, I've been told. Sunstroke, you know!''

''How careless of me.'' Embry's voice remained bland, but his eyes were as hard as stones, making the younger men squirm uncomfortably before, with a dangerously swift change of mood, he shrugged and said lightly: ''I suppose my fortunate escape from the dire consequences of being unwise enough to fall asleep in the hot sun calls for an offering to the Roman gods! Or better yet, a goddess. Venus, perhaps? I believe I've read that it was customary to visit her temple at least once every week, to give thanks, or to settle arguments.''

After he had sauntered back to the house, the twins exchanged uneasy glances. ''I say, do you think he *knows?* Didn't think we said anything significant, did you?''

''Of course we didn't!'' Myles said stoutly. ''Said nothing at all, really! But perhaps *we* should go along too, when *he* does. Just in case, you know. Can't have anyone we might know thinking we didn't keep our word.''

Once the two young men had decided that a second visit to that exclusive establishment known as the Temple of Venus was necessary in order to protect their honor as gentlemen, they could see no reason why *duty* could not be synonymous with pleasure on this occasion, and especially since they were supposed to return to London again within the next two days. In fact, they had no sooner despatched the customary note to Madame Orlanda that formally requested permission to call upon her that evening than they were already in the hands of their valets, and even had their carriage ordered for eight o'clock sharp, for there was no question in their minds that they would receive anything but a polite note of acceptance in reply.

By the time they had arrived at their destination and had been greeted by their hostess, the twin Viscounts were in fine fettle and had almost forgotten their reason for being here in the first place. They engaged in a lighthearted discussion as to the merits of redheaded women as opposed to blondes or brunettes, and whether they would reengage the twin redheads they had enjoyed before or seek variety this time, not making their choice so quickly. After all, their friend Giles had told them with a significant wink, that part of the fame of the Temple of Venus lay in the fact that they had only to state what they wished and it would be provided for their pleasure and enjoyment, even if it was "a make-believe kind of thing"—something like a charade but much more fun, as Giles had described it.

Told that they might feel free to roam about until they found whatever or *whoever* caught their fancy, both Roger and Myles decided to begin their exploration with the velvet-hung chamber that was whimsically known as the Theatre, and where, from their comfortable chairs visiting gentlemen could observe some of the priestesses of Venus as they bathed or played in pretended unawareness of their "audience" who watched from the darkness on the other side of the multicolored layers of gauze curtains.

Escorted to their seats by attentive "footmen" who were actually young women dressed in livery, their crystal glasses brimming with vintage champagne, both gentlemen had barely settled back with anticipation beginning to rise in their twin breasts when a drawling, rather sarcastic voice from the seat to the left of Roger gave them both an unpleasant start.

"Selby and Rowell. What a coincidence! You might

have mentioned that you two intended to come here tonight, and we might have shared one carriage. But tell me, are you still trying to settle that argument of yours?''

''Forgotten *which* argument you mean,'' Roger countered cleverly. ''Myles and I argue all the time, you know.''

''Hmm, yes, I suppose I *do* know,'' Viscount Embry said noncommittally, and left the subject alone as some of the scantily clad ''priestesses'' who had been disporting themselves in their sunken bath now decided to emerge in order to stretch their limbs gracefully before some of them reclined on marble slabs to be massaged and oiled by ''slaves'' and others wrapped themselves in thin silk robes after they had allowed themselves to be dried by their attendants.

The gauze curtains gave the whole enticing scene an effect of pastel unreality, as if they had been viewing it though a veil of mist; and most of those who watched seemed to be quite entranced as different young women arrived on the ''stage''—or left it, once they had been on view long enough to be chosen or not. Viscount Selby, his gaze still fixed, had held his glass up for a third time without realizing when it was filled by one of the attendants or how he had managed to drain it so fast until he felt himself nudged in the ribs by his twin.

''I *say,* Roger! Isn't *that*… Mean to say… Well, I *told* you, didn't I? Can't deny it now, can you?'' Although Myles had meant to speak in a whisper, his excitement at being able to prove his earlier assertion made his voice carry before his brother had a chance to nudge him back fiercely and cough. *He* had noticed how Embry, who had been lounging in the chair on his other side and had actually *yawned* a few times, had suddenly seemed to tense like a coiled spring, even though he had not changed his position at all. In any case, Roger thought after he'd blinked his eyes a few times, it had to be an illusion! No matter what Myles had thought or Embry might have imagined, it just wasn't possible to be *sure*—just because a shapely female who happened to have hair of an unusual shade of bronze shot through with gold, and skin that was only slightly lighter in color had climbed out of the sunken bath on the far side with her back to them and had almost immediately run off the stage all muffled up in the silk robe that had been handed to her. He held his glass up again to be filled, only to drain its contents immediately when he noticed that Viscount Embry had decided to leave. Quite at a loss, Selby was rescued by his brother, who pointed out reasonably that first of all Embry couldn't possibly know anything, and in any case what was the point of following him?

"Besides," Myles added with a sudden note of alertness in his voice, "I've just seen a real beauty! The small brunette with a birthmark on her hip. Want to watch her a while. And you know very well what Embry's like—always going off somewhere on his own. Sure we'll run into him later. Find out what he's been up to."

As a matter of fact, Nicholas Dameron, Viscount Embry, had left the voyeuristic pleasures of the theater with every intention of leaving the Temple of Venus itself. He was in a singularly unpleasant mood and angry with himself as well for having come here in the first place—only because of a few disjointed phrases overheard on a sleepy afternoon. For Christ's sake! Just because of that time in Naples and the sheer coincidence of learning that Sir John Travers, lately of the city of Colombo in the British Crown Colony of Ceylon, had rented the villa his drunken young companions had insisted upon visiting... What difference could it make to him anyway? None at all—not even if by an even stranger and completely unlikely coincidence that same Sir John Travers had happened to marry the young virago who had referred to him as her *uncle.* He had, with commendable self-control, put that incident quite out of his mind until this afternoon, when he had foolishly allowed himself to become slightly intrigued at the thought that the evil-tempered mermaid he'd been considerate enough to leave a virgin might have progressed within the space of a few months to wife, and then to whore. He was aware, of course, that the Temple of Venus was famous for being frequented by *ladies* who were either bored or restless or married to old men and who played at being harlots for the sheer enjoyment of it. What man granted entrée here was not? But even if the bronze-maned priestess of Venus he had only caught a glimpse of had been the same sea witch he'd captured briefly one moonlit night, it still made no difference to him. In fact, it was surprising that he could remember her at all, much less the colors captured in her hair.

The hell with her, no matter where she was or what she had become! Nicholas's hard mouth twisted in the travesty of a smile that mocked at his own idiocy before an equally wry thought stopped him as he approached the front door. Suppose that she *was* here after all, one of the bored women looking for excitement? This time he would have no reason to stop himself from taking her as he should have before, without scruples. And the best way to erase her annoying memory would be to take her and use her exactly as he had always wanted to from the first moment he had seen her swimming naked in the Governor's pool with the silver light reflecting off the wet silk of her skin and her hair floating about her like writhing tendrils of sea weed.

"I am disappointed that none of my lovely priestesses took your fancy tonight. But perhaps you are in the mood for something different—or *unusual,* perhaps?"

When Orlanda undertook to be charming, she could make herself almost sparkle, her teasing black eyes *suggesting* everything while promising nothing—yet! Now, sensing something of his mood, for all that his dark face showed her nothing beyond a lifted eyebrow, she put her ringed hand lightly on Nicholas Dameron's sleeve while she cocked her head a little to one side and let her mischievous smile become a challenge.

"For instance?" His lazy voice matched her challenge and made her laugh with genuine delight at the prospect of a contest which she knew she must win in the end.

"I said different or unusual, did I not? And as you must know, my lord, my Temple of Venus would not otherwise have attained its present...may I say *fame* instead of notoriety? What might your pleasure be tonight? Or your mood? Everyone who comes here has a reason for doing so—you agree? They are looking for something they cannot find elsewhere, and that 'something' is...whatever it is they desire."

"That could be a very rash promise to make, *signora.*" His voice seemed to hold a grim kind of humor in it as his eyes narrowed at hers. "For example—what if I happened to want, for just *this* night only, a woman with hair of a certain particular coloring that is quite uncommon? A—*married* woman?" Nicholas Dameron's dark green eyes watched her wickedly while he spoke, but Orlanda merely smiled and shrugged.

"Ah, I am no enchantress with a magic wand, as you well know, but perhaps in *your* case... Do you feel adventurous enough to follow me, my lord? I am going to take you to a particular room that is set apart from all the others, where anything may be discovered if you wish it hard enough. I call it the Chamber of True Dreams. And I can promise you that you will not be disappointed!"

It had not been the woman's ridiculous "promise" that

had decided Nicholas to follow her in the end but rather his own curiosity, coupled with the bored, restless feeling that had been plaguing him for the past few weeks while he'd lived *without* living, like a parasite, with nothing more important to challenge or occupy his mind than what clothes he should have his valet lay out for him on that particular day or which club or theater he might visit. In fact, he had been glad of the opportunity to visit Italy with the Marquess of Newbury, even if it meant keeping an eye on his relative's twin brothers-in-law for part of the time, because it had meant escaping from London for a breathing space he had begun to feel he sorely needed. But in the end the Marquess, who was deeply involved in politics, had made a hurried and secretive journey to meet with the King of Sardinia, and his restless heir was forced to cool his heels in Rome in the company of two extremely young men on their Grand Tour who were determined to see and experience *everything.*

Perhaps Roger and Myles would learn something in the Chamber of True Dreams, or even discover their secret fantasies. Lying on a wide, silk-covered bed that was piled with silken cushions that were meant to dream on, Nicholas found himself frowning up at the patterned ceiling while wreathing, sickly sweet smoke floated up to join the patterns already there and form new ones that kept moving and changing all the time. Presently, as he concentrated on watching the different shapes that seemed to emerge, Nicholas found himself unable to remember if he was smoking opium or hashish and decided that he did not really care which it was, for he had smoked both before and was aware of what effects they could produce. True Dreams. An exaggeratedly fanciful name. Dreams, perhaps. Rather pleasant, relaxing ones too; but hardly *true* dreams, whatever *those* were. In fact…

In fact even the small effort it took to turn his head

against the soft silk cushions seemed hardly worthwhile until he saw why he had suddenly felt impelled to glance at the door. It had opened, with a soft click of the latch, and now she had pushed it closed behind her, standing there poised on bare feet with her wet hair streaming down past her shoulders and her only garment a damp silk chemise that clung to every curve and hollow of her honey-skinned body. His mermaid-turned-whore in the flesh. Or was he only dreaming her?

''Nicholas?'' she said on a softly questioning note. ''That *is* what you prefer to be called, is it not?'' And then she lifted up her arms and began shaking out her hair, sending drops of water flying everywhere, each one like a miniature golden bubble in the orange lamplight and the lighted braziers in every corner of the room. ''Do you still like me better now than before?'' she said teasingly, with her fingers still in her hair and her lifted arms emphasizing her high, pointed breasts and the flatness of her belly below the arch of her rib cage. ''I've *changed,* you know, and I have learned so much since we last met, thanks to *you.* You left me with a thirst for more knowledge, I suppose.'' She smiled in a provocative, rather tantalizing manner before murmuring huskily, ''Would you like me to show you how *much* I have learned?''

The room had become musky and grey-veiled from smoke, for all that he had either dropped or laid aside the long-stemmed pipe before she had crossed the small space between them, to lie beside him on the silk-covered couch of pipe dreams. Strangely enough, Nicholas found that although he could not remember her name, he remembered her body and the silky texture of her skin and most of all her hair—a curtain falling across her face when she bent, and a mantle for her shoulders when she flung her head back.

"Don't you want me?" she whispered. "You did before. Would you rather have someone else to share your dream with?"

Moving with the smoky currents rather than try to fight against them, Nicholas heard himself laugh, the sound grating even in his own ears. "I apologize, mermaid. But I'm afraid that the pipe that sends pleasurable dreams also takes away certain physical urges. I wonder that you have not learned *that* yet, along with the rest of the knowledge you seem to have acquired. Perhaps *you* should seek out someone better able to slake your appetites tonight."

She had been lying almost *docilely* by him with her face resting against his shoulder and her firm breasts pushing against his ribs while one of her hands moved caressingly over his body. But now she reared up angrily like a female cobra ready to strike, becoming ever more furious when he only gave her a mocking half-smile and a shrug.

Alexa was sorely tempted to lose her temper completely and make him regret his indifference even if she had to scratch and bite to arouse some reaction from him. Was he telling the truth, or did he really not *want* her at all? And yet, while she was trying to curb her rage she felt his arm suddenly enclose her body against his, while his fingers seemed to become trapped in the tangled masses of her hair. She felt her pent-in breath released in a sigh as she did what suddenly seemed easier and let her head down against his shoulder again.

And now it was he who said almost angrily, "Don't you want to go hunting for a more satisfying prey before the night is over and you must return to hide behind your facade of respectability once more?"

"Do *you* want me to leave?"

His arm tightened, almost cutting off her breath as he said under his breath and in Spanish, "*Dios!* And how should I know what I want or do not want at this moment?

Stay if you will or go if you will. What difference can it make?'' His eyes had closed as if he meant to sleep, but his arm still held her close and his fingers remained caught in her hair, so that Alexa found she could hardly move her head without feeling that her hair might be torn out at the roots.

With her face pressed against his chest she could feel his heartbeat pulse against her cheek and the roughness of the hair on his chest against her nipples, making them erect and sensitive against her will, almost aching with the need to have his fingers touch them; his mouth claim them as he had done before. What was happening to her? ''Be careful, my dear,'' Orlanda had warned her earlier. ''Too often the body can betray the mind, and blind emotion override sensibility and *will.*'' Alexa had come here planning to seduce him while he was still half-dazed by the drug he had willingly indulged in, meaning to keep her mind clear and calculating while she cleverly inflamed his desire to the boiling point before she retreated. But instead of responding to all the techniques of lovemaking she had been instructed in, he had told her frankly and without embarrassment that he was incapable of making love to her under the circumstances. She should make some suitably cutting remarks and leave at once before he insulted her even further by falling asleep. Hadn't he told her to go or stay as she pleased? And at what point had she turned her body so close to his that she was almost lying on top of him, with one of her legs straddling his in a shameless fashion?

Moving her head cautiously again, Alexa noticed with mounting anger and resentment that his eyes were still closed and he was breathing quite evenly and peacefully. Had he actually forgotten her presence?

''I *hate* you, Nicholas Dameron!'' she almost growled between gritted teeth, adding passionately, ''and I will always hate you and despise you for the lying hypocrite that you are!"

Although she had hoped for some reaction from him, Alexa flinched instinctively at the strange, short laugh he gave. "*Do* you, *querida?*" he murmured half-mockingly in a drowsy voice, his eyes still closed. Alexa had opened her mouth to make some suitably acerbic retort when he said in the same half-slurred tone that seemed to deride himself as well as her: "You must not expect to surprise me with that kind of statement, you know. My pure virgin wife felt the very same way, or perhaps worse. I did take her virginity after all, and very clumsily too, I'm sure, to judge from the way she used to cower away from me if I came within a few inches of her mortified body." Again his short, humorless laugh made Alexa flinch in spite of the feeling of shock that had made her body stiffen. Then he said thoughtfully, "I suppose I should have had the sense to stick to whores and the Indian and Mexican women I met who wanted the same thing I did. But, Christ, did you ever know a young man under twenty with any sense at all?"

Alexa did not know why he was suddenly telling her all the sordid details of his past, unless he had managed to forget her presence and was talking almost to himself. Part of her revolted against his forcing her to hear any more; and yet another part of her wanted to hear *everything,* so that she would have even more reason to hate and despise him. Whores and women of even less than easy virtue. He should indeed have stayed at his own level.

"Why *did* you marry then?" she heard herself ask with surprise. "Since you are not a *female,* no one could have forced you into a marriage you did not want, surely?"

She thought for a few moments that he had either fallen asleep after all or chose not to reply to her question until he said with sudden bitterness: "No? Ah well, I suppose

I did not have a rifle pointed at my head or the threat of being shut up in a room to exist on bread and water to *make* me take a wife. But my father died before I was old enough to remember what he looked like, and I was brought up by the Spanish side of my family. They had already arranged a marriage for us when poor little Teresa was still playing happily in her cradle. *She* was not asked if she cared for the match or not, I'm sure, and *I* married because it was expected of me to produce heirs as quickly as possible in case either hostile Indians or a storm at sea finished me off—which would have been a stroke of good fortune for *her,* I'm sure. But..." Alexa felt his shrug against her and wondered why her mouth had suddenly become so dry as he said in a detached voice: "I suppose we were both unlucky in the end. I can feel sorry for her *now,* and I see too clearly what a clumsy brute I must have seemed to the poor girl. *She* hadn't been told anything at all about what she might expect to take place in a marriage bed, and I had had no experience with...I suppose it must be called *innocence,* for want of a better word, although ignorance was more like it. Hell...!"

He paused for so long that Alexa was on the point of bursting out at him to finish what he had begun, so that she need not be goaded into thinking about him merely because he had managed to arouse a certain amount of curiosity in her. Tilting her head back so that she could see the expression on his face, Alexa felt her heart give a sudden, nervous jolt when she encountered those dark, jungle-green eyes she remembered only too well, especially when they narrowed at her like the slitted eyes of a crouching black panther. Moistening her lips, she succeeded in forcing what she hoped would pass for a coy smile, while she ran one hand teasingly down from his shoulder until it rested on his thigh. Instead of displaying any evidence of desire, he frowned down at her before growling: "How the devil did *you* get here? Damn!'' Running tense fingers through his tousled dark hair, he seemed to wince; completely ignoring Alexa's growing anger in his preoccupation with himself, until at last he released her from the almost crushing embrace in which he'd held her locked against himself, saying in an insultingly casual tone of voice: ''Since the *signora* has been kind enough to provide me with a handmaiden to share my dream, would you be a good girl and bring me a glass of that cold wine from the bucket in the corner there? And while you're about it, you might as well light that pipe up for me again. It seems to have gone out.''

With a kind of *spring* that would have done any feline justice, Alexa leapt off the bed and stood glaring down at him while she wondered viciously exactly what he might do if she raked at him over and over again with her nails, especially since there was no body of water handy for him to try and drown her in. More annoyingly still, she noticed that he had levered himself up against a pile of cushions and closed his eyes again; although being part animal himself, she thought unpleasantly, he must have sensed the pent-up fury in her that was on the verge of eruption. Why else would he have thought to say without even looking at her: ''Listen here, my girl, if you're of a mind to throw a temper tantrum I should warn you that childish displays of that nature tend to bore instead of titillate me—if *that* was your object—and I presume that *is* why you're here?'' Ignoring Alexa's choked gasp, he continued in a bored and slightly weary tone of voice: ''Although I am not generally in the mood to give advice, I *will* do you the favor of warning you that if you hope to get ahead in your—ah—chosen profession, you should really learn to do as you're bid by your clients, with a smile and a *pretense* of enjoyment at least!''

''What?'' As Alexa's voice rose dangerously in pitch

he seemed to give an exaggerated shudder before he suggested rather impatiently that since she was obviously neither docile nor obliging, both qualities that he always insisted upon in women, she might just as well take herself off and have the *signora* send in one of her better-trained young ladies. ''Like... Oh, yes, the ravishing blonde. Maddalena, I believe her name was. Very much a *real* woman in every way. And please—before you begin to shriek again—let me assure you that I intend to pay the *signora* for the time you've spent with me, as well as for your earlier efforts to make yourself pleasing.''

Had he perhaps gone a little *too* far in teasing that dangerously volatile temper of hers he remembered almost *too* well? Regarding her through barely slitted eyes he screened with his lashes, Nicholas found himself hoping that she would manage to control herself this time at least, for the contents of that pipe had been very potent, and he still felt waves of that dreamlike feeling washing over him from time to time. Looking at her as she stood there like an angry young Amazon in that diaphanous apology for a chemise, with angry spots of color blazing in her cheeks and her lips parted as she literally gasped for breath, Nicholas wanted her almost as much as he did *not* want her. He had desired her from the very first time he'd set eyes on her; and now he damned her and the infernal chemistry that was like an invisible cord drawing him to her. For he had actually begun to want her now with his loins, although his mind despised and almost detested what she had so easily become, and the suspicious cynic in him mistrusted most of all the maneuvering she must have done to ''find'' him here tonight. And that was why, when he had somehow *known* with his senses that he was going to see her again, he had deliberately ensured that he could not make love to her even if he had wanted to. It was for the same reason that now, with an angrily muttered obscenity that would never be used within earshot of a *lady,* Nicholas pushed himself off the bed and strode over to one of the braziers to light his pipe. He noticed, quite interestedly, that she had at long last recovered at least some of her powers of speech.

"You...!" Alexa sputtered ragingly. "Oh, you...you unspeakable... Oh! If I only could...could..."

With legs crossed he had settled back against the cushions again, and now he gave her a curious look before he suggested disinterestedly that if she *wanted* to swear in any language she chose there was really no reason why she could *not,* was there? Especially now that she must be quite used to hearing all kinds of oaths and obscenities.

There was a dangerous moment, after she whirled around and almost ran to the other side of the room, when Nicholas thought she actually meant to pick up one of the red-hot braziers and throw it at him; but then she plucked open a door he had not noticed before and rushed through it with all the force and fury of a whirlwind, the door slamming heavily in her wake. Would she come back? Would she not? Obviously it would be the best thing for both of them if they never set eyes on each other again!

Nicholas stared morosely at the door while the smoke gradually and insidiously worked its sweet magic in his mind again, and he noticed that the door had on it the same pattern as the ceiling and that it even seemed to twist and change shapes in the same way. When he set the pipe aside and lay back again, he stopped wondering about *her* and began thinking about the decision he would have to make very soon that concerned another young woman and another dynastic marriage. His lips twisted ironically at that conceit. "Dynastic" certainly fit the attitude of the Dowager Marchioness of Newbury, who had already told him imperiously that she thought he'd do, after all, and that considering the elevated rank that would be his some day, he could do no better than to marry a girl young enough and healthy enough to bear lots of children and who was also *used* to the running of a large household and the correct etiquette and manner of doing things on any occasion that might arise.

"You have described the kind of paragon of all virtues who cannot possibly exist, Belle-Mère," he had challenged her quizzically, using the name she has asked him to use. And he had hardly expected her burst of gleeful laughter before she announced that she had in mind already exactly the kind of accomplished young woman she described—one who was reckoned a raving beauty as well.

"I see," Nicholas had said drily, not really believing that the old woman who seemed to rule all of her family with her iron will could actually be *serious* in discussing a wife for him in much the same fashion as she might have described the points and ancestry of a blooded thoroughbred mare. It was almost to humor her that he had added in much the same tone, "And might I ask the *name* of this paragon, or must that remain a mystery until our wedding day?"

"Tch, tch!" She had chided him, although there seemed to be a grudging twinkle in her sharp black eyes. "There's no need to sharpen your sarcasm on *me,* my boy. We're not primitive heathens, are we? And I'll tell you the name of the girl who will make you the perfect wife, just to show I don't take offence at *small* lapses."

When he had inclined his head in caustic acknowledgment, the dowager pronounced triumphantly: "Why, it's *Helen,* of course! Lady Helen Dameron, my granddaughter and your *very* distant cousin, fortunately. Wouldn't do if the relationship was *too* close, you know. And she's to come out this season; it's all been arranged. So there cannot possibly be any obstacles to an engagement by next spring, let's say, and the marriage..."

"Just a minute, if you please!" Even the dowager had looked a trifle startled at the sudden harshness of his voice, but by then Nicholas was past caring if he angered her or not. "I apologize for interrupting you, Belle-Mère...." He smoothed his voice out somewhat, although the rough edges were still there to hear. "But there is one thing that I feel we should settle quite clearly and definitely between us before we go on—and that is that I am used to ruling my own life and my own destiny, and I intend to go on doing so. In other words, my dearest Belle-Mère, I have no intentions of becoming yet another one of your puppets whose strings you seem to control with such ease; and when, or *if* I decide to marry again, *I* will do the choosing this time! I hope I have managed to insure that there will be no further misunderstandings between us?"

He had half expected her to fly into one of the formidable rages he had heard discussed in nervous whispers and had fully expected her to order him out of her house and her sight at the very least. Instead, to his amazement, she had thrown her head back and given vent to peal after peal of genuine laughter, after which, while she wiped her eyes, she announced that she was *damn* glad to find at least one Dameron with gumption and thought they were going to deal together very well indeed.

So he had taken a stand, and found no opposition once he had done so. What harm then, if he had been formally introduced to the blonde and lovely Lady Helen, who at the age of sixteen seemed to possess more poise and sophistication than many women over twice her age. And since they *were* distantly related, and he was constantly being asked to accompany the family here and there to meet all their friends and acquaintances, it had seemed quite natural to act as Helen's escort on a few of these occasions. The only problem was that the next thing he knew, all the gossips were buzzing and the whole of society expected their engagement to be announced officially at any time. Goddammit! Even through the peaceful haze that seemed to hold him in the middle of a puffy cloud, Nicholas could feel the lightning-jab of anger. There was nothing wrong with Helen, and he could even *like* her in a distant kind of way. Moreover, he was quite sure she'd make someone an excellent wife. The fact was that *he* could not feel that he was prepared to marry again. Not after Teresa, and the scars that refused to fade, even after all the years that had passed since then.

28

"Did you *see?*" Alexa cried angrily. "There is no need to try and make me feel better by saying I *tried,* I assure you; because even if I did—and I might as well tell you it was the most difficult thing in the whole world to pretend that I… Well, in any case I *failed!* First of all, he…he just was not interested in me in the very least. And then to make matters *worse* I had to lose my temper. And *then*… Could you hear the things he said to me? The even *worse* things he implied? Why, he all but said in so many words that he looked on me as a…a…"

"As a *whore?*" Orlanda inserted helpfully, making Alexa stop her pacing in mid-stride while her face reddened.

"Oh! I didn't mean… You know I did not mean to be… But it was his *attitude!* That smug, superior, patronizing manner of his! Not that any of that excuses my lamentable lack of self-control, of course, but…" Alexa's face tautened, her eyes slitting like those of a cat. "Do you know that he even dared suggest that he wanted *Maddalena* to…to replace *me?* 'That ravishing blonde,' he called her. Hah! 'A real woman,' I think, were his next words. And…"

"Please, my dear, please!" Orlanda held up a warding-off hand that seemed to droop from the weight of the rings she wore on it. "If you think that Maddalena might put our Viscount in a better frame of mind, then you ought to be practical and sensible about it, should you not? And since you seem to have an attraction—or is it a *weakness?*—for him, perhaps...?" Orlanda raised delicate eyebrows that implied everything she had left unsaid, and Alexa, who had opened her mouth to make a hot denial, suddenly started to bite her lip.

"Well?" Orlanda said encouragingly. "Shall I send for Maddalena and have *her* go to him? After all, my love, I have my *reputation* to consider, you know. Since *you* didn't suit him..."

"But *that* was only because I let him make me so *angry!*" Alexa said rather shamefacedly. "The *next* time...I mean... Well, I do not enjoy admitting defeat! And he is still here, is he not? This time *I* will be the victor, I promise you that, even if I have to swallow my own pride for the moment."

Nicholas had been almost asleep, or perhaps he *had* been asleep and dreaming. Between the sweet-smoke-filled room and the constantly moving patterns that formed faces and pictures and places he had been in and some scenes he didn't even want to remember, he had at some point *felt,* before he heard, the music. Only a guitar, which sounded very far away—so far as to almost be a part of his memories only; nothing he was really experiencing. He knew he had had too much of the pipe of deceitful dreams and that he should not have allowed himself to give in to weakness, but it was too late to think of that now, when he had reached the place where there was no boundary line between fantasy and reality. It was something like lying in the bottom of a boat and letting the current take you wherever it willed, not caring where or when the rocking motion would stop at journey's end.

Where was it, this journey's end? From here he would be going back to England, to ceremony and formality and rigid boundaries. Not his real world, which was something that not one of his recently acquired "friends" would ever understand, any more than they could ever have understood the kind of life and the *way* of life he had been brought up to. New Orleans—rich, sophisticated, aristocratic—and two years spent studying French and Castilian Spanish side by side with the art of dueling—pistols, rapiers or knives—had been an education in itself. Within the space of a few months he had taught himself how to get on and was accepted into the most exclusive circles. And in New Orleans he had met Teresa and had found it easy and convenient to fall in love with her and to agree with his uncles and his mother that it was not only time he married but an excellent match he was making as well, for Teresa's dowry included property in New Orleans, Texas and California.

"She was beautiful and very rich and you loved her into the bargain. I would agree with your family that it was an excellent match indeed! And if the poor thing was frightened of marriage at first, surely you could have been a little more patient and understanding with her?"

"Dammit, you don't understand! Patient hell! That first night, when I was drunk and knew damn well I was drunk, I left her alone after she started to cry. And I left her alone for a whole week after that because she seemed so terrified of me. But then there came the night when I…I suppose the house slaves talked—God, I don't remember now how it came about! But my father-in-law talked to me first, and then my two brothers-in-law, and then worse than that my friends, who even thought it was laughable that I hadn't yet introduced my wife to her conjugal duties.''

''And you *did,* I suppose—and she did not—enjoy what took place?''

''Why should she have enjoyed it? Neither of us did, I suppose. In any case I grew tired of seeing her shrink away and almost shrivel up with fear and hatred every time she saw me in private. I lay with her only once more, and having made myself drunk does not excuse the fact that it was against her will. So I went back to California and to my *ranch* there, and by the time a year had passed, the house I was building was ready and I sent for her. She didn't want to come to a wild, rough place like California, or to leave her family or friends and the softly cushioned life she was accustomed to in New Orleans; but *I* insisted and her family insisted, and so...''

''And so?'' the soft voice insisted from somewhere beyond him and somewhere close to him at the same time, and he shrugged slightly.

''It isn't a new story in that part of the country, especially if any of the Indian tribes decide to go on the rampage. She traveled with a large party, and they had soldiers with them as well as their own armed guards. I had sent some of my own most trusted *vaqueros* ahead as well, to guide them through the desert country, and it was one of them who survived long enough to relate what happened. They took her, you see, along with a few of the other women who were young and attractive enough; and they killed everyone else. I could have wished that they had killed *her* as well, especially knowing what I knew about the way that captive women are treated by the Apache.''

''But, for God's sake, did you not have a search made for her if you did not look for her yourself?''

''Did I not? And did *you* know that the life expectancy of a captive female is usually no more than three *months?*

Perhaps a few more if one of the warriors decided to take her as a wife; but *she* was so delicately nurtured and so—easily bruised! But I searched for her myself against the advice of *her* family as well as mine, and I offered rewards for her return; and in the end there was no trace to be found of her or any of the others, except the word of a *Comanchero*—one of those who trade with the Indians and buy their captured booty or exchange it for rifles and ammunition—who said she and two others had been sold to another tribe, he thought in Mexico perhaps. There was no point in searching after that....''

''But why, *why?* If she was alive and suffering, or if... Why, how can you be certain even now that she is not still alive?''

''Because I am certain she is dead. In fact, I made sure of it. And at the moment I am not sure why I have been dredging up some of the most unpleasant details of my sordid past for *your* benefit. Christ, I could have sworn you'd flounced off in a temper a long time ago—if I was not imagining that you were here in the first place!'' Sleepy green eyes squinted narrowly at Alexa, who was sitting on the carpeted floor with her feet curled under her and her elbows resting on the silk-sheeted bed while she asked her rather indignant questions and received answers she did not particularly care for. But now, rising to her feet in one fluid motion, she managed a smile and a wide-eyed look at the same time.

''But you sent me away to bring you more wine, do you not remember? And here it is, in a silver bucket. Shall I pour you out a glass now that you are awake? Or would you prefer to have something to eat first? Another freshly filled pipe?''

She was wearing, now, a very simple gown that fell straight down from her shoulders to her ankles and was caught just under her breasts by a green satin ribbon threaded through lace-trimmed eyelets—much in the style of the Directory period in France at the beginning of the century, and very becoming on her too, as Alexa well knew. She held her smile when his eyes, after he had seemed to blink them into focus, traveled over her slowly with a frowning and somehow *considering* look before he shuttered them, giving her an indifferent shrug.

"I suppose it's really not important whether I sent you away or you went of your own accord, for obviously I'm not at my best tonight. But since you're here I suppose you might as well join me in a glass of wine, if you wouldn't mind pouring it for both of us? And perhaps after that you could have some fruit and cheeses sent up—and order me a bath, unless men are permitted to join the lovely priestesses of Venus in theirs?"

Resisting the strong temptation to throw a glass of chilled wine in his sardonic face, Alexa handed him one instead; and when he held his glass up with a lifted black brow, she gritted her teeth and poured out a little of the wine into a glass for herself, glad of a chance to turn her back on him for a few moments.

"I think that perhaps you have misunderstood my position here," she said finally when she was ready to turn and face him once more, trying to keep her voice even. "I am not one of your priestesses, and neither am I a maid, although if you really need a bath and a cold repast I suppose I could try to arrange for both. Was there anything else?"

"Yes. You might hand me that bottle of wine you are so sparing with first, and then you can bring yourself and your glass with you and join me in this comfortable bed. Perhaps you might persuade me to tell you even more sordid details of my evil past, since it seems to be of interest to you for some morbid reason." Noticing her slight hesitation, Nicholas gave a harsh laugh. "By God! What in hell are you *afraid* of, if that is what accounts for your almost maidenly reluctance? If it's rape, I can assure you I am not quite ready for such an act yet. The hashish I have been smoking must be remarkably pure, because some of its effects have not left me yet. Well?''

''Well?'' Alexa countered lightly, seating herself just as lightly on the edge of the bed to prove to him that she was by no means afraid of him. What a ridiculous thought! ''And here is your wine,'' she added quickly, not liking the particularly caustic look he shot in her direction at that moment. ''I'll pour you some more...''

She had leaned forward, beginning to tilt the wine bottle over his glass, when he suddenly caught her wrist and held her there in mid-motion with her hair falling forward across her flushed cheeks and down past her breasts that were discreetly covered now, but by fine muslin and nothing else.

''I...I thought you wanted more wine,'' Alexa stammered stupidly, feeling herself at a disadvantage, especially when he laughed rather unpleasantly when she tried to tug her wrist free.

''And perhaps something more than just the wine? I would not want you to think that I was entirely unappreciative of the efforts you've made to please—or your proficiency in the arts of seduction, not to mention your *patience!*'' When Alexa only stared at him as if she had not guessed his meaning, he firmly removed the bottle of wine from her almost nerveless grasp and set it down on the table by the bed, looking down at her with a smile she liked even less than his earlier laugh.

''You are hurting my wrist!'' she whispered almost automatically, without knowing why she had to whisper it. And she repeated in a more normal tone, ''Patience! And what did you mean by *that?*''

''Why, only what is usually meant by the word, of

course—my erstwhile mermaid! I think I have been floating on the soft mist-clouds of pipe dreams for a long time, and you are still here—even though I had thought you gone, perhaps forever. And yet when I began to realize that I was no longer dreaming the sound of my own voice or the things that I had been telling you—why, I began to ask myself questions, even though that took almost too much effort in my rather euphoric state. Have *you* ever smoked hashish, by the way? I believe it is very commonly indulged in in certain parts of India and the Middle East, although in China opium is much preferred.... What is the matter with you now?"

"I told you before that you were hurting my wrist!" Alexa gritted out with a commendable effort at self-control. "There is no need to be so brutal in your treatment of me and in your subtly ugly insults either. One would almost think that *I* had done *you* some mortal injury meriting revenge!"

With his mind gradually clearing as it became emptied of smoky fantasies, Nicholas wondered himself why he troubled himself with her or took a strange, warped kind of pleasure out of watching his poisoned darts pierce her skin. She was right, after all. What had she ever done to injure him? Except—the dark demon side of him answered too promptly—except by marrying a very rich man who was too old to please her and finding her pleasure in playing the whore, bitch that she was. Not for the money—that at least would have been halfway excusable—but to satisfy her degraded appetites. And even so, why in hell should it matter to him?

He dropped her wrist as if it had suddenly begun to burn his fingers, and as she started to rub at it absently with her head bent and ripples of her dark bronze hair hiding her face from his cruelly probing eyes, he suddenly wondered again why she stayed and why she had come back to his borrowed bed here a second time. Suddenly, and before he had had enough time to change the direction of his thoughts, she flung up her head, shaking back her heavy hair to hang like a mane between her shoulders. And it was in that same flash of a moment that her eyes met his defiantly, their grey-smoke darkness pinpointed by leaping flame-reflections that made him want to find out if he could look all the way into them and through them to whatever lay in her devious little mind as she sat there returning his stare without once looking away.

In the end it was Nicholas who broke, almost compulsively, the strangely tautening silence between them. "Why are you *really* here, I wonder?" It sounded more like a question he asked of himself; and when Alexa did not answer immediately he gave an indifferent shrug and reached sideways to pour wine for himself first before directing an unreadable glance at her and refilling her glass too—handing it to her and almost forcing her to take it.

She watched him suspiciously as he held his glass up to catch the light before he drank at least half its contents in one swallow and set it down with a sarcastic question. "Is there something wrong with the wine that makes *you* afraid to drink it?"

Flushing angrily at the inference he had made, Alexa drank almost as much as he had before looking back at him defiantly; knowing, even as she did so, that she would be much better off to leave at once while she still retained some control over the anger he always seemed able to provoke her to. "There!" she said with as much coldness as she could muster, and could not stop herself from adding, "Although I cannot possibly imagine why you should suddenly imagine that your wine might be either poisoned or drugged. What a ridiculous thought!"

"I must confess to being an inordinately suspicious and *doubting* individual," he said with one of his twisted smiles that more closely resembled a sneer. "In fact, I was forced to realize quite early in my life that most people and things are not what they appear to be on the surface—and that hard-earned knowledge has even saved my life on occasion. But in spite of rather priding myself on being quite a good judge of human character and motivation, I have to admit that *you* succeed in puzzling me somewhat. Or was *that* your intention all along?"

"And now you really *are* being ridiculous!" Alexa said heatedly as she replaced her glass on the table with such careless haste that she knocked over his glass as well as hers, breaking one of them and spilling wine everywhere while she felt like crying with vexation.

"Oh! Oh, *now* look what you have made me do!" She would have leapt from the bed if he hadn't restrained her with a swift movement that took her so completely by surprise that she sprawled almost on top of him, with her face far too close to his for her comfort.

Alexa's first and purely instinctive reaction was to *escape,* but the movement she made only made his arm tighten about her waist to keep her an unwilling prisoner while his voice said harshly: "You stupid, thoughtless female! There are splintered shards of glass everywhere and you are barefooted. Unless you *meant* to have your feet cut and bleeding as a form of penance?" And then he growled almost threateningly, "Stop your wriggling about, dammit! Unless of course it's meant to be an inducement? Even if it is, I'm afraid you'll have to wait until I've had a few direct answers from you. I've made myself clear, I hope?"

None of the angry retorts she had been aching to let fly at him would emerge from Alexa's suddenly dry throat when she was forced to meet those hard green eyes of his by the deceptively gentle pressure of his fingers under her chin, fingers which then uncurled to cup her face and caress her cheek rather absently in a fashion that made her long to jerk her head away. "Good!" he said with infuriating satisfaction in a tone that indicated that he took her meek submission for granted, adding on a note of pretended solicitude, "But perhaps you are not quite comfortable as you are? I would not want your pretty neck to become stiff while we have our conversation, even if I *am* such a brute." And then, without any warning, he changed positions, taking her with him as he moved, so that she lay helplessly on her back with one of his legs thrown over her to keep her so while his fingers touched her face again and he said softly, "I wonder that your husband gives you such freedom and allows you to keep such late hours! Unless you manage to keep him drugged when it's convenient for you, the poor deluded man!"

No, I will *not* humiliate myself by struggling against his superior strength in a vain effort to get free, Alexa thought before she said with as much contempt as she could muster, "I only wish you would ask me these questions of yours that will not wait, and then set me free! And I will not answer any I consider too personal, or no concern of *yours,* not even if you..."

"Oh, but I can assure you that I have no intentions of resorting to torture, if that was what you were thinking of," he broke in derisively. "And as for setting you *free,* I do not recall having invited you here in the first place, you fire-haired *bruja!* Nor do I remember begging you to stay when you left earlier. Which brings me to the same question you have cleverly managed to evade each time I've asked it so far. Why did you choose to find me tonight? And how did you know I was here? No, don't look away like a cowardly bitch. Answer me, damn you; and then you can go, if that's still what you want—to hell, for all I care!"

His fingers were suddenly as cruel as his contemptuous

words, as they twisted thick strands of her hair into a rope that kept her head still and almost forced a cry of pain from her before she remembered her pride and bit her lip instead, her eyes shooting sparks of hate at him. "And if I do not choose to give you any answers?" she flared defiantly, even while she wondered if he would tug the hair from her scalp in retaliation as his eyes narrowed in a wickedly speculative way that almost made her shudder.

Bracing herself for the *worst,* Alexa sucked in her breath and instinctively squeezed her eyes shut without meaning to do so. What *would* he do to her now? The very last thing she had expected was to hear him laugh softly and (to her ears) dangerously. "Why, then, I suppose I will have to draw my own conclusions, and especially as to why you seem so afraid to answer a perfectly reasonable question. Why indeed are you here? In the first place, obviously because you wanted to be, although I don't wish to sound too conceited. But since you persist in being stubborn—or could it be *shyness* by some chance?—perhaps there is another way of finding out..."

Alexa felt his breath warmly against her face in the instant before he kissed her—unexpectedly, unfairly and quite ruthlessly, with no regard whatsoever for her feelings or the efforts she made to fend him off by pounding at his shoulders with her fists and trying to tear *his* hair out when that did not have any effect. Of *course* she must have struggled and fought against him until all her strength was expended! Why would she *not* have? Unless she had forced herself into calculated acquiescence when she remembered what she had meant to achieve by leading him on until he was all but driven crazy with desire for her, and then... Whatever it was she planned to do at *that* point, it seemed obvious that a *pretended* response to his kiss was quite in keeping with her plans and really much easier than continuing with a pointless struggle. Having made her decision with a feeling of relief, Alexa gave a sigh and allowed herself to *yield,* even going so far as to slip her hands under the embroidered Chinese robe he wore to touch his back and cling to his shoulders while his kiss, which had been relentlessly harsh and almost punishing at first, had suddenly turned into a whole barrage of kisses that explored her parted lips and every inch of her face—lingering over her temples and her ears and even her closed eyelids before concentrating on her mouth again, first lightly and then demandingly until she felt so strangely weak and breathless that she could not protest against anything he was doing—neither the kisses nor the way he tore her thin muslin gown apart from bodice to hem with a savage kind of impatience before his hand began its slow and almost teasing caressing of her flesh in a fashion she remembered only too well.

How and when had *he* begun to control what was taking place between them? Why had *she* not been more assertive from the beginning, using every trick and stratagem that she had learned recently with deliberate calculation while remaining quite detached herself? Alexa tried almost desperately to cut herself off from feeling and reaction to the insidiously treacherous encroachment of his hands as they roved all too surely and familiarly over her body by forcing her own hands to explore with equal boldness the length of his back and from there along his smoothly muscled thighs until she found the proof she sought. He *did* desire her after all, in spite of everything he had said to the contrary. And he would want her even more desperately when she touched him in certain ways and held him as she did now. She became slightly less unsure of herself when she felt his immediate reaction and the tensing of his body against hers. Only for moments; and then, with a decisive moment that shocked her with its suddenness, he freed himself from her and sat up, caressing one of her breasts quite casually while he first drank wine straight from the bottle and then held it out to her with a questioning lift of an eyebrow. "No?" he said in an overly pleasant voice, adding almost on the heels of that, "But perhaps you prefer to enjoy your wine in a more imaginative and adventurous fashion? Lie still, *mi querida.* It's only a little cold by now..."

Alexa gasped when he tilted the bottle and she felt the chill liquid trickle from her navel down to the vee of her parted thighs; and she gasped again when he bent his head, and his lips and tongue traced the wetness left by the wine until they had found where she was most sensitive, lingering there even when she cried out for him to stop...*no*...she didn't want...she did *not*...

"But you know that you do, little liar. Why continue to deny what you feel?" He looked up at her mockingly before he bent his head again; and this time, knowing she was completely lost to reason, Alexa pressed the back of one hand over her mouth to stop herself from screaming out loud—or begging him quite shamelessly not to stop what he was doing, not now, not yet, while it was just starting to happen to her. When he *did* stop she heard herself moan and heard him laugh—a short, ragged laugh that was not a real laugh at all before he swung his body to lie along the length of hers and poured the last of the wine over himself, his harsh, whispered words to her both promise and threat at the same time.

"I think you know already that this is only the first of the many times and the many ways in which I mean to have you, sea witch...for all that I wish I did not want you at all!"

"And I too," she whispered back before she caught him against herself and took him in the same way he was taking her again, without calculation or detachment, and in fact without making any attempt at all to force herself into thinking more rationally and sanely merely because that was what she *should* do. What she *wanted,* at this very moment, was exactly what was happening—the combined pleasures of both giving and receiving, heightening and intensifying every feeling and carrying her higher and higher still until she suddenly reached the highest pinnacle of all and stayed poised there for only moments before she let herself burst into a million star-fragments that floated very slowly and unwillingly back down to earth and the reality she did not want to wake up to yet. Oh please, not yet! Not until she'd had enough time to prepare herself for it! Still in a kind of daze, her eyes closed, Alexa was only half-aware of his movement of withdrawal until she felt the hard urgency of his hands on her thighs, parting them and holding them captive until he had positioned himself between them.

And then, before she had quite realized what he was about, it was already too late for protests. Her eyes flying open and dilating, Alexa felt a sharp, stabbing sensation that made her hips jerk involuntarily as she tried to escape; and over her own choked cry of pain she heard him swear harshly before his hands moved up from her writhing hips to hold her wrists pinioned.

''No! Stop it, you're *hurting* me! You were not supposed to… I didn't *know* it hurt this much! You brute, let me go!''

Alexa glared up at him, eyes swimming with tears as she continued to struggle, until he brought his face down to hers and said between his teeth: ''I'm in no mood to ask you for explanations *now,* you cheating little tease, but you might just as well get it through your head that since the damage is already done you might just as well decide to make the best of it! *I* certainly intend to!'' And with that unfeeling pronouncement he continued to ignore both her abusive epithets and her entreaties as he took full advantage of her helplessness, his movements slow and deliberate at first and almost *teasing* until Alexa could have screamed aloud with frustration and hate.

Afterwards she could not recall exactly when or how everything had changed. Was it at the time she suddenly realized that there was no more pain? Or after he had begun to kiss her breasts? Or when he slid one hand between their bodies to touch her in certain ways that made her catch her breath and arch herself even closer to him, beginning actually to want him even deeper inside her—to *want* him; meeting his kisses fiercely and moving with him until she felt it begin to happen for her again and her body began to shudder and she cried out without words at first and then his name, clasping him against herself even harder when she knew it was happening for him too.

What did *how* or *when* matter in any case? Drowsily content, Alexa lay snuggled against him with her lips against his shoulder and one leg over his, making murmuring sounds in her throat that were almost like purrs as his fingers stroked the length of her back and her thighs. She had *thought* she hated him for a little while but she didn't now. Ah, she didn't even want to *think* at this moment, only to go on feeling, without words or thoughts getting in the way.

29

Alexa had not *meant* to fall asleep. She remembered deciding that she would stay only as long as *he* did not destroy the new and strangely tenuous mood that held them both silent, and would leave quietly as soon as he slept. Hadn't she been told, after all, that men usually tended to sleep heavily once they had expended themselves? Perhaps it had been the warmth of the room and his body next to hers, the strangely soothing, sweetish scent of incense smoke curling up from the braziers. Or *had* it been something *other* than incense that had lulled her into a sleep that was almost insensibility?

''My lord, my lord, you know that I would not normally burst in on you in this fashion, but you *must* come at once, or there is likely to be a particularly ugly scandal that will certainly ruin us all! Only *you* might succeed in talking sense to the Marquess! Please, I beg you to hurry!''

Orlanda? Could that possibly be Orlanda's voice? And what on earth had she been talking of in such agitated tones? Alexa wanted to wake up to find out what it was all about, and yet at the same time she felt as if it was too much trouble and would rather have continued to dream her pleasant dreams in peace.

She heard a harsh masculine voice she recognized all

too well snarling oaths in Spanish and English and French as he demanded in turn where in hell his damned clothes were and why *he* was the only man who could stop Newbury from insanity? *Newbury?* Blinking her eyes determinedly, Alexa said in a sleep-fogged voice: "What on earth is happening and why is everyone making so much *noise?*" She wondered rather indignantly why *he* was already up and half-dressed when *she* was not and why he gave her such a darkly brooding, almost *hateful* kind of look before he *ordered* her to go back to sleep and wait for him because he had not finished with her yet, by any means!

"And let me remind you again that if you're foolish enough to try leaping out of bed in your usual impetuous fashion, you'll probably cut your feet badly enough to bleed to death!"

"But, Orlanda? Didn't I hear you say..."

Adding to her growing feelings of frustration and rage, Alexa saw that even Orlanda, whom she had considered a friend and *ally* up to now, was acting as if she did not even exist. In fact, she was holding the door open in what appeared to be a veritable frenzy of impatience while she cried out, "For God's *sake!* Even now it might be too late!" And then the door slammed heavily behind them, and Alexa found herself alone in the Chamber of True Dreams with only a man's dragon-embroidered Chinese robe and an unfamiliar ache and stickiness between her thighs to remind her of the reality of what had taken place and how easily he had managed to turn the tables on her in spite of all her careful planning.

It was *only* because he had been unscrupulous enough to use the advantage of his superior physical strength that he had managed to... No! She would not think of it yet; nor would she lie here on these silk sheets that were disgustingly stained now with her own blood. Go back to sleep and wait for him indeed! And what *else* had he had the audacity to add? He wasn't *finished* with her, indeed! Just as if she'd been some common prostitute he'd paid in advance for services *he* did not consider fully rendered yet! Well, she would make sure he received an unpleasant shock when he returned to an empty smoke-filled room, an empty blood-stained bed, and—an Accounting for the night which would include the extra charge that was normally asked for a virgin.

If she had dared stay longer, how much she would have enjoyed doing so, if only in order to see his face when he received it! But the sky had already begun to turn pink and all the usual early morning clattering and creaking of farmers delivering their produce and tradesmen preparing to open their businesses had already begun, making Alexa feel relieved that she had thought to arrive at the Temple of Venus in one of the plainest unmarked carriages owned by her friends. And even so she was still running the risk of being seen and recognized in spite of her hat and veil—arriving at the villa at *this* hour of the morning. How Bridget would scold and shake her head dolefully; but perhaps there would be no one else awake to see her—and Perdita had already assured her that both the coachman and footman were perfectly discreet.

In fact, they drove the small, closed carriage directly to the stables, from where a narrow, covered passageway led directly to one of the private side doors into the house. And Alexa had been given a key to that door....

Within a very few minutes now she would be safely in her room, ordering her poor Bridget to draw her a hot bath in the sunken marble tub. And *then* she would allow herself to think about everything and to remember... particularly those half-heard words and phrases that still continued to nag at her mind. *Had* Nicholas's abrupt departure, only half-dressed, and Orlanda's unmistakable agitation, really anything to do with the Marquess of Newbury? And if so... Ah, it was easier to concentrate on some thoughts rather than others.

Impatiently, Alexa felt the key turn silently in the lock before she pushed the door open, sighing with relief once she was through it and at the foot of the winding stone stairway that would take her to her chambers. The last person she had expected to find sitting there with her apron held up to her face was Bridget, who should have been waiting in her room instead.

"Oh...my lady, if you could only know how hard I've been praying and how many Rosaries I've said already! Ah, thank God you're here at last before the rest of them have had the time to start wondering. It was the Duchess herself who told me I'd best wait here for you and...and...be the first one to tell you."

Alexa did not need the evidence of Bridget's swollen eyes and blotched face nor the renewed sobbing she broke into now to tell her what had happened, and she need not have said aloud what her mind already *knew.* "It's...Sir John, isn't it? *When?*" Alexa heard her own voice, and it sounded flatly devoid of feeling; but she had reached out blindly for the support that the roughly mortared wall afforded her as she leaned against it.

Words. "Oh, ma'am, it was in his sleep and God's mercy to take him that way without any pain. It was Mr. Bowles who noticed first, when it was time for his medicine..."

More words, but they barely glanced off the surface of Alexa's mind, already beginning to spin in an inescapable vortex of grief and guilt and self-hate. "Alexa, darling, you must think only of *his* release. It would have made no difference, you know, whether you had been here or not."

"Ah yes, and you must also think that he would not have wanted you to grieve or to feel this... Ah, this quite ridiculous state of *blaming* one's self—and for why? It is not what your husband he try to teach you, eh?"

They were all so kind to her! Bridget, Perdita, Giusto. And even Orlanda, when she heard. Business matters, they all reminded her. She must not forget that she was now in total control of an enormous fortune and would be one of the richest women in England when she finally arrived there. ''Ah, my love, think how you are going to take all of London by storm! Once you are discovered by society you will find yourself positively *deluged* by invitations to *every* fashionable gathering.'' Perdita gave a nostalgic sigh before she brightened up enough to begin describing the London of *her* day, before everyone had become so stuffy and conventional; when the threat of Boney across the channel had only heightened one's pleasure in living each day to the fullest possible extent. ''Oh yes, you will *love* London once you've grown used to the weather. It is the greatest city in the whole world now, as everyone agrees.''

The London that was eulogized by all its foreign visitors as being the greatest city in the whole world was indeed filled with all kinds of wonders and opportunities for those who had enough money to spend. There were the fashionable shops of Regent Street, Burlington Arcade and Bond Street to tempt even those with the most fastidious tastes, and the magnificently laid out parks where even citizens of modest means could stroll about and watch the *beau monde* as they rode by on their blooded thoroughbreds or their carriages with gold-crested doors. All the major thoroughfares were illuminated by gaslight after dark; and from the great houses of Belgravia and St. James's crystal chandeliers spilled their brilliance through open windows and doorways as carriage after carriage drew up before them to discharge fashionably dressed gentlemen, wearing dashing velvet-collared capes and silk top hats, and elegantly gowned and bejeweled ladies wearing gold and silver ornaments in their hair.

This was London during the season, where those fortunate enough to possess titles in addition to wealth could keep themselves occupied both day and night with the pursuit of any kind of pleasure or excitement they might desire; and to young men fortunate enough to have large allowances to spend, such as the twin Viscounts Selby and Rowell, nothing could be more enjoyable than a London season, with so many entertainments to choose from. When one grew tired of the endless balls and receptions there was always the theater or the opera house, where all the Cyprians were to be observed, after which they could always visit Madame Olivier's or Mott's or Kate Hamilton's for what *they* always referred to laughingly as a "nightcap." But on *this* particularly warm and sunny afternoon, when they had already visited their hatter and their tailor before going to Hyde Park to watch the pretty horsebreakers show their mettle along Rotten Row, they had decided that nothing would taste better than the cream fruit ices sold at Gunter's, in Berkeley Square, where they were always certain to encounter several friends and acquaintances, not to mention relatives.

"Trouble with being related to *half* of London is *meeting* them everywhere," Selby said rather gloomily when he recognized the occupants of one of the open carriages stopped under the shade of some trees on the opposite side of the square.

"Worse when they happen to be sister Iris and her brood and you know they'll expect us to escort them back," his brother said just as gloomily as they rode over to join the ladies, who had seen them and waved. "Know too that *Helen* isn't finished questioning us about Rome and about Embry. Pity him in a way if the match *does* come off. Cold as a cucumber, our little niece!"

Cold or not, there was no question but that Lady Helen Dameron was indeed a beauty. Her hair was not merely blonde but *gold,* and her eyes were a pansy-blue. Her nose was straight, her mouth the perfect cupid's bow, her features cameo-perfect, as if they had been carved by a master sculptor from white and rose marble. And in addition to being a beauty at barely sixteen years of age, Lady Helen possessed the poise and self-possession of a mature woman, sometimes succeeding in rather overawing even her uncles.

For the past five minutes, however, Lady Helen had felt her poise slipping as her annoying twin uncles had neglected her completely to engage in some silly mumbled argument that took up so much of their concentration that they seemed not to hear any of the questions she asked them. She was not used to being ignored by any man, even if they happened to be relatives, and her cheeks became quite flushed with anger, causing her mother to ask anxiously if she was sure she was feeling quite *well.* ''You *cannot* miss the grand ball at Stafford House, my love, for it is to be *the* social event of the season. And even your father has promised to attend with us.'' Lady Iris ended on a distracted note as she wondered if her formidable mother-in-law might decide to go too, which would mean having to take a *second* carriage, unless Newbury decided, as he sometimes did, to drive himself, so that he could go out afterwards with some of his political acquaintances; and in *that* case of course he would sleep at his club and...

''Mama! Here's the waiter we sent for. May I have a strawberry-flavored ice this time, please?''

''Oh of course, dear, of course!'' Thankfully brought back to reality, Lady Iris beamed at her second daughter Ianthe, who took after her in personality as well as looks; whereas Helen was growing to be more and more like her grandmother the Dowager Marchioness and was just as determined to have her way. Sometimes Helen's *hardness* worried Lady Iris a little, but she had long ago given up trying to change anything about her oldest daughter.

''I have only asked you the same question *four* times already!''

Since no one, not even her mother, had ever heard such a *shrill* note in Lady Helen's usually soft and well-modulated voice, it was no wonder that they all looked at her in surprise, even the two Viscounts who had caused such loss of self-control.

"I *only* asked," Helen said in a softer and more controlled voice, "whether Embry is back from the country yet?" Her exquisite nose actually wrinkled slightly when she made a small moue of distaste. "I really cannot understand why he was not told by any of his *friends* that no one goes down to their country houses until it is past *August* and the season is over."

The twins exchanged meaningful glances before the Viscount Selby, who was usually their spokesman, said rather stiffly: "Think *we* didn't tell him? Deering too. Even Papa! Only raised that infernal eyebrow and told us he was going to look at horses. Didn't say exactly when he'd be back, I'm afraid."

"But if it was only for *horses*... Why, they have the best blooded stock at the Baker Street Bazaar in Marylebone, I've heard—even from *you!*"

"No need to nag at *us,* dear niece," the Viscount Rowell said bluntly with all the annoyingly privileged familiarity of an uncle, making Helen's color rise angrily even though she contrived to keep an otherwise placid look on her face. "Ought to know by now that Embry will always do exactly as *he* pleases! *You* might be sensible to remember that too. Doesn't like to be questioned, either. Found that out in Rome...eh, Roger old boy?"

Although Myles hastily changed his chuckle into a cough while his brother tried to change the subject by asking his older sister if they had gone shopping this morning—and where had they gone—Lady Helen at least had not failed to draw her own conclusions from that last sentence; and her feeling of angry frustration grew when it suddenly struck her to wonder for the first time if Nicholas

Dameron, Viscount Embry and her future *husband,* might actually decide to *stay* in the country for the rest of the season? Surely not! Why, he had *almost* promised her that he would be at the Sutherlands' ball at Stafford Hall, and her *humiliation* before the whole of society would be *unendurable* if at the last minute he did not appear. She must speak again to her grandmother, and perhaps even her usually remote father might be persuaded to use his influence. Why, *that* was the night on which she had planned he would propose to her at last! He *had* to be back in time, whatever she had to do to insure it.

It was unusual for Helen to remain silent for so long a time, and especially when the discussion had become centered on the ball at Stafford House and what everyone would be wearing there; and Myles could not help glancing at her rather uneasily while he hoped she would soon forget all about that infernally stupid remark of his about Rome. Women and their damned questions and curiosity!

Almost on the very heels of her uncle's rueful thought, Lady Helen asked an idle question of her mother that was meant to show them all how little interested she was in their conversation *or* the ball itself, for that matter.

"Is not that lady in the carriage that has just drawn up next to ours an acquaintance of yours, Mama? She seems to know everyone else."

Lady Iris, having turned her head, now smiled and bowed graciously in the direction of the lady her daughter had indicated before turning back to explain that it was Lady Margery, of course. She had *never* been able to recollect the name of the man the poor thing had married—*eloped* with, if the story was to be believed—although her husband *did* happen to be the younger son of some impoverished country baronet and a bit of a black sheep to boot. "But *she* of course was one of the Earl of Weymouth's daughters—the *last* Earl, I meant, of course. Impeccable background, and of course dear Margery is still received everywhere, even if I have not seen her out in society for at least five or six years, I'm sure."

"Such a pleasant-looking woman, for all that her gown is hardly quite *stylish,*" Helen murmured in a rather bored and condescending tone before adding in a positively syrupy voice: "And I see that my dear *uncles* seem to recognize Lady Margery's female companion as well, although it is certainly hard to make out her features because of her bonnet. Do you think she might be someone *we* should know, perhaps?" Her sharp eyes had not missed the fact that her uncles had exchanged almost incredulous glances before they had begun to clear their throats and begin low-voiced sentences they did not finish. Was it possible that the fashionably gowned young woman (at least she *seemed* to be quite young) was one of those *adventuresses* who lived on the fringes of society and were better known to young men than their mothers? What a scandal that could cause if poor Lady Margery was either duped or induced into introducing some *upstart* to her friends!

While her mind raced, Lady Helen managed to fix her uncles with a wide-eyed, guileless-seeming look that did not deceive them in the least despite their discomfort under it.

"Well it *is* a closed carriage, my love, and you're right about the newest style in bonnets, of course. I shudder to think of the day when I might cut one of my closest friends by mistake." Lady Iris played directly into Helen's hands by turning questioningly to her younger brothers. "*Do* you know the other occupant of Lady Margery's carriage?"

"Ah—er—were never *officially* introduced, you know! One of those things that can happen abroad—large *crowds* and all that—difficult sometimes to meet people. Not many people over *there* who know what *we* consider the correct thing. Hmm!" Viscount Selby found that he was sweating under his starched collar at the end of his speech.

"*Abroad,* you said? But what a coincidence this is, then.

Don't you think so, Mama? Why, it had to be Rome, then, for that is the last place you visited, is it not? And has Embry met your distant acquaintance, Uncle Myles?'' As Helen turned the battery of her blue-eyed stare on the Viscount Rowell, he reddened before almost rapping out, ''Don't think so. Wasn't there when *we* were. Anyway, no need to make mountains out of molehills, is there?''

''But, surely, if she moves in the same circles that *we* do you can at least tell us who she is?'' Helen persisted. ''Unless she is a *foreigner?*''

''Oh, do have the goodness to enlighten us all before you drive my poor girls quite mad with curiosity!'' Lady Iris joined in impatiently, and gave one of her commanding stares at her brothers, who seemed to find it necessary to exchange those telling looks again before Selby spoke up in a resigned sort of voice.

''Um—believe the name was Travers. Wasn't that it, Myles? Friends of *our* friend Damiano. Husband a Baronet or something of the sort, I believe—really a friend of Damiano's *father.* And that's all we know. Had no idea they were planning to visit London.''

''Oh, is she *married?* Well, I suppose that it is hardly likely we shall encounter each other at all, is it, Mama?'' Suddenly indifferent, Helen was able to settle back more comfortably against the cushions and look about again to see if any more of their friends had arrived. Even if she had been aware that *she* was being studied by at least one of the occupants of the carriage that had first attracted her curiosity, she would have taken it as a tribute to her beauty—something she had become quite accustomed to by now.

PART IV

30

During the past two months Alexa had developed more than a passing fondness for both Mr. Edwin Jarvis, her solicitor, and his wife, who had been born Lady Margery Davenish and still considered everything she had given up when she eloped with her husband well lost for love's sake. "A *coup de foudre,* my dear!" she had confided with a twinkle. "The magic thunderclap. And it *was* exactly like that for us both, you know. All I have to do is see my dearest love across a room filled with people and I feel quite weak at the knees, as I did that very first time I set eyes on him. I'm so very *lucky!*"

Lady Margery (as everyone called her) had accompanied her husband on his hurried journey to Rome and had immediately volunteered to take charge of Alexa and make sure she had *entrée* into London society. And it was she—rather than poor Perdita, who was too grief-stricken herself to be of much help or comfort—who had almost forced Alexa out of her daze of grief and self-recrimination, reminding her sternly that it was precisely what Sir John would *not* want her to feel and that only by *giving in* would she betray the confidence he had placed in her.

"But I feel as if I could have spent more *time* with

him,'' Alexa had whispered with her throat raw from weeping. ''Instead, I spent too much time *selfishly,* and even when he was *dying* and might have needed me I was...''

''What utter nonsense!'' Lady Margery had said strongly. ''You know very well indeed that your husband was so heavily drugged to keep him from feeling too much pain at the last that he would not even have known you. And my husband, who has known Sir John for over thirty years, says that *he* would have preferred it this way. What good does it do to surround a deathbed with loudly weeping friends or family who can only deprive one of the privilege of dying in peace, and with some dignity? Come, my dear child. Where is your backbone? After all, you are *not* quite alone, you know. My dear Edwin is one of the cleverest, most intelligent men alive, and *I* either know or am related to almost everyone mentioned in *Debrett's Peerage* or *Burke's Peerage.* Between the three of us I am sure that we shall contrive to manage very well.''

Since then...Alexa looked around herself and could hardly believe that she was where she was. In London, of all places, which had sounded to her only a year ago as distant as the stars she used to watch at night. And in none of her wildest flights of imagination could she have imagined *then* that she would ever be the mistress of an imposing house in Belgrave Square that she actually *owned,* in addition to owning a country manor in Yorkshire in the heart of the hunting district and her own horses and carriages and heaven knew what else, for her mind had not yet quite grasped the enormous extent of the wealth that she alone had full control over. It was almost frightening to think of sometimes, until she remembered a line in the letter that Sir John had left for her, reminding her that wealth represented *power* when it was used correctly.

Alexa had been pacing the newly and expensively carpeted floor of her book-lined library ever since she and Lady Margery had returned from their impulsive excursion to Gunter's to try their famous ices. She had not been expecting to catch her first glimpse of two of her half sisters and her father's second "wife" there, although she had always known that it would be only a matter of time until that very thing happened. And soon she would probably see her father for the first time since she had been an infant, perhaps her wicked grandmother as well. At least *she* was prepared and had made her plans in advance, giving herself the advantage over them.

As Alexa took yet another turn about the room Lady Margery said mildly: "I am sure it wasn't exactly a *pleasant* experience for you, my dear, but you must get used to the thought that more than likely you will start to run into them *everywhere,* especially after the Sutherlands' ball, where you will meet *everybody,* including the Queen and Prince Albert. There is no use in *making* yourself upset, you know. I'm sure we could think of better ways in which to occupy your time, such as a visit to the theater at Drury Lane if you care for Shakespeare or the Royal Opera House in the Haymarket, although I am afraid *that* area is rapidly becoming quite notorious!"

Had it been those innocently uttered words of Lady Margery's that had spurred her into an act of foolish defiance that might well cost her her *entrée* into polite society? Or was it merely a sense of boredom and her impatient nature combined that prompted Alexa to embark the very next day on a venture that both her new friends would have strongly disapproved of, had they only known of it?

In the end it had not been at all easy to accomplish her plan, which involved not only her faithful Bridget's unquestioning aid but a ride on one of the famous omnibuses every visitor to London talked about. In fact, since it had recently become quite fashionable, if a trifle "Bohemian," for almost everyone to be able to talk to their friends about having taken a ride on an *omnibus,* Alexa was provided with her excuse for leaving her house *on foot* with a drab brown pelisse that belonged to Bridget disguising her afternoon dress of dark green damasked cotton trimmed with bronze lace and green velvet ribbon; and wearing a bonnet that looked remarkably plain once she had ruthlessly cut off all of its expensive trimmings.

Although no longer easily shocked by any of her mistress's impulsive whims to do something quite out of the ordinary, even Bridget was driven to protest once they had been dropped off not far from the Haymarket and Alexa, acting as bold as brass, had actually hailed a hansom cab as if she was quite used to doing so. And when the driver had given them a very *peculiar* look upon being informed of the address he was to take them to, before venturing to suggest that perhaps they could have been given the wrong directions and would never want to go *there*—not two respectable-looking young women, surely—by then Bridget felt like wringing her hands fearfully, especially when Alexa said in her firm, crisp voice that she did *indeed* have the right address and would be pleased to be taken there as soon as possible.

"Please, ma'am, don't you think we should go back now? It certainly doesn't look like a very *nice* neighborhood for you to be in, and the way that man started looking us over really *funny* like..."

"Well, he stopped grumbling when he saw his tip, didn't he?" Alexa said in the same crisp voice she'd used before, adding almost consolingly when she saw Bridget's wan expression, "You have to admit it looks like quite a *nice,* smartly kept-up house from outside here, doesn't it? And for heaven's sake do try to stop looking like a lamb on its way to the slaughter house! We shall both be perfectly safe, I assure you!'' Ignoring a few curious loafers who stared too boldly, Alexa used the heavy brass knocker with force and was soon rewarded by the sound of footsteps just before the door was opened by an impassive-looking *butler,* of all things!

''May I help you young ladies?'' he said inquiringly, still standing there in the doorway until forced to move back when Alexa picked up her skirts and walked inside, with the timorous Bridget all but clinging to the back of her pelisse.

''Please be good enough to close the door behind us immediately,'' Alexa said composedly. ''And then you may tell Madame Olivier that her niece is calling upon her. I am her sister Victorine's daughter, in case she might have forgotten.''

''It's a good thing that you seem to have taken more after *me* than after your poor mother,'' Solange said frankly later when they were comfortably ensconced in her elegantly decorated parlor. ''But if you had taken after her you wouldn't be here, would you?'' She chuckled richly as her hazel eyes continued to appraise this unexpected visitor of hers. Her *niece,* by God, and a good-looking little piece she'd turned out to be too! ''You've got *brass,* haven't you, for all that you look like a fashionable lady and speak like one. It's really almost a pity that you aren't what I took you for at first, you know! You'd have gone far, my dear, although it can't compare to how much further you can go *now* as a rich widow. Ah, how much I'm going to enjoy thinking of it from now on!'' The rich contralto chuckle rang out again as Solange leaned forward to pour more champagne into Alexa's glass before refilling her own and glancing up quizzically. ''I suppose, since you have met my friend Orlanda, that you *know* everything?''

''*Almost* everything,'' Alexa said, and frowned slightly.

''There were *some* things, she told me, that would be better explained by you. That is, of course, if it will not upset you to have the past dredged up.''

''Ah, the past should *remain* the past, yes? If I was blind and a fool at one time, then I have only myself to blame for what I allowed to be done. You understand? Ah yes, I hate him! And hate that evil mother of his even more. But, again, it was I who made myself a victim by putting myself in their way; and one learns to be practical as one gets older. After I came back from Europe, having learned many more lessons while I was there, why, my dear, they were generous enough to help set me up in my present establishment once they were sure I had learned my lesson well. They are a strange family, you should be warned. The old witch is the worst and the most dangerous opponent of all, but the *men*—it is they you should be most guarded against, because they are all charming, and women usually find them quite fascinating. But they are just as evil and as twisted inside as *she* is. Be careful if one of them should seem to pursue you—never trust them! Me, I know all their secrets and the kind of *amusements* they enjoy in my establishment here, as well as in the *other* houses I run that cater to certain specialized perversions.'' After a glance at Alexa's face to discover if her expression had changed, Solange shrugged and shook her head, with its dyed chestnut curls, before awarding her niece an almost grudging smile. ''What a welcome surprise you have turned out to be. Especially since I have not been able to shock you yet. And now I think it is for *you* to tell me what I can do to help you, although I'm sure you understand by now that I can do nothing and say nothing openly. Also, you should be very careful indeed if you plan to visit me again—particularly after they've learned who you are.''

''Perhaps you can help me with your suggestions? For

I *would* like very much to come back and see you as often as I can—without their knowing that we have found each other, naturally."

"*Oui, naturellement!*" Solange affirmed and burst out laughing again at the drollness of it all. Perhaps she *would* finally have the revenge she had dreamed of for so many years. She emptied her fourth (or was it the fifth?) glass of champagne and rang for more, remembering how it had been when Gavin Dameron, Marquess of Newbury, and her *brother-in-law,* had grown weary of her throwing herself at him and had taken her as his mistress. Taken her to the little private villa he kept in St. John's Wood, with its stone wall around it for privacy and its pretty garden with a small pond and a fountain and even a sundial with a verse on it. Inside, the villa had been even prettier, and she had thought herself in heaven when he first took her there. Ah, *bon Dieu,* how passionately, how *insanely* she had loved him then! Enough to do anything he asked of her, *be* anything he wanted her to be for him, go to any lengths to please him. What an imbecile!

"I let myself become his slave, you see. No, not even that. I was his *thing.* Ah yes, I can see that you wonder how such a thing could happen to a woman as worldly-wise as I was even then—and *why!* But that must be because you have never believed yourself in love, my dear, and you should pray that such a foolishness will never happen with *you!*"

"If it is too painful for you..." Alexa began awkwardly, but her aunt brushed aside her words almost scornfully.

"Why should it be painful *now?* It has been over a long time, and I am free from that obsession that possessed even my soul for a time." After she had taken another sip of champagne Solange said: "It was after the time he spent in that Turkish prison that he changed. My sister never knew him the way *I* did later. He was a charming, rather reckless boy when they decided it would be a great adventure to get secretly married—he and my sister Victorine. He had plans to be a poet, like his idol Lord Byron. But when he came back—he was even more handsome in a harder way that made him seem all the more attractive to me, and that was all I saw at first. Later, when he would talk in his sleep sometimes and twist and turn and scream out loud with his nightmares, I began to guess what they had done to him.'' Solange laughed, but it was a bitter sound with none of the earlier richness in it. ''It was because of that, I suppose, that he did what he did with me—and does with the other women he keeps or buys for a night. You look horrified, my dear! I have learned since then that such things are quite common; and there are many other perversions men indulge in which are much worse. You may see for yourself, if you think your stomach is strong enough!''

For days afterwards Alexa herself had nightmares from which she would wake to find her body streaming with perspiration. Her *father!* Impossible to reconcile that earlier description of a laughing, golden young man who was an idealist and a poet with the cold, dissipated rake who found his real pleasure in inflicting pain and degradation on others. Although Orlanda had *hinted,* her aunt Solange had held nothing back from her, not even the very worst details.

''Here, unhook my gown for me,'' Solange had said abruptly, standing up. ''You'll soon discover why I can never wear a gown that exposes my back. And I used to have a very pretty back—all my lovers said so, even *he*—before he gave me those ugly scars you see. I suppose it is fortunate for me that there are certain men who find even scars an excitement!''

Was *this* a part of what her dear Sir John had wanted

her to learn early enough so that she could better protect herself? And were all men ugly and twisted and perverse behind their polite manners and charming smiles? Remembering against her will one particular smile that had never been meant to charm *her* at least, Alexa could not prevent herself from shuddering when she thought of how close she had come to succumbing to that frightening physical chemistry that her aunt had called *obsession.* But from now on, having been warned, she would take care to stay away from *that* particular Dameron at least. She had even made a point of finding out that he was away from London buying horses in the country and had informed nobody when he might return; which while being typically inconsiderate on *his* part, certainly made *her* plans easier to carry out. In fact, even now, as she admired the stylish cut of her new riding habit in the unusual shade known as "London smoke," Alexa hoped quite fervently that his horse-buying would keep him busy for the next few weeks. With a last glance at the mirror to make sure that her black silk hat with the chiffon veil that had been modelled after a man's top hat was still set on her head at exactly the right angle, Alexa ran downstairs to find her patient friend and tell her she was ready at last to go riding in the park for the first time.

31

"They *say* that she has her riding habits designed and tailored by Stultz himself. And the hats she wears with them are from Lock's, of course—boots from Medwin's. Recognize their touch anywhere."

"But those are *gentlemen's* establishments!"

"What's the difference, my dear? *All* the ladies will be going there now for their new riding habits, I suppose. Barlow was complaining his wife and daughters have already ordered everything new."

"I had it from the Countess herself that she has ordered most of her new gowns for the season from Mrs. Bell of Cleveland Row. And I had been wondering why she was always too busy of late."

"*I* have heard that she actually *owns* a house in Belgrave Square, next to Lord and Lady Morecambe's. *Do* you think we ought to leave cards? After all, if dear Lady Margery is vouching for her…"

"Some rich nabob's widow is what I heard, old boy. No *trade* involved, though. Husband had a title and all that—very old family, I understand. But *she's* worth a fortune, I'm told."

"Dammit! Join the fortune hunters myself if I was

younger! Fine horsewoman—good seat too. Showed up even our incomparable Miss Skittles on the Row this morning. Should have been there yourself."

Much to the annoyance of Lady Helen Dameron, who had looked forward to the "informal" levee they were attending that evening, it seemed as if everyone present could talk of nothing else but that *bold creature. "La Belle Inconnue,"* some silly romantic had called her, and everyone else had taken it up. Why were men so very gullible in some ways? A "horsebreaker"—wasn't that what they called women like Catherine Walters, who was known as "Skittles" of all things and flaunted herself and her wild, almost unmanageable horses on Rotten Row? A kept woman—bought and paid for. Helen was not supposed to know about such things, of course, but her grandmother had been quite straightforward with her when she had explained what men were like, even after they were married.

"Give 'em enough brats and they'll let you alone after that, my dear. Their harlots—Cyprians—whatever they call 'em *these* days. *They* see the ugly side of a man, and better them than *you;* remember that when you turn a blind eye."

She, this woman they were all talking about, was probably one of *those,* in spite of her so-called connections. Who else would have put on a public exhibition of her riding skills without knowing that everyone watching was comparing her with this Skittles creature, and even laying *wagers* on one or the other? Not a *lady,* certainly!

"What's the matter, sweet coz? Silent—wistful—not pining for the *country,* are you?" Helen had not noticed Charles, Viscount Deering, come up to them, flanked by her detestable uncles.

Helen made her smile sweeter as she acknowledged their bows and allowed them to kiss her small hands. "Why *should* I pine for the country when I am finding

London and my first season so exciting? Why, just the town *gossip* alone… And I've been sitting here alone with Mama while we tried to solve the great mystery puzzle tonight. Haven't we, Mama?''

Lady Iris, who had been looking for her friend Lady Stokes in the crush, gave a preoccupied assent, already beginning to wonder if they should leave early enough to attend the theater party given by the Ainslies.

''La Belle Inconnue,'' Helen said with a little laugh. ''Heavens, I think that is all we have heard this evening. It is almost as unusual a nickname as 'Skittles,' do you not think so?'' She looked from one to the other of the three gentlemen with pretended naiveté before giving a deprecating little shrug that showed off her sloping white shoulders to perfection. ''You cannot imagine the *things* people have been saying, and now I do wish that I had persuaded Mama to take one of *our* carriages to the park this morning to see everything. Were *you* there by chance? And was it really the same person we saw with Lady Margery at Gunter's the other day?''

While the two Viscounts kept finishing each other's incomplete sentences as they gave an exaggerated (Helen was sure) account of the lovely *young* Lady Travers, her impeccably cut riding habit (Stultz, of course!) and her magnificent chestnut thoroughbred, Helen's sharp eyes had not failed to make note of the fact that Lord Charles remained silent and unusually thoughtful through it all. Helen asked ingenuously: ''But if she is so much the *lady* and so enormously wealthy, why is it that no one knows her background or where she comes from? Unless she is Spanish or Italian or something like *that,* of course…''

Only then did Charles say in a strangely off-hand kind of voice: ''Oh—I have the feeling that Lady Travers comes from sturdy English stock, all right, although I arrived at the Row too late to catch more than a glimpse of her this morning.'' And try as she would, Helen could not get anything more out of him for the rest of the night.

''Well, my dear! It seems as if all of London is talking about you, although in the most flattering terms possible, of course. So *wise* of you, though, to remain slightly *mysterious,* at least until after the Stafford House ball. And—oh goodness! Look at all these cards! Now *that* is the real sign of acceptance, you know.''

Alexa and Lady Margery had just returned after a tiring morning and afternoon spent shopping at various establishments on Regent Street, and the silver tray in the entrance hall was already piled high with engraved cards that Alexa only frowned at with a slightly preoccupied air.

''I suppose Mr. Jarvis is right and I should employ a secretary,'' she said, leading the way into the pleasantly airy room she had just had redecorated for her use as a study and a retreat. ''But I have been sending out polite notes in reply to them all, and that is what has been keeping me busy almost every afternoon.'' She paused by one of the windows with her back half-turned to her friend before adding, as if it had been a casual afterthought: ''I see that there has been a great deal of activity going on across the square for the past few days. Bridget mentioned that it is all because the Dowager Marchioness of Newbury has decided to move in. Do you think perhaps that *she* might feel curious enough to have one of her footmen drop a card off here? I wonder what I should do in that case!''

Lady Margery, who had let herself sink into a chair with a sigh as soon as they had entered, now sighed again as she looked quizzically at the straight-backed young woman who had just turned about to face her. ''I would think, love, that it would depend on just what you mean to *achieve* in the end, if you know what it is yourself. You have made yourself *noticed* already and have them all buzzing with conjecture as to *who* you are and where you have appeared from. And there is no doubt in *my* mind that after you have made your formal social debut at Stafford House next week you will be firmly established in the best social circles, if that is indeed *all* you want?'' She moved her hand almost wearily at Alexa's look that mixed surprise and wariness. ''You don't *mind* my being frank? After all, we have all been quite open with each other from the beginning, have we not; and you know that I know as much as my husband does. The point is, my dear—and I hope you have thought about it very carefully, for you know how fond I am of you—are you really *sure?* Of what you want, what you might gain, and what you might *lose?*''

What *did* she hope to achieve in the end? Alexa had already asked herself the question many times; and as for having something to *lose,* why, that could be dismissed easily enough because she felt almost like the Spanish conquistador Cortez, who set fire to his own ships so that he and his followers could only go forward and never back. She herself had nothing and nowhere to go back to either. Nothing to lose, really, as *they* did.

She said as much as she walked slowly away from the windows to stand by her desk, running her fingers abstractedly over its polished surface while she considered everything else. Mr. Jarvis had already pointed out the ''perils and pitfalls'' as he put it. Her aunt's profession for one thing. Her husband's far too recent death. And most of all her own indiscretion (he had been kind enough not to call it ''stupidity,'' she thought wryly) that fateful night in Rome. *Men,* after all, were usually believed; and he could very easily spread the story that she was given to frequenting brothels for entertainment. *Would* he actually do so? Alexa had almost to shake the thought from her mind.

"You said yourself that they are *noticing* me," she said finally. "And *I* haven't made any overt moves in that direction, have I? Let *them* come to me first, when they begin to *wonder* and tie little facts together and ask themselves questions. Perhaps that is all I want—to see *them* suffer the torture of *suspense* and start to be afraid of consequences for a change. Oh, I don't know! Except that I want them all to know who I am! The Witch, my grandmother. Gavin Edward Dameron, Marquess of Newbury, and his bigamous wife and his bastard daughters. The *future* Marquess of Newbury. Do you think that he will be quite as anxious to marry the lovely Helen when he knows the truth? If no one else knows, let *them* know and try to live with the constant anticipation that I might topple them down from their high perches any time I choose to!"

"Well, love, do think everything over *very* carefully and do weigh every consequence, won't you?" And then, dropping her rather solemn tone as her eyes began to twinkle irrepressibly, Lady Margery added, "But I must admit that I can hardly wait until I see their faces when you make your curtsy to the Queen. And you must *promise* to be the soul of discretion until then at *least!*"

After her friend had left, Alexa wondered rather guiltily if Mr. Jarvis, who had connections everywhere and in every walk of life, might have learned that she had called on her aunt against his express advice and that, besides communicating with her by messenger twice since then, she planned to pay her aunt Solange another visit very soon. There was so much more she had to find out! Including… Alexa picked up the scrawled note that had accompanied one of the extravagant baskets of flowers she had received during the past few days. She had not mentioned *this* to Mr. Jarvis either, wanting to think it over for herself first. What *should* she do about Lord Charles Lawrence? She felt nothing for him any longer, of course—if she ever had. But he had seen her riding, and the name *Travers* had obviously touched a chord; he was *almost* sure she was the same Miss Alexandra *Howard* he had been privileged to become acquainted with in Ceylon last year. Alexa frowned again over his note.

> ...If I am mistaken, or presumptuous, I beg that you will forgive me. But if *La Belle Inconnue* and the young lady who has haunted my dreams ever since I was *forcibly* prevented from keeping our last appointment are one and the same...I am almost afraid to say more, except, again, I know that I know you, for there cannot be *two* women in this world blessed with the same expressive face and eyes and the same unique *hair* that magically seems to have entrapped all the changing colors of autumn. And so I remain in suspense until I know if you choose to acknowledge our previous acquaintance or not.
>
> Deering.

What a well-written and almost poetic note! Alexa thought a trifle cynically as she threw it down on her dressing table again. He had emphasized "*forcibly* prevented." Had it been *that* way indeed, and not the way Nicholas had told it? Nicholas *Dameron*—a liar too many times already. But she didn't want to think about *him,* especially while he was safely out of the way. Lord Charles. Her *cousin,* in fact sharing the same grandmother. What if she made him fall in love with her? It suddenly struck Alexa that *they* (as she had begun to say), even if they guessed at or *knew* her real identity, could not possibly know whether *she* was aware of her true antecedents or not, which made the whole situation even more deliciously ironic. And what if it was Lord Charles who made sure that she was properly introduced to *all* his relations, particularly on his *mother's* side? After that, and hearing of her name and background, there would be at least *two* of them who would begin to worry and wonder without being able to say anything openly.

If Lord Charles had hoped to receive some acknowledgment of his rather impetuous missive the next time he saw Lady Travers riding in the park, he was disappointed; for she rode with her friend Lady Margery again and spoke to no one except her companion and the Countess of Jersey, to whom she had just been introduced. What a magnificent horsewoman she was, as he should well remember from the many times they had ridden together in Colombo. Less than a year ago, as impossible as that seemed. And yet, in that short space of time she must have been both married and widowed! How much experience had she had? She was still as slim as a willow wand and did not *look* too much different, except for the way she wore her hair now and her modish, expensive clothes. And she had gained, since then, an almost indefinable air of self-assurance and poise along with the polish. *Lady* Travers. Was it really possible that she could have married that old man she used to refer to as her "uncle"? A Baronet—and very rich into the bargain, if he remembered correctly. And now all that wealth was hers to squander and enjoy, at least until she allowed herself to become entrapped by one of the fortune hunters the town was full of these days. Charles caught himself frowning at some of his closest friends who happened to be as impoverished as *he* was at the moment and feeling quite *protective* of her. Alexandra. "Alexa" that forbidding aunt of hers had called her. He had wanted her even then and had planned to bring her to England under his protection. *Would* have too, if Nicholas hadn't seen fit to interfere, damn him! But perhaps it *was* just as well after all, for *now*—by God, she was here in London and not only wealthy but *accepted* by everyone!

Deciding to be patient, Lord Charles made a point of riding in the Row every day at about the same time that *she* usually did. He told himself that she had doubtless become wary of fortune hunters already, which would account for her aloofness and reserve in public. Even the die-hard old dowagers were beginning to unbend enough to admit grudgingly that in spite of her obvious youth Lady Travers seemed to be a quiet and serious-minded young woman with both the knowledge and proper regard for the conventions; although he could not help smiling to himself when he suddenly thought of his grandmother the Dowager Marchioness of Newbury and what *her* reactions might be. Perhaps, since she had moved into what was referred to as "Old Newbury House" in Belgrave Square for the rest of the season, he should find out by calling and paying his dutiful respects. Such a coincidence that Lady Travers lived just opposite!

Since the Dowager insisted on strict observance of the formalities, Lord Charles decided to leave his card with her butler on his way to the park the next day. He found himself quite nonplussed when he was requested to wait in the library for a few minutes and relieved the next moment when his Uncle Newbury's third daughter, Philippa, came running down the stairs to announce gleefully that Belle-Mère had decided *he* could just as well escort them to watch the riders in the park, since their uncles were so late thcy had probably forgotten their promise, as usual. "And I am really quite glad, because I had much rather go with *you!*" Philippa added breathlessly before Helen could come downstairs and show her annoyance at having to be burdened with the presence of her younger sisters.

Lady Helen, however, had surprisingly been all smiles and sweetness when she joined them with her other sister in a surprisingly short time, explaining to her *dearest and most obliging* cousin that she and her sisters had been invited to spend a few days with Belle-Mère, who actually planned to give a ball for her. Wasn't it sweet and thoughtful? "And I am to help with the guest list and *all* the plans, of course; for after all, as Belle-Mère reminded me, it will not be long before I will be giving my *own* balls!" She gave one of her rather tinkling laughs before saying archly, with a sideways glance at her preoccupied-seeming cousin, "That is, of course, if I can hope to drag Embry up to London for the season!" She added with another small laugh: "I must admit though that for the *moment* I cannot help feeling quite *relieved* that Embry is busy with *purchasing* horses instead of *watching* them and their female riders like the rest of you besotted gentlemen, or becoming another adoring follower of this mystery lady! Has anyone learned anything more about her background yet?"

"Her background is quite respectable, I'm sure, sweet coz," Charles responded automatically as he scanned the crowd of elegantly dressed ladies and gentlemen who had arrived earlier to promenade up and down or ride or watch everyone else. "Will *you* not ride today?" he added almost maliciously, knowing how Helen hated to be outshone in anything. "I see several of your friends are here already and are waving at you. You are not nervous about riding that new Arab mare of Grandmother's, are you? Perhaps *I* should try her out first, unless Ianthe is ready to take the challenge?"

That was enough for Helen, whose archness dropped away for a few moments as she snapped: "I think that I am a good enough rider to handle almost any horse fit for riding, although I'm grateful for your concern. But is *your* mount too fresh and likely to be troublesome? Because in *that* case, of course I would be more than glad to forgo the pleasure of riding in Rotten Row to allow *you* to do so."

Instead of replying in kind as he was tempted to do, Lord Charles took a glance at the watch he had drawn from his vest pocket and shrugged instead as he advised his cousin to mount and be quick about it, before they were too late to see anyone.

Determined *not* to be observed losing her temper, Lady Helen followed his example in mounting one of the horses that had been brought along in the wake of their large open carriage, quite aware, as they cantered forward to join a group of acquaintances, that the silver-grey coat and darker mane of her mare formed a perfect complement to her charcoal-colored riding habit and her blonde and gold coloring. In fact, she received so many compliments from everyone they encountered that her smile became quite genuine and her cheeks a rose-pink that enhanced her beauty even more. *Everything* should have and *would* have gone off quite perfectly if they had not happened to meet with Lady Travers, who was riding a white-stockinged bay with a matching star on his forehead and was accompanied, for a change, by only her groom riding behind her. This time she was wearing a severely cut black cloth riding habit that was trimmed with black velvet, its severity relieved by white satin and silk and occasional intriguing glimpses of the white muslin *trousers* she had actually dared to wear beneath her skirts. Helen had *heard* that it was now considered quite the thing to do so, but it seemed to her that they could easily appear quite *vulgar* worn by certain persons—Lady Travers providing the perfect example.

It was on the tip of Helen's tongue to observe as much when a rather flashily dressed woman almost *flew* past them on a huge black brute of a horse that seemed not only wild but completely unmanageable as well, in spite of the fact that its rider was foolhardy enough to keep only one gloved hand on her reins while she lifted the other as she passed in an openly challenging salute.

"That Skittles!" an admiring masculine voice commented laughingly at about the same time that Helen's nervous grey mare reared up, almost unseating her rider, and decided to bolt in the opposite direction from that taken by the black. For some terror-filled, almost timeless moments, while she clung on with all her strength to reins and mane, Helen felt as if everything was whirling past her. Trees and shrubs and other horses and riders. Faces with open mouths and cries of alarm that were drowned out by the sound of the wind whistling in her ears and the pounding of hooves. And then, just as suddenly as it had all begun it was over, and Helen realized that she was actually *alive* and had been spared even the humiliation of being *thrown* in front of everyone. But she might have been *killed!* Helen had to force herself to sit erect again and wished she could stop her hands from shaking for long enough so that she could straighten her hat, with its ostrich plume that now covered her eyes and most of her face instead of curling jauntily about its brim. "Here, let me do that for you," a competent feminine voice offered, and before Helen had time to protest she found the offending feather no longer obscuring her vision as her silk hat was adjusted over the golden mass of curls it had taken her maid over two hours to arrange. The same matter-of-fact feminine voice said it was a very pretty hat indeed before adding that *any* horse might decide to run away at any time and they were hard to control if one was taken completely unawares as *she* had obviously been. "It has even happened to *me* on several occasions, and sometimes I have ended up taking the most ungraceful spills!"

As Helen's vision returned and she saw who had been

speaking to her, she could gladly have *cried* with vexation or...

"How can we ever thank you enough?" Lord Charles said fervently at that moment. "I suppose all the rest of us, even *I,* must have been paralyzed with shock for those few crucial moments during which only *you* were quick-witted enough to act! I..."

"*I* had almost decided far too rashly to take up the gauntlet that had just been thrown, I'm afraid!" Alexa said in a dry voice as she released her firm hold on the Arab mare's reins. "In fact, I had already started off, and that was why I was able to catch up so easily." She shrugged lightly. "There is really no need for thanks, you know. I'm sure someone else would have done the same if I had not got there first."

Helen, very much aware of all the curiously watching eyes that surrounded them and her own unfortunate obligation to the woman who had obviously managed to halt her runaway mount, had almost managed to force out her grudging little speech of thanks when she heard her cousin say in a *suppressed* kind of voice: "But *you* were the first to act! You were always such an excellent horsewoman, as I remember so clearly. Will you at least do me the honor of accepting my profound *gratitude,* even if you do not choose to accept my apologies for—certain things I had no control over?"

Only Alexa was aware of Lady Helen's icy blue gaze that went from one of them to the other, prompting her to give the bemused Lord Charles a smile that showed off her dimple before she said kindly: "I think I *did* have enough sense even *then* to guess at what might have happened. But as it turned out I did not stay in Colombo for much longer." She did not say more, but turned to her golden half sister with a commendably pleasant smile and a nod that seemed to dismiss Lord Charles politely.

"I do hope that the *rest* of your ride will be a much more pleasant experience for you. And now I really think that I should be..."

"Please! I am sorry if I seemed quite *speechless* earlier, but I suppose I *was* taken quite unawares. However, I do thank you very much indeed for—your help." Helen's halfhearted attempt at a speech of thanks made Alexa shrug lightly as she said, "*Por nada,* as a Spaniard would say. Do have a pleasant day!" Before Lord Charles could think of anything else to say she had whirled her horse about and was gone, leaving him staring after her in a bemused fashion while his cousin raged inside herself; her mind suddenly filled with all kinds of questions and suspicions.

32

"Oh, my lady, I'm quite sure there won't be another ball gown there tonight as beautiful as yours! It takes my breath away, it does!"

In spite of Bridget's raptures, Alexa continued to study herself critically in the mirrors that reflected her image from all angles. Her colors tonight were green and gold. Dark green velvet caught up in flounces by gold rosettes, revealing layers of green silk and gauze shot through with gold thread that created a shimmering effect whenever she moved. For jewels she had chosen emeralds set in gold. Around her throat, circling one wrist, dropping from her ears. And in her elaborately coiffed hair she wore delicately wrought gold "roses" with jade leaves. Real rose petals had provided the color that touched her cheekbones and her lips; every tiny detail helping to make her reflected image a stranger to herself. *Was* she beautiful? What would *they* think? Did she really *care* after all?

No matter how severe she was with herself and how coolly composed she managed to appear *outwardly,* Alexa could not help either the shortness of her breath or the racing of her pulses once they had actually arrived at Stafford House. In fact, she had to fight off the impulse to clutch tightly to Mr. Jarvis's arm for support, even after Lady Margery had begun to introduce her friend Lady Travers to all of *her* friends and acquaintances.

Names and faces—some friendly and some more curious than anything else. Eyes took in every detail of her ball gown, her magnificent jewels, and her *hair*....

"Ah, that hair! Know why you seemed familiar from a distance now. Adelina, of course. No one else in *our* day had hair quite the same shade, you know, and she made the most of it. Hah! Sure *you* do too. Related, are you?"

An embarrassed daughter-in-law whispered into the ancient Dowager's ear-trumpet, causing her to raise both her eyebrows and her lorgnette to study Alexa more closely before she pronounced irritably that no one could mistake that *hair*—and the young woman had Adelina's stubborn chin as well. "*You* never knew Adelina, did you? Well then, *you* couldn't know!" She gave a triumphant cackle. "Only reason *you* were born, my girl, is because Adelina tired of her flirtation with your papa and sent him back home. Didn't know *that* either, did you?"

"Let's move along, shall we?" Mr. Jarvis said firmly and proceeded to do just that, much to Alexa's disappointment, for she had been intrigued by the old lady's observations in spite of herself. At the next moment, however, she was terrified to realize that they were descending the stairway with a crowd of others; to be presented at last to the Duke and Duchess of Sutherland and their *most* distinguished guests—Queen Victoria and Prince Albert.

"So *that* is Lady Travers? I must say that she is not quite what I had expected. Gavin, what do *you* think?"

"My dear sister, why ask *me?* I'm sure my wife or my daughters would be better informed as to the background of the morals of the—er—*Lady* in question!" The Marquess of Newbury gave his sister one of his bored, cynical smiles before he continued on his way past her to join a small group of his cronies who were clustered by the doorway to one of the antechambers that led off the lower floor of the Great Hall. The kind of gossip that his sister habitually indulged in held no more interest for him than its present subject, at least, not until he found that even his politically-minded friends were discussing the same Lady Travers. It was only then that he deigned to cast a casual glance in her direction, expecting to see nothing out of the ordinary.

"Isn't that Deering standing closest to our latest beauty? Rich widow—*young* too, eh?"

If the world-weary Marquess did not choose to add his comments to the others, it was nothing out of the ordinary; and his silence was not remarked on by any of them either. He was usually uninterested in the latest beauties and the latest gossip, unless the gossip had to do with international affairs. There was, in fact, no change in his demeanor at all when he first looked at Alexa and in doing so met her eyes for less than a fleeting second before he turned deliberately and walked through the doorway and out of her sight.

Well, after all, what had she excepted? Her father—her *real* father—but a man, nonetheless, that she already knew almost too much about. She should concentrate on the knowledge that *she* had the advantage over him so far. Alexa was able to smile quite normally at Lord Charles when he appeared before her and even to introduce him to Mr. Jarvis and Lady Margery. So far, she had survived the worst part of the ordeal she had been dreading for the past two weeks. The Queen and her Consort had been more than kind and so had the Duke and Duchess of Sutherland. But most important, she had finally *seen* the Marquess of Newbury, and had found it easy not to like him—easier still to put his presence here out of her mind for the time being, while she was still feeling relieved that a certain *other* person had not seen fit to attend this particular function. At least, not *yet!*

They had decided to leave early, soon after the first quadrille, in fact. It was well known by now that the young Queen forbade the waltz at the small weekly dances she gave at the palace; and her friend the Duchess of Sutherland had tactfully arranged for *two* orchestras in this instance—one indoors in the grand ballroom for the Queen's entertainment and one *outdoors* (if one could call it that) under the green glass dome of her conservatory, where the waltz *was* permitted.

Alexa was partnered by Mr. Jarvis for the first dance, Lord Charles having been cunning enough to beg permission to ask Lady Margery to be *his* partner. And after that it seemed only courteous to give Mr. Jarvis the opportunity to dance with his wife at least *once* before they left.

"Do you really believe it is *wise* to leave Alexa alone with that young man? I did not like the way in which he *looked* at her when he thought *we* weren't watching."

"My dear, I am certain that Alexa is quite capable of keeping Deering at arm's length; no matter how languishingly he gazes at her! And in any case…"

"Ohh! And *now* it is not just a case of languishing glances, as you can see quite obviously!" Lady Margery was so upset that she almost forgot they were within a few feet of the Queen and Prince Albert until she felt the pressure of her husband's fingers over hers, reminding her to be cautious.

"I do not see how we can leave the floor without drawing far too much attention to everyone concerned," Mr. Jarvis said quietly. "In fact," he added, "I believe we might just as well sit down and wait it out, for whatever the outcome of *this,* I am certain it will be quite interesting, to say the least."

Interesting indeed! For a short, confusing space of time

Alexa found herself not quite aware of what was happening as one event followed too closely on the heels of another. She had been dancing with Lord Charles and relishing a feeling of *intrigue,* especially when she began to realize that he was steering her towards the open French windows that led outside. Should she let him lead her or not? Was she going to be *respectable* or not?

''You are adorable. And I remember everything—from our very first meeting to what *I* did not intend to be our last.''

''We had some very interesting conversations, did we not?'' Alexa said brightly at about the same time the voice she *least* wanted to hear spoke from somewhere behind her.

''Might I be excused for going from conversation to coincidence? My dear Charles—and—it *is* Lady Travers now, is it not? I would not interrupt for the world, except that Belle-Mère is here and is looking forward to meeting the *wife* of one of her very dearest friends, she says.''

Just as if he had deliberately arranged it, the music ended at that moment, leaving Alexa no alternative but to turn about and look him in the eyes. A mistake, she discovered within a few seconds before she purposefully looked away from him and back at Lord Charles, who was saying in a rather sullen voice, ''Embry! Didn't know you'd decided to tear yourself away from the country and *horses!* Kitty get too impatient, did she?''

Nicholas Dameron, Viscount Embry, displayed no embarrassment whatsoever at the blunt reference to the young woman otherwise known as ''Skittles''; merely lifting one shoulder in a careless shrug before drawling caustically: ''Kitty's already got the new horse I promised her and Belle-Mère's still waiting. As I just said, she's quite eager to meet Lady Travers. And naturally, so am I, especially since I've been told by Helen of her heroic rescue the other day.'' Leopard-green eyes bored coldly into hers when Alexa forced herself to look defiantly back at him, noticing how his mouth twisted in that travesty of a smile she remembered all too well as he inclined his dark head in what was meant to pass for a bow.

''I *do* hope you do not mind my singing your praises to my grandmother and my—cousin?'' Lady Helen's voice was honey-sweet as she came up to place her fingers lightly on Nicholas's black-clad arm, although her significant pause had conveyed exactly what it was meant to imply, and there was neither sweetness nor warmth in the cold blue eyes that flickered over Alexa from head to foot. Her *betrothed,* she had meant to say of course, before she had cut herself off. Perhaps it wasn't quite *official* yet? Not that it mattered one bit to her, Alexa thought furiously before it suddenly dawned on her that she had just received what amounted to a Royal Summons, precipitating a meeting she was not sure she was prepared for yet; although now that the challenge had been issued her pride and her stubbornness would not let her evade it.

''I'm afraid our grandmother—Belle-Mère, she prefers to be called—is a rather formidable person,'' Lord Charles said apologetically to Alexa. ''She is quite outspoken, I'm afraid, and you must not on any account feel that you are *obliged* to meet her.''

''After *that* description I wouldn't be surprised if poor Lady Travers is quite terrified at the thought,'' Nicholas said sardonically with a lift of one eyebrow, causing Alexa to grit her teeth before she announced in as cool and unconcerned a tone as she could manage that she quite looked forward to meeting the Dowager Marchioness of Newbury, of whom she'd heard such a great deal.

''Poor Lady Travers'' indeed! And she was hardly ''terrified'' either, even if *he* would like to think so.

''How very *kind* of you to be so *indulgent,*'' Helen said

with more forced sweetness. She gave a small laugh that was equally false. "I expect that Belle-Mère feels she must *thank* you for being so helpful to me the other day."

"You won't mind walking as far as the conservatory with us, will you?" Nicholas added in a tone of such smooth affability that Alexa shot him a suspicious glower as she placed her fingers lightly on Lord Charles's gallantly proffered arm; noticing as she did so that Helen positively *clung* to *her* escort's sleeve in an openly possessive fashion he did not seem to object to in the least. What gullible fools men could be! Alexa thought scornfully before she felt her pulse begin to race in the next instant when she recollected every warning she had received against the woman she was about to meet.

Danger and adventure...were they synonymous? Quite suddenly she could almost *hear* Sir John's voice cautioning her to keep her head no matter what the circumstances; for that was the only way she could remain in control of any situation in which she might find herself. Alexa caught a glimpse of herself in one of the many mirrors that lined the hallway through which they had to pass on their way to the conservatory, and her glance reassured her that she looked her best—enabling her to bestow smiles on *all* of them, even the detestable Nicholas.

The peculiarly *clashing* looks they exchanged might have been lost on Lord Charles, who was busy worrying about his grandmother's usually outspoken manner of speech; but it was *not* lost on Lady Helen, who had begun to wish she had not lagged behind to greet a friend while Embry walked ahead of her to find Charles and his partner. Had she missed some important part of their conversation? And if *Charles* had met this flamboyant Lady Travers before, was it possible that Embry had met her also? She wished that she could find out without making too obvious a point of it, and then consoled herself by thinking that no doubt Belle-Mère would soon find out all there was to know about this typically *nouveau riche* female and just as quickly demolish all her pretensions to gentility if she chose. And of course that was exactly why her grandmother had cleverly sent for the creature—to give her a public setdown from which she could never recover.

But in the meantime, much to Lady Helen's displeasure, their progress through the throng of dancers and those who observed the dancing in the conservatory was far too slow. There were too many friends and acquaintances who had to be acknowledged and then the inevitable introductions made. It disappointed Helen that Lady Travers managed to appear quite self-composed and not in the least nervous all through what *most* women might have considered an *ordeal,* especially if this was the first time she had had the privilege of mixing with *society.* During a short pause while they waited for some three or four couples to leave the floor as the orchestra struck up one of the latest waltzes, Helen said with condescending politeness, "I *know* my cousin Deering has already told me he has met you before, Lady Travers, but I must admit I have forgotten where, except that it was some foreign place..."

"It was in Ceylon—one of the crown colonies, of course," Lord Charles said quickly before Alexa had had a chance to reply. "Told you *several* times over, sweet coz. We were fortunate enough to be invited to a ball at the Governor's mansion, as I recall—among other things," he added with a rather dark look at the Viscount Embry, who merely shrugged in a careless fashion.

"What an excellent memory *you* must have, my dear Charles! I had almost forgotten the ball at Queen's House, although not the Governor's pool, or some of those particularly beautiful beaches."

Once again Helen felt herself strangely left out for some reason, and she had opened her mouth to inquire directly if indeed Embry and Lady Travers were already acquainted with each other when they reached the cozy alcove where the Dowager Marchioness of Newbury had chosen to ensconce herself.

"Ah! So *here* you are at last! Took your time, didn't you?"

"You cannot believe the *crush* inside, Belle-Mère."

"And of course we had to run into almost everyone we knew."

Helen and Lord Charles spoke almost at the same time, but the Dowager ignored them while her eyes, hooded and inscrutable, studied every detail of Alexa's appearance before she said shortly, "Well, now that you're all *here* at last, which one of you is going to perform the introductions? *My* generation knew their manners, at least! No, no, no!" She waved her ringed hand impatiently to silence Lord Charles and looked imperiously at Viscount Embry. "*You* do it, Nicholas. More *correct.* Well?"

Even while he performed the formally polite and perfunctory introduction that manners and custom demanded, Nicholas found himself wondering angrily why he should almost feel *sorry* for the teasing, calculating little bitch who was about to receive the setdown she richly deserved. In fact, he had been surprised at how easily and almost meekly she had agreed to accompany them here to what would surely prove the end to all her aspirations to being accepted by polite society. Dammit, she should have been more cautious—just as she should be more afraid at this minute. But instead she continued to smile naively as if she had not noticed the open, almost insulting way the Dowager looked her over before she deigned to speak.

"So *you're* the Lady Travers I've been hearing so much about. And you're very young, too! Never thought he'd marry, you know, especially not since he was so badly wounded that time in India—although I suppose *you* would have been only an infant at that time? It *was* Sir John Travers you were married to, wasn't it? And now you're a widow...you must tell all about it, and how you happened to meet. We were very old friends, Sir John and I."

"Oh, but of course I knew all that and had been quite longing to meet you too, ma'am. My husband spoke of you *so* often that I could almost begin to feel I *knew* you, if you'll forgive my presumption. And—oh yes, of *course,* how could I have forgotten—he also used to tell me about his early friendship with the present Marquess of Newbury, and..."

If the Dowager's hands had clenched themselves over the handle of her silver-topped cane, they were hidden by the folds of her silver and gold brocaded skirt so that nobody noticed; although even Helen could not help but sense the almost indefinable tension in the air while she wondered why Belle-Mère had not yet made one of her famous cutting comments instead of merely saying, "Ah, indeed? How *garrulous* men tend to become with age, and how they gossip, to be sure! But now that you have intrigued me you must tell me more, Miss...?"

"It's Lady Travers now, ma'am. But in Ceylon I was known as Miss Howard." Alexa discovered that she was actually able to manage a small laugh before she added, "I should not wish to *bore* everyone with the history of my family, however, fascinating *I* find it myself." Shrugging lightly, Alexa dared to smile as she said: "For instance, I've been told I take after my paternal grandmother in both coloring and *nature,* although I cannot be sure the latter was meant to be flattering since *she* was also known as a witch!"

"How interesting! I will have to hear more about this fascinating family of yours quite soon. Helen, my dear, you *have* sent Lady Travers an invitation to your ball next week, I hope? We're neighbors, I believe, and that should make matters convenient. You'll come?'' The Dowager's recovery from the barbed darts she had taken was remarkable, Alexa had to admit grudgingly, even as she inclined her head.

''I will have to look in my appointment book, of course, but I am sure I shall manage to be free on such a special occasion. How kind!''

33

Alexa had begun to feel a certain sense of elation at how easily that very first confrontation had gone, even while she reminded herself that she had not *won* any battles yet. True, the old Marchioness had *seemed* to retreat for the moment, but that was probably only in order to decide on the best form of attack. Be careful, Alexa warned herself as she felt some of her bravado melt away when the Dowager suddenly changed tactics in the most puzzling way possible and became *too* charming; insisting that Alexa must sit by her for a little while longer at least and tell her *all* about dear Sir John while Embry must find them another chair for Helen, and her grandson Charles must also make himself useful and...

"Better ask Helen to dance. Can't have everyone standing around here looking awkward, can we? Go on. Do as I say! And if your mama says anything, my dear, you may tell her *I* said so! *I* never missed a single waltz if I could help it—once it was considered permissible to do so."

Once the reluctant Helen and her equally reluctant cousin had obediently joined the rest of the dancers, Alexa was forced to meet a smile that did not reach stony eyes as the Dowager said questioningly: "Ceylon? A pleasantly warm climate there all year round, I believe. Don't you miss it? London must seem unpleasantly cold after the tropics, I suppose, and everything becomes extremely dull once the season is over, although I've heard that it is quite different in warmer countries such as Spain and Italy, for instance, or the south of France. Have you had the chance to see anything of Europe yet or did poor John keep you hidden?'' Without giving Alexa a chance to answer the Marchioness shook her head with pretended commiseration before continuing: ''You mustn't mind my frankness, for it's one of the few things considered excusable at my age. Such a gallant, idealistic man John Travers used to be, and quite a catch as well, even in those days before he became so rich. Until, of course… But *you* must know all too well what I am speaking of, unless you've had an overly protective upbringing. Ah, here's Embry, at last! My dear Nicholas, how rude of you to stay away so long and neglect your duty while I have been boring poor Lady Travers with ancient gossip. *Do* ask her to dance to make up for it! I've sent Helen and Charles off to dance already.''

He should not have felt himself obligated to ask her, and *she* should not have allowed him to take her hand on the heels of his curtly worded ''request'' that she do him the honor. *Except,* Alexa thought furiously, that he had not given her a chance to refuse him before she found herself led inexorably onto the floor and his arm encircled her waist to draw her far more closely against his arrogantly held body than *decency* permitted. Indeed, she would have made an attempt to escape if she had not been made to feel that her fingers would be crushed and *mangled* by his had she done so. In the end, all she could do was to demand, in a voice rendered slightly breathless and choked by the force of her emotions, that he release her *immediately* and allow her to rejoin the friends with whom she had arrived here, while *he* should surely return to his fiancée.

"Fiancée?" Alexa could not help but feel uneasy at the way he seemed to scrutinize her through dangerously narrowed eyes. "If you've been listening to gossip, Lady Travers, then you must surely be aware that there's been no official announcement yet."

"Official? Then an announcement is *expected,* of course. And I have *not* been listening to gossip at all—it was Charles who told me that..."

"*Charles?* If you'll accept the advice of an old friend, such familiar usage of Deering's first name might be misconstrued by the gossips and those who are sticklers for convention." His sarcastic drawl made hot color rise in Alexa's cheeks as she threw her head back to shoot him a daggerlike look.

"Your *advice,* my Lord Embry, is both unnecessary and uncalled for, I assure you! And you are not an old *friend. That* is surely the height of hypocrisy!"

"I beg your pardon, Lady Travers. I meant only to spare *you* the embarrassment you might have felt if I had substituted *lover* for *friend.*" His smile reminded Alexa of a tiger baring its teeth. "Is *Charles* understanding enough, do you think?"

"Is that any concern of *yours?*" Rallying, Alexa gritted her teeth and stared at him frostily before adding: "*Really,* my lord, I fail to understand this insulting assumption of familiarity on your part based upon no more than the *slightest* acquaintance, unless you hope to *frighten* or to threaten me for some incomprehensible reason. And now, if you will allow me to rejoin my friends...?"

"I'm sure Mr. Jarvis and his wife will not leave without you—hypocrite! And if you continue with your useless attempts to run away from me, let me assure you that you will only succeed in making yourself look foolish as well as conspicuous."

"You...you...!"

"Be careful, Lady Travers. You might be overhead by someone who does not understand you as well as I do."

Alexa said in a furious undertone, "Will you *stop* holding me so tightly? And we *are* no more than acquaintances. If you were really my friend you would not *force* this dance upon me!"

"My sweet, wanton nymph, you have already reminded me that I am *not* your friend! And I should certainly hope for *your* sake that you do not allow too many of your *other* acquaintances the same liberties you led *me* to take."

"*Led* you? Why..."

Viscount Embry said smoothly, and just loudly enough to be overheard by the few couples who were close enough: "But please allow me to lead you outside, Lady Travers. The fresh air will restore you, I am sure, and the feeling of dizziness will go away. You might also enjoy the sight of the fountains when they are illuminated...." Smiling down at her dangerously, he added in a softer voice: "Perhaps they might remind you of Rome? And if you do *not* come with me willingly then I will carry you if I have to, *cara! I* don't give a damn about gossip; but in your case...?"

She hardly needed his caustic reminder to make her realize that he was right, of course—and that *she,* being a female, would be the only one to be stigmatized by society if he carried out his threat. And in that case she would lose all the ground she had gained with such careful planning and slowness. *Damn* him! Alexa thought, trying valiantly to keep her head instead of exploding with rage. If she could only manage to concentrate her thoughts upon finding out what he wanted of her and exactly how much of a *threat* he could prove to be... In any case, it would never do to let him imagine she was *afraid* of him!

The conservatory opened out onto a covered terrace at one end, with steps leading down from there into a sylvan setting of lawns and shrubbery and shade trees. Rustic paths led to small groves with fountains splashing into lily ponds, or to marble gazebos surrounded by miniature moats crossed by pretty wooden bridges. At any other time, and with a different companion, Alexa would have enjoyed inspecting all the marvels she had heard so much of; but on this occasion she felt nothing but dismay when her first feeling of relief at seeing so many others on the small terrace was soon dispelled as she was practically *forced* down the steps and along a winding pathway screened by shrubbery with only dim illumination provided by lanterns hung from some of the trees.

"*Everyone* was staring at us, and God knows what they must be thinking! Will you *stop!* I cannot possibly walk as fast as you can, and... You don't have to *drag* me along! I don't want to go any further. Do you hear me?"

Where was he taking her? He must be quite insane, and so was she to have allowed herself to be intimidated by his threats. Alexa found herself gasping for breath and was quite incapable of speech by the time he paused at last; having forced her to walk across a damp stretch of grass that had probably ruined her thin dancing shoes as well as the hem of her gown. And it was *dark* here—with not even the dim glow of lantern light to see by.

By this time she might easily have fallen if he had not continued to hold her by the arm, as he had when he led her across the terrace and down all those steps, and then around the waist as well, once he had got her away from the curious stares. But *why?* Why had he done this? To drag *her* out here so publicly, when he was expected to marry Helen; and do so under Helen's haughty nose at that! If she had any spirit at all she would never agree to marry him *now!*

Perhaps the stream of jumbled thoughts that kept her mind so busy with unanswerable questions had been meant to barricade her from the kind of weakness she had given way to before. Or if he had not been so despicable as to take unfair advantage of the fact that she was hardly capable of *breathing,* let alone protesting, when he…

She must have come close to fainting and instinctively reached for support, Alexa thought dazedly some moments later. Why else would she be clinging to his shoulders? Her lips felt bruised from the punishing brutality of the kisses he had inflicted on her, and her breasts still tingled painfully from the roughly familiar way he had handled them. And she had *let* him! As sanity came back her clinging hands became fists that beat at him before he caught her wrists and forced them down and behind her back while he jerked her stiffly resisting body against his in the same motion; holding her pinioned there in spite of her furious demands that he release her this very instant or she would…she would…

"Would you really have the courage to scream and bring everyone running?" he inquired interestedly, pressing her even closer as if he actually enjoyed her useless struggles to free herself. "What will you tell them, I wonder?" And then, as if to taunt her even further, Nicholas bent his head and began to plant light, teasing kisses everywhere on her face, even while she twisted her head back and forth.

Alexa felt his lips burn her temples, her forehead, her cheeks and the corners of her mouth. Such falsely tender kisses he gave her, even while his hold on her wrists tightened so ruthlessly each time she attempted to free them, that she felt he might easily break them without scruple.

Almost sobbing with a mixture of rage and chagrin, she was forced into *pleading* with him to set her free.

"Don't! Please—haven't you done enough already? You have probably quite ruined my reputation as it is; was that your intention when you *forced* me out here with you? Must you continue to inflict further cruelties upon me to satisfy some warped side of your nature? You were *always* cruel towards me! Does it give you *pleasure* to inflict hurt and pain on a helpless woman? Is that one of the traits you possess in common with the Dameron whose title you hope to inherit some day, my Lord Viscount?"

There was a curious rigidity to his body that Alexa could not help but notice with a tinge of fear; and at the end of her angrily impulsive speech she could have sworn she heard the breath hiss between his teeth before he said in a curiously soft voice that made her even more apprehensive, "So you think that Newbury and I are much alike, do you? I find it interesting that you should think so! Or that you should know so much and yet so little. *Christ!*" The sudden fury in his voice made Alexa flinch, and the next moment she stumbled backward as he released her so suddenly that she might easily have fallen if she had not felt herself brought up short by a tree at her back. She wanted to run and knew she should run, but he stood there before her, close enough for her to almost feel the heat of his body yet not touching her this time. Forcing her to stand there and *listen* while he went on in a tone of barely leashed violence: "If you had any realization of all the different kinds of pain and degradation and abuse that can be and are inflicted on some human beings by others in the name of 'pleasure,' I do not think you'd have dared make your whining, hypocritical little complaints to me of cruelty and the infliction of pain—unless you meant it as a challenge? I understand that there are some women who actually enjoy such treatment. Is that what you need for *your* pleasure? Should I have slapped you instead of kissing you? Or used a whip on you before I took you for the first time—a virgin whore! Who could have expected it? Had you stayed longer you might have proved yourself worth the exorbitant price you put on your maidenhead, my sweet Lady Travers! And had I found you after you had run away that morning I might indeed have been sorely tempted to beat you, and would have taken a great deal of pleasure in doing so too! In fact, now that you've put the idea into my head..."

"Stop it! I don't want to hear any more!" Involuntarily, Alexa pressed her hands over her ears to cut off the sound of his drawling, sarcastic voice and the import of his words; but in spite of that she heard his harshly mocking laugh and his next words as well. "No? I had not thought that a *lady* given to frequenting bawdy houses could be either surprised or shocked by anything! But perhaps you've had some unpleasant experiences since our last meeting—besides losing a husband and gaining a fortune?"

"No!" Alexa said. "No, I won't stay to be cut to pieces by you in this way, damn you!" With a sudden agility born of sheer desperation she reacted like a cornered animal, taking Nicholas by surprise as she ducked under an overhanging branch and began to run—neither knowing nor caring that it was dark and she did not know her way.

"Alexa!" The angry sound of his voice, using her name for the first time, only made her lift up her skirts even higher in order to run even faster, regardless of shrubs that tore at her silk stockings and stones that bruised her feet. If only she could escape from him and the threat and the torment he represented! And for the first time she realized how it felt to be hunted instead of being the hunter; filled with almost mindless terror at the thought of being slowly and inexorably gained upon and far too frightened to turn her head and look back in case he might be there just behind her.

Run—run—run! Words pounding in her head in time with the blood pulsing in her temples and the trip-hammer beat of her heart. She was beyond reason by now and driven by purely primitive instinct alone. And when her headlong flight was abruptly halted by an arm around her waist, hauling her backward and almost off her feet, Alexa's choked scream of terror was just as instinctive as her desperate efforts to tear herself free.

"No—no! Let me go, let me *go!*"

"Stop fighting me like a damned wildcat then, and I will! What in hell got into you? If I hadn't caught up with you in time you'd have run right into a stream, you foolish, headstrong little..." Needing both his hands to hold her still and prevent her from clawing at him, there was only one way to stop her hysterical screeching, Nicholas thought grimly as he jammed his mouth down over hers. She was a bitch of the worst kind and a virago into the bargain, in addition to being a born whore. And he should have taught her a lesson by cutting her in public as if he'd never met her before or had forgotten that he had. But no—damn his own weakness—he'd allowed himself to yield to a senseless impulse and had led her down into the garden so that he could kiss her soft, corrupt, lying lips again—and again!

"I suppose I must look a frightful *mess!*" Alexa said after a while. "But I daresay *you* do too! How on earth shall we face everybody now? They are all probably *waiting* on the terrace until we return..."

"A second reception line. Do you think the Queen and Prince Albert will be there as well?"

"I cannot be sure about *them,*" Alexa returned thoughtfully before adding, "but I *am* sure that Lady Helen will be quite anxious by this time, aren't you?"

"And so will your devoted Lord Charles, I suppose; not to mention all your other admirers; I consider myself lucky that duels are no longer in fashion." The familiar caustic note had returned to Nicholas's voice, although Alexa pretended to ignore it as she tried to keep her tone light.

"I don't suppose *I* shall be quite as lucky in avoiding unpleasant consequences as you are, since I'm not a *man*. *You* will get the sly winks and ribald comments from your friends, and *I* will be considered a fallen woman, no doubt." She gave a rather shaky laugh. "At any rate I can console myself with the fact that I am *rich,* I suppose. And that I can live wherever I please and do whatever I please without worrying about *conventions* any longer!"

"I had no idea that you ever did," Nicholas said drily. "Swimming naked in the moonlight and frequenting bordellos for amusement...?"

"Oh, *stop* before you become nasty and *cutting* and make me hate you all over again!" Alexa had been content to stroll slowly with his arm encircling her waist and holding her close to his side, as if that last kiss that had held them locked together in a kind of spell had actually transformed them into lovers. But now she made an angry attempt to pull free, only to be thwarted when he swung her body before his and forcibly lifted her stubborn chin with one hand to make her face him.

"Did I actually manage to persuade you to *stop* hating me for a few minutes? You should tell me how I achieved such a miracle so that I can try to repeat it."

It was only after he had kissed her very thoroughly again and they had resumed their leisurely walk that Alexa thought to ask if he had any idea of where he was taking her *this* time.

"It must be getting quite late. Oh *dear!*" she said with belated concern for her unfortunate chaperones, who must by now be searching for her everywhere. And as to *their* reactions and the reactions of everyone else when they saw her disheveled appearance and drew their conclusions...well, *that* was something she was not ready to think of just yet.

In spite of her attitude of careless bravado, Alexa could not help hanging back when she saw the lights ahead of them. "Perhaps it might be best if I could go straight home. You could tell everyone that I had a fainting fit and you did not know what else to do. I really do not think that I..."

"We are going back to the house through a side door that leads directly into one of the guest apartments," Nicholas said as if he had not heard her fainthearted protests. "We can tidy ourselves in there before we go back to face the rest of the assembly and pretend we returned to the house almost at once by another route and have been here all along. Unless you prefer to have developed a headache that necessitated your lying down to rest for a while?"

34

It was inevitable, of course, that there would be gossip and even outright speculation as to how well Viscount Embry and the rich and recently widowed Lady Travers knew each other and for how long. And was it not *strange,* went some of the whispers over tea and dainty sandwiches and petit fours, that so many people had observed the couple leave off dancing to walk quite openly down to admire the garden, and no one could remember seeing them *return?*

"I *did* notice that Embry danced with the oldest Dameron girl. Lady Helen, is it? But that was quite some time afterwards, of course!"

"Can't say that I remember seeing Lady Travers during the early part of the evening either, not until we were ready to leave and all waiting for our carriages. Last time I saw her before *then* was with Atherton's younger son, Viscount Deering. Understand he's paying court in that direction."

"Adelina allows it?"

"My dear—Lady Travers was presented to Adelina, and did *not* receive one of her setdowns. Everyone was *waiting* for it of course, and you cannot imagine the surprise…!"

"*I* was most surprised when I heard that Newbury of

all people had condescended to be almost *agreeable!* Now *that,* you must agree, is quite unusual!''

Adelina, Dowager Marchioness of Newbury, was aware of all the whispers and all the sly questions that were being asked, for she had long made it a habit to be aware of *everything* in case she might be able to make use of some tidbit of gossip or information. Like a spider, she spun her webs, keeping in touch with her old ''friends'' and acquaintances only because they might prove useful to her some day. She had always despised the same gossips she milked dry while remaining contemptuously detached; and she had always made whatever decisions she felt she needed to make quickly and definitely and without stupid qualms. But now for the first time she was nonplussed; and the thought infuriated her enough to cause her to pace restlessly before the open window that looked out over the square to the house opposite—the one belonging to the very creature who was the cause of her present mood.

The Dowager almost snorted aloud. Lady Travers indeed! If poor John had become senile enough before he died to imagine that his fortune and name were enough to transform a chit of a girl into an adversary capable of matching wits with *her,* why then it was a pity he could not have lived long enough to find out how deluded he was. Just as deluded as he must have been all those years ago to imagine that she might still want him even after he was no longer a man. Her lips curled contemptuously at the memory. Silly fool! But then, so were most men, as she had discovered very early. When she had taken lovers it had only been to use them for her own pleasure; as and when she pleased. And none of them had ever guessed how easily she had led them to do her will and to serve her.

But the past was the past, and something had to be done *now* about John's widow before her hints became threats and she succeeded in causing an ugly scandal—which was her intention, no doubt, if John had tutored her. Her granddaughter? The Dowager stared thoughtfully out of the window. Whether she was or not made no difference at all to *her,* and why should it? Gavin had always been a romantically minded weakling, with his infatuations for poetry and Byron and women. He had been a whining, clinging child she had detested, and he had turned into exactly the kind of man she had expected. She might have ignored, if not tolerated, his marriage to that silly young French creature if he had not compounded his stupidity by getting a daughter by her and then chasing after Byron to Greece, where typically he had succeeded in getting himself captured instead of killed. There had been ransom notes. How she had laughed as she tore them up and tossed them in the fire, thinking that perhaps the hospitality of the Turks might teach him something of life's realities. But then… Ah, the cursed Fates! Embry, her strong, golden son had irritated her by dying and leaving Gavin the only surviving heir.

There was a desk in front of the window, and Adelina sat down abruptly, feeling the treacherous weakness in her legs. Damn old age! Damn her body for submitting to what her mind was not ready to admit! Her fingers played with a silver paper knife, sharper-edged than most. Gavin—who could only beget girls and had been all but turned into one himself by the Turks, who enjoyed young striplings more than they did women. At least he'd been ready to accept every one of her dictates after he had been returned. And he had accepted everything she had told him about his wife and their child. Such tragic deaths she had made up for them! Nothing left to chance. The brat was not to be told anything—she should have been safely married off to some planter by now and breeding brats of her own. There had been more than enough money to make sure of everything. There was *still* a regular sum of money deposited to the account of Martin Howard, which must be stopped, of course. Adelina remembered the girl's words that night of the Sutherlands' ball. "I am said to take after my grandmother; they say she's a witch." Ah yes, she remembered being called *that* too!

Still playing with her paper knife, the Dowager Marchioness frowned abstractedly. Get rid of her! As subtly as possible of course. And as quickly as possible. A pity that it couldn't have happened the other night, but there were other alternatives. Madame Olivier—*la belle tante?* Did the niece know? Her grandson, Charles—smitten by the woman or her fortune? Nicholas—ah, *he* was the only puzzle remaining for the moment—he, and his relationship with Lady Travers. But if there *was* a relationship between the two, she would find out, for the people she paid to follow them both were the best in that kind of business, and she had used them before. *Gavin?* Suddenly the Marchioness began to chuckle soundlessly to herself. Ah, yes—*Gavin.* And why not? The ultimate weapon in her hands. Charles—or Gavin. Or *both?* And as for Nicholas, he must marry Helen as soon as possible so that both she and the gossips might forget how openly and humiliatingly he had neglected her at the ball last week. In fact, the announcement of their engagement should be made at Helen's ball here. So many different situations might be arranged!

The old Marchioness was still at the window when she noticed that one of the carriages had been brought around to the front of the house that had occupied so much of her attention of late. Ah! So she had finally decided to venture abroad again, had she? And high time too!

Ironically enough, Lady Margery had said almost the same thing to Alexa the previous day. "My dear, it is quite *unlike* you to hide away from things, I cannot help feeling.

And your excuse of having contracted a slight cold and fever cannot serve you for too much longer, unless you decide to be dramatic enough to claim you have consumption. Do come and visit me at least, if you are bored with riding in the park, and we will think of something different to do."

Lady Margery was a dear, sweet soul, and she was perfectly right, of course, Alexa thought as she settled herself against the velvet cushions of the carriage. She had been a coward hiding behind excuses in the safety of her room, and it had done her no good since she could not escape from her thoughts.

"Oh, my lady! I've never seen so many letters and cards in my whole life! And the flowers and baskets of fruit and ladies and gentlemen coming to call on you... Why, even Mr. Bowles had to agree with me that *he's* never seen the like before!" Bridget had sounded quite awed as she brought all the calling cards and notes upstairs each day. And each day there had been the engraved card she had dreaded even when she had come to expect it—accompanying bloodred roses. "Newbury" was all the card said; and before she threw it into the fire and consigned the roses to Bridget, she would always look at it and shudder; remembering all she had been told about him and the strangely unexpected way they had met.

That memory always began with Nicholas Dameron, Viscount Embry—whom she was vastly better off not thinking about. There was a purely sensual, physical attraction between them that neither of them could deny and which was surely the best reason in the world for them to stay away from each other. *He,* at least, had made that clear when having "rescued" her from the awkward situation into which he'd been inconsiderate enough to put her in the first place, he had not only devoted all his attention to Lady Helen for the rest of the night but had made a point of avoiding Alexa as well. He was hateful, as she should have *remembered,* even if he *had* helped her with smoothing out her hair and her gown while he reassured her far too glibly that it was a *friend* of his who occupied the particular suite of rooms they had positively sneaked into, and she wouldn't mind it in the least if Alexa used her comb or her brush. *She!* And he knew exactly where the private entrance was and that the door would be left unlocked. It was only by exercising every ounce of willpower that Alexa kept herself from making several sarcastic comments, especially when he did not bother to pretend that he did not know where everything was kept.

It was Embry's suggestion that they leave the room separately and that he should go first to make sure there was no one about who might notice. And all he did afterwards was to stick his head back in the door and point in the direction where he said he had just seen Lady Margery. Having done what he must have considered selfishly to be his "duty," he had obviously ceased to concern himself with her or the thought that she might lose her way.

How could she have had any idea of how enormous and *rambling* Stafford House was, or how many rooms and corridors running into each other there might be? It had not taken Alexa very long to discover that she was hopelessly lost and might *never* find her way back unless she was fortunate enough to run into a servant or another guest.

How *thankful* she had felt when she had heard the faint sounds of music at last! Leaning her head back with her eyes closed, Alexa heard her own shuddering sigh before she breathed in deeply again. She had even thought she heard voices at last and had hurried forward, pausing before a set of double doors which she knew must lead into the ballroom with a sudden feeling of awkwardness as she pictured a sea of faces turning to study her and judge her when she walked in alone. And if she was asked questions, what were her answers to be?

A sudden sound (a muffled sob, a door opening and closing?) had made Alexa whirl about nervously, suddenly as tense as a cat in unfamiliar surroundings. And that was when she had found herself alone and face to face with her natural father, the Marquess of Newbury. How odd that, in spite of having at the time to fight back an irrational urge to turn and flee from his stoney-blue eyes that flickered over her without depth or expression, she could still remember every detail of his appearance; from his crimson and gold brocade waistcoat to the diamond buttons down his ruffled shirtfront and the diamond stickpin in his cravat.

"Forgive me if I startled you, but I did not expect..." Alexa must have made some slight movement of retreat that suddenly brought her directly under one of the gaslights, for it seemed to her as if his eyes had suddenly become riveted to her hair in a strangely concentrated manner that made her unaccountably nervous, so that she felt impelled to rush into speech.

"I...I had retired for a few moments and was foolish enough to get myself lost, I am afraid. I..."

"We have not been formally introduced, but your husband and I were once close friends. He was Sir John Travers? I am Newbury."

It was easy afterwards to think of how she might have responded, but to have said, "I am Alexa, your daughter by your *legal* wife, Victorine," would have been too hopelessly melodramatic, especially considering the circumstances and the occasion. And in any case, she had been caught quite unprepared. Alexa's slight nod of acknowledgment must have sufficed, and whatever else she *might* have thought of to say went unsaid as a positive *gush* of ladies burst through the doors at that moment in search of one of the retiring rooms that had been set aside for guests wishing to tidy themselves. From their looks it was obvious what conclusions they had leaped to immediately, and in fact one elaborately bejeweled matron went as far as to say brightly, "Why, my dear Lady Travers! *Here* you are after all, and I have just told Lady Margery that I saw you walk into the gardens with..." Her falsely apologetic trill of laughter had been interrupted by the Marquess saying in his smooth, cold voice that he had had the honor to show Lady Travers the Tapestry Room while they spoke of her late husband, who had been a very close friend of his. And after that Alexa had no option but to accept both his proffered arm and his escort into the Great Hall.

Newbury! Even on this unseasonably warm afternoon Alexa shivered slightly. For some reason she felt unnerved by both the Marquess himself and his strange actions. He was pursuing her, with his cards and his roses the color of blood, but coldly and dispassionately. Why? Alexa thought she knew enough about men by now to feel sure he had no feelings of *sexual* desire for her; so that if he paid her such assiduous attention it was for some *other* reason.

The carriage made slow progress along the crowded streets, where the noise of clattering traffic was sometimes unbearable, and the occupants of several other carriages remarked that poor Lady Travers *did* look as if she had been ill. That pallor! And she had appeared to be asleep in spite of the din. After those pitying remarks the ladies would usually fall to discussing with relish the latest *whispers* about Lady Travers and her many admirers. Viscount Deering, who had seemed to have the advantage until his cousin *Embry* had suddenly appeared on the scene. *Newbury* (that cold fish!) was supposed to send her flowers every day while poor Lady Iris pretended to know nothing, and the Dowager Marchioness of all people had actually invited Lady Travers to the ball she was giving for Newbury's oldest daughter! Everyone was cadging for invitations, of course, avidly waiting to observe everything At First Hand.

Alexa was by no means asleep, though she kept her eyes closed on purpose so that she would not have to spend every minute bowing or smiling at some acquaintance whose carriage had drawn abreast of hers instead of concentrating on what she should do next. Her hands clenched on her lap as she thought of Newbury—a man who enjoyed making women suffer. Was it possible that he *knew* who she was and how much of a threat she could prove to be to his career, his reputation and his present family? And if so… Oh, God, no! Alexa thought almost wearily. So many *possibilities,* and she had been over every one of them too many times already. Why do so again? All she should ponder was the thought that since *she* was a danger to them, then *they* could very well prove a danger to her. Hadn't she been warned by everyone? No, she could not and must not trust any one of them, not even Charles, who had always been unfailingly kind and pleasant to her. And certainly not Nicholas, who had called almost daily at the Dowager's house across the square where *Helen* happened to be staying, without *once* having the courtesy to call or drop his card off at *her* house. Not that she would have *seen* him, of course, Alexa reminded herself severely. In fact, she would much rather *not* have to meet him again.

In all likelihood, Alexa thought with silent, bitter laughter, he and the old witch together are planning how to get rid of me! Why, she would never have consented to dance with Nicholas if the old witch had not almost forced her into it; and it had probably been all planned between them that he would take Alexa into the garden and then… But he *had* taken her safely back to the house afterwards and had even tried to be quite *pleasant* to her for a change, not that that lasted! And he'd had no right to give her those dark, contemptuous looks just because she was obliged to dance once with Newbury.

With an impatient sigh Alexa sat up straighter and opened her eyes, observing with relief that she was almost at her destination. Since carriages were not permitted in Burlington Arcade and had to wait some distance away, Alexa soon found herself on her own as she strolled casually by all the boutiques with their treasure-trove windows that tempted customers inside. Almost *anything* one could think of could be purchased in the Arcade, from daring books in French at Jeff's Bookshop to boots and shoes, snuffboxes and filigree work, and wonderfully trimmed bonnets in all the latest styles. And of all the little millinery shops the most elegant by far was known as "Milady's," where every aristocratic visitor could request to be shown to a small private room with an assistant to wait upon her and help her try on all the very latest styles in bonnets and trimmings and decorations to be worn in the hair at evening functions. As Alexa pushed open the door a tiny silver bell tinkled overhead to summon Madame Louise, who always appeared immediately, her usual smile deepening when she recognized a regular customer.

"Ah! Milady Travers, such a pleasure always! And today especially, when I 'ave so many new creations to show. Some are just arrived from Paris, and these I *must* show to you myself for even *I* find them so chic, so out of the ordinary! And you would like your usual wine and some biscuits for refreshment? Ah, *oui*... and here is Hortense, who will see to everything while I shall take you upstairs to one of the larger rooms. You do not mind the stairs, I hope?"

Following Louise up a set of stairs carpeted in red plush that matched the curtains, Alexa did not feel the need to say anything at all until Louise had shown her into a comfortable room that was furnished like a parlor except for a red and gold patterned curtain drawn across the back of the room. "I will bring in the refreshments myself, and the hats; and I will make sure that you will not be disturbed," Louise whispered as she unlocked the door and let Alexa in. "And please to ring the bell if you should desire anything and I will come myself. The key, milady."

The door safely locked, Alexa had barely turned back to the room when the curtains were drawn apart to reveal another part of what must be an extremely large chamber, this particular section furnished as a bedroom, with a canopied and curtained bed, an elaborately mirrored dressing table, and two comfortable-looking chairs set on either side of a marble-topped table.

"I wondered if you had arrived already," Alexa said without surprise as she went forward to greet her aunt. "You look well, Tante Solange."

"*Tante* indeed! The way you look today we could easily pass as sisters! And *I,* my dear, had barely two hours' sleep last night." Solange's eyes studied Alexa with a professionally critical scrutiny. "I would not think that *you* have slept very much either. So?"

Alexa decided to be blunt. "The reason for my begging to see you? It is—Newbury. Ever since the night of the Sutherlands' ball he has been sending me red roses each day, accompanied only by his card. It's begun to worry me! I wondered if *you* might know what it means with him, if it means anything; or if..." Alexa had sat down opposite her aunt, but now she sprang up as if she could no longer contain herself and began to walk back and forth while she continued in a suppressed kind of voice, "If you might be able to advise me as to how...as to what I should do about it."

35

"If you will remember, my dear, I had warned you at our first meeting to be extremely careful. Do you think that because of your money and your position *you* could not be made to disappear 'mysteriously'? Best stay close to only those you can trust, and tell that lawyer of yours everything. Let *them* know it. And never forget either that she is probably having you followed."

It had been *that* part of her aunt's speech that had startled her most. *"Followed?"* Alexa echoed incredulously, and Solange lifted both shoulders before she gestured wearily with the cheroot she had just lit up.

"For God's sake, I should be disappointed to learn that you still retain some traces of *naiveté!* Followed—of course! There are people who make a profession of it. And there is no doubt that *she* would like to find out exactly what you are up to. In fact, I can imagine very well that the old witch would love to know if you and I have discovered each other's existence or have met. So you understand now—the precautions? Although…" and Solange had suddenly given a bawdy chuckle, "…I have been thinking that if you found my friend Orlanda's house interesting you might find *my* establishment even more so.

Perhaps I can arrange for a secret visit if you would care for it?"

In the end, although her aunt had not been able to tell her much more than she already had about the Marquess of Newbury, Alexa had learned a great many other interesting things besides the warning that she was probably being followed wherever she went.

Item: Solange had left by the private entrance, and for the sake of discretion Alexa was making a show of trying on bonnets between sips of wine. Wearing one particularly outrageous creation of grey ruched silk and feathers, she pulled a face at her reflection in the mirror. Item: all the rich and fashionable men visited Madame Olivier's establishment or rented private apartments from her for their secret assignations with *ladies.* The Viscount Deering particularly enjoyed virgins or demi-vierges and the Viscount *Embry* preferred older and more experienced women, usually blondes. The disgusting *libertine!* Alexa thought viciously and almost jabbed herself with a hatpin. By the time she left, she had spent far too much money on five bonnets that she might never wear, including the grey silk she had not even liked.

Trailed by one of Madame Louise's errand boys who was loaded down by hatboxes, Alexa found her steps becoming slower as she wondered if all the little millinery boutiques had private rooms upstairs for daytime use by those who needed a certain kind of privacy and could afford to pay for it. Private. Secret. How many secrets were *really* secrets? Pausing in front of one particular shop window that displayed rather daring books published in France, Alexa smiled to herself, wondering if every woman who visited the little millinery stores wondered about the others there. Perhaps whoever might have followed her to Milady's would wonder too if she had gone there for new bonnets or to meet a lover. About to move on, Alexa suddenly caught sight of the novel *Lelia* by George Sand, which she had not been able to find before. Ignoring the looks she received from two dowagers who happened to be passing, Alexa commanded the patient boy to wait for her and stepped boldly into the store, which was frequented almost entirely by men, only to be sorry she had done so a few moments later when she saw who was there. "Speak of the devil..." The old saying suddenly filled her mind as she inclined her head slightly before giving her attention to the clerk behind the counter and telling him exactly which book she had come to purchase in a brisk, matter-of-fact voice.

"Fashionable bonnets and French novels. A creature of opposites. Are you quite recovered from your cold?"

"Lord Embry! How very *kind* of you to inquire!" Having given him a forced smile that matched the tone of her voice, Alexa was happy of the chance to turn back to the clerk. "Thank you. That *is* exactly the book I am looking for. If you would be kind enough to inform me of the cost...?" She might have known, Alexa thought bitterly in the next instant, that he would not allow her to escape him so easily.

With a manner of easy familiarity that made her grit her teeth with rage, he reached across the counter to pick up her book and study it with a tilt of one dark brow. "George Sand? Surely you cannot be one of *her* followers? Somehow, I would have imagined that you would prefer a different type of novel."

"Indeed, my lord? I can only hope that your *imagination* did not picture me enthralled by the novels of Mrs. Gore, for instance. But then, there's no accounting for the tastes of different individuals, is there?" Alexa could only hope that both her voice and her attitude conveyed nothing more than cold indifference to his opinions, even while she wondered if he meant to continue fencing with her. To her relief, however, he tossed the book down on the counter with an irritatingly casual shrug before observing that if there was *one* thing he had learned it was that a gentleman never attempted to argue with a *lady.* She had not quite liked the unnecessary emphasis he had given that last word, and her brows drew together loweringly while she hunted for some suitable cutting retort; but at that moment a rotund little man emerged from some dusty corner bearing a large parcel that was neatly done up with brown paper and string and ornamented by several large red blobs of sealing wax.

"It's the books his Lordship the Marquess ordered last month, my lord—the rare editions. I hesitate to *send* them over in view of their value, my lord, but he did tell me most specifically that he wished to have them *at once*—in fact, the very day they arrived! So when I learned that Lord *Embry* was here I thought I might dare take the liberty of inquiring… That is…"

Happy that Embry's attention was directed elsewhere for a change, Alexa made haste to complete *her* purchase, wishing that the clerk who waited on her had not insisted almost indignantly that milady could not possibly walk out of the store with a book that was not nicely done up with paper and string. It was a *rule* and he had to abide by it or lose the position he had held for the past five years. And after all that, he was snail-slow into the bargain, and Alexa's foot began to tap angrily as she kept her eyes fixed in the direction of the door she longed to go through, pretending she could not overhear the conversation between Embry and that funny, gnomelike little man.

"To save you any further embarrassed stutters and apologies, Milliken, I'll take the damn books along with me and make sure that they are delivered to the Marquess and none other. And for God's sake spare me your thanks as well! I wouldn't do it unless it was convenient, as you well know.''

''Ah, your Lordship is too kind, too condescending. And I also meant to ask, of course, if your Lordship found everything that your Lordship was looking for upstairs? All was to your satisfaction? If there is any—um—particular edition your Lordship might wish me to find, in *any* language, I am sure I shall be able to oblige.''

What an oddly *obscure* kind of speech that had been, Alexa thought as she almost snatched up the small package the clerk handed to her grudgingly and made purposefully for the door. *Not* that it interested her in the *least,* even when Embry had deliberately lowered his voice before replying and there had been some talk of money paid by the month or every quarter. Not for books, surely? She could not see Nicholas of all people as a collector of rare editions.

''Do you happen to have your carriage waiting?'' Alexa had been so occupied with her thoughts that to hear his voice at her side startled her into a gasp before she recovered sufficiently to shoot him a coldly suspicious look, which he returned with a bland smile she found quite unusual for *him,* unless of course he had some devious objective in mind.

''If you meant to be kind enough to offer me conveyance back home, my lord, I must thank you for your consideration, but I did travel here in my own carriage, which is just…''

''What a stroke of luck! I hadn't realized how infernally *heavy* books can be, and I left my horse stabled several streets away. I was wondering in fact if you might not mind taking me in *your* carriage? You could set me down in Belgrave Square if that is the most convenient for you, for I had planned to call on Belle-Mère in any case. Ah,

Lady Acton! Always a pleasure. And you've met Lady Travers, of course?''

Alexa had no chance to say anything at all in reply to his aggravatingly impudent speech before they had come face to face with one of the *worst* gossips that Lady Margery had warned her against, one of the bulging-eyed matrons, in fact, who had caught her standing alone with Newbury in the corridor. Trailed by her two younger children and their subdued-looking governess, Lady Acton gave Alexa a smile that reminded her of a crocodile, while her sharp brown eyes went curiously from Embry to Alexa and back again. And since she had halted, they had no choice but to do the same as Lady Acton said archly: ''Ah! Been shopping, I see! But you must not worry—I will not ask for what and for whom. And I am so happy to see Lady Travers *quite* recovered from her cold. My dear, we have *all* worried about you, you know, and have missed seeing you riding in the Row. Shall we see you at the ball for dear Helen? But how silly of me to ask. Of course you will be there! *Such suspense!*'' Lady Acton gave an exaggerated sigh before she moved her gimlet gaze from Alexa's face to her companion's. ''I imagine that everyone is wondering the same thing. Will that particular night be the exciting occasion when a certain announcement we have all been waiting for is made at last? Such a lovely, well-mannered girl, and such a *perfect* choice. Even Acton said so, and he does not usually comment. Don't *you* agree with me, Lady Travers?''

''Oh *yes!* I've said the same thing myself, dear Lady Acton. The perfect choice, the perfect *match!*'' Ignoring Lady Acton's rather startled look, Alexa managed a guileless smile and widened her eyes before she added confidingly, ''But you know how *slow* men can be sometimes!''

''And I suppose that was meant to be another of your subtle feminine reprimands, my sweet Alexa?'' Before she could recover or utter any protest, Alexa felt her arm taken and gripped in a manner that warned her against her first instinctive impulse to wrench it away. Then Nicholas Dameron said in the same lazy drawl: "I'm sure it is safe to confide in as discreet a friend as *you* are, Lady Acton, that Lady Travers has been taking full advantage of being my close friend and confidante to subject me to almost daily sermons and advice on the very same topic." Even Lady Acton, her mouth slightly open, seemed incapable of speech for once as he continued with smooth hypocrisy that made Alexa take a deep breath of barely suppressed fury: "Ah, I had been hoping to find an ally in *you* at least, but since I find myself outnumbered by all you ladies who have decided I must become affianced very soon to a paragon of all the feminine virtues, how can a mere male argue? I can only hope that I will not disappoint your expectations!"

The hypocritical, despicable *bastard!* Searching in her mind for words, Alexa could find none that were sufficiently *descriptive* enough as she was forced, by the warning pressure of his fingers biting into the soft flesh of her arm, to stand there at his side with an artificial smile pasted onto her face while she heard him say that he was *sure* Lady Acton would excuse them both for the moment—he had promised to deliver Lady Travers *and* her new bonnets to Belgrave Square within the hour.

By the time he had handed her with a falsely overdone politeness into her carriage and had joined her in it, Alexa could feel herself almost bursting with pent-up fury. If not for *convention,* if not for the throngs of people in Burlington Arcade, if not for the presence of her coachman and footman when they had found her carriage, why, she would have told him to find himself a hansom or to *walk,* for all she cared! And the memory of Lady Acton's *face* as they had walked away… Oh God! How *could* he have said what he did? Lady Acton—one of the *worst* gossips in town!

No sooner had they started off than she turned on him like one of the Furies, her voice positively trembling with the force of her righteous anger. "Do you have any idea of what you *said?* Of what she might have *thought,* for God's sake? Lady Acton is… That *look* on her face when you said in that particular tone of voice… Do you know that you must be *mad?* Do you realize what you might have… What your *fiancée* might… What… That *look!* She was quite *speechless!* Her…" While attempting to control herself, Alexa caught Lord Embry's squinted look and wicked, almost little-boy grin by some mischance and broke into laughter, totally incapable of further speech. Each time she started to *recover,* the memory of that particular *look* on poor Lady Acton's face was enough to send her into more fits of hysterical laughter, until, inevitably, she could hardly breathe and tears streamed down her face.

Whenever she laughed too hard, Alexa would always develop the hiccups, and it was impossible to try to act *dignified* when one had the hiccups! It was the only reason, of course, for her not being able to either protest or *wrest* herself away when she suddenly became aware that Lord Embry was no longer sitting opposite her in the carriage but beside her instead, and worse still, was holding her in his arms with a degree of familiarity that was quite uncalled for.

In broad *daylight* on *Regent Street* with all the usual traffic that crowded it! If she could only fall into a swoon as easily and conveniently as some women seemed able to, Alexa would have done so with relief. Having driven her into hysterics, he could at least have shown enough consideration to draw the curtains over the carriage windows. But no. And by this evening not only Lady Acton but the rest of fashionable society would doubtless be buzzing with rumor and speculation and outright gossip. Unbearable! Especially since *he* did not seem at all concerned, Alexa thought angrily as she made a belated attempt to free herself, protesting in choked whispers.

"There was no need—to take advantage of... Stop!"

"You would have fallen off your seat if I had not kept you from doing so, you stubborn, silly... And since all I am attempting to do is dry your face with my last clean handkerchief—dammit!—you might as well stop gasping like a beached fish and keep *still;* do you hear me?" His voice was as grimly uncompromising as the ruthless manner in which he scrubbed at Alexa's face until her cheeks felt sore, and she almost cried again from sheer frustration and rage.

"A...a beached... How dare you! And I wasn't *gasping*, I was... Stop it, before you take all the skin off my face, you brute! Ohh...!" Alexa's voice had risen to a wail of exasperation when she became suddenly aware of the interested looks they were receiving from another carriage that had come up alongside hers. Not only the twin Viscounts Selby and Rowell but their formidable mother the Duchess—her lorgnette raised—and their two younger nieces Ianthe and Philippa as well. *Helen's* sisters who were also *her* half sisters Alexa thought, and almost began to laugh uncontrollably again at the looks on all of their faces.

She must have made some choked sound in her throat as her dilating eyes went back to meet Lord Embry's narrowed regard once more, for he said in a casually interested tone of voice, "Are you *often* subject to, er—strange fits of this nature? And is there any known cure for them?" But there was nothing either casual or even civilized about the way the green of his eyes seemed to darken as they dwelt upon her mouth; nor about the way his fingers tilted up her chin just before he kissed her, giving her no chance to speak or to resist as the arm that had been about her waist tightened so savagely as to almost cut off her breath.

"I *say,* what a collection of new bonnets and boots! There, on the other side of the street? Did you notice, Mama?" Roger, Viscount Selby, was as usual a little quicker in recovering his wits than his brother Myles. But unfortunately his youngest niece Philippa was not only observant but possessed of a particularly piercing voice as well, almost drowning out his attempt at being tactful.

"Isn't that *Embry?* But *I* thought he was supposed to marry Helen and *that* was why Belle-Mère is giving a ball—to announce their engagement!"

"Of course it isn't *Embry!*" Myles said in a pooh-poohing kind of voice that immediately made Philippa glare at him balefully before he added pacifically, "Don't you want to see all the new things in the shopwindows, Pippa? You *said* you did earlier, y'know."

His heart sank, however, when his mother raised her lorgnette before saying in her most *forbidding* tones, "That *is* Lady Travers—I am positive of *that* much at least, for one cannot mistake her *hair!* But as to the other *person* who is with her, one cannot quite..."

"But it *is* Embry, Grandmama!" Philippa persisted excitedly. "And he is *kissing* her, too! Won't Helen be just..."

Whatever else she had been about to say was interrupted by Ianthe who blurted, "Oh, *do* shut up, Pippa!" before bursting into tears.

It had been, Alexa reflected dreamily, almost like the excitement of first swimming underwater—holding her breath before she opened her eyes into green depths—and then, suddenly realizing what had just happened, she snatched her hands from around his neck and jerked erect, reaching futilely for the cord that would release the velvet carriage curtains. Already annoyed at her own display of weakness, his mocking laugh before he made the caustic comment that since at least half of London had seen them already he could only think of one other reason for her sudden desire for *privacy* only added more fuel to the fire already raging in Alexa's breast.

"Half of London, *including* Selby and Rowell!" Alexa snapped back vengefully. "And *not* to mention the Duchess of Atherton, as well as your fiancée's two younger sisters! I *would* have warned you, had you not been so recklessly precipitate! I do *not* suppose there'll be any 'Exciting Announcement' made at the ball under the circumstances, will there? Just think how *disappointed* all of society is going to be, although no doubt the relish they'll take in gossiping about the *reasons* will partially console them!"

She had flung each word at him like a barb, but to her angry amazement Alexa discovered none of the expressions she had *expected* to see on his darkly saturnine face—only a lifted eyebrow as he inquired if he was expected to apologize for making *her* a target for the gossips. With a far too casual shrug Nicholas continued in a matter-of-fact voice: "If you're really so much concerned for your reputation as you seem to be, my poor Alexa, we can formally announce *our* engagement tomorrow night and have it published in the *Times* the following day, to make it official. I had no intention, in any case, of offering for Helen; that was Belle-Mère's idea in the first place. But now that I think of it, becoming engaged to *you* instead should put an end to all *that* nonsense for good, thank God!"

At first, sure she could not possibly have heard correctly, Alexa could only stare at him as if she was stupefied. And then as he continued to look at her through those dark green eyes that darkened even further when he narrowed them, and in which she could discern no feeling or expression at all, the enormity of what he had just said struck her at last with all the force of an unexpected blow.

"I...I *beg* your pardon?" Alexa said in a husky voice that was a little above a whisper, and he repeated his suggestion (it had not even been couched as a *question!*) rather impatiently, adding that he certainly hoped she did not expect the hypocrisy of a more formal kind of proposal, with him going down on one knee and presenting her with a posy of violets or something equally ridiculous.

"And announcing an *engagement,* as you're well aware, does not necessarily mean that a marriage will follow, in case the idea makes you nervous. It will, however, insure that I'm no longer a target for matchmaking mamas and that you..." the pause was infinitesimal, but Alexa noted it for all that, "why, *you* will find it easier yourself to escape fortune hunters and—the other kind of hunter as well!"

Feeling hunted herself, Alexa shook her head violently, as if she was denying that she had heard correctly. "No! I cannot believe that I...that you... You must be *deranged* to...to..."

"To *propose* to you?" he taunted her with that strange, twisted smile she had hated from the first time she had seen it turned on her. "Do you place such a low value on yourself as to think a man has to be mad to offer you marriage, or is it that you would prefer receiving a different type of *proposition?*"

"It is hardly the value I place on *myself,* but my memory of the unfailingly brutal and callous manner in which *you* have always treated me that makes me feel you are merely playing some kind of cruel game with me!" Alexa blazed back at him. "Or could it be that your *pride* demands that you come up with a conveniently understanding fiancée you can produce for the world to see *before* Helen breaks off the understanding you two obviously had? Why should I let myself be used by you again?''

''The Spaniard,'' she remembered Charles Lawrence calling him laughingly in that long-ago time in Colombo. And at this moment there was none of the English Lord to be discerned in his harsh, high-planed dark features. Only the proud, vengeful Spaniard with twin white lines of barely checked fury on either side of his mouth and the slight, ominous flare of his nostrils that she remembered from before. Just as she recalled all too well the particularly throaty softness of his voice, reminding her unpleasantly of the low growl of a crouched black panther ready to spring.

''Have I *used* you indeed? Forgive me for pointing out that my recollection is quite different. In fact, almost the opposite! I think I had you—or *used* you, as you put it—for the first time and the only time at the bordello known as the Temple of Venus, and that you charged me quite an exorbitant price for your surprising virginity, which I paid! And I also recall quite clearly that I did not go there seeking you out in order to *use* you—quite the contrary, in fact. There I was, half-asleep in my hashish dream and perfectly content until I was disturbed by the intrusion of a priestess of Venus who—it soon became apparent—wished to make use of *me!* Should I go on?''

''No!'' Alexa said strongly, painfully aware of her warmly flushed face. ''No, I don't wish to be reminded of anything unpleasant, and I've no intention of entering into a pretended engagement to you only in order that you might *save face,* as they would say in the East!''

Having made her defiant speech, she was immeasurably relieved when the carriage jerked to a stop and she heard the announcement that they were *home* at last. The same sense of relief enabled her to turn to Lord Embry and say politely that her carriage was at his disposal, should he wish to be set down elsewhere.

"Thank you, my sweet, but later, perhaps? I believe there is still much to be discussed and decided between us."

36

Afterwards it was easy to tell herself that she should have been warned by the way his words sounded as if they had been bitten off, or to wonder why she hadn't kicked and struggled and screamed out aloud for help, even if he *had* had the insolence to whisper as he carried her out of the coach and up the steps of her house with the servants and poor Mr. Bowles staring, "If you'd prefer to 'save face,' as they say in the East, my darling Alexa, then you *will* let them all think that you are actually in a swoon, which is what I intend to say unless you'd rather have everyone think otherwise."

And then there was the other, more fatalistic part of her mind that told her he would have done what he meant to do in any case, no matter what her reactions might have been! But at first, however, even when he carried her upstairs and she heard him demand from Bridget where her room was, even then she had no *real* inkling of the outrageous, monstrous act he meant to perpetrate. Not even when she heard him say grimly to Bridget, "And *you* can stay *outside* this door, do you hear? And if you and that butler have any sense you'll keep the rest of the servants downstairs and out of sight!"

"But...oh, but my lord! If my Lady's ill someone should be seeing to her."

"*I'll* be seeing to your lady. And if you have to tell them something you might as well say we're discussing plans for our betrothal and wedding—in *private,* you understand?"

He had *dropped* her onto her bed to lie sprawling against the patterned brocade spread, just as he had once dropped her into the Indian Ocean, uncaring if she would sink or swim. And while Alexa continued to lie there in a daze of shock, her eyes wide and staring in disbelief, he locked and bolted her bedroom door quite calmly before turning back to survey her with an expression she neither liked nor trusted and did not wish to see. Squeezing her eyes tightly shut, she told herself that this was only a nightmare, nothing more. Not something that could actually happen to her—to the wealthy Lady Travers—in this civilized day and age. Why, when she opened her eyes again she would be able to laugh at herself for imagining...

"You can keep your eyes closed or open—it's all the same to me. And you can take off that ugly purple dress you're wearing, and all your damned petticoats and your corset as well—or if you prefer it, I'll rip the clothes off your body myself! But either way, my mermaid, I'll have you naked the way I first saw you; and I mean to *use* you, my virgin slut, as I should have done *then* and later. In every way and every fashion I see fit. *Bruja,* do you understand me? Is *this* the way you really want a man to take you?"

The purple taffeta ripped under his hands with a loud tearing noise that made Alexa flinch. The petticoats tore, and her shift; and she lay there with her teeth gritted together, *willing* herself not to cry out or beg him for mercy. She only flinched again when she felt the coldness of a knifeblade against her skin as he cut away her corset, although she kept her eyes closed and stayed unmoving even then.

She could hear her own breathing and his, and she felt the bed give and felt the warmth of his body as he leaned over hers; but she would *not* open her eyes and give either him or what he meant to do to her any recognition. She lay with her legs and her arms outspread like a whore and was as cold inside herself as a whore while only her mind screamed for him to *do* it—whatever he wished to do with her body—do it and be done, freeing her, by his act, of *himself* and his image in her mind and her blood and her flesh. Free of the terrible, frightening chemistry that had bound her to him all this time and still did and still would unless he was the one to wield the sword that would cut her away from him forever. The sword of his own flesh... Why in God's name didn't he do something?

Alexa's eyes flashed open to trap his unguarded for less than an instant before he shuttered them again and awarded her that one-sided, twisted smile she had come to know far too well. ''You remind me of a pagan sacrifice, you know,'' Nicholas said drily. ''What I *should* have done in the first place was chain you to the nearest rocks and let some poor unsuspecting dragon have you!''

''Does that mean that you are *not* going to rape me after all? I mean, after going to so much trouble and *exertion?*''

She *thought* she discerned the slightest twitch to his lips before he retorted: ''I was merely waiting until I had recovered my breath, as a matter of fact. You are no light weight, you know. Perhaps you should consider giving up puddings.''

''Oh!'' Alexa exclaimed, sitting upright, ''you're despicable!''

''So you've said before, quite often. And you, of course, are a teasing little bitch!''

Her sharply uttered ''No!'' was caught and lost against

the sudden, savage attack of his mouth over hers that opened her to him in the end—to his hands, charting her curves and hollows, and later to his lips and his tongue that savored and lingered over certain of her most sensitive parts. And she too let herself touch him where she wanted to touch him and put her mouth on him wherever she wanted to bestow it until at last he moved from her for just long enough to take her under the arms and slide her body up over his and against his until he tasted her mouth again and she tasted his. And in that time Alexa felt him both impale and fill her and make her hips arch fiercely and demandingly up against him, learning the counterpoint to each movement of his hard, man's body and the rippling feel of different muscles under his skin. Learning, feeling, rising and climbing as she grew tauter and tighter and more breathless until she moaned and whimpered against his shoulder while she felt eruptions everywhere before, fragmented into feather-light foam, she burst and scattered against the sky.

She should have been able to stay sky-flung like a star. Why couldn't she have? "Goe and Catch a Falling Star..." John Donne. Why did stars have to fall? Or the whirling of the Earth be capable of pulling her away from a star? Even if it *was* only a meteor, or two, or three! *More!* Oh, yes, infinitely more! Smiling to herself, Alexa sat up and stretched before falling back onto the bed with her arms spread wide and her imagination busy.

"Bridget, I think I'd like to sleep for a little while. But you'll wake me up by seven, won't you? Unless Lord Embry should call earlier, that is."

"Yes, milady. I won't forget, I promise."

Did I really say those words? Dear God, I'm as insane as *he* seemed to be, then. Turning over onto her stomach, Alexa buried her face against a pillow with an angry motion. Fool! She jeered at herself. Did he say anything about love? No, it had been *convenience* instead. And what had Harriet tried to teach her a long time ago? Logic and reason should always outweigh emotion—God, she must try to think that way always! Think how suddenly it had all come about. Think of… Supposing he already knew everything about her and had been made to realize what kind of threat she could turn out to be? Perhaps *that* was their plan—to make sure Alexa was kept tame and silent until they had decided how to deal with her. And if he actually went so far as to wed her, what would it mean and what would *he* have to lose? Perhaps a year or two at the most, before she met with a convenient *accident* that would free them all of the threat she represented. Just like poor Amy Robsart in Sir Walter Scott's novel *Kennilworth.* And if they were married, he'd own everything she now called her own. Wealth, possessions—even her body itself! She'd be completely at his mercy. At *their* mercy, in fact. Her grandmother knew very well who "Lady Travers" was and what she represented. Of *course* she would have to be got rid of, even if Helen had to wait a year or two for her husband. Her rich, *widowed* husband.

Soaking in a hot bath perfumed with Oil of Attar of Roses helped Alexa to relax somewhat after she had realized that she could not manage to fall asleep. With her hair bound up, she leaned her head back over the edge of the tub and closed her eyes, aware that her poor faithful Bridget was watching over her to prevent her falling asleep and drowning. Lying heavily between her breasts on her own gold chain was the signet ring that Nicholas Dameron, Lord Embry, had given her; so like the one Gavin Dameron had once given Victorine Bouvard that she had not been able to prevent the shiver that ran through her body when it was carelessly bestowed on her—almost as an afterthought.

"Oh, here! It's customary, I suppose, until I have bought you a proper engagement ring. You won't be able to wear it on your finger, but perhaps you have a plain gold chain to thread it on?" He had been half-dressed already when he had turned around to drop the heavy ring between her breasts. And *she* had still been floating somewhere in a delicious daze of contentment, not really paying too much attention to the ring while she was watching *him.*

"And what is supposed to happen next? Where are you going? I cannot recall having *agreed* to become engaged to marry you, you know. I had made up my mind that..."

"*Querida,* you might as well make up your mind that we're betrothed, and *you* are well and truly compromised. Think of Lady Acton and the Duchess of Atherton, not to mention your own servants, who are *not* above gossiping, I'm sure. And as for the rest, I do hope you will not take to asking me *questions!* I was advised that Helen was prepared to be a most *understanding* wife, the kind that any man would appreciate."

"Helen! Why didn't you compromise *her* instead? And I can only hope that *you* prove just as nobly *understanding* as you expect your *wife* to be!"

That, Alexa recalled, had been the point when he had bent over her and kissed her very thoroughly into silence, while he whispered against her mouth between kisses that *he* was not at all understanding and would strangle her and shoot any man he found her with. Oh God! What was she to think? Was he playing some secret game with her? And worst thought of all—was *this* the same way that Gavin Dameron had seduced her mother before he had abandoned her? Ah, but Victorine's daughter would not prove so easy.

The scent of roses followed her everywhere, even after she had dressed in one of her new gowns, which had quite a daringly low neckline that showed off her emeralds. Bridget was so upset she was almost sulking. "But, ma'am! I mean, milady, you're surely *not* going out to-night? You haven't *rested* properly yet, and there'll be the ball tomorrow. And what if Lord Embry should come by and ask for you?"

Alexa twirled around in her bronze silk gown with gold lace flounces and smiled brilliantly. "If Lord Embry *should* find enough time to call, why then you may tell him that I've gone to Sloane Square to Lady Fenton's card party and that I may go from there to Chelsea to visit the Carlyles, if it is not too late; or Cremorne Gardens, perhaps, if we can make up a party of sufficiently daring souls! He may find me easily enough if he wishes to, I'm sure."

The perfume of roses followed her all the way downstairs, and there were two silver vases of crimson roses standing on the table in the hallway, along with the silver tray piled with cards and envelopes. On the point of ordering the roses taken away immediately, Alexa heard Mr. Bowles say in a purposefully expressionless voice, "Lord *Deering* is already here and waiting for you, my Lady."

"Admit it! You had quite forgotten that you had agreed to my escorting you to Deirdre Fenton's card party."

"Oh, very well then. I *had* forgotten. But I am glad that *you* had not, because I would have hated to walk into such a crowd alone." Alexa turned her head to smile at her escort before looking about them and adding: "But I'm even *more* relieved that *you* are escorting me on my first visit to Cremorne Gardens, although I think it isn't really half as wicked as it's made out to be!" If her voice sounded slightly strained, Lord Charles did not seem to notice as he gave her elbow a small squeeze.

"How could *you* recognize evil when you are so *innocent* yourself? So innocent and so *open*—the first qualities I remarked and admired in you when we met. I remember dancing with you and riding with you and all the conversations we used to have, particularly those in French. And if you could only know how I have *suffered* since then, thinking of what might have been if only I had not been *drugged!* Lady Travers—Alexa..."

"Nicholas told me that your intentions were far from honorable, and that all you wanted was to have a virgin, until you tired of her and wanted another," Alexa said guilelessly, noting with relief that Lord Charles, about to gather her into his embrace, had let his hands drop and was staring at her with a mixture of hurt and indignation.

"*He* told you that? After everything he said to *me* about *you,* his insinuations..."

"Then he told you that he arrived in your place? He *did* leave me a virgin, however. Or did he take the trouble to mention it?" Alexa's voice sounded brittle, and she had forgotten her earlier apprehension at having been separated from the rest of the party they had arrived with here from the Carlyles' house. "Not that it matters at all to *me* what he says or leaves cunningly *unsaid,* of course," she added insouciantly, and had started to turn away when she felt Lord Charles take her by the elbow.

"If you honestly feel the emotions you have just expressed, then for God's sake tell me why you've agreed to *marry* him? How did he manage to coerce you into it? I had sworn to myself that I would keep silent since my motives could be misunderstood, but now I cannot for your sake hold back any longer. Be *careful.* Be on guard always. There are those, unfortunately, to whom money is everything—especially if they play for high stakes."

Alexa stared into his face as she said slowly and almost disbelievingly, "Are you telling me that *Embry* is in need of *money?* Why, I thought..."

"My grandmother pays him a handsome allowance as long as he flatters her and follows her dictates. *That* is all he has until whatever trouble it was that he got into in California is forgotten and he can safely return there, which cannot be, I'm sure, for many more years."

"What kind of trouble are you speaking of? Something very bad?"

"It was..."

Lord Charles hesitated and seemed to have difficulty choosing his words, and Alexa wondered impatiently why he was suddenly so *stiff* and reluctant, until she heard a voice say pleasantly from behind her: "It was the worst crime of all, wasn't it, Charles? Murder. In fact, I was accused of murdering my wife."

37

"How dare you act as if—I was—as if you *owned* me?" Alexa panted in a furious, almost breathless whisper. "I have never felt so *humiliated* in my entire life! And poor Charles—we were only... He was only trying to..."

"I can imagine quite easily what your 'poor Charles' had in mind once he thought you were convinced of *my* perfidy and opportunism," Lord Embry grated in an equally furious undertone as he dragged an angry and unwilling Alexa along by the wrist. His eyes, caught momentarily by gaslight, flashed with the dangerous green brilliance of those of a stalking Bengal tiger. "One of the dark alcoves, or perhaps even a private room, if he felt sure enough of you. Was *that* the kind of adventure you came seeking tonight in Cremorne Gardens?"

"You judge everyone else by your own vile standards, don't you? But I am not accountable to you or to anyone else for my actions! Do you *hear* me, damn you?" Alexa's words were blurted out vehemently between gasps. "I will *never* marry you! I refuse to be engaged to you either! Let *go* of me, you...you *murderer!*"

For a moment she thought it was because of what she had said that he halted so suddenly that she would have fallen against him if he had not at the same time released her aching wrist with a kind of backward *shove* that almost made her lose her balance. There was what felt like a rough-textured wall at her back and the innocuously soothing, splashing sound of a fountain nearby. And over all those sounds and sensations the awareness of the two burly men who had appeared from nowhere to block their path. Conversationally, one of them said, ''Seems to *me,* Jimmy m'boy, that this pretty lady was screaming for help.''

''A lady in distress, eh Bert? I'd say it's our Christian duty to come to the rescue, wouldn't you?''

''*I'd* say that when a little lady says 'no' a *real* gentleman wouldn't want to try and drag her off against her will! Course—there's a difference between a gentleman and a toff...''

''Bert's right. Now a gentleman would apologize for letting himself get carried away and walk off, wouldn't he, Bert? And then Bert and I will make sure her Ladyship's returned safe and sound to her *friends!*''

''Ah, but what happens if you are not dealing with a *gentleman?*'' Nicholas's voice was soft and almost pleasant, but with a certain undertone that suggested the *unpleasant* and made Alexa give an involuntary shudder as if she had just been chilled. It was partly the way he just *stood* there with his feet astride; such an easy-seeming and almost relaxed stance on the surface, while underneath she could almost feel like a physical *thing* the vibrating, couched tension of a wild beast ready to spring but waiting for its prey to move first.

While they had been speaking with each other the two men had begun, almost imperceptibly, to move apart, and one of them had a cudgel! ''There is really no *need...*'' Alexa had begun in the calmest tone of voice she could muster, when she was cut off by Nicholas's short ugly laugh. ''Obviously, my love, these *gentlemen* are anxious to be your knights-errant! Shall we joust for your fickle favors? They are most expensive to purchase, I should warn you two gallant knights! But if you *or* whoever paid you for your gallantry tonight should be prepared to pay the necessary price, then you might ask at Madame Olivier's for the lady in distress!'' As every intentionally brutal word assaulted her like stones meant to hurt and maim, Alexa felt herself grow cold, then hot, then cold again. And during those same slow seconds she saw the dull, dangerous gleam of the knife blade in his hand, remembering suddenly the way he had quickly disposed of her corset earlier that day.

''Well?'' Nicholas taunted as the two exchanged uneasy glances before turning wary eyes back on him. He smiled, but it was a feral baring of his teeth only as he said softly, ''It's been a long time since I've been in a *real* fight—or killed a man. Which one of you is first? Or shall it be both together?''

''You'll never take us both, toff, for all that bluster... *Ahh!*''

When had he moved? How fast, for it to happen in seconds like a blur before her eyes? He *must* have moved, because one man writhed on the ground fighting for breath, with his hands clasped over his belly, and the other one had dropped his club to clutch at his arm, blood dripping from between his fingers already.

''Christ! Ah, Jesus! I'm bleedin' to death! We didn't mean any harm, guv. I...I swear it! Just...just trying to help a lady, that's all! Bert, tell him I'm right, for... Ohmigawd!'' Bert, attempting painfully to sit up, was straightened out by a carefully placed kick that left him lying motionless almost at the same time that Nicholas said softly and savagely between his teeth, ''Who paid you?''

''For God's sake, guv! I've already told you—no...!'' There was a bloody line down the side of the bewhiskered, jowly face and across the back of the hand the man had lifted, and he had suddenly begun to make grotesquely whimpering noises through his open mouth as he started to back away with his eyes flickering from the knife blade to the hard, expressionless face and narrowed, deadly eyes that were like death looking back at him.

"I *could* take off an ear very easily, or slit your nostrils for you. And then there's always the belly, and yours is easy to find. You might live that way, with your guts spilling out, for a few days at least! I could give you lessons, my friend, on the uses of a knife and the many ways of carving a man up into bloody segments while he still lives. Must I show you or will you give me the name I asked for? I'm in too much of a hurry to ask again, so…?"

Unable to help herself, Alexa turned her head away and began to retch miserably, her hands sliding down the wall as she sank to her knees with her forehead pressed against the roughly uneven surface, her whole body shaking with revulsion. He had actually meant every coldly dispassionate threat he'd made—she did not doubt it now. Accused of murdering his *wife,* he'd admitted openly and even casually. And how had he killed *her?* Had she died slowly and painfully, poor miserable woman? And dear God, what was *she* doing with a man who could talk so calmly of *torturing* another human being? "I could give you lessons on the uses of a knife…" he had said and had gone on to elaborate on those uses of a knife. Alexa felt herself heave again and was even sicker this time, a cold sweat breaking out all over her body in spite of the chilly night air and the cashmere shawl she'd worn for protection against it.

"We had better go before someone else decides to stroll along this particular pathway. You are quite through with being sick, I hope?" Too weak to put up any resistance, Alexa allowed herself to be pulled none too gently to her feet again and made to walk beside him, her skirts brushing against the poor wretch who sat moaning weakly as he continued to clutch at his arm. Nicholas, she noticed, did not bother to spare the unfortunate fellow or his unconscious (or *dead?*) companion a second glance; and *that* evidence of heartlessness and hardness made her shudder again and press the back of one hand against her mouth to prevent herself from being sick once more.

"I had thought that since you used to go hunting and enjoyed it you would not collapse at the sight of a little blood," he said in a harsh voice, his fingers tightening over her arm as she almost stumbled.

"It...it wasn't the *blood* at all," Alexa managed to choke out through her dry, constricted throat. With an effort she swallowed hard. "It was *you!* What you did and what you *said.* I cannot even bear to talk about it yet! But you were...you were worse than an animal to do what you did to that poor devil. And what if you've killed his friend? Or if *he* should die from loss of blood? Dear God! I do not know you at all, do I? You could never force me to marry you! Do you think that I am so stupid and thoughtless as to let you marry me for my fortune and then arrange for my convenient demise? Or had you planned to murder me yourself, just as you murdered your first wife?"

She *thought* she heard his sharply indrawn breath as his grip on her arm tightened painfully enough to elicit a cry from her. But then he relaxed his hold almost at once and his voice seemed to hold nothing more than wry amusement as he said, "Do you imagine me as some Bluebeard? If you do, then perhaps you should remember never to wander inquisitively into locked chambers—or ask too many questions!"

"*That* will hardly happen since there is no question of our ever being *married!*" Alexa retorted heatedly. "And *what* did you mean by that filthy insinuation you dared make to those men? Why, if I had a knife or a pistol with which to defend myself I would have…''

''I'm under no illusions as to what you *would* have done given the chance, my sweet Alexa, despite the inevitable bloodletting! But as to the reference I made to Madame Olivier, she *is* your aunt, is she not? And considering your obvious fascination for bordellos and your knowledge of what goes on in such houses of pleasure, what other conclusion could be drawn?''

More flung stones, carefully aimed and meant to injure. And—he *knew!* For how long had he known and how *much?* Hell-bent on vengeance now, it was *that* knowledge that acted like a glass of cold water thrown in her face and made her choose her next words more carefully. But in her preoccupation Alexa had hardly noticed his handing her up into a carriage and climbing in beside her until she heard the door slammed shut and felt herself jerked back against padded velour as the coachman cracked his whip. Ostentatiously, Alexa moved as far away from him as she could while she pretended to stare with fascination out of the window, saying frostily over her shoulder without once turning her head, ''You really had no need to take the trouble to *hire* a vehicle to take me home, since I had my *own* carriage with me. *Now* I shall be obliged to…''

''You do not have to worry on that score, *mi corazón.* I sent your coachman and his sleepy attendant back to Belgrave Square when I first arrived, knowing how much we have to talk about in *private.* And although I appreciate your concern as to my financial capabilities, I should assure you that this carriage is mine, and not hired.''

''I don't in the least care…!'' As she turned back to face him Alexa could feel herself positively tremble with fury. ''How *dared* you *presume* enough to act in such a high-handed fashion! To take so much for granted… Ohh! I cannot wait to get back home and to be free of your presence! And *please,* I would prefer *not* to have any further conversation between us until then. I've made myself quite clear, I hope?''

As she turned her head around again, her shoulders squared and stiffly unyielding, Alexa heard his lazy, aggravating laugh, which this time contained an undercurrent of genuine amusement.

''Sweetheart, if you really *mean* that, you would be the perfect woman, you know. I have always thought the eternal babbling of a typical female a damned waste of time, especially if she has an adorably sensuous mouth that should be occupied with *deeds,* instead of senseless words.'' Alexa's back became even straighter as she used every ounce of self-control she could muster in order to keep silent in spite of the way he was *baiting* her. She kept her head stubbornly turned away and her lips pressed tightly together, even when his voice took on, surprisingly, a coaxing, almost caressing note as he murmured thoughtfully: ''You *do* have an adorable mouth, sweet witch. And an adorably rounded little bottom as well. Straight, long legs... Do you know how unusual and delightful that is? And as for your skin, it's like gold silk, *querida mía.* The kind of skin that a man could never tire of touching—or kissing.'' It was all Alexa could do to remain sitting there unmoving as she felt the warmth of his lips against the nape of her neck and where her neck and shoulder joined. She felt, unwillingly, the heat flood through her body as he murmured softly against her shoulder: ''And your sweet, pointed breasts with those coral nipples—you should be painted in the nude—as a sea nymph perhaps, but only by a great painter who could do you justice.'' His fingers brushed very lightly and almost tantalizingly across her breasts for just an instant, and Alexa gasped as if she had been burned by his touch.

''Stop! I don't want you to *touch* me again, do you hear? I...''

Almost to her surprise, Nicholas gave an indifferent shrug and leaned his shoulders against the opposite corner of the seat they shared. ''No? Very well, my love. In that case I will leave it all up to *you* without having to feel selfish. I'm sure you've learned a great deal more about pleasing a man than you've let *me* discover so far.''

Gritting her teeth together, Alexa managed to keep from uttering the heated words that were on the tip of her tongue. Damn him to hell! Why was it that he seemed to find some malicious satisfaction in taunting and insulting her and trying her patience and control to the utmost? Her head ached from all the thoughts that tumbled around in her mind, and she would have given anything to be safely at home in her own bed at this moment—*alone!* She needed to be able to *think* without distraction, and there were urgent decisions that had to be made, if only so that she could keep her own peace of mind.

When the carriage jerked to a halt at last, Alexa gave a heartfelt sigh of relief. She was *home* at last, and at this time of the night even *he* would not dare to force his way in as he had done before when he'd taken her unawares. *This* time, if he tried to use the same forceful tactics she would *scream* for help as loudly as she could.

As she gathered up her skirts to descend from the carriage, Lord Embry, who had come around to her side, put his hands on either side of her waist to lift her down; and it was only while she was in midair, so to speak, that Alexa realized with a sickening jolt that this was *not* Belgrave Square that he had brought her to after all.

Continuing to hold her before him, a stunned, unwilling captive, Nicholas said in the same dangerously soft voice that Alexa had already heard him use earlier: ''If you have any idea of making a *fuss* I hope you will be wise enough to put the notion out of your head at once. I would be sorry if you forced me to leave ugly scars on that lovely golden body of yours. *Comprende, mi dulce amor?*''

No doubt he would do exactly as he threatened without a qualm. Alexa had to *force* herself to stand still and tilt her face up to meet his unreadable look with a semblance, at least, of courageous defiance. ''Am I permitted at least to ask where you have brought me? And *why?*'' Despite her efforts her voice emerged as a husky whisper, but at least it did not shake.

''Why, I thought we might visit one of the establishments managed by your aunt! The two houses sit side by side. Or had you already noticed? One caters to what you might call the regular trade, and the other is for special purposes. And privacy of course. There are suites that are rented out—I keep one rented myself for occasions when I might find such accommodations useful. And I can assure you, my sweet, that you'll find *these* quarters much cleaner and more tastefully done up than the sleazy little *chambres de convenance* at Cremorne Gardens, or even those above certain little boutiques in Burlington Arcade. But you will be able to see for yourself in a few minutes and draw your own comparisons, won't you?''

38

Adelina, the Dowager Marchioness of Newbury, was in the habit of keeping late hours, as everyone in the family knew; and so, when her grandson Deering was announced by a sleepy-looking butler at well past eleven o'clock, she merely waved an impatient hand and said that the Viscount should be directed to come upstairs to her rooms. So, had Charles finally got up enough courage to tell her something that she already knew? She had only agreed to see him in case he happened to have learned something she was not yet aware of, and she would soon find out if that was the case or not.

"Obviously, my dear Charles, you were not successful. Oh, for heaven's sake, sit *down!* There—on the divan. And now you shall relate everything to me in detail, omitting nothing, if you please."

All through Charles's rather jerky recital and even for some time after he had stopped speaking, his grandmother continued to watch him in the rather unnerving fashion he remembered all too well from his childhood. Soul-searching, he had heard it called, and although he had always despised himself for being afraid of her and in fact almost *hated* her, he was unable to prevent himself from wanting her approval and fearing her disapproval. "I...what could I have *done,* after all? Embry of all people! Perhaps I took too much for granted, but, Belle-Mère, you said..."

"Ah yes, I know exactly what I said, Charles. That I would tell him some things that should change his mind about this ridiculous 'engagement' to our rich widow." She shrugged her shoulders. "Perhaps *that's* what is behind the rather *forceful* manner in which he took her away. Perhaps if you still want this particular wealthy bride—you should be more forceful yourself. That is probably why she allows *Embry* to *control* her! Hmm...I *wonder?*" The Dowager chuckled to herself, as if something had just occurred to her, and her grandson stiffened before leaning forward to say in a voice that held suppressed anger:

"Her *carriage* was sent back home by Embry some hours ago, as I understand it. And *she* went with him! If I *thought,* by God, that..."

In an exaggeratedly patient manner that managed to convey impatience as well, the Dowager Marchioness raised her eyebrows and said: "My dear *boy!* Even if Embry *is* bold enough to take her, and even if she managed to keep herself a virgin after poor Sir John passed away—or even *before,* for that matter, *he* could never have accomplished such a feat, poor man, as I've told you! For God's sake—are you such a *romantic* that you cannot think of a marriage as a matter of either convenience or expediency? Once a marriage has made you rich, why should you not be able to afford a virgin every week or every night for that matter? And how many females can you think of who are as rich as Lady Travers? My poor little fellow, you are not wise enough yet, obviously, to realize that enough money can buy you anything and everything you crave, including *power.* Is barely managing to keep up appearances, thanks to the goodwill of your creditors, your only goal? Well, good night, Charles. And perhaps Embry..."

Lord Charles leaped up from his seat, his handsome face flushed with a mixture of emotions, saying at the same time in a *suppressed* kind of voice, "I think I understand everything even more clearly *now,* and that from now on I shall be easily able to act in a more *detached* manner."

"I should certainly hope so for *your* sake, Charles, and especially since your mother has told me tearfully that your father will no longer be good for any of your gambling debts or for certain *other* expenses he does not approve of. And I am glad that at least you had enough sense not to ask *me!*" Although the tone of Adelina's voice was one of boredom, her eyes had not mistaken her grandson's response to her words. Anxious to dismiss him, she repeated, "And so, good night once more, Charles. I have just noticed how late it is. I shall see you again tomorrow night, I presume?"

"Tomorrow?" he said at the door, mildly surprising her by his vehemence.

"If you can *manage* such a feat cleverly enough, I *think* it should be before supper, just in case *Embry* might decide to make sure of her fortune before *you* do."

How she *needed,* yet at the same time despised, the *sheep* she had always found it so easy to *use!* Adelina thought contemptuously after Charles had left. While she had still been young and attractive enough it had been through the giving or the yielding—for a time at least—of her body, and through sighs and whispered half-promises. After that it was through *fear.* She knew every weakness and every guilty secret of them all, did she not? And coupled with that, they had all realized by now that she would always ensure that *her* will prevailed in the end. But how many of them had faced the reason *why?* Ah, the weak, silly *fools!* Almost without being aware of it, the

Marchioness had left her straight-backed chair to cross the room. And in front of her mirror she had courage enough to confront her own image without flinching—in fact, even with a little smile. Her youth and her looks had been useful enough while they lasted, of course, but the real reason for the power she wielded was and always had been her total dedication to getting her own way. *Amoral,* unscrupulous, witch… She had never bothered to concern herself with the words that had been used to describe her—and why should she? She was stronger than any of them precisely because she *despised,* and had never let herself be governed by all their so-called *ethics* and *morals* even though she had always been aware that it was necessary for her to *pretend* she did sometimes. *Fools!* she thought again, walking back to her desk and the blotter that was covered with splotched words and drawings she had made while she was listening to Charles's apologies for his lack of strength. The only one of them she could neither read nor manipulate was *Nicholas,* the grandson, ironically, of *her* Nicholas, who had been the only man she had known who had meant what he had said when he'd turned his back on her. The only one she'd actually *wept* over for a time; and she had only been fifteen or sixteen then.

Adelina had crossed the room again, this time to stand before the fireplace, where she dismissed all memory of weakness from her mind. If Nicholas had not reacted as she'd hoped he would, there were the *other* possibilities, of course. Charles, if he actually found enough courage or felt desperate enough to be resolute. But in case he did not move quickly or decisively enough, she had already taken the precaution of making certain alternative arrangements of her own that could not fail to take care of everything once and for all. By this time tomorrow night… As she pulled the cord that would summon her maid, the Dowager allowed herself the luxury of a cold, secret smile as she wondered idly if Nicholas was capable of treating a woman with the same coldly detached ruthlessness he had displayed earlier in disposing of two hired bullies sent to "rescue" a young woman; and what his *real* motives were in taking her off with him to a well-known bordello. But then tomorrow would give her the answer to that question too, and another reason for informing Newbury that she must see him before noon on urgent business that could not wait.

Filled with a sense of satisfaction, Adelina found it easy to fall asleep that night without the usual drops of laudanum in her cup of chocolate, her last drowsy thought a vindictive one. Silly, arrogant little upstart bitch! How sorry she was going to be for letting herself imagine she was capable of matching wits with *her...!*

Not knowing that she had already been contemptuously dismissed as an adversary, Alexa had been concentrating on keeping her wits about her and her defenses raised from the moment Nicholas had "escorted" her inside the house he seemed so familiar with, using a private entrance to which he possessed (naturally!) a key. And how openly, without any vestige of shame or embarrassment, he had proclaimed *his* lecherous habits before turning hypocrite and accusing *her* of...

"Is there something you find particularly fascinating about this rather depressing little entrance hall? The potted aspidistra perhaps?"

Managing to recover herself Alexa said, "It needs water, poor thing," and met the dangerously *measuring* look on his face with feigned insouciance before adding brightly, "and speaking of water reminds me of how extremely *thirsty* I am, not to mention being positively *famished* as well. You did not intend *starving* me, did you?"

"I thought, my sweet *accomplished* Alexa, that I had

already managed to make my intentions clear,'' Nicholas said between his teeth as he took her elbow with unnecessary firmness. ''But if not, then I shall endeavor to make myself *quite* clear—once we are upstairs.'' Without giving her a chance to protest, he had already begun to *force* her up a winding flight of red-carpeted stairs before he added caustically, ''And before you complain of *exhaustion* I should inform you that my apartments open off the first landing, so you have only a short climb.''

''How very convenient for your purposes and your weak female visitors,'' Alexa said acidly, and felt her temper begin to rise at his soft, amused laugh. ''*Especially*''—and here she managed to snatch her arm from his grip as she added with calculated scorn—''if you have to drag them all up here to your—your Den of Iniquity by *force!*''

They had already reached the landing by now, and it was fortunately a little better lighted than the stairs, so that Alexa was able to study his face for the effect of her cutting words. If he possessed any *remnant* of a conscience, he…

''*Den of Iniquity?*'' Nicholas repeated in a disbelieving voice. And then, as if to himself as he started to turn his key in the lock: ''Good *God!*''

Torn between the choices of stamping her feet or scratching his eyes out, Alexa remembered just in time her resolve *not* to let him provoke her and breathed deeply instead while she wondered what might happen if she made a run for it. And it was during that small moment of silence between them, just before he swung the door open, that Alexa heard another door bang somewhere below them and a *laugh* just before the screams began. ''No more—I *beg* you! Ahh! Help me—someone, please! Noooo!'' Feeling as if her blood had turned to ice, Alexa did not even realize that she had clutched at Nicholas's arm. ''The naughty wench, trying to run away 'stead of being *grateful* to your Lordship for everything! And shall I bring her to you now, milord, or truss the little bitch up again?'' The terrified, piteous screams that *pleaded* were suddenly cut off with the slam of a heavy door, and Alexa was suddenly conscious of the sound of her own breathing and the weakness in her knees before she was able to choke out, ''Oh God! How *can* such things *happen!* Please... Oh, please *do* be quick before they...they can...''

Those screams seemed to keep filling her ears and echoing in her head, so that it took her, in her overwrought state, some seconds to become aware that instead of responding to those desperate entreaties for help they had just heard, Nicholas had almost *flung* her into his own rooms, locking the door behind them purposefully.

She would have fallen if not for the couch. It was upholstered in a dark blue and gold plush that felt seductively soft under her hands, and as Alexa recovered her balance and turned back to see him watching her with his back to the door, it seemed to her as if his eyes had never looked so deeply green or so imperviously hard as they did at that moment. ''No, not even *you...!*'' Alexa said in what was almost a whisper. ''You *heard,* didn't you? They were... Oh dear *God!* You cannot possibly remain indifferent to the suffering and degradation of another human being? Nicholas? You heard what that horrible man said—you heard her crying out for help! *Begging* for someone to save her from...'' Her voice had risen without her being able to help it, and somehow, in spite of all she had said, he had not moved except to catch her by the wrists when she tried desperately to make for the door. ''Let *me* go, if you are too much of a coward! Let...'' He cut her off ruthlessly.

''Let you go *where?* And to what? Christ! I had not realized this tendency of yours to become overemotional!''

''Overemotional you call it? To want to rescue a poor,

tortured creature screaming aloud for help...?" Alexa began struggling wildly until she felt her wrist jerked painfully behind her back in the same motion that pulled her closely up against the length of his body.

"Your poor, tortured creature is probably screaming aloud in order to earn herself an extra pound or so. Are you so *naive* that you're not aware there are some women who *enjoy* that kind of treatment? And some poor whores on the streets outside who would submit to *anything*—any perversion or brutality required of them—for as little as five shillings?" The sound of his laugh was harsh and ugly in her ears. "Why, there is nothing at all that cannot be had—for the right price! From a genuine virgin to a child of either sex. If they are not old enough to sell themselves their parents will do so willingly enough. You must know, of course, of the specialized houses?" Feeling as if her throat was paralyzed, Alexa could only stare up at him speechlessly while he continued in the same hatefully cutting voice: "No? You continue to surprise me! But perhaps it's natural that *you* would not be particularly interested in infants, although some *men* are. They are usually between the ages of four to eleven, unless of course some rich customer..."

"Don't!" Alexa managed in a choked voice. "Please don't!" Children..."

"Male or female—a matter of personal preference. But of course the older they are the longer they are likely to survive. Would you rather I described some different perversion and how it is catered to?"

"No!" White-faced, Alexa flung her head back to glare at him, her eyes like darkly glowing coals. "You have already described too many of the disgusting, *inhuman* perversions that you seem all too familiar with." Her body stiffly unyielding against his, she drew in a sharp breath before almost spitting out, "Unless, of course, you want

to tell me what *your* particular preference—no, your *perversion*—happens to be?''

''Mine? Ah, I'm disappointed! I thought, *mi corazón,* that you understood my particular form of perverseness as well as I understand *yours.* Why do you think I brought you here tonight?''

''You are not only perverse, you are *obscure!*'' Alexa cried angrily. ''And you understand nothing—*nothing* about me! For if you did… Damn you! What do you think you're doing?''

''Giving in to my particular form of *vice,* I suppose,'' Nicholas said grimly as he carried her, kicking and struggling, past a heavy wooden door that stood ajar into a dimly lit room that was dominated by a bed on which he dropped her unceremoniously. ''While you are undressing, *querida,* I will ring for some chilled white wine—unless you'd prefer champagne? And in case we become hungry later on…''

''Did you bring me here by *force* in order to *rape* me? I suppose *that* must be your favorite form of vice.''

''My sweet Alexa,'' he said in a deceptively soft voice. ''I should apologize, I suppose, for not making it clear enough. It was not to *rape* you at all; quite the contrary. For tonight I had hoped that you would show me all the different ways in which a little virgin-whore is taught to make love to a man.''

''Oh!'' Alexa said with venomous sweetness, wishing that every word she uttered could have been a poisoned dagger. ''But do you want to be shown only what I learned while I was still virginal or what I have learned *since* then as well? And I really should tell you while I'm about it that *you're* the only man I thought of charging a fee! I suppose that's what it's called, and I suppose that *does* make me a…''

''I have always known what you are, sweetheart, so

there's no need to worry about disillusioning me. Although I must warn you that if you decide to put a price on your services tonight, I expect value for my money. It's understood?'' His laugh, as he bent for an instant to brush his fingers with suggestive familiarity across her breasts, was insolent. ''You have nice firm breasts, thank God, even if they're not very full. But I must say that you've the prettiest little bottom in the world, if I remember correctly, and I'll expect you to show it off after Dawes has brought up our wine and cold meats. Do undress quickly, won't you?''

''And if I do not choose to *undress* or...or...anything else?'' Alexa said in a carefully *calm* voice, even as her nails dug into her palms as she waited for his reply.

He had been looking through a mirrored armoire that was conveniently placed opposite the bed and turned back to toss a silk peignoir at her before saying as if he had not heard her, ''You might want to put this on later if you feel cold. Or at least while Dawes might be about.''

Alexa sat up in his bed with her clenched fists supporting her and said with quiet *violence,* ''Perhaps you did not understand what I said just now? I *said...*''

''A carefully couched hypothetical question, I think. You really need an answer?'' As he turned in the doorway with the light behind him, Alexa could not see his face or the expression on it when he said evenly: ''Well, then, *if* you want to play at being stubborn and coquettish and *if* I should feel impatient or aggravated, then I would instruct Dawes to see to it that you're made ready for me. He's quite used to dealing with recalcitrant females, I understand. He'd soon have you stripped of your pretty gown and all your petticoats, even your tightly laced corset and your silk stockings. That is, unless I tell him to leave you provocatively half-clad when he uses his softest leather straps to secure your wrists and your ankles. Hmm! Now that I've let my imagination picture the scene I must admit it's an alluring one. Especially if..."

"You filthy, rotten *bastard!* You..."

"If you should go on in *that* fashion you'd have to be gagged as well, since *I* don't particularly enjoy hearing a female screech. And now that I think of it, Dawes is supposed to be an expert in using a dog whip without marking up a delicate skin. A few swipes might do wonders in teaching you to hold your temper *and* your tongue, my love."

"Fiend!" Alexa cried after him as he started to walk away into the other room, her voice almost cracking with breathless fury. "You'd never *dare* to try such tactics on *me!* I'm not some frightened little whore you've picked up off the streets to threaten and browbeat, Lord Embry! I'd have you in *jail,* believe me, if you or anyone else so much as dared lay one hand on me. Damn you! How *dare* you threaten me!" As she swung her legs off the bed, still half-blinded by rage, Alexa's groping hand encountered a china comfit box on the night stand, and without thinking she threw it against the door he had left half-closed behind him (while she had still been *talking!*) with all the force she could muster. Hearing that satisfying *smash* made her feel better, and *stronger,* Alexa thought, grinding her teeth together as she sprang like a wild animal off the bed and ran to the dresser to seize a porcelain vase to throw in the same direction she had thrown the fragile china box. *That* explosive crash was even louder, and her only regret was that *he* had erupted through the doorway a split second too late. The blue-shaded lamp she grabbed for next was heavier than she had anticipated, and before she could lift it high enough she found it snatched out of her grasp and set down again; and in the very next moment, before she had time to catch her breath again, she was lifted and

thrown back on the bed as if she was of even less account than a *lamp*.

"You had better listen to me *very* closely this time, my darling," Nicholas grated between his teeth as he leaned over her, his face a hard, threatening mask. "Because after *that* temper tantrum of yours my patience is exhausted. No, you'd be wise not to say a word, *querida!*" It was the barely controlled way in which he took her face between the fingers of one hand, with his palm against her *throat* as he forced her to look up at him, that made Alexa catch back her angry words and fall unwillingly silent while he continued with cold deliberation: "I had just rung for Dawes before you began to screech and smash everything in sight like a virago. And I tell you *now* that if you are *not* undressed and wearing that silk wrap I handed you by the time he comes up... I think I have already told you what the other alternative is?" As he released her face and straightened, Alexa heard him add softly and almost contemplatively: "Of course, it might be that you derive some excitement from that kind of thing, and that is why you encourage Newbury. But in any case, I'm sure that we shall learn a great deal more about each other before the night is over, aren't you?"

After Nicholas had walked off into his dressing room, leaving her there on the bed without another glance, it took several moments before Alexa found she could think coherently again. How *dared* he! He was only trying to *frighten* her with his ridiculous threats, of course. To have her tied up and *beaten* as if she... And then like a glass of cold water thrown in her face she remembered all too vividly the screams she had heard earlier and the cruelly callous words uttered before the poor creature had been dragged off to face more agony. And Nicholas himself had not cared, had *dismissed* it casually. As casually as she had heard him say, "I was accused of killing my wife," and then a few minutes afterwards use his knife on a man with cold deliberation.

He was capable of any act of cruelty or violence. Alexa was suddenly positive of it, and the thought made her shiver with a cold chill that struck through her body and cooled some of the heated rage that had all but clouded her thinking so far. Dear God! she thought suddenly, what was the point in accumulating knowledge if she had not enough control over her emotions to *use* everything she had learned? Why, every time she let herself be provoked into losing her temper and her self-control with it she was only allowing herself to be bested; and even worse, manipulated! Dragging in a deep if rather ragged breath, Alexa set her jaw determinedly as she slid off the bed and stood up. Discretion, she had heard, was the better part of valor; and in this case, by remaining stubborn she would only heap more humiliation upon herself, whereas a pretense at least of conceding gracefully might even give her the advantage, for a change.

While she had been engaged in thinking and soul-searching Alexa had hardly been conscious of the faint sounds of splashing that came from behind the closed door to the dressing room; but now, as she struggled with the buttons running down the back of her gown, she became suddenly aware that the sounds had stopped. What was *he* doing? Changing his clothes in privacy while she was allowed none? As she stared balefully at that closed door Alexa had a sudden thought that made her lips curve wickedly for a moment before she composed her features again.

"Nicholas?" she managed to say rather timidly before she knocked at the door. "Nicholas, I...I'm afraid I need some help." Alexa thought she heard him swear softly before he opened the door to her second knock and she looked up to meet his scowl and his narrowed, suspicious eyes. He had already stripped down to the waist, she noticed, before her eyes fell on the razor he was holding, and she said with wide-eyed guilelessness: "Oh, goodness! You surely didn't think you might need to *defend* yourself from *me?* I only knocked to ask if you could help me with some buttons I cannot undo myself."

"I *happened,*" he said grimly as he wiped off traces of lather with the end of the towel he had slung about his neck, "to have been engaged in *shaving* myself just now."

"But don't you have a *valet* to look after you? I could never manage to do anything for myself without my maid to help me. I am sorry if I *interrupted* you, though... only..."

"Maldito sea!" Nicholas swore feelingly. "If the sight of a razor makes you so nervous you begin to babble inanities, I'll put it away immediately, I promise you! Where are these buttons? At the back? Then for God's sake turn yourself about if you want me to play lady's maid!"

He had positively *slammed* his razor down on a shelf by the door before wadding the towel up to throw it across the room, Alexa noted with almost smug satisfaction as she had turned around obediently to stand with her neck bowed and her hands clasped before her in an attitude of mock-submission meant to annoy rather than deceive him. All she had to do, she told herself now, was to remember *not* to fly into a rage again no matter how he tried to prod her into it. Why, *that* would probably frustrate him more than anything else!

39

The ubiquitous Mr. Dawes had not only swept the debris left scattered everywhere as mute evidence of an explosion of rage; he had also stoked the fires in both rooms and swiftly set a table with linen and silver and crystal before the fire in the sitting room, explaining as he did that Madame Olivier certainly never stinted on anything for her most valued customers. "And I hopes, milord, that the cold repast is to your liking? Everything you usually wants when you pull the cord three times, though o'course I'd gladly bring anything else...?"

When Dawes's words had suddenly trailed off, Nicholas had been standing directly before the fire and staring almost angrily into it. Then, as he looked up and followed the direction of the man's gaze, he found himself just as frozen with disbelief for an instant.

"Oh," Alexa said hesitantly as she paused effectively in the doorway of the bedroom. "I did not realize... You are not *angry* with me, are you? I...I only borrowed what looked like your *oldest* garments—*not* those made by Stultz, of course—because I wanted to *surprise* you."

"Did you?" A certain note in Nicholas's voice made Alexa rush quickly into speech before he could say more.

"Well, you see, darling, I really wanted to look attractive for you, but your *last* mistress must have been rather *bigger,* as well as *shorter* than I am and when I put on that peignoir and realized how *frightful* I looked...I had the idea from something my friend Leonie said to me once about men finding it *exciting* to see a woman dressed this way. Wasn't it true after all? Do I look too *mannish?*"

She had worn a pair of his trousers folded up at the bottom until they were several inches above her ankles, with a ribbon from one of *her* garments to hold them up around her slender waist, and a thin white linen shirt, rolled up at the sleeves and held together by a knot at the waist, instead of studs. And she did not look in the least mannish, as she doubtlessly knew quite well! The vixen! And why was it that she could make him want her and be enraged at her at the same moment? It was as if each encounter was like a fencing match of thrust, parry and riposte that continued to the next and the next. His long pause as he studied her appearance was meant to unnerve her, but she seemed to be able to keep her questioning pose without altering it—like a *Tableau Vivant,* Nicholas thought grimly.

"What is *your* opinion, Mr. Dawes?" Alexa said brightly as she turned her gaze quickly away from Nicholas's fire-shadowed face and ominous silence. Although her heart had begun to thud rather apprehensively she persisted in the same light tone, "I *know* of course that you could only be the same Mr. Dawes whose *efficiency* in every respect I've just heard praised so highly!"

"What *is* your frank opinion, Dawes?" Nicholas asked in a drawling kind of voice that held undertones Alexa did not particularly care for. "I would like to hear it."

"Well, milord, now that you've *asked...!*" Stony eyes flicked over Alexa again in a coldly considering way before Dawes said: "I've seen troublesome ones before—the kind you can't trust. And there's nothing like taking precautions, *just in case,* your Lordship! If I might be pardoned for making the suggestion. Sometimes just seeing the straps is enough to do the trick, milord. And if not…"

"I'm sure I may leave it up to you, Dawes, although you should keep in mind that I don't want her marked up. Not unless she's aggravating enough to make me tire of her."

It was partly stubborn pride and partly sheer cowardice that made Alexa bite back the righteously indignant words that had almost escaped her at *that.* It was only when he addressed her tauntingly with, "I certainly hope you haven't lost the power to move along with the power to speak, sweetheart!" that she was able to respond to his baiting of her at last in a voice that sounded almost even.

"I…forgive me, but I was only rather taken aback, I suppose. I had no idea that *your* inclinations were so like *Newbury's*—especially since you became so angry with me once for suggesting as much."

At that moment, with her hair loose and hanging over her breasts and down her back like a wild mane and the color blazing along her cheekbones, her curiously slaty eyes pinpointed by the reflected crimson of the fire, Nicholas was reminded of some female pirate who lacked only a pistol or a cutlass to make the image complete. Through the fine, thin linen of his favorite shirt her nipples were easily discernible and all the more tantalizing for being barely veiled. And the time she must have spent before the mirror in his dressing room had surely reassured her of the seductively intriguing image she presented. Damn her! Masculine attire, the way *she* wore it, only served to emphasize her femininity and to flaunt it. From hellcat to temptress—how surprising and unexpectedly swift the transition had been!

She had just made some ridiculous statement that was

meant to be provocative, hadn't she? Allowing the cynical side of his nature to prevail on this occasion, at least, Nicholas shrugged negligently before reminding her that *she* had been the one to announce herself famished and thirsty, had she not? Unless she had since changed her mind...? In the end he regretted the consideration he had displayed for her, especially when he realized that she actually ate with an almost peasant appetite and gusto instead of picking at her food in a ladylike, mannerly fashion. She consumed, with equal enthusiasm, cold roast beef and veal as well as capon stuffed with oysters and several different kinds of cheeses as well, washing everything down with the wine that he had been thoughtful enough to order. Tempted to make some caustic comment, Nicholas decided instead to sit back and watch her with fascination while he wondered annoyedly what made her as changeable and as unpredictable as the direction of the wind or the moods of the ocean.

"Oh *thank* you. You cannot imagine how *very* hungry I was!" Alexa said at length as she bit into an apple. "Mmm! And what a good apple too! This is the best way to *enjoy* any fruit, you know. Would you care for a bite? There's almost half left, and I don't think I can eat another bite of *anything!*"

"I was beginning to wonder when you might come to that conclusion," Nicholas said almost disbelievingly before adding, "but are you sure you have had quite enough, my dear?"

"Well...if we can have some cognac perhaps? I've found it does wonders for the digestion, as well as making me much more...well...passionate. That is, of course, unless you would prefer that I feign reluctance?" Alexa gave him a limpidly questioning look before resuming sweetly, "I *had* noticed of course that whenever I have been with *you,* it is that element of near-rape I remember the best.

But that is not *too* unusual, of course. I mean that particular..."

When he rose from the chair opposite where he'd been lounging negligently it was in one swiftly fluid motion that gave Alexa barely time in which to widen her eyes before he had leaned across the table and grabbed her onto her feet with such force that for a moment she thought he meant to haul her across the table. The fingerbowl she had been using went flying and her wineglass tipped over. A plate, left too near the edge, crashed to the floor.

"Alexa," Nicholas said in a softly polished voice, "you shall have your cognac and show me the extent of your passion in bed, I think, unless you want me to take you here and now, bent over the table or on the floor or in any other fashion you prefer. *So?*" When she managed to shake her head as she tried to swallow, he released her at last, sending her floundering back into her chair. "While I find two glasses for the cognac, why don't you wait for me in the bedroom? Unless, of course, I've mistaken your preference?" He hardly waited for her to start out of the chair as if she'd been pulled by strings before turning towards the sideboard. But over his shoulder, catching her almost in the doorway with his casually flung command, he said, "Take only the shirt off for the moment, *tesoro,* and don't get in bed yet, will you? Seeing those sweet little curves of yours so provocatively outlined has given me all kinds of intriguing notions, I must admit."

The sound of her swiftly indrawn breath seemed loud in the suddenly still air between them as Alexa whirled to face him on bare feet, her eyes blazing against the sudden whiteness of her taut face. "For God's sake! Haven't you wasted enough time already on your cruel little games? You have convinced me by now of the futility of resistance—why hesitate to be *blunt* again? Instruct me as to the nature and form of the performance you want from me, my lord, so that I might do whatever you say I must and have it done and over with as soon as I may. You wished your shirt returned and my breasts bared?'' Alexa's fingers had been tearing angrily at the knot while she was speaking, and now as it came loose she almost ripped the shirt from her own body and flung it contemptuously in his direction, standing there like a fiercely proud young Amazon in the firelight that tipped the gold of her breasts with crimson. ''And now, Lord Embry? What else do you require of me?'' Her voice had become quite breathless and shook slightly from the force of her emotions; but Alexa stood her ground without flinching, even when his long strides brought him up to her in a dangerously purposeful manner that could have meant he intended to strangle her.

Nicholas himself was not quite sure of his intentions until he had halted less than a foot away from where she stood with her hands clenched into fists at her sides and her long, slim legs set boldly apart; her eyes glaring hatred up at him like those of a trapped vixen. Trapped.... His girl-wife had had black Creole eyes that had looked at him almost in the same way. Dumb-animal eyes filled with fear and hate and frustration and revulsion, flickering away when they encountered his without realizing that he too had been caught in the same trap as she. And if fate had not intervened...? The fire flickered and the slate-dark eyes that raged into his held at least no fear, and no revulsion yet. Her breasts, high and pointed, had looked as if they have been brushed with silver by the moon, that first time he had seen her; but now as they moved with her quick, angry breathing they seemed to have borrowed some of the fire's gold to complement the bronze mane of hair she shook back angrily under his long, speculative look.

He had not said a word yet, Alexa thought. Did he hope to unnerve her by the way he looked her over appraisingly as if she had been a slave on the auction block? And what *did* he really want with her after all? What more?

"Turn around," Nicholas said startlingly, and her mouth dropped open as she stared up at him disbelievingly until he repeated it in a harsh, rather impatient tone. "My dear, your little breasts are quite charming, as you well know; but your—derriere, shall we say?—is your most enticing feature. Provocative too. Why don't you walk into the bedroom ahead of me, and I will tell you what I *require* next after we get there. Well? A few moments ago you sounded anxious to have your *performance* over and done with as quickly as possible, if I recall correctly."

With a visible effort Alexa managed to bite back the rebellious words she longed to fling at him and compressed her lips instead, giving him one last contemptuously hateful look before turning on her heel with her shoulders back and her head high, every inch the proud aristocrat on her way to execution.

"Stop there, exactly where you are standing now by the bed. You would have made a good soldier, my sweet. And do stay *as* you are too, so that I can admire the fetching picture you present. I really think that you should be painted this way—the pirate wench taken captive and disarmed, and following orders for a change. Tell me, does this ordeal seem to you as painful as walking a plank with an ocean filled with hungry sharks at its end?"

"Much worse, I assure you. And does my admission give your Lordship satisfaction?" Every word dripped acid, for all that Alexa felt her teeth sink into her lip soon afterwards when she felt that he had come up behind her. What did he really intend to do with her? Oh, God! How *easy* it had all sounded, and how detached from reality somehow—the lessons that had been intended to teach her how to play the whore. You did this and you did that, or you allowed a man to do thus and so—all carefully *cal-*

culated, the object being to find his weaknesses and play on them, so that in the end he would become slave to his own weaknesses and the woman who found out what they were. Delilah…Salome…Cleopatra…countless others. The great courtesans of the world who ruled through the men they made mad for them and then manipulated. None of *them* would be standing here as stiff and brittle as a dry twig that could be snapped in two without effort. Any one of them would, by now, have turned aggressor and had him in bed, an easy victim. Or…or they would give *in* in such a manner that pretended defeat turned out to be actual victory. The victor vanquished… *Think* about it, Alexa! she commanded herself. Think only of what you should have learned by now and use that knowledge.

It was as if she had become paralyzed while *he*—her enemy and her adversary—had somehow been able to sense her thoughts and act as *she* should have done. In *honor* of that travesty of a supper she had been forced to sit through, he had donned a shirt but without troubling to fasten any more than two or three buttons at the most. And now Alexa felt his bare chest press against her naked back as his arms seemed to surround her and hem her in like the columns of a conquering army; so sure of victory that already his hands had begun to move possessively and far too intimately over her captive body.

Her first, instinctive movement to escape was stilled when his hands moved from her breasts to between her thighs, holding her so closely against himself that she was forced to feel everything he meant her to feel and to wonder fearfully how far he meant to go. "And *now,*" he said softly in her ear, "untie that damned ribbon. You said you wanted a swift conclusion to this? Then show me some of the tricks you have learned from your recent lovers and the bordellos you're fond of frequenting, and perhaps you'll have your wish." Even while he was speaking he had brushed aside her clumsy fingers and had untied the ribbon himself before Alexa, feeling as if she was in a kind of daze, had realized what he was about.

"*No!*" she cried furiously, and then cried out again when she felt herself propelled forward to be almost flung face down across his bed with her arms caught up and twisted behind her back. His fingers held her wrists together like manacles and tightened mercilessly when she attempted, just once, to move. But this time she fought back her scream and only gasped instead, allowing him, without a struggle, to use his free hand to pull the trousers over her hips with savage force, so that they slid down to her ankles, trapping her and rendering her even more helpless than she was already with the weight of his body leaning over her.

"And now, perhaps, we can talk frankly to each other," Nicholas said pleasantly before adding: "Hold still, love, before I am forced to dislocate your arm and then force the bone back into its socket again—a very painful process, I'm afraid. So, I suggest that you do as you promised and perhaps even derive some enjoyment from this."

Even after he had released her, Alexa continued to lie still, with her fingers meshed tightly together above her head. Turn limp, she commanded herself. Or turn into wood. Why wouldn't her treacherous body obey the sensible, pragmatic orders given by her brain? Her arms ached almost intolerably, although she would not let him know that as she waited for him to hurt her again and thought fiercely, I hate him! I hate him! And please, let it be over with soon, and let him get no pleasure from it.

"The maiden sacrifice!" she heard him say sarcastically from somewhere above her before adding: "Will you send me an accounting for *another* maidenhead after tonight? Or have you already been thoroughly explored? Keep still, *querida,* while you think about your answer and I make you ready for some exploration of my own."

Roughly, he shoved a pillow under her hips to elevate them before he allowed his hands the license to rove, stroking gently and almost tenderly at first while Alexa pushed the back of one hand against her mouth and then, driven by pride, between her teeth to stop herself from crying out loud when the "exploration" he had threatened her with became painfully and humiliatingly intimate.

The almost involuntary movements she made to escape his probing fingers might have seemed to him, she thought afterwards, an eager and wanton response to his callous invasion of her body—her privacy—*herself.* In the end, in spite of herself, she *did* cry out against it and against the poised, waiting threat of his body lying now alongside hers while he stroked her breasts with one hand and continued to move and to feel and to go even more deeply inside her with the other, in spite of what *she* did or didn't want.

Until he left her abruptly Alexa had not realized that her ragged breaths had become loud sobs that made her whole body shudder. Rage and frustration and hate mingled with disgust at herself for showing such contemptible weakness and especially before *him.* She did not *want* to weep and could not help herself, and at the same time she felt, childishly, like kicking and screaming aloud to relieve her feelings.

"That's enough of your damned sniveling! Here, sit up and drink some wine to calm you down. For God's sake! One would think you were some startled little innocent who had never known a man's touch before."

Alexa felt herself caught under the shoulders and dragged upright before she was all but *forced* up against the ornately carved gilt headboard of the bed, a glass of wine thrust so roughly into her hands that some of it spilled over her, trickling coldly between her breasts and down her belly. She felt sore and debased and *used. Mis*-used was more like it; and he had done it with cold, cruel detachment in order to teach her a lesson in humility, no doubt. Trying to catch back her sobs, Alexa almost choked, both on the wine and her mortification. How she had begun to hate him and the harsh, caustic tone that usually entered his voice when he addressed her, as he did again now.

"One would imagine you've been violated, to judge from your piteous sobs. Don't tell me your *other* lovers have been so lacking in imagination as to let any part of such a tempting delectable body go neglected?" He laughed when she almost unconsciously drew her legs up under her, and taunted, "Modesty at this late stage? Or is it more pretense? Can it be, my sweet, shy Alexa, that you're disappointed that I did not take what was begun to a final conclusion? Should I now?"

Goaded, she turned on him with her cheeks still damp from the angry tears she had shed, wanting above all to hurt him wherever he was most vulnerable with her arrowed words. "If you treated your wife in the same callous fashion in which you've treated *me,* I am hardly surprised that she shrank from you. Perhaps she might even have found her second captivity vastly preferable to the *first.* Was that why you had to kill her?"

There was a silence that seemed to stretch forever, long enough for her to notice irrelevantly that the gas lamps had been turned down under their blue shades that matched the shades of the old-fashioned lamps on the dressing table. That the fire had burned down to red coals, and that the thin cigar he had been smoking gave off a most peculiar odor which she could not place.

He dragged on the cigar while she felt herself compelled to keep her eyes on his face; and while he seemed to hold the smoke he inhaled within himself for an interminable time, his eyes glittered at her like jagged shards of green glass until they were veiled at last by smoke. "Did I really bare my soul to you that night? How boring that must have been for you. In fact, I'm surprised that you decided to linger, especially in view of... But why *did* you stay? And why did you suddenly appear when you did, as my—ah, yes—true dream, I think it was. How is *your* memory? Can you remember all the bordellos you've been in, looking for whatever it is you were looking for?" He was so close to her that their shoulders almost touched, close enough so that Alexa could almost feel the violence that emanated from his body and stretched like taut strings under the surface calmness of his voice. If she *moved* now or even looked away he would probably put his hands about her neck and snap it. Encountering a leopard or a panther unexpectedly in the jungle when there were only a few feet separating you and no time in which to bring up a gun, you stood there very still and stared the predator down, ignoring the growls and the swishing tail and the narrowed green eyes. *This* was a different kind of predator that she faced now, one she found more frightening and more dangerous. She should never have let herself forget, Alexa thought, that this man only put on a surface show of being civilized—just as easily as he wore his London clothes and his title and his polite manners. But underneath there was the savage barbarian who carried a knife from force of habit and used it without hesitation, a cruel man raised in a savage, primitive land, with the dark Spanish blood of the ruthless conquistadores running in his veins. Besides his unfortunate wife, how many others had he killed?

"Here, dammit!" Nicholas said in a hard voice, and put his cigar to her lips. "Inhaling this ought to loosen your stubborn tongue, along with some of the prudishness you seem to have acquired quite suddenly."

"But I..." Alexa knew, even as she began to protest, that it would do her no good.

"If you're afraid of becoming sick, there's no need to worry. This is a different kind of 'cigar,' my dear innocent, and I'm surprised that you haven't tried this kind of thing before. Try to inhale it slowly, and hold the smoke in your lungs for as long as you can."

Alexa coughed and spluttered at first, but he remained inflexible; and at last she managed unwillingly to satisfy him, not daring to do otherwise. Her throat seemed to burn from the harshness of the smoke, and she drained the glass of wine he had given her, wondering the next moment how she happened to be holding another glass in her hand. How? Of course. It was *his* glass, and he had gone into the next room for more wine to get drunk on. Primitive man. Naked sculpture by Michelangelo come to life as he walked back to her. This time the smoke did not burn her throat and her lungs quite as much, and Alexa felt some of the tenseness in her body relax as she leaned her head back against the headboard and breathed in deeply. "It's not tobacco, is it?"

"This particular plant grows like a weed, and the medicine men swear it can cure almost every ailment known."

"I'm sure *that* claim is highly exaggerated! But I suppose..." Her voice trailed off rather vaguely as Alexa suddenly became aware of the effect of the blue lampshades. Except for the sullen, dark red coals everything was deep, dark blue, like diving deeply into the ocean and being able to live and breathe underwater in that dim blueness.

"And what do you suppose, Alexa?"

"I have forgotten what I supposed at first, so I'm sure it was nothing very important." Turning her head, Alexa met his shadowed look head on before she said thoughtfully, "But I *do* suppose, you know, that I would like to know if you really did murder your wife?"

"Are you admitting that you might actually have some *doubts!*" There was something underlying the sarcastic tone of his voice that almost puzzled her before she heard him say, without any inflection this time, "I did kill her, though. Call it murder, if you will; it's a word that fits the deed as well as any other. And does *that* satisfy your curiosity?"

40

"Marry her? My dear Nicholas, it's surely not that vast, *vulgar* fortune that attracts you, is it? If you are short of money..."

"I'm sure you are already well aware of my financial standing, Belle-Mère," he had answered her shortly, preparing to take his leave of her as politely and as quickly as possible. But it was then that the Dowager Marchioness of Newbury had taken him by surprise by crossing the room to put an urgent hand on his sleeve.

She had given a short, almost resigned sigh before saying quietly: "Very well, then. I had not meant to let too many family skeletons out of the closet all at once, but in this case... You will at least sit down, instead of continuing to stand there *towering* over me while I make my speech, I hope? Please, I find it difficult enough as it is."

Knowing how subtly cunning she could be, he had waited skeptically for the speech she had promised him; and although he had learned long ago to school his face so that it showed no reaction, he had responded to her concisely delivered *facts,* as she called them, in his gut. An explanation for everything, she had promised, and had not even spared herself in admitting baldly that after her husband who was so much older than she was had become bedridden with a stroke, she had taken lovers. And one of them had been Sir John Travers, Bart....

"He was young and handsome. A friend of Gavin's. I used to feel his eyes on me, following me everywhere. He worshiped me, he said. And was fool enough to go off to India to make a fortune—for *me,* he said, poor fool. And then he actually came back *with* his fortune but without his manhood, actually believing I would be content to play Beatrice to his Dante. Pure, unsullied love, he called it. Ah, I'm afraid I've never been one to mince words or be less than blunt. So, he took himself off, hating me as passionately as he swore he had once loved me, swearing dramatically that he would be revenged, even if it was from the grave."

"Poor fool indeed!" Nicholas remembered commenting drily before she had lifted an imperious hand.

"I had forgotten about the man until his *widow* turned up out of the blue. And would have ignored *her* had I not known her background and what she was—and had I not realized belatedly that John Travers had indeed meant what he said when he spoke of revenge."

"And what *is* her background?"

"You heard all the hints she dropped when she was presented to me? 'My grandmother, they tell me, is a witch,' she said." The Dowager gave a harsh laugh. "True enough, my dear Nicholas, I've been called that and worse by my enemies. And true enough too that I'm her grandmother on the wrong side of the blanket. She's one of Newbury's by-blows, you see. And I've been paying her foster-parents for her upkeep all these years. Martin and Victorine Howard. They took her off to Ceylon as their own brat, and I bought Martin Howard his coffee estate on condition she was never to be told that she was the bastard daughter of the Marquess of Newbury and one of his whores. That her real mother is, in fact, the woman supposed to be her *aunt*—a woman that every man in London knows well as Madame Olivier.''

There were more disclosures, of course. Belle-Mère was thorough as well as efficient, and had had Lady Travers followed and her many indiscretions noted. Meetings with Lord Deering, who was openly infatuated with her. Meetings with Madame Olivier, her ''aunt.'' A discreet chamber kept for her use over her favorite millinery boutique in Burlington Arcade.

''Knowing you, with that stony face of yours, you'll want to make sure of everything for yourself, won't you? And you'll learn even more than I know now, I'll be bound. But for God's sake realize at least that you'd be making a laughingstock as well as a fool out of yourself if you persist with this madness. She wants to make a big, ugly scandal of course. Why do you think she encourages Newbury to send her flowers every day? Her *father,* mind you, and she must know it. So this afternoon it was you, and tonight it will be poor Charles in one of those disgustingly sordid little cubbyholes they rent out in Cremorne Gardens. My *dear* Nicholas! Even if you are dead set against a match with Helen, at least consider the consequences of this *other!* The creature is out to use you—or Charles—or anyone else she can sink her claws into, for that matter. Men can be such fools over a pretty face and a pretty figure, and you can get *both,* as well as some lusty enjoyment, from any whore at Madame Olivier's!''

Although he was careful not to let Belle-Mère see it, Nicholas had surprised himself by the violence of the wrath he felt like an explosion in his brain when he had realized how devious and how conniving she really was—the little bitch! And cool as a cucumber, she had denied nothing he had accused her of yet. She was obviously a born harlot, and deserved to be treated like one. And as for her virginity—if she had not used some typical whore's stratagem to fool him, that was—he should remember that all whores were virgin to begin with, and that if he hadn't been the first some other man would have been. In fact, it was more than possible that she had "chosen" him that night because she had learned he was her father's heir.

He should have kept his mind detached earlier, while toying with her as he pleased, before taking her in the fashion he had planned to take her—instead of allowing her desperate-sounding sobs to deter him, Nicholas thought grimly now. No doubt, among her other talents she also possessed the facility to shed copious tears whenever it suited her. And then, to top it all, she had just had the cool effrontery to ask him if he had actually murdered his wife, conjuring up memories and images in his mind that he had been trying to forget. Damn her! His fingers itched to close around the slim column of her neck, but instead Nicholas said brusquely, "Here! And this time try to hold the smoke in for as long as possible—it's one way at least of keeping you silent!" Perhaps she had sensed the consequences that awaited her if she provoked him further, because Alexa obeyed him silently after one sideways glance at his face. And it was then, not being able to resist the impulse any longer, that he shot at her harshly, "Tell me, since we seem to be exchanging confidences at the moment, how did you fall into the habit of visiting bordellos for your amusement? Did your husband know you did it?"

For some illogical reason it infuriated him even more when, instead of flinching away from the blunt question, she was brazen enough to turn her head and look him squarely in the eyes while she answered him coolly.

"It was my husband's idea that I needed to learn as much as possible about human nature. He knew that he only had a few months to live when he married me, you see, and he wanted me to be prepared. Most women are *not,* poor things! When I first met *you,* for instance, how you must have laughed to yourself at my *naiveté.* I knew nothing, and understood nothing, even about my own body or the sensations that could too easily be aroused by someone unscrupulous—someone used to seducing young girls! But I have learned so much since then, Lord Embry, and from the best teachers in the world, I think.'' Alexa shrugged almost challengingly before she added thoughtfully: ''Of course, I have been finding out that it is one thing to be *told* things and even to watch, and quite different when it is actually happening to *you.* I don't think I would like to be dependent on a man's whims or his money to support me. I *prefer,* in fact, to make my own choices.''

''*Do* you? And that night in Rome, when you played priestess of Venus... I must admit it makes me curious as to why you happened to visit *me.* Or did you intend to try out your talents on as many men as possible? Christ!'' Nicholas gave a harsh laugh. ''I think I begin to understand now. The virgin-whore—knowledgeable, tantalizing, promising everything and giving nothing in the end. *That* was your intention when you suddenly appeared like an apparition out of a dream, wasn't it? As I remember it now you *did* prove that you had learned a great deal since the last time we had been together. And I must admit that I did not expect that you might still be clinging to your pure and virginal state. Did your *husband* enjoy watching you with other men? Did he instruct you as to how you might lead them up to a certain point before you made some excuse to leave—I'm sure you promised to come back as soon as possible!—and laugh to see how you had managed to fool them?''

''If you do not enjoy hearing the truth you should not

ask for it. And since you did not know my husband you have no right to say what you did! He...''

Her indignant protest was cut off when Alexa felt his fingers bite into her bare shoulders, twisting her body around so that she could not help falling against him.

''I am glad I did not know your husband, who used you for his own purposes. But I am still curious as to why, by some strange coincidence, you happened to turn up that evening.''

Resentfully, Alexa looked up at him with her eyes slitted. Whatever the drug was that he had forced her to take, it had made her free of fear. Her mind felt very clear and free, as if it floated separately from her body. And her words were clear and carefully pronounced. ''You want to know? I watched you make love with Maddalena in the room of mirrors one night, and I thought then that I wanted you. After all, it was *you* who first made me aware of sensuality and certain feelings that could be aroused in my *body,* in spite of the protests of my mind. Yes, *you!* If I had not been with you that night on the beach, then Sir John might not have had to save my reputation by telling everyone we had just become engaged. And...but what does it matter now? I lost my virginity and my husband on the same night, Nicholas Dameron! My *illusions* and my innocence I had lost a long time before.'' And then she said with a soft laugh that seemed to come from someone inside herself that wasn't even her at all: ''But what does all *that* matter? Now that we know the worst about each other and have played at question and answer, am I to find out for what other reason you brought me here or may I go home to sleep? I would not miss your Belle-Mère's ball and the announcement of your betrothal to Helen for the world.''

Face down the crouching, sleek-muscled predator.

Never turn your eyes away or let him sense fear, or you are lost....

There was a moment, as she looked deep into the green darkness of his eyes, that Alexa thought she saw what death looked like. And then, acting purely instinctively, she yielded to the tightening hold of his fingers on her shoulders and leaned more closely against him, letting her fingers trail teasingly down his chest and even further before he pushed her roughly backward with a muttered obscenity. And she laughed as she caught him closer and felt the smooth movement of muscles under his flesh and met the violence of his knife-plunge into her with the upward arch of her hips, *feeling* him inside her and against her with every sensitive nerve ending.

"*Puta!*" he whispered harshly with his lips only inches away from hers. "I can tell you've had plenty of practice." He put his hands under her to raise her against him and Alexa gasped, feeling and following the motion of his body as he turned and turned her with him so that she was astride his loins now, her long tangled mane of gold-streaked bronze hair hanging down to brush his face and his chest before she shook it back for a moment, leaning over him again; and their duel of thrust and counter-thrust continued.

"Aren't you glad of it? This practice that makes me a *puta?* Only you're mistaken, you know. I do not need to charge a fee for whatever gives *me* pleasure. I can choose for myself. Does this give *you* pleasure, your Lordship? Do you enjoy being my stallion?"

"As long as you ride me well and pleasingly, my Lady." Accepting her unexpected challenge, Nicholas laughed suddenly and thought, why not? She was certainly more appealing *this* way—willing and even slightly aggressive—than she had been as a sullen victim. After all, what had he expected or wanted from her that went beyond this? Why should it be of any account to him how many other men had been caressed by her and kissed by her and tempted by her? The sea nymph he had almost trapped and the trembling virgin he had foolishly left intact had only been illusive images he'd allowed his own mind to conjure up. The well-trained whore whose every movement was calculated and practiced was the real woman and had always been. It was he who should have known better, who had deceived himself.

It was like a jousting match, this unacknowledged contest of skills and wills between them; and the changing pattern of their bodies against rumpled sheets was reflected in the mirrors that had been carefully placed in the room for just such a purpose. "So you saw me with Maddalena? Did you enjoy what you saw, you sly little bitch?"

"You seemed to enjoy *her,*" Alexa returned a trifle tartly. "But to be honest, your performance with *me* did not match that earlier one. I was disappointed."

"You were far too argumentative to please me as well as Maddalena did, I'm afraid, and if you expect a better performance from me tonight *you* should try harder to excite *me* instead of boring me with your damned chattering!" Without warning Alexa found herself on her back as he withdrew himself from her, only to sit astride her and trap one of her hands in his. "Let me demonstrate to you, my sweet, what *might* have happened if I'd let Dawes at you first. And be quiet, or..."

She had to bite down on her lip in order not to let him hear her scream out loud with outrage as he used the soft leather straps that Dawes had thoughtfully left attached to the bedposts in order to secure her wrists above her head. Then he let his hands slide down her body in a leisurely and almost possessive fashion, lingering over her breasts for a moment or two before moving downward. Instinctively, angrily, Alexa pressed her thighs together. "Whatever you *think* you might achieve by the use of *force*... Stop!'' She kicked at him, trying to aim at the most vulnerable parts of his body. *Tried* to, until he had her ankles secured as well, to leave her open and helpless and now, at last, watchfully silent.

''I do not think, sweet slut, that I will need to use *force* on you. Why should I? But you have a sweet body that I would like to explore and use as I please, without restraint. And I should hate to have to go to the trouble of gagging you; so perhaps you will attempt to restrain yourself from crying out too loudly?'' To add to her almost unbearable sense of frustration he left her there spread out on the bed while he proceeded to add more coals to the fire and then light up another of his ''cigars,'' dragging deeply on it before he came back to stand looking down at her in a strangely disturbing manner before he said politely, ''You'll join me in indulging?'' And leaning down over her, held it to her lips with one hand while with the other he began to caress her with deceptive gentleness.

Even with her eyes squeezed tightly shut Alexa could almost see as well as feel the dark ocean-blue that surrounded her as she rose and sank and rose and sank like a rudderless ship controlled by the wind alone and by the way he was touching her, taking infinite time with her, just as if he had been an explorer who had discovered some new world that might be worth conquering. She felt as if she were a block of marble being sculpted into a statue, the sculptor's chisel forming every outline of muscle and vein and curve and hollow. And like a tautly spread canvas soaking up a painter's first light brushstrokes before he added, as he grew more confident, another and yet another layer until she was *his* picture, *his* marble statue, *his* conquered new continent.

There was no help for it, Alexa tried to tell herself. She was a helpless victim, subject to whatever torment he decided to inflict on her. And yet, when his hands molded her flesh, his fingers traced teasing patterns over her skin, his lips and tongue tasted her and tested her endurance—she wanted more. Cruelly, calculatedly, he made her *want* and then *need* the fulfillment he had made her crave. No longer ruled by reason, but by her senses alone, Alexa had never been so utterly, totally conscious of her body until now, when he had made her so. Or of feeling so *acutely,* with every inch of her burning, achingly sensitive skin, so many different kinds of touches and textures. And never before had she given herself up so unreservedly to sensation and pure sensuality and to her own sexuality.

There was no world but this bedroom, no time but now, and nothing she wanted more than this exquisite agony and exquisite pleasure mixed together. She wanted to experience everything, to know everything, to feel everything. To watch him make love to her body and to explore his in the same way. There was a mirror set cunningly into the molded ceiling above the bed, Alexa discovered when she slowly opened her eyes. Why hadn't she taken notice of it before? Pinned down in the center of the blue velvet twilight, the reflected image of her own body seemed to gleam back at her, sprawled across the white bedsheets, pale as ivory in contrast with his sunbrowned skin and dark head that was bent to her. She heard herself gasp and then moan out loud as she writhed against the sheets and against the straps that held her pinioned, forgetful of aching muscles and chafed skin and everything but a rising, expanding urgency that grew and kept growing until it was all she knew and all she felt.

Alexa's gasping moans had quickened until she was almost sobbing, and her head thrashed from side to side. ''Please, Nicholas. Oh, please, I...I *want...*'' Her voice was a strained and almost incoherent whisper forced out of her without her volition. ''Please. No! Don't...!''

If she could have done so Alexa would have pounded frantically at his chest when his body slid deliberately and teasingly up the length of hers until he had positioned himself between her thighs and she could feel the poised, hard length of him against her there and cried out again when he held her face between his palms and began to kiss her lightly while he whispered between kisses: "Have I made you want me, my sweet captive vixen? My lovely, corrupt Alexa—how easily and how sweetly you yield, and tempt, and plead. But for *what, mi corazón?* What *do* you desire? Tell me, Alexa. Open your eyes into mine when you tell me if you're willing to be my little whore for tonight—for a whore's price. And *will* you, my sweet?"

"Yes!" she sobbed out. "Yes, and I *want* you too! Damn you, Nicholas Dameron! I want you *inside* me—I want you to... I *want* you, do you understand? I..."

"*This* is what you want? And *this?*" Alexa's neck arched backward as a primitive, almost animal sound broke from her throat, and her indrawn breath seemed to have become trapped somewhere inside her body; deep inside her, as *he* was now, filling her so completely that there was no more room anywhere inside her—no empty spaces—ah, not even her mouth any longer as his possessed it fiercely and she was the center, the vortex of a whirlwind and only motion existed and she suddenly became the wind itself—a tightly wrapped spiral whirling higher and higher and higher until she whirled about the sun and became a billion glittering, scattered fragments of light falling through the sky as slowly as eternity.

Ripple after ripple of feeling made Alexa's body shake spasmodically for a long time afterwards, and she could not remember when he had finally slipped the straps from about her wrists until she realized that she was clinging tightly to him, as if she wished to clasp his body even more closely against hers.

"Don't go away from me yet; I want you to keep holding me," Alexa murmured protestingly when he disengaged her clinging arms. And then when she felt him free her ankles at last she said: "I suppose I'm all bruised now, you heartless brute! You did not have to go so far as to tie me down in order to do what you just did, you know, not after I had given *in.*"

"But *I* wanted more than 'giving in' from you, *mi tesoro.* I wanted you the way you were. Do you understand? Wanting and lusting and wild with longing, and that is how I had you in the end and will always have you whenever I feel so inclined. Have you learned that yet, *bruja?*"

Lifting her arms, Alexa slid her palms along his back with lingering slowness while she let a languorous smile curve her lips. "Oh, *yes!* And I've learned also that you want *me* just as much—which is only *fair,* is it not, my scowling demon-lover? And have you enjoyed my body as much as I enjoyed yours? Nicholas, I think I'd like very much to touch *your* body everywhere as you touched mine, and to make you want me all over again so that we could... Ah!" Suddenly tightening her arms about his neck, Alexa reached up to kiss his taut, unsmiling mouth before she lay back again and whispered: "Since I'm your more than willing whore tonight, you should let me try and prove that I am worth the price you offered to pay for my services, shouldn't you? And if I can please you more than once, perhaps you'll hire me again for another night or two?"

"Do you know, you taunting temptress-bitch, how many times tonight I have come close to choking you to death? Be careful with your barbed and teasing promises, sweet Alexa, in case I hold you to them and keep you locked in here naked and available to serve my needs at any time and in any fashion I wish! You might not enjoy being used and being forced to cater to *my* desires without *yours* being of any consideration at all to *me.* So, for your own sake, try not to provoke me any further, in case I make you sorry."

The abrasively warning note underlying the words he snarled down into her face should have made her thoughtful enough to lose at least some of her newly acquired brazenness, Nicholas thought wrathfully as he wrenched himself free of her false, clinging arms and the lying, suggestive invitation of her silk-skinned body pressing against his with bold, open wantonness while she whispered in a voice as warm and sweet as honey of being his *willing* whore and of showing him the ways she had learned of pleasing a man. How quickly and easily she gave way to the innate sensuality of her nature, and how dared she blame *him* for it! With long, angry strides he crossed the room and snatched up a bottle of wine, tilting his head back to pour cool, gold liquid down his throat straight from the bottle itself, like a Spanish peasant. Cleansing the taste of her from his tongue and erasing the feel and the textures of her from his lips. "I have learned that you want me just as much..." she had murmured, discovering his weakness as unerringly as any experienced harlot, curse her! And no wonder, considering her real origins.

"Are you going to finish *all* the wine without offering me any?" Although he kept his back turned to her Nicholas could not help but watch her in the mirror and see how she stretched with lazy, catlike satisfaction before sitting up against the bedhead with her legs crossed, not making any attempt to cover herself, even when she suddenly met his angry eyes in the mirror and smiled teasingly instead of cowering. "You are very much like a fierce, wild satyr when you are naked, you know. Most men are not as beautifully formed as *you* are under their clothes. I noticed your body that first time that I saw you in the Governor's pool, but I would have been far too shy to admit it *then,* of course. I didn't know anything at all at that time. Just think, if I had never met you I might actually have been married off to some dull young planter or civil servant or...or even *worse!*" Alexa gave a small shudder. "And then..." She looked back at his frozen reflection in the blue-edged mirror and said in a softer voice: "Then I might always have felt *stifled,* and even worse, might not even have known *why!* Nicholas? I am not *provoking* you by speaking honestly to you, am I? Have you decided yet what you are going to do with me now that you have me here at your mercy?" The way she deliberately and languorously stretched her arms above her head so that her perfectly formed, pointed breasts invited attention was, he told himself disagreeably, another typical whore's trick. First she had protested against everything and pretended to resist; and now, quite suddenly, it was quite the other way around and she was not only yielding but eager for more, the unpredictable little bitch.

Without saying a word to her, Nicholas drank again before he slammed the bottle down on the table, making the blue-shaded lamp tremble and the flame waver. Why should her calculated babble of words that were meant to disarm him have any effect on him? And why should he give a damn how many naked men she had seen and made love to—for *experience*— Hadn't that been her ridiculous excuse? The fact was...

Warm bare arms encircled him from behind, and a warm naked body pressed closely against his back. He felt the soft, practiced touch of her lips on his shoulder before Alexa laid her cheek against it and said questioningly: "Why won't you speak to me? Why do you always seem so *angry* with me every time we meet? And are you tired of me already or...or only embarrassed because you find that you cannot...? If that is all..."

"Alexa!" His voice held such cold menace that it silenced her and held her still. His fingers closed over her wrists and wrenched her arms apart before he released them and turned to face her, looking into her upturned, unflinching face and those witch-dark eyes that could be as opaque as slate or as deeply unfathomable as wells a man wanted to dive into, even if he might be lost forever in their cold, still depths. To Nicholas, fixing his eyes on her parted lips was both safer and wiser. Sweet, lying mouth still red from his kisses. The mouth of a whore. Before she could speak again he brushed the back of one hand across her mouth with careful, deceptive gentleness, leaving his fingers for long enough against her lips to feel the agitated flutter of her breath before he handed her the bottle of wine. ''Do you need a glass, *querida?* Or are you daring enough to drink this slightly warm wine from the bottle, as I did?'' He watched her glance at him somewhat doubtfully before she gave an insouciant shrug and tilted the bottle cautiously to her lips. Then he said, his voice steel blades sheathed in velvet: ''You have succeeded in making me feel rather guilty, you know. And of course your mouth—especially as I watch you with your head tilted back as you enjoy that wine from the bottle—how could I not remember your mouth as pure pleasure and delight?'' He smiled at her quite pleasantly as Alexa lowered the bottle, almost choking over the last swallow she had taken, and removed it firmly from her hand before he slid his hands up her arms to her shoulders, pulling her against him for a moment as he kissed her lingeringly but without passion of any kind.

When he lifted his head and held her away from him with his hands still holding her, Alexa tried to search his eyes; but they looked only at her mouth, and she tried to keep her lips from trembling when she said, ''Nicholas...?'' She wanted to be brave enough to let her thoughts tumble from her tongue as they flashed through her mind.

To say wisely and sanely, Why do we constantly try to hurt and scar each other like duelists in order to hide the truth? But in the end, as his fingers tightened over her shoulders and he looked at *her* at last, she said nothing, reading his dark thoughts through his eyes.

"I think you've made me yearn for the open, passionate rose of your mouth that promised me anything a short time ago and invites me to want everything *now,* Alexa, except speech. *Now,* and *here,* and in *this* manner."

41

Mr. Edwin Jarvis's little offices at Lincoln's Inn Fields had always seemed cozy and cheerful with the homelike touches added by his wife of fresh flowers in pottery vases and embroidered samplers on the walls; and there was always a teakettle on the simmer in one corner of the anteroom for waiting clients who might enjoy a cup of China tea with plenty of sugar and fresh cream, and shortbread biscuits to nibble on if they were hungry. Today, because it was grey and chilly outside with a sharp wind blowing, there was a small fire leaping merrily in the grate with a gaily colored crocheted rug thrown before it to cover the worn spots in the old carpeting; and a beaming young clerk led Alexa to the comfortable settle set at right angles to the fire, so that she could keep warm.

"I'll just pop my head in and tell Mr. Jarvis you're here, Lady Travers, although he *does* have another client with him at the moment, I'm afraid. If I had known that he was expecting you I would have made a point of reminding him."

"He wasn't expecting me. I suppose it was an impulse of mine, since I happened to be in the neighborhood and remembered that I had been wishing to speak quite urgently to Mr. Jarvis on several of my business matters. But if he is very busy, of course…''

''Oh, no, no, Lady Travers, I am *quite* sure he will want to see you as soon as he is… That is, if you would not mind…? I'm sure he won't be more than another fifteen minutes at the *most.* I'll tell Mr. Jarvis you're here now, and…''

Lady Travers, Mr. Meeks thought, wasn't looking at all her usual self this afternoon, poor young lady. Quite peaked, she looked, with those dark rings under her eyes as if she hadn't slept a wink all night, and even her voice had sounded strangely lifeless. He'd brought her a cup of nice hot tea, but although she'd managed a smile and thanked him for it, he could not help noticing, whenever he glanced up from his ledgers, that she hadn't taken one sip yet. Just kept staring into the fire as if she could see something in there....

She could see almost too much, her wide, unseeing eyes remaining fixed as if mesmerized by the constantly changing pattern and movement of dancing flames as her mind ran backward. Pictures—voices—words. A series of kaleidoscopic scenes, changing and running into each other, some of them etched in blue. Changing… Even her feelings kept changing, and her mind, until she no longer knew what to think or what she should do, or even what she *wanted.*

Want. Why must she remember herself saying it out loud last night? Alexa's pale cheeks flushed without her being aware of it. ''I want you…and I know that you want me just as much…'' she had said, and had proved it to both of them quite shamelessly. But was it only because she had played the whore so well and so willingly that he had wanted her again—and yet again. ''You should have been a waterfront doxy, servicing your customers in doorways and behind bales of cargo and making sure each one is satisfied as quickly as possible so that you can go on to the next.'' He had growled the words at her in an ugly voice, but the next moment he had pulled her up savagely by the hair to meet his punishing mouth before he carried her back to bed.

It had seemed, at least to *her,* as if some part of the barrier between them had crumbled after that, and there was suddenly no more need for hard and hateful words and actions meant both to punish and to defend. To *her,* Alexa thought again, and the thought was as bitter as gall to swallow. Perhaps *he* had merely decided to try different tactics meant to lull her into confiding in him and trusting him. But then, how was she to *know?* How could she begin to think in a clear and *detached* manner when she hadn't yet learned to sweep unwanted thoughts and images from her mind?

``Shake the kaleidoscope, Alexa, and now look through it again. What do you see?'' How old had she been when Sir John had given her that most marvelous toy? It was almost as much fun as the horse. So many different colors and patterns, and her imagination could turn them into anything in the world she wanted to see.

``Spin all your thoughts together. What do you see?'' The colors were all tinged with blue and the patterns were the way their bodies lay fitted together, even when they were both still. Lying on her side with the curve of her body following the curve of his and her head on his arm, feeling his breathing against her cheek. As easy and comfortable to talk as it was to lie close-wrapped without words.

Had the words been flattering lies when he had whispered, ``I think I desire you, Alexa, more than I have desired any other woman I have met.'' And she had said foolishly, ``Even more than you desired your…'' and could have bitten through her tongue the next moment.

"I never desired my wife as a woman. When I took her it was with lust, and even that was because in a drunken state it's easy to imagine doing anything to anyone. Didn't I tell you that in Rome when I related my life history to you? Is there anything else I omitted?"

"I'm sorry. I had no right to pry and I didn't really *mean* to. You always sound so *bitter* when you speak of her, though. As if you...as if you *hated* her, even though you blamed yourself for everything."

"And I suppose it was for *that* reason that I hated her. For making me feel guilty, for being taken by Indians, for everything, in fact, that the poor girl had no control over. And most of all—do you understand, damn you?—most of all for not dying long before, as she was supposed to. For surviving long enough—God knows why—until *I* had to be the one to kill her."

In spite of the fire's heat Alexa gave a slight shiver that made Mr. Meeks glance at her worriedly and wonder if she had a fever. How flushed her cheeks had become suddenly! He wished that his employer, who would certainly know what to do, would get rid of his long-winded country squire quickly, and wondered the next moment if he should inquire if there was something she needed. But it wasn't his place to intrude, of course. Especially when Lady Travers seemed so deep in thought that she seemed quite unaware of her surroundings as she continued to gaze fixedly into the fire. He wondered, before he turned back to his work with a sigh, what she saw in there, a woman as young and as pretty as she was. Was it a man's face, perhaps?

The face Alexa saw in her mind came so sharply etched into her memory that it seemed more familiar to her than the face of any other person she had ever known—the shade and color of his eyes, the hard line of his jaw, and the harshly uncompromising slant of his lips when he scowled. It was the hardest and sometimes the most cruel face she had seen, although she knew, and her fingers had traced, every line and plane of it. The face of a throwback to one of the ruthless Spanish conquistadores that did not belong here in London where gentlemen were supposed to abide by certain civilized conventions and rules. "The Spaniard," Charles had laughingly called him once. *He* had called himself a "Californio." And had admitted to being a murderer as well, although she had tried, belatedly, to stop him from telling her, not wanting to learn anything more—anything *worse.* But he had pulled her even more closely against him, arms tightening about her even while she protested again that she was sorry she had said anything to bring up what was obviously a most personal and painful subject.

"Why? After all, I suppose *I* was the one who first brought up the subject of my wife to you, and I can still detect some curiosity lurking in you, sweet Pandora. Surely you want to hear the end of that particular tragic tale?"

"Nicholas, please don't. You don't have to..."

"I don't *have* to, but perhaps I must." She remembered that he had an arm about her shoulders while he spoke and that she had turned her head slightly to press her face and her lips against it, and she remembered every word he had used as if they had been printed on a page in her brain.

"Did I tell you before how many years it had been? I suppose it doesn't matter. Sometimes I cannot remember myself! But after the first year and all the searching and the questions, she was already dead in my mind, poor creature—and in the minds of everyone else. Her family had masses read for the peace of her soul and added her name to those already engraved in the marble of the family crypt. And then, having been put to rest officially, she was forgotten—conveniently I suppose, and especially for me—until an unfortunate coincidence occurred. We have family connections in Mexico, and there had been a reward offered for any information. Only, who would have expected it to be claimed so many years later?'' Alexa could remember all too clearly the sound of his indrawn breath before his voice became suddenly devoid of all emotion, sounding flat and hard as he went on. ''When I saw her I felt relieved—and angry because I had had to postpone my plans to rush off on a wild goose chase. The woman I saw lying on a filthy straw pallet was a pitifully emaciated old hag with thin, greying hair chopped off short in the Comanche fashion; and she was dying. They had not even left her with clothing—whoever had owned her last. Only a dirty rag of a blanket that hardly covered... Then she said—my name. She had lost most of her teeth along with everything else, but she was *alive* and she was still my wife and here we were reunited in the middle of nowhere. An old mountain man's cabin with a makeshift lean-to, and it had taken me three days to get there from the nearest squalid town. I couldn't get near her for the stench, and I did not think I could bear to touch her. I looked at her and heard what she was trying to tell me through that sunken hole of a mouth and I wished her dead before I had ever arrived there. I didn't want to hear her story nor her moans of agony when the pain of her disease became strong. She had stayed alive until now in spite of every use and abuse she had been subjected to because she was afraid to kill herself. And now, since everything that had happened to her was *my* doing, she had her revenge at last when she begged *me* to do it for her. I suppose I should have had the sense to leave her to die on her own, as she would have. All I had to do was pay the old man who had traded a pelt or two for her enough money, and *he* might have done it himself. But instead I gave her enough of the rotgut whisky I had brought with me to put her to sleep and then I shot her through the temple.''

How could he have spoken so dispassionately, Alexa was able to think *now,* although at the time, while his words dropped against her one by one like cold pebbles, she had felt numb. And while she was still searching for words she couldn't find, he had said mockingly, "Sweet, tender Alexa! Had you imagined some dramatic, vastly different story filled with passion, jealousy and rage, perhaps? Are you disappointed?" And he had begun to caress her and to whisper Spanish words of love in her ear, and then to make love to her, just as if that terrible story he had related to her had been of no consequence at all. And perhaps that was true, and the only reason he had told her anything might have been to exonerate himself, since Lord Charles had already let it slip that he had killed his poor wife. The real story might be very different indeed; and she must keep firmly in her mind that Nicholas Dameron had, by his own admission, killed several unfortunate men in *duels* he had engaged in, a barbaric custom still popular in Louisiana and other backward places in America, she had been made to understand. She should also understand, Alexa reminded herself carefully, that he was a man who thought first of himself and what would best serve *his* ends, completely selfish where *he* was concerned and completely thoughtless of others. Why else would he have kept her out all night in a well-known house of assignation without the slightest consideration for her reputation? Worse still, he had let her fall asleep trustingly in his arms; and as soon as he was sure she slept soundly he had made a hasty departure, leaving her behind like a piece of discarded merchandise he had used and found flawed.

He had only meant to use her and had done it very cleverly too, her Aunt Solange had told her cuttingly—among other things. Blunt, ugly facts of life that Alexa had tried to ignore or gloss over because she... Oh God, why not admit it to herself at least? Because she could not help *wanting* him as strongly and as passionately as she felt she could hate him!

"You silly, stupid little *fool!* What were you thinking of to let him use you like a bloody whore without a brain in her head? *Brains*—intelligence—*merde!* Here's the rich Lady Travers with her big mansion in Belgrave Square with all its bedrooms and her maids to wait on her—and she spends the night *here,* where her fine gentleman brings all of his fancy pieces. Well, my dear, you must admit I'm an expert in that field, so why don't you climb out of that bed he left you in when he'd had enough of you and let me take a look at you! I could tell you how you compare with some of the others he's fancied, if you like."

Alexa winced slightly at the memory of opening her eyes when the covers were yanked off her body and seeing Solange looking down at her with angry disgust written all over her face. She had wished, in fact, that she could run and hide somewhere, if there was anywhere to hide from those scathing, accusing words that seemed to bare her to herself by stripping away all the excuses she had been using.

"You'd do better to stand up and face *me,* my girl, than lie there on your back with your legs spread just in case *he* might decide to return, because he won't today, I'll tell you that! But there's been others asking after you just in case you haven't had your fill yet. Ah! So he's left you with enough strength to stand up straight? And a pretty little bauble to remind you of last night—or in payment? He's generous, at least. I've heard he paid an extravagant price for your maidenhead without a squabble." Until *then* Alexa had forgotten about the gold chain that encircled her hips, thin, with flat links that seemed to flow into each other. Her night's wages in advance, he had told her as he fastened the catch. At the time it had seemed—part of the game they played. But when, under her aunt's cynical eyes, Alexa had glimpsed herself in a mirror, she saw a pagan symbol of slavery, a reminder that she was a possession of the man who had put it on her. Instinctively, her fingers had sought the clasp, and Solange had laughed harshly. "The only way you'll take *that* off is to have it sawn through by a goldsmith, *chérie.* I've seen a few like that before with those tricky clasps that can't be undone once they've been fastened. It must have amused him, I'm sure." And then, eyes narrowing as though she could see into her niece's mind, Solange said:

"*Ciel!* One hopes that in addition to *this* act of stupidity you have not completely lost all of your senses? There's nothing wrong with playing harlot for some man if it is what *you* enjoy also and you are suitably discreet. But to allow yourself to be guided not by your head but by what you have between your legs—that is unforgivable stupidity! And how the old witch your grandmother must be chuckling to find how easily gulled you were after all. Lord Embry brings you here openly and uses you for a night; and this morning, my dear, he's told Lord Deering and even *Newbury* that since you're here and obviously available *they* might just as well have the use of his latest whore too!"

"Lady Travers?"

"Oh!" Alexa did not realize that she had put her hands up to her ears until she heard her name repeated anxiously; and the sound of *another* voice startled her for an instant, until she thankfully recollected where she was and why. Poor Meeks was staring at her in a most peculiar fashion, his Adam's apple bobbing as he swallowed awkwardly before stuttering, "Oh, beg pardon I'm sure, Lady Travers, and I did not mean to...to..."

"Ah! My dear Alexa, you'll accept my apologies for keeping you waiting? *Some* of my clients need every detail explained at least three times over, and thank God *you're* not like that or I'd have retired before now and driven my poor wife into a nervous decline. Come in!''

There was a warm fire in his office too, and comfortable leather-covered chairs with plump cushions and extra comfort. With a conspiratorial wink, Mr. Jarvis offered her a small glass of sherry while he invited her not to bother with formality. ''We've been wondering how you were, you know. And *I've* had several matters I wanted to discuss with you, but Margery keeps telling me I should let you find your feet first and have enough time in which to enjoy yourself. You *have* been doing just that, I hope?'' The shrewd eyes that scanned her over gold-rimmed pince-nez were almost impossible to evade, and Alexa began to search frantically in her mind for words, or for a beginning at least. And then, taking some of the burden from her, Mr. Jarvis said in a gentler, more serious tone of voice: ''My dear, if there's anything *I* have learned from life it's to spit out what's bothering me, if you'll excuse the vulgar expression. And there *is* something the matter, is there not? And that is why you came?''

Once she had *started* to speak Alexa found it easier to continue with her somewhat jerky narrative. She *had* to speak to someone, *do* something, or go mad! And Mr. Jarvis, bless him, did nothing but nod his head occasionally to encourage her to go on and pour her more sherry when her throat seemed to become too dry. There was no condemnation in his attitude or his voice when he finally spoke; but he kept, thank God, the kind of objectivity she needed desperately. And he neither exaggerated nor played down the weakness she had shown and the foolish risks she had taken. In fact, his *calmness* immediately made her feel calmer and more self-confident.

''Well, as the saying goes, no use crying over spilt milk, is there? Which means, my dear, that no matter how foolish you've *been,* you're better off thinking and planning for what might be *ahead* of you as a consequence instead of wringing your hands over what's *done.* Now, let's think about the *worst* consequences first and then what we will do to prevent them, shall we?'' It was the only time, until then, that he had looked at her a trifle severely. ''You ought to have learned by now that *panicking* and showing you're afraid is the very *worst* thing. You've been out hunting wild game in the jungles, haven't you? Seen what can happen if a hunter loses his head when he's charged by his quarry? Ah, of course you have! *You* don't want to be the one to panic or start running, do you? If you've got something to face then my advice is face it at once, while they expect you to run. Be the one to attack *first,* but always remember to have some form of defense to fall back on.'' Leaning back in his chair, Mr. Jarvis gave Alexa a rather droll smile and a shake of his head. ''I get carried away, don't I? It's no wonder Margery tells me I should have been a general.''

''But how can I possibly *face* everyone? That is, if he…if I only *knew!* Was everything he said and did part of a carefully calculated plan? For God's sake, why did he give me his own signet ring and insist that we must be *engaged?* After all, there was no need…''

''Ah, but perhaps there was, eh? To keep you mollified and quiet until a final plan was decided upon? I don't believe in speculation, generally; I prefer to deal in facts. But it is a fact that the *Times* tomorrow is to carry an announcement of the engagement of Lady Helen Dameron to the Viscount Embry. And that *is* a fact, my dear, for the editor is a friend of mine. I'm sorry.''

There was a pause, then, while those words reechoed in Alexa's mind—and her aunt's words as well. ''You're only allowed *one* mistake, my dear, and that is if you're damn lucky. And if you don't learn from that, you deserve what you get. Mine was Newbury, and after that it was always the *thinking* side of me in control. The *best* whores, *chérie,* are those clever enough to *use* the men who think that *they* are the users. There is no room for sentimentality, and as for what is known as *love*—pah! It doesn't exist, my girl. You'll learn that soon enough if you haven't already.''

Finally Alexa lifted her head and looked steadily across the desk. ''Sorry? Why should you be? For telling me the truth? It makes everything fit in too, doesn't it? But what am I to do *now?* If Charles and Newbury know already...?''

''But don't forget that *you* hold the trump cards. Never forget it and never let *them* forget it either. And remember that on *their* side it's the Dowager Marchioness who directs everything. Now, you want to hear what *I* suggest? Only suggestions, mind, because *you're* the one to make the decisions every time.''

This time at least she *had* made some decisions. This time... God knows how many times she had told herself that and had allowed herself to be made weak. But never, *ever* again. She had made her one mistake and the next was not going to be *hers.* As the carriage made its way through streets that were as crowded as usual, Alexa wondered who was following her and what they looked like. But from now on she was prepared, and Mr. Jarvis was making arrangements that would insure she would be watched over at all times by men he knew and trusted and who had worked for him before. Not only that, but he had given her a small, prettily engraved pistol that would fit easily into a reticule and was capable of firing two shots. Tomorrow, she thought, she would buy one or two larger and more efficiently deadly pistols to keep beside her in the carriage and in her house. And she knew already what else she had to do to prevent a reoccurrence of what had happened.

By the time Mr. Jarvis's carriage, which he had kindly loaned her, had arrived in front of her own house, Alexa had a coldly determined set to her jaw and a composed facade that enabled her to sweep by those of her servants who were about to greet her. Her air of lofty assurance was considerably helped by the fact that Solange had relented sufficiently to provide her with a gown and a bonnet more suitable for the daytime than the evening finery she'd gone out in last night, even if the gown was plain enough to belong to a governess (as it probably had, Alexa thought a trifle grimly) and the bonnet a little too frivolous to match.

"My Lady! We did not know—especially when Lord Deering came by so late to look for you...."

"Oh, dear! You did *not* get my message then? How tiresome! But you *did* hear by this morning at least, I trust. Is Bridget upstairs? Good. I need my bath and a short rest before I have to begin dressing for the ball this evening. Were there any callers this morning?"

Mr. Bowles's voice held obvious disapproval as he said after clearing his throat significantly: "Lord Deering called *twice,* m'lady, and left a letter that is upstairs, I believe. The Marquess of Newbury also left a note. Hrrm! And Lord Embry called to inquire, he said, if you had returned yet."

"Did he indeed?" At the foot of the staircase, Alexa turned to say with cold, angry emphasis, "Please be sure to instruct *all* the servants, Mr. Bowles, that in future I am *not* at home to Embry. And if there are any notes or cards from him, they are *not* to be accepted!"

42

"You look magnificent!" Lord Deering said fervently as Alexa descended the curving stairway. And even *she,* studying herself critically in the mirror a few moments before, could see no signs of the previous night's lack of sleep or the carefully applied cosmetics she had used to make her look just as she did now. Just enough color in her lips and cheeks to look natural; and the dark smudges under her eyes seemed to have vanished, while her eyes themselves looked almost unnaturally large and brilliant. "Lovely!" Lord Charles repeated softly, as she paused with studied coquettishness on the bottom step to pose for him. Her mirror had already told her that she looked her best tonight, and her mirror at least was always uncompromisingly honest with her. The finest black lace trimmed with velvet over silver and gold brocade—full, flounced skirt spreading out from a tight basque bodice that came to a point at the waist. Her shoulders were bare, the low neckline of her gown trimmed with black and silver lace. And she wore diamonds about her throat, sparkling on each wrist, and in a magnificent tiara set in her bronze-gold hair. Ah yes, she *did* look well today, and she looked *rich,* as well.

"How kind of you to offer to escort me this evening," Alexa said in a low and purposefully meaningful voice as she looked up into his face for an instant before veiling her eyes behind long lashes. "I cannot tell you how grateful I was for your wonderfully understanding letter, without which... Oh, but I find *now* that I cannot put into words how lucky I am to have such a steadfast friend and ally."

"Oh, Alexa—Lady Travers—" Charles seized both of her hands spontaneously in his and held them tightly while he continued in the same low, vibrant voice, "Surely you know—you *must* know by now—what my *true* feelings are for you? What they have *always* been? I could only *wish*..." And then with an apologetic, self-deprecating laugh he released her hands to shake his head ruefully. "You have a way of making me forget my surroundings, I'm afraid. And even your stern-looking butler and at least three footmen who are standing behind us in the hall. What can I say?"

She knew by now of course what he wanted to say, and it meant that her first step forward was accomplished, or soon would be. And the next would be Newbury, whom she still could not bear to think of as her *father,* and after that... Ah yes, of course. Belle-Mère. But *this* time it must be done in a different way. A more open, and yet more diffident manner. But first there was Charles, and fortunately he was more than eager to help her scheme, as he glanced rather doubtfully at his watch. "Oh dear! I suppose I was so impatient to get here that I did not stop to think of time. It is still only eight-thirty and they are not receiving yet, but if you don't mind *that* I would be happy to think you might join the family in the small drawing room upstairs? I *wish* you would."

Alexa demurred, avowing that it would not be proper or convenient at all, and invited him to join her for a glass of sherry in her library, where he could inspect some of her latest purchases. And just as she had expected, no sooner had Bowles served them the sherry and departed than Lord Deering begged her to consent to marrying him.

"I…oh *dear,* Lord Deering…Charles…" As she hung her head and pretended to stammer, Alexa could not help thinking cynically how *easy* it was after all to be—what had her aunt said?—a *clever* whore, who pretended to promise everything without giving anything of herself. "I am *overcome,* you *must* know that I am. But how can I consent to your gallant offer after…*now?* If nothing had happened…if…but I cannot possibly consent to ruining *your* life and *your* position in society."

"*My* life? *My* position? Alexa! Ah, dear God!" Lord Charles had sprung up to pace about the room quite feverishly before he returned to stand before her and beg her to look at him and to tell him what answer she would have given him had he had the chance to ask her this same question yesterday while they were at Cremorne.

"I… Oh, it's impossible! What difference can it make *now?* I suppose I would have at least agreed to consider it. But—you *know* what happened. And I know your uncle knows, and—how should I know how many others? What happened was vile, disgusting. It was…only *look!*"

When she unfastened her diamond bracelets one by one and he saw the bruises encircling her wrists, she heard him suck in his breath. "My God! Alexa…!"

Looking down, she said in a whisper: "There are the same kind of bruises around my ankles too. And so now you see why it is impossible for me to take advantage of you. Oh *please,* Charles, do not ask me again, and let me try and forget it! I am forcing myself to go out tonight only because it will be worse if I don't face everybody *now.* If I hide away then everyone will think I am *guilty,* and if I do not, that I'm brazen. But I'd rather be called brazen than *guilty* when I know I am innocent!"

"If I had known the kind of man he is and how thin the veneer of *civilized* behavior he affects when it suits him, I would... Perhaps I *will* call him out, the unspeakable blackguard! That he dared treat a *lady* in such a fashion! That he... Oh, my poor darling girl, how you must have suffered! He...he took your virginity, did he not? Oh, I *know* your marriage to your "Uncle" John was one in name only! What does *that* matter in comparison to..."

"Charles, you must, you *must* promise me not to do anything so silly as to call him out. There'd be a worse scandal; and besides, he boasted to me of how many men he's killed in duels when he was in New Orleans! Please. If anything happened to you..."

"Then you must say you will marry me in order to protect me! Do you think I care for anything but *you?* Let *me* protect *you!*"

"Well?" the Dowager Marchioness of Newbury cried irritably when her daughter, Lavinia, almost burst into her private sitting room. "And *now* what is it, for God's sake? Is it tragedy or comedy this time?"

"Mama, it's Charles! Why he didn't *say* anything before, to his own *mother* at least... But he's just become *engaged,* he says, to a *widow.* And he said that *you* knew of his intentions and approved!"

"Lavvy," the Dowager said contemptuously, "you've always been a silly creature! Of course I approve. The woman's rich as Croesus, and quite young to boot. And remember that Charles needs money, Lavvy. The boy's got extravagant tastes. So, is *that* all?"

"I...well, *you* might laugh, Mama, but a mother always *knows* when something is amiss. All this *closeting* together of Charles and this female, and *Newbury* of all people. *I* should have the right to know what is going on with my own son, shouldn't I? *And* there's Embry stalking about with such an *ugly* look on his face that *I* for one feel quite afraid to go near him. He's quite ignoring poor Helen too, and it is beginning to look quite obvious, I'm afraid. Mama…"

When after a less than perfunctory knock her door was flung open again, the Dowager merely sighed this time and raised an elegant eyebrow. "My *dear* Nicholas! It's so obvious you didn't learn your manners anywhere on *this* continent!" And then, waving an impatient hand at her daughter, she said, "Oh very *well,* Lavvy, I'll be down to see to things myself since *Iris* obviously cannot manage—*after* Embry and I have the set-to I can see the dear boy is spoiling for."

With commendable patience Nicholas waited until the door had closed before he said between his gritted teeth, "More of your Machiavellian plotting and planning, Belle-Mère? And how is it that I can suddenly find myself engaged to a *very* young lady that I have *not* had the honor to propose to? By God…!"

"I wish you would stop being so *Spanish,* Nicholas, and at least sit down, so that I do not have to crane my neck to look up at you. And if you need explanations…"

"Oh indeed! I am waiting most anxiously to hear them!"

Giving him an exaggeratedly patient look, the Dowager folded her hands together on her lap and said, "And since I am needed downstairs to settle all kinds of crises, I shall try to be brief. In fact, dear boy, the announcement was made so suddenly for *your* sake." Catching his angry, incredulous look, she shook her head at him warningly and continued, "*Do* wait and hear me out before you start stamping around in a *pet.* And do *not* blame me for keeping it quiet, because to tell the truth I did not hear until *very* late last night that poor Deering and this Lady Travers had become secretly engaged and planned to make the official announcement as soon as her period of *mourning* is over.'' She looked at him severely. ''You behaved *quite* outrageously last night, you know. But that is Charles's business now, I suppose. And as for my poor Helen, you *have,* after all, appeared to be paying public court to the chit, so that it had become *expected.* So, if you've been foolishly reckless enough to tell any of your cronies that you expect to marry Lady Travers just before she announces that *she* happens to be engaged to Lord *Deering*... Oh dear, Nicholas! You are surely *not* so obtuse as to not realize the obvious? And as for Helen, for goodness' sake surely even *you* can't be cruel enough to embarrass her so? And not only Helen, but all the rest of the family as well. Carry it off for *her* sake at least for a month or two—until the season's ended at least. And then *she* can appear to have broken it off—don't you see?''

''No, I'm afraid I do *not,* Belle-Mère.'' He had been listening to her with his face hard and closed, and now he rose abruptly in one, almost feral motion, to stand looking down at her again while he said in a dangerously quiet voice: ''I warned you once that I do not intend to let myself be manipulated—not by you or by anyone else. And although I *might* agree for Helen's sake to let others think we are an engaged couple, I intend to tell Helen herself the truth, just so that there can be no future misunderstandings. I hope I make myself clear? And as for Alexa and *Charles,* you know he's after the money, don't you? Is *that* another of your cleverly arranged matches, Belle-Mère? Did someone in your confidence *happen* to tell her that *my* engagement to Helen was to be announced tonight?''

The Dowager's laugh tinkled like a high silver bell. ''Oh my *dear* Nicholas! You sound... Why, if I did not *think* I knew better I might imagine you had actually fallen in *love!* How very amusing!''

He had opened the door before he turned to look at her and say quietly, ''I do not think you know me at all, Belle-Mère.''

The door closed firmly, and Adelina's brow puckered in a thoughtful frown as she stared at it for some moments. And then, with a shrug, she gave an impatient tug at the bell cord. First things first! The ball and its minor attendant crises could wait for a few minutes longer, until she had talked to Newbury—and perhaps to Charles as well, in case his courage needed bolstering.

To the Dowager's advantage, although she did not know it yet, Charles and Alexa had started up the stairs when Nicholas came down with his face as black as thunder and quite as furious, almost cannoning into them before he halted on the step above, his eyes narrowing unpleasantly as they dwelt on Alexa, and going down from her swiftly averted face that had suddenly gone pale to her hand that was clasped firmly in Charles's. It was impossible for them to pass as long as he stood there deliberately barring their way, and of course he knew it, Charles thought furiously, his face reddening.

''What a coincidence, to be sure. How quickly the lady becomes engaged and disengaged! I've just been told. Or is it not *official* yet?''

''Embry, if it is your intention to make a scene…''

Nicholas drawled: ''A scene? But why on earth should *I* make a scene, and over what? I must admit, though, that since we are all such close friends I am hurt that you two did not confide in *me*. Or was this something very sudden?''

''If you don't mind, Alexa and I are going up to see my grandmother,'' Charles said stiffly.

''*Alexa* has not yet confirmed or denied anything, has she? And it is not like her to be so subdued and silent.

You must not feel guilty, sweet Alexa, for changing your mind, although you might have told me last night at least."

"Why, you...!" Charles had begun when Alexa, clinging frantically to his hand, looked defiantly up at her tormentor.

"Stop it! Stop this...this hypocritical farce at *once,* do you hear me! Go back to your own fiancée and leave me alone."

He ignored Charles as if he did not exist when he caught her hand clutched onto the banister, tugging it free. "Alexa, damn you, I want *you* to tell me the truth. You've decided to marry *Charles?* Just like that? Why, for God's sake?"

Her voice was close to the breaking point and sounded almost hysterical as she tried to tug her aching wrist free of his grasp.

"I...I *love* Charles, do you hear? I've—I've always loved him and I'm going to marry him. Is that enough for you? Is it? And *now* will you leave me alone? I wish I'd never have to *see* you again. I... Let *go* of me!"

"Isn't that enough of an answer for you, you blackguard?" Charles said furiously. "By God, if I had a pistol..."

"You don't, Deering. And *I* happen to have a knife, as *your* blackguards found out soon enough last night," Nicholas said in a dangerously pleasant voice. "And as for my answer—well, so as not to appear a bad loser, am I at least allowed to give the prospective bride a congratulatory kiss? Since I'm obviously not going to be invited to the wedding...!"

He had taken her by surprise—damn him, damn him!—dropping her wrist as suddenly as he caught her chin to tilt it up. And he hadn't kissed her for over a second or two either, just long enough to tell her something she didn't need reminding of, especially with his gold chain lying about her hips. He had known it too—although his face didn't move a muscle she had seen that dark flicker in the depths of his green eyes, like a crouching black panther—tail swishing. He *knew* how weak he made her, and she hated him for it and for his mocking farewell salute before he went past them. *"Hasta luego, mi mentirosilla!"* How dared he call her a little liar!

"Alexa, my dearest, never for the *world* would I have subjected you to such rudeness if I'd thought... You're shaking, my love! Does seeing him frighten you that much?"

"He... Of *course* the sight of him upsets me! Can you blame me for it? And you saw how he acted, how he treated me. Oh, how I *wish* sometimes, that I had been born a man instead of a female! It is only *our* reputations that can so easily be ruined by some unscrupulous male, and never *his,* no matter how glaring his crime. 'What a man boasts of, a woman *confesses!*' How true it is of our society, and how unfair!"

"There's trouble? Or is this only a lovers' quarrel?" The Marquess of Newbury stood at the foot of the staircase gazing up at them with his usual rather aloof expression, and Alexa could not help the flush that stained her cheeks when she wondered how much he might have seen or overheard.

While she sought for words it was Lord Deering who said furiously: "It's intolerable! You should have seen—and heard—how insolent he was just now with his hints and innuendoes and his complete lack of any trace of *conscience.* Not only did he speak without any show of respect, but he even went so far as to seize my fiancée forcibly by the wrist when she tried to evade him—and in front of *me,* mind you—and to force his so-called congratulatory kiss upon her as well. He has no idea, I tell you, of either civilized manners nor deportment! How can you, as head of the family, tolerate his outrageous behavior? It's an insult to us all.''

''I'm afraid Embry *is* rather inclined to either ignore or deliberately flout our social codes,'' the Marquess said rather absentmindedly. And then, quite obviously changing the subject, he said, ''But why don't we all go upstairs to my mother's rooms? I am quite sure she will have some ideas as to how this matter should be dealt with.'' He looked directly at Alexa for a moment before saying in a rather hard voice, ''And it *will* be dealt with too, I assure you, Lady Travers.''

Alexa had spoken earlier with the Marquess of Newbury and had found it easier than she had anticipated, since she had not had to look at him directly but had been able to turn her head away or look down while she related, with Charles prompting her, the story she had prepared for them all. At least he had assured her that he was flattered she had felt herself able to confide in him so frankly on a matter that he was sure must be unbearably painful for her to discuss. By not the slightest nuance in his speech or demeanor had he betrayed anything other than polite concern and *support* when she had virtually thrown herself on his mercy. And in no way had *she* allowed him to guess that she knew he had asked about her—*for* her, Solange had said—or that she was aware of the cellarlike apartment he kept at that discreet house of assignation and the purpose for which he used it. If she had let herself as much as *think* about it, she might have given herself away by shuddering each time he looked at her.

''You had better stop being such a greenhorn, my dear, if you mean to survive among these people you are dealing with!'' Solange had warned Alexa when she had angrily criticized her for allowing such horribly evil things to go on in her establishment. ''What did you think I was running here, anyway, an exclusive boarding school for girls?

Anything goes in *this* kind of school, and my customers get anything they are willing to pay through the nose for. If they did not they would go elsewhere for it, and I'd soon be out of business! Newbury lets me alone now, I'm too old for him and he had his fill of me a long time ago, but he patronizes my place and he pays damn well, so he can have what he wants and do as he pleases—you understand? If you saw life and human nature from *my* point of view it would soon make you think differently about a lot of things, and it would make you as hard as nails too, the way *I* am. So take my advice and learn fast—or else step aside and out of their way before you're stepped on and squashed like I was and your mother was too, in a way."

No, Alexa had thought then; and now again she told herself the same thing. No! She was different, and she had the weapons with which to fight back. Hadn't she already surprised them all by taking the war into their own camp, so to speak? Newbury couldn't very well pursue her any longer, since she had openly appealed to him as head of his family to protect her reputation. And her convenient engagement to Lord Charles had helped her outface and outwit even Nicholas and would surely keep him away from her at a safe enough distance so that he could no longer continue to take advantage of her own treacherous senses, her purely *physical* weakness for a man her *mind* hated and distrusted. Now there was only the Dowager Marchioness to be faced in the very boudoir where she sat like a spider spinning her webs of intrigue and treachery—the most dangerous and yet the most *telling* confrontation of all.

"So you're suddenly being clever, for a change," the Dowager said abruptly as soon as they were alone. She had insisted that the men must leave them together for a frank talk between *females* and sent a significant look at them both before they had left and she turned back to Alexa with a strange smile.

Was she supposed to let herself be taken aback by rudeness? Alexa smiled back deprecatingly and shook her head slightly before she said, "Oh, but not anywhere near as clever as *you* are, madame, although I am trying to learn from your example. *Are* we to be direct with each other?"

"Skirting the usual politeness usually saves time, I've found. So, let's have directness by all means! What do you want? If it's another title, poor Charles seems quite besotted by you and *he* has one. It cannot be *money,* for you have more than enough. Any so-called revelations you might think to gain something by making could only reflect for the worse on *you,* you must realize quite clearly. *And* on your unfortunate mother and the man who was kind enough to offer her bastard his name. I have also noticed that you haven't mentioned your ridiculous story to my son Newbury!"

"*Shall* I?" Alexa said sweetly. "Perhaps *he* might have some recollection of a marriage that took place some twenty years ago? And, madame, please don't think me *quite* so foolish as to hint at things without having *proof.* In fact, I have with me tonight facsimiles of a marriage certificate and a birth certificate taken from the original documents and attested to as such. And the original documents are in safekeeping, to be handed to no one but myself, unless of course something should befall me, in which case they are to be made public. *Very* public indeed, along with all the circumstances involved, which as you know were not exactly—savory or *moral,* to say the least! But then of course you have already realized that I am no poor little French *émigrée* who is easily intimidated. In fact, I think I take much more after you than I do my mother or even my father. Perhaps it is because I am beginning to think more as you do and to want..."

"Well, since you've come *this* far, you might as well go on! What *do* you think to gain from all this without being ruined yourself?"

"Power," Alexa said bluntly, and saw Adelina's eyes flicker. "Wasn't that what *you* always wanted and made sure you had? Power over the lives of everyone around you. The queen without a crown. But then even a queen is mortal and ages, until inevitably *'La Reine est morte; Vive la Reine!'* Who did you think to leave your kingdom to, after all? One of those same persons you could always lead and manipulate so easily?"

Adelina suddenly laughed harshly. "You're a bold hussy! My *kingdom* indeed! Was that meant as flattery? And if I had one—you think *you* should be my heir? Let me see these facsimiles you spoke of first, in case you might think I've grown trusting in my old age. And *then,* perhaps, we might go on being *direct* with each other."

Waiting, even after the papers she had produced had been carefully read and handed back to her, Alexa finally heard the Dowager say with a shrug that admitted nothing, "Well, so you've decided to marry Charles? Isn't that aiming too low in view of your ambitions for the future? With your *fortune,* after all..."

"There are also the fortune hunters that follow in droves. I know. And some of them have grander and older titles. But supposing I wanted—" Alexa cut herself off quickly, then continued, "*not* to allow anyone else control of those things that are already mine, such as my wealth and myself? I am engaged to Charles, and I care for him of course, but perhaps I should not rush into marriage too quickly."

"Charles will be much easier to manage than some man like...like *Embry,* for instance, who will always have everything *his* way. As he did last night, I gather. Were the accommodations your aunt offers comfortable or merely convenient?''

''Both, I suppose—for Lord Embry!'' Alexa said, and rose, smiling. ''You know what you know and arrange, and I know what *I* know and *could* arrange for. I have found our discussion interesting as well as instructive, *Grandmère,* but I suppose I must not be so rude as to keep you too long.'' She thought she did well, keeping both her smile and her voice light.

''Considerate. But since you are here already you might as well wait and accompany me downstairs, since it will look better for *you* in view of the gossip that must already be going the rounds. Better for Charles too, because if they see that *I* seem to have accepted you then they'll tend to discount the rumors. I suppose you'll be leaving for the country in a few days like everybody else?''

Clever Belle-Mère, Alexa thought when she found herself walking downstairs with the formidable Adelina. Always change the subject when it becomes unpleasant. But at least she was being affable for a change. As they reached the bottom of the stairway Alexa noticed Nicholas leaving the ballroom with Helen on his arm, and wondered why she suddenly felt so angry, particularly when everything was going so well.

43

When he took an icy Helen outside to look at the stars with him, Nicholas had not imagined it would be easy to be bluntly honest with her, nor had he thought she would quickly thaw and then as quickly heat to the boiling point, instead of showing relief when he informed her that she should plan on breaking off their engagement as soon as she possibly could once they were all safely off to the country.

''No! I won't have it as much as *thought* that you have *jilted* me! Why, you must have known that when you were constantly seen in my company everywhere you had already compromised me. And you are *older* than I am and much more experienced.'' Helen had actually begun to weep real tears as she continued between sobs: ''Like that...that *Lady* Travers, who must be quite as experienced as *you* are, I suppose, and you're lucky that *I* at least have enough self-discipline *not* to interfere with...with *that* side of a man's life! Have I ever acted jealous or questioned you? I've give you no reason to...to throw me aside so publicly! You cannot—you cannot—you cannot!''

''For God's sake, be calm! Stop acting like a spoiled child, Helen. Admit I never made you any promises or told you any lies, and don't ask me to either; just to save you from having hurt feelings. In any case, my dear, you'd do much better with a more malleable husband than I'd make; and I'm sure you can bring almost any man you wanted to the point of proposing if you turn the battery of your beauty on him."

In the end he had stayed out longer with Helen than he had intended to, because she was afraid of going back in with a reddened nose; and by the time they did so, Alexa had already escaped.

Escaped, he had thought. Damn her, from *what?* The same sexual tension that seemed to overtake them both when they were in each other's presence? For all he knew *she* might have the same feeling with every man she happened to be with at the time. Let Charles be the one to have to put up with her, since they were both hypocrites and deserved each other thoroughly.

"You will at least dance with me, won't you? Or they'll all think the very worst, I know they will." Helen, for a change, was almost childishly human; and in the end Nicholas danced with her at least three times before he ordered his carriage brought around and drove himself to the establishment of Madame Olivier, who might or might not be Alexa's true mother. Picking out two of her prettiest young "ladies," he kept them in his apartments all night for his pleasure and theirs as well. He had decided that tomorrow he would go out and arrange to *buy* one of the discreet villas in St. John's Wood, so that he could keep a regular mistress and have more privacy than his present apartments provided. The hell with Alexa! She was a clever little bitch who quickly made use of any advantage she could think of.

Nicholas caught a glimpse of her twice, out riding in Rotten Row, with Lord Deering, her fiancé, sticking as closely as a burr at her side; and then he heard that she had left town for the country earlier than usual, and that Lord Charles had gone too. He should, perhaps, have gone to find her at her house sometime and taken her as he had before, without too much serious argument; but perhaps this way was the best. And in the meantime London was getting foggy and quite chilly and he had begun to think not only of the country with its clean air but of California and the warm sun and ripening grapes and the smell of cattle and horses and drying hides and hay and the ocean all mixed in together on a puff of warm breeze, and to wonder sourly what he was doing here with a title that really meant nothing to him, living the kind of empty life he'd always despised.

In the end, since he had held back from positively committing himself to any of the hunts or shooting parties he had been invited to, Nicholas was able to make his own plans for moving to the country for a month or two before he left for warmer climes. And so when Newbury pressed him to accompany him to a meeting of the Judge and Jury Society which was presided over by a gentleman who styled himself the Lord Chief Baron Nicholson, he agreed that it might prove interesting to attend—to hear the "cases" and view the usual *poses plastiques* and *tableaux vivants* featuring scantily clad or nude young women in various "classical" poses.

"I hope you will not be misled by the *name* of the premises," the Marquess said when his carriage drew up before a gaslit sign advertising the Cider Cellars at Maiden Lane in Covent Garden. "They are quite well done up downstairs, and their cellars are actually well stocked with almost any kind of wine you may desire. It is really a very interesting kind of place, as you will discover, and quite unique, which is why I thought that you would enjoy a visit here before you leave London."

If Newbury had not felt it necessary to go into detail, his twin brothers-in-law, Roger and Myles, were more than happy to do so, especially when they learned that the Viscount Embry had not visited the Cider Cellars before.

"I *say* old man, if we'd had any idea you'd never even *heard* of the Judge and Jury Society, we'd have suggested a visit ourselves a long time ago. Quite interesting sometimes, don't *you* think so, Myles? Need to know the ropes, though. Myles and I will tell you if Newbury hasn't already."

"Last week it was Lord Truscott's divorce case they tried in here, you know. All the dirty linen they can't expose in the courts comes out *here,* and everything's described in the plainest terms, of course."

"Sometimes it's only the latest scandal in town, and *that's* usually more interesting than anything else. Apart from Nicholson, of course, all the other judges are usually played by *judges*—or actors in some cases. And you'll find some of the country's leading barristers participating as well. Jury's always a jury of the defendant's peers, of course."

"You forgot to tell him about being *picked,* Roger old boy! You see, they always pick out the jury and whoever is to play defendant at random—highest compliment. And one of the conditions of being able to *view,* is that you can't refuse if you're picked, although of course no one would want to, would they?"

"I think I am beginning to fall in love with Venus. Do you see how lovely she is, Myles? Look at that thick chestnut hair. I'd take a wager it falls to below her waist when it's undone."

"Taken. I think it'll do no more than brush her waist. But *Diana*—hair like gold threads, eh, old man? Graceful and elegant too. See how the bow she holds poised brings out some of *her* finer points? Think I'll choose to worship at the fair Diana's shrine tonight."

They had progressed through the *poses plastiques* and were now viewing several *tableaux vivants,* each of which was the subject of a short lecture delivered by none other than the Lord Chief Baron Nicholson. Already bored, Nicholas was finding it difficult to hide his yawns as one prettily posed female figure followed another on the oval-shaped stage that divided this one large room into two sections. But Diana the Huntress intrigued him against his will, and angrily he had to acknowledge why. Chaste Diana, goddess of the moon and of its female mysteries. Also known as Artemis, the horned goddess—with her priestesses who gave themselves once a year to any man who desired them.

"Ah, that's a pretty Helen of Troy torn between her husband and her lover." Thank God that was to be the last of the *tableaux,* Nicholas thought. He found himself wishing that he didn't have to stay on for the second half of the evening, which would no doubt turn out to be just as boring as the first had been. Where had Newbury disappeared to? "Ah, I see some friends of mine," he had said before he had excused himself. "I will find you afterward, Nicholas, and I'm sure that in the meantime Selby and Rowell will manage to entertain you."

Selby and Rowell had hardly stopped talking since then, either engaged in their private and endless arguments or relating to him some of the unexpurgated details that had been revealed during some of these "trials."

"If there's enough time they usually have two—a divorce and a rape, perhaps. Or sometimes even some scandal that'll never reach a courtroom. Remember Mrs. Pardoe? Colonel's wife—pretty little thing with fire in her eye too. Ended up being kept by some shopkeeper after going the rounds."

"She'd been too open in her liaison with the poor colonel's youngest subaltern, and *he* happened to be a cousin of ours. Half her age at least. So they tried her in absentia through *him*—or at least, the appointed defendant supposed to *be* him—and after that she was fair game, you know."

"Oyez, oyez, oyez. Be it known to all of ye here present that the court..."

The "courtroom" was more like the set on a theater stage than anything else, with its layered curtains that showed only outlines of bodies and not faces, and its makeshift furniture and scenery. One could see, from a vantage point in the "audience" below the stage, that there was a judges' bench big enough to hold a panel of five judges and a jury box and witness box and even a box for the defendants. But no one could see each other because of the curtains, which added an air of mystery.

"You see these numbered cards they have given each of us? Presently a servant will come by to look at the number on each card, and if it corroborates with any of the numbers *he* has been given, that person is one of the chosen few and will be led to one of those boxes to perform his function for the evening."

"It sounds most intriguing," Nicholas drawled when he saw the twins' faces turned to him expectantly. Dammit, what else could he say? Some new adult game combining playacting and charades which everyone would cheer heartily when it was over. And he for one wished it might be over soon.

He had begun to feel relieved when "Barlow vs. Barlow" was over in less than a half hour; the guilt of *Mrs.* Barlow, who had run off with her rich shopkeeper husband's groom, having been firmly established—especially after the gentleman who played the groom had described several instances in which *he'd* done the riding of Mrs.

Barlow in extreme and gross detail, bringing loud guffaws of laughter from the audience.

"Well, everyone knew how *that* would turn out," Roger said before adding, "but *now* is the time for the very latest scandal or piece of gossip to be aired, you know, even if *names* are never used. And then you will see how everyone begins to *guess,* and how many wagers are taken as to the outcome."

"The number on your card please, sir? Ah, *yes,* sir—you're one of the lucky ones, you are. If you'll follow me please, sir?"

"Oh, *hell!*" Nicholas swore, only half under his breath, when he realized *he* was supposed to be one of the "lucky ones." An unwilling and obstinate juror, probably, and he had never enjoyed either watching or engaging in parlor games. He had not expected to be shown into the defendant's box either.

One thing was for certain—they took themselves seriously, especially when it came to the formalities! "Prisoner at the Bar…you shall be permitted to speak in your own defense…and you will solemnly swear to answer all questions asked by this court with the truth and nothing but the truth…." So now he was supposed to become an *actor,* for God's sake!

"We have before us a case—a case of proclaimed rape, and of force used—and on a lady, yet! Let all hear the evidence and weigh it, and let all hear what is *accused* and what is *explained* and consider every fact carefully before the jury decides and the judges sentence."

"Ah…this is a case of honor put in question, gentlemen. Bear with me. And we shall, with much probing for the Truth, find out if a lady is a whore—or if it's the whore who plays at being a lady!"

"My Lords—gentlemen—shall we first hear all the evidence that has been presented to us in support of the complaint before we question the defendant?''

''Yes, let us by all means; and let not the smallest detail be spared in the descriptions of the acts that the prisoner-defendant is accused of perpetrating on this—was it lady-whore or whore-lady?''

The purpose of their game of charades and impromptu playacting was apparent enough by now, Nicholas thought grimly, but not its real significance—not yet. They wanted salacious detail to relish and lick their lips over and called up their faceless ''witnesses'' to describe what they thought they had seen or heard, with the explanation that they were reading, for the benefit of the jury, actual statements that had been made. And for a time it was almost impossible to determine *who* was actually on trial, the prisoner at the bar or the lady he was accused of misusing.

'''Tis said, your honors, that *she,* the lovely Lady Anonymous, enjoys exposing her naked body to the sun and to the eyes of servants and gardeners. Ah, but there's no story of rape *there,* where one might say that some provocation existed.''

''There's some talk of an affinity for bordellos, but only in foreign climes, so we've heard; and there's no proof of that either.''

''Ah, but we *do* have the proof of our eyes and our own powers of discernment, do we not? The Lady Anonymous is rich, rich, rich! Good manners and deportment in public, good seat on a horse. Carefully well-behaved—*chaperoned,* even. No scandals and no gossip until…''

Nicholas thought he recognized that voice. Perhaps most of the voices he had heard. Politicians and barristers—actors and painters. But apart from their enjoyment of scandal and ribald tale-telling, what else were they after in this instance? He had no doubts left when, quite abruptly, they began to question *him* and press him for more *details.*

"And so, prisoner at the bar, you are now called upon to defend yourself from the charges brought against you. To wit, and most seriously, that you did, with malice aforethought, deliberately seek to turn a lady into a whore by treating her as such. That you did all this against her will and in spite of her pleas, and went to the extent of using force in order to rape her. Even worse, that said lady was in fact still a virgin until you had her."

"Oh, and still more!" With a strangely high-pitched giggle a voice Nicholas had heard several times that same evening carried on the recital of the "charges" against him while seeming to savor each one. "That not only did you carry her upstairs in her own home to rape her in her own bedroom—did she fight you *very* hard?—but that you took her off quite publicly to the apartment you keep in a famous brothel and there had to use restraints on her before you could have your way. Did you keep them on her all night? Did you persuade her *not* to fight in the end?"

"Yes, tell us! How many times did you have this poor abused lady? Did you strip her yourself or have it done for you? Was she also gagged, or not?"

"*How* did you have her, and was it only you? You kept her there all night, did you not? Was she easily persuaded to obedience in the end?"

"*Why* did you do it? Did you feel yourself *encouraged* to take such bold steps—to make such a public display of her?"

"Give the prisoner a chance to speak, I say! And to answer all our questions!"

A gavel was banged down twice, bringing with it a certain amount of silence, and into the silence Nicholas said inquiringly, "Have I a barrister to defend me and advise me?"

There was a sudden silence before a whispering kind of

voice said, "Your barrister advises you that—the Truth shall set you free."

The truth? Why the *hell* had Newbury brought him here tonight? Was it to hear something he *wanted* to hear? He had been tricked against his will into participating in this comedy of theirs, and he'd be damned if he was going to play along tamely for their titillation merely because he seemed to have caused a great scandal as a result of his stupidly precipitate actions a few days ago. "She was fair game after that, of course!" "After she'd gone the rounds." The little she-cat had really brought it on herself by acting the pious hypocrite and crying rape like Potiphar's wife; but then *he* should have left her alone in the first place.

"Prisoner at the bar! Where are your answers? We're waiting."

"Perhaps he needs to be prompted. Prisoner, was the lady willing or unwilling when you took her? Was she truly virgin? And the restraints—did you have to use them on her?"

"*Yes!* To all your questions. Were there any more?"

"He's insolent. He should be hanged by the neck until he's dead, dead, dead!"

"Gentlemen of the jury?"

"Guilty...guilty...guilty..."

"It is our solemn duty now to pass sentence upon you, and our sentence shall be in accordance with the nature of the heinous offense you have committed against innocent womanhood and against the mores of society."

"Details, details! We're supposed to delve into *how* and with whom and with *what,* and *he* hasn't told us anything yet, dash it!"

"I know that I, for one, asked a lot more questions. How's it over so soon? Didn't have time to find out too much, and *I* wanted to know particularly how many times she was… What's that? Pleaded *guilty,* you say? Without even… Why, the bounder! Deserves to be shot! Hard labor at the very least, *I* would say. Touch of the cat to teach good manners, eh?''

While his ''judges'' were still arguing the point Nicholas said an obscenity under his breath and walked away, past the man who had escorted him and might almost have attempted to bar his way if he had not seen Lord Embry's *look;* and down a somewhat labyrinthine passage that took him *eventually* past the dressing room allotted to the Greek and Roman goddesses who had posed for them earlier that evening, finally arriving in the lounge known as the ''Cyder Room,'' where he stayed with two of the girls and a newfound friend until Newbury discovered him there an hour or so later.

44

"You were amused by this evening's entertainment?" Newbury murmured in his usual rather bored tones, as the obsequious attendant handed them their hats and canes and a pretty female who had been in one of the *poses plastiques* earlier made a lingering task of adjusting velvet-collared evening capes on their shoulders. He tossed a coin at the girl and turned back to Nicholas as if hearing his answer did not really interest him.

"I found it very interesting, I must say." Nicholas's voice was tightly controlled as they turned to climb the steps leading outside. "Tell me, are these—*mock* trials did you call them?—held very often?"

"Ah—" Newbury's shrug was a slight lift of one shoulder. "That depends, I think, on the latest scandals. The proceedings can become quite ribald at times."

"So I found. And the—er—female defendants? Do they ever get the chance to file their own defense before they are sentenced?"

"Seldom, I'm afraid! As you will have noticed, it is not a club where one can take females, although in these meetings of the Judge and Jury Society you will find the women ably represented. Did you not think so tonight?"

"I thought," Nicholas said bluntly, "that it was rather strange that an invited *guest* such as myself, who is not a member of the society, should have been chosen to play the part of the defendant in this particular case. A coincidental accident, you think, sir?" As they came to the top of the steps the night air had a welcome chill to it after the smoke-filled, overheated atmosphere they had just left.

"Life is full of coincidences—and of accidents, I suppose," Newbury said rather absentmindedly as he seemed to look about for their carriage. "So, the season is all but over again. You're still off to the country tomorrow?"

So the subject had been dropped, and changed? Still thoughtful, Nicholas said shortly, "Yes. London has begun to bore me and I could use some fresh air. I've already sent my man off ahead with what luggage I shall be needing. When do *you* go down?"

"A week or two perhaps. I have business to attend to in town. But I believe my family will also be leaving for Merfield within the next day or two. Deering's already left, of course."

"Has he? Along with Lady Travers? I had *heard* so, but by another strange coincidence I could have sworn I recognized his voice today among my accusers!"

"*Did* you think so? But if he's decided to come back into town for some reason perhaps we might run into him later at the club, or… Ah, there's the damned carriage at last."

"I'm sorry, milord. It's the fog, you see, and people everywhere on the streets where they ain't even lit…"

Fog hung like a thin, yellowish pall that blurred and softened everything and seemed to curl in wispy spirals around each lamppost, making even the gaslights waver and shiver. "Infernal nuisance, the fog!" Newbury said shortly as they settled back under the laprobes that his footman had handed them. "Seems to make it colder than usual as well as making distances seem longer. Ah yes. Thank you, Evans! A stirrup cup is just what we need on a night like this. Nicholas?'' As Evans held up a silver tray that held two large pewter mugs steamingly redolent with the mingled odors of spices and rum, Newbury used one of the damask napkins conveniently folded on the tray to hand one to Nicholas before picking up his own gold-crested mug. ''It's a recipe from Jamaica, I understand. Excellent blend of coffees too. Evans makes sure to procure it from downstairs just before we start out, so that it's still hot.''

The Marquess was more talkative and affable tonight than Nicholas had ever known him to be in the past, and he found himself wondering why. Did he intend to broach the subject of Helen again? Or was it something else he meant to bring up sooner or later? Sipping at his drink rather cautiously, Nicholas found it rather bitter and perhaps a trifle too sweet, although the fragrant spices and liberal spiking with rum made up for that. At least it was hot and strong and warmed the belly. ''Turkish coffee. Have you ever tried it the way the Turks have it? It's a taste that most other people find it hard to acquire. Of course the coffee we are drinking is not quite as strong, nor half as bitter.''

''You've been to Turkey, sir?'' Nicholas said for the sake of making innocuous conversation, while his mind dwelt on the earlier part of the evening with its Shakespearean overtones. And only a Portia had been missing to spring to *his* defense! Christ, Nicholas thought suddenly, it was a good thing that it had only been a *mock* trial, considering the ''sentence'' that had been passed on him. He realized suddenly that Newbury was responding to his polite question and came back to attention with a slight jolt of surprise.

''I've been in Turkey, yes,'' Newbury said in that expressionless voice of his as he leaned back negligently. "But that was many years ago, of course, in the 'twenties and not under the most pleasant of circumstances. I was their prisoner-of-war—one of the idealistic young idiots who followed poor Byron to glory and found... Ah well! Turkish prisons are meant to reduce men from human status to that of crawling, abject animals! But then prisons and punishment are all supposed to teach a lesson in the discipline of life to those who need such lessons, I suppose. And—I have some rum here in this flask to refill our cups with once we've done with the coffee."

It seemed outside of reality to imagine that the cold, distant Marquess of Newbury could ever have been young and idealistic, let alone a prisoner of the Turks; and even more surprising that he should have mentioned what was obviously a little-known fact during a casual conversation, unless he hoped to encourage some similar confidence in return.

As the fog seemed to grow denser and close off the carriage windows, Nicholas drained his cup almost automatically, following Newbury's example, grimacing slightly at the bitterness of the dregs. Altogether it had been a strange kind of evening, and not entirely pleasant either, although it had given him a lot to think about. The coffee mixed with rum had made him feel too warm, and he shrugged off his heavy cape, wishing he could, with politeness, have refused the rum that Newbury was pouring for them both. The jarring, rocking motion of the carriage and the suddenly stifling closeness of the atmosphere was making his head ache, for some stupid reason.

"Ah, there's nothing like Jamaican rum! But my dear Embry—it's not to your liking?"

"Who was the barrister for the defense?"

"Why, *I* was, of course. I thought you might have recognized it from the start. You must admit, though, that *you* were not very helpful.''

''I thought... Damn!'' Nicholas ran his fingers irritably through his hair, wondering why his thoughts were hard to collect. ''If *she* was on trial too, then who...''

''My dear fellow, I thought that should have been explained. I was *her* prosecutor at the same time! Although unfortunately... But is there something wrong...?''

How long Newbury's voice seemed to go on echoing. Like the other voice that had pronounced so solemnly, ''Prisoner at the bar, you are hereby sentenced...'' Sentenced to what? It had been nothing more than a grotesque, silly piece of game-playing. Charades...childish games...spin-the-bottle... spinning top...spinning...

His head seemed to be spinning too, each time he tried to move it. Dammit, he must have had too much to drink. That damn Jamaican rum of Newbury's. Lie still and breathe deeply before you open your eyes—someone had taught him that when he was very young and just starting to drink. But he had not felt this way in years, and the thought that a few drinks in one evening could... As he lay there unmoving with his eyes still closed, Nicholas could sense the gradual seeping-in of different sounds and sensations through thin cracks in his consciousness. All unfamiliar, making remembering where he was difficult, even if it did not seem too important yet. Damp, river smells. Mildew and other indefinable odors. Cold—that was it. He had waked up because he was cold and he was lying on something hard and lumpy with no covering and no... Opening his eyes wasn't much better. Blackness. Void. Perhaps he was still in the grip of some strange nightmare! In any case his head ached, so closing his eyes and going back to sleep was more sensible. And when he finally did wake up it would be to daylight and the smell of coffee. But it was strange, all the same, how weighted down he felt, somehow.

"Your Lordship? You should have had a nice long sleep by now, sir. Long enough to sleep off everything, eh? But you've got to wake up now. It's almost time."

Time? Nicholas opened his eyes into the single orange eye of a lantern that moved and then was hung up with a click of metal against metal as two men, bulky shapes against the light at first, moved forward. "Thought you might like to take a look around, sir. Always helps, in the beginning, to know where you are. I'm Brown and this is Partridge, and it's both of us or either of us you'll be seeing as long as you're here. And there's no need for your Lordship to worry about your clothes or your wallet and such. They've all been put away and duly accounted for, and you'll get 'em back, sir, when it's time for you to leave here."

"Here?" Nicholas said carefully.

He tried to sit up, and the man who had spoken—Brown?—sprang forward solicitously to help him, saying apologetically, "You'll get used to it after a day or two, sir. Except for certain times, you'll be able to move as far as the other wall there."

"He *might* get used to it!" the other man, speaking for the first time, said judiciously. "Some don't. Not if they're used to the soft life. Being locked up in a prison cell's hard to take for any bloke, even if he ain't had it easy."

His *cell* was a boxlike space enclosed by three brick walls and a heavily barred door, the only tiny light that penetrated the gloomy darkness coming from a tiny grating set high against the ceiling. The "bed" was a raised cement block against one wall, covered by a thin mattress filled with straw and nothing else. A slop bucket across from the bed and straw scattered on the floor—the bare essentials. What the hell else did he expect? It was hard, at first, not to burst into a shout of bitter laughter. It was hard to believe that this was the reality he had awakened to.

With difficulty, Nicholas swung his feet down to the floor, the length of chain between them heavy. He had already noticed that his wrists were manacled too, with a two-foot length of chain separating them. And as bedposts two cement pipes at the head and foot of the bed bore convenient manacles as well. He must obviously be considered a dangerous criminal! He looked up to find both men watching him with understandable curiosity tinged with cautiousness, and wondered what in hell they thought he could do, especially under the circumstances, since the chain between his wrists happened to be attached to a sort of pulley set into the ceiling so that by a tug on the *other* end by the cell door any movement he made could be limited. *Or...?* It was an unpleasant thought, and one he'd rather not face just yet. What exactly had he been "sentenced" to at that so-called mock trial? And how did they—whoever *they* were—think to get away with *this?* Unless they meant to kill him. And there suddenly flashed into his mind the memory of a high-pitched voice chanting, "Hanged by the neck until he's dead, dead, dead!"

Brown and Partridge. Better to concentrate on his—what did they call them here in England?—jailers? "Am I allowed to ask questions?" Nicholas said at last in a carefully controlled voice.

"There's some that we can't answer, milord. But you can ask away all you like! Helps, I should think." That was Brown, the talkative one, moonfaced, with a reddish fringe of hair and a mustache to match. Partridge was smaller and had a full head of brown hair and a large nose.

"This is a prison? Which prison? And where?"

"It's a prison all right, sir. Can't say any more'n that, though."

"And would you happen to know just *why* I am here? And for how long?" Nicholas added grimly as more memories came flooding back, "I think I can remember *how* I happened to be brought here." Newbury, of course, and that damn coffee that must have been spiked with more than rum alone. But for God's sake, why?

"Well, sir..." Brown scratched at the bald spot in the center of his head. "All *we're* told is what *our* duties are, you see. But I'll be fetching you a piece of paper that was left, sir. It's supposed to tell you the whys and wherefores of your being here, I think. And..." Brown shifted from one foot to the other a trifle awkwardly before he added. "Everything else, sir. You'll be supposed to read it each time—before, your Lordship."

The lantern flame seemed to dance and waver as if a draft had come into the cell. They had given him prison trousers to wear, complete with stripes. No matching shirt. Perhaps he shouldn't ask his next question and leave whatever came next as a surprise. But then, he rather liked Brown and hated to disappoint that expectant cherubic face. "Before what?" Nicholas said, and waited until Brown stopped looking at the tips of his thick boots and looked up again, carefully avoiding his eyes while he cleared his throat.

"Before you're flogged, sir." And then he added awkwardly, "I'm sorry, sir. One of the duties I don't much care for, 'specially when it's a gentleman like you who stays calmlike and don't fuss. But it's my job, you see."

He hadn't realized he'd been holding his breath until he heard himself expel it sharply. Not a mockery, not a game after all. They were obviously after blood. And what else? A plea for the "court's" mercy? A retraction of some things he'd admitted to? *Damn* them! "I think I do see," Nicholas said quietly enough. And then he laughed harshly and said to Brown's startled face, "There's nothing I can very well do about it under the circumstances, is there? Although I can't promise to grin and bear it either. *When?* And how…"

He was ashamed of his hesitation over that until Brown's unhappy reply wiped everything but shock from his mind.

"Well, sir, every day, sir. I really am…"

"Jesus Christ! And for how long? Until I break? Or until I'm dead, dead, dead…?" And then, violently, "*Fuck* them!"

"It's not *that* bad, your Lordship, I promise you. Maybe the first time, when you ain't used to it; but after that it won't be too many lashes each day, and I won't lay 'em on real hard the days there's no one to watch it done. You seem like a good sport, your Lordship, and it's a shame, but…"

"Christ!" He had to stop himself from laughing bitterly again, although it was almost funny. A travesty of a trial and the purging of his sins. Would they give him absolution afterwards and take him back into the fold if he survived this particular trial by ordeal? By God, it really *was* funny, but if he laughed now poor Brown would blame himself for driving him insane with terror. Poor Brown, who had to perform his daily duties whether he enjoyed them or not.

He wished suddenly that he could have something to drink. Brandy—rotgut—anything. But that was probably against the rules. He was saved from asking the question he felt almost compelled against his will to ask by Partridge, who suddenly took an important-looking watch out of his pocket and looked up at Brown to say, "It's almost time. Better have everything done with and ready before *they* arrive."

Like a puppet pulled by a string, he had to move when the length of rope attached to his manacles was tugged through the pulley until he was balanced on the soles of his feet, ankles double-shackled to those convenient iron pipes, arms above his head. To make it even worse he had to be blindfolded like a felon facing a firing squad in spite of the fact that his back was to the barred cell door. *Damn* them! Nicholas thought again, and in the darkness before his eyes and in his soul he concentrated his thinking only on what he planned to do to them all, one by one, if he was ever set free or managed to free himself. There were certain methods of torture perfected by the Comanche and Apache Indians that *these* arrogant, *civilized,* self-styled gentlemen had no conception of.

He refused the wooden bit that Brown offered him and clamped his jaws together instead; and because he had refused to read that ridiculous "sentence" out loud from the piece of paper Brown had diffidently handed him, his punishment tonight would be doubled, he'd been warned. Let it! Let them kill him and answer to the consequences before a real judge and jury if the hypocritical bastards dared. "You may begin now." Newbury's voice? How many of them were here to watch and gloat? Charles for one, no doubt. The lash wrapped itself around his torso in a stinging caress that made breath hiss through his teeth as his body flinched from it involuntarily. No, damn them, no! If they waited for him to cry for pity, for mercy, they'd see him in hell first! Only his body moved, and that without his being able to help it as he felt that first biting stroke of the lash repeated over and over and over until he lost count and concentrated only on breathing in and out and keeping his jaws locked together; feeling the sweat trickling down his arm and down his face and his sides while he waited for it to be over or to lose consciousness or...

Pain was nothing—did not exist. The old padres who had walked the Camino Real to establish their chain of missions had scourged themselves to mortify flesh and release the pure soul. Every day. Every single day—for the soul. The flesh meant nothing. Everything became louder; each sound magnified. The crack of the whip reminded him of the mule skinners he'd ridden beside, watching them practice their art with careless ease, getting a fly on the tip of a mule's ear. Brown, if it was Brown, should become a mule skinner. Agony faded in and out, and the worst pain was in his arms as they were slowly pulled out of their sockets. He wanted to be able to stand on his feet, but his legs wouldn't hold him....

"I think that is enough for one day." Had he heard it or only imagined it? But suddenly everything stopped except the sound of his breathing, which was so loud that it sounded as if he'd been running a race uphill. "Very well, you can let him down now." "He's either an arrant fool or a stubborn knave, I wonder which?" "It might be difficult to..." Now the voices faded in and out of each other, and suddenly he was lying flat on his face and still alive, with his back aching atrociously; the only thing that kept him at least semiconscious.

"Has he had any water?"

"No sir, I didn't know... He asked questions, mostly."

"Ah! Well that was to be expected, I suppose. You can do something about that sore back later. Give him some water now. I want to hear him talk, if he can."

Some of the water trickled into his mouth and some escaped down the side of Nicholas's face. Newbury. He knew *that* voice, even if he still wore the damned bandage over his eyes. Newbury doing the talking, but someone else as well. All of them, perhaps, inspecting his cuts and weals. And the hell with them!

"Nicholas..." A sigh. "A pity you insist upon being so stubborn. This is not exactly enjoyable for any of us."

"My noble counsel for the defense? Enjoyable—for *you,* I'm sure. What you bloody English would call your—

cup of tea, isn't it, Newbury? Goddamn your hypocritical soul!''

''Your bitterness is understandable, I suppose! But you have to understand that you are no longer in some wild section of the United States, dear boy. Whatever you wanted to do should have been done less publicly. And it's precisely as your counsel for the defense that I am here, believe it or not. You might not have to go through this ordeal day after day if you decide to be sensible instead of *noble* and relate the *real* story.'' When Nicholas remained silent the Marquess sighed again. ''My dear Nicholas, you were extraordinarily *stolid* today, but tomorrow is going to be almost unendurable; and the day after *that*...I know, you see, what the lash can do when it's applied regularly and to what lengths you will go, in the end, to avoid it! If you don't enjoy being whipped like a dog for pretending you did not mount a willing bitch—and one, by the way, who is the cause for your present predicament—you could save yourself a great deal of unnecessary pain by being truthful. No? Ah well, in that case I'll leave you to the ministrations of the good Brown, then. *À demain!*''

45

Newbury had been right. The second time *was* much worse than the first, and the time after that worse still. Worst of all, though, were the times when he had to suffer the application of what smelled like horse liniment and burned worse than the knife-blade kiss of the lash that was all he had to look forward to each day. That—and Newbury's visits. And after a while he grew to sense when Newbury was alone and when he was not.

It was his raging anger and what they had called his stubbornness that sustained him those first few days when he was beaten first and then alternately cajoled and taunted. Alex—Alexa. He heard her name mentioned so often that he could sometimes hear it sounding in his mind like a tolling bell. Alexa—sweet Alexa, false, lying, treacherous Alexa! Did she know and gloat over the hell she had delivered him into? Alexa lying with Charles. Did she offer to be *his* willing whore and parade naked before him decked in jewels? Discreetly, of course. *Privately.* Ah, Alexa! What had happened to the sea-drenched, moon-kissed mermaid with her innocent honesty? Alexa with the undressed hair and the dimple when she smiled; with nails stabbing like knives when she turned vixen. Weeping with her mouth open like a bawling child. Had he really been the cause of the change in her? "After *you...!*" she had accused and she was probably right. If she was a bitch ripe and ready to be mounted, it must have been he who had shown her that lying with a man could be a pleasure instead of a distasteful duty. Bitch—whore—manufacturing sobs and moans of ecstasy as she pleased. Did she too come to watch and wait for the day when he would break? Did she know that Newbury wanted her and waited patiently for that day too? *"And sometimes, why an honest whore's the lady and 'tis the lady who's the dishonest whore!" "Ah, but how to tell, sir, which is which?"* He remembered that much clearly out of all the mummery of that night, although he had forgotten by now how long ago that had been.

It was indeed the lady who was the whore, and a dishonest one into the bargain. But—deliver his one-time mermaid and his willing virgin to Newbury? *Was* he her father? It probably did not matter to Newbury, because he wanted too much to put scars on that silken gold skin while she screamed, and if it happened it would be, again, because of *him.*

"How many of them come?" he asked Brown one day. "Are there women among them too?"

"Well, my lord, I'm not supposed to tell, as you know, but as long as I don't tell *who,* I don't suppose... Sometimes it's only the gentleman you *know,* sir. Sometimes there's another gentleman too, and sometimes there's three or four of them. And twice, sir, there was a lady, but she was all muffled up in a cloak with a hood so that no one could really see what she looked like."

"Thank you, Brown. You're an honest man, at least."

"Sir... Sir, if you'd only..."

"No. It's gone too far for that now, don't you see that? It's too late." He laughed suddenly, and the sound of that laugh made Brown's skin crawl, as he told Partridge later. "You see, Brown, I've realized that this is really purgatory, and I'm here to be cleansed of all my sins and the weight of the guilt of them. Christ, I might as well be in a fucking monastery, don't you think? *Being* scourged instead of taking it upon myself to do so."

And now, instead of pacing about the cell like a restless animal, Nicholas had taken to spending hours lying face down on his mattress without moving, except for the rise and fall of his breathing. He thought of things he hadn't thought of for years and remembered incidents that had happened when he was a very young child, as well as certain other incidents in his life. And as for the whippings, when it was time he let them pull him upright and let what had to happen happen; and the pain meant nothing to him now, although sometimes he felt sorry for poor Brown, who seemed to feel the pain for *him* and always had to blow his nose heavily afterwards.

"You're a fool, Nicholas," Newbury said irritably on one of his visits. "All this for a woman—a bitch who deserves to be whipped instead of using you as her whipping boy. Do you enjoy this?"

"Did *you* enjoy being whipped in your Turkish prison, Newbury? And what did *you* do to try and save yourself?" Nicholas's voice held only a faint curiosity, but to his surprise Newbury answered the question. "I did not enjoy being thrashed while the women standing behind their screens in Abdul Hakim's seraglio giggled in their shrill voices and asked that the bastinado be laid on harder to make me scream and writhe more. No, I did not enjoy it—nor Abdul Hakim himself, nor the fact that I knew that my *mother*—my loving, tenderhearted mother—knew where I was and *how* I was and would not send the money for my ransom—*my* money—until she knew I was the only son left to inherit the title of Marquess of Newbury and to give her the money she needed to live on as she felt she needed to live. And *then* my ransom was paid, and I was expected to be grateful for that for the rest of my life—which *she* arranges for me. The great whore of Babylon, my Belle-Mère, who took lovers from among my friends while my poor old fool of a father was still alive and sucked them dry of their manhood before she spat them out like orange pips. Do you understand that, Nicholas? Have you not discovered yet what they are? Women who laugh while a man suffers and think themselves clever for arranging such a thing. And worst of all are the lady-whores, as *you* should know only too well. Like your Alexa, with that hair of hers that is as bronze shot through with gold and has eyes that can look as black as burning pitch, and has a soul to match, I'm sure. How she laughs as she twists and turns in bed with my besotted nephew and does to him everything she has done with you! She has taken a house close to his in the country, and he is more at her house and more often in *her* bed than he is in his own. Did she take away *your* manhood too and turn you into a eunuch?''

''Perhaps *you* have already seen to that, Newbury. You are obsessed with whores and lady-whores, and particularly with *this* one because she's so like your mother, whom you hate and cannot touch. It was your *mother* you were describing just now as your words painted the portrait she has hanging in her room. You are far too fanatic, my dear Newbury! But how can I, in the position in which you have placed me, prove whether the whore is a lady or the lady a whore? It's not a puzzle that concerns me any longer, you see.'' Nicholas's short laugh held something almost akin to amusement. ''Why, I have become like a monk in a monastery who is scourged daily to drive out the devil in him. You should find yourself another more willing and able scapegoat, or be daring and try her yourself. It should be easy, to judge from what *you* tell me!''

Indifferently, Nicholas turned his head to the wall and might have been asleep in spite of the loudness of Newbury's harsh breathing.

His bitch-mother. His *mother!* She had come here herself to enjoy the righteous sport of watching an uncivilized American being taught to mind his manners until she, like the others, had tired of waiting for their entertainment to become sport. She had mentioned recently that it had gone on long enough and there should be *other* ways to take care of the upstart little bitch—once she had married Charles and he had control of her money, of course. And even his friends who were members of the Judge and Jury Society had begun to look rather sheepish and pull at their whiskers as they said offhandedly that dash it all, old man, the fellow had more than paid his dues and had shown he had backbone, at least. "After all, old chap, we can't commit *murder,* can we? And sooner or later there are questions bound to be asked, and it could be a deuced awkward situation for all of us, couldn't it?"

Much to Brown's surprise, Newbury sat there, almost as unmoving as Nicholas himself, for over an hour after any conversation between them had ceased. And *now* what? Brown asked himself uneasily when the Marquess, still without a word, picked up his hat and cane and departed. For God's sake, now what?

Until his carriage had started on, the Marquess of Newbury managed to restrain his fury and even his thoughts, as well. Nicholas Dameron, his heir, was nothing more than a poor, besotted fool with more stubbornness than good sense and therefore to be despised as he deserved! He had, however, managed to point out something that he, Newbury, had surprisingly not realized for himself. The remarkable resemblance in coloring and even slightly in features between the two bitches, his mother and Alexa. Could she possibly be a by-blow of a by-blow of one of his dear uncles? Not *im*possible at all. But how the old bitch would hate it if he could tell her so and prove it! No wonder they seemed pressed from the same mold—both greedy, scheming, cunning *users* who hungered for power over people like the hungry needed food. Ah, no wonder the once-fair Adelina wanted her younger rival out of the way. And Alexa wanted another titled husband. Newbury gave vent to a sudden, soundless chuckle that curled his fastidious lips. Why not? Play the bitches against each other, and perhaps they'd destroy each other in the end! But *one* of them, at least, he would have and use and make into his slave in the end like all the other fawning bitches he'd broken and brought to heel. In the end they *all* came obediently and even willingly to lick his hand and beg for his favors, his *love!* The sluts—*wanting* to delude themselves that the kind of treatment he meted out to them was indeed that. Love! If he had ever been capable of that particular weakness in his life it had been his feeling for Victorine, the wife that *he* had chosen for himself; and for the infant daughter she had suffered untold agonies to bear for him. And his mother, his witch-mother, God rot her soul, had destroyed them too. Had laughed when she said to him, "My dear Gavin, they *said* it was the flu, you know. But perhaps she killed herself and your brat as well when she saw *this!*" putting a cutting from the newspaper that listed him dead before him. And from then he had allowed himself no weakness or vulnerability that could be used on him like a goad.

He thought suddenly of Iris—a poor, *suitable* brood-cow found for Adelina's son, the Marquess, who had suddenly stopped breeding—and let his lips twist. Ah yes, how he'd enjoyed telling the old bitch *that* happy piece of news. He neither liked or disliked his bovine Marchioness, who had no idea from whom, or after what kind of stimulations, he came to her bed for the minute or two that was necessary in order to deposit his sperm in her; and he was immensely relieved when *that* effort was no longer needed. And as for his three daughters, he tolerated them and provided for all their needs as long as they did not make any demands for a show of affection from *him*—until they were ready to be married off to suitable husbands who would be chosen, no doubt, by his mother.

Knowing his Uncle Newbury's habits and guessing where he spent at least a short part of his recent evenings, Lord Deering was quite taken aback when the Marquess was announced quite unexpectedly.

"What an unexpected surprise and a *pleasure* to see you venture so far into the countryside, sir," Charles stammered.

"Well, I certainly hope you *will* be pleased in the end, my dear Charles," the Marquess rejoined drily as he surrendered his outerwear to a servant and went to stand by the fire. "But why is it you're at *your* house this evening? I had quite expected the opportunity of calling on the charming Lady Travers in order to find you."

Noticing his nephew's flush and tightened lips, the Marquess raised an eyebrow as Charles said sulkily: "It's because *she* decided she needed an evening to herself, the teasing bitch! By God, I'm beginning to learn that she knows all the tricks of a born cocotte in leading a man on without once committing herself to anything. If we had been *married* I would have..."

"Well then, put forward the date for your nuptials, my dear boy. And *then* you'll be able to teach her quickly! Perhaps she's tired of being kept dangling by *you*."

"Kept dangling by *me?*" Charles ejaculated furiously, leaping to the carefully angled bait. "Why, it's the other way around, you know? For *now* she says she's not *ready* for another marriage so soon after her husband's death, and in the meantime my creditors have begun to dun me, since the announcement of our wedding has not yet been published. Why, I'm beginning to think that she only meant to *use* me from the very beginning, to get her revenge on *Embry,* I suppose; as well as being protected from the gossipmongers by announcing her engagement to me! She's been making a fool of me, that's what she's done! Begging me to come down to the country with her because she would positively pine away if she did not have my company every day, and then…"

"Spare me, I beg you!" Newbury said in a pained voice as he held up his hand, cutting his nephew off in midsentence before he continued in his usual bored tone: "Of *course* she's making a fool of you, my dear *young* nephew. All women will try to do so if you *let* them, you know. But *one* way of keeping them busy as well as more malleable is to bed them more often and more—um—*forcefully,* or so I've often observed. Try having her outdoors, for a change—in a hayloft like a milkmaid or in the stable if she likes the smell of horses and grooms. Come, Charles, come! Your lack of initiative quite disappoints me, you know." He had been studying Lord Deering's sullen and rather *thwarted* expression as he spoke, and now after an infinitesimal pause the Marquess said in a softer voice, "You *do* bed her, don't you, Charles? *Have* you done so?"

"Only *once,* damn her!" Charles admitted angrily, his face reddening again as he went on furiously: "And *then* she only lay there stiffer than a poker and twice as cold. Why, even a harlot would have done better! She will hardly even allow me the rare *privilege* of kissing her dainty lips, you know, and yet when that swine *Embry* kissed her before me that night I might have sworn… Why, damnation, she has only to hear the bastard's *name* mentioned and there's a change in her face at once. In fact, to tell you the truth, I've started to wonder if she didn't *enjoy* being used by him and playing his whore! Why hasn't she taken off that damn gold chain he hung around her hips as if she was his tame bitch? Told *me* it was only because it meant going to a jeweler to get it sawn through and she was too embarrassed. But *I* think she's a lying little bitch. Why, if Embry *himself* had not admitted he'd put restraints on her because she would not..." And then, as if he'd suddenly been dumbfounded, Lord Charles said in a disbelieving whisper, "No! Not *Embry* of all... *He'd* never be such a quixotic idiot as to...do you *think?*"

"Ah," the Marquess said in his silkiest tones, "if you really wish to know what *I* think, my dear nephew, I believe we should try to search out the *real* truth for *ourselves,* don't you? And after we have discovered it I am quite certain that your shy little fiancée will be more than happy to marry you as soon as you like!"

46

How controlled by *seasons* everyone was here, Alexa thought as she turned away from her bedroom window with a light shiver. The London season was followed by a mass exodus to country estates or shooting boxes, and then it was Europe and the fashionable spas before it was time to return to London and the same old round again. She had to allow herself a rueful smile at that. ''Same old round.'' As if she was so used to it as to become bored already. She caught sight of herself in the mirror above the fireplace and made a grimace to replace the smile. Bored! Yes, that had to be it, of course, accounting for her strangely tense and uncertain moods of late. She was bored with the country, with fox hunting, with evenings spent listening to amateurish piano playing and shaky soprano voices after heavy six- and seven-course dinners, and—oh God—most of all she was bored with poor Charles.

Walking over to the fireplace, Alexa could not suppress an involuntary shudder of distaste when she recalled what a fiasco that night two weeks ago had turned out to be, despite the care she had given to planning and atmosphere once she had made up her mind that she should and *must,* for her own peace of mind, follow her aunt's cynical but nevertheless quite logical advice and "allow" him to take her to bed.

"My dear, a woman *always* thinks that the first man she gives herself to is the *only* one she could ever love—until she finds out that there is no better way of judging men than by comparison! I hope for *your* sake that you have not compounded your foolishness by imagining that you are *in love!*"

In love indeed! Hadn't she decided a long time ago that she would never, *ever* give in to such a foolish, weakening product of the imagination? And Charles had actually *saved* her by asking her to marry him in spite of the scandalous rumors she had brought upon herself. He said he had always loved her, that he worshipped her and wanted only to please her. Such a difference from... Alexa found herself worrying her lower lip with her teeth, wishing that she was able to prevent herself from thinking about him. Nicholas Dameron, Viscount Embry, who in spite of his "*hasta luego*" had apparently found it all too easy to put her out of his life without another thought.

"But where on earth is Embry these days?" she had heard one lady query rather petulantly at a dinner party a week ago. "I thought he was supposed to be here for the hunt." And someone else, with a chuckle, had interjected, "Probably paying attention to his pretty little fiancée for a change, I should imagine. Wonder when *that* wedding will be announced?" Of course he must be with Helen at Newbury's country estate near Scotland, Alexa had thought, and wondered why she felt so angry all of a sudden. After all, *she* was engaged to Charles and Nicholas was engaged, as he had always intended, to Helen.

"I *do* hope we are not going to run into Lord Embry at any of the functions we go to?" she had said to Charles soon after that, and he'd reassured her quickly by saying he *believed* Embry was visiting friends in France, or some such thing. He wasn't even in the country then, thank goodness. But nonetheless it did not stop her from dreaming about him against her will, or stop Charles Lawrence from boring her either. What was the matter with her? She didn't know herself *how* she felt or why. She had thought that learning all the arts and techniques of a courtesan could help her to perform if she had to and remain detached, and yet with Charles she had only felt revolted. And far from being able to bind him to her more closely by pretending a passionate response, she had barely managed to lie with him and let him use her body while she tried to close her mind off from the unpleasantness that was taking place. Ah, Solange was right! In spite of the "lessons" she had been supposed to learn well enough to practice, she could never have succeeded as a courtesan or even as a kept light o' love!

Back to the window she paced and then back to the mirror again. Perhaps *she* too needed a holiday abroad! Anywhere but here, facing interminable boredom and Charles's sulks. Perhaps she should take advantage of Perdita's repeated invitations and go back to Rome for a while. Perhaps... And then, as suddenly and as vividly as a blow she saw a picture of *his* face in her mind, and when she put her hands up to her face she remembered that *he* had done so, very gently, before he kissed her with almost painful tenderness. Oh God—Nicholas! Alexa thought, and put the back of one hand against her parted lips to stop herself from speaking his name out loud. How had it all happened? *What* had happened? She didn't want Charles; she could never marry Charles, never share his bed. She wanted... She continued to yearn, as most people did, for what she could not and should not have—against all logic and all reason. And what she should be grateful for and had in the palm of her hand, she was bored with! Looking up, the face of the woman she saw in a gold-framed mirror was far too pale and almost *tormented.* Alexa? she thought uncertainly, and almost reached out to touch the stranger that stared back at her through eyes that seemed hollowed into her face. An elegantly gowned stranger with carefully arranged hair and a tight-lipped, frustrated look, who knew inside herself what she wanted, but who did not have the courage to break out of the bounds that other people had set for her in order to seize it. *Harriet!* she thought suddenly. Poor Harriet, who hadn't grasped what she wanted in time because she played the game of coyness that was customary and fashionable. The lovely, vibrant young woman in the sketch she still had and the embittered, cynical old woman she had known were such opposites!

"Tell me where is fancy bred; in the heart or in the head?" Shakespeare had written of life as a series of tragedies and a series of comedies—cards falling face down on the table, and you held your breath and picked one, wondering, which? which? Or you refused to accept a chance decision made for you on a falling card, and you *tried!* Why not? What a fool, what a *fool!* Why, less than a whole season in London and she had begun to think like everyone else, swayed by *their* opinions, feeling she needed *their* approval, dreading their disapproval, whereas—dear God! As if a blinding light had exploded in her brain to cut her thoughts free, Alexa suddenly had a sensation of dizzy soaring that so exhilarated her that she wanted to laugh out loud. What had happened to her clearness and her directness and her honesty? She, who had too often expressed her disdain for hypocrisy and for *masks,* had donned one herself, and all too easily. Society—a set of people whose arrogance intimidated the weak and whose good manners and adherence to "convention" hid every kind of vice and debauchery. Why had she ever thought she had to have their approval? She, who had been warned solemnly against being swayed and influenced,

against being *used,* had let those very people who issued such warnings influence her actions against her own instincts, and in doing so had lost something of herself, including her courage and her truthfulness. She did not *need* them. Why, she did not even *like* them! She felt stifled, she was bored and pretended to enjoy herself. She did not dare to lie naked in the sun, because a naked body offended *them* and at the same time, because they had made everything that was natural and good unnatural and *bad,* they encouraged lies and deceit and prurience. She had fallen into the very trap and in with the very people she had always despised.

Look at my hair! Alexa thought, and now she did laugh at herself and her dimple creased her cheek. How I *hate* these tortured ringlets I affect just because everyone else does their hair this way! Perhaps if I appear somewhere with my hair loose and say it is the very *latest* thing in Paris they will all be doing it the next day. And why do I go to the houses of people who are boring and stuffy, and why do I go to balls and soirées and levees and routs, and why do I *have* to be seen here and seen there when I really don't enjoy any of it? And why do I wear corsets that cut off my breath and so many layers of petticoats and... Her laughter stopped as she thought suddenly and almost fiercely, And why was I so afraid of gossip, and why didn't I face *him* with all my doubts and trust him with the truth when he asked for it? When he cut through all their silly conventions and customs and carried me off with him, why didn't I accept it naturally and joyously? What *he* did was not through calculation but through *instinct.* And he never did *use* me as just a female body and a receptacle as Charles did; he made *love* to me and thought of *my* pleasure before taking his. And why was I so blind and so bigoted as to pretend for *them* that I felt nothing when actually I felt *everything,* and I should have known, if I had not let my instincts become dulled, that *he* felt the same?

She remembered, as she started to pull the pins and false braids out of her hair, that afternoon in her bedroom when she had waited stiffly for him to rape her, and he had not. And the exquisite ecstasy she had felt when he had made love to every part of her body after he had secured her wrists and ankles, not to degrade her but to teach her that loving and the act of love itself was something that was *felt* and could never be learned from text books or demonstrations by experts, because *emotion* was nothing calculated or clinical or pretended. He had pursued her openly and obviously, in spite of the gossips and in spite of Helen and in spite of her grandmother the witch; and that should have told her something if she had not been so preoccupied with fighting herself.

Oh, she had not felt so *light* and so carefree for months, Alexa thought happily as she kicked herself free of petticoats and pantalettes and finally her fashionable gown and even her corset.

"Oh, but, milady—!" Bridget protested despairingly while Alexa rummaged through closets and trunks stowed away in an attic until she found the riding costume she had worn in Ceylon that had shocked all the proper planters' wives. "You cannot go out riding like *that* surely? Oh ma'am—if Lord Deering should… Ohh!"

"Oh Bridget! Do you know that I have suddenly grown tired of *conforming* and doing everything I don't care to do just to please other people? Think—why should I? I am rich enough to go where I please and to do only as I please, and I am *free,* Bridget, I am *free!*" Not even bothering to braid her hair, Alexa tied it back from her face with a ribbon and let the ends hang down as loosely as her hair; and when she looked in the mirror again she liked the wild untrammeled creature that she saw. Turning around she said severely: "Bridget, we are going to please ourselves from now on. *I,* for instance, am going riding exactly as I am; and tomorrow or the day after I am going to find out where Lord Embry is hiding himself, and then I am going to hunt him down!" Throwing back her head, she laughed again at the expression on poor Bridget's face before she said teasingly: "And if you *really* like Mr. Bowles, then I think that you should try being a little forward sometimes. A little more self-confident, even if you don't feel so inside yourself. And perhaps we'll trap them both at the same time! Oh Bridget, don't look so horrified, for I am only a *little* mad this morning, you know! And it's only from...I think it is like being light-headed from the thin air at the very peak of a high mountain, or like being able to swim without any clothes on, or...it is *almost* like being made love to, but not quite. And don't *faint!* You might as well get used to it, because when I *find* him... Do you think I might need a pistol in order to make sure?"

Unable to help herself, Bridget sat down abruptly on a satin-covered chair, and kept sitting there with her mouth hanging open while her mistress ran out of the room and banged the door shut behind her like a high-spirited child.

Oh dear! she thought. Oh dear, and *now* what will we do next? Before Lady Travers had become engaged to Lord Deering and *seemed* to become more subdued, poor Mr. Bowles had been hinting darkly that he might have to give his notice. But now... And then suddenly Bridget got up with her face flushed and studied herself in the mirror as the thought, Why shouldn't *I* be the one to hang back and play coy for a change? And why shouldn't it be *my* feelings that come first? Hah! I'd like to see *him* find some female who'd listen to those long stories of his *and* to his sermons as well. "What people might say" indeed! And who cares? With a toss of her head, Bridget proceeded to sweep confidently downstairs, giving the pretty parlormaid she had always disliked a sweet smile as she passed her. Men *were* inclined to be slow as well as a trifle obtuse sometimes; which meant that sometimes, if a woman did not take the initiative, *he* might never find out what he was missing.

I'm *happy,* Alexa thought. I'm happy! How comfortable and natural it felt to ride astride a horse instead of side-saddle, and how pleasant it was to go out riding alone for a change without a groom trailing behind her or Charles beside her to hold her back. She was tired of conversations that consisted of banal trivialities and masked real feelings, and eyes that assessed and bored into her above mouths that smiled politely; and above all tired of *pretending!*

For a while it was enough to ride almost without thinking, letting her thoroughbred mare take her wherever she would. There was the feel of the crisp autumn air against her skin, blowing through her hair, and the autumn smells of fallen leaves and ripe fruit and newly mown hay, and distant sounds blended in with the air and carried along its currents to form part of the same *feeling.* And how sensuous was the feeling of feeling free and of yielding for a time to nothing else but that.

It was with a sense of shock and intrusion that Alexa suddenly became aware that her name was being called, and discovered resentfully that it was Charles and that he had somebody else with him. Since there was no help for it, she reined up and waited until he had caught up with her, all the muscles in her face tightening to form a smooth, hard mask. "Alexa! We have been wondering where you had ridden off to all alone. I would not have come to call without sending word ahead, you know, but it is not often my Uncle Newbury pays a visit to these parts, and he has insisted that he must see you."

Everything she had been hoping to lose seemed to gather around her again as the two men cantered up. What difference does it make if he is here? Alexa tried to tell herself. Charles is his nephew, after all; it's quite normal that he should decide to pay a visit. And yet, why did she always feel the constriction in the pit of her stomach when she saw this particular man? Her *father!* But no matter how many times she told herself that, she could not prevent the tension and the watchfulness that almost amounted to fear from spreading through every nerve in her body.

"My Lord, I'm flattered! But I must apologize for the informality of my attire this morning. I didn't expect..."

"But of course it is *I* who must apologize for this unexpected intrusion on your privacy." And then suddenly, as if he had somehow been able to read her thoughts a little earlier, the Marquess said: "I've often wondered why we waste time in unnecessary small talk! And since we have complete privacy out here in the open, you do not object if I bring up a certain subject that might prove an unpleasant reminder of certain painful incidents? I do not particularly enjoy doing so, of course; but your fiancé has reminded me that it is perhaps your *right* to know that within our *family,* at least, we do not take blatant infractions against the code of ethics that supposedly binds all *gentlemen*—not as lightly as some may think."

Alexa looked from one face to the other and could only read in Charles's face a *suppressed* kind of look as if he was holding back some strong emotion. The Marquess of Newbury looked no different, although his eyes watched her carefully in the same manner that had always made her so uncomfortable. "I do not think that I..." she began before Charles spoke in an urgent voice.

"Do you remember when you spoke to my uncle on the night of the ball for Helen's birthday? The same night that..." Before she could prevent it he had leaned forward to seize one of her hands and press it ardently. "I remember how you looked when you confided in me. How resolute and yet how shaken and wounded. And then when I saw for myself the way he dared treat you in front of *me*... My dearest, there are certain insults that cannot and will not be tolerated."

The tightness inside her seemed to constrict her breathing and cut off her power of speech, and Alexa suddenly heard the dull thud-thud of her heartbeats in her ears and in her head as if they had been magnified a hundred times. There was something here that she felt she did not want to understand or even to know about. Something crouched and evil and *waiting*.

"I'm afraid that my nephew has a way of skirting *around* the point without quite *coming* to it," the Marquess said in his usual detached tone of voice, forcing Alexa to turn her eyes and her attention to him against her will. "The powers of darkness..." She had time to wonder why that particular phrase should have suddenly entered her mind when she heard him say in the same almost disinterested voice, "Have you heard anything at all about the Judge and Jury Society, I wonder?"

47

As if in preparation for winter, the fog seemed to wrap its long, cold arms about London more and more closely each afternoon and each night while the air itself grew colder and damper. Close to the river the cold and the dampness seemed intensified, and the fog came earlier and stayed longer than it did in other parts of the city.

It only meant more darkness and a renewed awareness of pain, as the chilled air seemed to eat into his sore and lacerated back like acid. It was a reminder, perhaps, that he was still capable of feeling and still, almost impossibly, alive—although he had stopped asking himself *why* long before. It was easier, he had found, to crawl inside himself and dwell there in privacy and in silence like a Trappist monk, even while his body suffered the agonies of the damned. And whether it was as penance or punishment did not seem important any longer, because his will had been taken from him; and if he had had any choices in the beginning he had none left now, except to endure whatever they decided he must endure, for as long as his body decided to remain alive.

''I wonder if you have learned anything from this, Nicholas?''

For some reason even his power of speech felt rusty from being unused for the past few days while he lay there unmoving and in silence. It was not the eighteenth century, and he had not been thrown in the Bastille on the authority of the King's *lettre de cachet,* but he might as well have been. Except for Newbury, he was forgotten, just as if he had never existed at all. Newbury?

"I thought—that you might have gone—abroad for the sun by now." Turning his head was even more of an effort than speaking, although Nicholas found that he could manage both creditably enough in the end.

"Did you miss me?" Newbury asked somewhat ironically before he repeated his first question, this time with a slight degree of curiosity. "Well, Nicholas? I suppose I cannot *force* you to answer me, since you have already shown how foolishly and *pointlessly* stubborn you can be, but I must confess it's something I'd like to find out. Have you learned anything? Nothing?"

"Since you have been my instructor and mentor in this particular course, why shouldn't I answer your question? Why then, I suppose I have learned, among other things, obedience, humility and chastity. Oh yes, and patience too. Does it please you? If not, I must beg you to feed me the answers you prefer over honesty, and I will try to give them back to you. Ah, for God's sake! Why don't you put an end to this game of yours? Or if *you* don't have the stomach for it, instruct the good Brown accordingly. The river's not too far from here, is it? I think—I think that I should have paid more than in full for my crimes by now, if my honorable judge and jury are pleased to agree."

"Very eloquently spoken indeed, my dear Nicholas," the Marquess said affably as he rose from his chair and signaled to Brown. "But you see, even if you—poor, stupid, *used* fool that you've shown yourself to be—even if *you* have paid for stubbornness and stupidity I am still fair-minded enough to realize that in the end justice should and must win out, and the *truth,* my poor misguided fellow, must eventually prevail. I almost dislike having to tell you how *wasted* your noble sacrifice has been, although perhaps you might come to see it as another lesson you have been forced to learn."

"Oh *Christ!*" Nicholas said between his teeth when he felt himself hoisted onto his feet again. "And this is *yet* another lesson, I presume? What else must I learn in order to satisfy your sense of justice?"

"You don't *enjoy* being flogged?" Newbury said caustically from behind him. "I should have thought you did, from your cringing willingness to submit to such treatment rather than being strong enough to save yourself merely by uttering the truth, once I had offered you an alternative. You had a choice, you know!"

He had learned, by now, to let the taunts and the challenges flow over him and past him, and how to shut his mind off from what they forced upon him. And so he said only,. "It makes no difference whether I want or don't want, enjoy or don't enjoy—does it? So, as usual, I *submit* and am of course your most humble and obedient servant, your Lordship."

"I'm glad to hear it," Newbury said briefly and gave Brown an order that somewhat surprised the man. "The lantern, Brown. I want it hung from the hook up there, where it'll shed more light. It's really far too dim in here to see very clearly. In fact—ah yes—I think another lantern hung up *there*—excellent! And now we have our stage set well-lighted for the benefit of our audience. You do not mind being kept waiting until they arrive, Nicholas? No, I'm sure that you will not in *this* instance, since you might well have something *more* to anticipate than your daily lesson in discipline. Have I made you curious?"

"I suppose I should be curious to find out what offense

I am supposed to have committed *now* to have earned a second disciplining for the day, unless you mean to speed matters along. But I'm afraid I seem to have lost the capacity for being curious, my Lord Newbury, since I've learned that there is only what is inevitable, and *that* must be faced in any case.''

''You have become quite the philosopher of late, haven't you, my boy? I trust you'll continue along those lines in the future as well. Such detachment from baser human emotions can only build strength of character in the end. Perhaps I shall be proud of you yet.''

Oh God, I am so *tired* of all this, Nicholas thought dully. Today had been one of the worst days, with the pain eating into him until it became almost impossible to ignore and became agony so great when they applied that vile-smelling ''medication'' to his cuts that he had become sick from it, unable to stop himself from retching over and over again. And now he would have to face going through it all over again—and have time in which to anticipate what it would be like. Why couldn't they have hanged him instead? Why couldn't they take him out and hang him now to provide a spectacle for Newbury and his friends like the public hangings at Tyburn a century ago?

Nicholas hadn't realized that Newbury had been speaking until the Marquess had raised his voice to say severely, ''Really, Nicholas, you might pay a little more attention when you're spoken to. Quite ungrateful of you, considering the time and efforts I have expended to bring about an end to your—er—incarceration.''

''Then I am sorry, sir,'' Nicholas said wearily. ''But I was meditating on the wages of sin, you might say.'' He added more slowly in a colorless voice, ''And I am thankful to you for all your—efforts, of course.'' An end, Newbury had said. It had almost ceased to matter how and in what manner it would be ended.

"I should certainly think you ought to be, since I had to go all the way down to the country in order to exert my powers of diplomacy and persuasion. Successfully, I'm happy to report. And as soon as our *guests* arrive here, why I feel almost certain that the lady whose *honor* you violated might consider you've paid for your misdeeds and are now a repentant sinner deserving to be pardoned. A few groans and moans might help too. You know what softhearted creatures women can be if you excite their pity rather than their vindictiveness. And by all means do not forget to beg her pardon and assure her of your repentance. You *do* repent, do you not, Nicholas?"

How strange that he had almost forgotten how he had come to be here and *why,* as he existed from one hour to the next and had his days separated only by his regularly delivered "punishment." He existed through habit and nothing else and had lost his will to apathy, and he answered Newbury's question through habit also, as he said in a tiredly indifferent voice, "I am penitent indeed, a *Penitente* whose sins have been scourged out of him. She might believe it this time and grant me absolution if I ask for it humbly enough, I suppose!"

"Oh, I don't doubt it," Newbury said in his silkiest voice. "Why, she might even go so far as to feel some pangs of—*conscience,* perhaps? Women are such unpredictable creatures, after all!"

And men could be fools when they let themselves believe what they wanted to believe and not what they were told. Alexa. Sweet Alexa, loved and lost. And more than amply revenged by now for whatever she had lost or had suffered at his hands, by seeing him properly chastised and chastened. Did she know in what manner he was forced to wait for her arrival so that the performance might begin—and then finally be ended—and was that *why* she was deliberately tardy? A sudden draft of cold air made Nicholas shiver involuntarily, and even that small movement was enough to make him grit his teeth with pain. Ah, Alexa! If she needed the satisfaction of hearing him groan she might easily get her wish tonight, for his body had become weak and he did not think he could take very much more. Where was she?

She was cold, in spite of her warm cashmere pelisse lined with silk and trimmed with ermine, and in spite of all the petticoats she had worn under her dark green velvet gown. Alexa felt that she had never been so cold in her whole life as she was now, inside and out. If she had not kept her teeth gritted together she could not have stopped them from chattering. Where was Charles taking her? And worst of all, what would she find when they arrived? It was easier to keep her mind occupied with circumventing any sly plans Newbury might have for *her* instead of dwelling on any other alternatives; particularly the thought that he might actually have spoken the truth.

"Charles! How much further do we have to go? We're quite near the river, aren't we?" Her voice sounded almost strident in her own ears before she controlled it sufficiently to say more quietly: "I feel chilled by the cold dampness here, and I cannot say that I enjoy having to wear a blindfold either. Are you sure you and your uncle are not creating an overly exaggerated *drama* out of this Judge and Jury Society you are so mysterious about? Who *are* they and how dared they make me and my affairs the subject of one of these mock trials of theirs?"

"But, my dearest Alexa, I have already explained as much as I could to you, and so has my Uncle Newbury." Charles's voice held a note of exaggerated patience that vexed her even more. "The trial was held to vindicate *you* from censure and from any possibility of being thought of as fair prey for any crude advances by other men. I know from the stubborn set of your lips that you do not like to hear such things, but surely you must realize the *truth* of what I've said? And as for Embry, why, once he had shown his true colors and his obvious contempt for the code of ethics and morality that governs us all, who knows what further outrages he might have committed? My poor cousin had a fortunate escape indeed!''

It was strange how behind a blindfold all the other senses seemed intensified as if in compensation, Alexa thought, and clenched her hands together tightly in her ermine muff. Even though she could not see Charles's face to gauge his expression, there had been a certain nuance in his voice that made her feel that his whole speech had been a hypocritical sham to cover something *else.* Was *she* meant to be put on trial now? Or was this excursion she had agreed to a ruse to get her out of the way by shipping her off somewhere as they had done with her Aunt Solange before? But no! Not even *they* would dare try to get away with anything so obvious, especially since her servants knew whom she was with and that her hurried return to London had something to do with Newbury's visit to her. She had even taken the precaution of sending off a letter to Mr. Jarvis informing him of everything she had been told and what she planned to do. In fact—and it made her feel safer—he *had* promised to make sure she was followed everywhere for her protection. Safe? Alexa repeated the word in her mind and sat up straighter. She would *not* let herself be afraid. No matter…no matter what.

''You should have warned me, Charles, that these corridors are so narrow, and I would not have worn my new crinoline,'' Alexa said as she felt her wide skirts brushing against walls on either side of them. Whatever this place was that they had finally arrived at, it felt damp and cold and had a strange, almost moldy odor that made her flesh creep when she imagined moss creeping up crevices in old stone walls and spider webs hugging dark corners or covering windows and doorways. Not to mention scuttling mice and huge, gaunt rats with angry red eyes. Perhaps it *was* just as well she still wore that black silk bandage over her eyes so that she couldn't see where Charles was leading her. "And you might have been thoughtful enough to warn me we had so far to walk, so that I could have worn some suitable shoes," Alexa added quickly to ward off the uneasy, even apprehensive feeling that seemed to grow stronger and stronger with every step she took.

"I am sorry for the blindfold, but you will understand when I am able to remove it that it was for your own protection," Charles had said earlier, and now he repeated his apology as he promised it would not be long now and she would soon have a chance to see everything for herself.

"See for myself? Is it another one of these mock trials, which I'm to be allowed to watch this time? And..." Alexa found she swallowed drily before she went on carefully, "And what has all *this* got to do with...with what you said about Embry?"

Her heart had begun to thump alarmingly for some reason as Charles drew her to an abrupt halt, and she was about to tear the silken bandage away herself when he stopped her with his hand laid warningly on her arm as he whispered, "Please be patient for just a minute or two longer, my dear. My uncle has planned a little entertainment especially for you this evening, and you would not wish to spoil his surprise, would you?"

"I..." Alexa had begun when she heard the Marquess of Newbury say affably, "Ah! So there you are at last. We have been ready and waiting for at least a half hour or more. And, Lady Travers, I thank you for gracing us with your presence tonight and for your forbearance so far." She felt her cold hand picked up and the touch of his cold, dry lips on its back before he said, "But first—

the overture before, so to speak, the curtain rises. Brown? You may begin now.''

At first she did not understand at all what that sound was or what it meant, and she stood there frozen while she listened to that regular cracking noise that was being repeated over and over and over with a steady rhythm. It was only when she heard a gasp and Nicholas said almost violently after that, ''Oh damn. Damn!'' as he felt his head spin sickly and knew he was going to faint or be sick again, that Alexa was able to move again and tore clawingly at the black silk that prevented her from seeing…horror and the interior of hell itself, as her glazed eyes were able to focus once more.

''Ah,'' Newbury said pleasantly, ''so you were too impatient to wait? But it doesn't matter, my dear Lady Travers, because *this* you see, is what happens to transgressors; and *this* is your revenge, which has been and *is* being exacted on your behalf. You must not look so… Do support her, Charles, there's a good fellow, in case she… I'm sorry, Lady Travers, for not thinking that the sight of blood might make you feel faint, but first and foremost I wanted you to know that your accusations did not go unheard and were not ignored by *some* of us at least!'' And then while Alexa fought to make her paralyzed throat and tongue function again as the room seemed to lurch back and forth with the swinging lanterns, the Marquess turned back to Brown and said in a tone of bored irritation, ''I think some cold water will revive him *this* time, Brown. And then you may continue again.''

''No,'' Alexa whispered, and then in a scream that seemed to echo and reecho from every wall, ''No...o...o...o!'' She ran against the barred door and shook it, then slid down the bars to her knees with her face contorted like that of a demented woman while she choked out, ''Oh *God!* Oh God—you *monsters,* what have you *done* to him?'' She barely heard the Marquess say reproachfully, ''*I,* madam? I was but the *instrument* of the justice that *you* condemned this poor wretch to when you accused him of abduction and forcible rape. Did I not make that sufficiently *clear?* If I did not, I'm sorry.''

''No, no! Please, I *beg* you not to...he didn't...he never *did*...I was...''

She was gasping so hard she could hardly speak by now, and Newbury said smoothly: ''But, my dear Lady Travers, surely you won't allow the natural softness of your heart to influence you into accusing *yourself?* No, it won't do, will it, Charles? Why, Embry admitted at his trial to the truth of what you said. Taking you to a bordello against your will, using restraints to keep you tied down and helpless while he ravished your body as he pleased...''

''At least he had *that* much decency left in him,'' Charles said, and added, ''Unless, of course, he meant to *boast* of his despicable actions.''

''Perhaps he'll be able to tell us himself. He's stirring again, I see. Well, Nicholas? Are you back with us or will you have to be taught your manners all over again?''

''Newbury—you will—as usual—teach me anything—it—pleases you to—teach me, I suppose,'' Nicholas said in a strained whisper he had to force out while he felt his body shudder with the cold chills that overtook it as water dripped into his eyes and even his mouth. ''But I wish—that—you would not—'' He held his own despairing words back just in time when he realized that he had been about to *plead,* and said when Newbury asked him in his smooth voice to finish what he had been about to say, ''Nothing—or—I've forgotten—'' And this time could not prevent from gasping out loud when the lash descended again, without warning.

Alexa had felt, while they were all talking over her and around her, as if all her muscles—even those that controlled her breathing and those in her throat—had somehow become paralyzed, like her fingers locked tight over the coldness of iron bars, and her eyes, and her open mouth, and her mind and the thoughts in it as well. Frozen in place—like everything else and everyone else in this ghastly tableau—until suddenly she became aware of the pressure of Charles's hand on her shoulder and saw the strange look that Newbury sent over her head before he turned calmly back to watch the continuance of the carnage he had already begun.

She had been holding in her breath because she could not breathe, and everything was trapped in her head until it was filled to the bursting point.... And then, on the sharp gust of her expelled breath, she heard herself cry out wildly as she felt for one inexplicable instant *his* pain as well as her own combined in agony so unendurable that she almost fainted from it.

"Alexa! Good God, for a moment...!"

"My dear Charles, you should have warned me that your *fiancée* had such a delicate constitution. Unless it is a little more than that, and you have made her that way?"

She heard Charles and she heard Newbury's sneering voice, and when she lifted her bent head she saw that the Marquess stood just on the other side of the bars, looking down at her with that expression in his eyes that she had always found terrifying before. And she had been right to be frightened because now, catching him unawares, she understood what it meant and why all of this was being enacted and how he had planned and manipulated and must have waited for this moment. Yet strangely enough it was this sudden, intuitive feeling that made Alexa lose her fear of him, and her blind desperation as well; enabling her to meet his eyes steadily and hold them until he suddenly drew in his breath and looked below her eyes, saying in a falsely solicitous voice, "Ah, your lovely velvet gown must be quite ruined,'' before he turned away abruptly and murmured questioningly, ''My good Brown, do you think we could find out exactly what his Lordship might have *forgotten?* I have a feeling...''

''Oh, stop! For God's sake, haven't you done enough? Gone far enough? You know, as you always knew very well...'' Alexa drew in a shuddering breath and started to pull herself erect, but Charles had both his hands on her shoulders now and would not let her, as he leaned over her to say softly, ''My dearest, you are still distraught, aren't you?''

''Do let her finish speaking, Charles. I am curious to find out what I have always known.''

Alexa said steadily: ''Nicholas never *raped* me. Never. I lied. I lied because I was so angry with him, but I never thought... How could I have known to what ugly lengths you would go? You...'' she felt rising anger stiffen her as she spat straight in his smiling face. ''You whoreson! Butcher! If anyone should be put on trial, it is *you!*''

Newbury laughed shortly and without mirth as he said mockingly, ''And so it's proven that the lady's a whore, or a whore playing a lady. You admit? On your knees like a Christian saint, or a repentant sinner?''

''I have already admitted to what you brought me here to admit, and I will repeat it if it pleases you. I lied. I lied! There was no force, no rape. I was most willing. And I do not have to kneel before anyone as depraved and as evil as *you!*'' Panting, Alexa fought to be free of the weight of Charles's hands pressing her down, and when his fingers tightened as he swore angrily at her, she sunk her nails into one hand and her teeth into the other; and then, before he could strike her as he meant to, she took advantage of his momentarily being thrown off-balance and pushed him as hard as she could, sending him staggering backward as she sprang to her feet and faced him defiantly.

It was Newbury's warning voice that halted Lord Deering before he could carry out the threat implicit in the ugly expression on his usually handsome face. "Charles! No! *That* will do no good, you know."

"Did you see what the bitch did to me? She deserves..."

"Charles!" Newbury said again in a sharper voice that silenced him. He looked back at Alexa and smiled. "So you *are* quite capable of defending yourself—when you want to? And when you choose to, you'll let any man bed you? Ah, there's nothing worse than a *depraved,* wanton bitch who's a liar into the bargain! Look what you have done to my poor nephew, who treated you *honorably* and offered you marriage. And then, of course...shall we ask our silent Nicholas what *he* thinks? After all, we must not forget that *he* has been the one to suffer the most for his misguidedly foolish notion that *you* might need protection from... Well, at any rate, instead of speaking the truth in his own defense he chose to uphold *your* lie in yours. And all for nothing, as it turns out. Such a wasted, useless sacrifice. Being chained like a dog to be flogged daily..."

Her face turning white, Alexa repeated in a stunned whisper, "To be... Oh God, no! Every *day? Why?* Why wasn't I *told?* Why wasn't *I* put on trail and questioned also? If I had thought..."

"Why," Charles said behind her in a voice filled with vindictiveness, "you *were* on trail in a way. It all depended on what Embry might say, you see. And had he told the truth, why then, my dear Lady Travers, I might have had you many more times by now, but under vastly different circumstances; especially since you seem to enjoy frequenting brothels and receiving your payment in gold chains to flaunt about your hips. And *I* would not have been the only one to mount you either, bitch!"

"Charles, Charles! She's your fiancée, after all, and we

must remember that the trial is over and the sentence has been passed but not yet fully executed. It's not pleasant to be made whipping boy for a confessed whore, is it, Nicholas? Tell me again, do you enjoy being flogged?''

''No!'' Alexa cried out frantically, pulling at the door. ''Oh don't! Don't!'' But Newbury had already looked at Brown and nodded, and she had to watch all over again and feel her own body flinch as if the lash had embraced it too at the same time.

''Well? That was enjoyable?''

''No. Damn you, no! I—do not find it—enjoyable in the least. Does that please you?''

He'd had to force the words out. He was in agony, and his torment was all because of *her*. I cannot stand it, Alexa thought. I cannot *stand* it! How can *he?* She saw Newbury watching her again as if he waited, and knew what he waited for.

''What are your conditions?'' This time it was her turn to force words to emerge from her dry throat. ''Tell me what they are and I will meet them, damn you! But if all you needed was my admission that I lied deliberately, then you have it already and you can let us *go*.''

''*Us?* Why *you're* quite free to leave when you please, of course, but there is unfinished business here, I'm afraid. I'm sure my nephew will be glad to loan you his carriage, if not his escort as well.''

''And the alternative?'' It was a question she had not really needed to ask, and as he answered it and the door was unlocked for her Alexa was conscious of their eyes on her. Not Nicholas, who had never once acknowledged her presence there; but the man Newbury called Brown—and Charles—and another man who was introduced as Partridge, of all things—and Newbury himself, her whoreson father. All of them on one side of the scale and on the other herself—her body and her wits staked in a last, desperate gamble that might still lose her the only prize that *she* wanted above all.

"Nicholas?" She had not dared to touch him, seeing the way he flinched almost instinctively when she had stretched out her hands to him. "Please, try to understand? Please—I could not stand..."

He was sitting on the floor where they had left him, with his knees drawn up; and his newly bearded face, concealed by his clasped hands, rested on his knees as he remained hunched over and silent. Until she said on a despairing note, "Please, I...I love you, Nicholas!"

And then, without lifting his head, he said indifferently: "Then I'm sorry for you, poor Alexa, for there's not much of me left that is as I was, and that not worth the marring of your soft and silken skin. I have had enough time to grow used to the whip, and you should have let them finish what they started and thought only of yourself. Two fools are worse than one, I think."

"Brown!" She felt herself suddenly grasped around the waist from behind and carried roughly backward until she was set on her feet in the center of the floor, gasping from having her breath cut off. "I said a minute, and *you* said you were more than willing. I'm impatient to find out if you're still as great a liar as before." Alexa heard Charles whisper something and Newbury laughed. "Strip her for us, Brown. She's bashful as well as being slow."

"Two fools are worse than one," Nicholas had said without troubling to lift his head. But *now* he had. Was the thought of seeing her forcibly stripped of her clothing what it took to make him notice her? As Brown, a grin on his face, approached her, Alexa flung her head up and looked challengingly at Newbury. "I can do it myself, and you would enjoy it better if I did! Besides, I did say 'willingly,' didn't I?"

Would he remember, in spite of everything, that she had once told him she could not undress herself? It was for Nicholas that she defiantly removed her clothing now, item by item and layer by layer. The green velvet gown that she had bought only because that particular shade of deep green reminded her of the color of his eyes. Five petticoats and a crinoline—corded, lined with horsehair and finished with braid straw at the hem. The very latest thing, she had been told; but perhaps men did not appreciate such things. Removing her tightly laced corset was more difficult than all the rest, and in the end Alexa had to call on Brown to help her. Why was the human body supposed to be kept hidden? Was it only for the secret excitement of the prurient, since anything natural and open was no longer exciting? It felt *good* to be rid of her clothes again, even if she had to shiver slightly from the cold. Let him see her now as he had seen her for the first time and still remain indifferent, if he could!

''Well, gentlemen?'' The gold chain encircling her hips caught the light from the lantern and turned bronze to match Alexa's hair. It seemed strange to her how her mood of bravado had actually turned into fearlessness, Alexa thought as she found herself posing for their inspection.

''Bravo!'' Newbury applauded sarcastically. ''And now, I hope, there will be no last-minute regrets?'' It seemed as if Brown, like a well-trained dog, responded to every slight signal his master gave.

''Come along, milady,'' he said, grasping her wrists firmly before her, and felt a momentary pang of regret at being forced to put scars on such magnificent golden skin. But then, perhaps she was one of those who might enjoy being treated like a bitch. What a bold and brassy piece of goods she'd proved to be so far, stripping her clothes off without seeming to turn a hair. But how long would *that* last once his Lordship wanted her whipped in certain different ways? Ah, it was almost a pity indeed, until he got to thinking about it. They wanted her looking at them to begin with, and allowed enough slack to squirm—and *that* was always fun.

48

She had undone her hair as well as her clothes, and it fell almost to her waist in a rippling bronze river. He hated the color of her hair to the same degree that it made him desire her—desire to have her subjugated and cringing. All the more *now,* since the bitch had managed to surprise him and leave his poor nephew gasping like a beached fish. He should, in fact, start her first lesson off by allowing Brown and Partridge to explore and handle her thoroughly until she lost some of her arrogance. And it was, of course, partly that arrogant air of hers that reminded him of his mother, along with her hair.

"Tie up her damned hair or cut it off!" the Marquess said irritably to Brown, who seemed to be taking an unconscionably long time to make sure she was secured—by the ankles first, and then by the wrists above her head—leaving her helpless and, by now, probably quite frightened. "I love you, Nicholas!" he had heard her whisper, and Nicholas, well-trained by *him,* had not shown any reaction except indifference. The Marquess smiled suddenly, an ugly smile. Brown seemed to be having difficulty with her hair. Why not...? He had already given Nicholas a swig of brandy from his silver flask, and now Newbury insisted that he must have another and get to his feet.

"I thank you for the brandy, but I'm afraid that I cannot, Newbury. Your disciplines for the good of my soul have made me weak. Don't you have another and more willing victim to play with now?"

"I watched you watching her body as it emerged from her clothes," Newbury said softly. "Didn't the sight of it arouse some emotion in you? Even *pity,* perhaps?"

"She has a beautiful body and a skin like gold silk that it would be a shame to spoil, but you will do as you will, I suppose. Why ask *me* for an opinion when you have taught me that I should have none of my own? Perhaps she enjoys putting herself on exhibition. Why should I care?" And then, pushing his fingers through his hair almost angrily, Nicholas said, "Oh damn! I have not had brandy to drink for so long that I'm probably a little drunk; and if I must be on my feet to please you, then you will have to help me."

"Tie up her hair so that it will not get in the way," the Marquess had instructed him. "Brown does not seem able to manage, and you, I am sure, have had some experience with it. And if *you* cannot either, then we will cut it off, although that would be a shame, don't you think?"

Everything about her was familiar, from the faint trace of her perfume to the high, pointed breasts he had loved so well. She stood as he had stood every day for what now seemed like his whole life, waiting for that first and least expected scorpion sting of the lash and anticipating each stroke after that. *He* had been afraid. Why wasn't she? And then he closed his mind off to any thought that meant feeling, because his arms ached from having been almost dragged out of their sockets and his back and chest felt as if someone had dragged a lighted brand across them. He managed, fumblingly, to make a clumsy knot in the lantern-bright hair that hung against the nape of her neck.

"Nicholas?" she said softly. "Nicholas, is it very bad? Why...?"

"Ask Newbury your questions, for God's sake, and let me go back to my meditations," he said roughly, and left her, walking carefully until he was able to let himself down to the almost reviving coldness of the stone floor again. She *wanted* this. Standing there with every contour of her body outlined in the orange light for them all to see—although Charles had no doubt seen her naked body often enough for it to be no novelty. Any minute now, Brown would come up behind her and look at Newbury for a signal before he raised his arm, and then *she,* no doubt, would scream and he... Why had she done it? Why hadn't she let things be at this late stage when it hardly mattered? Newbury had been right all along, of course, and he'd been the fool. But Christ, what did it matter now? If they'd begun with him, they might as well finish with him, and there was no point in her making herself a goddamned martyr for *his* sake.

"Well?" Newbury said silkily. "You are tolerably comfortable at least?" He noticed from the corner of his eye that Brown had moved up quietly, and he smiled; and noticing his smile, Alexa's teeth bit into her lip for an instant as she looked at him with a fixed kind of concentration that almost threw him off until he seized on something he had been mildly curious about ever since he had been reminded how much like his bitch-mother she was. "By the way, our mutual friend Embry pointed out to me recently that there is a decided resemblance between you and the Dowager Marchioness. Do you know your parentage?"

If he had not asked a question she would have asked one of him that would have led to the same reply she meant to give him—in front of too many witnesses for him to be able to evade. And yet in a certain part of her mind she had wondered what might happen if she did not speak at once but waited to see how terrible it felt to feel a leather thong against taut, bare skin, punishment for all the torture she had made *him* suffer. Perhaps, most of all, to find out what Nicholas might or might not do. But now?

"I know my parentage very well," Alexa said in a steady voice. "Although I did not know who my real father was until recently. But why do you ask?"

"Idle curiosity." They had brought in chairs for him and for Charles, and the Marquess lounged back in his, still smiling. "Are we distantly related by some chance? It might add a decided *piquancy* to what takes place tonight, I think."

This time she had to take in a deep breath before she was able to answer him without a change in her voice. "Not *distantly* related, I am sorry to say, my Lord Newbury, but far too closely for *my* liking at least. My grandmother, your mother, did not tell you, then?"

"Tell *me*—? Ah, my clever little bitch, if you think to put me off by crying 'incest' as you announce you're one of my bastards by a whore I've encountered, I should tell *you* that you're barking up the wrong tree. I've always made sure, before I've done with a woman, that she will not bear any fruit of *mine,* at least—as I will do with you when I've done with you."

Alexa saw his eyes flicker and sucked in her breath again, this time with a feeling of panic. Thank God she managed *not* to scream when she felt a streak of liquid fire wrap itself around her hips, although the breath she expelled sounded like a sob.

"Ah," Newbury said smilingly, "and now do you think you might change your story? Because no matter whose bastard you are, my dear, you are certainly not mine."

"I'm not your *bastard!* Was Victorine Bouvard your

legal wife, as the marriage certificate in my possession testifies, or did you always make a habit of marrying a second wife while the first was still alive? Do you remember that you had a daughter by my mother, poor soul, and that she was christened Alexandra Victoria after the Princess of Kent? Or was it more convenient, perhaps, to let my mother believe you had been killed in Greece, so that you could marry the daughter of a Duke and breed your bastards off *her?*''

''Someone... Curse you, bitch! Someone has told you all this! Solange! Yes, Solange! Confess it!''

''I might confess to anything, I admit, if I'm beaten hard enough, but it'll do you and your family no good when the documents that prove what I say are produced! Do you remember Harriet Howard? *Martin,* who was her brother? A sketch portfolio? A book of poems with an inscription to your beloved 'Rina'? A signet ring bearing your crest outlined by diamonds? Gavin Edward Dameron, Viscount Dare, presently Marquess of Newbury. And how I've hated the thought that *you* of all men are my father! I can only think of you as Newbury, you know. Does *that* make incest any easier to stomach, my lord?''

The silence that followed was almost a tangible tightness that seemed to expand and swell until it seemed as if the small space that enclosed them all was filled to smothering point before it was abruptly broken by a burst of jarring laughter.

''*Por Dios!*'' Nicholas Dameron said. ''And now I could almost feel sorry for *you,* Newbury. It seems as if the women of your line are even more cunning and vindictive than the men! Do you find yourself hoist by your own petard?''

There was a second or two after that when no one was certain of what Newbury, who had remained white-faced and staring as if he had turned to stone, might do when he rose very slowly from his chair. Alexa's heart had begun to thump almost painfully again when he said in a very soft voice to Brown, "Give me the whip." And then, when the man stared at him as if he was still in a mesmeric trance, he almost snarled, "Give me the damned whip, I say!"

"You can easily persuade her to tell you where she has hidden all those papers," Charles said in an urgent, almost gloating voice. "Whip her a few times and she'll crack. And after we're married and *she's* safely locked up in the place Belle-Mère told me of, there'll be no more danger of scandal, will there?"

"Ah yes, my mother," Newbury said in that same quiet voice. "My clever, scheming, vindictive mother. It would be much like her to… Sit down again, Charles. And be silent unless I speak to you, yes? And Nicholas, perhaps I shall yet have to teach you that in *some* cases silence has its virtues. You understand, I hope." The only sign that the Marquess had come close to losing his control showed in the harshness of his breathing in the stillness that held them all again until he let down the rope through the pulley himself, and taking up his heavy cloth cloak, threw it roughly over Alexa's suddenly cold body. "Here, cover yourself! And now you shall repeat this story of yours and answer my questions, and I hope for your sake that you have the correct answers. But first, tell me what you meant earlier when you said that my—that the Dowager Marchioness *knew* everything?"

The Marquess of Newbury showed no loss of his usual composure as he casually handed his silk hat and his coat to the sleepy butler at his mother's house in Belgrave Square; and his manner was just as politely distant as he dropped his gloves and cane on a table before turning away to stand with his back to the fire.

She had greeted him with a sarcastic lift of her eyebrows and a trace of irritation in her voice as she said, "My dear Gavin. Such a surprise on a night like this, and at such an hour! Darley tells me that you noticed a light in my room…?"

"Ah yes. I was dropping Alexandra—Lady Travers, that is—off at *her* house when I saw it and thought you might still be up."

He smiled at her in a manner that actually made her slightly uneasy, so that she snapped: "*Alexandra,* is it? I should have thought that your *nephew* would be the one to escort her home. Or did you have other news to give me? Because if not—it has been quite a tiring day for me and I am planning, as you know, to leave for Spain the day after tomorrow. Please come to the point, if you will."

"Ah, but the point, my dear mother, is that I do not think you are going to find it convenient to be leaving for Spain when I am counting on your help with all the tiresome preparations for a wedding. In fact, I thought you might wish to give a small prewedding reception here, and then arrange for the reception *after* the ceremony itself to be held at *my* residence. You have always been so good at *arranging* things, after all."

For once he had managed to surprise her. The Dowager actually stopped rocking back and forth in her chair to frown up at him before she said crossly, "Wedding? It's too late at night for me to be interested in solving riddles. *Whose* wedding can you possibly be speaking of?"

"You don't mind if I help myself to some of your excellent brandy, Mother?" Without waiting for her answer, he had already opened the sideboard and was pouring out a drink of her best Napoleon cognac for himself, with a deplorable lack of manners. What had got into him? She was not comfortable with this new mood of his, nor with the strangely measuring way in which his eyes seemed to study her and almost force her to repeat her last question, this time with unconcealed irritation.

"Whose? Why your granddaughter's, of course. To Embry. She insisted upon him as her choice of a bridegroom, I'm afraid. Although it seems only just, don't you agree, that my *daughter* should be the next Marchioness of Newbury?"

"And when did all *this* take place, and since when have *you* interested yourself in such things?" the Dowager cried petulantly. "*I* should have been told if Helen had changed her mind about breaking off her engagement to Embry, and you should also have informed me that you had decided to set him free. Unless..." She sat up straighter in her chair and her eyes began to brighten. "Unless you finally had the truth from both of them? Ah, is *that* why you're really here? To tell me that you finally did as I suggested and forced matters?"

"Dear, clever, *inventive* mother." The Marquess raised his glass to her in a mocking toast and sipped from it pensively before he lowered it and said: "I suppose that you could, if you would, say that I contrived almost by accident to force matters. To force secrets, rotten with worms and maggots, out into the open to be examined. But as to your earlier question—did I not say my *daughter? Your granddaughter?* Helen, poor girl, is only one of my three bastard daughters by my bigamous wife, as you always knew, dear Mother. I was speaking of the wedding that is to take place between my *legitimate* daughter and my only heir. I thought you would have guessed already, unless your age is beginning to muddle your thinking. It would be a pity if *that* should happen or you should make me think so, in case I should have to commit you to the exclusive sanitarium you recommended to my nephew Charles for his future wife's lodging. Ah!" His sudden cold laugh made the Marchioness, who had never been frightened in her life, suddenly cringe back in her rocking chair and lick her dry lips as he came a few steps closer to stand gazing down at her before he said mockingly: "But why do you suddenly look so white, *ma belle-mère?* We both know you do not possess a conscience, so it cannot be that, can it? Well then? You are not usually speechless, and I had been looking forward to hearing some comments from you since you are so good at *planning.* Just as you planned for my removal from my wife and my child and for my extended stay in Turkey; and as you planned so cleverly for poor Victorine with the help of the Howards. And again for Embry to be punished and warned to conform to what *you* dictated, just as *I* was; and for me to take and use my own daughter in the same fashion as you know and encourage me to use my whores! The list is almost endless, is it not? You do not wish me to tire us both by going on, do you? My bitch-whore-mother?"

"You cannot speak to me so! How *dare* you! And all on the word of a cunning bitch who means to use us all? If she's your daughter—you could have bred her on Solange—don't you see it all, and how they've planned to dupe you? There was no wedding certificate. That poor foolish creature who claimed you married her could not even prove it. Gavin, you are too easily *led* by your emotions. If you were not you'd see that everything I've done was for *your* good! Look where you are now—the position you hold in the government, the way you are respected. If *I* had not made sure that you were protected from certain of your foolish mistakes, you would be...a nobody! Nothing, and nowhere, do you understand? You are the Marquess of Newbury, and the name means something—*family* means something! With a little French upstart... Hah! People who are weak need somebody to lead them, my dear Gavin, and you were a weakling until I decided you should be made stronger. And now, be good enough to leave my house so that I can seek my bed, for I do not choose to entertain you any longer. Why don't you go across the street and let that little bitch you call your 'daughter' accommodate your moods for a change?''

Face flushed with anger, the Dowager Marchioness made as if to rise from her chair, only to find herself pushed back into it with so much force that she gasped with fear and outrage. ''You have forgotten yourself completely now! How dare you treat *me* in such a fashion? Leave *now,* Gavin, before I ring for my servants to remove you.''

''My dear *mother!*'' Instead of obeying her or looking chastened he threw back his head and laughed, and she suddenly noticed that he was playing with the silver-topped cane he had brought in with him. And then the laughter was wiped from his voice and his face as he leaned over her and said distinctly: ''This is not *your* house, and the servants who staff it are not *your* servants. Do you understand? *I* am the Marquess of Newbury and *I* own this place and everything else I pay for from *my* income. *You* are dependent on what *I* choose to allow you—and what you may do or not do is also dependent upon *my* permission, since I am the head of this family. It is high time you realized it, I think! Why, Madame Mother, in less than a half hour I could pay five doctors enough money to put you away and out of my sight forever; and under conditions you'd hardly enjoy. And...'' As he twisted one end of the cane the silver knob came off, and he shook free five leather thongs that were knotted along their length and held them over her face while he said: ''Do you see my little toy? It would give me pleasure to use it on you while I think of all your vicious meddling and the havoc it has caused in so many lives. Who would know? Who would *care?* You are not loved, Belle-Mère. You *were* feared once, perhaps, but no longer, no longer!

No more intriguing—I'm seeing to it that in future you'll have to beg me for every penny I allow you, if I choose to. The spies you employ are to be paid off immediately, and it is *you* who will be watched and *guarded* from now on. Think on it, and remember that at any time I please I can turn this pleasant life of luxury you lead into an *unpleasant* nightmare! For I happen to be spawned by you and am what you turned me and twisted me into! Be warned, therefore, and do nothing to thwart or annoy me!''

For long after her son had left her the Marchioness sat in her chair trembling as if she had the ague and was ashamed to ring for her maid because of it. And for the first time in her life she felt helpless and afraid and wholly at the mercy of another person. Why did it have to happen? Why to *her?* ''The Queen is dead!'' she suddenly remembered that strong voice saying. ''Long live the Queen!'' And so power passed, and now it was the young Queen who had it. But for how long? And how and to what end would she use it?

49

Most of the fashionable town houses in London had been closed up when the season ended, but almost as many had been reopened again during the last week in October for the Wedding. After all, it was the most intriguing and unexpected event of the year, and there were so many *questions* that no one seemed to know the answers to.

"*Adelina* is actually sponsoring her, my dear; and they say that Newbury of all people is to give her away. I wonder how it all came about so suddenly? And what happened to poor Deering?"

"What *I* wonder is where Embry has been hiding himself all this time—and if this sudden change of heart has anything to do with the fact that Helen jilted him."

"But didn't you hear the whispers that were going the rounds just before we left London? Something to do with Embry *abducting* her for a reckless, stolen night, while all the time they were both engaged to other people."

"I fear you have a far too romantic turn of mind, love. Reckless, stolen night indeed! You're too young to know about such things, even if they did happen. *I'm* going to this wedding out of pure curiosity; because I *don't* know why or how it came about and I'd like to."

* * *

"I never *wanted* this kind of a wedding. How did it all come about? They're all coming because they're curious, that's all. And my *grandmother* has been like a crocodile, all smiles. I do not trust her like that. I am no longer sure of anything, not even myself. Ah, it was so easy to be bold that night when I was desperate and it was the only course left to me. I knew what I wanted then and I was determined to have it too, and that helped. But now... Do you understand what I am saying? Now I feel as if everything is being decided *for* me and I'm helpless. And vulnerable too, because I have thrown all my javelins and have no more weapons left to lose. *Lose!* Did you hear what I said? 'Lose' instead of 'use.' Does that mean...why am I suddenly so nervous and afraid? I wish I had been more *firm* about not wearing a wedding gown and about not being married in a church. I wish that this ivory lace and satin was not so close to *white* as to almost be a travesty. I wish..."

"Well, my dear," Lady Margery said mildly as Alexa took her third or fourth turn about the room with her voluminous skirts held up almost as high as her knees, "I must only hope for your sake then that you are not like *some* people, who do not want what they have wished for once they are sure of getting it, and that you are marrying this time for *love* and for no other reason."

There were some things she could not bear to speak about even with as dear and as close a friend as Margery had become. How could she say: "I am *afraid* of love because I've seen and felt how it, or even the lack of it, can hurt. What good will it do *me* to admit I'm marrying for love if the man I'm marrying does not love *me?*" Alexa had always suffered from an excess of *pride;* and so she managed a smile and a noncommittal apology for her silly attack of nerves and appeared quite calm by the time

Bridget came up to tell her that the carriages were ready and the Marquess of Newbury and his mother both awaited her downstairs.

''My love, you have nothing to worry about,'' Lady Margery said reassuringly when she caught the suddenly unguarded expression on Alexa's face. ''You look perfectly lovely, and your bridal gown is the most exquisite creation in the world. Your...Newbury was quite right to insist that this must be a formal and very public wedding, you know. Edwin explained it all to me! They'll all come to look and of course they'll speculate, but that will be *all,* since you'll have faced them down—all of you. And just think, within an hour or two you will have your rightful name to keep. You will be *Lady Alexa Dameron,* Viscountess Embry, and some day you will be the Marchioness of Newbury. I'm so glad everything turned out so perfectly *this* way, and you did not feel obliged to...well, that no innocent persons are being *hurt.* And it was almost too generous of you to make such a very large settlement on Lord Deering to pay his debts and keep him comfortably off just because you might have injured his feelings. *Edwin* didn't approve of it, of course, but I reminded him that females are naturally more sensitive than men are, and that it is still *your* money after all. Oh, dear! I didn't mean to keep you here listening to my chattering...!''

Everything taken care of—Alexa had an excuse to remain silent behind her Mechlin lace veil, which was embroidered with seed pearls to match her headdress. And time to think, before they had reached the church; although perhaps trying *not* to think would be not only preferable but wiser if she wished to retain her composure.

They were all silent. The Marquess and Alexa in one carriage, and the Dowager Marchioness and Lady Margery in another.

It was clever of her to choose Embry over Charles in

the end, Adelina thought. The chit *was* quite clever after all. Power, she had said. But the old queen wasn't dead yet and they needed her support. It had been *her* clever suggestion that Alexa should settle an income on Charles to keep him quiet as well as indebted. And at least the girl had brains enough to realize she needed advice as well as public backing in order to build up a facade of respectability. Power by proxy—why not? She could make her help and her guidance more and more necessary until in the end it would be *her* influence that would prevail. And sooner or later she would see to it that the incongruous friendship Alexa had formed with Lady Margery would dwindle off into a casual acquaintance.

The Dowager straightened her back and pretended to adjust the plumes on her elegant bonnet. Most important of all, she must try to make sure that Alexa never became weak enough to be influenced or *ruled* by her husband; and being a woman of decision, the Marchioness had already taken several steps in that direction without letting Newbury know anything about it. Oh no—he might have frightened her with his threats in the beginning, but she was far from finished yet!

"And here we are!" Lady Margery said with forced brightness, for she had never trusted nor cared for Adelina. "Goodness, it seems as if we're back at the height of the season, doesn't it? All the carriages!"

There was a larger crowd of hangers-on than usual waiting to see the bride, perhaps because it had turned out to be such a surprisingly clear and balmy day for late autumn. A ragged cheer went up when a splendid-looking equipage finally came to a smart halt; and again when the bride herself appeared. "Coo, ain't *she* a beauty!" "Did you get to see her face, Jenny?" "Never saw such a pretty dress in all my life, I'm sure!"

Alexa heard the comments without knowing what she

heard. Under her short white kid gloves her hands felt frozen. I'm afraid…I'm afraid…thoughts beating like live wings against the surface of her mind. What am I doing here? *Why?* He's a stranger, and I'm a damned fool to give myself to him, to *offer* myself to him, in fact. *Will* he be here? How *unreal…!* I have not even seen him since that night.…

That night still haunted her memory. Lamplight and candlelight and red glow of coals from a brazier one of the men had brought in for warmth. "You had best be married as soon as possible, in case…" "Only to the man *I* choose." Had she chosen only because she continued to believe *she* had been chosen? Or because she was too prideful and too stubborn to admit defeat?

"You will find it easier to walk down the aisle holding my arm, I think," the Marquess of Newbury reminded her drily, and puppetlike, Alexa obeyed his suggestion. The aisle stretched endlessly before her, and each step she took was punctuated by faces turning—a sea of faces on either side of her, parting like the Red Sea. A blur of candlelight waited ahead of her. There was even an organ playing loudly enough to drown out all the whispers that arose like leaves rustling in a sharp breeze; but not loud enough to drown the remembered half-tone of his voice saying huskily, "You can make a better choice than the dregs of *me,* sweet clever Alexa! I admire your sense of drama and timing exceedingly, of course, but not strongly enough for *marriage*—and its duties.…" *Duties?* And yet he had sent her, some days later, a short and rather stilted letter containing a formal proposal of marriage and asking that his absence while he recovered from an *illness* be excused.

Had she been relieved or not? How did she feel *now* when there was no turning back? Afraid? No! This had been *her* choice and *her* decision and his also in the beginning, and…

Holding her head higher above the leaf-rustling, Alexa could see now that he was waiting for her, his thick, dark hair catching some of the candlelight. He had grown a mustache that made his dark face look harder and more like that of a stranger; and even when she came up close and was standing beside him, there was nothing to be read in his eyes, which merely seemed to *watch* her instead of *feeling* her in the way she remembered.

She must have made the correct responses, although afterwards Alexa could not recall having done so. At some point during the ceremony Nicholas took off her glove and put a ring on her finger, and she knew they had knelt side by side only because he took her hand again to help her rise. What brought her back to the consciousness of sharp-edged reality was perhaps the perfunctory brush of his lips at the corner of her mouth before he lifted his head again and asked her politely if she was ready for the crowds once more; proffering his arm in the same formally polite manner. The organ sounds swelled again, and this time there were voices and words to acknowledge until her lips felt tired from smiling and her neck ached from nodding.

"I believe we are supposed to go from here into the vestry and sign our names in a book to make it all completely legal." Nicholas had bent his dark head down to hers as if he meant to whisper some love words in her ear; and it was foolish of her to expect anything of the kind, because he, Alexa realized, must be just as tense as she was. It was the strangeness of everything, the *newness,* that made them both so awkward with each other.

"You will not do her any injury," the Marquess stated softly at Nicholas's side while they both stood and watched Alexa's bent bronze head as she signed the register.

"If it would please you better I can give you my word

that I won't so much as lay a finger on your daughter my *wife,* sir.'' The Viscount Embry's twisted smile met Newbury's cold eyes; and Adelina, catching that small piece of byplay between the two, stored what she had heard in her mind until she could consider how it might be used by her later.

''We...that is, Margery and Edwin Jarvis wanted to hold a small and very private reception for us afterwards, but since their house is so small I offered...Nicholas, you do not mind? I sent you a letter asking what you thought of the idea, but when I did not hear, I had to make some decision on my own.'' Was it only her imagination or had he actually winced slightly when he gave her that indifferent shrug?

''Why not? I'm sure you have become used to making all decisions on your own and have good reasons for them as well. Have you decided where we are to spend our honeymoon yet?''

She had been holding his arm as they left the vestry, but now Alexa had to fight back her instinct to turn on him with her nails and her loudest virago shriek, just to see what his reaction would be. How dared he resent her because she had shown herself to be *strong?*

She might have said as much, and more perhaps, if they had not been greeted by a hail of rice and confetti at that moment as the waiting crowd of the curious and the well-wishers pressed in about them, forcing politeness on them both, so that they stood almost back to back like duelists who had to interrupt their private quarrel to defend themselves from an enemy army.

''*Where* is this reception of yours being held?'' Nicholas shot at her under his breath at one point, and through her fixed smile she whispered back, ''At *my...our* house in Belgrave Square, of course!'' wishing that her whispered words could have been darts instead.

"Such an exquisite gown, my dear."

"Wish you both well."

She hardly knew any of these people. Among strangers, mummers and actors, she had even become a stranger to herself; taking on the coloration of her surroundings and those who surrounded her like a chameleon. It didn't seem possible or even quite *real* that she had, only a few moments ago, signed herself and the fortune that had been her independence into the keeping of her *husband.* How short a time it had taken to forget everything poor Harriet had tried to teach her, and Sir John, and...*Harriet?* Somewhere in that sea of anonymous, staring faces she must have seen, out of the corner of her eye, a woman who reminded her of Harriet but could not possibly be. Alexa became aware that she was being guided forward now by Nicholas's hand on one arm and Mr. Jarvis's on the other; and that a carriage was waiting for her, the horses restive in that crowd of people and other equipages. But all the same, she had to look again, her head turning as she pulled back slightly, her eyes widening and looking suddenly very black in her pale face.

It couldn't be, but it *was!* How could she mistake that tall, angular figure or that somewhat forbidding face with lines pulling the mouth down at the corners to give it a perpetually caustic expression?

"Aunt Harry? *Harriet?* It *is* you, but why didn't you write to me? Why did you not let me know that you were in London?"

"My dear Alexa," Harriet said later in the familiarly acid tone that Alexa recalled so well, "I am surprised that you *still* persist in asking so many questions all at once! How on earth do you expect to get any answers?" And then, relenting slightly, she said rather gruffly, "I only meant to see you as a bride from a distance, you know. I suppose I should have been strong enough to resist the temptation.''

''And *I* cannot understand why you should say such a thing, when it was *you* who taught me to be, of all things, *direct.* It is wonderful that you are here, and especially at this time, but how is it possible that you *are?* Is there anything wrong? The last time we talked...''

''Ah yes. Since then Martin made a remarkable recovery and decided in the end... Well, there was a young Eurasian woman he had begun to see quite regularly, and after she had borne him a second child he *married* her. Naturally the household was hers to run, and her ways were different from mine; that was only to be expected! So...''

Poor Harriet. ''Belle-Mère''? Her doing to bring Harriet here, probably, but whatever she had meant to achieve was of no account *now.* Everything had been taken care of already, including Alexa herself—married into the *family,* no less. An advantageous and obviously *sensible* alliance that no one could take exception to, not even Harriet herself. Poetic justice, no less.

Still, it came as a surprise when Nicholas suggested offhandedly that perhaps Harriet might care to come and stay with them in the country for a week or so, until they decided where in Europe they would spend the rest of the winter and the spring. In fact, he was sure his wife would be happy to have a female companion during the next few weeks, while he would probably be busy.

Busy? Alexa asked herself, and decided soon afterwards *not* to ask the question out loud. In any case, she *did* want to become reacquainted with Harriet, who had been responsible for her bringing up and much of her present philosophy as well. The strangest thing of all, she thought a little later, was the meeting between Harriet and the Marquess of Newbury. She had wondered belatedly if there might not be some resentment; some coldness or even anger because of Harriet's part in the pretense that had sent them all to Ceylon. But instead, it was almost a shock to see them begin to talk as if there had not been so many years between their last meeting and this one.

"I cannot understand why you and your mother have suddenly decided to take such an interest in this...in the former Lady Travers," the Marchioness of Newbury protested to her husband in a rather petulant voice. "And as to your actually offering to give her *away,* that in itself is bound to cause comment, you know. And now this so-called aunt of hers whom you happen to know so well..."

"There was a time, my dear Iris, when I might actually have been foolhardy enough to *marry* Harriet Howard if she had been less independent," the Marquess said in his indifferent fashion. "However, she did not admire Byron as I did—an almost insurmountable barrier at that time." He did not mention his passion for Victorine, which may or may not have arisen because of Harriet's continued indifference; and Lady Iris did not pursue the subject, although she still harbored some resentment at being practically *forced* into coming up to London to attend Embry's wedding to a young female who had contrived to throw everyone's plans awry, besides being far too careless of her reputation. Almost unwillingly she found herself forced to wonder again if it could be possible that Embry's new bride was rather *too* closely related to the Dowager Marchioness Adelina through one of her brothers. Although *that* might account for everything, of course. Sometimes it was better and far more comfortable *not* to know too much.

Harriet Howard, on the other hand, still saw Gavin, Marquess of Newbury, as the young man she had toyed with so many years ago when she had been too sure of him, and had regretted losing when it had been too late. And now, not knowing anything about him as he *was,* she was able to converse quite naturally with the man she remembered, not knowing anything about the man he had since become.

Altogether, the small private reception passed off very well, with everyone present setting out to be charmingly polite to everyone else. A success, they would all say later. Catered by Gunter's, of course, and everything done in the best of taste, from the flower arrangements to the wines. Adelina, the Dowager Marchioness of Newbury, had seen to all *those* arrangements, while her son the Marquess had made up the guest list, which included some of the most distinguished and influential names and titles in the country. Even the old Duke of Wellington had made an appearance; and her Gracious Majesty the Queen had sent a gift accompanied by a personally written note offering her felicitations. No newly married couple could have asked for a more auspicious beginning to their life together; and no one observing Lord Embry and his radiantly smiling bride would have thought them anything but happy and exceptionally blessed by both fortune and circumstances, especially considering the unqualified support they had received from both the Marquess of Newbury and his formidable mother.

Fate, the Marquess thought. Kismet. His former masters the Turks had believed in the inevitable. Alexandra Victoria, his daughter by his girl-wife would be one day, as her mother should have been, the Marchioness of Newbury. And the old bitch-goddess, *his belle-mère* had been defeated at last. He did not trust her when she appeared to be so uncommonly obliging; but then *he* held the reins of power firmly in his grip now, and he could look forward to the pleasure of reminding her of that fact quite frequently. His mind toyed with the idea of retiring her to the country with a companion to watch over her who would be answerable only to him. Ah, how she would hate that!

And especially if that companion happened to be the outspoken Miss Harriet Howard. An interesting thought, and one he intended to pursue later. In the meantime, he allowed Lady Iris to babble on of her plans for *Helen's* wedding next year, the grand reception they must hold for her, and the new wardrobe she would need in order that she might outshine every other fashionable young lady next season. "And personally," Lady Iris went on, "I am really quite relieved that the dear child decided to break off her engagement to Embry. I have always thought that there was something rather wild and *dissolute* about him, you know. And not quite polished either, which is unfortunate, since he's your heir. I can only hope for the sake of his bride that the thought of getting him on the rebound, so to speak, does not begin to rankle after a while! Although for *Helen's* sake I cannot help but feel happy that she has decided on Worley, despite his age. He dotes on her, at least, and she will have everything in the world she desires, in addition to being a Countess. I am so glad that you gave your consent at once and that even your mother approves of the match."

The Dowager Marchioness had hardly paid any attention to her daughter-in-law's excited announcement of Helen's engagement to the Earl of Worley, a man at least twenty years older than the girl. She had always been sure that Helen would marry well and suitably. No, it was *this* match, which had been forced on her, that occupied her full attention for the moment—even after she had returned to her own house. She had always been adept at reading people and finding out their weaknesses so that she could use them to her advantage. And in this case, for her own protection she meant to make an ally of the new Lady Embry, her granddaughter. Lovers! Ah yes, that was it. Encourage her to take lovers, find them for her, offer, *understandingly,* to provide her with alibis any time she needed them. And then… Why, there were so many delicious alternatives to be weighed and measured. But first Alexa must be put under obligation to her, must eventually come to *need* her help and connivance. And to that end, it might help to cultivate Harriet Howard, who must surely know more about Alexa than anyone else. After all, both Harriet and her weak fool of a brother were unquestionably in *her* debt, and a subtle reminder when Miss Howard came to tea the next day might prove helpful. Ah, if Gavin thought he could defeat her and break her so easily, he'd find in the end that he was mistaken. A man with a flawed character was always vulnerable, and he must be made to remember that she knew all his flaws, his weaknesses and his vices far too well.

50

"Wedding nerves, same as all brides. *That's* all it is. And I *might* add that I'm glad for all our sakes that there *was* a wedding after all."

Mr. Bowles looked significantly at Bridget, who immediately took fire and snapped back: "Indeed, Mr. Bowles? *I* had never thought that there was any *doubt* that there'd be a wedding in the end. And don't you *dare* try to tell me that's the only reason that my poor Lady Alexa's walking up and down her room by herself in her pretty green silk negligee while his Lordship's already asleep in his *own* room, and on their wedding night, no less! It's not natural, nor normal either; *that's* what I was starting off to say. But you're a *man,* of course, and I should have known better than to think you might understand."

The fiercely partisan Bridget would have stayed to guard her mistress's locked door if she had not been dismissed to her own room and to her own bed several hours before Alexa was able to fall asleep. She had hoped that *he* would come knocking at her door so that she could have the vindictive pleasure of ignoring him, half fearing and half expecting that he might decide to break her door down if she did not let him in. It must have been past midnight when she finally slept. And when she woke up it was past twelve in the afternoon, and she was lying on top of her bedcovers, curled up like an infant, and still alone.

It was Bridget who woke her, cheeks redder than usual from embarrassment. Bridget who informed her that her husband had stayed in the library for two hours or more before retiring to his own room.

"His Lordship said... He told me you weren't to be disturbed before noon, my lady. And I was to start packing for you, for the country...?"

Alexa discovered that all her limbs felt stiff and that she was enraged, at the same time. How dared he give orders to her servants in her house! And indirectly to *her* as well? She drew in a deep breath, meaning to send back an icy message by Bridget; and then it suddenly dawned on her that she was *married,* and everything that had been hers was now *his.* Including herself, even if he had not bothered to avail himself of his conjugal rights on their wedding night. Was *that* why Bridget seemed unable to meet her eyes this morning? The scorned bride. She had locked her door last night, but it was Bridget and not her husband who had awakened her by knocking at her door.

"I believe we *are* supposed to spend a week or so in the country before we travel to Europe," Alexa said as she forced herself to stretch, hoping that Bridget could not see her face when she added: "But how *considerate* of Lord Embry to make sure I was to sleep late! Is *he* already awake, Bridget? If he is, please do tell him that I have to consult with him before we can be completely packed. I cannot quite remember if we are supposed to go first to Spain or to Germany, you know."

His Lordship, Alexa was informed soon afterwards, had called for a carriage and departed over an hour ago. He had left word for Lady Alexa that he had several urgent business matters that needed his immediate attention and would keep him away until shortly before eight that night, at which time he planned to join her and their guests at dinner.

It was only by a determined exercise of her willpower that Alexa was able to continue pinning up her hair while she said with studied casualness, "Oh? I suppose I had forgotten in all the turmoil yesterday. Did his Lordship happen to leave me a guest list, by any chance?"

"Oh *yes,* ma'am," Bridget said quickly. "He had given it to Mr. Bowles before he left—in case you might have forgotten, he said—and I have it here with me. And Cook would like to talk with you about the menu as soon as it's convenient for you, my lady."

Damn him, damn him! What kind of a cruel game was he playing with her now? Formality, politeness, and *distance.* He was *avoiding* her, that much was obvious. And by inviting guests to dinner on the night after they had been married, he was making it clear that he did not care to be alone with her. Did it also mean that she would spend another night alone in her own bed? Alexa gritted her teeth together and glared with narrowed eyes at her own reflection in the mirror. She meant to have it out with him and get everything straight between them as soon as he entered the house again, whether he liked it or not—guests or no guests. Just because they were married now, how dared he treat her with such detached indifference, as if she had suddenly become no more than a *housekeeper?* She snatched up the guest list that Bridget had cautiously laid on the dresser before her and frowned angrily over it. Nicholas's writing was almost as impossible as *he* was. Except for a few names that were familiar to her, the list was barely legible. Ten people—most of them strangers to her—and she would have to play the gracious, smiling hostess. It was hard not to give in to her impulse to tear the piece of paper she held into little shreds, or to pick up the crystal bottles ranged before her and send them smashing one by one into the mirror; and Alexa might even have given in to her impulses if one of the footmen had not knocked at the door to her sitting room and offered her a square parchment envelope borne on a silver tray.

"I'll read it in here, Bridget," she called to the girl in her most controlled voice. "And you might as well send for Cook at the same time, I suppose." But her mind stayed angry until some of her rage was replaced with curiosity after she had read the note from Adelina, Dowager Marchioness of Newbury, intimating that there were several private matters of some urgency she wished to discuss with her *dear* Alexa—this same afternoon, if possible.

"What a very pretty gown, my dear," the Marchioness commented when Alexa had been shown into her private sitting room. "That particular shade of brown suits your coloring very well, and I like the gold ribbon trimming. I was fond of browns and golds myself when I was younger. Would you care for tea? Or coffee, perhaps? Or," waving Alexa impatiently into a chair, "that I should come as quickly as possible to the point?

"Fortunately—or perhaps unfortunately—I think we are enough alike, you and I, to appreciate *directness,*" the Dowager began bluntly after her maid had left them. "And you've certainly proved that you're quick-witted as well as ambitious." She gave a cackle of laughter. "At least, thank God, you're not a milksop like the rest of them. You know what you want and go after it, don't you? Well, grudgingly or not I have to give you credit for that. But to have *real* power—and that's what you said you were after, wasn't it?—well, to have *that,* my dear, you need to know a lot of things about a lot of people; and that's where *I* have the advantage over you, because I know everybody that matters and everything about them too. And I've played the game a lot longer than you have, and succeeded—until *you* came along.'' Even though Alexa had not spoken, the Dowager waved an impatient, beringed hand in a silencing gesture before she went on with a shrug: ''But, if there's anything I've learned it's to accept what *has* to be accepted, even if I don't like it. There's no use the two of us being enemies, is there, if we can *use* each other? And by that I mean that I can help *you* gain whatever ends you're after, my dear, and at the same time you can help *me!* And we don't have to interfere with each other either, do we? I think you've a logical enough mind to realize the *sense* of what I'm proposing, don't you?''

Alexa said cautiously, ''And that is…? You must forgive me if I don't quite see how *I* can be of any help to you, ma'am.''

''You don't? Well I'll tell you how. And it could have advantages for you too, as you'll find out.'' Surprisingly, the Dowager gave vent to another harsh crow of laughter as she studied Alexa's face before saying: ''You don't trust me, do you? Well, that's clever of you too, I suppose. I wouldn't do you any favors unless it was to my advantage, because I've always looked out for myself first. How else d'you think I've survived and done so well for myself in a man's world? If you want power, my dear, you can't allow yourself the luxury of being swayed by your emotions. You'd best learn instead how to arouse the emotions of *others* for your own purposes. I married an old, rich man with a title, and I had my pick of young lovers when I wanted them and discarded them when I was tired of them, just like *men* do with the women who give in too easily. They can't resist a woman who's stronger than they are and controls a relationship. They're not used to being used themselves, you see, and they never see it, the poor fools! And when you're a married woman it's easy enough to break off an affair whenever you choose to and keep them still hungering after you; as I'm sure you'll find out soon enough for yourself if you haven't been stupid enough to develop an emotional attachment for your husband. And in that case everything I've been telling you was a waste of time, because you'll end up being nothing but a poor silly brood cow with no say about anything, not even the use of what used to be *your* fortune—which he'll spend on his mistresses, no doubt! But I, my dear, managed to keep *my* husband my adoring slave—and a cuckold, until the day he died.''

Alexa had found this sudden, blunt openness on the part of her grandmother quite surprising, although she had not let herself become disarmed by such unexpected frankness. But the *last* part of the Dowager's speech had struck home all the same, because she knew it was no more than a repetition of everything she'd been told before and warned against before—by Harriet first, and then all the other worldly-wise instructors Sir John had taken the trouble to find for her. Hadn't even her Aunt Solange told her the same thing in cruder terms? ''You'd better start thinking with your head, my girl, and not with what you've got between those pretty legs of yours!'' she'd said. And hadn't she seen and heard for herself how *base* men were and how unfeeling towards women they could too easily rule; and how easy it was to transform those same men into slaves begging for favors *if* a woman knew enough and was clever enough to keep herself *detached?* It was *acting* and not feeling that counted. Why hadn't she learned that yet?

As if she had been able to read minds, the Dowager leaned forward in her chair and said startlingly: ''There's already a strain between you and Nicholas, isn't there? You're not going to bother denying it if you're intelligent enough. *I* saw it clearly if no one else did. And I'm not asking you to confide in me, if that's what you're afraid of, although I *could* give you some advice if you need it in order to make him easier to manage. You'll find, sooner or later, that men are all the same and quite as easy to fool as to keep happy—once you have discovered what their weaknesses are."

Alexa found that all the muscles in her face felt stiff from the effort of keeping it composed, even her lips. But now, somehow, she managed to smile and to say quite lightly: "I must rehearse myself until I am a better actress, I suppose. But the strain you noticed is due, I think, to the circumstances leading up to our marriage, of which you're aware, and also to the fact that neither of us is *used* to having our freedom restricted. I daresay we shall both manage to come to an understanding sooner or later, and perhaps getting away from London and all the soot and smoke and fog will help."

"Ah!" Adelina exclaimed with satisfaction. "That is *exactly* what I wished to speak to you about in the first place. Newbury has become very difficult of late and has actually been raising objections to my leaving London for Spain and Portugal as I usually do every year. He's suggested the *country*—but I detest being cooped up there for the winter, and so would *you,* I'm sure! Servants' parties for Christmas, and visits to and from neighboring squires and parsons and their wives—and before *that* all the men are usually off to Scotland or the moors for the shooting. I hope you're not naive enough to think that because you're newly wed your husband's going to miss all the fun to stay with *you* and have all the other men make jokes behind his back and call him henpecked? *I've* always believed that if a man's entitled to his amusements so is a woman, although *we* are forced to be more discreet than they are."

"I beg your pardon," Alexa said rather constrainedly, "but I'm afraid that I..."

"I am suggesting, my dear Alexa, that you would probably find the south of Spain with its warm sun and salubrious climate much more exciting than being snowbound in an English country estate. I know that *I* certainly do. And if *you* were to mention to Newbury that since you are used to a tropical climate you cannot stand the thought of a cold, damp winter and would much rather spend that time in Spain or Portugal with *me* as a suitable chaperone, why, I'm sure it would raise no objections from anyone and might prove a most interesting experience for you as well. *Do* consider all the possibilities as well as the advantages to you before you make up your mind, won't you? Or better still, try the country for a week or two *first!*"

Choices or decisions—there were always those to be made. Alexa returned to her own home in a strangely uncertain mood that kept her tense and on edge for the rest of the afternoon while she tried to clear her mind of the clutter of emotion in order to think rationally and calmly. Weighing everything. Preparing herself and the questions she had to ask like an actress rehearsing her lines while she waited and watched a fine drizzle wet the street outside her window until it blurred her view and she turned back to the welcoming warmth of the fire in her sitting room. She would be cool. She would be perfectly objective and reasonable and would not under any circumstances allow him to make her lose her temper. She would point out that it would be much more convenient for them both if they could come to some understanding from the very beginning of their marriage of what each of them could expect from the other. But in the end nothing turned out as she had expected and she could remember none of her carefully prepared speeches and attitudes when she most needed the armor they might have provided.

Perhaps it was the dinner party composed of strangers

and casual acquaintances that he had arranged without consulting her first. Or perhaps it was the rankling knowledge that he had not returned to the house to change for dinner until just before the first guests had arrived, leaving *her* to entertain them until he sauntered downstairs at last with his perfunctory apologies. Or had it been the seemingly interminable time that the men had spent over their port and cigars and their ribald jokes while six women who scarcely knew each other and had nothing in common sat in strained silence between equally strained efforts at making polite conversation? All that Alexa was conscious of by the time the last guests had left was her steadily mounting rage, which was aggravated by the fact that at least *two* of the "ladies" she had been forced to entertain were in fact "seclusives"—well-known courtesans who were kept by their protectors in pretty villas in St. John's Wood and who later would no doubt laugh over having been entertained by Viscount Embry and his *wife* in fashionable Belgrave Square. Laugh at *her* for being forced into it.

While Bowles was locking the front door Alexa turned abruptly to her husband, who had actually dared to yawn. "I must speak with you in private, if you please, my lord."

Sarcasm dripped from every word she uttered, but he had the temerity to stifle another yawn before he inquired if it could not wait until some other time when he was not so sleepy and could give her his full attention. "And if it's about money and what kind of allowance you desire, I have already taken care of *that* through your own solicitor, Mr. Jarvis. I'm sure he'll be able to explain everything to you much better than I can. You will have no reason to feel deprived."

The thought, as bitter as gall, that she might be expected to thank him for being generous enough to allow her to spend some of her own fortune almost choked her as Alexa looked up into his dark, impenetrable face and met his clouded-green eyes that showed her nothing at all, except, perhaps, bored indifference. And *that* she could not and did not intend to tolerate.

"If that was all that concerned you, then I hope that you'll excuse me?" He had actually made a motion to turn away from her when Alexa put her hand on his arm. She was aware that Mr. Bowles was watching them both while he pretended to fiddle with the bolts on the door, but by now she was past caring.

"There is a great deal *more* that concerns me and *must* be discussed tonight," Alexa said in a low, suppressed voice that vibrated with the force of anger raging in her.

This time she was awarded a quizzical upward tilt of a black eyebrow as Nicholas drawled, "*Must* be? I'm hardly in the mood for *discussions* of any kind tonight, I'm afraid, or for anything but rest. Is it urgent?" And then he must have seen something in her face that made him think better than to try and evade her, for he gave a resigned shrug before saying, "I can see you're determined to be insistent, so—shall we use the study or the library for this discussion? And will you promise me it will be brief?"

There was already a fire lit in the library, because some of the gentlemen had repaired there earlier to find a book that would settle an argument they'd had. Mr. Bowles added more coal to make the flames leap to life again before he left them alone with a decanter of cognac, two glasses, and the wary silence between them that continued while the Viscount Embry poured a large amount of cognac into each glass before handing one to his new bride.

"*Salud, Marquesa.*" With a rather mocking gesture he lifted his glass to her. "There was something urgent you had to discuss with me?"

In the end she could hardly fault him for *not* being honest with her after she had demanded it. And she could not accuse him of being purposely cruel either. She had asked for the truth and he had given it to her, like an arrow sent straight to the heart.

"Oh Christ, Alexa! I tried to tell you before that marrying me would be no good for you any longer, if you remember. But you insisted, and your father the Marquess insisted, and after I had been urged to consider the alternatives in a most persuasive fashion, marriage to you and my freedom seemed to become infinitely the easier of the choices I was given. I find it hard to believe that you did not *know*—but perhaps you didn't, and in that case I apologize to you for thinking so and also for what I am not able to give you, if you expected more from this marriage than my name and the title of Marchioness of Newbury that will be yours some day."

By then the white heat of anger that had made her hurl her questions at him had been replaced by a growing coldness inside her that even the cognac she swallowed far too fast could not stop from spreading, until she felt as if she had been turned into a statue carved out of ice. And still she had persisted with her questioning, just as if she needed to have her wound probed to see if she was still capable of feeling anything at all. "*Why?* Nicholas, at least tell me *why?* I think...perhaps I could understand better if you could *explain...?*"

"You might find my explanation difficult to understand, I'm afraid."

Afterwards, when she was lying on her back in her bed staring at the moving shapes and shadows thrown on the ceiling by the fire, Alexa found that she could remember every word he had said and the sound of his voice and his profile against the reddish fireglow as he stood with one elbow leaning on the mantelpiece and *told* her, actually in a detached kind of way, as if what he was telling her was no longer of any consequence to him, or had happened to somebody else.

"There's a point, after some time, when you know you have to find some way of escaping from the pain, and I escaped by going inside myself and separating what was in my mind from what was happening to my body. I had to stop *feeling,* Alexa. It was the only way. And after that it really didn't seem to matter, you see. There were times when my body felt pain and protested; but it had nothing to do with me, because I lived in my mind. But you don't really see at all, do you?" He had turned his fire-shadowed face towards her then and reached out to touch one of the curled ringlets that hung down to frame her face. "I'm sorry if I've proved a disappointing husband, my dear, but I'm sure that once you've had time to think of the advantages of this kind of polite marriage, you'll end up considering yourself lucky."

51

Her husband had already left the house to conduct more mysterious business arrangements when Alexa had herself driven to Lincoln's Inn Fields to see her solicitor regarding an annulment of her marriage on grounds of nonconsummation. It was a farce, a sham. And worst humiliation of all, it had been *forced* upon him—*she* had been forced upon him—and he had made it quite clear that he neither wanted nor desired her and preferred to spend as much time as possible away from her. It was intolerable, and all she wanted was her freedom again.

Used to nothing but understanding and sympathy from Mr. Jarvis, Alexa was understandably taken aback when he told her bluntly that he must, in all good conscience, advise her not to be a fool. And so would any other person, lawyer or friend.

"But I do not think, then, that I have managed to make myself quite clear!" Alexa cried indignantly. "How can you expect me to live under such conditions? And last night—the day after our wedding, mind you—he had the bad taste to invite two well-known courtesans to dinner in *my* home, and I was forced to be gracious to them while he and his newfound cronies lingered over their after-dinner port. Do you think me foolish not to accept *that?* And all he said when I spoke to him on the subject was...'' Alexa had to force herself to pause and breathe deeply before she could continue, ''was that he felt *sorry* for me because I had changed into a pious hypocrite like all the others! Must I put up with his insults too in addition to everything else?'' Without thinking of what she was doing, Alexa had sprung out of her chair to begin prowling about the small room until Mr. Jarvis's mild voice checked her.

''*Please,* Lady Alexa, I must beg you to resume your seat so that I do not give myself a stiff neck trying to follow you about the room. And if you will only listen to what *I* have to say *in extenso* before you... Ah, thank you.'' As Alexa subsided stiff-backed into her chair again Mr. Jarvis gave her an old-fashioned inclination of his head before he went on to say quite firmly: ''My dear Lady Alexa, I feel it is my *duty* to advise you that in this case you have everything to gain by remaining married to Viscount Embry—and everything to lose if you are too precipitate. Divorce is an impossible thing for a *woman,* you know, unfair as it may be; and to obtain an annulment can sometimes be almost as impossible in some cases when it can be proven that—ahem!—that the wife is no longer *virgo intacta* if you take my meaning! And, as reluctant as I am to mention such a delicate subject, there remains the possibility that you might be with child. No, no, please allow me to finish.'' Alexa had opened her mouth to protest angrily but now she bit her lip instead and forced herself to listen to a speech she did not care to hear, as Mr. Jarvis steepled his fingers and continued in his dry voice: ''*Most* men, you know, would not be so fair-minded and gentlemanly as to ensure that all of the monies left to you by your *late* husband be legally settled on you once more with only a few small conditions attached—once they had already gained control of everything that was yours through marriage. I must tell you that I consider Lord Embry's decision most generous under the circumstances."

"You call him *generous* to give me back what is rightfully mine and *dare* attach *conditions* to his doing so? *What* conditions? Oh, I am afraid, Mr. Jarvis, that I have other words that fit better than 'generous'!" Alexa leaned forward with her eyes flashing and her teeth clenched together in a manner that reminded Mr. Jarvis uncomfortably of a wildcat ready to pounce, as she repeated between her teeth, "*What* conditions?"

He said hastily: "Only two, my dear Lady Alexa, only two. The first is that you do not *give* away any money or property hereafter, such as was the case with Lord Deering, you remember. And the second is that if you—hem—happen to take a *lover,* well then—control of the money, of *everything,* goes back to your lawful husband. Although of course in the case of his *death* he has taken the precaution to make provision that it will then revert to you again without any conditions at all. And if you will consider everything in the light of *reason* you will realize for yourself that..."

Unable to bear any more, Alexa erupted onto her feet again as she exclaimed in a voice shaking with infuriation: "Oh, but I have already realized quite clearly what he is about, I assure you. *He* doesn't want me, but nobody else can have me either, isn't that it? Why, the *bastard!* The vile, conniving... No, I *won't* offend your ears again by *swearing,* Mr. Jarvis, but if Lord Embry thinks to keep me tame and as *celibate* as *he* says *he* is, why then..." Alexa gave vent to a burst of wild, almost hysterical laughter that made Mr. Jarvis blanch before she said in a softer tone of voice that seemed even more menacing for that very reason: "Then he will have to follow me everywhere I go, Mr. Jarvis, to make sure of me. And I'll make it as difficult as I can for him to do so, and I will take as many lovers as I please all the same. If he catches me *in flagrante delicto*—you see, I remember my Latin—then I lose my money; but I shall make myself rich again by my own efforts. I wonder how my husband Viscount Embry will like the idea that his wife has become a whore? Oh yes, Mr. Jarvis, I assure you that I would make a very good harlot if I put my mind to it. Perhaps my aunt will help me to get started? Or…"

"For God's sake!" the usually imperturbable Mr. Jarvis was shocked into saying. "I implore you to be careful of saying such things, even if you don't mean them. If you will only take the time to reflect quietly and soberly… I was too blunt perhaps and might have seemed lacking in understanding for your plight, but you must understand that I was only stating facts and reminding you of what the law is. If there is anything I could do…"

"There is nothing that you can do, Mr. Jarvis, and I appreciate both your uncomfortable position and your frank relation of certain *facts,*" Alexa said quietly as she began drawing on her gloves. "But all the same I intend to do exactly as I just stated if he drives me to it; and *that* is a fact too. Thank you for your time, and please remember to give my regards to Lady Margery. You might tell her that I am planning to go off to Spain in search of the warm sun with my grandmother as my chaperone. The thought of a cold English winter and an even colder bed holds no appeal for me! Good afternoon, Mr. Jarvis."

It seemed as if all her rage and all the hurt it covered had suddenly turned into one cold, solid mass that occupied all the space inside her, so that in the strangest way she could almost understand what Nicholas had tried to explain to her last night even though she could not forgive him for what he had done to her. Cajoled her, coaxed her, pursued her and wooed her; taught her what *passion* meant and what ecstasy was—made her want him and long for everything he could make her feel, even if it was against her will. And then, he had rejected her. Not for revenge, not out of hate. She could have understood those strong emotions and accepted them with better grace than she could deal with his *indifference.* Hamlet—she had always despised his eternal vacillation even if she enjoyed his soliloquies. "Get thee to a nunnery...go!" How casually he had dismissed poor Ophelia, whom he had once courted ardently; and how easy *her* husband had found it to force her into a nunlike existence, or so he must have thought. Let him continue to think so while he lived his detached existence inside himself that was centered around himself, until such time as she chose to let him discover what *she* was up to.

In her present mood, Alexa found that she no longer cared who might see her or what they might say when she sent her own carriage back home and took a hansom cab to visit her Aunt Solange.

If Madame Olivier did not profess herself overjoyed to see her wayward niece again, she did not reprove her for arriving without warning either, her only comment at first being: "Well! I had hardly expected to see you here again after getting yourself remarried—with Newbury giving you away and the old witch herself in attendance, so I'm told. You deserve to be congratulated for managing such a coup."

Later, after they had each had a second glass of the excellent champagne she always kept on hand for her best customers, Solange said brusquely: "Well, hadn't you better come out with it? You didn't expect to pull any wool over *my* eyes with your light and airy chatter, I should hope." But when Alexa told her what she planned to do if she was forced to it her aunt burst into rich, genuine laughter. "*Ma pauvre petite!* Where is your head? Pah, if you worked for *me* I can guarantee you wouldn't last long.

I told you before that you'd never make a good whore because you're not detached enough. And for all you *think* you've learned, my girl, you know nothing at all of the reality of doing it yourself with a different man every hour, which is a lot different from talking about *how* to do it or watching other people do it, as you'd find out at once. Listen, and I'll give you some free advice for the last time. Why don't you face up to the truth you're trying to hide from yourself? You're a fool, that's evident, and you're in love with the bastard you're married to—like the idea or not. *Merde!* If that's the way it is why don't you stop acting like a spoiled little child throwing a tantrum to get attention and go after what you really want instead? That's what I would do.''

No! Alexa told herself rebelliously when she was on her way back home. No, no, no! She felt like screaming it out loud. How could her Aunt Solange, who had never known her until a few months ago, pretend to understand her well enough to divine her deepest emotions? She was *not* in love with Nicholas Dameron; she never had been. All she had felt for him was something she had already admitted—want. Physical desire. An animal craving that had affected her body, perhaps, but never her mind. All the same, by the time Mr. Bowles had opened the door for her with a reproachful look, Alexa's mood had become more thoughtful than defiant, although she had not changed her mind, she told herself. Not about anything.

''His Lordship came back and left less than a half hour ago, my lady. He asked me to remind you that you had asked a Miss Howard from Ceylon to dinner tonight and desired that you offer his apologies for his absence since he had a previous engagement to dine at his club. Also, Cook wishes to know…''

''Thank you, Bowles. You may send Cook upstairs to me in fifteen minutes. And please be sure to send a carriage for Miss Howard at seven precisely. I will give you her direction before then.''

There was no point in dissolving into tears or throwing temper tantrums that would do her no good. *He* had decisively set the pattern of their relationship and had made it clear what it was to be. And as Harriet reminded her later, now that she was a *married* woman she must be prepared to entertain and make calls and keep herself busy running her household and fulfilling social obligations. There was also charity work....

''Oh, for heaven's sake, Aunt Harry! What you are advising me to do, in other words, is to keep myself busily immersed in complete *dullness,* until I myself become dull and stupefied and won't care about anything any longer!''

''Well, my dear, you must admit that it beats moping about being discontented and *vinegarish!* And the reason I brought the subject up is because it's quite obvious to me that *something's* not right with you *and* with your marriage when a young and newly wed couple feel more comfortable with a chaperone about. Now, why else would you both positively beg me to come down to the country with you when you're still supposed to be on your honeymoon?''

Alexa had sipped her wine and given a lift of one bare shoulder at that, hoping that she had not given too much away earlier. ''It's because *honeymoons*... That kind of thing is so old-fashioned, after all. And my marriage to Embry is a matter of convenience for us both—a *mariage de convenance* in the modern style where we each have our own friends and pursue our own interests. Why, I plan to go very soon to Spain—perhaps to Portugal and the south of France as well—*without* Embry, of course. I think the Dowager Marchioness Adelina will accompany me as my chaperone. Do you not find that quite ironic and amusing?'' She had managed a light, gay laugh at Harriet's sourly foreboding expression and said coaxingly: ''*Please,* Aunt Harry. Why don't *you* come along too? Then I shall have *two* chaperones, and we'll have such a capital time, I'm sure. Adelina knows *everyone* of any consequence there, and we shall be staying at castles and private villas and...oh, you would love it, I'm sure. Besides, I do trust you and I don't *her*—not one bit. We only *use* each other and my...and Newbury won't let *her* go this year unless *I* do, so you see...''

''I see that you are sailing in very dangerous waters, my dear, and I can only hope that you'll be very careful indeed. What does your husband think of this plan of yours?''

''Embry? Why, I haven't told him yet, but *he* won't care a fig anyhow—he's always so busy with *business* and his own amusements. Please say you'll come, Aunt Harry. And if I become too foolish you can advise me.''

''We'll see, we'll see,'' Harriet said in the end when Alexa kept on begging her to come. But she didn't like any of it. She was glad, however, that she *had* agreed to go down to the country with the girl, because she obviously needed some stable companionship. There was a brittle quality to the brilliance of her smile and the gaiety of her manner that hid nerves strung tight. Something was very, very wrong; but she could hardly ask bluntly what it was while they were still becoming reacquainted. Perhaps, after they had spent enough time together, Alexa might feel ready to confide in her and there might be something she could do to help. Harriet had not been able to shake off her feelings of guilt for what *had* happened and had *almost* happened that time in Ceylon; although as to what had led up to it all—she had always thought that what she had done was for the best.

52

It was the routine. To the country for the shooting season and the hunt until winter had well and truly set in; and then soon after Christmas, plans were already being made for visits to Europe; traveling about to kill the time until the next London season began. It was like living by a clock—by a sundial.

Alexa and Harriet traveled down to the house in one of the carriages. In spite of the fine drizzle that was falling, Lord Embry had preferred to drive himself in the phaeton. It took three other carriages and a heavy, rather old-fashioned traveling coach to carry all of their baggage and those of the servants who were to accompany them to the country. Alexa had worn three flannel petticoats under the others she usually wore, and her warmest fur-trimmed cashmere pelisse over a fine wool dress of warm golden brown trimmed with dark orange and flame. Autumn colors, her dressmaker had told her. Even Harriet had complimented her on her looks and the color in her face, little suspecting that it was not natural but due to artificial aids.

''I'm afraid I'll never get used to this English weather again,'' Harriet commented, shivering a little as they started out. ''My dear, I think it must be back to Ceylon for me, after all. Martin's being more than generous, and I can afford to take a small house in Colombo or in Kandy, I think. It's the *damp* here that is so hard on old joints and old bones."

"Then you should come with me next month to Spain. At least you can go with us there *first,* can't you? You'll miss the worst of the Bay of Biscay that way; and I believe there are always ships on their way to Ceylon and India that stop in at Lisbon and *Cádiz* for cargo *and* passengers. At least, do think about it, won't you? I don't intend to be buried away in the country for more than a week or ten days at the very *most* and expect to be warm and enjoying myself *thoroughly* again before the end of November."

"Well, I certainly *hope* so," Harriet said in a rather noncommittal voice as she drew her fleece-lined lap robe more closely about her. "But, my dear, I don't know if *I* am up to life in high circles and the constant running around you're bound to be doing. And my wardrobe will hardly pass muster as you well know, so either way I'd feel like a fish out of water."

"But if I took a small villa of my own, so that we could just lie and bake in the sun and explore—at least for a while?"

"Well, we'll see! But perhaps Embry might decide to accompany you? After all, modern marriage or not, every man desires an heir to inherit his name and his title, if he has one. Surely..."

"Since you are going to live in the same house with us, Aunt Harriet, I suppose it's best that *I* explain something to you before you find out for yourself—or from the servants." Harriet had never heard such a cold bitterness in Alexa's voice before as she continued with only the curling and uncurling of her fingers over the handle of her reticule betraying emotion: "My husband does not visit my room nor my bed and in fact chooses to avoid me as much as possible. I do not think he cares if he has an heir or not, as long as it's not by *me.* And he does not care where I go or how I amuse myself as long as I...well, *that* is not too important. The point is that he is completely indifferent to me. You will see it for yourself, I'm sure."

What Harriet did see during the next few days was that Alexa was desperately unhappy, for all of her pretended insouciance and surface gaiety and lightheartedness. She hardly saw Lord Embry at all except at dinnertime, for he usually went out riding for most of the day or else stayed closeted in his study or his bedroom. This was a strange marriage indeed, and Harriet wondered how it had come about in the first place.

The sun had not shown itself for three days now, and although there had been invitations to dinners and musical evenings or whist at the houses of some of the local gentry, Alexa had pleaded tiredness and the nuisance of having to supervise the unpacking of their baggage as her excuse for not going out. She spent the dreary sunless days in the house or in her own rooms, where she could pace until she felt tired enough to be able to sleep; and she played chess with Harriet and wrote letters and poured tea. And saw *him* across the dinner table from her, met him sometimes on the stairs where they exchanged polite greetings, or saw him from her window as he left on his rides mounted on a big black stallion with a white star on its forehead that *she* would have loved to ride—and saw him come back soaked to the skin; knowing by now that he would stay to dry himself off in the stables while he talked to the grooms and the stablehands and they drank brandy together. She knew *that* because Bridget had reported it to her. Mr. Bowles, Bridget said, did *not* think it was proper for his Lordship to hobnob with his servants!

This afternoon Alexa did not turn away from the window as she usually did but remained staring outside as the light gradually changed from one shade of grey to another until it was dark, with the orange lantern-glow blooming from the windows of the stables and the head groom's quarters above it; and she found herself wondering what they talked about and why he seemed to enjoy the company of those rough, simple men enough to spend so much time with them. What am I to do? she thought, watching the water run down from the eaves in long streams that reminded her of the heavy monsoon rains in Ceylon. I have everything I once thought I wanted, and nothing I want *now.*

"My dear, you really cannot go on making excuses to all your neighbors forever," Harriet reminded her as they sat in the smaller drawing room waiting for dinner to be announced. "Even if you *do* plan to go away soon you should perhaps make their *acquaintance* at least; so that next year..."

Next year? And then the year after that and the year after that, with Europe to look forward to next, before London. Her lovers would be carefully chosen and discreetly met, and she would change them if she grew tired of them or if they showed signs of becoming too intense. No doubt her grandmother would advise her! And soon she would be armored against emotion or weakness and would not even *feel* the emptiness inside herself.

"Alexa? My dear, are you dressed warmly enough? You shivered just now as if you'd felt a cold draught on you. You're not sickening for something, are you?"

Alexa gave one of her new, brittle laughs. "Someone must have walked over my grave just then. Isn't that what the superstitious say?"

That night over dinner Lord Embry said casually: "The weather is expected to clear by tomorrow, according to one old farmer I encountered today. Perhaps you ladies might want to take one of the carriages and make some calls?

Our closest neighbors are the local squire and his wife, and Mrs. Eden is quite young and would be glad of company of someone her age, I'm sure. She's also quite an excellent horsewoman, and has a friendly, vivacious personality."

Since Alexa had just taken a taste of her game pie and could hardly answer him yet, Harriet said, "Then we should certainly make that the first of our calls, since Alexa too has always loved to ride and is quite a horsewoman herself—although I'm sure you know that already."

"*Did* you ever watch me when I used to ride in the Row almost every day, Embry? Why, at first they could not decide if I was one of the pretty horsebreakers or not, and *then* everyone began taking wagers on who was the better rider, your friend 'Skittles' or I!"

For just an instant Alexa thought she saw some tiny spark of amusement in his eyes, and then he raised his napkin to his lips before saying indifferently: "Really? In that case, my dear, I must hope that *you* came off the winner. You'll find, though, that riding in Rotten Row is very different from riding about in the countryside, especially if you don't know your way about. And you should be sure that the hack you choose is not easily startled. Perhaps Mary Eden might be able to give you some advice and show you which paths and bridle trails are safest for riding."

They're dueling now, Harriet thought with a sense of foreboding. And after *that* cut she waited for Alexa's temper to show. But surprisingly the explosion she dreaded did not come, and instead Alexa said with surprising calmness: "It is always wisest to know one's way about in a strange place, of course, and even more pleasant to have such an obliging and *knowledgeable* neighbor as this Mrs. Mary Eden. But do tell me something about her husband to prepare me. Does *he* ride too?"

Her answer was delivered shortly. ''Squire Eden used to be Master of the Hunt some years back, until he took a bad fall and injured his spine in some way. He's confined to a chair or his bed now.''

''Oh, how very *sad* for him. And for his wife, of course, but at least *she* can still go riding, so I suppose she must count herself fortunate to have such an *understanding* husband who does not tie her to his side.''

Intervening quickly, Harriet put in, ''But under the circumstances, do you think it might be too much of a strain or even an embarrassment for the poor gentleman to have to receive callers who are strangers to him?''

''They both enjoy company tremendously, I assure you, and your visit would be very welcome if you'd care to go?''

''I'll send a letter over tomorrow to inquire when it would be convenient for the Edens to receive us, of course. Since we have not met before it would hardly be proper to show up unannounced, I'm sure, unless people in this part of the country are more informal. Or were *you* planning to escort us and perform introductions?''

''As a matter of fact, I visited Eden Manor earlier today to look at a thoroughbred yearling they've decided to sell,'' Nicholas said deliberately. ''So they are halfway expecting you—unless you'd prefer not to go, or feel you might be bored by people who prefer the country to London and are down to earth and quite simple, in their way, I suppose. No, the Edens are too natural and honest to stand on ceremony or insist upon formalities, I'm afraid, if that is what you expect. And more often than not they do not even bother to get dressed for dinner. They have three or four courses at the most, and Mary Eden enjoys cooking a meal herself sometimes. If you wish to seek their acquaintance you'll find that what they appear to be is what they *are* and that they accept other people in the same way.'' Suddenly, as if he had realized he'd said too much, he shrugged and added carelessly: ''But you must do as you please, of course. I'll say no more on the subject.''

Glancing at Alexa, Harriet thought she looked as if she'd been struck, her eyes like dark pools in her pale face until she shielded them by looking down at her plate to make a pretense of eating. When she looked up again she had composed her features into a mask that gave nothing away, like the sound of her voice as she said, ''My goodness! All I asked you, after all, was whether you planned to go with us if we visit your friends tomorrow. I had no *idea*...''

''I beg your pardon.'' By now he too was composed. ''I should have mentioned it earlier, I suppose, but I have made plans to visit a horse fair at a small village close to Basingstoke with one of the grooms who was born there. I shall probably be away until some time tomorrow, or perhaps the day after if I do not find any horses worth buying and decide to go up to London for a day.''

''My dear,'' Harriet said when the ladies had retired, ''is *that* what is making you so unhappy? The thought that there might be another woman involved?''

If she let herself *laugh* as she almost felt tempted to, Alexa thought, then she would not be able to stop and would end up in hysterics, which would never do. ''Another Woman''—the way poor Harriet had *said* it! Mary Eden, whose company he sought out instead of hers and whose praises he'd just sung? He'd cut himself off from all *feeling*, he'd told her, but had he omitted to tell her that he had only cut himself off from feeling anything for *her?* Why couldn't *she* do the same thing?

''Alexa!'' Harriet said sharply to hide her alarm when instead of answering her the young woman had merely stared at her with dilated, empty eyes, her hands going up to push against her temples in an almost mindless gesture.

"Now listen to me, my girl, I won't allow you to fall to pieces, d'you hear? It's not going to do you any good. Where's that stubbornly resolute fighting spirit you used to possess? And have you forgotten how to use your *mind* and the intelligence God gave you! I don't care if you don't want to tell me what's at the root of all this, but all I can say is that you'd be better off using your energy on some kind of *positive* action instead of wasting it on *fluttering*—like a silly little moth against a lampshade! What happened to your backbone, for heaven's sake? You ought to have learned by now that the sooner you face facts and look them squarely in the eye instead of trying to run away from them, the better off you'll be." Leaning forward in her chair to transfix Alexa with her most *quelling* look, Harriet added, "And *that* is why I suggest that while your husband is off at his horse fair tomorrow, you and I should make a point of calling on the Edens; even if it's only out of curiosity and nothing else."

Idle curiosity. What else? It was only being cooped up indoors for three long, boring days that had unhinged her slightly, Alexa told herself later while Bridget was helping her undress for bed. She certainly wasn't *jealous* of this Mary Eden, who was such a paragon of all the *simple* virtues, according to her husband—who was certainly more familiar with vices than virtues to judge from *her* experiences with him! Still, it would do no harm to go out of the house for a change and to find out for herself why he sought *them* out while he took pains to avoid *her*. Or was it only *Mary* Eden's company that he sought?

Bridget had taken to country hours already and was trying to cover her yawns when Alexa dismissed her impatiently. Only ten o'clock—not quite that—and everyone was in bed. She found it impossible to fall asleep so early and usually read for a while; but tonight, upon picking up the book on her night stand, Alexa was reminded that she had finished reading it last night and had forgotten to bring up another book from the library before she came upstairs. For some moments she hesitated, undecided; and then, not wanting to lie awake in her bed with only her thoughts for company, she snatched up the quilted satin robe that matched her peach-colored nightgown from the back of the chair where Bridget had left it and went resolutely downstairs, with a candlestick to light her way. One of Miss Austen's novels would suit her mood tonight, if she could find one that she had not read yet. Or perhaps what shc needed tonight was to read some philosopher who would put things in perspective for her before he put her to sleep.

There was still a lighted fire in the book-lined room to keep it warm—but surely the efficient Mr. Bowles should have made sure that the wood brought in was not wet? The room was full of smoke, and it was only after a few seconds that Alexa recognized that the particularly sweetish-acrid odor was familiar and felt herself freeze in the center of the room at about the same time *his* voice drawled, "For God's sake, don't drop it or you're likely to start a fire! And what in hell are *you* doing down here so long past your bedtime?"

The unpleasant note in his voice stiffened her spine as Alexa turned around slowly to discover him sprawled negligently in one of the wing chairs that were placed on either side of the fireplace, long legs extended before him.

"I suppose I could ask *you* the same question, but since I've already guessed the answer I'll let it pass. And if your Lordship has no objections I will try to find the book I was looking for as soon as possible and make haste to leave you to escape into your pipe dreams once more." Almost blinded by a mixture of emotions she had no time to try and analyze, Alexa reached upward and pulled out the first book her groping fingers discovered, and had already reached the door when she swung about to face the red glow of the pipe as he drew on it; and because her hands had begun to shake she first set down her candlestick on a table that stood there before she said in a voice that shook with the force of all that was inside her: "How dare you call *others* hypocrites and cowards when you are the worst of all? How *glad* I am that I came here tonight to realize for myself what you really are! *This* has become your reality, has it not? You find it easier to hide behind your puffs of smoke than to deal with feelings or emotions or anything that might pull you off your lofty perch of detachment from humanity, don't you? Well then, *stay* hidden safely in your selfish little world of you and yourself with your dream pipe for a lover! And you need not go to all the trouble of trying to avoid me in the future, I assure you, my lord, because...because I intend taking pains to stay out of *your* way as much as possible! Good night to you—and enjoy your dreams!"

He could not know, of course, that once she was back in her bedroom she had thrown the book she carried against the wall as hard as she could before flinging herself across her bed to pound on her pillows in a paroxysm of sheer frustration before the tears came like a flood and brought her the release she needed, until worn out, she fell asleep still sobbing like a lost child. And once asleep, Alexa slept so soundly that she did not hear her door being opened or feel the gentle, almost tentative touch of fingers against her damp cheek; brushing back the unruly strands of hair that seemed to have become pasted against it.

Lying there with most of her face burrowed into her pillow and her arms wrapped around it as if for solace, she looked childish and vulnerable. His poor little tear-drenched mermaid who should have stayed an innocent child of nature in her fairy kingdom. Had it really been he who had made the first breach in the walls and tempted her outside? Remembering the first time he had seen her weep without wanting to, Nicholas swore softly under his breath and pulled the covers over her curled-up body, half-glad and half-sorry that he had found her sleeping so soundly. He had not meant to enter her room at all, nor even to pause outside her closed door instead of passing it without a glance as he usually did. But tonight it was as if her scathing little speech had pricked at him and irritated him just enough to let loose a demon of perversity that prompted him to try her door to find out if she had really meant everything she'd said. And then, when the handle had turned easily he had walked in without thinking or wondering why he did so. Probably just as well it had turned out this way. She seemed to have adapted herself very well to her new environment, which was probably what she had always wanted. The best thing *he* could do for her was probably to let things be as they were—and to let *her* be. When the door closed softly behind him, Alexa stirred slightly but did not wake, although for a little while she did dream.

Perhaps it was those half-remembered dreams and what they had evoked in her that made Alexa so silent and so pensive for most of the day. Dreams—or regrets, maybe. For what had been and for what was and for everything yearned for that could never be attained.

Harriet thought Alexa was coming down with a cold and suggested, regretfully, that they should not think of venturing out in that case. "I'm not getting a *cold;* it was just that I had some horribly depressing dream and woke up *crying,* although afterwards I could not even remember what it was about," Alexa improvised glibly. She did not tell Harriet that she had burst into tears again a short time before when she had discovered that short of suffocating to death and in spite of all Bridget's efforts her corset could *not* be laced up tightly enough to allow her to wear one of her favorite gowns. Nor did she mention to Harriet the frightening possibility that had suddenly entered her mind, especially after she had caught Bridget's unhappy and commiserating look. What would be the point of burdening Harriet with yet another of her problems at this particular moment? It was something she should have thought of herself and would have to deal with herself, even though she longed to have someone she could confide in who would truly understand the predicament she suddenly found herself in—or even a strong shoulder to lean against and a pair of strong arms to hold her tightly without any words needing to be said.

It was sheer weakness to allow herself to indulge in such pointless fantasies, Alexa reminded herself sternly after a while, suggesting brightly to Harriet that they might just as well take advantage of the break in the weather while they could and pay a call on Squire Eden and his wife Mary.

53

"Well, my dear," Harriet said later that night, "I certainly don't think that you have anything to worry about in *that* direction. She's a pretty enough woman with a passable figure, I'll admit, but *not* the flighty type, by any means. And I don't think her devotion to her husband is put on; nor his for her. *I* sensed that they're very happy together. What did *you* think?"

"Mary Eden and I are going riding tomorrow if the rain holds off again," Alexa said without answering directly. "I thought they seemed quite comfortable and contented in the world they've made for themselves, but it'll be easier to tell for certain when she and I have had time alone, I think. Anyhow, I *did* find that I liked her; and she does know a great deal about horses, I must admit. Good night, Aunt Harry." She went up to bed, leaving Harriet staring thoughtfully after her.

Once, when Alexa had been about ten years old, a genial visitor with a red face and fearsome mustache had taught her card tricks. Simple ones, of course. But the one that had taken the most concentration for her, because of her impatience, was trying to lean one card up against another very carefully until the whole deck of cards became a snake—and if you touched just the one card you'd begun with it was enough to make everything collapse and leave the snake no more than a tired skin. You could do it with dominoes too, she had learned much later; but she never forgot the cards and how easy it was to demolish the result of all that careful concentration with no more than the lightest flick of her little finger. And once it was started there was nothing you could do to stop it—nothing. Until the whole had collapsed and you sat staring at it dolefully, wondering if you had enough energy and concentration and patience to build it all up again—just to see the same thing happen all over again. That was how the next day seemed in retrospect, although when she woke that morning and saw that it was not raining and there were breaks in the grey clouds that still hung overhead, Alexa felt quite lighthearted at the prospect of being able to ride again after what seemed an age.

''I don't think we should stay out too long today,'' Mary Eden said before they started out. ''Guy made me promise I'd get back home before the rain, and you should too. It can be awfully treacherous in some spots when it's so wet and you can't see your way too well. So please forgive me if I cut our ride short, won't you? I know we're going to have a few more nice days soon before the winter really sets its teeth in.''

Alexa had had her heart set on riding the black stallion at least once, just to *show* him, but Mr. Grubb, the head groom, was old and crusty and quite adamant that Nero was not to be ridden by anyone save the master himself—and that was that. It did not help Alexa's rising sense of frustration when Mary Eden murmured apologetically at her side: ''I *hate* to seem as if I am taking sides, you know, but he *is* right. Nero can be dangerous and even vicious at times; and he'd be impossible to manage in weather like this, I promise you, even if you were the best horsewoman in the world. Please *do* take one of the other hacks instead. They're all such beauties, and all spirited and a joy to ride.''

In the end Alexa picked a beautifully marked bay mare with more than a touch of Arab in her and was immediately informed by Mr. Grubb that she was not only descended from the famous thoroughbred ''Eclipse'' but tended to be frisky and a mite headstrong as well—like some *women* were. And if *he* had been asked his opinion he would have suggested one of the hunters who was a good jumper as well, knowing the countryside hereabouts as well as *he* happened to, having been brought up here from boyhood!

''Oh Mr. Grubb, I am *quite* sure Lady Embry knows exactly what kind of mount she wants, and of *course* she's not going to try and *jump* her. In any case, I only mean to show Lady Embry the shortcut to the Manor so that she can visit us whenever she cares to.''

Grumbling under his breath, Grubb finally did as he was told and actually helped Alexa to mount; his parting shot being that the mare was probably with foal and shouldn't be ridden too hard.

''*Thank* you, Mr. Grubb,'' Alexa said sweetly. ''I shall certainly try to remember all of your advice.''

''I'm afraid he *is* used to having his own way, and dreadfully outspoken,'' Mary offered deprecatingly once they had set off. ''But he's been here for simply *years,* since the last Marquess of Newbury was still quite *young,* I believe. And he *does* understand horses and can do anything with them. Why, he's the best horse doctor for miles around! So *please* excuse his lack of polite manners, won't you?''

After Alexa had vowed insincerely that of course she understood and did not in the least mind his gruff manners, their ride actually became quite a pleasant experience in spite of the grey skies overhead. The mare tested her rider with a show of spirit and then settled down very well; and Mary pointed out different landmarks that might prove useful if Alexa ever needed to find her way home. She also pointed out one or two different paths that would make the journey between their houses even shorter, but added doubtfully that she did not think Alexa should attempt to try them yet because they tended to become slippery in wet weather and because falling tree branches could also prove quite a hazard.

"I am so *very* glad that Nicholas married someone like you," Mrs. Eden said suddenly, and then flushed as she added hesitantly: "You don't mind that I call him that, do you? Only Guy and I came to know him so well that it seemed quite ridiculous to be so *formal* after a while. But you see, he's always seemed so *alone!* Or as if he must always keep himself off at a distance as an *observer,* instead of… But how forward you must think me to say all this to you about your husband when you must know him so much better."

"Alone?" Alexa found herself echoing, seizing on that one word for some reason.

"Well, yes. And I'm sure *you* know as well as I do that sometimes one is never more lonely than in the midst of a crowd of people, especially in an unfamiliar environment. *Guy* noticed it first, when they began talking about California and exchanging stories, and then it became obvious to me too. And then when Guy *asked* quite bluntly what the *deuce* he was doing here in such an artificial setting that didn't suit him in the very least…" Mary shot an apologetic glance in Alexa's direction as she murmured: "I'm afraid that my husband tends to be *very* blunt sometimes, but only if he really likes you, of course! Well, it was only *then* that Nicholas—your husband, that is—admitted he'd never meant to stay this long or to get—

'sucked in,' I believe he said. And *that* is why I'm so glad that he met you in *time,* before he goes back. And—please forgive me for being so *emotional*—it's a habit of mine I *deplore* but cannot seem to eradicate. But I'm just so happy that he's found a woman who's willing to give up all the glitter and the silk-cushioned comforts of London and Europe to go with the man she loves to *his* real home." Mary's eyes were shining with real tears that she brushed away with the back of her hand before she leaned forward to give Alexa's cold cheek a spontaneous kiss, adding soon afterwards, "But I *do* hope we can spend some time together before you two have to leave. Do you promise you will?"

"Of course I promise. As soon as I can manage it!" Alexa said the words mechanically as she concentrated all her attention upon schooling her face *not* to show any of her whirling, confused, and *angry* thoughts. He had confided in *Mary* and her husband. Everything except one tiny detail that he must have deliberately omitted. *Her.* His *wife.* The wife he had been forced to marry and intended to desert as soon as possible. Oh God, *God!* Only let her have the strength not to *show* anything, but to *act* as well as *he* could when it suited whatever devious purposes he had in mind. She must, she *must!* Otherwise she would die from the humiliation and the bitterness and the pain that twisted so hard and so deep inside her that she could have screamed aloud from it—and from rage as well.

Aloud, she said with careful attention to the inflection of her voice: "I'm sorry now that I could not have been here earlier, at the very beginning of autumn. There is no change of seasons in Ceylon, where I was brought up, and I have not yet seen the snow. Can you imagine that?" "Words, words, words"—like Hamlet. Words to cover and to disguise those things inside that went too deep and were too dark to be put into superficial words.

"Oh, but you'll be able to see snow in California. Snow in the mountains, with the burning desert sands as a contrast. But the southern part of California has a very pleasant and mild climate, so I understand. Perhaps you'll come and visit us next year?"

And then like a miracle sent to save her, Alexa felt the first few drops of rain spatter on her taut-white knuckles and heard Mary say with dismay, "Oh no! I've been so engrossed in our talk that I did not even *think*...what must you think of me? Please, you *will* come home with me, won't you? We'll both get rather wet, but..."

"Heavens, no," Alexa said lightly. "I've always loved riding in the rain and *this* ride will be such fun. My aunt will be frantic if I don't return; and anyhow, I want to prove to my husband that I am quite as hardy as *he* is. I *know* you'll understand."

While Mary Eden was still hesitating, Alexa flashed her a smile before she turned the mare around and called teasingly, "Go on. *You* hurry back home and face your husband. I'm sure *mine* cannot be back yet, so I can take my time and be *careful.* And thank you for your honesty, Mary Eden."

Was *that* the first flick of her fingernail against a carefully balanced card? Had it already happened before, or did it happen afterwards, when the wildness took possession of her with the rain blowing in her face and the mare becoming a part of her and a tree branch snatching her hat away so that the wind had its will of her hair and it streamed behind her in the end like a wet banner and she screamed all her raging fury out loud into the sky and into the earth and into the fierce wind itself until she could feel even the trees and the shrubs about her answer her while the rain flowed into her mouth and soaked her through every layer and every garment she had worn until it reached her skin and stayed to caress it with every miniature rivulet and stream that flowed over her and about her as if she were a continent and a storm and at the same time made out of the dust from all the stars and the stars themselves and even the empty spaces between them?

For some time she had been completely insane, of course. Or had somehow left her body like the yogis who were advanced enough were supposed to do, letting herself be taken and carried in whirling spirals by a mighty wind that took her higher and higher and even higher yet until she no longer felt the branches whipping against her face or tearing at her hair and heard nothing but her own keening scream surrounding her until it echoed and echoed through all the vastness of the sky and touched against every star before it came back to her at last. But by then she had already begun it. And even if in a part of her mind she watched in horror and despair the slow-fall of the cards and knew the empty, crumpled ending, she knew also that she could not halt anything now. Not even if he called to her and called for her with a note of *something* in his voice she had never heard in it before. Never...never...never...!

It was dark, and the rain still beat against her and ran down her face to mix with and disguise the tears that poured from her eyes. There were sounds—screaming—and a voice that called, "Alexa! Alexa! Damn you, *answer* me!"

How had he known how to track her down and where to find her as she lay cushioned on moss in the shelter of the trees that guarded her? But in the end when some vestige of sanity came back to her, it was because of the poor, beautiful, gallant little mare she had ridden so thoughtlessly that she lay screaming in agony somewhere close by. It was for *her,* poor creature, that Alexa answered in a voice that was so hoarse she could not recognize it as her own.

"Here!" that voice said. "I'm *here!* But first...oh

please, for God's sake do something for *her!* Do something, I beg you, I *beg* you...*do something* to stop her suffering!''

He was as wet as she was, but he had a lantern sheltered under the heavy wool cloak that he dropped over her inert, shivering body after he had felt for broken bones and bumps first, in spite of her protests that there was nothing wrong with *her.*

''Please, Nicholas, *please!* You must—you must!''

''Don't move, then. You had damned well better not move an inch before I get back to you. Do you understand?''

Without waiting for his reply, she heard him move away and after she had waited for what seemed an interminable time that awful screaming that tortured her and lacerated every nerve in her body was abruptly stilled; and she was able to make out, at last, other sounds in the greater silence that followed.

When he came back to her Alexa grabbed at his wet shoulders without thinking as she choked, ''*Did* you—? *How* did you—? There was no shot...''

''Even if I'd carried a gun with me it wouldn't have been any damned good by now. You want to know how? With a *knife!* That's how I had to do it. Is that *enough* for you?''

''I'm sorry! I'm sorry, I'm sorry! If I'd listened to Grubb, if I'd had enough sense to... Why couldn't I have broken my neck? Do you think I'll *ever* be able to forgive myself?''

For a few minutes she felt comfortable and almost secure inside the circle of his arms while he held her against him as if she had been a child who needed comfort. And then she remembered too much and tried to pull away from him. ''I...I'm all *right* now. There's no need...I'm...all in one piece...I'm afraid...!''

"Are you sure? Do you know how long you've been lying here?" His voice was brusque and impersonal as he said: "Do you think you can stand? I had to borrow one of the Edens' horses to come out here after you. Jesus Christ, Alexa! Don't you possess *any* common sense at all, tucked away in some corner of that shallow, empty little head of yours? It's high time you started to grow up and begin acting like an adult for a change, instead of like a goddamned spoiled little brat who must always have things *her* way, no matter what the cost! Dammit—can you stand up or do I have to carry you?"

It seemed strange and almost funny for her to be saying what she started to say now and yet, once the cards started falling in her head she had to go on with it and have it over with.

"No! Not yet. There's something I want to tell you now that I should have told you before, I suppose, only you made it…difficult to…"

"I suppose you're wondering about my plans to go to California?" Incongruously enough, he was still holding her against himself—so close that she could even hear the beating of his heart before he said quietly, "I'm sorry I didn't say anything before you had to hear it from someone else, Alexa."

"It's true, though? Isn't it?"

"Yes, it's true. I should have had my fun and tasted what I wanted to taste of London as Lord Embry, heir to the Marquess of Newbury. Good God!" His laughter sounded harshly in her ears as he said: "I knew from the start of the adventure that I didn't fit in—and that there were limits to what I could stomach; and whatever happened is my own damned fault for procrastinating and putting off the inevitable. Christ, I'd smother if I stayed here any longer, moving in circles like a rider on an eternal carousel until I get so dazed and so dizzied that I forget how to get off the damned thing! I meant to tell you when I came back today, Alexa, although I can't blame you for thinking—whatever the hell it is you're thinking. But whether you believe it or not, I *was* going to tell you. And—dammit..."

"Don't! I... *Please,* I only wish you would not find it necessary to—to tell me any more lies or...or make me any more apologies, or...just *don't,* do you hear me?" Still held in his arms, Alexa turned her head upward to talk into the dark blur that was thankfully all she could see of his face; and she heard words again coming from somewhere removed from herself—pouring down on them both like the incessant dripping of the rain. "I *tried* to tell you before, I just said. I tried to tell you that I had already made up my mind—that I want to belong only to *myself* again, and to live only for myself and to do only as *I* please, and *when!* I am going to Spain in two weeks' time. I'm going with—Belle-Mère. She needs me now, you see, and she has persuaded me that I might need her. We shall use each other for a while, I suppose! But I want to take lovers if I choose to do so, and I feel I must tell you that I *will,* if I want to! Do you hear me, Nicholas? Do you hear me? I don't give a damn...not a *damn* what you threaten me with or...or...even what you might *do* to me! I don't care. You made me... You made me not..." Racked by sobs, she had begun to pound furiously against him while she tried to force more words out and could not. Until she finally had no more strength left in her wrists, and instead of beating against him her fingers now clung to the wet fabric of his shirt and she lay there crouched with her face against his heart, sobbing helplessly.

"Ah *hell,* Alexa! You poor, tormented little bitch! You can stop your damned weeping now. And you can take your lovers and have them or discard them—as many as you want. Why not? I suppose you're right, and it is only fair after all. And I don't want any of your goddamned money—it was yours to begin with and it always has been yours, whether you knew it or not! Does that satisfy you and make you feel better? Will it stop your damned caterwauling?"

When she could not make herself stop he swore violently under his breath and finally had to carry her to where he had tethered his shivering mount. And so, holding her in the saddle before him, he brought her back and left *her* to answer all of Harriet's questions, while he took the horse to the stables and sent to the house for enough brandy to make them all drunk as well as warm.

54

How fast all the cards could collapse, one over the other, until there was not one left standing. And once you'd done with that deck, of course you'd start on another—that is, if you had enough patience to go on and on with the same game that was only, when one looked at it sensibly, building up in order to tear down again.

No. There would be no more card-castles or card-soldiers standing all in a row as they waited for a flick of the nail against the first card. No more dream castles; although one learned from those in some ways. Here, lying naked in the sunlight that had already started to turn her skin golden again, Alexa watched the clouds that floated in the distance and let herself remember, as her mind made pictures and faces out of the puffy cloud-shapes that stayed far enough away for her to feel safe, that they would not come between her and the hot golden honey of the sunlight.

England was already a dim, pastel blur in her mind—like the elusive mountain mists that vanished as soon as the sun touched them. Packing. Bridget crying. Mr. Bowles putting on his stiffest upper lip and most regal air until he'd actually turned quite human at the last minute, although he'd made sure that her Ladyship understood that it was *he* who was doing *her* a favor by following her all the way to one of the colonies.

She could almost see Harriet's uncompromising profile carved onto the edge of one of those clouds. Thank God for Harriet and *her* unqualified support at least, even if she had made it quite clear from the first that she did *not* understand at all why two *supposedly* sane people who also happened to be married to each other should act like idiots or sulking children who turned their backs on each other instead of *talking* everything out like adults. But there were some things she could not tell Harriet and did not want to admit to herself, perhaps.

Well, Alexa, you've made your bed and now you must lie in it! *Alone,* if need be. For all of her hysterical rantings, she had taken no lovers, in the end; nor had she desired any of the handsome, polished, Spanish Dukes, Counts and Marquesses that she had been introduced to and encouraged to lie with by her grandmother. Eventually she had spent only two weeks in Spain, and had stayed that long only because she wanted to be sure of passage on one of the fastest sailing ships afloat; built in one of the New England shipyards of North America and purchased by one of the richest shipowners in England. Newbury had arranged *that* for her, and almost casually he had handed her another gift too on that last occasion they had met just before she had embarked for Spain.

"So it's the heat of the sun and, I must presume, the heated Spanish passions as well that you're after with my dearest viper of a mother as your guide through those dangerous shoals? I am hardly cut out to play the paternal role, my dear Alexandra, but I do hope you are—*aware?*"

"I'm aware that she thinks to use me by encouraging me to use her," Alexa had said calmly. "But I'm hardly interested in lovers at this point, since... Oh, I suppose you must have noticed the thickening of my waist already, since you seem to notice *most* things."

"Indeed? I'm flattered you give me credit." Newbury gave her one of his measuring looks before he said softly, "But there's a glaring omission here, is there not? Does the infant you're obviously carrying not have a *father?*"

"It's *my* doing entirely!" Alexa had said heatedly, and then added, looking him straight in the eye: "*I* sent Nicholas away and told him when I did that I intended to do as I please and take as many lovers as I pleased. And that I only wanted to be *free* of obligations. Oh damn! I beg your pardon, but it is only my condition that makes me so stupidly *tearful!*"

"I should hope so," Newbury said, and continued in an interested voice, "But do you mean to give me an answer to this riddle? As *I* recall you were quite mad for Embry not very long ago. And so?"

She flushed, beginning to play with her handkerchief. "Yes! Yes I was, and I…you see, I cannot be *quite* sure if Nicholas is the father, or…or Charles. And I *cannot* be so… Well, Nicholas doesn't *know.* And I do not *want* him to know either. I *hope* that is understood. All I want is that he should be *happy* with… *Merde!* How I hate and *despise* weeping women!"

Someone was calling through a megaphone that it was time for all visitors to go ashore; and when Alexa, having dabbed fiercely at her eyes, had turned them on the man who was by some freak of fate her natural father, she caught his faintly caustic smile as he said in his usual bored voice: "Well, Alexandra Victoria, I can only say that for a short time you actually succeeded in *surprising* me, as well as adding a certain amount of *intrigue* into my otherwise quite boring existence. In fact, I have often thought of what might have happened if I'd ordered you *gagged* after you had played Lady Godiva and…bared your all, so to speak. Noble, my dear, noble! The Amazon come to the rescue of her mate. But then it's too bad that most men who are not quite as depraved and lacking in illusions as *I* am, cannot accept such a gesture in the spirit it is meant. There was your lover, beaten and tortured by the wicked villain—and I am *very* good at that kind of thing, by the way. But he defends *you* and takes the blame upon himself, *almost* to the end, in fact. I *do* believe that if you had not revealed your—*our*—secret when you did, the idiot might have done something absolutely stupid and senseless in order to rescue you! But then, of course—and fortunately for *both* of you, I might add—*you* did the rescuing. And very well carried out too, with suspense to the last minute while the evil Marquess, like Bluebeard, slavers over his latest prospective victim. Ah, what energy, what planning and what scheming and, in fact, what a lot of trouble you put me to for nothing! But at least it shows you've got *some* modicum of sense left. Lovers should always part while they still love each other, I believe—before the gold is tarnished and turns to dross. So you and Nicholas will always love each other, and you will each compare the other loves that come along with the one perfect, bittersweet union. My God! I do believe I might even write a play some day, if my excesses do not catch up with me first and poor Nicholas willy-nilly finds himself the next Marquess of Newbury!''

Alexa had been by turns indignant, angry, wondering and—God help her now at *this* late stage—elated! She met Newbury's raised eyebrow as he made her an old-fashioned bow and told him in a severe undertone: ''You *know* you are a thoroughly corrupt, evil, *wicked* man; and you will probably end up getting the clap one day, which will put an end to your *nasty* goings on—and it would serve you right too. But all the same, I am glad that I have had the chance to *understand* some things about you.

Good-bye—father!'' Surprising herself more than she shocked Newbury, Alexa stood on her toes to give him a swift kiss on the cheek before he could brush her away, and stepped backward to stand against the rail and watch all the visitors leave. She had not expected Newbury to turn and wave to her and nor did he. But for a moment she had thought that he looked almost...frightened!

We're all the same way, after all, Alexa thought, and turned lazily onto her side. Frightened to show feeling, frightened *of* feeling because it means exposing ourselves to pain.

''For heaven's *sake,* Alexa! Haven't you had enough sun for one day? And you know how *slow* you are about getting dressed these days. Please *do* hurry! Bridget already has your bath waiting for you, so you have no more excuse for dawdling.''

Hurry, hurry, hurry! Harriet was worse than a Company Sergeant Major ordering around the newest recruit in the regiment, but Alexa had to admit she *needed* it or she'd become far too lazy.

The house that had been Sir John's house was hers now but she could sometimes feel his warmly understanding presence here. She had turned herself into a kind of recluse since she had come back to Ceylon, but it was really only because she so needed to lie naked under the sun again and to draw its warmth inside herself after all the months of deprivation when she had almost turned into—one of *them!* The kind of cold, judgmental, rigidly encased creatures who cared only for certain rules of etiquette and what *convention* decreed, with no thought at all for feelings. And *now* at last she understood what Nicholas had tried to tell her that night in the rain when she had told him bitterly how much she despised him even while he kept her warmly in his arms. That was one of the thoughts she could not bear when she recalled how *narrow* her mind had become and how stubbornly she had refused to see beyond herself and the tiny margins *she* had set for him—as well as herself. Margins that left no room for stretching or expanding or stepping out of those self-made boundaries. How could he have cared or continued to care for the self-righteous, unhearing *prig* she had let herself become? Well, no use crying over spilt milk, was there? And then Alexa started to laugh. Mrs. Langford! Good God, she had almost turned into a Mrs. Langford with a proverb or a motto to suit every occasion and every situation!

''Alexa! It would be the absolute *height* of bad manners, not to mention bad *taste,* to be late for dinner on an occasion such as this.''

''I'm ready—I'm coming—yes, at once!''

''The Governor and Mrs. Mackenzie have *always* been so kind to you and so *fond* of you. Just a little gratitude shown in return...'' Aunt Harry had taken up her lecture as soon as they were in their carriage, and Alexa wondered idly why she felt so tense. But then, she had always been fond of the Mackenzies and of Mrs. Mackenzie in particular, and it was sad to think that the jovial, hospitable man she remembered so well was in such bad health that he had tendered his resignation as Governor of the Crown Colony of Ceylon and would be replaced by Sir Colin Campbell, who had been one of the Duke of Wellington's aides.

How everything changed—especially people! ''Now my *dear* Alexa, I know how much you detest anything so vulgar as *name*-dropping, but in this case you know how they are all longing to hear everything they can about England, so I do hope you'll be gracious. And...'' Why did she feel so strongly that this had all happened before? *Déjà vu!* But she had suddenly had the feeling, because of her thoughts earlier, of course, and because of the last time she had sat in a carriage with Aunt Harriet on their way to the Queen's

House on the occasion of her eighteenth birthday celebration. There had even been a moon that night, like the moon that would be rising soon. Oh, but this was silly! Wishful thinking, pipe dreams. She or her other priggish self had said that once, Alexa thought, and then promptly closed her eyes to make a wish on the first star she saw. Venus, the evening star, named after the Roman goddess of love.

"Well, thank *goodness* we actually arrived here. Only five minutes early. That is quite excusable."

Dinner had been planned for such an unusually early hour, Alexa found, because all of the children had begged to be allowed to dine with the grown-ups just this once—all seven sons and four daughters, a natural phenomenon that made Alexa positively blanch when Harriet sent her a *speaking* look. But in the end, dinner *en famille* did not turn out to be quite the ordeal she had expected it might be, and they spent a pleasantly informal evening playing charades and even silly games like Hide-and-Seek and Sardines, until one by one the children were either packed off to bed, or excused themselves politely if they were older.

"You're not tired?" Alexa was asked considerately by Mrs. Mackenzie before being invited to take a turn about the gallery, and she felt a painful kind of throb when she remembered another night and another year. At least, she thought, they were polite enough not to ask inquisitive questions about her *husband,* Lord Embry, and where *he* might be while his wife was expecting their first child.

"Look, there's the moon. Almost full, isn't it?"

"I suppose we'll miss the tropics in a way, but at least we'll be home while the children are in school, and not so far away as *this.*"

Alexa leaned her elbows on the railing and looked out toward the ocean, barely able to make out the riding lights of the ship that had arrived late and would have to ride an anchor until morning. *Déjà vu* again. Or was it merely *yearning* that swept her back to the newness and innocence of the past with its possibilities for fresh beginnings? She let the conversation of the others flow around her and past her until she heard herself sigh and then forced herself back to the present once more.

"Well, I suppose it's the last dinner party I'll give here at Queen's House," the Governor said, and puffed at his cigar. Mrs. Mackenzie, Alexa remembered suddenly, smoked a hookah. Hashish. It was quite fashionable with the older generation, and even with *this* one, she supposed.

Ah, she felt almost smothered by her memories! *Déjà vu*—nostalgia—even the faint scent of sadness for what might have been, drifting up to her from the jasmine and honeysuckle and gardenias.

"We have your old room ready for you. Wanted this night to bring back memories of younger, happier times, you know, if you'll forgive an old man's fancifulness!"

No, Alexa thought. No... It would be too much; I *cannot*... And then suddenly she saw the faces turned towards her, watching her, and she said nothing. Why not? Whispered in her mind, in her ears, on the sighing rustle of the coconut palms bending before each tiny breath of a sea breeze. And in her pulses—racing, racing until she could hear them in her temples. Why not? Why not? She had wished on the first star and perhaps there was magic at work tonight, and she'd never know if magic was *real* unless she let herself be swept along with the tide of the night itself—let herself float on a dark, star-specked barge with the moon at its helm. Why not? And then—yes!

"Once upon a time..." There had been a fairy tale she'd read very long ago about six princesses who carried their dainty dancing slippers in their hands and crept out at night, past the watchdogs and past the guards the king had set, to find their princes and dance with them all night. This too had happened before, as the magic tide took her on her bare feet with a thin cotton camboy that covered her from her breasts to just below her knees, her only garment. Only this time Menika led the way and then held back, her teeth white against her copper skin in the moonlight. She murmured some soft words in Sinhalese that Alexa could hardly catch, although she thought she understood them—enough to know there was no translating them into English in her mind. The cotton cloth fell away from her body, from the swelling breasts and the gently burgeoning, rounded belly that last year had been as flat as a young athlete's. But it didn't matter. Wasn't that one of the things she had learned at last? She was herself, Alexa, *inside.* And when she dived into the moving, silver-peaked blackness of the Governor's pool she swam underwater for a while and became, for some seconds perhaps, a mermaid—a wild child of the ocean with a golden comb for her hair that hung down past her breasts, and a silver tail to reflect the moon by on a magic night like this one when all the boundaries between reality and unreality could be dissolved by only a thought in one's mind—and if that was strong enough *it* became reality. Believe. No doubts. *Know* what is real! And at the last second and her last breath she felt the beating and the movement of the water around her as she shot to the surface and breathed air again while she treaded water and took her time about pushing the heavy strands of hair from over her eyes and her lips because she *knew*...she knew even before she felt his arms go about her and felt his salt-wet kiss taste the salt of her lips. And only then did she open her eyes to his voice saying huskily, "Oh God...oh *God,* my moon-witch, how much I have wanted you! And how much I want you *now!*" Not only her hungry eyes but her fingers traced the contours of his face and the feel of his wet black hair and felt him against her thighs and then between them until she heard him say in a voice that was half groan and half caress, "I don't want to drown in your enchanted pool, mermaid, sea witch, sweet Alexa, with your eyes like night that trap the moon in them just as you trapped me that first night I saw you...."

The grass was soft and sweet smelling under them as the wildness of urgency gave way to touching and tasting and reexploring, and rose very slowly and very gradually until their longing for each other and the aching, agonizing need for each other became like a wind, like an ocean gathered into one wave, like dying and being reborn again. And they lay together there, he, on his side behind her, holding her so closely and yet so gently that it almost *hurt* being so happy, and she had to turn her head to make sure it was he, and he had not left her. And in the end she had to turn to face him and touch him and hold him and tell him in naked words what she had always felt for him and had fought with all her strength and could not help; because some people, as the ancient Greek legend had it, were but two halves of a single whole, separated by some jealous god and condemned to search the earth forever until they found, at last, the other half with whom, when joined together, they made the perfect whole. And some things were not to be questioned but only accepted gladly and joyfully, so that their resting here together with the child that would be theirs between them was like reaching a plateau at the top of a mountain they had had to climb with their hands and their knees and their feet until they had had to shed everything else but the one fact that they loved each other. "I love you, I love you, I love you!" Alexa said fiercely. "Oh Nicholas, *why* did you let me go? Why did you go away before I could take back all the horrible, ugly, *lying* things I said to hurt you? And oh if you hadn't come...if you hadn't come I would have come looking for you, you know! With our baby carried in a pack on my back, if I had to. It *is* our baby, you know.

Bridget…oh, thank God for Bridget, because *she* kept count of certain dates even if *I* did not!''

He started to laugh then, and the laugh creases at the corners of his eyes and his mouth made him look younger and wiped from his face the hard and twisted look he used to wear most of the time before. ''Alexa, my sweet Alexa, did you think I would have *cared? Do* you, my love?'' And when she looked at his face in the moonlight before shaking her head decisively, the last barrier fell and she leaned her face contentedly against his shoulder while he told her that it was Newbury of all people who had told him the truth in his bored, slightly jeering fashion.

''Oh, *Nicholas!* I can't *bear* to think that *I*…'' Alexa shuddered against him until he tilted up her chin and kissed her fiercely.

''It's done. And I *learned* from what happened, strangely enough. Perhaps it taught me to *think* of what consequences my own selfish actions might have on other people.'' He kissed her eyelids and the tip of her nose before his lips traveled very slowly to hers and brushed against them lightly as he whispered: ''Especially a certain hot-tempered, reckless, sharp-tongued virago that I had fallen in love with in spite of myself. And do you know why? Because the first time I saw her the little witch of the sea put her invisible silver net about me, and I was trapped forever in the net of her enchantment until…''

''Go on. You're not going to stop now, are you?''

''You have a bad habit of interrupting, my dearest love, which I *might* have to…'' Holding his mouth teasingly a mere inch from hers, Nicholas whispered, ''Until I *bought* a goddamned ship, which had better be a *magic* ship that flies many times from New York and Boston to China and back in the future, let me tell you, or I'll be reduced to borrowing money from my rich heiress bride!''

''The story!''

"Well, I guess the story has a good witch in it like all such stories, and her name happens to be Harriet. So we plotted and planned with a considerable amount of help from high places, I might add, until at last when the night was just right and the moon and the tide and my wicked enchantress was swimming in her pool, I caught *her* in my own invisible net of gold. And you're trapped forever, sweet witch, just as I am—so I suppose we might just as well make the best of it, don't you think?"

"Why not?" Slipping from his reluctant arms, Alexa poised herself on the edge of the pool before turning back to him with one hand on her hip, just above the golden chain he had put on her once. "Will you come and swim with me in my enchanted pool once more, my darling? I've heard that two silver nets are *much* stronger than one, and I mean to keep you in my thrall forever and ever, you know!"